PENGUIN BOOKS

THE YOUNG HORNBLOWER

C. S. Forester was born in Cairo in 1899, where his father was stationed as a government official. He studied medicine at Guy's Hospital and, leaving Guy's without a degree, he turned to writing as a career. His first success was *Payment Deferred*, a novel written at the age of twenty-four and later dramatized and filmed with Charles Laughton in the leading role. In 1932 Forester was offered a Hollywood contract, and from then until 1939 he spent thirteen weeks of every year in America. On the outbreak of war he entered the Ministry of Information and later he sailed with the Royal Navy to collect the material for *The Ship*. He made a voyage to the Bering Sea to gather material for a similar book on the United States Navy, and during this trip, he was stricken with arteriosclerosis, a disease which left him crippled. However, he continued to write and in Captain Hornblower created the most renowned sailor in contemporary fiction. C. S. Forester died in 1966.

C. S. FORESTER

The Young Hornblower

Comprising

MR. MIDSHIPMAN HORNBLOWER
LIEUTENANT HORNBLOWER
HORNBLOWER AND THE HOTSPUR

PENGUIN BOOKS

PENGUIN BOOKS

Published by the Penguin Group
Penguin Books Ltd, 27 Wrights Lane, London W8 5TZ, England
Penguin Putnam Inc., 375 Hudson Street, New York, New York 10014, USA
Penguin Books Australia Ltd, Ringwood, Victoria, Australia
Penguin Books Canada Ltd, 10 Alcorn Avenue, Toronto, Ontario, Canada M4V 3B2
Penguin Books (NZ) Ltd, Private Bag 102902, NSMC, Auckland, New Zealand

Penguin Books Ltd, Registered Offices: Harmondsworth, Middlesex, England

Mr. Midshipman Hornblower first published by Michael Joseph 1950
Copyright 1950 by Cassette Productions SA
Lieutenant Hornblower first published by Michael Joseph 1952
Copyright 1952 by Cassette Productions SA
Hornblower and the 'Hotspur' first published by Michael Joseph 1962
Copyright © Cassette Productions Ltd, 1962
All rights reserved

This omnibus edition first published by Michael Joseph 1964
Published in Penguin Books 1989
13

Printed in England by Clays Ltd, St Ives plc

*

Mr. Midshipman
Hornblower

THE EVEN CHANCE

A January gale was roaring up the Channel, blustering loudly, and bearing in its bosom rain squalls whose big drops rattled loudly on the tarpaulin clothing of those among the officers and men whose duties kept them on deck. So hard and so long had the gale blown that even in the sheltered waters of Spithead the battleship moved uneasily at her anchors, pitching a little in the choppy seas, and snubbing herself against the tautened cables with unexpected jerks. A shore boat was on its way out to her, propelled by oars in the hands of two sturdy women; it danced madly on the steep little waves, now and then putting its nose into one and sending a sheet of spray flying aft. The oarswoman in the bow knew her business, and with rapid glances over her shoulder not only kept the boat on its course but turned the bows into the worst of the waves to keep from capsizing. It slowly drew up along the starboard side of the *Justinian*, and as it approached the mainchains the midshipman of the watch hailed it.

"Aye aye," came back the answering hail from the lusty lungs of the woman at the stroke oar; by the curious and ages-old convention of the Navy the reply meant that the boat had an officer on board—presumably the huddled figure in the sternsheets looking more like a heap of trash with a boat-cloak thrown over it.

That was as much as Mr. Masters, the lieutenant of the watch, could see; he was sheltering as best he could in the lee of the mizzen-mast bitts, and in obedience to the order of the midshipman of the watch the boat drew up towards the mainchains and passed out of his sight. There was a long delay; apparently the officer had some difficulty in getting up the ship's side. At last the boat reappeared in Masters' field of vision; the women had shoved off and were setting a scrap of lug-sail, under which the boat, now without its passenger, went swooping back towards Portsmouth, leaping on the waves like a steeplechaser. As it departed Mr. Masters became aware of the near approach of someone along the quarterdeck; it was the new arrival under the escort of the midshipman of the watch, who, after pointing Masters out, retired to the mainchains again. Mr. Masters had served in the Navy until his hair was white; he was lucky to have received his commission as lieutenant, and he had long known that he would never receive one as

9

captain, but the knowledge had not greatly embittered him, and he diverted his mind by the study of his fellow men.

So he looked with attention at the approaching figure. It was that of a skinny young man only just leaving boyhood behind, something above middle height, with feet whose adolescent proportions to his size were accentuated by the thinness of his legs and his big half-boots. His gawkiness called attention to his hands and elbows. The newcomer was dressed in a badly fitting uniform which was soaked right through by the spray; a skinny neck stuck out of the high stock, and above the neck was a white bony face. A white face was a rarity on the deck of a ship of war, whose crew soon tanned to a deep mahogany, but this face was not merely white; in the hollow cheeks there was a faint shade of green —clearly the newcomer had experienced seasickness in his passage out in the shore boat. Set in the white face were a pair of dark eyes which by contrast looked like holes cut in a sheet of paper; Masters noted with a slight stirring of interest that the eyes, despite their owner's seasickness, were looking about keenly, taking in what were obviously new sights; there was a curiosity and interest there which could not be repressed and which continued to function notwithstanding either seasickness or shyness, and Mr. Masters surmised in his far-fetched fashion that this boy had a vein of caution or foresight in his temperament and was already studying his new surroundings with a view to being prepared for his next experiences. So might Daniel have looked about him at the lions when he first entered their den.

The dark eyes met Masters', and the gawky figure came to a halt, raising a hand selfconsciously to the brim of his dripping hat. His mouth opened and tried to say something, but closed again without achieving its object as shyness overcame him, but then the newcomer nerved himself afresh and forced himself to say the form of words he had been coached to utter.

"Come aboard, sir."

"Your name?" asked Masters, after waiting for it for a moment.

"H-Horatio Hornblower, sir. Midshipman," stuttered the boy.

"Very good, Mr. Hornblower," said Masters, with the equally formal response. "Did you bring your dunnage aboard with you?"

Hornblower had never heard that word before, but he still had enough of his wits about him to deduce what it meant.

"My sea chest, sir. It's—it's forrard, at the entry port."

Hornblower said these things with the barest hesitation; he knew that at sea they said them, that they pronounced the word "forward" like that, and that he had come on board through the "entry port", but it called for a slight effort to utter them himself.

"I'll see that it's sent below," said Masters. "And that's where you'd better go, too. The captain's ashore, and the first lieutenant's orders were that he's not to be called on any account before eight bells, so I advise you, Mr. Hornblower, to get out of those wet clothes while you can."

"Yes, sir," said Hornblower; his senses told him, the moment he said it, that he had used an improper expression—the look on Masters' face told him, and he corrected himself (hardly believing that men really said these things off the boards of the stage) before Masters had time to correct him.

"Aye aye, sir," said Hornblower, and as a second afterthought he put his hand to the brim of his hat again.

Masters returned the compliment and turned to one of the shivering messengers cowering in the inadequate shelter of the bulwark. "Boy! Take Mr. Hornblower down to the midshipmen's berth."

"Aye aye, sir."

Hornblower accompanied the boy forward to the main hatchway. Seasickness alone would have made him unsteady on his feet, but twice on the short journey he stumbled like a man tripping over a rope as a sharp gust brought the *Justinian* up against her cables with a jerk. At the hatchway the boy slid down the ladder like an eel over a rock; Hornblower had to brace himself and descend far more gingerly and uncertainly into the dim light of the lower gundeck and then into the twilight of the 'tweendecks. The smells that entered his nostrils were as strange and as assorted as the noises that assailed his ear. At the foot of each ladder the boy waited for him with a patience whose tolerance was just obvious. After the last descent, a few steps—Hornblower had already lost his sense of direction and did not know whether it was aft or forward—took them to a gloomy recess whose shadows were accentuated rather than lightened by a tallow dip spiked onto a bit of copper plate on a table round which were seated half a dozen shirt-sleeved men. The boy vanished and left Hornblower standing there, and it was a second or two before the whiskered man at the head of the table looked up at him.

"Speak, thou apparition," said he.

Hornblower felt a wave of nausea overcoming him—the after effects of his trip in the shore boat were being accentuated by the incredible stuffiness and smelliness of the 'tweendecks. It was very hard to speak, and the fact that he did not know how to phrase what he wanted to say made it harder still.

"My name is Hornblower," he quavered at length.

"What an infernal piece of bad luck for you," said a second man at the table, with a complete absence of sympathy.

At that moment in the roaring world outside the ship the wind veered sharply, heeling the *Justinian* a trifle and swinging her round to snub at her cables again. To Hornblower it seemed more as if the world had come loose from its fastenings. He reeled where he stood, and although he was shuddering with cold he felt sweat on his face.

"I suppose you have come," said the whiskered man at the head of the table "to thrust yourself among your betters. Another soft-headed ignoramus come to be a nuisance to those who have to try to teach you your duties. Look at him," the speaker with a gesture demanded the attention of everyone at the table—"look at him, I say! The King's latest bad bargain. How old are you?"

"S-seventeen, sir," stuttered Hornblower.

"Seventeen!" the disgust in the speaker's voice was only too evident. "You must start at twelve if you ever wish to be a seaman. Seventeen! Do you know the difference between a head and a halliard?"

That drew a laugh from the group, and the quality of the laugh was just noticeable to Hornblower's whirling brain, so that he guessed that whether he said "yes" or "no" he would be equally exposed to ridicule. He groped for a neutral reply.

"That's the first thing I'll look up in Norie's *Seamanship*," he said.

The ship lurched again at that moment, and he clung on to the table.

"Gentlemen," he began pathetically, wondering how to say what he had in mind.

"My God!" exclaimed somebody at the table. "He's seasick!"

"Seasick in Spithead!" said somebody else, in a tone in which amazement had as much place as disgust.

But Hornblower ceased to care; he was not really conscious of what was going on round him for some time after that. The nervous excitement of the last few days was as much to blame, perhaps, as the journey in the shore boat and the erratic behaviour of the *Justinian* at her anchors, but it meant for him that he was labelled at once as the midshipman who was seasick in Spithead, and it was only natural that the label added to the natural misery of the loneliness and homesickness which oppressed him during those days when that part of the Channel Fleet which had not succeeded in completing its crews lay at anchor in the lee of the Isle of Wight. An hour in the hammock into which the messman hoisted him enabled him to recover sufficiently to be able to report himself to the first lieutenant; after a few days on board he was able to find his way round the ship without (as happened at first) losing his sense of direction below decks, so that he did not know whether he was facing forward or aft. During that period his brother officers ceased to have faces which were mere blurs and came to take on personalities; he came painfully to learn the stations allotted him when the ship was at quarters, when he was on watch, and when hands were summoned for setting or taking in sail. He even came to have an acute enough understanding of his new life to realize that it could have been worse

—that destiny might have put him on board a ship ordered immediately to sea instead of one lying at anchor. But it was a poor enough compensation; he was a lonely and unhappy boy. Shyness alone would long have delayed his making friends, but as it happened the midshipmen's berth in the *Justinian* was occupied by men all a good deal older than he; elderly master's mates recruited from the merchant service, and midshipmen in their twenties who through lack of patronage or inability to pass the necessary examination had never succeeded in gaining for themselves commissions as lieutenants. They were inclined, after the first moments of amused interest, to ignore him, and he was glad of it, delighted to shrink into his shell and attract no notice to himself.

For the *Justinian* was not a happy ship during those gloomy January days. Captain Keene—it was when he came aboard that Hornblower first saw the pomp and ceremony that surrounds the captain of a ship of the line—was a sick man, of a melancholy disposition. He had not the fame which enabled some captains to fill their ships with enthusiastic volunteers, and he was devoid of the personality which might have made enthusiasts out of the sullen pressed men whom the press gangs were bringing in from day to day to complete the ship's complement. His officers saw little of him, and did not love what they saw. Hornblower, summoned to his cabin for his first interview, was not impressed—a middle-aged man at a table covered with papers, with the hollow and yellow cheeks of prolonged illness.

"Mr. Hornblower," he said formally "I am glad to have this opportunity of welcoming you on board my ship."

"Yes, sir," said Hornblower—that seemed more appropriate to the occasion than "Aye aye, sir," and a junior midshipman seemed to be expected to say one or the other on all occasions.

"You are—let me see—seventeen?" Captain Keene picked up the paper which apparently covered Hornblower's brief official career.

"Yes, sir."

"July 4th, 1776," mused Keene, reading Hornblower's date of birth to himself. "Five years to the day before I was posted as captain. I had been six years as lieutenant before you were born."

"Yes, sir," agreed Hornblower—it did not seem the occasion for any further comment.

"A doctor's son—you should have chosen a lord for your father if you wanted to make a career for yourself."

"Yes, sir."

"How far did your education go?"

"I was a Grecian at school, sir."

"So you can construe Xenophon as well as Cicero?"

"Yes, sir. But not very well, sir."

"Better if you knew something about sines and cosines. Better if you could foresee a squall in time to get t'gallants in. We have no use for ablative absolutes in the Navy."

"Yes, sir," said Hornblower.

He had only just learned what a topgallant was, but he could have told his captain that his mathematical studies were far advanced. He refrained nevertheless; his instincts combined with his recent experiences urged him not to volunteer unsolicited information.

"Well, obey orders, learn your duties, and no harm can come to you. That will do."

"Thank you, sir," said Hornblower, retiring.

But the captain's last words to him seemed to be contradicted immediately. Harm began to come to Hornblower from that day forth, despite his obedience to orders and diligent study of his duties, and it stemmed from the arrival in the midshipmen's berth of John Simpson as senior warrant officer. Hornblower was sitting at mess with his colleagues when he first saw him—a brawny good-looking man in his thirties, who came in and stood looking at them just as Hornblower had stood a few days before.

"Hullo!" said somebody, not very cordially.

"Cleveland, my bold friend," said the newcomer, "come out from that seat. I am going to resume my place at the head of the table."

"But—"

"Come out, I said," snapped Simpson.

Cleveland moved along with some show of reluctance, and Simpson took his place, and glowered round the table in reply to the curious glances with which everyone regarded him.

"Yes, my sweet brother officers," he said. "I am back in the bosom of the family. And I am not surprised that nobody is pleased. You will all be less pleased by the time I am done with you, I may add."

"But your commission—?" asked somebody, greatly daring.

"My commission?" Simpson leaned forward and tapped the table, staring down the inquisitive people on either side of it. "I'll answer that question this once, and the man who asks it again will wish he had never been born. A board of turnip-headed captains has refused me my commission. It decided that my mathematical knowledge was insufficient to make me a reliable navigator. And so Acting-Lieutenant Simpson is once again Mr. Midshipman Simpson, at your service. At your service. And may the Lord have mercy on your souls."

It did not seem, as the days went by, that the Lord had any mercy at all, for with Simpson's return life in the midshipmen's berth ceased to be one of passive unhappiness and became one of active misery. Simpson had apparently always been an ingenious tyrant, but now, embittered and humiliated by his failure to pass his examination for his commission, he was a worse tyrant, and his ingenuity had multiplied itself. He may have been weak in mathematics, but he was diabolically clever at making other people's lives a burden to them. As senior officer in the mess he had wide official powers; as a man with a blistering tongue and a morbid sense of mischief he would have been powerful anyway, even if the *Justinian* had possessed an alert and masterful first lieutenant to keep him in check, while Mr. Clay was neither. Twice midshipmen rebelled against Simpson's arbitrary authority, and each time Simpson thrashed the rebel, pounding him into insensibility with his huge fists, for Simpson would have made a successful prize-fighter. Each time Simpson was left unmarked; each time his opponent's blackened eyes and swollen lips called down the penalty of mast heading and extra duty from the indignant first lieutenant. The mess seethed with impotent rage. Even the toadies and lickspittles among the midshipmen— and naturally there were several—hated the tyrant.

Significantly, it was not his ordinary exactions which roused the greatest resentment—his levying toll upon their sea chests for clean shirts for himself, his appropriation of the best cuts of the meat served, nor even his taking their coveted issues of spirits. These things could be excused as understandable, the sort of thing they would do themselves if they had the power. But he displayed a whimsical arbitrariness which reminded Hornblower, with his classical education, of the freaks of the Roman emperors. He forced Cleveland to shave the whiskers which were his inordinate pride; he imposed upon Hether the duty of waking up Mackenzie every half hour, day and night, so that neither of them was able to sleep—and there were toadies ready to tell him if Hether ever failed in his task. Early enough he had discovered Hornblower's most vulnerable points, as he had with everyone else. He knew of Hornblower's shyness; at first it was amusing to compel Hornblower to recite verses from Gray's "Elegy in a Country Churchyard" to the assembled mess. The toadies could compel Hornblower to do it; Simpson would lay his dirk-scabbard on the table in front of him with a significant glance, and the toadies would close round Hornblower, who knew that any hesitation on his part would mean that he would be stretched across the table and the dirk-scabbard applied; the flat of the scabbard was painful, the edge of it was agonizing, but the pain was nothing to the utter humiliation of it all. And the torment grew worse when Simpson instituted what he aptly called "The Proceedings of the Inquisition" when Hornblower was submitted to a slow and methodical questioning regarding his homelife and his boyhood. Every question had to be answered, on pain of the dirk-scabbard; Hornblower could fence and prevaricate, but he had to answer and sooner or later the relentless questioning would draw from him some simple admission which would rouse a peal of laughter from his audience. Heaven knows that in Hornblower's lonely childhood there was nothing to be ashamed of, but boys are odd creatures, especially reticent ones like Hornblower, and are ashamed of things no one else would think twice about. The ordeal would leave him weak and sick; someone less solemn might have clowned his way out of his difficulties and even into popular favour, but Hornblower at seventeen was too ponderous a person to clown. He had to endure the persecution, experiencing all the black misery which only a seventeen-year-old can experience; he never wept in public, but at night more than once he shed the bitter tears of seventeen. He often thought about death; he often even thought about desertion, but he realized that desertion would lead to something worse than death, and then his mind would revert to death, savouring the thought of suicide. He came to long for death, friendless as he was, and brutally ill-treated, and lonely as only a boy among men—and a very reserved boy—can be. More and more he thought about ending it all the easiest way, hugging the secret thought of it to his friendless bosom.

If the ship had only been at sea everyone would have been kept busy enough to be out of mischief; even at anchor an energetic captain and first lieutenant would have kept all hands hard enough at work to obviate abuses, but it was Hornblower's hard luck that the *Justinian* lay at anchor all through that fatal January of 1794 under a sick captain and an inefficient first lieutenant. Even the activities which were at times enforced often worked to Hornblower's disadvantage. There was an occasion when Mr. Bowles, the master, was holding a class in navigation for his mates and for the midshipmen, and the captain by bad luck happened by and glanced through the results of the problem the class had individually been set to solve. His illness made Keene a man of bitter tongue, and he cherished no liking for Simpson. He took a single glance at Simpson's paper, and chuckled sarcastically.

"Now let us all rejoice," he said, "the sources of the Nile have been discovered at last."

"Pardon, sir?" said Simpson.

"Your ship," said Keene, "as far as I can make out from your illiterate scrawl, Mr. Simpson, is in Central Africa. Let us now see what other *terrae incognitae* have been opened up by the remaining intrepid explorers of this class."

It must have been Fate—it was dramatic enough to be art and not an occurrence in real life; Hornblower knew what was going to happen even as Keene picked up the other papers, including his. The result he had obtained was the only one which was correct; everybody else had added the correction for refraction instead of subtracting it, or had worked out the multiplication wrongly, or had, like Simpson, botched the whole problem.

"Congratulations, Mr. Hornblower," said Keene. "You must be proud to be alone successful among this crowd of intellectual giants.

You are half Mr. Simpson's age, I fancy. If you double your attainments while you double your years, you will leave the rest of us far behind. Mr. Bowles, you will be so good as to see that Mr. Simpson pays even further attention to his mathematical studies."

With that he went off along the 'tweendecks with the halting step resulting from his mortal disease, and Hornblower sat with his eyes cast down, unable to meet the glances he knew were being darted at him, and knowing full well what they portended. He longed for death at that moment; he even prayed for it that night.

Within two days Hornblower found himself on shore, and under Simpson's command. The two midshipmen were in charge of a party of seamen, landed to act along with parties from the other ships of the squadron as a press gang. The West India convoy was due to arrive soon; most of the hands would be pressed as soon as the convoy reached the Channel, and the remainder, left to work the ships to an anchorage, would sneak ashore, using every device to conceal themselves and find a safe hiding-place. It was the business of the landing parties to cut off this retreat, to lay a cordon along the waterfront which would sweep them all up. But the convoy was not yet signalled, and all arrangements were completed.

"All is well with the world," said Simpson.

It was an unusual speech for him, but he was in unusual circumstances. He was sitting in the back room of the Lamb Inn, comfortable in one armchair with his legs on another, in front of a roaring fire and with a pot of beer with gin in it at his elbow.

"Here's to the West India convoy," said Simpson, taking a pull at his beer. "Long may it be delayed."

Simpson was actually genial, activity and beer and a warm fire thawing him into a good humour; it was not time yet for the liquor to make him quarrelsome; Hornblower sat on the other side of the fire and sipped beer without gin in it and studied him, marvelling that for the first time since he had boarded the *Justinian* his unhappiness should have ceased to be active but should have subsided into a dull misery like the dying away of the pain of a throbbing tooth.

"Give us a toast, boy," said Simpson.

"Confusion to Robespierre," said Hornblower lamely.

The door opened and two more officers came in, one a midshipman while the other wore the single epaulette of a lieutenant—it was Chalk of the *Goliath*, the officer in general charge of the press gangs sent ashore. Even Simpson made room for his superior rank before the fire.

"The convoy is still not signalled," announced Chalk. And then he eyed Hornblower keenly. "I don't think I have the pleasure of your acquaintance."

"Mr. Hornblower—Lieutenant Chalk," introduced Simpson. "Mr.

Hornblower is distinguished as the midshipman who was seasick in Spithead."

Hornblower tried not to writhe as Simpson tied that label on him. He imagined that Chalk was merely being polite when he changed the subject.

"Hey, potman! Will you gentlemen join me in a glass? We have a long wait before us, I fear. Your men are all properly posted, Mr. Simpson?"

"Yes, sir."

Chalk was an active man. He paced about the room, stared out of the window at the rain, presented his midshipman—Caldwell—to the other two when the drinks arrived, and obviously fretted at his enforced inactivity.

"A game of cards to pass the time?" he suggested. "Excellent! Hey, potman! Cards and a table and another light."

The table was set before the fire, the chairs arranged, the cards brought in.

"What game shall it be?" asked Chalk, looking round.

He was a lieutenant among three midshipmen, and any suggestion of his was likely to carry a good deal of weight; the other three naturally waited to hear what he had to say.

"Vingt-et-un? That is a game for the half-witted. Loo? That is a game for the wealthier half-witted. But whist, now? That would give us all scope for the exercise of our poor talents. Caldwell, there, is acquainted with the rudiments of the game, I know. Mr. Simpson?"

A man like Simpson, with a blind mathematical spot, was not likely to be a good whist player, but he was not likely to know he was a bad one.

"As you wish, sir," said Simpson. He enjoyed gambling, and one game was as good as another for that purpose to his mind.

"Mr. Hornblower?"

"With pleasure, sir."

That was more nearly true than most conventional replies. Hornblower had learned his whist in a good school; ever since the death of his mother he had made a fourth with his father and the parson and the parson's wife. The game was already something of a passion with him. He revelled in the nice calculation of chances, in the varying demands it made upon his boldness or caution. There was even enough warmth in his acceptance to attract a second glance from Chalk, who—a good card player himself—at once detected a fellow spirit.

"Excellent!" he said again. "Then we may as well cut at once for places and partners. What shall be the stakes, gentlemen? A shilling a trick and a guinea on the rub, or is that too great? No? Then we are agreed."

For some time the game proceeded quietly. Hornblower cut first Simpson and then Caldwell as his partner. Only a couple of hands were necessary to show up Simpson as a hopeless whist player, the kind who would always lead an ace when he had one, or a singleton when he had four trumps, but he and Hornblower won the first rubber thanks to overwhelming card strength. But Simpson lost the next in partnership with Chalk, cut Chalk again as partner, and lost again. He gloated over good hands and sighed over poor ones; clearly he was one of those un-enlightened people who looked upon whist as a social function, or as a mere crude means, like throwing dice, of arbitrarily transferring money. He never thought of the game either as a sacred rite or as an intellectual exercise. Moreover, as his losses grew, and as the potman came and went with liquor, he grew restless, and his face was flushed with more than the heat of the fire. He was both a bad loser and a bad drinker, and even Chalk's punctilious good manners were sufficiently strained so that he displayed a hint of relief when the next cut gave him Hornblower as a partner. They won the rubber easily, and another guinea and several shillings were transferred to Hornblower's lean purse; he was now the only winner, and Simpson was the heaviest loser. Hornblower was lost in the pleasure of playing the game again; the only attention he paid to Simpson's writhings and muttered objurgations was to regard them as a distracting nuisance; he even forgot to think of them as danger signals. Momentarily he was oblivious to the fact that he might pay for his present success by future torment.

Once more they cut, and he found himself Chalk's partner again. Two good hands gave them the first game. Then twice, to Simpson's unconcealed triumph, Simpson and Caldwell made a small score, approaching game, and in the next hand an overbold finesse by Hornblower left him and Chalk with the odd trick when their score should have been two tricks greater—Simpson laid his knave on Hornblower's ten with a grin of delight which turned to dismay when he found that he and Caldwell had still only made six tricks; he counted them a second time with annoyance. Hornblower dealt and turned the trump, and Simpson led—an ace as usual, assuring Hornblower of his re-entry. He had a string of trumps and a good suit of clubs which a single lead might establish. Simpson glanced muttering at his hand; it was extra-ordinary that he still had not realized the simple truth that the lead of an ace involved leading a second time with the problem no clearer. He made up his mind at last and led again; Hornblower's king took the trick and he instantly led his knave of trumps. To his delight it took the trick; he led again and Chalk's queen gave them another trick. Chalk laid down the ace of trumps and Simpson with a curse played the king. Chalk led clubs of which Hornblower had five to the king queen—it was significant that Chalk should lead them, as it could not be a singleton lead when Hornblower held the remaining trumps. Hornblower's queen took the trick; Caldwell must hold the ace, unless Chalk did. Hornblower led a small one; everyone followed suit, Chalk playing the knave, and Caldwell played the ace. Eight clubs had been played, and Hornblower had three more headed by the king and ten —three certain tricks, with the last trumps as re-entries. Caldwell played the queen of diamonds, Hornblower played his singleton, and Chalk produced the ace.

"The rest are mine," said Hornblower, laying down his cards.

"What do you mean?" said Simpson, with the king of diamonds in his hand.

"Five tricks," said Chalk briskly. "Game and rubber."

"But don't I take another?" persisted Simpson.

"I trump a lead of diamonds or hearts and make three more clubs," explained Hornblower. To him the situation was as simple as two and two, a most ordinary finish to a hand; it was hard for him to realize that foggy-minded players like Simpson could find difficulty in keeping tally of fifty-two cards. Simpson flung down his hand.

"You know too much about the game," he said. "You know the backs of the cards as well as the fronts."

Hornblower gulped. He recognized that this could be a decisive moment if he chose. A second before he had merely been playing cards, and enjoying himself. Now he was faced with an issue of life or death. A torrent of thought streamed through his mind. Despite the comfort of his present surroundings he remembered acutely the hideous misery of the life in the *Justinian* to which he must return. This was an opportunity to end that misery one way or the other. He remembered how he had contemplated killing himself, and into the back of his mind stole the germ of the plan upon which he was going to act. His decision crystallized.

"That is an insulting remark, Mr. Simpson," he said. He looked round and met the eyes of Chalk and Caldwell, who were suddenly grave; Simpson was still merely stupid. "For that I shall have to ask satisfaction."

"Satisfaction?" said Chalk hastily. "Come, come. Mr. Simpson had a momentary loss of temper. I am sure he will explain."

"I have been accused of cheating at cards," said Hornblower. "That is a hard thing to explain away."

He was trying to behave like a grown man; more than that, he was trying to act like a man consumed with indignation, while actually there was no indignation within him over the point in dispute, for he understood too well the muddled state of mind which had led Simpson to say what he did. But the opportunity had presented itself, he had determined to avail himself of it, and now what he had to do was to play the part convincingly of the man who has received a mortal insult.

"The wine was in and the wit was out," said Chalk, still determined on keeping the peace. "Mr. Simpson was speaking in jest, I am sure. Let's call for another bottle and drink it in friendship."

"With pleasure," said Hornblower, fumbling for the words which would set the dispute beyond reconciliation. "If Mr. Simpson will beg my pardon at once before you two gentlemen, and admit that he spoke without justification and in a manner no gentleman would employ."

He turned and met Simpson's eyes with defiance as he spoke, metaphorically waving a red rag before the bull, who charged with gratifying fury.

"Apologize to *you*, you little whippersnapper!" exploded Simpson, alcohol and outraged dignity speaking simultaneously. "Never this side of Hell."

"You hear that, gentlemen?" said Hornblower. "I have been insulted and Mr. Simpson refuses to apologize while insulting me further. There is only one way now in which satisfaction can be given."

For the next two days, until the West India convoy came in, Hornblower and Simpson, under Chalk's orders, lived the curious life of two duellists forced into each other's society before the affair of honour. Hornblower was careful—as he would have been in any case—to obey every order given him, and Simpson gave them with a certain amount of self-consciousness and awkwardness. It was during those two days that Hornblower elaborated on his original idea. Pacing through the dockyards with his patrol of seamen at his heels he had plenty of time to think the matter over. Viewed coldly—and a boy of seventeen in a mood of black despair can be objective enough on occasions—it was as simple as the calculations of the chances in a problem at whist. Nothing could be worse than his life in the *Justinian*, not even (as he had thought already) death itself. Here was an easy death open to him, with the additional attraction that there was a chance of Simpson dying instead. It was at that moment that Hornblower advanced his idea one step further—a new development, startling even to him, bringing him to a halt so that the patrol behind him bumped into him before they could stop.

"Beg your pardon, sir," said the petty officer.

"No matter," said Hornblower, deep in his thoughts.

He first brought forward his suggestion in conversation with Preston and Danvers, the two master's mates whom he asked to be his seconds as soon as he returned to the *Justinian*.

"We'll act for you, of course," said Preston, looking dubiously at the weedy youth when he made his request. "How do you want to fight him? As the aggrieved party you have the choice of weapons."

"I've been thinking about it ever since he insulted me," said

Hornblower temporising. It was not easy to come out with his idea in bald words, after all.

"Have you any skill with the small-sword?" asked Danvers.

"No," said Hornblower. Truth to tell, he had never even handled one.

"Then it had better be pistols," said Preston.

"Simpson is probably a good shot," said Danvers. "I wouldn't care to stand up before him myself."

"Easy now," said Preston hastily. "Don't dishearten the man."

"I'm not disheartened," said Hornblower, "I was thinking the same thing myself."

"You're cool enough about it, then," marvelled Danvers.

Hornblower shrugged.

"Maybe I am. I hardly care. But I've thought that we might make the chances more even."

"How?"

"We could make them exactly even," said Hornblower, taking the plunge. "Have two pistols, one loaded and the other empty. Simpson and I would take our choice without knowing which was which. Then we stand within a yard of each other, and at the word we fire."

"My God!" said Danvers.

"I don't think that would be legal," said Preston. "It would mean one of you would be killed for certain."

"Killing is the object of duelling," said Hornblower. "If the conditions aren't unfair I don't think any objection can be raised."

"But would you carry it out to the end?" marvelled Danvers.

"Mr. Danvers—" began Hornblower; but Preston interfered.

"We don't want another duel on our hands," he said. "Danvers only meant he wouldn't care to do it himself. We'll discuss it with Cleveland and Hether, and see what they say."

Within an hour the proposed conditions of the duel were known to everyone in the ship. Perhaps it was to Simpson's disadvantage that he had no real friend in the ship, for Cleveland and Hether, his seconds, were not disposed to take too firm a stand regarding the conditions of the duel, and agreed to the terms with only a show of reluctance. The tyrant of the midshipmen's berth was paying the penalty for his tyranny. There was some cynical amusement shown by some of the officers; some of both officers and men eyed Hornblower and Simpson with the curiosity that the prospect of death excites in some minds, as if the two destined opponents were men condemned to the gallows. At noon Lieutenant Masters sent for Hornblower.

"The captain has ordered me to make inquiry into this duel, Mr. Hornblower," he said. "I am instructed to use my best endeavours to compose the quarrel."

"Yes, sir."

"Why insist on this satisfaction, Mr. Hornblower? I understand there were a few hasty words over wine and cards."

"Mr. Simpson accused me of cheating, sir, before witnesses who were not officers of this ship."

That was the point. The witnesses were not members of the ship's company. If Hornblower had chosen to disregard Simpson's words as the ramblings of a drunken ill-tempered man, they might have passed unnoticed. But as he had taken the stand he did, there could be no hushing it up now, and Hornblower knew it.

"Even so, there can be satisfaction without a duel, Mr. Hornblower."

"If Mr. Simpson will make me a full apology before the same gentlemen, I would be satisfied, sir."

Simpson was no coward. He would die rather than submit to such a formal humiliation.

"I see. Now I understand you are insisting on rather unusual conditions for the duel?"

"There are precedents for it, sir. As the insulted party I can choose any conditions which are not unfair."

"You sound like a sea lawyer to me, Mr. Hornblower."

The hint was sufficient to tell Hornblower that he had verged upon being too glib, and he resolved in future to bridle his tongue. He stood silent and waited for Masters to resume the conversation.

"You are determined, then, Mr. Hornblower, to continue with this murderous business?"

"Yes, sir."

"The captain has given me further orders to attend the duel in person, because of the strange conditions on which you insist. I must inform you that I shall request the seconds to arrange for that."

"Yes, sir."

"Very good, then, Mr. Hornblower."

Masters looked at Hornblower as he dismissed him even more keenly than he had done when Hornblower first came on board. He was looking for signs of weakness or wavering—indeed, he was looking for any signs of human feeling at all—but he could detect none. Hornblower had reached a decision, he had weighed all the pros and cons, and his logical mind told him that having decided in cold blood upon a course of action it would be folly to allow himself to be influenced subsequently by untrustworthy emotions. The conditions of the duel on which he was insisting were mathematically advantageous. If he had once considered with favour escaping from Simpson's persecution by a voluntary death it was surely a gain to take an even chance of escaping from it without dying. Similarly, if Simpson were (as he almost certainly was) a better swordsman and a better pistol shot than him, the even chance was again mathematically advantageous. There was nothing to regret about his recent actions.

All very well; mathematically the conclusions were irrefutable, but Hornblower was surprised to find that mathematics were not everything. Repeatedly during that dreary afternoon and evening Hornblower found himself suddenly gulping with anxiety as the realization came to him afresh that tomorrow morning he would be risking his life on the spin of a coin. One chance out of two and he would be dead, his consciousness at an end, his flesh cold, and the world, almost unbelievably, would be going on without him. The thought sent a shiver through him despite himself. And he had plenty of time for these reflections, for the convention that forbade him from encountering his destined opponent before the moment of the duel kept him necessarily in isolation, as far as isolation could be found on the crowded decks of the *Justinian*. He slung his hammock that night in a depressed mood, feeling unnaturally tired; and he undressed in the clammy, stuffy dampness of the 'tween-decks feeling more than usually cold. He hugged the blankets round himself, yearning to relax in their warmth, but relaxation would not come. Time after time as he began to drift off to sleep he woke again tense and anxious, full of thoughts of the morrow. He turned over wearily a dozen times, hearing the ship's bell ring out each half hour, feeling a growing contempt at his cowardice. He told himself in the end that it was as well that his fate tomorrow depended upon pure chance, for if he had to rely upon steadiness of hand and eye he would be dead for certain after a night like this.

That conclusion presumably helped him to go to sleep for the last hour or two of the night, for he awoke with a start to find Danvers shaking him.

"Five bells," said Danvers. "Dawn in an hour. Rise and shine!"

Hornblower slid out of his hammock and stood in his shirt; the 'tweendecks was nearly dark and Danvers was almost invisible.

"Number One's letting us have the second cutter," said Danvers. "Masters and Simpson and that lot are going first in the launch. Here's Preston."

Another shadowy figure loomed up in the darkness.

"Hellish cold," said Preston. "The devil of a morning to turn out. Nelson, where's that tea?"

The mess attendant came with it as Hornblower was hauling on his trousers. It maddened Hornblower that he shivered enough in the cold for the cup to clatter in the saucer as he took it. But the tea was grateful, and Hornblower drank it eagerly.

"Give me another cup," he said, and was proud of himself that he could think about tea at that moment.

It was still dark as they went down into the cutter.

"Shove off," said the coxswain, and the boat pushed off from the ship's side. There was a keen cold wind blowing which filled the dipping lug as the cutter headed for the twin lights that marked the jetty.

"I ordered a hackney coach at the George to be waiting for us," said Danvers. "Let's hope it is."

It was there, with the driver sufficiently sober to control his horse moderately well despite his overnight potations. Danvers produced a pocket flask as they settled themselves in with their feet in the straw.

"Take a sip, Hornblower?" he asked, proffering it. "There's no special need for a steady hand this morning."

"No thank you," said Hornblower. His empty stomach revolted at the idea of pouring spirits into it.

"The others will be there before us," commented Preston. "I saw the quarter boat heading back just before we reached the jetty."

The etiquette of the duel demanded that the two opponents should reach the ground separately; but only one boat would be necessary for the return.

"The sawbones is with them," said Danvers. "Though God knows what use he thinks he'll be today."

He sniggered, and with overlate politeness tried to cut his snigger off short.

"How are you feeling, Hornblower?" asked Preston.

"Well enough," said Hornblower, forbearing to add that he only felt well enough while this kind of conversation was not being carried on.

The hackney coach levelled itself off as it came over the crest of the hill, and stopped beside the common. Another coach stood there waiting, its single candle-lamp burning yellow in the growing dawn.

"There they are," said Preston; the faint light revealed a shadowy group standing on frosty turf among the gorse bushes.

Hornblower, as they approached, caught a glimpse of Simpson's face as he stood a little detached from the others. It was pale, and Hornblower noticed that at that moment he swallowed nervously, just as he himself was doing. Masters came towards them, shooting his usual keen inquisitive look at Hornblower as they came together.

"This is the moment," he said, "for this quarrel to be composed. This country is at war. I hope, Mr. Hornblower, that you can be persuaded to save a life for the King's service by not pressing this matter."

Hornblower looked across at Simpson, while Danvers answered for him.

"Has Mr. Simpson offered the proper redress?" asked Danvers.

"Mr. Simpson is willing to acknowledge that he wishes the incident had never taken place."

"That is an unsatisfactory form," said Danvers. "It does not include an apology, and you must agree that an apology is necessary, sir."

"What does your principal say?" persisted Masters.

"It is not for any principal to speak in these circumstances," said Danvèrs, with a glance at Hornblower, who nodded. All this was as inevitable as the ride in the hangman's cart, and as hideous. There could be no going back now; Hornblower had never thought for one moment that Simpson would apologize, and without an apology the affair must be carried to a bloody conclusion. An even chance that he did not have five minutes longer to live.

"You are determined, then, gentlemen," said Masters. "I shall have to state that fact in my report."

"We are determined," said Preston.

"Then there is nothing for it but to allow this deplorable affair to proceed. I left the pistols in the charge of Doctor Hepplewhite."

He turned and led them towards the other group—Simpson with Hether and Cleveland, and Doctor Hepplewhite standing with a pistol held by the muzzle in each hand. He was a bulky man with the red face of a persistent drinker; he was actually grinning a spirituous grin at that moment, rocking a little on his feet.

"Are the young fools set in their folly?" he asked; but everyone very properly ignored him as having no business to ask such a question at such a moment.

"Now," said Masters. "Here are the pistols, both primed, as you see, but one loaded and the other unloaded, in accordance with the conditions. I have here a guinea which I propose to spin to decide the allocation of the weapons. Now, gentlemen, shall the spin give your principals one pistol each irrevocably—for instance, if the coin shows heads shall Mr. Simpson have this one—or shall the winner of the spin have choice of weapons? It is my design to eliminate all possibility of collusion as far as possible."

Hether and Cleveland and Danvers and Preston exchanged dubious glances.

"Let the winner of the spin choose," said Preston at length.

"Very well, gentlemen. Please call, Mr. Hornblower."

"Tails!" said Hornblower as the gold piece spun in the air.

Masters caught it and clapped a hand over it.

"Tails it is," said Masters, lifting his hand and revealing the coin to the grouped seconds. "Please make your choice."

Hepplewhite held out the two pistols to him, death in one hand and life in the other. It was a grim moment. There was only pure chance to direct him; it called for a little effort to force his hand out.

"I'll have this one," he said; as he touched it the weapon seemed icy cold.

"Then now I have done what was required of me," said Masters. "The rest is for you gentlemen to carry out."

"Take this one, Simpson," said Hepplewhite. "And be careful how you handle yours, Mr. Hornblower. You're a public danger."

The man was still grinning, gloating over the fact that someone else was in mortal danger while he himself was in none. Simpson took the pistol Hepplewhite offered him and settled it into his hand; once more his eyes met Hornblower's, but there was neither recognition nor expression in them.

"There are no distances to step out," Danvers was saying. "One spot's as good as another. It's level enough here."

"Very good," said Hether. "Will you stand here, Mr. Simpson?"

Preston beckoned to Hornblower, who walked over. It was not easy to appear brisk and unconcerned. Preston took him by the arm and stood him up in front of Simpson, almost breast to breast—close enough to smell the alcohol on his breath.

"For the last time, gentlemen," said Masters loudly. "Cannot you be reconciled?"

There was no answer from anybody, only deep silence, during which it seemed to Hornblower that the frantic beating of his heart must be clearly audible. The silence was broken by an exclamation from Hether.

"We haven't settled who's to give the word!" he said. "Who's going to?"

"Let's ask Mr. Masters to give it," said Danvers.

Hornblower did not look round. He was looking steadfastly at the grey sky past Simpson's right ear—somehow he could not look him in the face, and he had no idea where Simpson was looking. The end of the world as he knew it was close to him—soon there might be a bullet through his heart.

"I will do it if you are agreed, gentlemen," he heard Masters say.

The grey sky was featureless; for this last look on the world he might as well have been blindfolded. Masters raised his voice again.

"I will say 'one, two, three, fire'," he announced, "with those intervals. At the last word, gentlemen, you can fire as you will. Are you ready?"

"Yes," came Simpson's voice, almost in Hornblower's ear, it seemed.

"Yes," said Hornblower. He could hear the strain in his own voice.

"One," said Masters, and Hornblower felt at that moment the muzzle of Simpson's pistol against his left ribs, and he raised his own.

It was in that second that he decided he could not kill Simpson even if it were in his power, and he went on lifting his pistol, forcing himself to look to see that it was pressed against the point of Simpson's shoulder. A slight wound would suffice.

"Two," said Masters. "Three. Fire!"

Hornblower pulled his trigger. There was a click and a spurt of smoke from the lock of his pistol. The priming had gone off but no more—his was the unloaded weapon, and he knew what it was to die. A tenth of a second later there was a click and spurt of smoke from Simpson's pistol against his heart. Stiff and still they both stood, slow to realize what had happened.

"A miss-fire, by God!" said Danvers.

The seconds crowded round them.

"Give me those pistols!" said Masters, taking them from the weak hands that held them. "The loaded one might be hanging fire, and we don't want it to go off now."

"Which was the loaded one?" asked Hether, consumed with curiosity.

"That is something it is better not to know," answered Masters, changing the two pistols rapidly from hand to hand so as to confuse everyone.

"What about a second shot?" asked Danvers, and Masters looked up straight and inflexibly at him.

"There will be no second shot," he said. "Honour is completely satisfied. These two gentlemen have come through this ordeal extremely well. No one can now think little of Mr. Simpson if he expresses his regret for the occurrence, and no one can think little of Mr. Hornblower if he accepts that statement in reparation."

Hepplewhite burst into a roar of laughter.

"Your faces!" he boomed, slapping his thigh. "You ought to see how you all look! Solemn as cows!"

"Mr. Hepplewhite," said Masters, "your behaviour is indecorous. Gentlemen, our coaches are waiting on the road, the cutter is at the jetty. And I think all of us would be the better for some breakfast; including Mr. Hepplewhite."

That should have been the end of the incident. The excited talk which had gone round the anchored squadron about the unusual duel died away in time, although everyone knew Hornblower's name now, and not as the midshipman who was seasick in Spithead but as the man who was willing to take an even chance in cold blood. But in the *Justinian* herself there was other talk; whispers which were circulated forward and aft.

"Mr. Hornblower has requested permission to speak to you, sir," said Mr. Clay, the first lieutenant, one morning while making his report to the captain.

"Oh, send him in when you go out," said Keene, and sighed.

Ten minutes later a knock on his cabin door ushered in a very angry young man.

"Sir!" began Hornblower.

"I can guess what you're going to say," said Keene.

"Those pistols in the duel I fought with Simpson were not loaded!"

"Hepplewhite blabbed, I suppose," said Keene.

"And it was by your orders, I understand, sir."

"You are quite correct. I gave those orders to Mr. Masters."

"It was an unwarrantable liberty, sir!"

That was what Hornblower meant to say, but he stumbled without dignity over the polysyllables.

"Possibly it was," said Keene patiently, rearranging, as always, the papers on his desk.

The calmness of the admission disconcerted Hornblower, who could only splutter for the next few moments.

"I saved a life for the King's service," went on Keene, when the spluttering died away. "A young life. No one has suffered any harm. On the other hand, both you and Simpson have had your courage amply proved. You both know you can stand fire now, and so does every one else."

"You have touched my personal honour, sir," said Hornblower, bringing out one of his rehearsed speeches, "for that there can only be one remedy."

"Restrain yourself, please, Mr. Hornblower." Keene shifted himself in his chair with a wince of pain as he prepared to make a speech. "I must remind you of one salutary regulation of the Navy, to the effect that no junior officer can challenge his superior to a duel. The reasons for it are obvious—otherwise promotion would be too easy. The mere issuing of a challenge by a junior to a senior is a court-martial offence, Mr. Hornblower."

"Oh!" said Hornblower feebly.

"Now here is some gratuitous advice," went on Keene. "You have fought one duel and emerged with honour. That is good. Never fight another—that is better. Some people, oddly enough, acquire a taste for duelling, as a tiger acquires a taste for blood. They are never good officers, and never popular ones either."

It was then that Hornblower realized that a great part of the keen excitement with which he had entered the captain's cabin was due to anticipation of the giving of the challenge. There could be a morbid desire for danger—and a morbid desire to occupy momentarily the centre of the stage. Keene was waiting for him to speak, and it was hard to say anything.

"I understand, sir," he said at last.

Keene shifted in his chair again.

"There is another matter I wanted to take up with you, Mr. Hornblower. Captain Pellew of the *Indefatigable* has room for another midshipman. Captain Pellew is partial to a game of whist, and has no good fourth on board. He and I have agreed to consider favourably your application for a transfer should you care to make one. I don't have to point out that any ambitious young officer would jump at the chance of serving in a frigate."

"A frigate!" said Hornblower.

Everybody knew of Pellew's reputation and success. Distinction, promotion, prize money—an officer under Pellew's command could hope for all these. Competition for nomination to the *Indefatigable* must be intense, and this was the chance of a lifetime. Hornblower was on the point of making a glad acceptance, when further considerations restrained him.

"That is very good of you, sir," he said. "I do not know how to thank you. But you accepted me as a midshipman here, and of course I must stay with you."

The drawn, apprehensive face relaxed into a smile.

"Not many men would have said that," said Keene. "But I am going to insist on your accepting the offer. I shall not live very much longer to appreciate your loyalty. And this ship is not the place for you —this ship with her useless captain—don't interrupt me—and her worn-out first lieutenant and her old midshipmen. You should be where there may be speedy opportunities of advancement. I have the good of the service in mind, Mr. Hornblower, when I suggest you accept Captain Pellew's invitation—and it might be less disturbing for me if you did."

"Aye aye, sir," said Hornblower.

THE CARGO OF RICE

The wolf was in among the sheep. The tossing grey water of the Bay of Biscay was dotted with white sails as far as the eye could see, and although a strong breeze was blowing every vessel was under perilously heavy canvas. Every ship but one was trying to escape; the exception was His Majesty's frigate *Indefatigable*, Captain Sir Edward Pellew. Farther out in the Atlantic, hundreds of miles away, a great battle was being fought, where the ships of the line were thrashing out the question as to whether England or France should wield the weapon of sea power; here in the Bay the convoy which the French ships were intended to escort was exposed to the attack of a ship of prey at liberty to capture any ship she could overhaul. She had come surging up from leeward, cutting off all chance of escape in that direction, and the clumsy merchant ships were forced to beat to windward; they were all filled with the food which revolutionary France (her economy disordered by the convulsion through which she was passing) was awaiting so anxiously, and their crews were all anxious to escape confinement in an English prison. Ship after ship was overhauled; a shot or two, and the newfangled tricolour came fluttering down from the gaff, and a prize-crew was hurriedly sent on board to conduct the captive to an English port while the frigate dashed after fresh prey.

On the quarterdeck of the *Indefatigable* Pellew fumed over each necessary delay. The convoy, each ship as close to the wind as she would lie, and under all the sail she could carry, was slowly scattering, spreading farther and farther with the passing minutes, and some of these would find safety in mere dispersion if any time was wasted. Pellew did not wait to pick up his boat; at each surrender he merely ordered away an officer and an armed guard, and the moment the prize-crew was on its way he filled his main-topsail again and hurried off after the next victim. The brig they were pursuing at the moment was slow to surrender. The long nine-pounders in the *Indefatigable's* bows bellowed out more than once; on that heaving sea it was not so easy to aim accurately and the brig continued on her course hoping for some miracle to save her.

"Very well," snapped Pellew. "He has asked for it. Let him have it."

The gunlayers at the bow chasers changed their point of aim, firing at the ship instead of across her bows.

"Not into the hull, damn it," shouted Pellew—one shot had struck the brig perilously close to her waterline. "Cripple her."

The next shot by luck or by judgment was given better elevation. The slings of the foretopsail yard were shot away, the reefed sail came down, the yard hanging lopsidedly, and the brig came up into the wind for the *Indefatigable* to heave to close beside her, her broadside ready to fire into her. Under that threat her flag came down.

"What brig's that?" shouted Pellew through his megaphone.

"*Marie Galante* of Bordeaux," translated the officer beside Pellew as the French captain made reply. "Twenty-four days out from New Orleans with rice."

"Rice!" said Pellew. "That'll sell for a pretty penny when we get her home. Two hundred tons, I should say. Twelve of a crew at most. She'll need a prize-crew of four, a midshipman's command."

He looked round him as though for inspiration before giving his next order.

"Mr. Hornblower!"

"Sir!"

"Take four men of the cutter's crew and board that brig. Mr. Soames will give you our position. Take her into any English port you can make, and report there for orders."

"Aye aye, sir."

Hornblower was at his station at the starboard quarter-deck carronades—which was perhaps how he had caught Pellew's eye—his dirk at his side and a pistol in his belt. It was a moment for fast thinking, for anyone could see Pellew's impatience. With the *Indefatigable* cleared for action, his sea chest would be part of the surgeon's operating table down below, so that there was no chance of getting anything out of it. He would have to leave just as he was. The cutter was even now clawing up to a position on the *Indefatigable's* quarter, so he ran to the ship's side and hailed her, trying to make his voice sound as big and as manly as he could, and at the word of the lieutenant in command she turned her bows in towards the frigate.

"Here's our latitude and longitude, Mr. Hornblower," said Soames, the master, handing a scrap of paper to him.

"Thank you," said Hornblower, shoving it into his pocket.

He scrambled awkwardly into the mizzen-chains and looked down into the cutter. Ship and boat were pitching together, almost bows on to the sea, and the distance between them looked appallingly great; the bearded seaman standing in the bows could only just reach up to the chains with his long boat-hook. Hornblower hesitated for a long second; he knew he was ungainly and awkward—book learning was of no use when it came to jumping into a boat—but he had to make the leap, for Pellew was fuming behind him and the eyes of the boat's crew and of the whole ship's company were on him. Better to jump and hurt himself, better to jump and make an exhibition of himself, than to delay the ship. Waiting was certain failure, while he still had a choice if he jumped. Perhaps at a word from Pellew the *Indefatigable's* helmsman allowed the ship's head to fall off from the sea a little. A somewhat diagonal wave lifted the *Indefatigable's* stern and then passed on, so that the cutter's bows rose as the ship's stern sank a trifle. Hornblower braced himself and leaped. His feet reached the gunwale and he tottered there for one indescribable second. A seaman grabbed the breast of his jacket and he fell forward rather than backward. Not even the stout arm of the seaman, fully extended, could hold him up, and he pitched headforemost, legs in the air, upon the hands on the second thwart. He cannoned onto their bodies, knocking the breath out of his own against their muscular shoulders, and finally struggled into an upright position.

"I'm sorry," he gasped to the men who had broken his fall.

"Never you mind, sir," said the nearest one, a real tarry sailor, tattooed and pigtailed. "You're only a featherweight."

The lieutenant in command was looking at him from the sternsheets.

"Would you go to the brig, please, sir?" he asked, and the lieutenant bawled an order and the cutter swung round as Hornblower made his way aft.

It was a pleasant surprise not to be received with the broad grins of tolerantly concealed amusement. Boarding a small boat from a big frigate in even a moderate sea was no easy matter; probably every man on board had arrived headfirst at some time or other, and it was not in the tradition of the service, as understood in the *Indefatigable*, to laugh at a man who did his best without shirking.

"Are you taking charge of the brig?" asked the lieutenant.

"Yes, sir. The captain told me to take four of your men."

"They had better be topmen, then," said the lieutenant, casting his eyes aloft at the rigging of the brig. The foretopsail yard was hanging precariously, and the jib halliard had slacked off so that the sail was flapping thunderously in the wind. "Do you know these men, or shall I pick 'em for you?"

"I'd be obliged if you would, sir."

The lieutenant shouted four names, and four men replied.

"Keep 'em away from drink and they'll be all right," said the lieutenant. "Watch the French crew. They'll recapture the ship and have you in a French gaol before you can say 'Jack Robinson' if you don't."

"Aye aye, sir," said Hornblower.

The cutter surged alongside the brig, white water creaming between the two vessels. The tattooed sailor hastily concluded a bargain with another man on his thwart and pocketed a lump of tobacco—the men were leaving their possessions behind just like Hornblower—and sprang for the mainchains. Another man followed him, and they stood and waited while Hornblower with difficulty made his way forward along the plunging boat. He stood, balancing precariously, on the forward thwart. The mainchains of the brig were far lower than the mizzenchains of the *Indefatigable*, but this time he had to jump upwards. One of the seamen steadied him with an arm on his shoulder.

"Wait for it, sir," he said. "Get ready. Now jump, sir."

Hornblower hurled himself, all arms and legs, like a leaping frog, at the mainchains. His hands reached the shrouds, but his knee slipped off, and the brig, rolling, lowered him thigh deep into the sea as the shrouds slipped through his hands. But the waiting seamen grabbed his wrists and hauled him on board, and two more seamen followed him. He led the way onto the deck.

The first sight to meet his eyes was a man seated on the hatch cover, his head thrown back, holding to his mouth a bottle, the bottom pointing straight up to the sky. He was one of a large group all sitting round the hatch cover; there were more bottles in evidence; one was passed by one man to another as he looked, and as he approached a roll of the ship brought an empty bottle rolling past his toes to clatter into the scuppers. Another of the group, with white hair blowing in the wind, rose to welcome him, and stood for a moment with waving arms and rolling eyes, bracing himself as though to say something of immense importance and seeking earnestly for the right words to use.

"Goddam English," was what he finally said, and, having said it, he sat down with a bump on the hatch cover and from a seated position proceeded to lie down and compose himself to sleep with his head on his arms.

"They've made the best of their time, sir, by the Holy," said the seaman at Hornblower's elbow.

"Wish we were as happy," said another.

A case still a quarter full of bottles, each elaborately sealed, stood on the deck beside the hatch cover, and the seaman picked out a bottle to look at it curiously. Hornblower did not need to remember the lieutenant's warning; on his shore excursions with press gangs he had already had experience of the British seaman's tendency to drink. His boarding party would be as drunk as the Frenchmen in half an hour if he allowed it. A frightful mental picture of himself drifting into the Bay of Biscay with a disabled ship and a drunken crew rose in his mind and filled him with anxiety.

"Put that down," he ordered.

The urgency of the situation made his seventeen-year-old voice crack like a fourteen-year-old's, and the seaman hesitated, holding the bottle in his hand.

"Put it down, d'ye hear?" said Hornblower, desperate with worry. This was his first independent command; conditions were absolutely novel, and excitement brought out all the passion of his mercurial temperament, while at the same time the more calculating part of his mind told him that if he were not obeyed now he never would be. His pistol was in his belt, and he put his hand on the butt, and it is conceivable that he would have drawn it and used it (if the priming had not got wet, he said to himself bitterly when he thought about the incident later on), but the seaman with one more glance at him put the bottle back into the case. The incident was closed, and it was time for the next step.

"Take these men forrard," he said, giving the obvious order. "Throw 'em into the forecastle."

"Aye aye, sir."

Most of the Frenchmen could still walk, but three were dragged by their collars, while the British herded the others before them.

"Come alongee," said one of the seamen. "Thisa waya."

He evidently believed a Frenchman would understand him better if he spoke like that. The Frenchman who had greeted their arrival now awakened, and, suddenly realizing he was being dragged forward, broke away and turned back to Hornblower.

"I officer," he said, pointing to himself. "I not go wit' zem."

"Take him away!" said Hornblower. In his tense condition he could not stop to debate trifles.

He dragged the case of bottles down to the ship's side and pitched them overboard two at a time—obviously it was wine of some special vintage which the Frenchmen had decided to drink before the English could get their hands on it, but that weighed not at all with Hornblower, for a British seaman could get drunk on vintage claret as easily as upon service rum. The task was finished before the last of the Frenchmen disappeared into the forecastle, and Hornblower had time to look about him. The strong breeze blew confusingly round his ears, and the cease-less thunder of the flapping jib made it hard to think as he looked at the ruin aloft. Every sail was flat aback, the brig was moving jerkily, gathering sternway for a space before her untended rudder threw her round to spill the wind and bring her up again like a jibbing horse. His mathematical mind had already had plenty of experience with a well-handled ship, with the delicate adjustment between after sails and head-sails. Here the balance had been disturbed, and Hornblower was at work on the problem of forces acting on plane surfaces when his men came trooping back to him. One thing at least was certain, and that was that the precariously hanging foretopsail yard would tear itself free to do all sorts of unforeseeable damage if it were tossed about much more. The ship must be properly hove to, and Hornblower could guess how to set about it, and he formulated the order in his mind just in time to avoid any appearance of hesitation.

"Brace the after yards to larboard," he said. "Man the braces, men."

They obeyed him, while he himself went gingerly to the wheel; he had served a few tricks as helmsman, learning his professional duties under Pellew's orders, but he did not feel happy about it. The spokes felt foreign to his fingers as he took hold; he spun the wheel experi-mentally but timidly. But it was easy. With the after yards braced round the brig rode more comfortably at once, and the spokes told their own story to his sensitive fingers as the ship became a thing of logical con-struction again. Hornblower's mind completed the solution of the pro-blem of the effect of the rudder at the same time as his senses solved it empirically. The wheel could be safely lashed, he knew, in these con-ditions, and he slipped the becket over the spoke and stepped away from the wheel, with the *Marie Galante* riding comfortably and taking the seas on her starboard bow.

The seamen took his competence gratifyingly for granted, but Horn-blower, looking at the tangle on the foremast, had not the remotest idea of how to deal with the next problem. He was not even sure about what was wrong. But the hands under his orders were seamen of vast experi-ence, who must have dealt with similar emergencies a score of times.

The first—indeed the only—thing to do was to delegate his responsibility.

"Who's the oldest seaman among you?" he demanded—his determination not to quaver made him curt.

"Matthews, sir," said someone at length, indicating with his thumb the pigtailed and tattooed seaman upon whom he had fallen in the cutter.

"Very well, then. I'll rate you petty officer, Matthews. Get to work at once and clear that raffle away forrard. I'll be busy here aft."

It was a nervous moment for Hornblower, but Matthews put his knuckles to his forehead.

"Aye aye, sir," he said, quite as a matter of course.

"Get that jib in first, before it flogs itself to pieces," said Hornblower, greatly emboldened.

"Aye aye, sir."

"Carry on, then."

The seaman turned to go forward, and Hornblower walked aft. He took the telescope from its becket on the poop, and swept the horizon. There were a few sails in sight; the nearest ones he could recognize as prizes, which, with all sail set that they could carry, were heading for England as fast as they could go. Far away to windward he could see the *Indefatigable's* topsails as she clawed after the rest of the convoy—she had already overhauled and captured all the slower and less weatherly vessels, so that each succeeding chase would be longer. Soon he would be alone on this wide sea, three hundred miles from England. Three hundred miles—two days with a fair wind; but how long if the wind turned foul?

He replaced the telescope; the men were already hard at work forward, so he went below and looked round the neat cabins of the officers; two single ones for the captain and the mate, presumably, and a double one for the bos'un and the cook or the carpenter. He found the lazarette, identifying it by the miscellaneous stores within it; the door was swinging to and fro with a bunch of keys dangling. The French captain, faced with the loss of all he possessed, had not even troubled to lock the door again after taking out the case of wine. Hornblower locked the door and put the keys in his pocket, and felt suddenly lonely—his first experience of the loneliness of the man in command at sea. He went on deck again, and at sight of him Matthews hurried aft and knuckled his forehead.

"Beg pardon, sir, but we'll have to use the jeers to sling that yard again."

"Very good."

"We'll need more hands than we have, sir. Can I put some o' they Frenchies to work?"

"If you think you can. If any of them are sober enough,"

"I think I can, sir. Drunk or sober."

"Very good."

It was at that moment that Hornblower remembered with bitter self-reproach that the priming of his pistol was probably wet, and he had not scorn enough for himself at having put his trust in a pistol without repriming after evolutions in a small boat. While Matthews went forward he dashed below again. There was a case of pistols which he remembered having seen in the captain's cabin, with a powder flask and bullet bag hanging beside it. He loaded both weapons and reprimed his own, and came on deck again with three pistols in his belt just as his men appeared from the forecastle herding half a dozen Frenchmen. He posted himself in the poop, straddling with his hands behind his back, trying to adopt an air of magnificent indifference and understanding. With the jeers taking the weight of yard and sail, an hour's hard work resulted in the yard being slung again and the sail reset.

When the work was advancing towards completion, Hornblower came to himself again to remember that in a few minutes he would have to set a course, and he dashed below again to set out the chart and the dividers and parallel rulers. From his pocket he extracted the crumpled scrap of paper with his position on it—he had thrust it in there so carelessly a little while back, at a time when the immediate problem before him was to transfer himself from the *Indefatigable* to the cutter. It made him unhappy to think how cavalierly he had treated that scrap of paper then; he began to feel that life in the Navy, although it seemed to move from one crisis to another, was really one continuous crisis, that even while dealing with one emergency it was necessary to be making plans to deal with the next. He bent over the chart, plotted his position, and laid off his course. It was a queer uncomfortable feeling to think that what had up to this moment been an academic exercise conducted under the reassuring supervision of Mr. Soames was now something on which hinged his life and his reputation. He checked his working, decided on his course, and wrote it down on a scrap of paper for fear he should forget it.

So when the foretopsail yard was re-slung, and the prisoners herded back into the forecastle, and Matthews looked to him for further orders, he was ready.

"We'll square away," he said. "Matthews, send a man to the wheel."

He himself gave a hand at the braces; the wind had moderated and he felt his men could handle the brig under her present sail.

"What course, sir?" asked the man at the wheel, and Hornblower dived into his pocket for his scrap of paper.

"Nor'-east by north," he said, reading it out.

"Nor'-east by north, sir," said the helmsman; and the *Marie Galante*, running free, set her course for England.

Night was closing in by now, and all round the circle of the horizon there was not a sail in sight. There must be plenty of ships just over the horizon, he knew, but that did not do much to ease his feeling of loneliness as darkness came on. There was so much to do, so much to bear in mind, and all the responsibility lay on his unaccustomed shoulders. The prisoners had to be battened down in the forecastle, a watch had to be set—there was even the trivial matter of hunting up flint and steel to light the binnacle lamp. A hand forward as a lookout, who could also keep an eye on the prisoners below; a hand aft at the wheel. Two hands snatching some sleep—knowing that to get in any sail would be an all-hands job—a hasty meal of water from the scuttle-butt and of biscuit from the cabin stores in the lazarette—a constant eye to be kept on the weather. Hornblower paced the deck in the darkness.

"Why don't you get some sleep, sir?" asked the man at the wheel.

"I will, later on, Hunter," said Hornblower, trying not to allow his tone to reveal the fact that such a thing had never occurred to him.

He knew it was sensible advice, and he actually tried to follow it, retiring below to fling himself down on the captain's cot; but of course he could not sleep. When he heard the lookout bawling down the companionway to rouse the other two hands to relieve the watch (they were asleep in the next cabin to him) he could not prevent himself from getting up again and coming on deck to see that all was well. With Matthews in charge he felt he should not be anxious, and he drove himself below again, but he had hardly fallen onto the cot again when a new thought brought him to his feet again, his skin cold with anxiety, and a prodigious self-contempt vying with anxiety for first place in his motions. He rushed on deck and walked forward to where Matthews was squatting by the knightheads.

"Nothing has been done to see if the brig is taking in any water," he said—he had hurriedly worked out the wording of that sentence during his walk forward, so as to cast no aspersion on Matthews and yet at the same time, for the sake of discipline, attributing no blame to himself.

"That's so, sir," said Matthews.

"One of those shots fired by the *Indefatigable* hulled her," went on Hornblower. "What damage did it do?"

"I don't rightly know, sir," said Matthews. "I was in the cutter at the time."

"We must look as soon as it's light," said Hornblower, "and we'd better sound the well now."

Those were brave words; during his rapid course in seamanship aboard the *Indefatigable* Hornblower had had a little instruction every-where, working under the orders of every head of department in rota-tion. Once he had been with the carpenter when he sounded the well—whether he could find the well in this ship and sound it he did not know.

"Aye aye, sir," said Matthews, without hesitation, and strolled aft to the pump. "You'll need a light, sir. I'll get one."

When he came back with the lantern he shone it on the coiled sound-ing line hanging beside the pump, so that Hornblower recognized it at once. He lifted it down, inserted the three-foot weighted rod into the aperture of the well, and then remembered in time to take it out again and make sure it was dry. Then he let it drop, paying out the line until he felt the rod strike the ship's bottom with a satisfactory thud. He hauled out the line again, and Matthews held the lantern as Hornblower with some trepidation brought out the timber to examine it.

"Not a drop, sir!" said Matthews. "Dry as yesterday's pannikin."

Hornblower was agreeably surprised. Any ship he had ever heard of leaked to a certain extent; even in the well-found *Indefatigable* pump-ing had been necessary every day. He did not know whether this dry-ness was a remarkable phenomenon or a very remarkable one. He wanted to be both noncommittal and imperturbable.

"Hm," was the comment he eventually produced. "Very good, Matthews. Coil that line again."

The knowledge that the *Marie Galante* was making no water at all might have encouraged him to sleep, if the wind had not chosen to veer steadily and strengthen itself somewhat soon after he retired again. It was Matthews who came down and pounded on his door with the un-welcome news.

"We can't keep the course you set much longer, sir," concluded Matthews. "And the wind's coming gusty-like."

"Very good, I'll be up. Call all hands," said Hornblower, with a testiness that might have been the result of a sudden awakening if it had not really disguised his inner quaverings.

With such a small crew he dared not run the slightest risk of being taken by surprise by the weather. Nothing could be done in a hurry, as he soon found. He had to take the wheel while his four hands laboured at reefing topsails and snugging the brig down; the task took half the night, and by the time it was finished it was quite plain that with the wind veering northerly the *Marie Galante* could not steer north-east by north any longer. Hornblower gave up the wheel and went be-low to the chart, but what he saw there only confirmed the pessimistic decision he had already reached by mental calculation. As close to the wind as they could lie on this tack they could not weather Ushant. Short-handed as he was he did not dare continue in the hope that the wind might back; all his reading and all his instruction had warned him of the terrors of a lee shore. There was nothing for it but to go about; he returned to the deck with a heavy heart.

"All hands wear ship," he said, trying to bellow the order in the manner of Mr. Bolton, the third lieutenant of the *Indefatigable*.

They brought the brig safely round, and she took up her new course, close hauled on the starboard tack. Now she was heading away from the dangerous shores of France, without a doubt, but she was heading nearly as directly away from the friendly shores of England—gone was all hope of an easy two days' run to England; gone was any hope of sleep that night for Hornblower.

During the year before he joined the Navy Hornblower had attended classes given by a penniless French émigré in French, music, and dancing. Early enough the wretched émigré had found that Hornblower had no ear for music whatever, which made it almost impossible to teach him to dance, and so he had endeavoured to earn his fee by concentrating on French. A good deal of what he had taught Hornblower had found a permanent resting place in Hornblower's tenacious memory. He had never thought it would be of much use to him, but he discovered the contrary when the French captain at dawn insisted on an interview with him. The Frenchman had a little English, but it was a pleasant surprise to Hornblower to find that they actually could get along better in French, as soon as he could fight down his shyness sufficiently to produce the halting words.

The captain drank thirstily from the scuttlebutt; his cheeks were of course unshaven and he wore a bleary look after twelve hours in a crowded forecastle, where he had been battened down three parts drunk.

"My men are hungry," said the captain; he did not look hungry himself.

"Mine also," said Hornblower. "I also."

It was natural when one spoke French to gesticulate, to indicate his men with a wave of the hand and himself with a tap on the chest.

"I have a cook," said the captain.

It took some time to arrange the terms of a truce. The Frenchmen were to be allowed on deck, the cook was to provide food for everyone on board, and while these amenities were permitted, until noon, the French would make no attempt to take the ship.

"Good," said the captain at length; and when Hornblower had given the necessary orders permitting the release of the crew he shouted for the cook and entered into an urgent discussion regarding dinner. Soon smoke was issuing satisfactorily from the galley chimney.

Then the captain looked up at the grey sky, at the close reefed topsails, and glanced into the binnacle at the compass.

"A foul wind for England," he remarked.

"Yes," said Hornblower shortly. He did not want this Frenchman to guess at his trepidation and bitterness.

The captain seemed to be feeling the motion of the brig under his feet with attention.

"She rides a little heavily, does she not?" he said.

"Perhaps," said Hornblower. He was not familiar with the *Marie Galante,* nor with ships at all, and he had no opinion on the subject, but he was not going to reveal his ignorance.

"Does she leak?" asked the captain.

"There is no water in her," said Hornblower.

"Ah!" said the captain. "But you would find none in the well. We are carrying a cargo of rice, you must remember."

"Yes," said Hornblower.

He found it very hard at that moment to remain outwardly unperturbed, as his mind grasped the implications of what was being said to him. Rice would absorb every drop of water taken in by the ship, so that no leak would be apparent on sounding the well—and yet every drop of water taken in would deprive her of that much buoyancy, all the same.

"One shot from your cursed frigate struck us in the hull," said the captain. "Of course you have investigated the damage?"

"Of course," said Hornblower, lying bravely.

But as soon as he could he had a private conversation with Matthews on the point, and Matthews instantly looked grave.

"Where did the shot hit her, sir?" he asked.

"Somewhere on the port side, forrard, I should judge."

He and Matthews craned their necks over the ship's side.

"Can't see nothin', sir," said Matthews. "Lower me over the side in a bowline and I'll see what I can find, sir."

Hornblower was about to agree and then changed his mind.

"I'll go over the side myself," he said.

He could not analyse the motives which impelled him to say that. Partly he wanted to see things with his own eyes; partly he was influenced by the doctrine that he should never give an order he was not prepared to carry out himself—but mostly it must have been the desire to impose a penance on himself for his negligence.

Matthews and Carson put a bowline round him and lowered him over. He found himself dangling against the ship's side, with the sea bubbling just below him; as the ship pitched the sea came up to meet him, and he was wet to the waist in the first five seconds; and as the ship rolled he was alternately swung away from the side and bumped against it. The men with the line walked steadily aft, giving him the chance to examine the whole side of the brig above water, and there was not a shot hole to be seen. He said as much to Matthews when they hauled him on deck.

"Then it's below the waterline, sir," said Matthews, saying just what was in Hornblower's mind. "You're sure the shot hit her, sir?"

"Yes, I'm sure," snapped Hornblower.

Lack of sleep and worry and a sense of guilt were all shortening his temper, and he had to speak sharply or break down in tears. But he had already decided on the next move—he made up his mind about that while they were hauling him up.

"We'll heave her to on the other tack and try again," he said.

On the other tack the ship would incline over to the other side, and the shot-hole, if there was one, would not be so deeply submerged. Hornblower stood with the water dripping from his clothes as they wore the brig round; the wind was keen and cold, but he was shivering with expectancy rather than cold. The heeling of the brig laid him much more definitely against the side, and they lowered him until his legs were scraping over the marine growths which she carried there between wind and water. They then walked aft with him, dragging him along the side of the ship, and just abaft the foremast he found what he was seeking.

"Avast, there!" he yelled up to the deck, mastering the sick despair that he felt. The motion of the bowline along the ship ceased. "Lower away! Another two feet!"

Now he was waist-deep in the water, and when the brig swayed the water closed briefly over his head, like a momentary death. Here it was, two feet below the waterline even with the brig hove to on this tack —a splintered, jagged hole, square rather than round, and a foot across. As the sea boiled round him Hornblower even fancied he could hear it bubbling into the ship, but that might be pure fancy.

He hailed the deck for them to haul him up again, and they stood eagerly listening for what he had to say.

"Two feet below the waterline, sir?" said Matthews. "She was close hauled and heeling right over, of course, when we hit her. But her bows must have lifted just as we fired. And of course she's lower in the water now."

That was the point. Whatever they did now, however much they heeled her, that hole would be under water. And on the other tack it would be far under water, with much additional pressure; yet on the present tack they were headed for France. And the more water they took in, the lower the brig would settle, and the greater would be the pressure forcing water in through the hole. Something must be done to plug the leak, and Hornblower's reading of the manuals of seamanship told him what it was.

"We must fother a sail and get it over that hole," he announced. "Call those Frenchmen over."

To fother a sail was to make something like a vast hairy doormat out of it, by threading innumerable lengths of half-unravelled line through it. When this was done the sail would be lowered below the ship's bottom and placed against the hole. The inward pressure would then force the hairy mass so tightly against the hole that the entrance of water would be made at least much more difficult.

The Frenchmen were not quick to help in the task; it was no longer their ship, and they were heading for an English prison, so that even with their lives at stake they were somewhat apathetic. It took time to get out a new topgallant sail—Hornblower felt that the stouter the canvas the better—and to set a party to work cutting lengths of line, threading them through, and unravelling them. The French captain looked at them squatting on the deck all at work.

"Five years I spent in a prison hulk in Portsmouth during the last war," he said. "Five years."

"Yes," said Hornblower.

He might have felt sympathy, but he was not only preoccupied with his own problems but he was numb with cold. He not only had every intention if possible of escorting the French captain to England and to prison again but he also at that very moment intended to go below and appropriate some of his spare clothing.

Down below it seemed to Hornblower as if the noises all about him —the creaks and groans of a wooden ship at sea—were more pronounced than usual. The brig was riding easily enough hove-to, and yet the bulkheads down below were cracking and creaking as if the brig were racking herself to pieces in a storm. He dismissed the notion as a product of his over-stimulated imagination, but by the time he had towelled himself into something like warmth and put on the captain's best suit it recurred to him; the brig was groaning as if in stress.

He came on deck again to see how the working party was progressing. He had hardly been on deck two minutes when one of the Frenchmen, reaching back for another length of line, stopped in his movement to stare at the deck. He picked at a deck seam, looked up and caught Hornblower's eye, and called to him. Hornblower made no pretence of understanding the words; the gestures explained themselves. The deck seam was opening a little; the pitch was bulging out of it. Hornblower looked at the phenomenon without understanding it—only a foot or two of the seam was open, and the rest of the deck seemed solid enough. No! Now that his attention was called to it, and he looked further, there were one or two other places in the deck where the pitch had risen in ridges from out of the seams. It was something beyond his limited experience, even beyond his extensive reading. But the French captain was at his side staring at the deck too.

"My God!" he said "The rice! The rice!"

The French word "riz" that he used was unknown to Hornblower, but he stamped his foot on the deck and pointed down through it.

"The cargo!" he said in explanation. "It—it grows bigger."

Matthews was with them now, and without knowing a word of French he understood.

"Didn't I hear this brig was full of rice, sir?" he asked.

"Yes."

"That's it, then. The water's got into it and it's swelling."

So it would. Dry rice soaked in water would double or treble its volume. The cargo was swelling and bursting the seams of the ship open. Hornblower remembered the unnatural creaks and groans below. It was a black moment; he looked round at the unfriendly sea for inspiration and support, and found neither. Several seconds passed before he was ready to speak, and ready to maintain the dignity of a naval officer in face of difficulties.

"The sooner we get that sail over that hole the better, then," he said. It was too much to be expected that his voice should sound quite natural. "Hurry those Frenchmen up."

He turned to pace the deck, so as to allow his feelings to subside and to set his thoughts running in an orderly fashion again, but the French captain was at his elbow, voluble as a Job's comforter.

"I said I thought the ship was riding heavily," he said. "She is lower in the water."

"Go to the devil," said Hornblower, in English—he could not think up the French for that phrase.

Even as he stood he felt a sudden sharp shock beneath his feet, as if someone had hit the deck underneath them with a mallet. The ship was springing apart bit by bit.

"Hurry with that sail!" he yelled, turning back to the working party. and then was angry with himself because the tone of his voice must have betrayed undignified agitation.

At last an area five feet square of the sail was fothered, lines were rove through the grommets, and the working party hurried forward to work the sail under the brig and drag it aft to the hole. Hornblower was taking off his clothes, not out of regard for the captain's property but so as to keep them dry for himself.

"I'll go over and see that it's in place," he said. "Matthews, get a bowline ready for me."

Naked and wet, it seemed to him as if the wind blew clear through him; rubbing against the ship's side as she rolled he lost a good deal of skin, and the waves passing down the ship smacked at him with a boisterous lack of consideration. But he saw the fothered sail placed against the hole, and with intense satisfaction he saw the hair mass suck into position, dimpling over the hole to form a deep hollow so that he could be sure that the hole was plugged solid. They hauled him up again when he hailed, and awaited his orders; he stood naked, stupid with cold and fatigue and lack of sleep, struggling to form his next decision.

"Lay her on the starboard tack," he said at length.

If the brig were going to sink, it hardly mattered if it were one hundred or two hundred miles from the French coast; if she were to stay afloat he wanted to be well clear of that lee shore and the chance of recapture. The shot hole with its fothered sail would be deeper under water to increase the risk, but it seemed to be the best chance. The French captain saw them making preparations to wear the brig round, and turned upon Hornblower with voluble protests. With this wind they could make Bordeaux easily on the other tack. Hornblower was risking all their lives, he said. Into Hornblower's numb mind crept, uninvited, the translation of something he had previously wanted to say. He could use it now.

"Allez au diable," he snapped, as he put the Frenchman's stout woollen shirt on over his head.

When his head emerged the Frenchman was still protesting volubly, so violently indeed that a new doubt came into Hornblower's mind. A word to Matthews sent him round the French prisoners to search for weapons. There was nothing to be found except the sailors' knives, but as a matter of precaution Hornblower had them all impounded, and when he had dressed he went to special trouble with his three pistols, drawing the charges from them and reloading and repriming afresh. Three pistols in his belt looked piratical, as though he were still young enough to be playing imaginative games, but Hornblower felt in his bones that there might be a time when the Frenchmen might try to rise against their captors, and three pistols would not be too many against twelve desperate men who had makeshift weapons ready to hand, belaying pins and the like.

Matthews was awaiting him with a long face.

"Sir," he said "begging your pardon, but I don't like the looks of it. Straight, I don't. I don't like the feel of her. She's settlin' down and she's openin' up, I'm certain sure. Beg your pardon, sir, for saying so."

Down below Hornblower had heard the fabric of the ship continuing to crack and complain; up here the deck seams were gaping more widely. There was a very likely explanation; the swelling of the rice must have forced open the ship's seams below water, so that plugging the shot-hole would have only eliminated what would be by now only a minor leak. Water must still be pouring in, the cargo still swelling, opening up the ship like an overblown flower. Ships were built to withstand blows from without, and there was nothing about their construction to resist an outward pressure. Wider and wider would gape the seams, and faster and faster the sea would gain access to the cargo.

"Look'e there, sir!" said Matthews suddenly.

In the broad light of day a small grey shape was hurrying along the weather scuppers; another one followed it and another after that. Rats! Something convulsive must be going on down below to bring them on deck in daytime, from out of their comfortable nests among the unlimited food of the cargo. The pressure must be enormous. Hornblower felt another small shock beneath his feet at that moment, as something further parted beneath them. But there was one more card to play, one last line of defence that he could think of.

"I'll jettison the cargo," said Hornblower. He had never uttered that word in his life, but he had read it. "Get the prisoners and we'll start."

The battened-down hatch cover was domed upwards curiously and significantly; as the wedges were knocked out one plank tore loose at one end with a crash, pointing diagonally upwards, and as the working party lifted off the cover a brown form followed it upwards—a bag of rice, forced out by the underlying pressure until it jammed in the hatch way.

"Tail onto those tackles and sway it up," said Hornblower.

Bag by bag the rice was hauled up from the hold; sometimes the bags split, allowing a torrent of rice to pour onto the deck, but that did not matter. Another section of the working party swept rice and bags to the lee side and into the ever-hungry sea. After the first three bags the difficulties increased, for the cargo was so tightly jammed below that it called for enormous force to tear each bag out of its position. Two men had to go down the hatchway to pry the bags loose and adjust the slings. There was a momentary hesitation on the part of the two Frenchmen to whom Hornblower pointed—the bags might not all be jammed and the hold of a tossing ship was a dangerous place wherein a roll might bury them alive—but Hornblower had no thought at that moment for other people's human fears. He scowled at the brief check and they hastened to lower themselves down the hatchway. The labour was enormous as it went on hour after hour; the men at the tackles were dripping with sweat and drooping with fatigue, but they had to relieve periodically the men below, for the bags had jammed themselves in tiers, pressed hard against the ship's bottom below and the deck beams above, and when the bags immediately below the hatchway had been swayed up the surrounding ones had to be pried loose, out of each tier. Then when a small clearance had been made in the neighbourhood of the hatchway, and they were getting deeper down into the hold, they made the inevitable discovery. The lower tiers of bags had been wetted, their contents had swelled, and the bags had burst. The lower half of the hold was packed solid with damp rice which could only be got out with shovels and a hoist. The still intact bags of the upper tiers, farther away from the hatchway, were still jammed tight, calling for much labour to free them and to manhandle them under the hatchway to be hoisted out.

Hornblower, facing the problem, was distracted by a touch on his elbow when Matthews came up to speak to him.

"It ain't no go, sir," said Matthews. "She's lower in the water an' settlin' fast."

Hornblower walked to the ship's side with him and looked over. There could be no doubt about it. He had been over the side himself and could remember the height of the waterline, and he had for a more exact guide the level of the fothered sail under the ship's bottom. The brig was a full six inches lower in the water—and this after fifty tons of rice at least had been hoisted out and flung over the side. The brig must be leaking like a basket, with water pouring in through the gaping seams to be sucked up immediately by the thirsty rice.

Hornblower's left hand was hurting him, and he looked down to discover that he was gripping the rail with it so tightly as to cause him pain, without knowing he was doing so. He released his grip and looked about him, at the afternoon sun, at the tossing sea. He did not want to give in and admit defeat. The French captain came up to him.

"This is folly," he said. "Madness, sir. My men are overcome by fatigue."

Over by the hatchway, Hornblower saw, Hunter was driving the French seamen to their work with a rope's end, which he was using furiously. There was not much more work to be got out of the Frenchmen; and at that moment the *Marie Galante* rose heavily to a wave and wallowed down the further side. Even his inexperience could detect the sluggishness and ominous deadness of her movements. The brig had not much longer to float, and there was a good deal to do.

"I shall make preparations for abandoning the ship, Matthews," he said.

He poked his chin upwards as he spoke; he would not allow either a Frenchman or a seaman to guess at his despair.

"Aye aye, sir," said Matthews.

The *Marie Galante* carried a boat on chocks abaft the mainmast; at Matthews' summons the men abandoned their work on the cargo and hurried to the business of putting food and water in her.

"Beggin' your pardon, sir," said Hunter aside to Hornblower, "but you ought to see you have warm clothes, sir. I been in an open boat ten days once, sir."

"Thank you, Hunter," said Hornblower.

There was much to think of. Navigating instruments, charts, compass—would he be able to get a good observation with his sextant in a tossing little boat? Common prudence dictated that they should have all the food and water with them that the boat could carry; but—Hornblower eyed the wretched craft dubiously—seventeen men would fill it to overflowing anyway. He would have to leave much to the judgment of the French captain and of Matthews.

The tackles were manned and the boat was swayed up from the chocks and lowered into the water in the tiny lee afforded on the lee quarter. The *Marie Galante* put her nose into a wave, refusing to rise to it; green water came over the starboard bow and poured aft along the deck before a sullen wallow on the part of the brig sent it into the scuppers. There was not much time to spare—a rending crash from below told that the cargo was still swelling and forcing the bulkheads. There was a panic among the Frenchmen, who began to tumble down into the boat with loud cries. The French captain took one look at Hornblower and then followed them; two of the British seamen were already over the side fending off the boat.

"Go along," said Hornblower to Matthews and Carson, who still lingered. He was the captain; it was his place to leave the ship last.

So waterlogged was the brig now that it was not at all difficult to step down into the boat from the deck; the British seamen were in the sternsheets and made room for him.

"Take the tiller, Matthews," said Hornblower; he did not feel he was competent to handle that over-loaded boat. "Shove off, there!"

The boat and the brig parted company; the *Marie Galante*, with her helm lashed, poked her nose into the wind and hung there. She had acquired a sudden list, with the starboard side scuppers nearly under water. Another wave broke over her deck, pouring up to the open hatchway. Now she righted herself, her deck nearly level with the sea, and then she sank, on an even keel, the water closing over her, her masts slowly disappearing. For an instant her sails even gleamed under the green water.

"She's gone," said Matthews.

Hornblower watched the disappearance of his first command. The *Marie Galante* had been entrusted to him to bring into port, and he had failed, failed on his first independent mission. He looked very hard at the setting sun, hoping no one would notice the tears that were filling his eyes.

THE PENALTY OF FAILURE

Daylight crept over the tossing waters of the Bay of Biscay to reveal a small boat riding on its wide expanses. It was a very crowded boat; in the bows huddled the French crew of the sunken brig *Marie Galante*, amidships sat the captain and his mate, and in the stern-sheets sat Midshipman Horatio Hornblower and the four English seamen who had once constituted the prize-crew of the brig. Hornblower was seasick, for his delicate stomach, having painfully accustomed itself to the motion of the *Indefatigable*, rebelled at the antics of the small boat as she pitched jerkily to her sea-anchor. He was cold and weary as well as seasick after his second night without sleep—he had been vomiting spasmodically all through the hours of darkness, and in the depression which seasickness brings he had thought gloomily about the loss of the *Marie Galante*. If he had only remembered earlier to plug that shot-hole! Excuses came to his mind only to be discarded. There had been so much to do, and so few men to do it with—the French crew to guard, the damage aloft to repair, the course to set. The absorbent qualities of the cargo of rice which the *Marie Galante* carried had deceived him when he had remembered to sound the well. All this might be true, but the fact remained that he had lost his ship, his first command. In his own eyes there was no excuse for his failure.

The French crew had wakened with the dawn and were chattering like a nest of magpies; Matthews and Carson beside him were moving stiffly to ease their aching joints.

"Breakfast, sir?" said Matthews.

It was like the games Hornblower had played as a lonely little boy, when he had sat in the empty pig-trough and pretended he was cast away in an open boat. Then he had parcelled out the bit of bread or whatever it was which he had obtained from the kitchen into a dozen rations, counting them carefully, each one to last a day. But a small boy's eager appetite had made those days very short, not more than five minutes long; after standing up in the pig-trough and shading his eyes and looking round the horizon for the succour that he could not discover, he would sit down again, tell himself that the life of a castaway was hard, and then decide another night had passed and that it was time to eat another ration from his dwindling supply. So here under Hornblower's eye the French captain and mate served out a biscuit of hard bread to each person in the boat, and filled the pannikin for each man in turn from the water breakers under the thwarts. But Hornblower when he sat in the pig-trough, despite his vivid imagination, never thought of this hideous seasickness, of the cold and the cramps, nor of how his skinny posterior would ache with its constant pressure against the hard timbers of the stern-sheets; nor, in the sublime self-confidence of childhood, had he ever thought how heavy could be the burden of responsibility on the shoulders of a senior naval officer aged seventeen.

He dragged himself back from the memories of that recent childhood to face the present situation. The grey sky, as far as his inexperienced eye could tell, bore no presage of deterioration in the weather. He wetted his finger and held it up, looking in the boat's compass to gauge the direction of the wind.

"Backing westerly a little, sir," said Matthews, who had been copying his movements.

"That's so," agreed Hornblower, hurriedly going through in his mind his recent lessons in boxing the compass. His course to weather Ushant was nor'-east by north, he knew, and the boat close hauled would not lie closer than eight points off the wind—he had lain-to to the sea-anchor all night because the wind had been coming from too far north to enable him to steer for England. But now the wind had backed. Eight points from nor'-east by north was nor'-west by west, and the wind was even more westerly than that. Close hauled he could weather Ushant and even have a margin for contingencies, to keep him clear of the lee shore, which the seamanship books and his own common sense told him was so dangerous.

"We'll make sail, Matthews," he said; his hand was still grasping the biscuit which his rebellious stomach refused to accept.

"Aye aye, sir."

A shout to the Frenchmen crowded in the bows drew their attention; in the circumstances it hardly needed Hornblower's halting French to direct them to carry out the obvious task of getting in the sea-anchor. But it was not too easy, with the boat so crowded and hardly a foot of freeboard. The mast was already stepped, and the lug sail bent ready to hoist. Two Frenchmen, balancing precariously, tailed onto the halliard and the sail rose up the mast.

"Hunter, take the sheet," said Hornblower. "Matthews, take the tiller. Keep her close hauled on the port tack."

"Close hauled on the port tack, sir."

The French captain had watched the proceedings with intense interest from his seat amidships. He had not understood the last, decisive order, but he grasped its meaning quickly enough when the boat came round and steadied on the port tack, heading for England. He stood up, spluttering angry protests.

"The wind is fair for Bordeaux," he said, gesticulating with clenched fists. "We could be there by tomorrow. Why do we go north?"

"We go to England," said Hornblower.

"But—but—it will take us a week! A week even if the wind stays fair. This boat—it is too crowded. We cannot endure a storm. It is madness."

Hornblower had guessed at the moment the captain stood up what he was going to say, and he hardly bothered to translate the expostulations to himself. He was too tired and too seasick to enter into an argument in a foreign language. He ignored the captain. Not for anything on earth would he turn the boat's head towards France. His naval career had only just begun, and even if it were to be blighted on account of the loss of the *Marie Galante* he had no intention of rotting for years in a French prison.

"Sir!" said the French captain.

The mate who shared the captain's thwart was protesting too, and now they turned to their crew behind them and told them what was going on. An angry movement stirred the crowd.

"Sir!" said the captain again "I insist that you head towards Bordeaux."

He showed signs of advancing upon them; one of the crew behind him began to pull the boat-hook clear, and it would be a dangerous weapon. Hornblower pulled one of the pistols from his belt and pointed it at the captain, who, with the muzzle four feet from his breast, fell back before the gesture. Without taking his eyes off him Hornblower took a second pistol with his left hand.

"Take this, Matthews," he said.

"Aye aye, sir," said Matthews, obeying; and then, after a respectful pause, "Beggin' your pardon, sir, but hadn't you better cock your pistol, sir?"

"Yes," said Hornblower, exasperated at his own forgetfulness.

He drew the hammer back with a click, and the menacing sound made more acute still the French captain's sense of his own danger, with a cocked and loaded pistol pointed at his stomach in a heaving boat. He waved his hands desperately.

"Please," he said, "point it some other way, sir."

He drew farther back, huddling against the men behind him.

"Hey, avast there, you," shouted Matthews loudly—a French sailor was trying to let go the halliard unobserved.

"Shoot any man who looks dangerous, Matthews," said Hornblower.

He was so intent on enforcing his will upon these men, so desperately anxious to retain his liberty, that his face was contracted into a beast-like scowl. No one looking at him could doubt his determination for a moment. He would allow no human life to come between him and his decisions. There was still a third pistol in his belt, and the Frenchmen could guess that if they tried a rush a quarter of them at least would meet their deaths before they overpowered the Englishmen, and the French captain knew he would be the first to die. His expressive hands, waving out from his sides—he could not take his eyes from the pistol—told his men to make no further resistance. Their murmurings died away, and the captain began to plead.

"Five years I was in an English prison during the last war," he said. "Let us reach an agreement. Let us go to France. When we reach the shore—anywhere you choose, sir—we will land and you can continue your journey. Or we can all land, and I will use all my influence to have you and your men sent back to England under cartel, without exchange or ransom. I swear I will."

"No," said Hornblower.

England was far easier to reach from here than from the French Biscay coast; as for the other suggestion, Hornblower knew enough about the new government washed up by the revolution in France to be sure that they would never part with prisoners on the representation of a merchant captain. And trained seamen were scarce in France; it was his duty to keep these dozen from returning.

"No," he said again, in reply to the captain's fresh protests.

"Shall I clout 'im on the jaw, sir?" asked Hunter, at Hornblower's side.

"No," said Hornblower again; but the Frenchman saw the gesture and guessed at the meaning of the words, and subsided into sullen silence.

But he was roused again at the sight of Hornblower's pistol on his knee, still pointed at him. A sleepy finger might press that trigger.

"Sir," he said, "put that pistol away, I beg of you. It is dangerous."

Hornblower's eye was cold and unsympathetic.

"Put it away, please. I will do nothing to interfere with your command of this boat. I promise you that."

"Do you swear it?"

"I swear it."

"And these others?"

The captain looked round at his crew with voluble explanations, and grudgingly they agreed.

"They swear it too."

"Very well, then."

Hornblower started to replace the pistol in his belt, and remembered to put it on half-cock in time to save himself from shooting himself in the stomach. Everyone in the boat relaxed into apathy. The boat was rising and swooping rhythmically now, a far more comfortable motion than when it had jerked to a sea-anchor, and Hornblower's stomach lost some of its resentment. He had been two nights without sleep. His head lowered on his chest, and then he leaned sideways against Hunter, and slept peacefully, while the boat, with the wind nearly abeam, headed steadily for England. What woke him late in the day was when Matthews, cramped and weary, was compelled to surrender the tiller to Carson, and after that they kept watch and watch, a hand at the sheet and a hand at the tiller and the others trying to rest. Hornblower took his turn at the sheet, but he would not trust himself with the tiller, especially when night fell; he knew he had not the knack of keeping the boat on her course by the feel of the wind on his cheek and the tiller in his hand.

It was not until long after breakfast the next day—almost noon in fact—that they sighted the sail. It was a Frenchman who saw it first, and his excited cry roused them all. There were three square topsails coming up over the horizon on their weather bow, nearing them so rapidly on a converging course that each time the boat rose on a wave a considerably greater area of canvas was visible.

"What do you think she is, Matthews?" asked Hornblower, while the boat buzzed with the Frenchmen's excitement.

"I can't tell, sir, but I don't like the looks of her," said Matthews doubtfully. "She ought to have her t'gallants set in this breeze—and her courses too, an' she hasn't. An' I don't like the cut of her jib, sir. She—she might be a Frenchie to me, sir."

Any ship travelling for peaceful purposes would naturally have all possible sail set. This ship had not. Hence she was engaged in some belligerent design, but there were more chances that she was British than that she was French, even in here in the Bay. Hornblower took a long look at her; a smallish vessel, although ship-rigged. Flush-decked, with a look of speed about her—her hull was visible at intervals now, with a line of gunports.

"She looks French all over to me, sir," said Hunter. "Privateer, seemly."

"Stand by to jibe," said Hornblower.

They brought the boat round before the wind, heading directly away from the ship. But in war as in the jungle, to fly is to invite pursuit and attack. The ship set courses and topgallants and came tearing down upon them, passed them at half a cable's length and then hove-to, having cut off their escape. The ship's rail was lined with a curious crowd —a large crew for a vessel that size. A hail came across the water to the boat, and the words were French. The English seamen subsided into curses, while the French captain cheerfully stood up and replied, and the French crew brought the boat alongside the ship.

A handsome young man in a plum-covered coat with a lace stock greeted Hornblower when he stepped on the deck.

"Welcome, sir, to the *Pique*," he said in French. "I am Captain Neuville, of this privateer. And you are—?"

"Midshipman Hornblower, of His Britannic Majesty's ship *Indefatigable*," growled Hornblower.

"You seem to be in evil humour," said Neuville. "Please do not be so distressed at the fortunes of war. You will be accommodated in this ship, until we return to port, with every comfort possible at sea. I beg of you to consider yourself quite at home. For instance, those pistols in your belt must discommode you more than a little. Permit me to relieve you of their weight."

He took the pistols neatly from Hornblower's belt as he spoke, looked Hornblower keenly over, and then went on.

"That dirk that you wear at your side, sir. Would you oblige me by the loan of it? I assure you that I will return it to you when we part company. But while you are on board here I fear that your impetuous youth might lead you into some rash act while you are wearing a weapon which a credulous mind might believe to be lethal. A thousand thanks. And now might I show you the berth that is being prepared for you?"

With a courteous bow he led the way below. Two decks down, presumably at the level of a foot or two below the water line, was a wide bare 'tweendecks, dimly lighted and scantily ventilated by the hatchways.

"Our slave deck," explained Neuville carelessly.

"Slave deck?" asked Hornblower.

"Yes. It is here that the slaves were confined during the middle passage."

Much was clear to Hornblower at once. A slave ship could be readily converted into a privateer. She would already be armed with plenty of guns to defend herself against treacherous attacks while making her purchases in the African rivers; she was faster than the average merchant ship both because of the lack of need of hold space and because with a highly perishable cargo such as slaves speed was a desirable quality, and she was constructed to carry large numbers of men and the great quantities of food and water necessary to keep them supplied while at sea in search of prizes.

"Our market in San Domingo has been closed to us by recent events, of which you must have heard, sir," went on Neuville "and so that the *Pique* could continue to return dividends to me I have converted her into a privateer. Moreover, seeing that the activities of the Committee of Public Safety at present make Paris a more unhealthy spot even than the West Coast of Africa, I decided to take command of my vessel myself. To say nothing of the fact that a certain resolution and hardihood are necessary to make a privateer a profitable investment."

Neuville's face hardened for a moment into an expression of the grimmest determination, and then softened at once into its previous meaningless politeness.

"This door in this bulkhead," he continued, "leads to the quarters I have set aside for captured officers. Here, as you see, is your cot. Please make yourself at home here. Should this ship go into action—as I trust she will frequently do—the hatches above will be battened down. But except on those occasions you will of course be at liberty to move about the ship at your will. Yet I suppose I had better add that any harebrained attempt on the part of prisoners to interfere with the working or wellbeing of this ship would be deeply resented by the crew. They serve on shares, you understand, and are risking their lives and their liberty. I would not be surprised if any rash person who endangered their dividends and freedom were dropped over the side into the sea."

Hornblower forced himself to reply; he would not reveal that he was almost struck dumb by the calculating callousness of this last speech.

"I understand," he said.

"Excellent! Now is there anything further you may need, sir?"

Hornblower looked round the bare quarters in which he was to suffer lonely confinement, lit by a dim glimmer of light from a swaying slush lamp.

"Could I have something to read?" he asked.

Neuville thought for a moment.

"I fear there are only professional books," he said. "But I can let you have Grandjean's *Principles of Navigation,* and Lebrun's *Handbook on Seamanship* and some similar volumes, if you think you can understand the French in which they are written."

"I'll try," said Hornblower.

Probably it was as well that Hornblower was provided with the materials for such strenuous mental exercise. The effort of reading French and of studying his profession at one and the same time kept his mind busy during the dreary days while the *Pique* cruised in search of prizes. Most of the time the Frenchmen ignored him—he had to force himself upon Neuville once to protest against the employment of his four British seamen on the menial work of pumping out the ship, but he had to retire worsted from the argument, if argument it could be called, when Neuville icily refused to discuss the question. Hornblower went back to his quarters with burning cheeks and red ears, and, as ever, when he was mentally disturbed, the thought of his guilt returned to him with new force.

If only he had plugged that shot-hole sooner! A clearer-headed officer, he told himself, would have done so. He had lost his ship, the *Indefatigable*'s precious prize, and there was no health in him. Sometimes he made himself review the situation calmly. Professionally, he might not—probably would not—suffer for his negligence. A midshipman with only four for a prize-crew, put on board a two-hundred-ton brig that had been subjected to considerable firing from a frigate's guns, would not be seriously blamed when she sank under him. But Hornblower knew at the same time that he was at least partly at fault. If it was ignorance—there was no excuse for ignorance. If he had allowed his multiple cares to distract him from the business of plugging the shot-hole immediately, that was incompetence, and there was no excuse for incompetence. When he thought along those lines he was overwhelmed by waves of despair and of self-contempt, and there was no one to comfort him. The day of his birthday, when he looked at himself at the vast age of eighteen, was the worst of all. Eighteen and a discredited prisoner in the hands of a French privateersman! His self-respect was at its lowest ebb.

The *Pique* was seeking her prey in the most frequented waters in the world, the approaches to the Channel, and there could be no more vivid demonstration of the vastness of the ocean than the fact that she cruised day after day without glimpsing a sail. She maintained a triangular course, reaching to the north-west, tacking to the south, running under easy sail north-easterly again, with lookouts at every masthead, with nothing to see but the tossing waste of water. Until the morning when a high-pitched yell from the foretopgallant masthead attracted the attention of everybody on deck, including Hornblower, standing lonely in the waist. Neuville, by the wheel, bellowed a question to the lookout, and Hornblower, thanks to his recent studies, could translate the answer. There was a sail visible to windward, and next moment the lookout reported that it had altered course and was running down towards them.

That meant a great deal. In wartime any merchant ship would be suspicious of strangers and would give them as wide a berth as possible; and especially when she was to windward and therefore far safer. Only someone prepared to fight or possessed of a perfectly morbid curiosity would abandon a windward position. A wild and unreasonable hope filled Hornblower's breast; a ship of war at sea—thanks to England's maritime mastery—would be far more probably English than French. And this was the cruising ground of the *Indefatigable*, his own ship, stationed there specially to fulfil the double function of looking out for French commerce-destroyers and intercepting French blockade-runners. A hundred miles from here she had put him and his prize crew on board the *Marie Galante*. It was a thousand to one, he exaggerated despairingly to himself, against any ship sighted being the *Indefatigable*. But—hope reasserted itself—the fact that she was coming down to investigate reduced the odds to ten to one at most. Less than ten to one.

He looked over at Neuville, trying to think his thoughts. The *Pique* was fast and handy, and there was a clear avenue of escape to leeward. The fact that the stranger had altered course towards them was a suspicious circumstance, but it was known that Indiamen, the richest prizes of all, had sometimes traded on the similarity of their appearance to that of ships of the line, and by showing a bold front had scared dangerous enemies away. That would be a temptation to a man eager to make a prize. At Neuville's orders all sail was set, ready for instant flight or pursuit, and, close-hauled, the *Pique* stood towards the stranger. It was not long before Hornblower, on the deck, caught a glimpse of a gleam of white, like a tiny grain of rice, far away on the horizon as the *Pique* lifted on a swell. Here came Matthews, red-faced and excited, running aft to Hornblower's side.

"That's the old *Indefatigable*, sir," he said. "I swear it!" He sprang onto the rail, holding on by the shrouds, and stared under his hand.

"Yes! There she is, sir! She's loosing her royals now, sir. We'll be back on board of her in time for grog!"

A French petty officer reached up and dragged Matthews by the seat of his trousers from his perch, and with a blow and a kick drove him forward again, while a moment later Neuville was shouting the orders that wore the ship round to head away directly from the *Indefatigable*. Neuville beckoned Hornblower over to his side.

"Your late ship, I understand, Mr. Hornblower?"

"Yes."

"What is her best point of sailing?"

Hornblower's eyes met Neuville's.

"Do not look so noble," said Neuville, smiling with thin lips. "I could undoubtedly induce you to give me the information. I know of ways. But it is unnecessary, fortunately for you. There is no ship on earth—especially none of His Britannic Majesty's clumsy frigates—that can outsail the *Pique* running before the wind. You will soon see that."

He strolled to the taffrail and loooked aft long and earnestly through his glass, but no more earnestly than did Hornblower with his naked eye.

"You see?" said Neuville, proffering the glass.

Hornblower took it, but more to catch a closer glimpse of his ship than to confirm his observations. He was homesick, desperately homesick, at that moment, for the *Indefatigable*. But there could be no denying that she was being left fast behind. Her topgallants were out of sight again now, and only her royals were visible.

"Two hours and we shall have run her mastheads under," said Neuville, taking back the telescope and shutting it with a snap.

He left Hornblower standing sorrowful at the taffrail while he turned to berate the helmsman for not steering a steadier course; Hornblower heard the explosive words without listening to them, the wind blowing into his face and ruffling his hair over his ears, and the wake of the ship's passage boiling below him. So might Adam have looked back at Eden; Hornblower remembered the stuffy dark midshipmen's berth, the smells and the creakings, the bitter cold nights, turning out in response to the call for all hands, the weevilly bread and the wooden beef, and he yearned for them all, with the sick feeling of hopeless longing. Liberty was vanishing over the horizon. Yet it was not these personal feelings that drove him below in search of action. They may have quickened his wits, but it was a sense of duty which inspired him.

The slave-deck was deserted, as usual, with all hands at quarters. Beyond the bulkhead stood his cot with the books upon it and the slush lamp swaying above it. There was nothing there to give him any inspiration. There was another locked door in the after bulkhead. That opened into some kind of boatswain's store; twice he had seen it unlocked and paint and similar supplies brought out from it. Paint! That gave him an idea; he looked from the door up to the slush lamp and back again, and as he stepped forward he took his claspknife out of his pocket. But before very long he recoiled again, sneering at himself. The door was not panelled, but was made of two solid slabs of wood, with the cross-beams on the inside. There was the keyhole of the lock, but it presented no point of attack. It would take him hours and hours to cut through that door with his knife, at a time when minutes were precious.

His heart was beating feverishly—but no more feverishly than his mind was working—as he looked round again. He reached up to the lamp and shook it; nearly full. There was a moment when he stood hesitating, nerving himself, and then he threw himself into action. With a ruthless hand he tore the pages out of Grandjean's *Principes de la Navigation,* crumpling them up in small quantities into little loose balls which he laid at the foot of the door. He threw off his uniform coat and dragged his blue woollen jersey over his head; his long powerful fingers tore it across and plucked eagerly at it to unravel it. After starting some loose threads he would not waste more time on it, and dropped the garment onto the paper and looked round again. The mattress of the cot! It was stuffed with straw, by God! A slash of his knife tore open the ticking, and he scooped the stuff out by the armful; constant pressure had almost solidified it, but he shook it and handled it so that it bulked out far larger in a mass on the deck nearly up to his waist. That would give him the intense blaze he wanted. He stood still, compelling himself to think clearly and logically—it was impetuosity and lack of thought which had occasioned the loss of the *Marie Galante*, and now he had wasted time on his jersey. He worked out the successive steps to take. He made a long spill out of a page of the *Manuel de Matelotage*, and lighted it at the lamp. Then he poured out the grease—the lamp was hot and the grease liquid—over his balls of paper, over the deck, over the base of the door. A touch from his taper lighted one ball, the flame travelled quickly. He was committed now. He piled the straw upon the flames, and in a sudden access of insane strength he tore the cot from its fastenings, smashing it as he did so, and piled the fragments on the straw. Already the flames were racing through the straw. He dropped the lamp upon the pile, grabbed his coat and walked out. He thought of closing the door, but decided against it—the more air the better. He wriggled into his coat and ran up the ladder.

On deck he forced himself to lounge nonchalantly against the rail, putting his shaking hands into his pockets. His excitement made him weak, nor was it lessened as he waited. Every minute before the fire could be discovered was important. A French officer said something to him with a triumphant laugh and pointed aft over the taffrail, presumably speaking about leaving the *Indefatigable* behind. Hornblower smiled bleakly at him; that was the first gesture that occurred to him, and then he thought that a smile was out of place, and he tried to assume a sullen scowl. The wind was blowing briskly, so that the *Pique* could only just carry all plain sail; Hornblower felt it on his cheeks, which were burning. Everyone on deck seemed unnaturally busy and preoccupied; Neuville was watching the helmsman with occasional glances aloft to see that every sail was doing its work; the men were at the guns, two hands and a petty officer heaving the log. God, how much longer would he have?

Look there! The coaming of the after hatchway appeared distorted wavering in the shimmering air. Hot air must be coming through it. And was that, or was it not, the ghost of a wreath of smoke? It was! In that moment the alarm was given. A loud cry, a rush of feet, an instant bustle, the loud beating of a drum, high-pitched shouts—"Au feu! Au feu!"

The four elements of Aristotle, thought Hornblower insanely—earth, air, water, and fire—were the constant enemies of the seaman, but the lee shore, the gale, and the wave, were none of them as feared in wooden ships as fire. Timbers many years old and coated thick with paint burnt fiercely and readily. Sails and tarry rigging would burn like fireworks. And within the ship were tons and tons of gunpowder waiting its chance to blast the seamen into fragments. Hornblower watched the fire parties flinging themselves into their work, the pumps being dragged over the decks, the hoses rigged. Someone came racing aft with a message for Neuville, presumably to report the site of the fire. Neuville heard him, and darted a glance at Hornblower against the rail before he hurled orders back at the messenger. The smoke coming up through the after hatchway was dense now; at Neuville's orders the after guard flung themselves down the opening through the smoke. And there was more smoke, and more smoke; smoke caught up by the following wind and blown forward in wisps—smoke must be pouring out of the sides of the ship at the waterline.

Neuville took a stride towards Hornblower, his face working with rage, but a cry from the helmsman checked him. The helmsman, unable to take his hands from the wheel, pointed with his foot to the cabin skylight. There was a flickering of flame below it. A side pane fell in as they watched, and a rush of flame came through the opening. That store of paint, Hornblower calculated—he was calmer now, with a calm that would astonish him later, when he came to look back on it—must be immediately under the cabin, and blazing fiercely. Neuville looked round him, at the sea and the sky, and put his hands to his head in a furious gesture. For the first time in his life Hornblower saw a man literally tearing his hair. But his nerve held. A shout brought up another portable pump; four men set to work on the handles, and the clank-clank clank-clank made an accompaniment that blended with the roar of the fire. A thin jet of water was squirted down the gaping skylight. More men formed a bucket chain, drawing water from the sea and passing it from hand to hand to pour in the skylight, but those buckets of water were less effective even than the stream from the pumps. From below came the dull thud of an explosion, and Hornblower caught his breath as he expected the ship to be blown to pieces. But no further explosion followed; either a gun had been set off by the flames or a cask had burst violently in the heat. And then the bucket line suddenly disintegrated; beneath the feet of one of the men a seam had gaped in a broad red smile from which came a rush of flame. Some officer had seized Neuville by the arm and was arguing with him vehemently, and Hornblower could see Neuville yield in despair. Hands went scurrying aloft to get in the foretopsail and forecourse, and other hands went to the main braces. Over went the wheel, and the *Pique* came up into the wind.

The change was dramatic, although at first more apparent than real; with the wind blowing in the opposite direction the roar of the fire did not come so clearly to the ears of those forward of it. But it was an immense gain, all the same; the flames, which had started in the steerage in the farthest after-part of the ship, no longer were blown forward, but were turned back upon timber already half consumed. Yet the after-part of the deck was fully alight; the helmsman was driven from the wheel, and in a flash the flames took hold of the driver and consumed it utterly—one moment the sail was there, and the next there were only charred fragments hanging from the gaff. But, head to wind, the other sails did not catch, and a mizzen-trysail hurriedly set kept the ship bows on.

It was then that Hornblower, looking forward, saw the *Indefatigable* again. She was tearing down towards them with all sail set; as the *Pique* lifted he could see the white bow wave foaming under her bowsprit. There was no question about surrender, for under the menace of that row of guns no ship of the *Pique's* force, even if uninjured, could resist. A cable's length to windward the *Indefatigable* rounded-to, and she was hoisting out her boats before even she was fully round. Pellew had seen the smoke, and had deduced the reason for the *Pique's* heaving to, and had made his preparations as he came up. Longboat and launch had each a pump in their bows where sometimes they carried a carronade; they dropped down to the stern of the *Pique* to cast their jets of water up into the flaming stern without more ado. Two gigs full of men ran straight aft to join in the battle with the flames, but Bolton, the third lieutenant, lingered for a moment as he caught Hornblower's eye.

"Good God, it's you!" he exclaimed. "What are you doing here?"

Yet he did not stay for an answer. He picked out Neuville as the captain of the *Pique*, strode aft to receive his surrender, cast his eyes aloft to see that all was well there, and then took up the task of combating the fire. The flames were overcome in time, more because they had consumed everything within reach of them than for any other reason; the *Pique* was burnt from the taffrail forward for some feet of her length right to the water's edge, so that she presented a strange spectacle when viewed from the deck of the *Indefatigable*. Nevertheless, she was in no immediate danger; given even moderate good fortune and a little hard work she could be sailed to England to be repaired and sent to sea again.

But it was not her salvage that was important, but rather the fact that she was no longer in French hands, would no longer be available to prey on English commerce. That was the point that Sir Edward Pellew made in conversation with Hornblower, when the latter came on board to report himself. Hornblower had begun, at Pellew's order, by recounting what had happened to him from the time he had been sent as prize master on board the *Marie Galante*. As Hornblower had expected—perhaps as he had even feared—Pellew had passed lightly over the loss of the brig. She had been damaged by gunfire before surrendering, and no one now could establish whether the damage was small or great. Pellew did not give the matter a second thought. Hornblower had tried to save her and had been unsuccessful with his tiny crew—and at that moment the *Indefatigable* could not spare him a larger crew. He did not hold Hornblower culpable. Once again, it was more important that France should be deprived of the *Marie Galante's* cargo than that England should benefit by it. The situation was exactly parallel to that of the salvaging of the *Pique*.

"It was lucky she caught fire like that," commented Pellew, looking across to where the *Pique* lay, still hove-to with the boats clustering about her but with only the thinnest trail of smoke drifting from her stern. "She was running clean away from us, and would have been out of sight in an hour. Have you any idea how it happened, Mr. Hornblower?"

Hornblower was naturally expecting that question and was ready for it. Now was the time to answer truthfully and modestly, to receive the praise he deserved, a mention in the *Gazette*, perhaps even appointment to acting-lieutenant. But Pellew did not know the full details of the loss of the brig, and might make a false estimate of them even if he did.

"No, sir," said Hornblower. "I think it must have been spontaneous combustion in the paint-locker. I can't account for it otherwise."

He alone knew of his remissness in plugging that shot-hole, he alone could decide on his punishment, and this was what he had chosen. This alone could re-establish him in his own eyes, and when the words were spoken he felt enormous relief, and not one single twinge of regret.

"It was fortunate, all the same," mused Pellew.

THE MAN WHO FELT QUEER

This time the wolf was prowling round outside the sheepfold. H.M. frigate *Indefatigable* had chased the French corvette *Papillon* into the mouth of the Gironde, and was seeking a way of attacking her where she lay at anchor in the stream under the protection of the batteries at the mouth. Captain Pellew took his ship into shoal water as far as he dared, until in fact the batteries fired warning shots to make him keep his distance, and he stared long and keenly through his glass at the corvette. Then he shut his telescope and turned on his heel to give the order that worked the *Indefatigable* away from the dangerous lee shore —out of sight of land, in fact. His departure might lull the French into a sense of security which, he hoped, would prove unjustified. For he had no intention of leaving them undisturbed. If the corvette could be captured or sunk not only would she be unavailable for raids on British commerce, but also the French would be forced to increase their coastal defences at this point and lessen the effort that could be put out elsewhere. War is a matter of savage blow and counter blow, and even a forty-gun frigate could strike shrewd blows if shrewdly handled.

Midshipman Hornblower was walking the lee side of the quarter-deck, as became his lowly station as the junior officer of the watch, in the afternoon, when Midshipman Kennedy approached him. Kennedy took off his hat with a flourish and bowed low as his dancing master had once taught him, left foot advanced, hat down by the right knee. Hornblower entered into the spirit of the game, laid his hat against his stomach, and bent himself in the middle three times in quick succession. Thanks to his physical awkwardness he could parody ceremonial solemnity almost without trying.

"Most grave and reverend signor," said Kennedy. "I bear the compliments of Captain Sir Ed'ard Pellew, who humbly solicits Your Gravity's attendance at dinner at eight bells in the afternoon watch."

"My respects to Sir Edward," replied Hornblower, bowing to his knees at the mention of the name, "and I shall condescend to make a brief appearance."

"I am sure the captain will be both relieved and delighted," said Kennedy. "I will convey him my felicitations along with your most flattering acceptance."

Both hats flourished with even greater elaboration than before, but at that moment both young men noticed Mr. Bolton, the officer of the watch, looking at them from the windward side, and they hurriedly put their hats on and assumed attitudes more consonant with the dignity of officers holding their warrants from King George.

"What's in the captain's mind?" asked Hornblower.

Kennedy laid one finger alongside his nose.

"If I knew that I should rate a couple of epaulettes," he said. "Something's brewing, and I suppose one of these days we shall know what it is. Until then all that we little victims can do is to play unconscious of our doom. Meanwhile, be careful not to let the ship fall overboard."

There was no sign of anything brewing while dinner was being eaten in the great cabin of the *Indefatigable*. Pellew was a courtly host at the head of the table. Conversation flowed freely and along indifferent channels among the senior officers present—the two lieutenants, Eccles and Chadd, and the sailing master, Soames. Hornblower and the other junior officer—Mallory, a midshipman of over two years' seniority—kept silent, as midshipmen should, thereby being able to devote their undivided attention to the food, so vastly superior to what was served in the midshipmen's berth.

"A glass of wine with you, Mr. Hornblower," said Pellew, raising his glass.

Hornblower tried to bow gracefully in his seat while raising his glass. He sipped cautiously, for he had early found that he had a weak head, and he disliked feeling drunk.

The table was cleared and there was a brief moment of expectancy as the company awaited Pellew's next move.

"Now, Mr. Soames," said Pellew, "let us have that chart."

It was a map of the mouth of the Gironde with the soundings; somebody had pencilled in the positions of the shore batteries.

"The *Papillon*," said Sir Edward (he did not condescend to pronounce it French-fashion) "lies just here. Mr. Soames took the bearings."

He indicated a pencilled cross on the chart, far up the channel.

"You gentlemen," went on Pellew, "are going in with the boats to fetch her out."

So that was it. A cutting-out expedition.

"Mr. Eccles will be in general command. I will ask him to tell you his plan."

The grey-haired first lieutenant with the surprisingly young blue eyes looked round at the others.

"I shall have the launch," he said, "and Mr. Soames the cutter. Mr. Chadd and Mr. Mallory will command the first and second gigs. And Mr. Hornblower will command the jolly boat. Each of the boats except Mr. Hornblower's will have a junior officer second in command."

That would not be necessary for the jolly boat with its crew of seven. The launch and cutter would carry from thirty to forty men each, and the gigs twenty each; it was a large force that was being despatched—nearly half the ship's company.

"She's a ship of war," explained Eccles, reading their thoughts. "No merchantman. Ten guns a side, and full of men."

Nearer two hundred men than a hundred, certainly—plentiful opposition for a hundred and twenty British seamen.

"But we will be attacking her by night and taking her by surprise," said Eccles, reading their thoughts again.

"Surprise," put in Pellew, "is more than half the battle, as you know, gentlemen—please pardon the interruption, Mr. Eccles."

"At the moment," went on Eccles, "we are out of sight of land. We are about to stand in again. We have never hung about this part of the coast, and the Frogs'll think we've gone for good. We'll make the land after nightfall, stand in as far as possible, and then the boats will go in. High water tomorrow morning is at four-fifty; dawn is at five-thirty. The attack will be delivered at four-thirty so that the watch below will have had time to get to sleep. The launch will attack on the starboard quarter, and the cutter on the larboard quarter. Mr. Mallory's gig will attack on the larboard bow, and Mr. Chadd's on the starboard bow. Mr. Chadd will be responsible for cutting the corvette's cable as soon as he has mastered the forecastle, and the other boats' crews have at least reached the quarterdeck."

Eccles looked round at the other three commanders of the large boats, and they nodded understanding. Then he went on.

"Mr. Hornblower with the jolly boat will wait until the attack has gained a foothold on the deck. He will then board at the main chains, either to starboard or larboard as he sees fit, and he will at once ascend the main rigging, paying no attention to whatever fighting is going on on deck. He will see to it that the maintopsail is loosed and he will sheet it home on receipt of further orders. I myself, or Mr. Soames in the event of my being killed or wounded, will send two hands to the wheel and will attend to steering the corvette as soon as she is under way. The tide will take us out, and the *Indefatigable* will be awaiting us just out of gunshot from the shore batteries."

"Any comments, gentlemen?" asked Pellew.

That was the moment when Hornblower should have spoken up— the only moment when he could. Eccles' orders had set in motion sick feelings of apprehension in his stomach. Hornblower was no maintop- man, and Hornblower knew it. He hated heights, and he hated going aloft. He knew he had none of the monkey-like agility and self-confid- ence of the good seaman. He was unsure of himself aloft in the dark even in the *Indefatigable*, and he was utterly appalled at the thought of going aloft in an entirely strange ship and finding his way among strange rigging. He felt himself quite unfitted for the duty assigned to him, and he should have raised a protest at once on account of his un- fitness. But he let the opportunity pass, for he was overcome by the matter-of-fact way in which the other officers accepted the plan. He looked round at the unmoved faces; nobody was paying any attention to him, and he jibbed at making himself conspicuous. He swallowed; he even got as far as opening his mouth, but still no one looked at him, and his protest died stillborn.

"Very well, then, gentlemen," said Pellew. "I think you had better go into the details, Mr. Eccles."

Then it was too late. Eccles, with the chart before him, was pointing out the course to be taken through the shoals and mudbanks of the Gir- onde, and expatiating on the position of the shore batteries and on the influence of the lighthouse of Cordouan upon the distance to which the *Indefatigable* could approach in daylight. Hornblower listened, trying to concentrate despite his apprehensions. Eccles finished his remarks and Pellew closed the meeting.

"Since you all know your duties, gentlemen, I think you should start your preparations. The sun is about to set and you will find you have plenty to do."

The boats crews had to be told off; it was necessary to see that the men were armed, and that the boats were provisioned in case of emer- gency. Every man had to be instructed in the duties expected of him.

And Hornblower had to rehearse himself in ascending the main shrouds and laying out along the main topsail yard. He did it twice, forcing himself to make the difficult climb up the futtock shrouds, which, projecting outwards from the mainmast, made it necessary to climb several feet while hanging back downwards, locking fingers and toes into the ratlines. He could just manage it, moving slowly and carefully, although clumsily. He stood on the footrope and worked his way out to the yard-arm—the footrope was attached along the yard so as to hang nearly four feet below it. The principle was to set his feet on the rope with his arms over the yard, then holding the yard in his armpits, to shuffle sideways along the footrope to cast off the gaskets and loose the sail. Twice Hornblower made the whole journey, battling with the disquiet of his stomach at the thought of the hundred-foot drop below him. Finally, gulping with nervousness, he transferred his grip to the brace and forced himself to slide down it to the deck—that would be his best route when the time came to sheet the topsail home. It was a long perilous descent; Hornblower told himself—as indeed he had said to himself when he had first seen men go aloft—that similar feats in a circus at home would be received with "ohs" and "ahs" of appreciation. He was by no means satisfied with himself even when he reached the deck, and at the back of his mind was a vivid mental picture of his missing his hold when the time came for him to repeat the performance in the *Papillon*, and falling headlong to the deck—a second or two of frightful fear while rushing through the air, and then a shattering crash. And the success of the attack hinged on him, as much as on any-one—if the topsail were not promptly set to give the corvette steerage way she would run aground on one of the innumerable shoals in the river mouth to be ignominiously recaptured, and half the crew of the *Indefatigable* would be dead or prisoners.

In the waist the jolly boat's crew was formed up for his inspection. He saw to it that the oars were properly muffled, that each man had pistol and cutlass, and made sure that every pistol was at half cock so that there was no fear of a premature shot giving warning of the attack. He allocated duties to each man in the loosening of the top sail, laying stress on the possibility that casualties might necessitate unrehearsed changes in the scheme.

"I will mount the rigging first," said Hornblower.

That had to be the case. He had to lead—it was expected of him. More than that; if he had given any other order it would have excited comment—and contempt.

"Jackson," went on Hornblower, addressing the coxswain, "you will quit the boat last and take command if I fall."

"Aye aye, sir."

It was usual to use the poetic expression "fall" for "die", and it was only after Hornblower had uttered the word that he thought about its horrible real meaning in the present circumstances.

"Is that all understood?" asked Hornblower harshly; it was his mental stress that made his voice grate so.

Everyone nodded except one man.

"Begging your pardon, sir," said Hales, the young man who pulled stroke oar, "I'm feeling a bit queer-like."

Hales was a lightly built young fellow of swarthy countenance. He put his hand to his forehead with a vague gesture as he spoke.

"You're not the only one to feel queer," snapped Hornblower.

The other men chuckled. The thought of running the gauntlet of the shore batteries, of boarding an armed corvette in the teeth of opposition, might well raise apprehension in the breast of a coward. Most of the men detailed for the expedition must have felt qualms to some extent.

"I don't mean that, sir," said Hales indignantly. " 'Course I don't."

But Hornblower and the others paid him no attention.

"You just keep your mouth shut," growled Jackson. There could be nothing but contempt for a man who announced himself sick after being told off on a dangerous duty. Hornblower felt sympathy as well as contempt. He himself had been too much of a coward even to give voice to his apprehensions—too much afraid of what people would say about him.

"Dismiss," said Hornblower. "I'll pass the word for all of you when you are wanted."

There were some hours yet to wait while the *Indefatigable* crept inshore, with the lead going steadily and Pellew himself attending to the course of the frigate. Hornblower, despite his nervousness and his miserable apprehensions, yet found time to appreciate the superb seamanship displayed as Pellew brought the big frigate in through these tricky waters on that dark night. His interest was so caught by the procedure that the little tremblings which had been assailing him ceased to manifest themselves; Hornblower was of the type that would continue to observe and to learn on his deathbed. By the time the *Indefatigable* had reached the point off the mouth of the river where it was desirable to launch the boats, Hornblower had learned a good deal about the practical application of the principles of coastwise navigation and a good deal about the organization of a cutting-out expedition—and by self analysis he had learned even more about the psychology of a raiding party before a raid.

He had mastered himself to all outside appearance by the time he went down into the jolly boat as she heaved on the inky-black water, and he gave the command to shove off in a quiet steady voice. Hornblower took the tiller—the feel of that solid bar of wood was reassuring, and it was old habit now to sit in the stern sheets with hand and elbow upon it, and the men began to pull slowly after the dark shapes of the four big boats; there was plenty of time, and the flowing tide would take them up the estuary. That was just as well, for on one side of them lay the batteries of St. Dye, and inside the estuary on the other side was the fortress of Blaye; forty big guns trained to sweep the channel, and none of the five boats—certainly not the jolly boat—could withstand a single shot from one of them.

He kept his eyes attentively on the cutter ahead of him. Soames had the dreadful responsibility of taking the boats up the channel, while all he had to do was to follow in her wake—all, except to loose that maintopsail. Hornblower found himself shivering again.

Hales, the man who had said he felt queer, was pulling stroke oar; Hornblower could just see his dark form moving rhythmically back and forward at each slow stroke. After a single glance Hornblower paid him no more attention, and was staring after the cutter when a sudden commotion brought his mind back into the boat. Someone had missed his stroke; someone had thrown all six oars into confusion as a result. There was even a slight clatter.

"Mind what you're doing, blast you, Hales," whispered Jackson, the coxswain, with desperate urgency.

For answer there was a sudden cry from Hales, loud but fortunately not too loud, and Hales pitched forward against Hornblower's and Jackson's legs, kicking and writhing.

"The bastard's having a fit," growled Jackson.

The kicking and writhing went on. Across the water through the darkness came a sharp scornful whisper.

"Mr. Hornblower," said the voice—it was Eccles putting a world of exasperation into his sotto voce question—"cannot you keep your men quiet?"

Eccles had brought the launch round almost alongside the jolly boat to say this to him, and the desperate need for silence was dramatically demonstrated by the absence of any of the usual blasphemy; Hornblower could picture the cutting reprimand that would be administered to him tomorrow publicly on the quarterdeck. He opened his mouth to make an explanation, but he fortunately realized that raiders in open boats did not make explanations when under the guns of the fortress of Blaye.

"Aye aye, sir," was all he whispered back, and the launch continued on its mission of shepherding the flotilla in the tracks of the cutter.

"Take his oar, Jackson," he whispered furiously to the coxswain, and he stooped and with his own hands dragged the writhing figure towards him and out of Jackson's way.

"You might try pouring water on 'im, sir," suggested Jackson hoarsely, as he moved to the afterthwart. "There's the baler 'andy."

Seawater was the seaman's cure for every ill, his panacea; seeing how often sailors had not merely wet jackets but wet bedding as well they should never have a day's illness. But Hornblower let the sick man lie. His struggles were coming to an end, and Hornblower wished to make no noise with the baler. The lives of more than a hundred men depended on silence. Now that they were well into the actual estuary they were within easy reach of cannon shot from the shore—and a single cannon shot would rouse the crew of the *Papillon,* ready to man the bulwarks to beat off the attack, ready to drop cannon balls into the boats alongside, ready to shatter approaching boats with a tempest of grape.

Silently the boats glided up the estuary; Soames in the cutter was setting a slow pace, with only an occasional stroke at the oars to maintain steerage way. Presumably he knew very well what he was doing; the channel he had selected was an obscure one between mudbanks, impracticable for anything except small boats, and he had a twenty-foot pole with him with which to take the soundings—quicker and much more silent than using the lead. Minutes were passing fast, and yet the night was still utterly dark, with no hint of approaching dawn. Strain his eyes as he would Hornblower could not be sure that he could see the flat shores on either side of him. It would call for sharp eyes on the land to detect the little boats being carried up by the tide.

Hales at his feet stirred and then stirred again. His hand, feeling round in the darkness, found Hornblower's ankle and apparently examined it with curiosity. He muttered something, the words dragging out into a moan.

"Shut up!" whispered Hornblower, trying, like the saint of old, to make a tongue of his whole body, that he might express the urgency of the occasion without making a sound audible at any distance. Hales set his elbow on Hornblower's knee and levered himself up into a sitting position, and then levered himself further until he was standing, swaying with bent knees and supporting himself against Hornblower.

"Sit down, damn you!" whispered Hornblower, shaking with fury and anxiety.

"Where's Mary?" asked Hales in a conversational tone.

"Shut up!"

"Mary!" said Hales, lurching against him. "Mary!"

Each successive word was louder. Hornblower felt instinctively that Hales would soon be speaking in a loud voice, that he might even soon be shouting. Old recollections of conversations with his doctor father stirred at the back of his mind; he remembered that persons emerging from epileptic fits were not responsible for their actions, and might be, and often were, dangerous.

"Mary!" said Hales again.

Victory and the lives of a hundred men depended on silencing Hales, and silencing him instantly. Hornblower thought of the pistol in his belt, and of using the butt, but there was another weapon more conveniently to his hand. He unshipped the tiller, a three-foot bar of solid oak, and he swung it with all the venom and fury of despair. The tiller crashed down on Hales' head, and Hales, an unuttered word cut short in his throat, fell silent in the bottom of the boat. There was no sound from the boat's crew, save for something like a sigh from Jackson, whether approving or disapproving Hornblower neither knew nor cared. He had done his duty, and he was certain of it. He had struck down a helpless idiot; most probably he had killed him, but the surprise upon which the success of the expedition depended had not been imperilled. He reshipped the tiller and resumed the silent task of keeping in the wake of the gigs.

Far away ahead—in the darkness it was impossible to estimate the distance—there was a nucleus of greater darkness, close on the surface of the black water. It might be the corvette. A dozen more silent strokes, and Hornblower was sure of it. Soames had done a magnificent job of pilotage, leading the boats straight to that objective. The cutter and launch were diverging now from the two gigs. The four boats were separating in readiness to launch their simultaneous converging attack.

"Easy!" whispered Hornblower, and the jolly boat's crew ceased to pull.

Hornblower had his orders. He had to wait until the attack had gained a foothold on the deck. His hand clenched convulsively on the tiller; the excitement of dealing with Hales had driven the thought of having to ascend strange rigging in the darkness clear out of his head, and now it recurred with redoubled urgency. Hornblower was afraid.

Although he could see the corvette, the boats had vanished from his sight, had passed out of his field of vision. The corvette rode to her anchor, her spars just visible against the night sky—that was where he had to climb! She seemed to tower up hugely. Close by the corvette he saw a splash in the dark water—the boats were closing in fast and someone's stroke had been a little careless. At the same moment came a shout from the corvette's deck, and when the shout was repeated it was echoed a hundred fold from the boats rushing alongside. The yelling was lusty and prolonged, of set purpose. A sleeping enemy would be bewildered by the din, and the progress of the shouting would tell each boat's crew to the extent of the success of the others. The British seamen were yelling like madmen. A flash and a bang from the corvette's deck told of the firing of the first shot; soon pistols were popping and muskets banging from several points of the deck.

"Give way!" said Hornblower. He uttered the order as if it had been torn from him by the rack.

The jolly boat moved forward, while Hornblower fought down his feelings and tried to make out what was going on on board. He could see no reason for choosing either side of the corvette in preference to the other, and the larboard side was the nearer, and so he steered the boat to the larboard main chains. So interested was he in what he was doing that he only remembered in the nick of time to give the order, "In oars". He put the tiller over and the boat swirled round and the bowman hooked on. From the deck just above came a noise exactly like a tinker hammering on a cooking-pot—Hornblower noted the curious noise as he stood up in the stern sheets. He felt the cutlass at his side and the pistol in his belt, and then he sprang for the chains. With a mad leap he reached them and hauled himself up. The shrouds came into his hands, his feet found the ratlines beneath them, and he began to climb. As his head cleared the bulwark and he could see the deck the flash of a pistol shot illuminated the scene momentarily, fixing the struggle on the deck in a static moment, like a picture. Before and below him a British seaman was fighting a furious cutlass duel with a French officer, and he realized with vague astonishment that the kettle-mending noise he had heard was the sound of cutlass against cutlass—that clash of steel against steel that poets wrote about. So much for romance.

The realization carried him far up the shrouds. At his elbow he felt the futtock shrouds and he transferred himself to them, hanging back downward with his toes hooked into the ratlines and his hands clinging like death. That only lasted for two or three desperate seconds, and then he hauled himself onto the topmast shrouds and began the final ascent, his lungs bursting with the effort. Here was the topsail yard, and Hornblower flung himself across it and felt with his feet for the footrope. Merciful God! There was no footrope—his feet searching in the darkness met only unresisting air. A hundred feet above the deck he hung, squirming and kicking like a baby held up at arm's length in its father's hands. There was no footrope; it may have been with this very situation in mind that the Frenchmen had removed it. There was no footrope, so that he could not make his way out to the yardarm. Yet the gaskets must be cast off and the sail loosed—everything depended on that. Hornblower had seen daredevil seamen run out along the yards standing upright, as though walking a tightrope. That was the only way to reach the yardarm now.

For a moment he could not breathe as his weak flesh revolted against the thought of walking along that yard above the black abyss. This was fear, the fear that stripped a man of his manhood, turning his bowels to water and his limbs to paper. Yet his furiously active mind continued to work. He had been resolute enough in dealing with Hales. Where he personally was not involved he had been brave enough; he had not hesitated to strike down the wretched epileptic with all the strength of his arm. That was the poor sort of courage he was capable of displaying. In the simple vulgar matter of physical bravery he was utterly wanting. This was cowardice, the sort of thing that men spoke about behind their hands to other men. He could not bear the thought of that in himself—it was worse (awful though the alternative might be) than the thought of falling through the night to the deck. With a gasp he brought his knee up onto the yard, heaving himself up until he stood upright. He felt the rounded, canvas-covered timber under his feet, and his instincts told him not to dally there for a moment.

"Come on, men!" he yelled, and he dashed out along the yard.

It was twenty feet to the yardarm, and he covered the distance in a few frantic strides. Utterly reckless by now, he put his hands down on the yard, clasped it, and laid his body across it again, his hands seeking the gaskets. A thump on the yard told him that Oldroyd, who had been detailed to come after him, had followed him out along the yard—he had six feet less to go. There could be no doubt that the other members of the jolly boat's crew were on the yard, and that Clough had led the way to the starboard yardarm. It was obvious from the rapidity with which the sail came loose. Here was the brace beside him. Without any thought of danger now, for he was delirious with excitement and triumph, he grasped it with both hands and jerked himself off the yard. His waving legs found the rope and twined about it, and he let himself slide down it.

Fool that he was! Would he never learn sense and prudence? Would he never remember that vigilance and precaution must never be relaxed? He had allowed himself to slide so fast that the rope seared his hands, and when he tried to tighten his grip so as to slow down his progress it caused him such agony that he had to relax it again and slide on down with the rope stripping the skin from his hands as though peeling off a glove. His feet reached the deck and he momentarily forgot the pain as he looked round him.

There was the faintest grey light beginning to show now, and there were no sounds of battle. It had been a well-worked surprise—a hundred men flung suddenly on the deck of the corvette had swept away the anchor watch and mastered the vessel in a single rush before the watch below could come up to offer any resistance. Chadd's stentorian voice came pealing from the forecastle.

"Cable's cut, sir!"

Then Eccles bellowed from aft.

"Mr. Hornblower!"

"Sir!" yelled Hornblower.

"Man the halliards!"

A rush of men came to help—not only his own boat's crew but every man of initiative and spirit. Halliards, sheets and braces; the sail was trimmed round and was drawing full in the light southerly air, and the

Papillon swung round to go down with the first of the ebb. Dawn was coming up fast, with a trifle of mist on the surface of the water.

Over the starboard quarter came a sullen bellowing roar, and then the misty air was torn by a series of infernal screams, supernaturally loud. The first cannon balls Hornblower ever heard were passing him by.

"Mr. Chadd! Set the headsails! Loose the foretops'l. Get aloft, some of you, and set the mizzen tops'l."

From the port bow came another salvo—Blaye was firing at them from one side, St. Dye from the other, now they could guess what had happened on board the *Papillon*. But the corvette was moving fast with wind and tide, and it would be no easy matter to cripple her in the half light. It had been a very near-run thing; a few seconds' delay could have been fatal. Only one shot from the next salvo passed within hearing, and its passage was marked by a loud snap overhead.

"Mr. Mallory, get that forestay spliced!"

"Aye aye, sir!"

It was light enough to look round the deck now; he could see Eccles at the break of the poop, directing the handling of the corvette, and Soames beside the wheel conning her down the channel. Two groups of red-coated marines, with bayonets fixed, stood guard over the hatchways. There were four or five men lying on the deck in curiously abandoned attitudes. Dead men; Hornblower could look at them with the callousness of youth. But there was a wounded man, too, crouched groaning over his shattered thigh—Hornblower could not look at him as disinterestedly, and he was glad, maybe only for his own sake, when at that moment a seaman asked for and received permission from Mallory to leave his duties and attend to him.

"Stand by to go about!" shouted Eccles from the poop; the corvette had reached the tip of the middle ground shoal and was about to make the turn that would carry her into the open sea.

The men came running to the braces, and Hornblower tailed on along with them. But the first contact with the harsh rope gave him such pain that he almost cried out. His hands were like raw meat, and fresh-killed at that, for blood was running from them. Now that his attention was called to them they smarted unbearably.

The headsail sheets came over, and the corvette went handily about.

"There's the old *Indy*!" shouted somebody.

The *Indefatigable* was plainly visible now, lying-to just out of shot from the shore batteries, ready to rendezvous with her prize. Somebody cheered, and the cheering was taken up by everyone, even while the last shots from St. Dye, fired at extreme range, pitched sullenly into the water alongside. Hornblower had gingerly extracted his handkerchief from his pocket and was trying to wrap it round his hand.

"Can I help you with that, sir?" asked Jackson.

Jackson shook his head as he looked at the raw surface.

"You was careless, sir. You ought to 'a gone down 'and over 'and," he said, when Hornblower explained to him how the injury had been caused. "Very careless, you was, beggin' your pardon for saying so, sir. But you young gennelmen often is. You don't 'ave no thought for your necks, nor your 'ides, sir."

Hornblower looked up at the maintopsail yard high above his head, and remembered how he had walked along that slender stick of timber out to the yardarm in the dark. At the recollection of it, even here with the solid deck under his feet, he shuddered a little.

"Sorry, sir. Didn't mean to 'urt you," said Jackson, tying the knot. "There, that's done, as good as I can do it, sir."

"Thank you, Jackson," said Hornblower.

"We got to report the jolly boat as lost, sir," went on Jackson.

"Lost?"

"She ain't towing alongside, sir. You see, we didn't leave no boat-keeper in 'er. Wells, 'e was to be boatkeeper, you remember, sir. But I sent 'im up the rigging a'ead o' me, seeing that 'Ales couldn't go. We wasn't too many for the job. So the jolly boat must 'a come adrift, sir, when the ship went about."

"What about Hales, then?" asked Hornblower.

" 'E was still in the boat, sir."

Hornblower looked back up the estuary of the Gironde. Somewhere up there the jolly boat was drifting about, and lying in it was Hales, probably dead, possibly alive. In either case the French would find him, surely enough, but a cold wave of regret extinguished the warm feeling of triumph in Hornblower's bosom when he thought about Hales back there. If it had not been for Hales he would never have nerved himself (so at least he thought) to run out to the maintopsail yardarm; he would at this moment be ruined and branded as a coward instead of basking in the satisfaction of having capably done his duty.

Jackson saw the bleak look in his face.

"Don't you take on so, sir," he said. "They won't 'old the loss of the jolly boat agin you, not the captain and Mr. Eccles, they won't."

"I wasn't thinking about the jolly boat," said Hornblower. "I was thinking about Hales."

"Oh, 'im?" said Jackson. "Don't you fret about 'im, sir. 'E wouldn't never 'ave made no seaman, not no 'ow."

THE MAN WHO SAW GOD

Winter had come to the Bay of Biscay. With the passing of the Equinox the gales began to increase in violence, adding infinitely to the labours and dangers of the British Navy watching over the coast of France; easterly gales, bitter cold, which the storm-tossed ships had to endure as best they could, when the spray froze on the rigging and the labouring hulls leaked like baskets; westerly gales, when the ships had to claw their way to safety from a lee shore and make a risky compromise between gaining sufficient sea-room and maintaining a position from which they could pounce on any French vessel venturing out of harbour. The storm-tossed ships, we speak about. But those ships were full of storm-tossed men, who week by week and month by month had to endure the continual cold and the continual wet, the salt provisions, the endless toil, the boredom and misery of life in the blockading fleet. Even in the frigates, the eyes and claws of the blockaders, boredom had to be endured, the boredom of long periods with the hatches battened down, with the deck seams above dripping water on the men below, long nights and short days, broken sleep and yet not enough to do.

Even in the *Indefatigable* there was a feeling of restlessness in the air, and even a mere midshipman like Hornblower could be aware of it as he was looking over the men of his division before the captain's regular weekly inspection.

"What's the matter with your face, Styles?" he asked.

"Boils, sir. Awful bad."

On Styles' cheeks and lips there were half a dozen dabs of sticking plaster.

"Have you done anything about them?"

"Surgeon's mate, sir, 'e give me plaister for 'em, an' 'e says they'll soon come right, sir."

"Very well."

Now was there, or was there not, something strained about the expressions on the faces of the men on either side of Styles? Did they look like men smiling secretly to themselves? Laughing up their sleeves? Hornblower did not want to be an object of derision; it was bad for discipline—and it was worse for discipline if the men shared some secret unknown to their officers. He glanced sharply along the line again.

75

Styles was standing like a block of wood, with no expression at all on his swarthy face; the black ringlets over his ears were properly combed, and no fault could be found with him. But Hornblower sensed that the recent conversation was a source of amusement to the rest of his division, and he did not like it.

After divisions he tackled Mr. Low the surgeon, in the gunroom.

"Boils—" said Low. "Of course the men have boils. Salt pork and split peas for nine weeks on end—what d'you expect but boils? Boils —gurry sores—blains—all the plagues of Egypt."

"On their faces?"

"That's one locality for boils. You'll find out others from your own personal experience."

"Does your mate attend to them?" persisted Hornblower.

"Of course."

"What's he like?"

"Muggridge?"

"Is that his name?"

"He's a good surgeon's mate. Get him to compound a black draught for you and you'll see. In fact, I'd prescribe one for you—you seem in a mighty bad temper, young man."

Mr. Low finished his glass of rum and pounded on the table for the steward. Hornblower realized that he was lucky to have found Low sober enough to give him even this much information, and turned away to go aloft so as to brood over the question in the solitude of the mizzen-top. This was his new station in action; when the men were not at their quarters a man might find a little blessed solitude there—something hard to find in the crowded *Indefatigable*. Bundled up in his peajacket, Hornblower sat in the mizzen-top; over his head the mizzen-topmast drew erratic circles against the grey sky; beside him the topmost shrouds sang their high-pitched note in the blustering gale, and below him the life of the ship went on as she rolled and pitched, standing to the northward under close reefed topsails. At eight bells she would wear to the southward again on her incessant patrol. Until that time Hornblower was free to meditate on the boils on Styles' face and the covert grins on the faces of the other men of the division.

Two hands appeared on the stout wooden barricade surrounding the top, and as Hornblower looked up with annoyance at having his meditations interrupted a head appeared above them. It was Finch, another man in Hornblower's division, who also had his station in action here in the mizzen-top. He was a frail little man with wispy hair and pale blue eyes and a foolish smile, which lit up his face when, after betraying some disappointment at finding the mizzen-top already occupied, he recognized Hornblower.

"Beg pardon, sir," he said. "I didn't know as how you was up here."

Finch was hanging on uncomfortably, back downwards, in the act of transferring himself from the futtock shrouds to the top, and each roll threatened to shake him loose.

"Oh come here if you want to," said Hornblower, cursing himself for his soft-heartedness. A taut officer, he felt, would have told Finch to go back whence he came and not bother him.

"Thank 'ee, sir. Thank 'ee," said Finch, bringing his leg over the barricade and allowing the ship's roll to drop him into the top.

He crouched down to peer under the foot of the mizzen-topsail forward to the mainmast head, and then turned back to smile disarmingly at Hornblower like a child caught in moderate mischief. Hornblower knew that Finch was a little weak in the head—the all embracing press swept up idiots and landsmen to help man the fleet—although he was a trained seaman who could hand, reef and steer. That smile betrayed him.

"It's better up here than down below, sir," said Finch, apologetically.

"You're right," said Hornblower, with a disinterested intonation which would discourage conversation.

He turned away to ignore Finch, settled his back again comfortably, and allowed the steady swing of the top to mesmerize him into dreamy thought that might deal with his problem. Yet it was not easy, for Finch was as restless almost as a squirrel in a cage, peering forward, changing his position, and so continually breaking in on Hornblower's train of thought, wasting the minutes of his precious half-hour of freedom.

"What the devil's the matter with you, Finch?" he rasped at last, patience quite exhausted.

"The Devil, sir?" said Finch. "It isn't the Devil. He's not up here, begging your pardon, sir."

That weak mysterious grin again, like a mischievous child. A great depth of secrets lay in those strange blue eyes. Finch peered under the topsail again; it was a gesture like a baby's playing peep-bo.

"There!" said Finch. "I saw him that time, sir. God's come back to the maintop, sir."

"God?"

"Aye indeed, sir. Sometimes He's in the maintop. More often than not, sir. I saw Him that time, with His beard all a-blowing in the wind. 'Tis only from here that you can see Him, sir."

What could be said to a man with that sort of delusion? Hornblower racked his brains for an answer, and found none. Finch seemed to have forgotten his presence, and was playing peep-bo again under the foot of the mizzen-topsail.

"There He is!" said Finch to himself. "There He is again! God's in the maintop, and the Devil's in the cable tier."

"Very appropriate," said Hornblower cynically, but to himself. He had no thought of laughing at Finch's delusions.

"The Devil's in the cable tier during the dog watches," said Finch again to no one at all. "God stays in the maintop for ever."

"A curious timetable," was Hornblower's sotto voce comment.

From down on the deck below came the first strokes of eight bells, and at the same moment the pipes of the bosun's mates began to twitter, and the bellow of Waldron the bos'un made itself heard.

"Turn out the watch below! All hands wear ship! All hands! All hands! You, master-at-arms, take the name of the last man up the hatchway. All hands!"

The interval of peace, short as it was, and broken by Finch's disturbing presence, was at an end. Hornblower dived over the barricade and gripped the futtock shrouds; not for him was the easy descent through the lubber's hole, not when the first lieutenant might see him and reprimand him for unseamanlike behaviour. Finch waited for him to quit the top, but even with this length start Hornblower was easily outpaced in the descent to the deck, for Finch, like the skilled seaman he was, ran down the shrouds as lightly as a monkey. Then the thought of Finch's curious illusions was temporarily submerged in the business of laying the ship on her new course.

But later in the day Hornblower's mind reverted inevitably to the odd things Finch had been saying. There could be no doubt that Finch firmly believed he saw what he said he saw. Both his words and his expression made that certain. He had spoken about God's beard—it was a pity that he had not spared a few words to describe the Devil in the cable tier. Horns, cloven hoof, and pitchfork? Hornblower wondered. And why was the Devil only loose in the cable tier during the dog watches? Strange that he should keep to a timetable. Hornblower caught his breath as the sudden thought came to him that perhaps there might be some worldly explanation. The Devil might well be loose in the cable tier in a metaphorical fashion during the dog watches. Devil's work might be going on there. Hornblower had to decide further on what was expedient. He could report his suspicions to Eccles, the first lieutenant; but after a year of service Hornblower was under no illusions about what might happen to a junior midshipman who worried a first lieutenant with unfounded suspicions. It would be better to see for himself first, as far as that went. But he did not know what he would find—if he should find anything at all—and he did not know how he should deal with it if he found anything. Much worse than that, he did not know if he would be able to deal with it in officer-like fashion. He could make a fool of himself. He might mishandle whatever situation he found, and bring down obloquy and derision upon his head, and he might imperil the discipline of the ship—weaken the slender thread of allegiance that bound officers and men together, the discipline which kept three hundred men at the bidding of their captain suffering untold hardship without demur; which made them ready to face death at the word of command. When eight bells told the end of the afternoon watch and the beginning of the first dog watch it was with trepidation that Hornblower went below to put a candle in a lantern and make his way forward to the cable tier.

It was dark down here, stuffy, odorous; and as the ship heaved and rolled he found himself stumbling over the various obstacles that impeded his progress. Yet forward there was a faint light, a murmur of voices. Hornblower choked down his fear that perhaps mutiny was being planned. He put his hand over the horn window of the lantern, so as to obscure its light, and crept forward. Two lanterns swung from the low deck-beams, and crouching under them were a score or more of men—more than that, even—and the buzz of their talk came loudly but indistinguishably to Hornblower's ears. Then the buzz increased to a roar, and someone in the centre of the circle rose suddenly to as near his full height as the deck-beams allowed. He was shaking himself violently from side to side for no apparent reason; his face was away from Hornblower, who saw with a gasp that his hands were tied behind him. The men roared again, like spectators at a prize-fight, and the man with his hands tied swung round so that Hornblower could see his face. It was Styles, the man who suffered from boils; Hornblower knew him at once. But that was not what made the most impression on Hornblower. Clinging to the man's face, weird in the shifting meagre light, was a grey writhing shape, and it was to shake this off that Styles was flinging himself about so violently. It was a rat; Hornblower's stomach turned over with horror.

With a wild jerk of his head Styles broke the grip of the rat's teeth and flung the creature down, and then instantly plunged down on his knees, with his hands still bound behind him, to pursue it with his own teeth.

"Time!" roared a voice at that moment—the voice of Partridge, bosun's mate. Hornblower had been roused by it often enough to recognize it at once.

"Five dead," said another voice. "Pay all bets of evens or better."

Hornblower plunged forward. Part of the cable had been coiled down to make a rat pit ten feet across in which knelt Styles with dead and living rats about his knees. Partridge squatted beside the ring with a sandglass—used for timing the casting of the log—in front of him.

"Six dead," protested someone. "That 'un's dead."

"No, he ain't."

" 'Is back's broken. 'E's a dead 'un."

" 'E ain't a dead 'un," said Partridge.

The man who had protested looked up at that moment and caught sight of Hornblower, and his words died away unspoken; at his silence the others followed his glance and stiffened into rigidity, and Hornblower stepped forward. He was still wondering what he should do; he was still fighting down the nausea excited by the horrible things he had seen. Desperately he mastered his horror, and, thinking fast, took his stand on discipline.

"Who's in charge here?" he demanded.

He ran his eye round the circle. Petty officers and second-class warrant officers, mainly; bosun's mates, carpenter's mates. Muggridge, the surgeon's mate—his presence explained much. But his own position was not easy. A midshipman of scant service depended for his authority on board largely on the force of his own personality. He was only a warrant officer himself; when all was said and done a midshipman was not nearly as important to the ship's economy—and was far more easily replaced—than, say, Washburn, the cooper's mate over there, who knew all about the making and storage of the ship's water barrels.

"Who's in charge here?" he demanded again, and once more received no direct reply.

"We ain't on watch," said a voice in the background.

Hornblower by now had mastered his horror; his indignation still flared within him, but he could appear outwardly calm.

"No, you're not on watch," he said coldly. "You're gambling."

Muggridge took up the defence at that.

"Gambling, Mr. Hornblower?" he said. "That's a very serious charge. Just a gentlemanly competition. You'll find it hard to sub—substantiate any charges of gambling."

Muggridge had been drinking, quite obviously, following perhaps the example of the head of his department. There was always brandy to be got in the medical stores. A surge of wrath made Hornblower tremble; the effort necessary to keep himself standing stock still was almost too much for him. But the rise in internal pressure brought him inspiration.

"Mr. Muggridge," he said icily, "I advise you not to say too much. There are other charges possible, Mr. Muggridge. A member of His Majesty's forces can be charged with rendering himself unfit for service, Mr. Muggridge. And similarly there might be charges of aiding and abetting which might include *you*. I should consult the Articles of War if I were you, Mr. Muggridge. The punishment for such an offence is flogging round the fleet I believe."

Hornblower pointed to Styles, with the blood streaming from his bitten face, and gave more force to his argument by the gesture. He had met the men's arguments with a more effective one along the same lines; they had taken up a legalistic defence and he had legalistically beaten it down. He had the upper hand now and could give vent to his moral indignation.

"I could bring charges against every one of you," he roared. "You could be court martialled—disrated—flogged—every man Jack of you. By God, one more look like that from you, Partridge, and I'll do it. You'd all be in irons five minutes after I spoke to Mr. Eccles. I'll have no more of these filthy games. Let those rats loose there, you, Oldroyd, and you, Lewis. Styles, get your face plastered up again. You, Partridge, take these men and coil this cable down properly again before Mr. Waldron sees it. I'll keep my eye on all of you in future. The next hint I have of misbehaviour and you'll all be at the gratings. I've said it, and by God I mean it!"

Hornblower was surprised both at his own volubility and at his self-possession. He had not known himself capable of carrying off matters with such a high hand. He sought about in his mind for a final salvo with which to make his retirement dignified, and it came to him as he turned away so that he turned back to deliver it.

"After this I want to see you in the dog watches skylarking on deck, not skulking in the cable tiers like a lot of Frenchmen."

That was the sort of speech to be expected of a pompous old captain, not a junior midshipman, but it served to give dignity to his retirement. There was a feverish buzz of voices as he left the group. Hornblower went up on deck, under the cheerless grey sky dark with premature night, to walk the deck to keep himself warm while the *Indefatigable* slashed her way to windward in the teeth of a roaring westerly, the spray flying in sheets over her bows, the straining seams leaking and her fabric groaning; the end of a day like all the preceding ones and the predecessor probably of innumerable more.

Yet the days passed, and with them came at last a break in the monotony. In the sombre dawn a hoarse bellow from the lookout turned every eye to windward, to where a dull blotch on the horizon marked the presence of a ship. The watch came running to the braces as the *Indefatigable* was laid as close to the wind as she would lie. Captain Pellew came on deck with a peajacket over his nightshirt, his wigless head comical in a pink nightcap; he trained his glass on the strange sail—a dozen glasses were pointing in that direction. Hornblower, look-through the glass reserved for the junior officer of the watch saw the grey rectangle split into three, saw the three grow narrow, and then broaden again to coalesce into a single rectangle again.

"She's gone about," said Pellew. "Hands 'bout ship!"

Round came the *Indefatigable* on the other tack; the watch raced aloft to shake out a reef from the topsails while from the deck the officers looked up at the straining canvas to calculate the chances of the gale which howled round their ears splitting the sails or carrying away a spar. The *Indefatigable* lay over until it was hard to keep one's footing on the streaming deck; everyone without immediate duties clung to the weather rail and peered at the other ship.

"Fore- and maintopmasts exactly equal," said Lieutenant Bolton to Hornblower, his telescope to his eye. "Topsails white as milady's fingers. She's a Frenchie all right."

The sails of British ships were darkened with long service in all weathers; when a French ship escaped from harbour to run the blockade her spotless unweathered canvas disclosed her nationality without real need to take into consideration less obvious technical characteristics.

"We're weathering on her," said Hornblower; his eye was aching with staring through the glass, and his arms even were weary with holding the telescope to his eye, but in the excitement of the chase he could not relax.

"Not as much as I'd like," growled Bolton.

"Hands to the mainbrace!" roared Pellew at that moment.

It was a matter of the most vital concern to trim the sails so as to lie as close as possible to the wind; a hundred yards gained to windward would count as much as a mile gained in a stern chase. Pellew was looking up at the sails, back at the fleeting wake, across at the French ship, gauging the strength of the wind, estimating the strain on the rigging, doing everything that a lifetime of experience could suggest to close the gap between the two ships. Pellew's next order sent all hands to run out the guns on the weather side; that would in part counteract the heel and give the *Indefatigable* more grip upon the water.

"Now we're walking up to her," said Bolton with grudging optimism.

"Beat to quarters!" shouted Pellew.

The ship had been expecting that order. The roar of the marine bandsmen's drums echoed through the ship; the pipes twittered as the bosun's mates repeated the order, and the men ran in disciplined fashion to their duties. Hornblower, jumping for the weather mizzen shrouds, saw the eager grins on half a dozen faces—battle and the imminent possibility of death were a welcome change from the eternal monotony of the blockade. Up in the mizzen-top he looked over his men. They were uncovering the locks of their muskets and looking to the priming; satisfied with their readiness for action Hornblower turned his attention to the swivel gun. He took the tarpaulin from the breech and the tompion from the muzzle, cast off the lashings which secured it, and saw that the swivel moved freely in the socket and the trunnions freely in the crotch. A jerk of the lanyard showed him that the lock was sparkling well and there was no need for a new flint. Finch came climbing into the top with the canvas belt over his shoulder containing the charges for the gun; the bags of musket balls lay handy in a garland fixed to the barricade. Finch rammed home a cartridge down the short muzzle;

Hornblower had ready a bag of balls to ram down onto it. Then he took a priming-quill and forced it down the touchhole, feeling sensitively to make sure the sharp point pierced the thin serge bag of the cartridge. Priming-quill and flintlock were necessary up here in the top, where no slow match or port-fire could be used with the danger of fire so great and where fire would be so difficult to control in the sails and the rigging. Yet musketry and swivel-gun fire from the tops were an important tactical consideration. With the ships laid yardarm to yardarm Hornblower's men could clear the hostile quarterdeck where centred the brains and control of the enemy.

"Stop that, Finch!" said Hornblower irritably; turning, he had caught sight of him peering up at the maintop and at this moment of tension Finch's delusions annoyed him.

"Beg your pardon, sir," said Finch, resuming his duties.

But a moment later Hornblower heard Finch whispering to himself.

"Mr. Bracegirdle's there," whispered Finch, "an' Oldroyd's there, an' all those others. But *He's* there too, so He is."

"Hands wear ship!" came the shouted order from the deck below.

The old *Indefatigable* was spinning round on her heel, the yards groaning as the braces swung them round. The French ship had made a bold attempt to rake her enemy as she clawed up to her, but Pellew's prompt handling defeated the plan. Now the ships were broadside to broadside, running free before the wind at long cannon shot.

"Just look at 'im!" roared Douglas, one of the musket men in the top. "Twenty guns a side. Looks brave enough, doesn't he?"

Standing beside Douglas Hornblower could look down on the Frenchman's deck, her guns run out with the guns' crews clustering round them, officers in white breeches and blue coats walking up and down, the spray flying from her bows as she drove headlong before the wind.

"She'll look braver still when we take her into Plymouth Sound," said the seaman on the far side of Hornblower.

The *Indefatigable* was slightly the faster ship; an occasional touch of starboard helm was working her in closer to the enemy, into decisive range, without allowing the Frenchman to headreach upon her. Hornblower was impressed by the silence on both sides; he had always understood that the French were likely to open fire at long range and to squander ineffectively the first carefully loaded broadside.

"When's he goin' to fire?" asked Douglas, echoing Hornblower's thoughts.

"In his own good time," piped Finch.

The gap of tossing water between the two ships was growing narrower. Hornblower swung the swivel gun round and looked along the sights. He could aim well enough at the Frenchman's quarter-deck, but it was much too long a range for a bag of musket balls—in any case he dared not open fire until Pellew gave permission.

"Them's the men for us!" said Douglas, pointing to the Frenchman's mizzen-top.

It looked as if there were soldiers up there, judging by the blue uniforms and the crossbelts; the French often eked out their scanty crews of trained seamen by shipping soldiers; in the British Navy the marines were never employed aloft. The French soldiers saw the gesture and shook their fists, and a young officer among them drew his sword and brandished it over his head. With the ships parallel to each other like this the French mizzen-top would be Hornblower's particular objective should he decide on trying to silence the firing there instead of sweeping the quarter-deck. He gazed curiously at the men it was his duty to kill. So interested was he that the bang of a cannon took him by surprise; before he could look down the rest of the Frenchman's broadside had gone off in straggling fashion, and a moment later the *Indefatigable* lurched as all her guns went off together. The wind blew the smoke forward, so that in the mizzen-top they were not troubled by it at all. Hornblower's glance showed him dead men flung about on the *Indefatigable*'s deck, dead men falling on the Frenchman's deck. Still the range was too great—very long musket shot, his eye told him.

"They're shootin' at us, sir," said Herbert.

"Let 'em," said Hornblower.

No musket fired from a heaving masthead at that range could possibly score a hit; that was obvious—so obvious that even Hornblower, madly excited as he was, could not help but be aware of it, and his certainty was apparent in his tone. It was interesting to see how the two calm words steadied the men. Down below the guns were roaring away continuously, and the ships were nearing each other fast.

"Open fire now, men!" said Hornblower. "Finch!"

He stared down the short length of the swivel gun. In the coarse V of the notch on the muzzle he could see the Frenchman's wheel, the two quartermasters standing behind it, the two officers beside it. He jerked the lanyard. A tenth of a second's delay, and then the gun roared out. He was conscious, before the smoke whirled round him, of the firing quill, blown from the touchhole, flying past his temple. Finch was already sponging out the gun. The musket balls must have spread badly; only one of the helmsmen was down and someone else was already running to take his place. At that moment the whole top lurched frightfully; Hornblower felt it but he could not explain it. There was too much happening at once. The solid timbers under his feet jarred him as he stood—perhaps a shot had hit the mizzen-mast. Finch was ramming in the cartridge; something struck the breech of the gun a heavy blow and left a bright splash of metal there—a musket bullet from the

Frenchman's mizzen-top. Hornblower tried to keep his head; he took out another sharpened quill and coaxed it down into the touchhole. It had to be done purposefully and yet gently; a quill broken off in the touchhole was likely to be a maddening nuisance. He felt the point of the quill pierce the cartridge; Finch rammed home the wad on top of the musket balls. A bullet struck the barricade beside him as Hornblower trained the gun down, but he gave it no thought. Surely the top was swaying more even than the heavy sea justified? No matter. He had a clear shot at the enemy's quarterdeck. He tugged at the lanyard. He saw men fall. He actually saw the spokes of the wheel spin round as it was left untended. Then the two ships came together with a shattering crash and his world dissolved into chaos compared with which what had gone before was orderly.

The mast was falling. The top swung round in a dizzy arc so that only his fortunate grip on the swivel saved him from being flung out like a stone from a sling. It wheeled round. With the shrouds on one side shot away and two cannon balls in its heart the mast tottered and rolled. Then the tug of the mizzen-stays inclined it forward, the tug of the other shrouds inclined it to starboard, and the wind in the mizzen-topsail took charge when the back stays parted. The mast crashed forward; the topmast caught against the mainyard and the whole structure hung there before it could dissolve into its constituent parts. The severed butt-end of the mast must be resting on the deck for the moment; mast and topmast were still united at the cap and the trestle-trees into one continuous length, although why the topmast had not snapped at the cap was hard to say. With the lower end of the mast resting precariously on the deck and the topmast resting against the mainyard, Hornblower and Finch still had a chance of life, but the ship's motion, another shot from the Frenchman, or the parting of the over-strained material could all end that chance. The mast could slip outwards, the topmast could break, the butt-end of the mast could slip along the deck—they had to save themselves if they could before any one of these imminent events occurred. The maintopmast and everything above it was involved in the general ruin. It too had fallen and was dangling, sails spars and ropes in one frightful tangle. The mizzen-topsail had torn itself free. Hornblower's eyes met Finch's; Finch and he were clinging to the swivel gun, and there was no one else in the steeply inclined top.

The starboard side mizzen-topmast shrouds still survived; they, as well as the topmast, were resting across the mainyard, strained taut as fiddle strings, the mainyard tightening them just as the bridge tightens the strings of a fiddle. But along those shrouds lay the only way to safety —a sloping path from the peril of the top to the comparative safety of the mainyard.

The mast began to slip, to roll, out towards the end of the yard. Even if the mainyard held, the mizzen-mast would soon fall into the sea alongside. All about them were thunderous noises—spars smashing, ropes parting; the guns were still bellowing and everyone below seemed to be yelling and screaming.

The top lurched again, frightfully. Two of the shrouds parted with the strain, with a noise clearly audible through the other din, and as they parted the mast twisted with a jerk, swinging further round the mizzen-top, the swivel gun, and the two wretched beings who clung to it. Finch's staring blue eyes rolled with the movement of the top. Later Hornblower knew that the whole period of the fall of the mast was no longer than a few seconds, but at this time it seemed as if he had at least long minutes in which to think. Like Finch's, his eyes stared round him, saw the chance of safety.

"The mainyard!" he screamed.

Finch's face bore its foolish smile. Although instinct or training kept him gripping the swivel gun he seemingly had no fear, no desire to gain the safety of the mainyard.

"Finch, you fool!" yelled Hornblower.

He locked a desperate knee round the swivel so as to free a hand with which to gesticulate, but still Finch made no move.

"Jump, damn you!" raved Hornblower. "The shrouds—the yard. Jump!"

Finch only smiled.

"Jump and get to the maintop! Oh, Christ—!" Inspiration came in that frightful moment. "The maintop! God's there, Finch! Go along to God, quick!"

Those words penetrated into Finch's addled brain. He nodded with sublime unworldliness. Then he let go of the swivel and seemed to launch himself into the air like a frog. His body fell across the mizzen-topmast shrouds and he began to scramble along them. The mast rolled again, so that when Hornblower launched himself at the shrouds it was a longer jump. Only his shoulders reached the outermost shroud. He swung off, clung, nearly lost his grip, but regained it as a counterlurch of the leaning mast came to his assistance. Then he was scrambling along the shrouds, mad with panic. Here was the precious mainyard, and he threw himself across it, grappling its welcome solidity with his body, his feet feeling for the footrope. He was safe and steady on the yard just as the outward roll of the *Indefatigable* gave the balancing spars their final impetus, and the mizzen-topmast parted company from the broken mizzen-mast and the whole wreck fell down into the sea alongside. Hornblower shuffled along the yard, whither Finch had preceded him, to be received with rapture in the maintop by Midshipman Bracegirdle. Bracegirdle was not God, but as Hornblower leaned across the breastwork of the maintop he thought to himself that if he had not spoken about God being in the maintop Finch would never have made that leap.

"Thought we'd lost you," said Bracegirdle, helping him in and thumping him on the back. "Midshipman Hornblower, our flying angel."

Finch was in the top, too, smiling his fool's smile and surrounded by the crew of the top. Everything seemed mad and exhilarating. It was a shock to remember that they were in the midst of a battle, and yet the firing had ceased, and even the yelling had almost died away. He staggered to the side of the top—strange how difficult it was to walk —and looked over. Bracegirdle came with him. Foreshortened by the height he could make out a crowd of figures on the Frenchman's deck. Those check shirts must surely be worn by British sailors. Surely that was Eccles, the *Indefatigable's* first lieutenant on the quarterdeck with a speaking trumpet.

"What has happened?" he asked Bracegirdle, bewildered.

"What has happened?" Bracegirdle stared for a moment before he understood. "We carried her by boarding. Eccles and the boarders were over the ship's side the moment we touched. Why, man, didn't you see?"

"No, I didn't see it," said Hornblower. He forced himself to joke. "Other matters demanded my attention at that moment."

He remembered how the mizzen-top had lurched and swung, and he felt suddenly sick. But he did not want Bracegirdle to see it.

"I must go on deck and report," he said.

The descent of the main shrouds was a slow, ticklish business, for neither his hands nor his feet seemed to wish to go where he tried to place them. Even when he reached the deck he still felt insecure. Bolton was on the quarterdeck supervising the clearing away of the wreck of the mizzen-mast. He gave a start of surprise as Hornblower approached.

"I thought you were overside with Davy Jones," he said. He glanced aloft, "You reached the mainyard in time?"

"Yes, sir."

"Excellent. I think you're born to be hanged, Hornblower." Bolton turned away to bellow at the men. " 'Vast heaving, there! Clynes, get down into the chains with that tackle! Steady, now, or you'll lose it."

He watched the labours of the men for some moments before he turned back to Hornblower.

"No more trouble with the men for a couple of months," he said. "We'll work 'em 'til they drop, refitting. Prize crew will leave us short-handed, to say nothing of our butcher's bill. It'll be a long time before they want something new. It'll be a long time for you, too, I fancy, Hornblower."

"Yes, sir," said Hornblower.

THE FROGS AND THE LOBSTERS

"They're coming," said Midshipman Kennedy.

Midshipman Hornblower's unmusical ear caught the raucous sounds of a military band, and soon, with a gleam of scarlet and white and gold, the head of the column came round the corner. The hot sunshine was reflected from the brass instruments; behind them the regimental colour flapped from its staff, borne proudly by an ensign with the colour guard round him. Two mounted officers rode behind the colour, and after them came the long red serpent of the half-battalion, the fixed bayonets flashing in the sun, while all the children of Plymouth, still not sated with military pomp, ran along with them.

The sailors standing ready on the quay looked at the soldiers marching up curiously, with something of pity and something of contempt mingled with their curiosity. The rigid drill, the heavy clothing, the iron discipline, the dull routine of the soldier were in sharp contrast with the far more flexible conditions in which the sailor lived. The sailors watched as the band ended with a flourish, and one of the mounted officers wheeled his horse to face the column. A shouted order turned every man to face the quayside, the movements being made so exactly together that five hundred boot-heels made a single sound. A huge sergeant-major, his sash gleaming on his chest, and the silver mounting of his cane winking in the sun, dressed the already perfect line. A third order brought down every musket-butt to earth.

"Unfix—bayonets!" roared the mounted officer, uttering the first words Hornblower had understood.

Hornblower positively goggled at the ensuing formalities, as the fuglemen strode their three paces forward, all exactly to time like marionettes worked by the same strings, turned their heads to look down the line, and gave the time for detaching the bayonets, for sheathing them, and for returning the muskets to the men's sides. The fuglemen fell back into their places, exactly to time again as far as Hornblower could see, but not exactly enough apparently, as the sergeant-major bellowed his discontent and brought the fuglemen out and sent them back again.

"I'd like to see him laying aloft on a stormy night," muttered Kennedy. "D'ye think he could take the maintops'l earring?"

"These lobsters!" said Midshipman Bracegirdle.

The scarlet lines stood rigid, all five companies, the sergeants with their halberds indicating the intervals—from halberd to halberd, the line of faces dipped down and then up again, with the men exactly sized off, the tallest men at the flanks and the shortest men in the centre of each company. Not a finger moved, not an eyebrow twitched. Down every back hung rigidly a powdered pigtail.

The mounted officer trotted down the line to where the naval party waited, and Lieutenant Bolton, in command, stepped forward with his hand to his hat brim.

"My men are ready to embark, sir," said the army officer. "The baggage will be here immediately."

"Aye aye, major," said Bolton—the army title and the navy reply in strange contrast.

"It would be better to address me as 'My lord'," said the major.

"Aye aye, sir—my lord," replied Bolton, caught quite off his balance.

His Lordship, the Earl of Edrington, major commanding this wing of the 43rd Foot, was a heavily built young man in his early twenties. He was a fine soldierly figure in his well-fitting uniform, and mounted on a magnificent charger, but he seemed a little young for his present responsible command. But the practice of the purchase of commissions was liable to put very young men in high command, and the Army seemed satisfied with the system.

"The French auxiliaries have their orders to report here," went on Lord Edrington. "I suppose arrangements have been made for their transport as well?"

"Yes, my lord."

"Not one of the beggars can speak English, as far as I can make out. Have you got an officer to interpret?"

"Yes, sir. Mr. Hornblower!"

"Sir!"

"You will attend to the embarkation of the French troops."

"Aye aye, sir."

More military music—Hornblower's tone-deaf ear distinguished it as making a thinner noise than the British infantry band—heralded the arrival of the Frenchmen farther down the quay by a side road, and Hornblower hastened there. This was the Royal, Christian, and Catholic French Army, or a detachment of it at least—a battalion of the force raised by the émigré French nobles to fight against the Revolution. There was the white flag with the golden lilies at the head of the column, and a group of mounted officers to whom Hornblower touched his hat. One of them acknowledged his salute.

"The Marquis of Pouzauges, Brigadier General in the service of His

Most Christian Majesty Louis XVII," said this individual in French by way of introduction. He wore a glittering white uniform with a blue ribbon across it.

Stumbling over the French words, Hornblower introduced himself as an aspirant to his Britannic Majesty's Marine, deputed to arrange the embarkation of the French troops.

"Very good," said Pouzauges. "We are ready."

Hornblower looked down the French column. The men were standing in all attitudes, gazing about them. They were all well enough dressed, in blue uniforms which Hornblower guessed had been supplied by the British government, but the white crossbelts were already dirty, the metal-work tarnished, the arms dull. Yet doubtless they could fight.

"Those are the transports allotted to your men, sir," said Hornblower, pointing. "The *Sophia* will take three hundred, and the *Dumbarton*—that one over there—will take two hundred and fifty. Here at the quay are the lighters to ferry the men out."

"Give the orders, M. de Moncoutant," said Pouzauges to one of the officers beside him.

The hired baggage carts had now come creaking up along the column, piled high with the men's kits, and the column broke into chattering swarms as the men hunted up their possessions. It was some time before the men were reassembled, each with his own kit-bag; and then there arose the question of detailing a fatigue party to deal with the regimental baggage, and the men who were given the task yielded up their bags with obvious reluctance to their comrades, clearly in despair of ever seeing any of the contents again. Hornblower was still giving out information.

"All horses must go to the *Sophia*," he said. "She has accommodation for six chargers. The regimental baggage—"

He broke off short, for his eye had been caught by a singular jumble of apparatus lying in one of the carts.

"What is that, if you please?" he asked, curiosity overpowering him.

"That, sir," said Pouzauges, "is a guillotine."

"A guillotine?"

Hornblower had read much lately about this instrument. The Red Revolutionaries had set one up in Paris and kept it hard at work. The King of France, Louis XVI himself, had died under it. He did not expect to find one in the train of a counter-revolutionary army.

"Yes," said Pouzauges, "we take it with us to France. It is in my mind to give those anarchists a taste of their own medicine."

Hornblower did not have to make reply, fortunately, as a bellow from Bolton interrupted the conversation.

"What the hell's all this delay for, Mr. Hornblower? D'you want us to miss the tide?"

It was of course typical of life in any service that Hornblower should be reprimanded for the time wasted by the inefficiency of the French arrangements—that was the sort of thing he had already come to expect, and he had already learned that it was better to submit silently to reprimand than to offer excuses. He addressed himself again to the task of getting the French aboard their transports. It was a weary midshipman who at last reported himself to Bolton with his tally sheets and the news that the last Frenchman and horse and pieces of baggage were safely aboard, and he was greeted with the order to get his things together quickly and transfer them and himself to the *Sophia,* where his services as interpreter were still needed.

The convoy dropped quickly down Plymouth Sound, rounded the Eddystone, and headed down channel, with H.M.S. *Indefatigable* flying her distinguishing pennant, the two gun-brigs which had been ordered to assist in convoying the expedition, and the four transports— a small enough force, it seemed to Hornblower, with which to attempt the overthrow of the French republic. There were only eleven hundred infantry; the half battalion of the 43rd and the weak battalion of Frenchmen (if they could be called that, seeing that many of them were soldiers of fortune of all nations) and although Hornblower had enough sense not to try to judge the Frenchmen as they lay in rows in the dark and stinking 'tweendecks in the agonies of seasickness he was puzzled that anyone could expect results from such a small force. His historical reading had told him of many small raids, in many wars, launched against the shores of France, and although he knew that they had once been described by an opposition statesman as "Breaking windows with guineas" he had been inclined to approve of them in principle, as bringing about a dissipation of the French strength—until now, when he found himself part of such an expedition.

So it was with relief that he heard from Pouzauges that the troops he had seen did not constitute the whole of the force to be employed —were indeed only a minor fraction of it. A little ·pale with seasickness, but manfully combating it, Pouzauges laid out a map on the cabin table and explained the plan.

"The Christian Army," explained Pouzauges, "will land here, at Quiberon. They sailed from Portsmouth—these English names are hard to pronounce—the day before we left Plymouth. There are five thousand men under the Baron de Charette. They will march on Vannes and Rennes."

"And what is your regiment to do?" asked Hornblower.

Pouzauges pointed to the map again.

"Here is the town of Muzillac," he said. "Twenty leagues from Quiberon. Here the main road from the south crosses the river Marais, where the tide ceases to flow. It is only a little river, as you see, but its banks·are marshy, and the road passes it not only by a bridge but by a long causeway. The rebel armies are to the south, and on their northward march must come by Muzillac. We shall be there. We shall destroy the bridge and defend the crossing, delaying the rebels long enough to enable M. de Charette to raise all Brittany. He will soon have twenty thousand men in arms, the rebels will come back to their allegiance, and we shall march on Paris to restore His Most Christian Majesty to the throne."

So that was the plan. Hornblower was infected with the Frenchmen's enthusiasm. Certainly the road passed within ten miles of the coast, and there, in the broad estuary of the Vilaine, it should be possible to land a small force and seize Muzillac. There should be no difficulty about defending a causeway such as Pouzauges described for a day or two against even a large force. That would afford Charette every chance.

"My friend M. de Moncoutant here," went on Pouzauges, "is Lord of Muzillac. The people there will welcome him."

"Most of them will," said Moncoutant, his grey eyes narrowing. "Some will be sorry to see me. But I shall be glad of the encounter."

Western France, the Vendée and Brittany, had long been in a turmoil, and the population there, under the leadership of the nobility, had risen in arms more than once against the Paris government. But every rebellion had ended in defeat; the Royalist force now being convoyed to France was composed of the fragments of the defeated armies —a final cast of the dice, and a desperate one. Regarded in that light, the plan did not seem so sound.

It was a grey morning—a morning of grey sky and grey rocks—when the convoy rounded Belle Ile and stood in towards the estuary of the Vilaine river. Far to the northward were to be seen white topsails in Quiberon Bay—Hornblower, from the deck of the *Sophia,* saw signals pass back and forth from the *Indefatigable* as she reported her arrival to the senior officer of the main expedition there. It was a proof of the mobility and ubiquity of naval power that it could take advantage of the configuration of the land so that two blows could be struck almost in sight of each other from the sea yet separated by forty miles of roads on land. Hornblower raked the forbidding shore with his glass, reread the orders for the captain of the *Sophia,* and stared again at the shore. He could distinguish the narrow mouth of the Marais river and the strip of mud where the troops were to land. The lead was going in the chains as the *Sophia* crept towards her allotted anchorage, and the ship was rolling uneasily; these waters, sheltered though they were, were a bedlam of conflicting currents that could make a choppy sea even in a calm. Then the anchor cable rumbled out through the hawse-hole and the *Sophia* swung to the current, while the crew set to work hoisting out the boats.

"France, dear beautiful France," said Pouzauges at Hornblower's side.

A hail came over the water from the *Indefatigable*.

"Mr. Hornblower!"

"Sir!" yelled Hornblower back through the captain's megaphone.

"You will go on shore with the French troops and stay with them until you receive further orders."

"Aye aye, sir."

So that was the way in which he was to set foot on foreign soil for the first time in his life.

Pouzauges' men were now pouring up from below; it was a slow and exasperating business getting them down the ship's side into the waiting boats. Hornblower wondered idly regarding what was happening on shore at this moment—without doubt mounted messengers were galloping north and south with the news of the arrival of the expedition, and soon the French Revolutionary generals would be parading their men and marching them hurriedly towards this place; it was well that the important strategic point that had to be seized was less than ten miles inland. He turned back to his duties; as soon as the men were ashore he would have to see that the baggage and reserve ammunition were landed, as well as the horses, now standing miserably in improvised stalls forward of the mainmast.

The first boats had left the ship's side; Hornblower watched the men stagger up the shore through mud and water, the French on the left and the red-coated British infantry on the right. There were some fishermen's cottages in sight up the beach, and Hornblower saw advance parties go forward to seize them; at least the landing had been effected without a single shot being fired. He came on shore with the ammunition, to find Bolton in charge of the beach.

"Get those ammunition boxes well above high-water mark," said Bolton. "We can't send 'em forward until the Lobsters have found us some carts for 'em. And we'll need horses for those guns too."

At that moment Bolton's working party was engaged in manhandling two six-pounder guns in field carriages up the beach; they were to be manned by seamen and drawn by horses commandeered by the landing party for it was in the old tradition that a British expeditionary force should always be thrown on shore dependent for military necessities on the countryside. Pouzauges and his staff were waiting impatiently for their chargers, and mounted them the moment they had been coaxed out of the boats onto the beach.

"Forward for France!" shouted Pouzauges, drawing his sword and raising the hilt to his lips.

Moncoutant and the others clattered forward to head the advancing infantry, while Pouzauges lingered to exchange a few words with Lord Edrington. The British infantry was drawn up in a rigid scarlet line; farther inland occasional red dots marked where the light company had been thrown forward as pickets. Hornblower could not hear the conversation, but he noticed that Bolton was drawn into it, and finally Bolton called him over.

"You must go forward with the Frogs, Hornblower," he said.

"I'll give you a horse," added Edrington. "Take that one—the roan. I've got to have someone I can trust along with them. Keep your eye on them and let me know the moment they get up to any monkey tricks —God knows what they'll do next."

"Here's the rest of your stores coming ashore," said Bolton. "I'll send 'em up as soon as you send some carts back to me. What the hell's *that*?"

"That's a portable guillotine sir," said Hornblower. "Part of the French baggage."

All three turned and looked at Pouzauges, sitting his horse impatiently during this conversation, which he did not understand. He knew what they were referring to, all the same.

"That's the first thing to be sent to Muzillac," he said to Hornblower. "Will you have the goodness to tell these gentlemen so?"

Hornblower translated.

"I'll send the guns and a load of ammunition first," said Bolton. "But I'll see he gets it soon. Now off you go."

Hornblower dubiously approached the roan horse. All he knew about riding he had learned in farmyards, but he got his foot up into the stirrup and climbed in the saddle, grabbing nervously at the reins as the animal started to move off. It seemed as far down to the ground from there as it did from the maintopgallant yard. Pouzauges wheeled his horse about and started up the beach, and the roan followed its example, with Hornblower hanging on desperately, spattered by the mud thrown up by the French horse's heels.

From the fishing hamlet a muddy lane, bordered by green turf banks, led inland, and Pouzauges trotted smartly along it, Hornblower jolting behind him. They covered three or four miles before they overtook the rear of the French infantry, marching rapidly through the mud, and Pouzauges pulled his horse to a walk. When the column climbed a slight undulation they could see the white banner far ahead. Over the banks Hornblower could see rocky fields; out on the left there was a small farmhouse of grey stone. A blue-uniformed soldier was leading away a white horse pulling a cart, while two or three more soldiers were holding back the farmer's frantic wife. So the expeditionary force had secured some of its necessary transport. In another field a soldier was prodding a cow along with his bayonet—Hornblower could not imagine with what motive. Twice he heard distant musket shots to which no one seemed to pay any attention. Then, coming down the road, they encountered two soldiers leading bony horses towards the beach; the jests hurled at them by the marching column had set the men's faces in broad grins. But a little way farther on Hornblower saw a plough standing lonely in a little field, and a grey bundle lying near it. The bundle was a dead man.

Over on their right was the marshy river valley, and it was not long before Hornblower could see, far ahead, the bridge and the causeway which they had been sent to seize. The lane they were following came down a slight incline into the town, passing between a few grey cottages before emerging into the highroad along which there lay the town. There was a grey stone church, there was a building that could easily be identified as an inn and postinghouse with soldiers swarming round it, a slight broadening of the highroad, with an avenue of trees, which Hornblower assumed must be the central square of the town. A few faces peered from upper windows, but otherwise the houses were shut and there were no civilians to be seen except two women hastily shuttering their shops. Pouzauges reined up his horse in the square and began issuing orders. Already the horses were being led out of the posthouse, and groups of men were bustling to and fro on seemingly urgent errands. In obedience to Pouzauges one officer called his men together —he had to expostulate and gesticulate before he succeeded—and started towards the bridge. Another party started along the highway in the opposite direction to guard against the possible surprise attack from there. A crowd of men squatted in the square devouring the bread that was brought out from one of the shops after its door had been beaten in, and two or three times civilians were dragged up to Pouzauges and at his orders were hurried away again to the town jail. The seizure of the town of Muzillac was complete.

Pouzauges seemed to think so, too, after an interval, for with a glance at Hornblower he turned his horse and trotted towards the causeway. The town ended before the road entered the marshes, and in a bit of waste ground beside the road the party sent out in this direction had already lighted a fire, and the men were gathered round it, toasting on their bayonets chunks of meat cut from a cow whose half-flayed corpse lay beside the fire. Farther on, where the causeway became the bridge over the river, a sentry sat sunning himself, with his musket leaning against the parapet of the bridge at his back. Everything was peaceful enough. Pouzauges trotted as far as the crown of the bridge, with Hornblower beside him, and looked over the country on the farther side. There was no sign of any enemy, and when they returned there was a mounted red-coated soldier waiting for them—Lord Edrington.

"I've come to see for myself," he said. "The position looks strong enough in all conscience here. Once you have the guns posted you should be able to hold this bridge until you can blow up the arch. But there's a ford, passable at low water, half a mile lower down. That is where I shall station myself—if we lose the ford they can turn the whole position and cut us off from the shore. Tell this gentleman—what's his name?—what I said."

Hornblower translated as well as he could, and stood by as interpreter while the two commanders pointed here and there and settled their respective duties.

"That's settled, then," said Edrington at length. "Don't forget, Mr. Hornblower, that I must be kept informed of every development."

He nodded to them and wheeled his horse and trotted off. As he left a cart approached from the direction of Muzillac, while behind it a loud clanking heralded the arrival of the two six-pounders, each drawn painfully by a couple of horses led by seamen. Sitting upon the front of the cart was Midshipman Bracegirdle, who saluted Hornblower with a broad grin.

"From quarterdeck to dung cart is no more than a step," he announced, swinging himself down. "From midshipman to captain of artillery."

He looked along the causeway and then around him.

"Put the guns over there and they'll sweep the whole length," suggested Hornblower.

"Exactly," said Bracegirdle.

Under his orders the guns were wheeled off the road and pointed along the causeway, and the dung cart was unloaded of its contents, a tarpaulin spread on the ground, the gunpowder cartridges laid on it and covered with another tarpaulin. The shot and the bags of grape were piled beside the guns, the seamen working with a will under the stimulus of their novel surroundings.

"Poverty brings strange bedfellows," said Bracegirdle. "And wars strange duties. Have you ever blown up a bridge?"

"Never," said Hornblower.

"Neither have I. Come, and let us do it. May I offer you a place in my carriage?"

Hornblower climbed up into the cart with Bracegirdle, and two seamen led the plodding horse along the causeway to the bridge. There they halted and looked down at the muddy water—running swiftly with the ebb—craning their heads over the parapet to look at the solid stone construction.

"It is the keystone of the arch which we should blow out," said Bracegirdle.

That was the proverbial recipe for the destruction of a bridge, but as Hornblower looked from the bridge to Bracegirdle and back again the idea did not seem easy to execute. Gunpowder exploded upwards and had to be held in on all sides—how was that to be done under the arch of the bridge?

"What about the pier?" he asked tentatively.

"We can but look and see," said Bracegirdle, and turned to the seaman by the cart. "Hannay, bring a rope."

They fastened the rope to the parapet and slid down it to a precarious foothold on the slippery ledge round the base of the pier, the river gurgling at their feet.

"That seems to be the solution," said Bracegirdle, crouching almost double under the arch.

Time slipped by fast as they made their preparations; a working party had to be brought from the guard of the bridge, picks and crowbars had to be found or extemporized, and some of the huge blocks with which the pier was built had to be picked out at the shoulder of the arch. Two kegs of gunpowder, lowered gingerly from above, had to be thrust into the holes so formed, a length of slow match put in at each bunghole and led to the exterior, while the kegs were tamped into their caves with all the stones and earth that could be crammed into them. It was almost twilight under the arch when the work was finished, the working party made laboriously to climb the rope up to the bridge and Bracegirdle and Hornblower left to look at each other again.

"I'll fire the fuses," said Bracegirdle. "You go next, sir."

It was not a matter for much argument. Bracegirdle was under orders to destroy the bridge, and Hornblower addressed himself to climbing up the rope while Bracegirdle took his tinderbox from his pocket. Once on the roadway of the bridge Hornblower sent away the cart and waited. It was only two or three minutes before Bracegirdle appeared, frantically climbing the rope and hurling himself over the parapet.

"Run!" was all that was said.

Together they scurried down the bridge and halted breathless to crouch by the abutment of the causeway. Then came a dull explosion, a tremor of the earth under their feet, and a cloud of smoke.

"Let's come and see," said Bracegirdle.

They retraced their steps towards where the bridge was still shrouded in smoke and dust.

"Only partly—" began Bracegirdle as they neared the scene and the dust cleared away.

And at that moment there was a second explosion which made them stagger as they stood. A lump of the roadbed hit the parapet beside them and burst like a shell, spattering them with fragments. There was a rumble and a clatter as the arch subsided into the river.

"That must have been the second keg going off," said Bracegirdle wiping his face. "We should have remembered the fuses were likely to be of different lengths. Two promising careers might have ended suddenly if we had been any nearer."

"At any rate, the bridge is gone," said Hornblower.

"All's well that ends well," said Bracegirdle.

Seventy pounds of gunpowder had done their work. The bridge was cut clear across, leaving a ragged gap several feet wide, beyond which the roadway reached out towards the gap from the farther pier as a witness to the toughness of the mortar. Beneath their feet as they peered over they could see the river bed almost choked with lumps of stone.

"We'll need no more than an anchor watch tonight," said Bracegirdle.

Hornblower looked round to where the roan horse was tethered; he was tempted to return to Muzillac on foot, leading the animal, but shame forbade. He climbed with an effort into the saddle and headed the animal back up the road; ahead of him the sky was beginning to turn red with the approach of sunset.

He entered the main street of the town and rounded the slight bend to the central square, to see something that made him, without his own volition, tug at his reins and halt his horse. The square was full of people, townsfolk and soldiers, and in the centre of the square a tall narrow rectangle reached upwards towards the sky with a glittering blade at its upper end. The blade fell with a reverberating thump, and the little group of men round the base of the rectangle dragged something to one side and added it to the heap already there. The portable guillotine was at work.

Hornblower sat sick and horrified—this was worse than any flogging at the gratings. He was about to urge his horse forward when a strange sound caught his ear. A man was singing, loud and clear, and out from a building at the side of the square emerged a little procession. In front walked a big man with dark curly hair, wearing a white shirt and dark breeches. At either side and behind him walked soldiers. It was this man who was singing; the tune meant nothing to Hornblower but he could hear the words distinctly—it was one of the verses of the French revolutionary song, echoes of which had penetrated even across the Channel.

"Oh, sacred love of the Fatherland . . ." sang the man in the white shirt; and when the civilians in the square heard what he was singing, there was a rustle among them and they dropped to the knees, their heads bowed and their hands crossed upon their breasts.

The executioners were winding the blade up again, and the man in the white shirt followed its rise with his eyes while he still sang without a tremor in his voice. The blade reached the top, and the singing ceased at last as the executioners fell on the man with the white shirt and led him to the guillotine. Then the blade fell with another echoing crash.

It seemed that this was to be the last execution, for the soldiers began to push the civilians back towards their homes, and Hornblower urged his horse forward through the dissolving crowd. He was nearly thrown from his saddle when the animal plunged sideways, snorting furiously—it had scented the horrid heap that lay beside the guillotine. At the side of the square was a house with a balcony, and Hornblower looked up at it in time to see Pouzauges still standing there, wearing his white uniform and blue ribbon, his staff about him and his hands on the rail. There were sentries at the door, and to one of them Hornblower handed over his horse as he entered; Pouzauges was just descending the stairs.

"Good evening, sir," said Pouzauges with perfect courtesy. "I am glad you have found your way to headquarters. I trust it was without trouble? We are about to dine and will enjoy your company. You have your horse, I suppose? M. de Villiers here will give orders for it to be looked after, I am sure."

It was all hard to believe. It was hard to believe that this polished gentleman had ordered the butchery that had just ended; it was hard to believe that the elegant young men with whom he sat at dinner were staking their lives on the overthrow of a barbarous but lusty young republic. But it was equally hard to believe, when he climbed into a fourposter bed that night, that he, Midshipman Horatio Hornblower, was in imminent deadly peril himself.

Outside in the street women wailed as the headless corpses, the harvest of the executions, were carried away, and he thought he would never sleep, but youth and fatigue had their way, and he slept for most of the night, although he awoke with the feeling that he had just been fighting off a nightmare. Everything was strange to him in the darkness, and it was several moments before he could account for the strangeness. He was in a bed and not—as he had spent the preceding three hundred nights—in a hammock; and the bed was steady as a rock instead of swaying about with the lively motion of a frigate. The stuffiness about him was the stuffiness of bed curtains, and not the stuffiness of the midshipmen's berth with its compound smell of stale humanity and stale bilgewater. He was on shore, in a house, in a bed, and everything about him was dead quiet, unnaturally so to a man accustomed to the noises of a wooden ship at sea.

Of course; he was in a house in the town of Muzillac in Brittany. He was sleeping in the headquarters of Brigadier General the Marquis de Pouzauges, commanding the French troops who constituted part of this expedition, which was itself part of a larger force invading Revolutionary France in the royalist cause. Hornblower felt a quickening of the pulse, a faint sick feeling of insecurity, as he realized afresh that he was now in France, ten miles from the sea and the *Indefatigable* with only a rabble of Frenchmen—half of them mercenaries only nominally Frenchmen at that—around him to preserve him from death or captivity. He regretted his knowledge of French—if he had had none he would not be here, and good fortune might even have put him among the British half-battalion of the 43rd guarding the ford a mile away.

It was partly the thought of the British troops which roused him out of bed. It was his duty to see that liaison was kept up with them, and the situation might have changed while he slept. He drew aside the bed curtains and stepped down to the floor; as his legs took the weight of his body they protested furiously—all the riding he had done yesterday had left every muscle and joint aching so that he could hardly walk. But he hobbled in the darkness over to the window, found the latch of the shutters, and pushed them open. A three-quarter moon was shining down into the empty street of the town, and looking down he could see the three-cornered hat of the sentry posted outside, and the bayonet reflecting the moonlight. Returning from the window, he found his coat and his shoes and put them on, belted his cutlass about him, and then he crept downstairs as quietly as he could. In the room off the entrance hall a tallow dip guttered on the table, and beside it a French sergeant slept with his head on his arms, lightly, for he raised his head as Hornblower paused in the doorway. On the floor of the room the rest of the guard off duty were snoring stertorously, huddled together like pigs in a sty, their muskets stacked against the wall.

Hornblower nodded to the sergeant, opened the front door and stepped out into the street. His lungs expanded gratefully as he breathed in the clean night air—morning air, rather, for there to the east the sky was assuming a lighter tinge—and the sentry, catching sight of the British naval officer, came clumsily to attention. In the square there still stood the gaunt harsh framework of the guillotine reaching up to the moonlit sky, and round it the black patch of the blood of its victims. Hornblower wondered who they were, who it could have been that the Royalists should seize and kill at such short notice, and he decided that they must have been petty officials of the Revolutionary government—the mayor and the customs officer and so on—if they were not merely men against whom the émigrés had cherished grudges since the days of the Revolution itself. It was a savage, merciless world, and at the moment he was very much alone in it, lonely, depressed, and unhappy.

He was distracted from these thoughts by the sergeant of the guard emerging from the door with a file of men; the sentry in the street was relieved, and the party went on round the house to relieve the others. Then across the street he saw four drummers appear from another house, with a sergeant commanding them. They formed into a line, their drumsticks poised high before their faces, and then at a word from the sergeant, the eight drumsticks fell together with a crash, and the drummers proceeded to march slowly along the street beating out a jerky exhilarating rhythm. At the first corner they stopped, and the drums rolled long and menacingly, and then they marched on again, beating out the previous rhythm. They were beating to arms, calling the men to their duties from their billets, and Hornblower, tone-deaf but highly sensitive to rhythm, thought it was fine music, real music. He turned back to headquarters with his depression fallen away from him. The sergeant of the guard came marching back with the relieved sentries; the first of the awakened soldiers were beginning to appear sleepily in the streets, and then, with a clatter of hoofs, a mounted messenger came riding up to headquarters, and the day was begun.

A pale young French officer read the note which the messenger brought, and politely handed it to Hornblower to read; he had to puzzle over it for a space—he was not accustomed to hand-written French—but its meaning became clear to him at length. It implied no new development; the main expeditionary force, landed yesterday at Quiberon, would move forward this morning on Vannes and Rennes while the subsidiary force to which Hornblower was attached must maintain its position at Muzillac, guarding its flank. The Marquis de Pouzauges, immaculate in his white uniform and blue ribbon, appeared at that moment, read the note without comment, and turned to Hornblower with a polite invitation to breakfast.

They went back to the big kitchen with its copper cooking pans glittering on the walls, and a silent woman brought them coffee and bread. She might be a patriotic Frenchwoman and an enthusiastic counter-revolutionary, but she showed no signs of it. Her feelings, of course, might easily have been influenced by the fact that this horde of men had taken over her house and were eating her food and sleeping in her rooms without payment. Maybe some of the horses and wagons seized for the use of the army were hers too—and maybe some of the people who had died under the guillotine last night were her friends. But she brought coffee, and the staff, standing about in the big kitchen with their spurs clinking, began to breakfast. Hornblower took his cup and a piece of bread—for four months before this his only bread had been ship's biscuit—and sipped at the stuff. He was not sure if he liked it, he had only tasted coffee three or four times before. But the second time he raised his cup to his lips he did not sip; before he could do so, the distant boom of a cannon made him lower his cup and stand stock still. The cannon shot was repeated, and again, and then it was echoed by a sharper, nearer note—Midshipman Bracegirdle's six-pounders on the causeway.

In the kitchen there was instant stir and bustle. Somebody knocked a cup over and sent a river of black liquid swirling across the table.

Somebody else managed to catch his spurs together so that he stumbled into somebody else's arms. Everyone seemed to be speaking at once. Hornblower was as excited as the rest of them; he wanted to rush out and see what was happening, but he thought at that moment of the disciplined calm which he had seen in H.M.S. *Indefatigable* as she went into action. He was not of this breed of Frenchmen, and to prove it he made himself put his cup to his lips again and drink calmly. Already most of the staff had dashed out of the kitchen shouting for their horses. It would take time to saddle up; he met Pouzauges' eye as the latter strode up and down the kitchen, and drained his cup—a trifle too hot for comfort, but he felt it was a good gesture. There was bread to eat, and he made himself bite and chew and swallow, although he had no appetite; if he was to be in the field all day, he could not tell when he would get his next meal, and so he crammed a half loaf into his pocket.

The horses were being brought into the yard and saddled; the excitement had infected them, and they plunged and sidled about amid the curses of the officers. Pouzauges leapt up into his saddle and clattered away with the rest of the staff behind him, leaving behind only a single soldier holding Hornblower's roan. That was as it had better be —Hornblower knew that he would not keep his seat for half a minute if the horse took it into his head to plunge or rear. He walked slowly out to the animal, which was calmer now when the groom petted him, and climbed with infinite slowness and precaution into the saddle. With a pull at the bit he checked the brute's exuberance and walked it sedately into the street and towards the bridge in the wake of the galloping staff. It was better to make sure of arriving by keeping his horse down to a walk than to gallop and be thrown. The guns were still booming and he could see the puffs of smoke from Bracegirdle's six-pounders. On his left, the sun was rising in a clear sky.

At the bridge the situation seemed obvious enough. Where the arch had been blown up a few skirmishers on either side were firing at each other across the gap, and at the far end of the causeway, across the Marais, a cloud of smoke revealed the presence of a hostile battery firing slowly and at extreme range. Beside the causeway on this side were Bracegirdle's two six-pounders, almost perfectly covered by a dip in the ground. Bracegirdle, with his cutlass belted round him, was standing between the guns which his party of seamen were working, and he waved his hand lightheartedly at Hornblower when he caught sight of him. A dark column of infantry appeared on the distant causeway. Bang—bang went Bracegirdle's guns. Hornblower's horse plunged at the noise, distracting him, but when he had time to look again, the column had disappeared. Then suddenly the causeway parapet near him flew into splinters; something hit the roadbed beside his horse's feet a tremendous blow and passed on with a roar—that was the closest so far in his life that a cannon shot had missed him. He lost a stirrup during the resultant struggle with his horse, and deemed it wiser, as soon as he regained moderate control, to dismount and lead the animal off the causeway towards the guns. Bracegirdle met him with a grin.

"No chance of their crossing here," he said. "At least, not if the Frogs stick to their work, and it looks as if they're willing to. The gap's within grapeshot range, they'll never bridge it. Can't think what they're burning powder for."

"Testing our strength, I suppose," said Hornblower, with an air of infinite military wisdom.

He would have been shaking with excitement if he had allowed his body to take charge. He did not know if he were being stiltedly unnatural, but even if he were that was better than to display excitement. There was something strangely pleasant, in a nightmare fashion, in standing here posing as a hardened veteran with cannon balls howling overhead; Bracegirdle seemed happy and smiling and quite master of himself, and Hornblower looked sharply at him, wondering if this were as much a pose as his own. He could not tell.

"Here they come again," said Bracegirdle. "Oh, only skirmishers."

A few scattered men were running out along the causeway to the bridge. At long musket range they fell to the ground and began spasmodic firing; already there were some dead men lying over there and the skirmishers took cover behind the corpses. On this side of the gap the skirmishers, better sheltered, fired back at them.

"They haven't a chance, here at any rate," said Bracegirdle. "And look there."

The main body of the Royalist force, summoned from the town, was marching up along the road. While they watched it, a cannon shot from the other side struck the head of the column and ploughed into it—Hornblower saw dead men flung this way and that, and the column wavered. Pouzauges came riding up and yelled orders, and the column, leaving its dead and wounded on the road, changed direction and took shelter in the marshy fields beside the causeway.

With nearly all the Royalist force assembled, it seemed indeed as if it would be utterly impossible for the Revolutionaries to force a crossing here.

"I'd better report on this to the Lobsters," said Hornblower.

"There was firing down that way at dawn," agreed Bracegirdle.

Skirting the wide marsh here ran a narrow path through the lush grass, leading to the ford which the 43rd were guarding. Hornblower led his horse onto the path before he mounted; he felt he would be more sure in that way of persuading the horse to take that direction. It was not long before he saw a dab of scarlet on the river bank—pickets thrown out from the main body to watch against any unlikely attempt to cross the marshes and stream round the British flank. Then he saw the cottage that indicated the site of the ford; in the field beside it was a wide patch of scarlet indicating where the main body was waiting for developments. At this point the marsh narrowed where a ridge of slightly higher ground approached the water; a company of redcoats was drawn up here with Lord Edrington on horseback beside them. Hornblower rode up and made his report, somewhat jerkily as his horse moved restlessly under him.

"No serious attack, you say?" asked Edrington.

"No sign of one when I left, sir."

"Indeed?" Edrington stared across the river. "And here it's the same story. No attempt to cross the ford in force. Why should they show their hand and then not attack?"

"I thought they were burning powder unnecessarily, sir," said Hornblower.

"They're not fools," snapped Edrington, with another penetrating look across the river. "At any rate, there's no harm in assuming they are not."

He turned his horse and cantered back to the main body and gave an order to a captain, who scrambled to his feet to receive it. The captain bellowed an order, and his company stood up and fell into line, rigid and motionless. Two further orders turned them to the right and marched them off in file, every man in step, every musket sloped at the same angle. Edrington watched them go.

"No harm in having a flank guard," he said.

The sound of a cannon across the water recalled them to the river; on the other side of the marsh a column of troops could be seen marching rapidly along the bank.

"That's the same column coming back, sir," said the company commander. "That or another just like it."

"Marching about and firing random shots," said Edrington. "Mr. Hornblower, have the émigré troops any flank guard out towards Quiberon?"

"Towards Quiberon, sir?" said Hornblower, taken aback.

"Damn it, can't you hear a plain question? Is there, or is there not?"

"I don't know, sir," confessed Hornblower miserably.

There were five thousand émigré troops at Quiberon, and it seemed quite unnecessary to keep a guard out in that direction.

"Then present my compliments to the French émigré general, and suggest he posts a strong detachment up the road, if he has not done so."

"Aye aye, sir."

Hornblower turned his horse's head back up the path towards the bridge. The sun was shining strongly now over the deserted fields. He could still hear the occasional thud of a cannon shot, but overhead a lark was singing in the blue sky. Then as he headed up the last low ridge towards Muzillac and the bridge he heard a sudden irregular outburst of firing; he fancied he heard screams and shouts, and what he saw as he topped the rise, made him snatch at his reins and drag his horse to a halt. The fields before him were covered with fugitives in blue uniforms with white crossbelts, all running madly towards him. In among the fugitives were galloping horsemen, whirling sabres that flashed in the sunshine. Farther out to the left a whole column of horsemen were trotting fast across the fields, and farther back the sun glittered on lines of bayonets moving rapidly from the high road towards the sea.

There could be no doubt of what had happened; during those sick seconds when he sat and stared, Hornblower realized the truth; the Revolutionaries had pushed in a force between Quiberon and Muzillac, and, keeping the émigrés occupied by demonstrations from across the river, had rushed down and brought off a complete surprise by this attack from an unexpected quarter. Heaven only knew what had happened at Quiberon—but this was no time to think about that. Hornblower dragged his horse's head round and kicked his heels into the brute's sides, urging him frantically back up the path towards the British. He bounced and rolled in his saddle, clinging on madly, consumed with fear lest he lose his seat and be captured by the pursuing French.

At the clatter of hoofs every eye turned towards him when he reached the British post. Edrington was there, standing with his horse's bridle over his arm.

"The French!" yelled Hornblower hoarsely, pointing back. "They're coming!"

"I expected nothing else," said Edrington.

He shouted an order before he put his foot in the stirrup to mount. The main body of the 43rd was standing in line by the time he was in the saddle. His adjutant went galloping off to recall the company from the water's edge.

"The French are in force, horse, foot, and guns, I suppose?" asked Edrington.

"Horse and foot at least, sir," gasped Hornblower, trying to keep his head clear. "I saw no guns."

"And the émigrés are running like rabbits?"

"Yes, sir."

"Here come the first of them."

Over the nearest ridge a few blue uniforms made their appearance, their wearers still running while stumbling with fatigue.

"I suppose we must cover their retreat, although they're not worth saving," said Edrington. "Look there!"

The company he had sent out as a flank guard was in sight on the crest of a slight slope: it was formed into a tiny square, red against the green, and as they watched they saw a mob of horsemen flood up the hill towards it and break into an eddy around it.

"Just as well I had them posted there," remarked Edrington calmly. "Ah, here comes Mayne's company."

The force from the ford came marching up. Harsh orders were shouted. Two companies wheeled round while the sergeant-major with his sabre and his silver-headed cane regulated the pace and the alignment as if the men were on the barrack square.

"I would suggest you stay by me, Mr. Hornblower," said Edrington.

He moved his horse up into the interval between the two columns, and Hornblower followed him dumbly. Another order, and the force began to march steadily across the valley, the sergeant calling the step and the sergeant-major watching the intervals. All round them now were fleeing émigré soldiers, most of them in the last stages of exhaustion—Hornblower noticed more than one of them fall down on the ground gasping and incapable of further movement. And then over the low slope to the right appeared a line of plumes, a line of sabres—a regiment of cavalry trotting rapidly forward. Hornblower saw the sabres lifted, saw the horses break into a gallop, heard the yells of the charging men. The redcoats around him halted; another shouted order, another slow, deliberate movement, and the half-battalion was in a square with the mounted officers in the centre and the colours waving over their heads. The charging horsemen were less than a hundred yards away. Some officer with a deep voice began giving orders, intoning them as if at some solemn ceremony. The first order brought the muskets from the men's shoulders, and the second was answered by a simultaneous click of opened priming pans. The third order brought the muskets to the present along one face of the square.

"Too high!" said the sergeant-major. "Lower, there, number seven."

The charging horsemen were only thirty yards away; Hornblower saw the leading men, their cloaks flying from their shoulders, leaning along their horses' necks with their sabres pointed forward at the full stretch of their arms.

"Fire!" said the deep voice.

In reply came a single sharp explosion as every musket went off at once. The smoke swirled round the square and disappeared. Where Hornblower had been looking, there were now a score of horses and men on the ground, some struggling in agony, some lying still. The cavalry regiment split like a torrent encountering a rock and hurtled harmlessly past the other faces of the square.

"Well enough," said Edrington.

The deep voice was intoning again; like marionettes all on the same string the company that had fired now reloaded, every man biting out his bullet at the same instant, every man ramming home his charge, every man spitting his bullet into his musket barrel with the same instantaneous inclination of the head. Edrington looked keenly at the cavalry collecting together in a disorderly mob down the valley.

"The 43rd will advance!" he ordered.

With solemn ritual the square opened up again into two columns and continued its interrupted march. The detached company came marching up to join them from out of a ring of dead men and horses. Someone raised a cheer.

"Silence in the ranks!" bellowed the sergeant-major. "Sergeant, take that man's name."

But Hornblower noticed how the sergeant-major was eyeing keenly the distance between the columns; it had to be maintained exactly so that a company wheeling back filled it to make the square.

"Here they come again," said Edrington.

The cavalry were forming for a new charge, but the square was ready for them. Now the horses were blown and the men were less enthusiastic. It was not a solid wall of horses that came down on them, but isolated groups, rushing first at one face and then at another, and pulling up or swerving aside as they reached the line of bayonets. The attacks were too feeble to meet with company volleys; at the word of command sections here and there gave fire to the more determined groups. Hornblower saw one man—an officer, judging by his gold lace —rein up before the bayonets and pull out a pistol. Before he could discharge it, half a dozen muskets went off together; the officer's face became a horrible bloody mask, and he and his horse fell together to the ground. Then all at once the cavalry wheeled off, like starlings over a field, and the march could be resumed.

"No discipline about these Frogs, not on either side," said Edrington.

The march was headed for the sea, for the blessed shelter of the *Indefatigable*, but it seemed to Hornblower as if the pace was intolerably slow. The men were marching at the parade step, with agonizing deliberation, while all round them and far ahead of them the fugitive émigrés poured in a broad stream towards safety. Looking back, Hornblower saw the fields full of marching columns—hurrying swarms, rather—of Revolutionary infantry in hot pursuit of them.

"Once let men run, and you can't do anything else with them," commented Edrington, following Hornblower's gaze.

Shouts and shots over to the flank caught their attention. Trotting over the fields, leaping wildly at the bumps, came a cart drawn by a lean horse. Someone in a seaman's frock and trousers was holding the reins; other seamen were visible over the sides firing muskets at the horsemen hovering about them. It was Bracegirdle with his dung cart; he might have lost his guns but he had saved his men. The pursuers dropped away as the cart neared the columns; Bracegirdle, standing up in the cart, caught sight of Hornblower on his horse and waved to him excitedly.

"Boadicea and her chariot!" he yelled.

"I'll thank you, sir," shouted Edrington with lungs of brass, "to go on and prepare for our embarkation."

"Aye aye, sir!"

The lean horse trotted on with the cart lurching after it and the grinning seamen clinging on to the sides. At the flank appeared a swarm of infantry, a mad, gesticulating crowd, half running to cut off the 43rd retreat. Edrington swept his glance round the fields.

"The 43rd will form line!" he shouted.

Like some ponderous machine, well oiled, the half battalion fronted towards the swarm; the columns became lines, each man moving into his position like bricks laid on a wall.

"The 43rd will advance!"

The scarlet line swept forward, slowly, inexorably. The swarm hastened to meet it, officers to the front waving their swords and calling on their men to follow.

"Make ready!"

Every musket came down together; the priming pans clicked.

"Present!"

Up came the muskets, and the swarm hesitated before that fearful menace. Individuals tried to get back into the crowd to cover themselves from the volley with the bodies of their comrades.

"Fire!"

A crashing volley; Hornblower, looking over the heads of the British infantry from his point of vantage on horseback, saw the whole face of the swarm go down in swathes. Still the red line moved forward, at each deliberate step a shouted order brought a machine-like response as the men reloaded; five hundred mouths spat in five hundred bullets, five hundred right arms raised five hundred ramrods at once. When the muskets came to the present the red line was at the swathe of dead and wounded, for the swarm had withdrawn before the advance, and shrank back still further at the threat of the volley. The volley was fired; the advance went on. Another volley; another advance. Now the swarm was shredding away. Now men were running from it. Now every man had turned tail and fled from that frightful musketry. The hillside was as black with fugitives as it had been when the émigrés were fleeing.

"Halt!"

The advance ceased; the line became a double column, and the retreat began again.

"Very creditable," remarked Edrington.

Hornblower's horse was trying jerkily to pick its way over a carpet of dead and wounded, and he was so busy keeping his seat, and his brain was in such a whirl, that he did not immediately realize that they had topped the last rise, so that before them lay the glittering waters of the estuary. The strip of muddy beach was packed solid with émigrés. There were the ships riding at anchor, and there, blessed sight, were the boats swarming towards the shore. It was high time, for already the boldest of the Revolutionary infantry were hovering round the columns, taking long shots into them. Here and there a man fell.

"Close up!" snapped the sergeants, and the files marched on stolidly, leaving the wounded and dead behind them.

The adjutant's horse suddenly snorted and plunged, and then fell first to its knees, and, kicking, to its side, while the freckle-faced adjutant freed his feet from the stirrups and flung himself out of the saddle just in time to escape being pinned underneath.

"Are you hit, Stanley?" asked Edrington.

"No, my lord. All safe and sound," said the adjutant, brushing at his scarlet coat.

"You won't have to foot it far," said Edrington. "No need to throw out skirmishers to drive those fellows off. This is where we must make our stand."

He looked about him, at the fishermen's cottages above the beach, the panic-stricken émigrés at the water's edge, and the masses of Revolutionary infantry coming up in pursuit, leaving small enough time for preparation. Some of the redcoats poured into the cottages, appearing a moment later at the windows; it was fortunate that the fishing hamlet guarded one flank of the gap down to the beach while the other was guarded by a steep and inaccessible headland on whose summit a small block of redcoats established themselves. In the gap between the two points the remaining four companies formed a long line just sheltered by the crest of the beach.

The boats of the squadron were already loading with émigrés among the small breakers below. Hornblower heard the crack of a single pistol-shot; he could guess that some officer down there was enforcing his orders in the only possible way to prevent the fear-driven men from pouring into the boats and swamping them. As if in answer came the roar of cannon on the other side. A battery of artillery had unlimbered just out of musket range and was firing at the British position, while all about it gathered the massed battalions of the Revolutionary infantry. The cannon balls howled close overhead.

"Let them fire away," said Edrington. "The longer the better."

The artillery could do little harm to the British in the fold of ground that protected them, and the Revolutionary commander must have realized that as well as the necessity for wasting no time. Over there the drums began to roll—a noise of indescribable menace—and then the columns surged forward. So close were they already that Hornblower could see the features of the officers in the lead, waving their hats and swords.

"43rd, make ready!" said Edrington, and the priming pans clicked as one. "Seven paces forward—march!"

One—two—three—seven paces, painstakingly taken, took the line to the little crest.

"Present! Fire!"

A volley nothing could withstand. The columns halted, swayed, received another smashing volley, and another, and fell back in ruin.

"Excellent!" said Edrington.

The battery boomed again; a file of two redcoat soldiers was tossed back like dolls, to lie in a horrible bloody mass close beside Hornblower's horse's feet.

"Close up!" said a sergeant, and the men on either side had filled the gap.

"43rd, seven paces back—march!"

The line was below the crest again, as the redcoated marionettes withdrew in steady time. Hornblower could not remember later whether it was twice or three times more that the Revolutionary masses came on again, each time to be dashed back by that disciplined musketry. But the sun was nearly setting in the ocean behind him when he looked back to see the beach almost cleared and Bracegirdle plodding up to them to report.

"I can spare one company now," said Edrington in reply but not taking his eyes off the French masses. "After they are on board, have every boat ready and waiting."

One company filed off; another attack was beaten back—after the preceding failures it was not pressed home with anything like the dash and fire of the earlier ones. Now the battery was turning its attention to the headland on the flank, and sending its balls among the redcoats there, while a battalion of French moved over to the attack at that point.

"That gives us time," said Edrington. "Captain Griffin, you can march the men off. Colour party, remain here."

Down the beach went the centre companies to the waiting boats, while the colours still waved to mark their old position, visible over the crest to the French. The company in the cottages came out, formed up, and marched down as well. Edrington trotted across to the foot of

the little headland; he watched the French forming for the attack and
the infantry wading out to the boats.

"Now, grenadiers!" he yelled suddenly. "Run for it! Colour party!"

Down the steep seaward face of the headland came the last company, running, sliding, and stumbling. A musket, clumsily handled,
went off unexpectedly. The last man came down the slope as the colour
party reached the water's edge and began to climb into a boat with its
precious burden. A wild yell went up from the French, and their whole
mass came rushing towards the evacuated position.

"Now, sir," said Edrington, turning his horse seawards.

Hornblower fell from his saddle as his horse splashed into the shallows. He let go of the reins and plunged out, waist deep, shoulder deep,
to where the longboat lay on its oars with its four-pounder gun in its
bows and Bracegirdle beside it to haul him in. He looked up in time
to see a curious incident; Edrington had reached the *Indefatigable's*
gig, still holding his horse's reins. With the French pouring down the
beach towards them, he turned and took a musket from the nearest
soldier, pressed the muzzle to the horse's head, and fired. The horse
fell in its death agony in the shallows; only Hornblower's roan remained
as prize to the Revolutionaries.

"Back water!" said Bracegirdle, and the longboat backed away from
the beach; Hornblower lay in the eyes of the boat feeling as if he had
not the strength to move a limb, and the beach was covered with shouting, gesticulating Frenchmen, lit redly by the sunset.

"One moment," said Bracegirdle, reaching for the lanyard of the
four-pounder, and tugging at it smartly.

The gun roared out in Hornblower's ear, and the charge cut a swathe
of destruction on the beach.

"That was canister," said Bracegirdle. "Eighty-four balls. Easy, port!
Give way, starboard!"

The longboat turned, away from the beach and towards the welcoming ships. Hornblower looked back at the darkening coast of France.
This was the end of an incident; his country's attempt to overturn the
Revolution had met with a bloody repulse. Newspapers in Paris would
exult; the *Gazette* in London would give the incident five cold lines.
Clairvoyant, Hornblower could foresee that in a year's time the world
would hardly remember the incident. In twenty years it would be entirely forgotten. Yet those headless corpses up there in Muzillac; those
shattered redcoats; those Frenchmen caught in the four-pounder's blast
of canister—they were all as dead as if it had been a day in which history had been changed. And he was just as weary. And in his pocket
there was still the bread he had put there that morning and forgotten
all about.

THE SPANISH GALLEYS

The old *Indefatigable* was lying at anchor in the Bay of Cadiz at the time when Spain made peace with France. Hornblower happened to be midshipman of the watch, and it was he who called the attention of Lieutenant Chadd to the approach of the eight-oared pinnace, with the red and yellow of Spain drooping at the stern. Chadd's glass made out the gleam of gold on epaulette and cocked hat, and bellowed the order for sideboys and marine guard to give the traditional honours to a captain in an allied service. Pellew, hurriedly warned, was at the gangway to meet his visitor, and it was at the gangway that the entire interview took place. The Spaniard, making a low bow with his hat across his stomach, offered a sealed envelope to the Englishman.

"Here, Mr. Hornblower," said Pellew, holding the letter unopened, "speak French to this fellow. Ask him to come below for a glass of wine."

But the Spaniard, with a further bow, declined the refreshment, and, with another bow, requested that Pellew open the letter immediately. Pellew broke the seal and read the contents, struggling with the French which he could read to a small extent although he could not speak it at all. He handed it to Hornblower.

"This means the Dagoes have made peace, doesn't it?"

Hornblower struggled through twelve lines of compliments addressed by His Excellency the Duke of Belchite (Grandee of the First Class, with eighteen other titles ending with Captain-General of Andalusia) to the Most Gallant Ship-Captain Sir Edward Pellew, Knight of the Bath. The second paragraph was short and contained only a brief intimation of peace. The third paragraph was as long as the first, and repeated its phraseology almost word for word in a ponderous farewell.

"That's all, sir," said Hornblower.

But the Spanish captain had a verbal message with which to supplement the written one.

"Please tell your captain," he said, in his lisping Spanish-French, "that now as a neutral power, Spain must enforce her rights. You have already been at anchor here for twenty-four hours. Six hours from now"—the Spaniard took a gold watch from his pocket and glanced at it—

112

"if you are within range of the batteries at Puntales there they will be given orders to fire on you."

Hornblower could only translate the brutal message without any attempt at softening it, and Pellew listened, white with anger despite his tan.

"Tell him—" he began, and then mastered his rage. "Damme if I'll let him see he has made me angry."

He put his hat across his stomach and bowed in as faithful an imitation of the Spaniard's courtliness as he could manage, before he turned to Hornblower.

"Tell him I have received his message with pleasure. Tell him I much regret that circumstances are separating him from me, and that I hope I shall always enjoy his personal friendship whatever the relations between our countries. Tell him—oh, you can tell him the sort of thing I want said, can't you, Hornblower? Let's see him over the side with dignity. Sideboys! Bosun's mates! Drummers!"

Hornblower poured out compliments to the best of his ability, and at every phrase the two captains exchanged bows, the Spaniard withdrawing a pace at each bow and Pellew following him up, not to be outdone in courtesy. The drums beat a ruffle, the marines presented arms, the pipes shrilled and twittered until the Spaniard's head had descended to the level of the maindeck, when Pellew stiffened up, clapped his hat on his head, and swung round on his first lieutenant.

"Mr. Eccles, I want to be under way within the hour, if you please."

Then he stamped down below to regain his equanimity in private.

Hands were aloft loosing sail ready to sheet home, while the clank of the capstan told how other men were heaving the cable short, and Hornblower was standing on the portside gangway with Mr. Wales the carpenter, looking over at the white houses of one of the most beautiful cities in Europe.

"I've been ashore there twice," said Wales. "The wine's good—vino, they calls it—if you happens to like that kind o' muck. But don't you ever try that brandy, Mr. Hornblower. Poison, it is, rank poison. Hello! We're going to have an escort, I see."

Two long sharp prows had emerged from the inner bay, and were pointing towards the *Indefatigable*. Hornblower could not restrain himself from giving a cry of surprise as he followed Wales' gaze. The vessels approaching were galleys; along each side of them the oars were lifting and falling rhythmically, catching the sunlight as they feathered. The effect, as a hundred oars swung like one, was perfectly beautiful. Hornblower remembered a line in a Latin poet which he had translated as a schoolboy, and recalled his surprise when he discovered that to a Roman the "white wings" of a ship of war were her oars. Now the simile was plain; even a gull in flight, which Hornblower had always looked upon until now as displaying the perfection of motion, was not more beautiful than those galleys. They lay low in the water, immensely long for their beam. Neither the sails nor the lateen yards were set on the low raking masts. The bows blazed with gilding, while the waters of the bay foamed round them as they headed into the teeth of the gentle breeze with the Spanish red and gold streaming aft from the masthead. Up—forward—down—went the oars with unchanging rhythm, the blades not varying an inch in their distance apart during the whole of the stroke. From the bows of each two long guns looked straight forward in the direction the galleys pointed.

"Twenty-four pounders," said Wales. "If they catch you in a calm, they'll knock you to pieces. Lie off on your quarter where you can't bring a gun to bear and rake you till you strike. An' then God help you —better a Turkish prison than a Spanish one."

In a line-ahead that might have been drawn with a ruler and measured with a chain the galleys passed close along the port side of the *Indefatigable* and went ahead of her. As they passed the roll of the drum and the call of the pipes summoned the crew of the *Indefatigable* to attention out of compliment to the flag and the commission pendant going by, while the galleys' officers returned the salute.

"It don't seem right, somehow," muttered Wales under his breath, "to salute 'em like they was a frigate."

Level with the *Indefatigable's* bowsprit the leader backed her starboard side oars, and spun like a top, despite her length and narrow beam, across the frigate's bows. The gentle wind blew straight to the frigate from the galley, and then from her consort as the latter followed; and a foul stench came back on the air and assailed Hornblower's nostrils, and not Hornblower's alone, clearly, for it brought forth cries of disgust from all the men on deck.

"They all stink like that," explained Wales. "Four men to the oar an' fifty oars. Two hundred galley slaves, that is. All chained to their benches. When you goes aboard one of them as a slave you're chained to your bench, an' you're never unchained until they drop you overside. Sometimes when the hands aren't busy they'll hose out the bilge, but that doesn't happen often, bein' Dagoes an' not many of 'em."

Hornblower as always sought exact information.

"How many, Mr. Wales?"

"Thirty, mebbe. Enough to hand the sails if they're making a passage. Or to man the guns—they strike the yards and sails, like now, before they goes into action, Mr. Hornblower," said Wales, pontifical as usual, and with that slight emphasis on the "Mister" inevitable when a warrant officer of sixty with no hope of further promotion addressed a warrant officer of eighteen (his nominal equal in rank) who might some day be an admiral. "So you see how it is. With no more than thirty of a crew an' two hundred slaves they daren't let 'em loose, not ever."

The galleys had turned again, and were now passing down the *Indefatigable's* starboard side. The beat of the oars had slowed very noticeably, and Hornblower had ample time to observe the vessels closely, the low forecastle and high poop with the gangway connecting them along the whole length of the galley; upon that gangway walked a man with a whip. The rowers were invisible below the bulwarks, the oars being worked through holes in the sides closed, as far as Hornblower could see, with sheets of leather round the oar-looms to keep out the sea. On the poop stood two men at the tiller and a small group of officers, their gold lace flashing in the sunshine. Save for the gold lace and the twenty-four-pounder bow chasers Hornblower was looking at exactly the same sort of vessel as the ancients used to fight their battles. Polybius and Thucydides wrote about galleys almost identical with these—for that matter it was not much more than two hundred years since the galleys had fought their last great battle at Lepanto against the Turks. But those battles had been fought with hundreds of galleys a side.

"How many do they have in commission now?" asked Hornblower.

"A dozen, mebbe—not that I knows for sure, o' course. Cartagena's their usual station, beyond the Gut."

Wales, as Hornblower understood, meant by this through the Strait of Gibraltar in the Mediterranean.

"Too frail for the Atlantic," Hornblower commented.

It was easy to deduce the reasons for the survival of this small number—the innate conservatism of the Spaniards would account for it to a large extent. Then there was the point that condemnation to the galleys was one way of disposing of criminals. And when all was said and done a galley might still be useful in a calm—merchant ships becalmed while trying to pass the Strait of Gibraltar might be snapped up by galleys pushing out from Cadiz or Cartagena. And at the very lowest estimate there might be some employment for galleys to tow vessels in and out of harbour with the wind unfavourable.

"Mr. Hornblower!" said Eccles. "My respects to the captain, and we're ready to get under way."

Hornblower dived below with his message.

"My compliments to Mr. Eccles," said Pellew, looking up from his desk, "and I'll be on deck immediately."

There was just enough of a southerly breeze to enable the *Indefatigable* to weather the point in safety. With her anchor catted she braced round her yards and began to steal seaward; in the disciplined stillness which prevailed the sound of the ripple of water under her cutwater was clearly to be heard—a musical note which told nothing, in its innocence, of the savagery and danger of the world of the sea into which she was entering. Creeping along under her topsails the *Indefatigable* made no more than three knots, and the galleys came surging past her again, oars beating their fastest rhythm, as if the galleys were boasting of their independence of the elements. Their gilt flashed in the sun as they overtook to windward, and once again their foul stench offended the nostrils of the men of the *Indefatigable*.

"I'd be obliged if they'd keep to leeward of us," muttered Pellew, watching them through his glass. "But I suppose that's not Spanish courtesy. Mr. Cutler!"

"Sir!" said the gunner.

"You may commence the salute."

"Aye aye, sir."

The forward carronade on the lee side roared out the first of its compliments, and the fort of Puntales began its reply. The sound of the salute rolled round the beautiful bay; nation was speaking to nation in all courtesy.

"The next time we hear those guns they'll be shotted, I fancy," said Pellew, gazing across at Puntales and the flag of Spain flying above it.

Indeed, the tide of war was turning against England. Nation after nation had retired from the contest against France, some worsted by arms, and some by the diplomacy of the vigorous young republic. To any thinking mind it was obvious that once the step from war to neutrality had been taken, the next step would be easy, from neutrality to war on the other side. Hornblower could foresee, close at hand, a time when all Europe would be arrayed in hostility to England, when she would be battling for her life against the rejuvenescent power of France and the malignity of the whole world.

"Set sail, please, Mr. Eccles," said Pellew.

Two hundred trained pairs of legs raced aloft; two hundred trained pairs of arms let loose the canvas, and the *Indefatigable* doubled her speed, heeling slightly to the gentle breeze. Now she was meeting the long Atlantic swell. So were the galleys; as the *Indefatigable* overtook them, Hornblower could see the leader put her nose into a long roller so that a cloud of spray broke over her forecastle. That was asking too much of such frail craft. Back went one bank of oars; forward went the other. The galleys rolled hideously for a moment in the trough of the sea before they completed their turn and headed back for the safe waters of Cadiz Bay. Someone forward in the *Indefatigable* began to boo, and the cry was instantly taken up through the ship. A storm of boos and whistles and catcalls pursued the galleys, the men momentarily quite out of hand while Pellew spluttered with rage on the quarterdeck and the petty officers strove in vain to take the names of the offenders. It was an ominous farewell to Spain.

Ominous indeed. It was not long before Captain Pellew gave the news to the ship that Spain had completed her change-over; with the treasure convoy safely in she had declared war against England; the revolutionary republic had won the alliance of the most decayed monarchy in Europe. British resources were now stretched to the utmost; there was another thousand miles of coast to watch, another fleet to blockade, another horde of privateers to guard against, and far fewer harbours in which to take refuge and from which to draw the fresh water and the meagre stores which enabled the hard-worked crews to remain at sea. It was then that friendship had to be cultivated with the half savage Barbary States, and the insolence of the Deys and the Sultans had to be tolerated so that North Africa could provide the skinny bullocks and the barley grain to feed the British garrisons in the Mediterranean—all of them beleaguered on land—and the ships which kept open the way to them. Oran, Tetuan, Algiers wallowed in unwontedly honest prosperity with the influx of British gold.

It was a day of glassy calm in the Straits of Gibraltar. The sea was like a silver shield, the sky like a bowl of sapphire, with the mountains of Africa on the one hand, the mountains of Spain on the other as dark serrations on the horizon. It was not a comfortable situation for the *Indefatigable,* but that was not because of the blazing sun which softened the pitch in the deck seams. There is almost always a slight current setting inwards into the Mediterranean from the Atlantic, and the prevailing winds blow in the same direction. In a calm like this it was not unusual for a ship to be carried far through the Straits, past the Rock of Gibraltar, and then to have to beat for days and even weeks to make Gibraltar Bay. So that Pellew was not unnaturally anxious about his convoy of grain ships from Oran. Gibraltar had to be revictualled—Spain had already marched an army up for the siege—and he dared not risk being carried past his destination. His orders to his reluctant convoy had been enforced by flag and gun signals, for no shorthanded merchant ship relished the prospect of the labour Pellew wished to be executed. The *Indefatigable* no less than her convoy had lowered boats, and the helpless ships were now all in tow. That was backbreaking, exhausting labour, the men at the oars tugging and straining, dragging the oar blades through the water, while the towlines tightened and bucked with superhuman perversity and the ships sheered freakishly from side to side. It was less than a mile an hour that the ships made in this fashion, at the cost of the complete exhaustion of the boats' crews, but at least it postponed the time when the Gibraltar current would carry them to leeward, and similarly gave more chance for the longed-for southerly wind—two hours of a southerly wind was all they wished for—to waft them up to the Mole.

Down in the *Indefatigable's* longboat and cutter the men tugging

at their oars were so stupefied with their toil that they did not hear the
commotion in the ship. They were just tugging and straining, under
the pitiless sky, living through their two hours' spell of misery, but they
were roused by the voice of the captain himself, hailing them from the
forecastle.

"Mr. Bolton! Mr. Chadd! Cast off there, if you please. You'd better
come and arm your men at once. Here come our friends from
Cadiz."

Back on the quarterdeck, Pellew looked through his glass at the hazy
horizon; he could make out from here by now what had first been reported from the masthead.

"They're heading straight for us," he said.

The two galleys were on their way from Cadiz; presumably a fast
horseman from the lookout point at Tarifa had brought them the news
of this golden opportunity, of the flat calm and the scattered and helpless convoy. This was the moment for galleys to justify their continued
existence. They could capture and at least burn, although they could
not hope to carry off, the unfortunate merchant ships while the *Indefatigable* lay helpless hardly out of cannon's range. Pellew looked round
at the two merchant ships and the three brigs; one of them was within
half a mile of him and might be covered by his gunfire, but the others
—a mile and a half, two miles away—had no such protection.

"Pistols and cutlasses, my lads!" he said to the men pouring up
from overside. "Clap onto that stay tackle now. Smartly with that carronade, Mr. Cutler!"

The *Indefatigable* had been in too many expeditions where minutes
counted to waste any time over these preparations. The boats' crews
seized their arms, the six-pounder carronades were lowered into the
bows of the cutter and long-boat, and soon the boats, crowded with
armed men, and provisioned against sudden emergency, were pulling
away to meet the galleys.

"What the devil d'you think you're doing, Mr. Hornblower?"

Pellew had just caught sight of Hornblower in the act of swinging
out of the jolly boat which was his special charge. He wondered what
his midshipman thought he could achieve against a war-galley with a
twelve-foot boat and a crew of six.

"We can pull to one of the convoy and reinforce the crew, sir," said
Hornblower.

"Oh, very well then, carry on. I'll trust to your good sense, even
though that's a broken reed."

"Good on you, sir!" said Jackson ecstatically, as the jolly boat shoved
off from the frigate. "Good on you! No one else wouldn't never have
thought of that."

Jackson, the coxswain of the jolly boat, obviously thought that Hornblower had no intention of carrying out his suggestion to reinforce the crew of one of the merchant ships.

"Those stinking Dagoes," said stroke oar, between his teeth.

Hornblower was conscious of the presence in his crew of the same feeling of violent hostility toward the Spanish galleys as he felt within himself. In a fleeting moment of analysis, he attributed it to the circumstances in which they had first made the galleys' acquaintance, as well as to the stench which the galleys trailed after them. He had never known this feeling of personal hatred before; when previously he had fought it had been as a servant of the King, not out of personal animosity. Yet here he was gripping the tiller under the scorching sky and leaning forward in his eagerness to be at actual grips with this enemy.

The longboat and cutter had a long start of them, and even though they were manned by crews who had already served a spell at the oars they were skimming over the water at such a speed that the jolly boat with all the advantage of the glassy-smooth water only slowly caught up to them. Overside the sea was of the bluest, deepest blue until the oar blades churned it white. Ahead of them the vessels of the convoy lay scattered where the sudden calm had caught them, and just beyond them Hornblower caught sight of the flash of oar blades as the galleys came sweeping down on their prey. Longboat and cutter were diverging in an endeavour to cover as many vessels as possible, and the gig was still far astern. There would hardly be time to board a ship even if Hornblower should wish to. He put the tiller over to incline his course after the cutter; one of the galleys at that moment abruptly made its appearance in the gap between two of the merchant ships. Hornblower saw the cutter swing round to point her six-pounder carronade at the advancing bows.

"Pull, you men! Pull!" he shrieked mad with excitement.

He could not imagine what was going to happen, but he wanted to be in the fray. That six-pounder popgun was grossly inaccurate at any range longer than musket shot. It would serve to hurl a mass of grape into a crowd of men, but its ball would have small effect on the strengthened bows of a war galley.

"Pull!" shrieked Hornblower again. He was nearly up to them, wide on the cutter's quarter.

The carronade boomed out. Hornblower thought he saw the splinters fly from the galley's bow, but the shot had no more effect on deterring her than a peashooter could stop a charging bull. The galley turned a little, getting exactly into line, and then her oars' beat quickened. She was coming down to ram, like the Greeks at Salamis.

"Pull!" shrieked Hornblower.

Instinctively, he gave the tiller a touch to take the jolly boat out into a flanking position.

"Easy!"

The jolly boat's oars stilled, as their way carried them past the cutter. Hornblower could see Soames standing up in the sternsheets looking at the death which was cleaving the blue water towards him. Bow to bow the cutter might have stood a chance, but too late the cutter tried to evade the blow altogether. Hornblower saw her turn, presenting her vulnerable side to the galley's stem. That was all he could see, for the next moment the galley herself hid from him the final act of the tragedy. The jolly boat's starboard side oars only just cleared the galley's starboard oars as she swept by. Hornblower heard a shriek and a crash, saw the galley's forward motion almost cease at the collision. He was mad with the lust of fighting, quite insane, and his mind was working with the rapidity of insanity.

"Give way, port!" he yelled, and the jolly boat swung round under the galley's stern. "Give way all!"

The jolly boat leaped after the galley like a terrier after a bull.

"Grapple them, damn you, Jackson!"

Jackson shouted an oath in reply, as he leaped forward, seemingly hurdling the men at the oars without breaking their stroke. In the bows Jackson seized the boat's grapnel on its long line and flung it hard and true. It caught somewhere in the elaborate gilt rail on the galley's quarter. Jackson hauled on the line, the oars tugged madly in the effort to carry the jolly boat up to the galley's stern. At that moment Hornblower saw it, the sight which would long haunt his dreams—up from under the galley's stern came the shattered forepart of the cutter, still with men clinging to it who had survived the long passage under the whole length of the galley which had overrun them. There were straining faces, empurpled faces, faces already relaxing in death. But in a moment it was past and gone, and Hornblower felt the jerk transmitted through the line to the jolly boat as the galley leaped forward.

"I can't hold her!" shouted Jackson.

"Take a turn round the cleat, you fool!"

The galley was towing the jolly boat now, dragging her along at the end of a twenty-foot line close on her quarter, just clear of the arc of her rudder. The white water bubbled all around her, her bows were cocked up with the strain. It was a bad moment, as though they had harpooned a whale. Some one came running aft on the Spaniard's poop, knife in hand to cut the line.

"Shoot him, Jackson!" shrieked Hornblower again.

Jackson's pistol cracked, and the Spaniard fell to the deck out of sight—a good shot. Despite his fighting madness, despite the turmoil of rushing water and glaring sun, Hornblower tried to think out his next move. Inclination and common sense alike told him that the best plan was to close with the enemy despite the odds.

"Pull up to them, there!" he shouted—everyone in the boat was shouting and yelling. The men in the bows of the jolly boat faced forward and took the grapnel line and began to haul in on it, but the speed of the boat through the water made any progress difficult, and after a yard or so had been gained the difficulty became insurmountable, for the grapnel was caught in the poop rail ten or eleven feet above water, and the angle of pull became progressively steeper as the jolly boat neared the stern of the galley. The boat's bow cocked higher out of the water than ever.

"Belay!" said Hornblower, and then, his voice rising again, "Out pistols, lads!"

A row of four or five swarthy faces had appeared at the stern of the galley. Muskets were pointing into the jolly boat, and there was a brief but furious exchange of shots. One man fell groaning into the bottom of the jolly boat, but the row of faces disappeared. Standing up precariously in the swaying sternsheets, Hornblower could still see nothing of the galley's poop deck save for the tops of two heads, belonging, it was clear, to the men at the tiller.

"Reload," he said to his men, remembering by a miracle to give the order. The ramrods went down the pistol barrels.

"Do that carefully if you ever want to see Pompey again," said Hornblower.

He was shaking with excitement and mad with the fury of fighting, and it was the automatic, drilled part of him which was giving these level-headed orders. His higher faculties were quite negatived by his lust for blood. He was seeing things through a pink mist—that was how he remembered it when he looked back upon it later. There was a sudden crash of glass. Someone had thrust a musket barrel through the big stern window of the galley's after cabin. Luckily having thrust it through he had to recover himself to take aim. An irregular volley of pistols almost coincided with the report of the musket. Where the Spaniard's bullet went no one knew; but the Spaniard fell back from the window.

"By God! That's our way!" screamed Hornblower, and then, steadying himself. "Reload."

As the bullets were being spat into the barrels he stood up. His unused pistols were still in his belt; his cutlass was at his side.

"Come aft, here," he said to stroke oar; the jolly boat would stand no more weight in the bows than she had already. "And you, too."

Hornblower poised himself on the thwarts, eyeing the grapnel line and the cabin window.

"Bring 'em after me one at a time, Jackson," he said.

Then he braced himself and flung himself at the grapnel line. His feet grazed the water as the line sagged, but using all his clumsy strength his arms carried him upwards. Here was the shattered window at his side; he swung up his feet, kicked out a big remaining piece of the pane, and then shot his feet through and then the rest of himself. He came down on the deck of the cabin with a thud; it was dark in here compared with the blinding sun outside. As he got to his feet, he trod on something which gave out a cry of pain—the wounded Spaniard, evidently—and the hand with which he drew his cutlass was sticky with blood. Spanish blood. Rising, he hit his head a thunderous crash on the deckbeams above, for the little cabin was very low, hardly more than five feet, and so severe was the blow that his senses almost left him But before him was the cabin door and he reeled out through it, cutlass in hand. Over his head he heard a stamping of feet, and shots were fired behind him and above him—a further exchange, he presumed, between the jolly boat and the galley's stern rail. The cabin door opened into a low half-deck, and Hornblower reeled along it out into the sunshine again. He was on the tiny strip of maindeck at the break of the poop. Before him stretched the narrow gangway between the two sets of rowers; he could look down at these latter—two seas of bearded faces, mops of hair and lean sunburned bodies, swinging rhythmically back and forward to the beat of the oars.

That was all the impression he could form of them at the moment. At the far end of the gangway at the break of the forecastle stood the overseer with his whip; he was shouting words in rhythmic succession to the slaves—Spanish numbers, perhaps, to give them the time. There were three or four men on the forecastle; below them the half-doors through the forecastle bulkhead were hooked open, through which Hornblower could see the two big guns illuminated by the light through the port holes out of which they were run almost at the water level. The guns' crews were standing by the guns, but numerically they were far fewer than two twenty-four pounders would demand. Hornblower remembered Wales' estimate of no more than thirty for a galley's crew. The men of one gun at least had been called aft to defend the poop against the jolly boat's attack.

A step behind him made him leap with anxiety and he swung round with his cutlass ready to meet Jackson stumbling out of the half deck, cutlass in hand.

"Nigh on cracked my nut," said Jackson.

He was speaking thickly like a drunken man, and his words were chorused by further shots fired from the poop at the level of the top of their heads.

"Oldroyd's comin' next," said Jackson. "Franklin's dead."

On either side of them a companion ladder mounted to the poop deck. It seemed logical, mathematical, that they should each go up one but Hornblower thought better of it.

"Come along," he said, and headed for the starboard ladder, and, with Oldroyd putting in an appearance at that moment, he yelled to him to follow.

The handropes of the ladder were of twisted red and yellow cord —he even could notice that as he rushed up the ladder, pistol in hand and cutlass in the other. After the first step, his eye was above deck level. There were more than a dozen men crowded on the tiny poop, but two were lying dead, and one was groaning with his back to the rail, and two stood by the tiller. The others were looking over the rail at the jolly boat. Hornblower was still insane with fighting madness. He must have leaped up the final two or three steps with a bound like a stag's, and he was screaming like a maniac as he flung himself at the Spaniards. His pistol went off apparently without his willing it, but the face of the man a yard away dissolved into bloody ruin, and Hornblower dropped the weapon and snatched the second, his thumb going to the hammer as he whirled his cutlass down with a crash on the sword which the next Spaniard raised as a feeble guard. He struck and struck and struck with a lunatic's strength. Here was Jackson beside him shouting hoarsely and striking out right and left.

"Kill 'em! Kill 'em!" shouted Jackson.

Hornblower saw Jackson's cutlass flash down on the head of the defenceless man at the tiller. Then out of the tail of his eye he saw another sword threaten him as he battered with his cutlass at the man before him, but his pistol saved him as he fired automatically again. Another pistol went off beside him—Oldroyd's, he supposed— and then the fight on the poop was over. By what miracle of ineptitude the Spaniards had allowed the attack to take them by surprise Hornblower never could discover. Perhaps they were ignorant of the wounding of the man in the cabin, and had relied on him to defend that route; perhaps it had never occurred to them that three men could be so utterly desperate as to attack a dozen; perhaps they never realized that three men had made the perilous passage of the grapnel line; per- haps—most probably—in the mad excitement of it all, they simply lost their heads, for five minutes could hardly have elapsed altogether from the time the jolly boat hooked on until the poop was cleared. Two or three Spaniards ran down the companion to the maindeck, and for- ward along the gangway between the rows of slaves. One was caught against the rail and made a gesture of surrender, but Jackson's hand was already at his throat. Jackson was a man of immense physical strength; he bent the Spaniard back over the rail, farther and farther, and then caught him by the thigh with his other hand and heaved him over. He fell with a shriek before Hornblower could interpose. The poop deck was covered with writhing men, like the bottom of a boat filled with flapping fish. One man was getting to his knees when Jackson and Oldroyd seized him. They swung him up to toss him over the rail.

"Stop that!" said Hornblower, and quite callously they dropped him again with a crash on the bloody planks.

Jackson and Oldroyd were like drunken men, unsteady on their feet, glazed of eye and stertorous of breath; Hornblower was just coming out of his insane fit. He stepped forward to the break of the poop, wiping the sweat out of his eyes while trying to wipe away the red mist that tinged his vision. Forward by the forecastle were gathered the rest of the Spaniards, a large group of them; as Hornblower came forward, one of them fired a musket at him but the ball went wide. Down below him the rowers were still swinging rhythmically, forward and back, forward and back, the hairy heads and the naked bodies moving in time to the oars; in time to the voice of the overseer, too, for the latter was still standing on the gangway (the rest of the Spaniards were clustered behind him) calling the time—"Seis, siete, ocho."

"Stop!" bellowed Hornblower.

He walked to the starboard side to be in full view of the starboard side rowers. He held up his hand and bellowed again. A hairy face or two was raised, but the oars still swung.

"Uno, dos, tres," said the overseer.

Jackson appeared at Hornblower's elbow, and levelled a pistol to shoot the nearest rower.

"Oh, belay that!" said Hornblower testily. He knew he was sick of killings now. "Find my pistols and reload them."

He stood at the top of the companion like a man in a dream—in a nightmare. The galley slaves went on swinging and pulling; his dozen enemies were still clustered at the break of the forecastle thirty yards away; behind him the wounded Spaniards groaned away their lives. Another appeal to the rowers was as much ignored as the preceding ones. Oldroyd must have had the clearest head or have recovered himself quickest.

"I'll haul down his colours, sir, shall I?" he said.

Hornblower woke from his dream. On a staff above the taffrail fluttered the yellow and red.

"Yes, haul 'em down at once," he said.

Now his mind was clear, and now his horizon was no longer bounded by the narrow limits of the galley. He looked about him, over the blue, blue sea. There were the merchant ships; over there lay the *Indefatigable*. Behind him boiled the white wake of the galley—a curved wake. Not until that moment did he realize that he was in control of the tiller, and that for the last three minutes, the galley had been cutting over the blue seas unsteered.

"Take the tiller, Oldroyd," he ordered.

Was that a galley disappearing into the hazy distance? It must be, and far in its wake was the longboat. And there, on the port bow, was the gig, resting on her oars—Hornblower could see little figures standing waving in bow and stern, and it dawned upon him that this was in acknowledgment of the hauling down of the Spanish colours. Another musket banged off forward, and the rail close at his hip was struck a tremendous blow which sent gilded splinters flying in the sunlight. But he had all his wits about him again, and he ran back over the dying men; at the after end of the poop he was out of sight of the gangway and safe from shot. He could still see the gig on the port bow.

"Starboard your helm, Oldroyd."

The galley turned slowly—her narrow length made her unhandy if the rudder were not assisted by the oars—but soon the bow was about to obscure the gig.

"Midships!"

Amazing that there, leaping in the white water that boiled under the galley's stern, was the jolly boat with one live man and two dead men still aboard.

"Where are the others, Bromley?" yelled Jackson.

Bromley pointed overside. They had been shot from the taffrail at the moment that Hornblower and the others were preparing to attack the poop.

"Why in hell don't you come aboard?"

Bromley took hold of his left arm with his right; the limb was clearly useless. There was no reinforcement to be obtained here, and yet full possession must be taken of the galley. Otherwise it was even conceivable that they would be carried off to Algeciras; even if they were masters of the rudder the man who controlled the oars dictated the course of the ship if he willed. There was only one course left to try.

Now that his fighting madness had ebbed away, Hornblower was in a sombre mood. He did not care what happened to him; hope and fear had alike deserted him, along with his previous exalted condition. It might be resignation that possessed him now. His mind, still calculating, told him that with only one thing left to do to achieve victory he must attempt it, and the flat, dead condition of his spirits enabled him to carry the attempt through like an automaton, unwavering and emotionless. He walked forward to the poop rail again; the Spaniards were still clustered at the far end of the gangway, with the overseer still giving the time to the oars. They looked up at him as he stood there. With the utmost care and attention he sheathed his cutlass, which he had held in his hand up to that moment. He noticed the blood on his coat and on his hands as he did so. Slowly he settled the sheathed weapon at his side.

"My pistols, Jackson," he said.

Jackson handed him the pistols and with the same callous care he thrust them into his belt. He turned back to Oldroyd, the Spaniards watching every movement fascinated.

"Stay by the tiller, Oldroyd. Jackson, follow me. Do nothing without my orders."

With the sun pouring down on his face, he strode down the companion ladder, walked to the gangway, and approached the Spaniards along it. On either side of him the hairy heads and naked bodies of the galley slaves still swung with the oars. He neared the Spaniards; swords and muskets and pistols were handled nervously, but every eye was on his face. Behind him Jackson coughed. Two yards only from the group, Hornblower halted and swept them with his glance. Then, with a gesture, he indicated the whole of the group except the overseer; and then pointed to the forecastle.

"Get forrard, all of you," he said.

They stood staring at him, although they must have understood the gesture.

"Get forrard," said Hornblower with a wave of his hand and a tap of his foot on the gangway.

There was only one man who seemed likely to demur actively, and Hornblower had it in mind to snatch a pistol from his belt and shoot him on the spot. But the pistol might misfire, the shot might arouse the Spaniards out of their fascinated dream. He stared the man down.

"Get forrard, I say."

They began to move, they began to shamble off. Hornblower watched them go. Now his emotions were returning to him, and his heart was thumping madly in his chest so that it was hard to control himself. Yet he must not be precipitate. He had to wait until the others were well clear before he could address himself to the overseer.

"Stop those men," he said.

He glared into the overseer's eyes while pointing to the oarsmen; the overseer's lips moved, but he made no sound.

"Stop them," said Hornblower, and this time he put his hand to the butt of his pistol.

That sufficed. The overseer raised his voice in a high-pitched order, and the oars instantly ceased. Strange what sudden stillness possessed the ship with the cessation of the grinding of the oars in the tholes. Now it was easy to hear the bubbling of the water round the galley as her way carried her forward. Hornblower turned back to hail Oldroyd.

"Oldroyd! Where away's the gig?"

"Close on the starboard bow, sir!"

"How close?"

"Two cable's lengths, sir. She's pulling for us now."

"Steer for her while you've steerage way."

"Aye aye, sir."

How long would it take the gig under oars to cover a quarter of a mile? Hornblower feared anticlimax, feared a sudden revulsion of feeling among the Spaniards at this late moment. Mere waiting might occasion it, and he must not stand merely idle. He could still hear the motion of the galley through the water, and he turned to Jackson.

"This ship carries her way well, Jackson, doesn't she?" he said, and he made himself laugh as he spoke, as if everything in the world was a matter of sublime certainty.

"Aye, sir, I suppose she does, sir," said the startled Jackson; he was fidgeting nervously with his pistols.

"And look at the man there," went on Hornblower, pointing to a galley slave. "Did you ever see such a beard in your life?"

"No—no, sir."

"Speak to me, you fool. Talk naturally."

"I—I dunno what to say, sir."

"You've no sense, damn you, Jackson. See the welt on that fellow's shoulder? He must have caught it from the overseer's whip not so long ago."

"Mebbe you're right, sir."

Hornblower was repressing his impatience and was about to make another speech when he heard a rasping thump alongside and a moment later the gig's crew was pouring over the bulwarks. The relief was inexpressible. Hornblower was about to relax when he remembered appearances. He stiffened himself up.

"Glad to see you aboard, sir," he said, as Lieutenant Chadd swung his legs over and dropped to the maindeck at the break of the forecastle.

"Glad to see *you*," said Chadd, looking about him curiously.

"These men forrard are prisoners, sir," said Hornblower. "It might be well to secure them. I think that is all that remains to be done."

Now he could not relax; it seemed to him as if he must remain strained and tense for ever. Strained and yet stupid, even when he heard the cheers of the hands in the *Indefatigable* as the galley came alongside her. Stupid and dull, making a stumbling report to Captain Pellew, forcing himself to remember to commend the bravery of Jackson and Oldroyd in the highest terms.

"The Admiral will be pleased," said Pellew, looking at Hornblower keenly.

"I'm glad, sir," Hornblower heard himself say.

"Now that we've lost poor Soames," went on Pellew, "we shall need another watch-keeping officer. I have it in mind to give you an order as acting-lieutenant."

"Thank you, sir," said Hornblower, still stupid.

Soames had been a grey-haired officer of vast experience. He had sailed the seven seas, he had fought in a score of actions. But, faced with a new situation, he had not had the quickness of thought to keep his boat from under the ram of the galley. Soames was dead, and acting-lieutenant Hornblower would take his place. Fighting madness, sheer insanity, had won him this promise of promotion. Hornblower had never realized the black depths of lunacy into which he could sink. Like Soames, like all the rest of the crew of the *Indefatigable,* he had allowed himself to be carried away by his blind hatred for the galleys, and only good fortune had allowed him to live through it. That was something worth remembering.

THE EXAMINATION FOR LIEUTENANT

H.M.S. *Indefatigable* was gliding into Gibraltar Bay, with Acting-Lieutenant Horatio Hornblower stiff and self-conscious on the quarter-deck beside Captain Pellew. He kept his telescope trained over toward Algeciras; it was a strange situation, this, that major naval bases of two hostile powers should be no more than six miles apart, and while approaching the harbour it was as well to keep close watch on Algeciras, for there was always the possibility that a squadron of Spaniards might push out suddenly to pounce on an unwary frigate coming in.

"Eight ships—nine ships with their yards crossed, sir," reported Hornblower.

"Thank you," answered Pellew. "Hands 'bout ship."

The *Indefatigable* tacked and headed in toward the Mole. Gibraltar harbour was, as usual, crowded with shipping, for the whole naval effort of England in the Mediterranean was perforce based here. Pellew clewed up his topsails and put his helm over. Then the cable roared out and the *Indefatigable* swung at anchor.

"Call away my gig," ordered Pellew.

Pellew favoured dark blue and white as the colour scheme for his boat and its crew—dark blue shirts and white trousers for the men, with white hats with blue ribbons. The boat was of dark blue picked out with white, the oars had white looms and blue blades. The general effect was very smart indeed as the drive of the oars sent the gig skimming over the water to carry Pellew to pay his respects to the port admiral. It was not long after his return that a messenger came scurrying up to Hornblower.

"Captain's compliments, sir, and he'd like to see you in his cabin."

"Examine your conscience well," grinned Midshipman Bracegirdle. "What crimes have you committed?"

"I wish I knew," said Hornblower, quite genuinely.

It is always a nervous moment going in to see the captain in reply to his summons. Hornblower swallowed as he approached the cabin door, and he had to brace himself a little to knock and enter. But there was nothing to be alarmed about; Pellew looked up with a smile from his desk.

"Ah, Mr. Hornblower, I hope you will consider this good news. There will be an examination for lieutenant tomorrow, in the *Santa Barbara* there. You are ready to take it, I hope?"

Hornblower was about to say "I suppose so, sir," but checked himself.

"Yes, sir," he said—Pellew hated slipshod answers.

"Very well, then. You report there at three P.M. with your certificates and journals."

"Aye aye, sir."

That was a very brief conversation for such an important subject. Hornblower had Pellew's order as acting-lieutenant for two months now. Tomorrow he would take his examination. If he should pass the admiral would confirm the order next day, and Hornblower would be a lieutenant with two months' seniority already. But if he should fail! That would mean he had been found unfit for lieutenant's rank. He would revert to midshipman, the two months' seniority would be lost, and it would be six months at least before he could try again. Eight months' seniority was a matter of enormous importance. It would affect all his subsequent career.

"Tell Mr. Bolton you have my permission to leave the ship tomorrow, and you may use one of the ship's boats."

"Thank you, sir."

"Good luck, Hornblower."

During the next twenty-four hours Hornblower had not merely to try to read all through Norie's *Epitome of Navigation* again, and Clarke's *Complete Handbook of Seamanship,* but he had to see that his number one uniform was spick and span. It cost his spirit ration to prevail on the warrant cook to allow the gunroom attendant to heat a flatiron in the galley and iron out his neck handkerchief. Bracegirdle lent him a clean shirt, but there was a feverish moment when it was discovered that the gunroom's supply of shoe blacking had dried to a chip. Two midshipmen had to work it soft with lard, and the resultant compound, when applied to Hornblower's buckled shoes, was stubbornly resistant to taking a polish; only much labour with the gunroom's moulting shoebrush and then with a soft cloth brought those shoes up to a condition of brightness worthy of an examination for lieutenant. And as for the cocked hat—the life of a cocked hat in the midshipman's berth is hard, and some of the dents could not be entirely eliminated.

"Take it off as soon as you can and keep it under your arm," advised Bracegirdle. "Maybe they won't see you come up the ship's side."

Everybody turned out to see Hornblower leave the ship, with his sword and his white breeches and his buckled shoes, his bundle of journals under his arm and his certificates of sobriety and good conduct in his pocket. The winter afternoon was already far advanced as he was rowed over to the *Santa Barbara* and went up the ship's side to report himself to the officer of the watch.

The *Santa Barbara* was a prison hulk, one of the prizes captured in Rodney's action off Cadiz in 1780 and kept rotting at her moorings, mastless, ever since, a storeship in time of peace and a prison in time of war. Redcoated soldiers, muskets loaded and bayonets fixed, guarded the gangways; on forecastle and quarterdeck were carronades, trained inboard and depressed to sweep the waist, wherein a few prisoners took the air, ragged and unhappy. As Hornblower came up the side he caught a whiff of the stench within, where two thousand prisoners were confined. Hornblower reported himself to the officer of the watch as come on board, and for what purpose.

"Whoever would have guessed it?" said the officer of the watch—an elderly lieutenant with white hair hanging down to his shoulders—running his eye over Hornblower's immaculate uniform and the portfolio under his arm. "Fifteen of your kind have already come on board, and—Holy Gemini, see there!"

Quite a flotilla of small craft was closing in on the *Santa Barbara.* Each boat held at least one cocked-hatted and white-breeched midshipman, and some held four or five.

"Every courtesy young gentleman in the Mediterranean Fleet is ambitious for an epaulette," said the lieutenant. "Just wait until the examining board sees how many there are of you! I wouldn't be in your shoes, young shaver, for something. Go aft, there, and wait in the portside cabin."

It was already uncomfortably full; when Hornblower entered, fifteen pairs of eyes measured him up. There were officers of all ages from eighteen to forty, all in their number one's, all nervous—one or two of them had Norie's *Epitome* open on their laps and were anxiously reading passages about which they were doubtful. One little group was passing a bottle from hand to hand, presumably in an effort to keep up their courage. But no sooner had Hornblower entered than a stream of newcomers followed him. The cabin began to fill, and soon it was tightly packed. Half the forty men present found seats on the deck, and the others were forced to stand.

"Forty years back," said a loud voice somewhere, "my grandad marched with Clive to revenge the Black Hole of Calcutta. If he could but have witnessed the fate of his posterity!"

"Have a drink," said another voice, "and to hell with care."

"Forty of us," commented a tall, thin, clerkly officer, counting heads. "How many of us will they pass, do you think? Five?"

"To hell with care," repeated the bibulous voice in the corner, and lifted itself in song. "Begone, dull care; I prithee be gone from me—"

"Cheese it, you fool!" rasped another voice. "Hark to that!"

The air was filled with the long-drawn twittering of the pipes of the bos'n's mates, and someone on deck was shouting an order.

"A captain coming on board," remarked someone.

An officer had his eye at the crack of the door. "It's Dreadnought Foster," he reported.

"He's a tail twister if ever there was one," said a fat young officer, seated comfortably with his back to the bulkhead.

Again the pipes twittered.

"Harvey, of the dockyard," reported the lookout.

The third captain followed immediately. "It's Black Charlie Hammond," said the lookout. "Looking as if he'd lost a guinea and found sixpence."

"Black Charlie?" exclaimed someone, scrambling to his feet in haste and pushing to the door. "Let's see! So it is! Then here is one young gentleman who will not stay for an answer. I know too well what that answer would be. 'Six months more at sea, sir, and damn your eyes for your impertinence in presenting yourself for examination in your present state of ignorance.' Black Charlie won't ever forget that I lost his pet poodle overside from the cutter in Port-o'-Spain when he was first of the *Pegasus*. Goodbye, gentlemen. Give my regards to the examining board."

With that he was gone, and they saw him explaining himself to the officer of the watch and hailing a shore boat to take him back to his ship. "One fewer of us, at least," said the clerkly officer. "What is it, my man?"

"The board's compliments, sir," said the marine messenger, "an' will the first young gentleman please to come along?"

There was a momentary hesitation; no one was anxious to be the first victim.

"The one nearest the door," said an elderly master's mate. "Will you volunteer, sir?"

"I'll be the Daniel," said the erstwhile lookout desperately. "Remember me in your prayers."

He pulled his coat smooth, twitched at his neckcloth and was gone, the remainder waiting in gloomy silence, relieved only by the glug-

glug of the bottle as the bibulous midshipman took another swing. A full ten minutes passed before the candidate for promotion returned, making a brave effort to smile.

"Six months more at sea?" asked someone.

"No," was the unexpected answer. "Three! ... I was told to send the next man. It had better be you."

"But what did they ask you?"

"They began by asking me to define a rhumb line. ... But don't keep them waiting, I advise you." Some thirty officers had their textbooks open on the instant to reread about rhumb lines.

"You were there ten minutes," said the clerkly officer, looking at his watch. "Forty of us, ten minutes each—why, it'll be midnight before they reach the last of us. They'll never do it."

"They'll be hungry," said someone.

"Hungry for our blood," said another.

"Perhaps they'll try us in batches," suggested a third, "like the French tribunals."

Listening to them, Hornblower was reminded of French aristocrats jesting at the foot of the scaffold. Candidates departed and candidates returned, some gloomy, some smiling. The cabin was already far less crowded; Hornblower was able to secure sufficient deck space to seat himself, and he stretched out his legs with a nonchalant sigh of relief, and he no sooner emitted the sigh than he realized that it was a stage effect which he had put on for his own benefit. He was as nervous as he could be. The winter night was falling, and some good Samaritan on board sent in a couple of purser's dips to give a feeble illumination to the darkening cabin.

"They are passing one in three," said the clerkly officer, making ready for his turn. "May I be the third."

Hornblower got to his feet again when he left; it would be his turn next. He stepped out under the halfdeck into the dark night and breathed the chill fresh air. A gentle breeze was blowing from the southward, cooled, presumably, by the snow-clad Atlas Mountains of Africa across the strait. There was neither moon nor stars. Here came the clerkly officer back again.

"Hurry," he said. "They're impatient."

Hornblower made his way past the sentry to the after cabin; it was brightly lit, so that he blinked as he entered, and stumbled over some obstruction. And it was only then that he remembered that he had not straightened his neckcloth and seen to it that his sword hung correctly at his side. He went on blinking in his nervousness at the three grim faces across the table.

"Well, sir?" said a stern voice. "Report yourself. We have no time to waste."

"H-Hornblower, sir. H-Horatio H-Hornblower. M-Midshipman—I mean Acting-Lieutenant, H.M.S. *Indefatigable*."

"Your certificates, please," said the right-hand face.

Hornblower handed them over, and as he waited for them to be examined, the left-hand face suddenly spoke. "You are close-hauled on the port tack, Mr. Hornblower, beating up channel with a noreasterly wind blowing hard, with Dover bearing north two miles. Is that clear?"

"Yes, sir."

"Now the wind veers four points and takes you flat, aback. What do you do, sir? What do you do?"

Hornblower's mind, if it was thinking about anything at all at that moment, was thinking about rhumb lines; this question took him as much aback as the situation it envisaged. His mouth opened and shut, but there was no word he could say.

"By now you're dismasted," said the middle face—a swarthy face; Hornblower was making the deduction that it must belong to Black Charlie Hammond. He could think about that even if he could not force his mind to think at all about his examination.

"Dismasted," said the left-hand face, with a smile like Nero enjoying a Christian's death agony. "With Dover cliffs under your lee. You are in serious trouble, Mr.—ah—Hornblower."

Serious indeed. Hornblower's mouth opened and shut again. His dulled mind heard, without paying special attention to it, the thud of a cannon shot somewhere not too far off. The board passed no remark on it either, but a moment later there came a series of further cannon shots which brought the three captains to their feet. Unceremoniously they rushed out of the cabin, sweeping out of the way the sentry at the door. Hornblower followed them; they arrived in the waist just in time to see a rocket soar up into the night sky and burst in a shower of red stars. It was the general alarm; over the water of the anchorage they could hear the drums rolling as all the ships present beat to quarters. On the portside gangway the remainder of the candidates were clustered speaking excitedly.

"See there!" said a voice.

Across half a mile of dark water a yellow light grew until the ship there was wrapped in flame. She had every sail set and was heading straight into the crowded anchorage.

"Fire ships!"

"Officer of the watch! Call my gig!" bellowed Foster.

A line of fire ships was running before the wind, straight at the crowd of anchored ships. The *Santa Barbara* was full of the wildest bustle as the seamen and marines came pouring on deck, and as captains and candidates shouted for boats to take them back to their ships. A line of orange flame lit up the water, followed at once by the roar of a broadside; some ship was firing her guns in the endeavour to sink a fire ship. Let one of those blazing hulls make contact with one of the anchored ships, even for a few seconds, and the fire would be transmitted to the dry, painted timber, to the tarred cordage, to the inflammable sails, so that nothing would put it out. To men in highly combustible ships filled with explosives fire was the deadliest and most dreaded peril of the sea.

"You shore boat, there!" bellowed Hammond suddenly. "You shore boat! Come alongside! Come alongside, blast you!"

His eye had been quick to sight the pair-oar rowing by.

"Come alongside or I'll fire into you!" supplemented Foster. "Sentry, there, make ready to give them a shot!"

At the threat the wherry turned and glided towards the mizzen chains.

"Here you are, gentlemen," said Hammond.

The three captains rushed to the mizzen chains and flung themselves down into the boat. Hornblower was at their heels. He knew there was small enough chance of a junior officer getting a boat to take him back to his ship, to which it was his bounden duty to go as soon as possible. After the captains had reached their destinations he could use this boat to reach the *Indefatigable*. He threw himself off into the sternsheets as she pushed off, knocking the breath out of Captain Harvey, his sword scabbard clattering on the gunwale. But the three captains accepted his uninvited presence there without comment.

"Pull for the *Dreadnought*," said Foster.

"Dammit, I'm the senior!" said Hammond. "Pull for *Calypso*."

"*Calypso* it is," said Harvey. He had his hand on the tiller, heading the boat across the dark water.

"Pull! Oh, pull!" said Foster, in agony. There can be no mental torture like that of a captain whose ship is in peril and he not on board.

"There's one of them," said Harvey.

Just ahead, a small brig was bearing down on them under topsails; they could see the glow of the fire, and as they watched the fire suddenly burst into roaring fury, wrapping the whole vessel in flames in a moment, like a set piece in a fireworks display. Flames spouted out of the holes in her sides and roared up through her hatchways. The very water around her glowed vivid red. They saw her halt in her career and begin to swing slowly around.

"She's across *Santa Barbara*'s cable," said Foster.

"She's nearly clear," added Hammond. "God help 'em on board there. She'll be alongside her in a minute."

Hornblower thought of two thousand Spanish and French prisoners battened down below decks in the hulk.

"With a man at her wheel she could be steered clear," said Foster. "We ought to do it!"

Then things happened rapidly. Harvey put the tiller over. "Pull away!" he roared at the boatmen.

The latter displayed an easily understood reluctance to row up to that fiery hull.

"Pull!" said Harvey.

He whipped out his sword from its scabbard, and the blade reflected the red fire as he thrust it menacingly at the stroke oar's throat. With a kind of sob, stroke tugged at his oar and the boat leaped forward.

"Lay us under her counter," said Foster. "I'll jump for it."

At last Hornblower found his tongue. "Let me go, sir. I'll handle her."

"Come with me, if you like," replied Foster. "It may need two of us."

His nickname of Dreadnought Foster may have had its origin in the name of his ship, but it was appropriate enough in all circumstances. Harvey swung the boat under the fire ship's stern; she was before the wind again now, and just gathering way, just heading down upon the *Santa Barbara*.

For a moment Hornblower was the nearest man in the boat to the brig and there was no time to be lost. He stood up on the thwart and jumped; his hands gripped something, and with a kick and a struggle he dragged his ungainly body up onto the deck. With the brig before the wind, the flames were blown forward; right aft here it was merely frightfully hot, but Hornblower's ears were filled with the roar of the flames and the crackling and banging of the burning wood. He stepped forward to the wheel and seized the spokes, the wheel was lashed with a loop of line, and as he cast this off and took hold of the wheel again he could feel the rudder below him bite into the water. He flung his weight on the spoke and spun the wheel over. The brig was about to collide with the *Santa Barbara*, starboard bow to starboard bow, and the flames lit an anxious gesticulating crowd on the *Santa Barbara*'s forecastle.

"Hard over!" roared Foster's voice in Hornblower's ear.

"Hard over it is!" said Hornblower, and the brig answered her wheel at that moment, and her bow turned away, avoiding the collision.

An immense fountain of flame poured out from the hatchway abaft the mainmast, setting mast and rigging ablaze, and at the same time a flaw of wind blew a wave of flame aft. Some instinct made Hornblower while holding the wheel with one hand snatch out his neckcloth with the other and bury his face in it. The flame whirled round him and was gone again. But the distraction had been dangerous; the brig had continued to turn under full helm, and now her stern was swinging in to bump against the *Santa Barbara*'s bow. Hornblower desperately spun the wheel over the other way. The flames had driven Foster aft to the taffrail, but now he returned.

"Hard-a-lee!"

The brig was already responding. Her starboard quarter bumped the *Santa Barbara* in the waist, and then bumped clear.

"Midships!" shouted Foster.

At a distance of only two or three yards the fire ship passed on down the *Santa Barbara*'s side; an anxious group ran along her gangways keeping up with her as she did so. On the quarterdeck another group stood by with a spar to boom the fire ship off; Hornblower saw them out of the tail of his eye as they went by. Now they were clear.

"There's the *Dauntless* on the port bow," said Foster. "Keep her clear."

"Aye aye, sir."

The din of the fire was tremendous; it could hardly be believed that on this little area of deck it was still possible to breathe and live. Hornblower felt the appalling heat on his hands and face. Both masts were immense pyramids of flame.

"Starboard a point," said Foster. "We'll lay her aground on the shoal by the Neutral Ground."

"Starboard a point," responded Hornblower.

He was being borne along on a wave of the highest exaltation; the roar of the fire was intoxicating, and he knew not a moment's fear. Then the whole deck only a yard or two forward of the wheel opened up in flame. Fire spouted out of the gaping seams and the heat was utterly unbearable, and the fire moved rapidly aft as the seams gaped progressively backward.

Hornblower felt for the loopline to lash the wheel, but before he could do so the wheel spun idly under his hand, presumably as the tiller ropes below him were burned away, and at the same time the deck under his feet heaved and warped in the fire. He staggered back to the taffrail. Foster was there.

"Tiller ropes burned away, sir," reported Hornblower.

Flames roared up beside them. His coat sleeve was smouldering.

"Jump!" said Foster.

Hornblower felt Foster shoving him—everything was insane. He heaved himself over, gasped with fright as he hung in the air, and then felt the breath knocked out of his body as he hit the water. The water closed over him, and he knew panic as he struggled back to the surface. It was cold—the Mediterranean in December is cold. For the moment the air in his clothes supported him, despite the weight of the sword at his side, but he could see nothing in the darkness, with his eyes still dazzled by the roaring flames. Somebody splashed beside him.

"They were following us in the boat to take us off," said Foster's voice. "Can you swim?"

"Yes, sir. Not very well."

"That might describe me," said Foster; and then he lifted his voice to hail, "Ahoy! Ahoy! Hammond! Harvey! Ahoy!"

He tried to raise himself as well as his voice, fell back with a splash, and splashed and splashed again, the water flowing into his mouth cutting short something he tried to say. Hornblower, beating the water with increasing feebleness, could still spare a thought—such were the vagaries of his wayward mind—for the interesting fact that even captains of much seniority were only mortal men after all. He tried to unbuckle his sword belt, failed, and sank deep with the effort, only just succeeding in struggling back to the surface. He gasped for breath, but in another attempt he managed to draw his sword half out of its scabbard, and as he struggled it slid out the rest of the way by its own weight; yet he was not conscious of any noticeable relief.

It was then that he heard the splashing and grinding of oars and loud voices, and he saw the dark shape of the approaching boat, and he uttered a spluttering cry. In a second or two the boat was up to them, and he was clutching the gunwale in panic.

They were lifting Foster in over the stern, and Hornblower knew he must keep still and make no effort to climb in, but it called for all his resolution to make himself hang quietly onto the side of the boat and wait his turn. He was interested in this overmastering fear, while he despised himself for it. It called for a conscious and serious effort of willpower to make his hands alternately release their death-like grip on the gunwale, so that the men in the boat could pass him round to the stern. Then they dragged him in and he fell face downward in the bottom of the boat, on the verge of fainting. Then somebody spoke in the boat, and Hornblower felt a cold shiver pass over his skin, and his feeble muscles tensed themselves, for the words spoken were Spanish—at any rate an unknown tongue, and Spanish presumably.

Somebody else answered in the same language. Hornblower tried to struggle up, and a restraining hand was laid on his shoulder. He rolled over, and with his eyes now accustomed to the darkness, he could see the three swarthy faces with the long black moustaches. These men were not Gibraltarians. On the instant he could guess who they were —the crew of one of the fire ships who had steered their craft in past the Mole, set fire to it, and made their escape in the boat. Foster was sitting doubled up, in the bottom of the boat, and now he lifted his face from his knees and stared round him.

"Who are these fellows?" he asked feebly—his struggle in the water had left him as weak as Hornblower.

"Spanish fire ship's crew, I fancy sir," said Hornblower. "We're prisoners."

"Are we indeed!"

The knowledge galvanized him into activity just as it had Hornblower. He tried to get to his feet, and the Spaniard at the tiller thrust him down with a hand on his shoulder. Foster tried to put his hand away, and raised his voice in a feeble cry, but the man at the tiller was standing no nonsense. He brought out, in a lightning gesture, a knife from his belt. The light from the fire ship, burning itself harmlessly out on the shoal in the distance, ran redly along the blade, and Foster ceased to struggle. Men might call him Dreadnought Foster, but he could recognize the need for discretion.

"How are we heading?" he asked Hornblower, sufficiently quietly not to irritate their captors.

"North, sir. Maybe they're going to land on the Neutral Ground and make for the Line."

"That's their best chance," agreed Foster.

He turned his neck uncomfortably to look back up the harbour.

"Two other ships burning themselves out up there," he said. "There were three fire ships came in, I fancy."

"I saw three, sir."

"Then there's no damage done. But a bold endeavour. Whoever would have credited the Dons with making such an attempt?"

"They have learned about fire ships from us, perhaps, sir," suggested Hornblower.

"We may have 'nursed the pinion that impelled the steel' you think?"

"It is possible, sir."

Foster was a cool enough customer, quoting poetry and discussing the naval situation while being carried off into captivity by a Spaniard who guarded him with a drawn knife. Cool might be a too accurate adjective; Hornblower was shivering in his wet clothes as the chill night air blew over him, and he felt weak and feeble after all the excitement and exertions of the day.

"Boat ahoy!" came a hail across the water; there was a dark nucleus in the night over there. The Spaniard in the sternsheets instantly dragged the tiller over, heading the boat directly away from it, while the two at the oars redoubled their exertions.

"Guard boat—" said Foster, but cut his explanation short at a further threat from the knife.

Of course there would be a boat rowing guard at this northern end of the anchorage; they might have thought of it.

"Boat ahoy!" came the hail again. "Lay on your oars or I'll fire upon you!"

The Spaniard made no reply, and a second later came the flash and report of a musket shot. They heard nothing of the bullet, but the shot would put the fleet—towards which they were heading again—on the alert. But the Spaniards were going to play the game out to the end. They rowed doggedly on.

"Boat ahoy!"

This was another hail, from a boat right ahead of them. The Spaniards at the oars ceased their efforts in dismay, but a roar from the steersman set them instantly to work again. Hornblower could see the new boat almost directly ahead of them, and heard another hail from it as it rested on its oars. The Spaniard at the tiller shouted an order, and the stroke oar backed water and the boat turned sharply; another order, and both rowers tugged ahead again and the boat surged forward to ram. Should they succeed in overturning the intercepting boat they might make their escape even now, while the pursuing boat stopped to pick up their friends.

Everything happened at once, with everyone shouting at the full pitch of his lungs, seemingly. There was the crash of the collision, both boats heeling wildly as the bow of the Spanish boat rode up over the British boat but failed to overturn it. Someone fired a pistol, and the next moment the pursuing guard boat came dashing alongside, its crew leaping madly aboard them. Somebody flung himself on top of Hornblower, crushing the breath out of him and threatening to keep it out permanently with a hand on his throat. Hornblower heard Foster bellowing in protest, and a moment later his assailant released him, so that he could hear the midshipman of the guard boat apologizing for this rough treatment of a post captain of the Royal Navy. Someone unmasked the guard boat's lantern, and by its light Foster revealed himself, bedraggled and battered. The light shone on their sullen prisoners.

"Boats ahoy!" came another hail, and yet another boat emerged from the darkness and pulled towards them.

"Cap'n Hammond, I believe!" hailed Foster, with an ominous rasp in his voice.

"Thank God!" they heard Hammond say, and the boat pulled into the faint circle of light.

"But no thanks to you," said Foster bitterly.

"After your fire ship cleared the *Santa Barbara* a puff of wind took you on faster than we could keep up with you," explained Harvey.

"We followed as fast as we could get these rock scorpions to row," added Hammond.

"And yet it called for Spaniards to save us from drowning," sneered Foster. The memory of his struggle in the water rankled, apparently. "I thought I could rely on two brother captains."

"What are you implying, sir?" snapped Hammond.

"I make no implications, but others may read implications into a simple statement of fact."

"I consider that an offensive remark, sir," said Harvey, "addressed to me equally with Captain Hammond."

"I congratulate you on your perspicacity, sir," replied Foster.

"I understand," said Harvey. "This is not a discussion we can pursue with these men present. I shall send a friend to wait on you."

"He will be welcome."

"Then I wish you a very good night, sir."

"And I, too, sir," said Hammond. "Give way there."

The boat pulled out of the circle of light, leaving an audience openmouthed at this strange freak of human behaviour, that a man saved first from death and then from captivity should wantonly thrust himself into peril again. Foster looked after the boat for some seconds before speaking; perhaps he was already regretting his rather hysterical outburst.

"I shall have much to do before morning," he said, more to himself than to anyone near him, and then addressed himself to the midshipman of the guard boat, "You, sir, will take charge of these prisoners and convey me to my ship."

"Aye aye, sir."

"Is there anyone here who can speak their lingo? I would have it explained to them that I shall send them back to Cartagena under cartel, free without exchange. They saved our lives, and that is the least we can do in return." The final explanatory sentence was addressed to Hornblower.

"I think that is just, sir."

"And you, my fire-breathing friend. May I offer you my thanks? You did well. Should I live beyond tomorrow, I shall see that authority is informed of your actions."

"Thank you, sir." A question trembled on Hornblower's lips. It called for a little resolution to thrust it out, "And my examination, sir? My certificate?"

Foster shook his head. "That particular examining board will never reassemble, I fancy. You must wait your opportunity to go before another one."

"Aye aye, sir," said Hornblower, with despondency apparent in his tone.

"Now lookee here, Mr. Hornblower," said Foster, turning upon him. "To the best of my recollection, you were flat aback, about to lose your spars and with Dover cliffs under your lee. In one more minute you would have been failed—it was the warning gun that saved you. Is not that so?"

"I suppose it is, sir."

"Then be thankful for small mercies. And even more thankful for big ones."

NOAH'S ARK

Acting-Lieutenant Hornblower sat in the sternsheets of the longboat beside Mr. Tapling of the diplomatic service, with his feet among bags of gold. About him rose the steep shores of the Gulf of Oran, and ahead of him lay the city, white in the sunshine, like a mass of blocks of marble dumped by a careless hand upon the hillsides where they rose from the water. The oar blades, as the boat's crew pulled away rhythmically over the gentle swell, were biting into the clearest emerald green, and it was only a moment since they had left behind the bluest the Mediterranean could show.

"A pretty sight from here," said Tapling, gazing at the town they were approaching, "but closer inspection will show that the eye is deceived. And as for the nose! The stinks of the true believers have to be smelt to be believed. Lay her alongside the jetty there, Mr. Hornblower, beyond those xebecs."

"Aye aye, sir," said the coxswain, when Hornblower gave the order.

"There's a sentry on the waterfront battery here," commented Tapling, looking about him keenly, "not more than half asleep, either. And notice the two guns in the two castles. Thirty-two pounders, without a doubt. Stone shot piled in readiness. A stone shot flying into fragments on impact effects damage out of proportion to its size. And the walls seem sound enough. To seize Oran by a coup de main would not be easy, I am afraid. If His Nibs the Bey should choose to cut our throats and keep our gold it would be long before we were avenged, Mr. Hornblower."

"I don't think I should find any satisfaction in being avenged in any case, sir," said Hornblower.

"There's some truth in that. But doubtless His Nibs will spare us this time. The goose lays golden eggs—a boatload of gold every month must make a dazzling prospect for a pirate Bey in these days of convoys."

"Way 'nough," called the coxswain. "Oars!"

The longboat came gliding alongside the jetty and hooked on neatly. A few seated figures in the shade turned eyes at least, and in some cases even their heads as well, to look at the British boat's crew. A number of swarthy Moors appeared on the decks of the xebecs and gazed down at them, and one or two shouted remarks to them.

"No doubt they are describing the ancestry of the infidels," said Tapling. "Sticks and stones may break my bones, but names can never hurt me, especially when I do not understand them. Where's our man?"

He shaded his eyes to look along the waterfront.

"No one in sight, sir, that looks like a Christian," said Hornblower.

"Our man's no Christian," said Tapling. "White, but no Christian. White by courtesy at that—French-Arab-Levantine mixture. His Britannic Majesty's Consul at-Oran pro tem., and a Mussulman from expediency. Though there are very serious disadvantages about being a true believer. Who would want four wives at any time, especially when one pays for the doubtful privilege by abstaining from wine?"

Tapling stepped up onto the jetty and Hornblower followed him. The gentle swell that rolled up the Gulf broke soothingly below them, and the blinding heat of the noonday sun was reflected up into their faces from the stone blocks on which they stood. Far down the Gulf lay the two anchored ships—the storeship and H.M.S. *Indefatigable*— lovely on the blue and silver surface.

"And yet I would rather see Drury Lane on a Saturday night," said Tapling.

He turned back to look at the city wall, which guarded the place from seaborne attack. A narrow gate, flanked by bastions, opened onto the waterfront. Sentries in red caftans were visible on the summit. In the deep shadow of the gate something was moving, but it was hard with eyes dazzled by the sun to see what it was. Then it emerged from the shadow as a little group coming towards them—a half-naked Negro leading a donkey, and on the back of the donkey, seated sideways far back towards the root of the tail, a vast figure in a blue robe.

"Shall we meet His Britannic Majesty's Consul halfway?" said Tapling. "No. Let him come to us."

The Negro halted the donkey, and the man on the donkey's back slid to the ground and came towards them—a mountainous man, waddling straddle-legged in his robe, his huge clay-coloured face topped by a white turban. A scanty black moustache and beard sprouted from his lip and chin.

"Your servant, Mr. Duras," said Tapling. "And may I present Acting-Lieutenant Horatio Hornblower, of the frigate *Indefatigable*?"

Mr. Duras nodded his perspiring head.

"Have you brought the money?" he asked, in guttural French; it took Hornblower a moment or two to adjust his mind to the language and his ear to Duras' intonation.

"Seven thousand golden guineas," replied Tapling, in reasonably good French.

"Good," said Duras, with a trace of relief. "Is it in the boat?"

"It is in the boat, and it stays in the boat at present," answered Tapling. "Do you remember the conditions agreed upon? Four hundred fat cattle, fifteen hundred fanegas of barley grain. When I see those in the lighters, and the lighters alongside the ships down the bay, then I hand over the money. Have you the stores ready?"

"Soon."

"As I expected. How long?"

"Soon—very soon."

Tapling made a grimace of resignation.

"Then we shall return to the ships. Tomorrow, perhaps, or the day after, we shall come back with the gold."

Alarm appeared on Duras' sweating face.

"No, do not do that," he said, hastily. "You do not know His Highness the Bey. He is changeable. If he knows the gold is there he will give orders for the cattle to be brought. Take the gold away, and he will not stir. And—and—he will be angry with me."

"Ira principis mors est," said Tapling, and in response to Duras' blank look obliged by a translation. "The wrath of the prince means death. Is not that so?"

"Yes," said Duras, and he in turn said something in an unknown language, and stabbed at the air with his fingers in a peculiar gesture; and then translated, "May it not happen."

"Certainly we hope it may not happen," agreed Tapling with disarming cordiality. "The bowstring, the hook, even the bastinado are all unpleasant. It might be better if you went to the Bey and prevailed upon him to give the necessary orders for the grain and the cattle. Or we shall leave at nightfall."

Tapling glanced up at the sun to lay stress on the time limit.

"I shall go," said Duras, spreading his hands in a deprecatory gesture. "I shall go. But I beg of you, do not depart. Perhaps His Highness is busy in his harem. Then no one may disturb him. But I shall try. The grain is here ready—it lies in the Kasbah there. It is only the cattle that have to be brought in. Please be patient. I implore you. His Highness is not accustomed to commerce, as you know, sir. Still less is he accustomed to commerce after the fashion of the Franks."

Duras wiped his streaming face with a corner of his robe.

"Pardon me," he said. "I do not feel well. But I shall go to His Highness. I shall go. Please wait for me."

"Until sunset," said Tapling implacably.

Duras called to his Negro attendant, who had been crouching huddled up under the donkey's belly to take advantage of the shade it cast. With an effort Duras hoisted his ponderous weight onto the donkey's hind quarters. He wiped his face again and looked at them with a trace of bewilderment.

"Wait for me," were the last words he said as the donkey was led away back into the city gate.

"He is afraid of the Bey," said Tapling watching him go. "I would rather face twenty Beys than Admiral Sir John Jervis in a tantrum. What will he do when he hears about this further delay, with the Fleet on short rations already? He'll have my guts for a necktie."

"One cannot expect punctuality of these people," said Hornblower with the easy philosophy of the man who does not bear the responsibility. But he thought of the British Navy, without friends, without allies, maintaining desperately the blockade of a hostile Europe, in face of superior numbers, storms, disease, and now famine.

"Look at that!" said Tapling pointing suddenly.

It was a big grey rat which had made its appearance in the dry storm gutter that crossed the waterfront here. Regardless of the bright sunshine it sat up and looked round at the world; even when Tapling stamped his foot it showed no great signs of alarm. When he stamped a second time it slowly turned to hide itself again in the drain, missed its footing so that it lay writhing for a moment at the mouth of the drain, and then regained its feet and disappeared into the darkness.

"An old rat, I suppose," said Tapling meditatively. "Senile, possibly. Even blind, it may be."

Hornblower cared nothing about rats, senile or otherwise. He took a step or two back in the direction of the longboat and the civilian officer conformed to his movements.

"Rig that mains'l so that it gives us some shade, Maxwell," said Hornblower. "We're here for the rest of the day."

"A great comfort," said Tapling, seating himself on a stone bollard beside the boat, "to be here in a heathen port. No need to worry in case any men run off. No need to worry about liquor. Only about bullocks and barley. And how to get a spark on this tinder."

He blew through the pipe that he took from his pocket, preparatory to filling it. The boat was shaded by the mainsail now, and the hands sat in the bows yarning in low tones, while the others made themselves as comfortable as possible in the sternsheets; the boat rolled peacefully in the tiny swell, the rhythmic sound as the fendoffs creaked between her gunwale and the jetty having a soothing effect while city and port dozed in the blazing afternoon heat. Yet it was not easy for a young man of Hornblower's active temperament to endure prolonged inaction. He climbed up on the jetty to stretch his legs, and paced up and down; a Moor in a white gown and turban came staggering in the sunshine along the waterfront. His gait was unsteady, and he walked with his legs well apart to provide a firmer base for his swaying body.

"What was it you said, sir, about liquor being abhorred by the Moslems?" said Hornblower to Tapling down in the sternsheets.

"Not necessarily abhorred," replied Tapling, guardedly. "But anathematized, illegal, unlawful, and hard to obtain."

"Someone here has contrived to obtain some, sir," said Hornblower.

"Let me see," said Tapling, scrambling up; the hands, bored with waiting and interested as ever in liquor, landed from the bows to stare as well.

"That looks like a man who has taken drink," agreed Tapling.

"Three sheets in the wind, sir," said Maxwell, as the Moor staggered.

"And taken all aback," supplemented Tapling, as the Moor swerved wildly to one side in a semicircle.

At the end of the semicircle he fell with a crash on his face; his brown legs merged from the robe a couple of times and were drawn in again, and he lay passive, his head on his arms, his turban fallen on the ground to reveal his shaven skull with a tassel of hair on the crown.

"Totally dismasted," said Hornblower.

"And hard aground," said Tapling.

But the Moor now lay oblivious of everything.

"And here's Duras," said Hornblower.

Out through the gate came the massive figure on the little donkey; another donkey bearing another portly figure followed, each donkey being led by a Negro slave, and after them came a dozen swarthy individuals whose muskets, and whose pretence at uniform, indicated that they were soldiers.

"The Treasurer of His Highness," said Duras, by way of introduction when he and the other had dismounted. "Come to fetch the gold."

The portly Moor looked loftily upon them; Duras was still streaming with sweat in the hot sun.

"The gold is there," said Tapling, pointing. "In the sternsheets of the longboat. You will have a closer view of it when we have a closer view of the stores we are to buy."

Duras translated this speech into Arabic. There was a rapid interchange of sentences, before the Treasurer apparently yielded. He turned and waved his arms back to the gate in what was evidently a prearranged signal. A dreary procession immediately emerged—a long line of men, all of them almost naked, white, black and mulatto, each man staggering along under the burden of a sack of grain. Overseers with sticks walked with them.

"The money," said Duras, as a result of something said by the Treasurer.

A word from Tapling set the hands to work lifting the heavy bags of gold onto the quay.

"With the corn on the jetty I will put the gold there too," said Tapling to Hornblower. "Keep your eye on it while I look at some of those sacks."

Tapling walked over to the slave gang. Here and there he opened a sack, looked into it, and inspected handfuls of the golden barley grain; other sacks he felt from the outside.

"No hope of looking over every sack in a hundred ton of barley," he remarked, strolling back again to Hornblower. "Much of it is sand, I expect. But that is the way of the heathen. The price is adjusted accordingly. Very well, Effendi."

At a sign from Duras, and under the urgings of the overseers, the slaves burst into activity, trotting up to the quayside and dropping their sacks into the lighter which lay there. The first dozen men were organized into a working party to distribute the cargo evenly into the bottom of the lighter, while the others trotted off, their bodies gleaming with sweat, to fetch fresh loads. At the same time a couple of swarthy herdsmen came out through the gate driving a small herd of cattle.

"Scrubby little creatures," said Tapling, looking them over critically, "but that was allowed for in the price, too."

"The gold," said Duras.

In reply Tapling opened one of the bags at his feet, filled his hand with golden guineas, and let them cascade through his fingers into the bag again.

"Five hundred guineas there," he said. "Fourteen bags, as you see. They will be yours when the lighters are loaded and unmoored."

Duras wiped his face with a weary gesture. His knees seemed to be weak, and he leaned upon the patient donkey that stood behind him.

The cattle were being driven down a gangway into another lighter, and a second herd had now appeared and was waiting.

"Things move faster than you feared," said Hornblower.

"See how they drive the poor wretches," replied Tapling sententiously. "See! Things move fast when you have no concern for human flesh and blood."

A coloured slave had fallen to the ground under his burden. He lay there disregarding the blows rained on him by the sticks of the overseers. There was a small movement of his legs. Someone dragged him out of the way at last and the sacks continued to be carried to the lighter. The other lighter was filling fast with cattle, packed into a tight, bellowing mass in which no movement was possible.

"His Nibs is actually keeping his word," marvelled Tapling. "I'd 'a settled for the half, if I had been asked beforehand."

One of the herdsmen on the quay had sat down with his face in his hands; now he fell over limply on his side.

"Sir—" began Hornblower to Tapling, and the two men looked

at each other with the same awful thought occurring to them at the same moment.

Duras began to say something; with one hand on the withers of the donkey and the other gesticulating in the air it seemed that he was making something of a speech, but there was no sense in the words he was roaring out in a hoarse voice. His face was swollen beyond its customary fatness and his expression was wildly distorted, while his cheeks were so suffused with blood as to look dark under his tan. Duras quitted his hold of the donkey and began to reel about in half circles, under the eyes of Moors and Englishmen. His voice died away to a whisper, his legs gave way under him, and he fell to his hands and knees and then to his face.

"That's the plague!" said Tapling. "The Black Death! I saw it in Smyrna in '96."

He and the other Englishmen had shrunk back on the one side, the soldiers and the Treasurer on the other, leaving the palpitating body lying in the clear space between them.

"The plague, by St. Peter!" squealed one of the young sailors. He would have headed a rush to the longboat.

"Stand still, there!" roared Hornblower, scared of the plague but with the habits of discipline so deeply engrained in him by now that he checked the panic automatically.

"I was a fool not to have thought of it before," said Tapling. "That dying rat—that fellow over there who we thought was drunk. I should have known!"

The soldier who appeared to be the sergeant in command of the Treasurer's escort was in explosive conversation with the chief of the overseers of the slaves, both of them staring and pointing at the dying Duras; the Treasurer himself was clutching his robe about him and looking down at the wretched man at his feet in fascinated horror.

"Well, sir," said Hornblower to Tapling, "what do we do?"

Hornblower was of the temperament that demands immediate action in face of a crisis.

"Do?" replied Tapling with a bitter smile. "We stay here and rot."

"Stay *here*?"

"The fleet will never have us back. Not until we have served three weeks of quarantine. Three weeks after the last case has occurred. Here in Oran."

"Nonsense!" said Hornblower, with all the respect due to his senior startled out of him. "No one would order that."

"Would they not? Have you ever seen an epidemic in a fleet?"

Hornblower had not, but he had heard enough about them—fleets where nine out of ten had died of putrid fevers. Crowded ships with twenty-two inches of hammock space per man were ideal breeding places for epidemics. He realized that no captain, no admiral, would run that risk for the sake of a longboat's crew of twenty men.

The two xebecs against the jetty had suddenly cast off, and were working their way out of the harbour under sweeps.

"The plague can only have struck today," mused Hornblower, the habit of deduction strong in him despite his sick fear.

The cattle herders were abandoning their work, giving a wide berth to that one of their number who was lying on the quay. Up at the town gate it appeared that the guard was employed in driving people back into the town—apparently the rumour of plague had spread sufficiently therein to cause a panic, while the guard had just received orders not to allow the population to stream out into the surrounding country. There would be frightful things happening in the town soon. The Treasurer was climbing on his donkey; the crowd of grain-carrying slaves was melting away as the overseers fled.

"I must report this to the ship," said Hornblower; Tapling as a civilian diplomatic officer, held no authority over him. The whole responsibility was Hornblower's. The longboat and the longboat's crew were Hornblower's command, entrusted to him by Captain Pellew whose authority derived from the King.

Amazing, how the panic was spreading. The Treasurer was gone; Duras' Negro slave had ridden off on his late master's donkey; the soldiers had hastened off in a single group. The waterfront was deserted now except for the dead and dying; along the waterfront, presumably, at the foot of the wall, lay the way to the open country which all desired to seek. The Englishmen were standing alone, with the bags of gold at their feet.

"Plague spreads through the air," said Tapling. "Even the rats die of it. We have been here for hours. We were near enough to—that—" he nodded at the dying Duras—"to speak to him, to catch his breath. Which of us will be the first?"

"We'll see when the time comes," said Hornblower. It was his contrary nature to be sanguine in the face of depression; besides, he did not want the men to hear what Tapling was saying.

"And there's the fleet!" said Tapling bitterly. "This lot,"—he nodded at the deserted lighters, one almost full of cattle, the other almost full of grain sacks—"this lot would be a Godsend. The men are on two-thirds rations."

"Damn it, we can do something about it," said Hornblower. "Maxwell, put the gold back in the boat, and get that awning in."

The officer of the watch in H.M.S. *Indefatigable* saw the ship's longboat returning from the town. A slight breeze had swung the frigate and the *Caroline* (the transport brig) to their anchors, and the longboat, instead of running alongside, came up under the *Indefatigable's* stern to leeward.

"Mr. Christie!" hailed Hornblower, standing up in the bows of the longboat.

The officer of the watch came aft to the taffrail.

"What is it?" he demanded, puzzled.

"I must speak to the Captain."

"Then come on board and speak to him. What the devil—?"

"Please ask the Captain if I may speak to him."

Pellew appeared at the after-cabin window; he could hardly have helped hearing the bellowed conversation.

"Yes, Mr. Hornblower?"

Hornblower told him the news.

"Keep to loo'ard, Mr. Hornblower."

"Yes, sir. But the stores—'

"What about them?"

Hornblower outlined the situation and made his request.

"It's not very regular," mused Pellew. "Besides—"

He did not want to shout aloud his thoughts that perhaps everyone in the longboat would soon be dead of plague.

"We'll be all right, sir. It's a week's rations for the squadron."

That was the point, the vital matter. Pellew had to balance the possible loss of a transport brig against the possible gain of supplies, immeasurably more important, which would enable the squadron to maintain its watch over the outlet to the Mediterranean. Looked at in that light Hornblower's suggestion had added force.

"Oh, very well, Mr. Hornblower. By the time you bring the stores out I'll have the crew transferred. I appoint you to the command of the *Caroline*."

"Thank you, sir."

"Mr. Tapling will continue as passenger with you."

"Very good, sir."

So when the crew of the longboat, toiling and sweating at the sweeps, brought the two lighters down the bay, they found the *Caroline* swinging deserted at her anchors, while a dozen curious telescopes from the *Indefatigable* watched the proceedings. Hornblower went up the brig's side with half a dozen hands.

"She's like a blooming Noah's Ark, sir," said Maxwell.

The comparison was apt; the *Caroline* was flush-decked, and the whole available deck area was divided by partitions into stalls for the cattle, while to enable the ship to be worked light gangways had been laid over the stalls into a practically continuous upper deck.

"An' all the animiles, sir," said another seaman.

"But Noah's animals walked in two by two," said Hornblower.

"We're not so lucky. And we've got to get the grain on board first. Get those hatches unbattened."

In ordinary conditions a working party of two or three hundred men from the *Indefatigable* would have made short work of getting in the cargo from the lighters, but now it had to be done by the longboat's complement of eighteen. Luckily Pellew had had the forethought and kindness to have the ballast struck out of the holds, or they would have had to do that weary job first.

"Tail onto those tackles, men," said Hornblower.

Pellew saw the first bundle of grain sacks rise slowly into the air from the lighter, and swung over and down the *Caroline's* hatchway.

"He'll be all right," he decided. "Man the capstan and get under way, if you please, Mr. Bolton."

Hornblower, directing the work on the tackles, heard Pellew's voice come to him through the speaking trumpet.

"Good luck, Mr. Hornblower. Report in three weeks at Gibraltar."

"Very good, sir. Thank you, sir."

Hornblower turned back to find a seaman at his elbow knuckling his forehead.

"Beg pardon, sir. But can you hear those cattle bellerin', sir? 'Tis mortal hot, an' 'tis water they want, sir."

"Hell," said Hornblower.

He would never get the cattle on board before nightfall. He left a small party at work transferring cargo, and with the rest of the men he began to extemporize a method of watering the unfortunate cattle in the lighter. Half *Caroline's* hold space was filled with water barrels and fodder, but it was an awkward business getting water down to the lighter with pump and hose, and the poor brutes down there surged about uncontrollably at the prospect of water. Hornblower saw the lighter heel and almost capsize; one of his men—luckily one who could swim—went hastily overboard from the lighter to avoid being crushed to death.

"Hell," said Hornblower again, and that was by no means the last time.

Without any skilled advice he was having to learn the business of managing livestock at sea; each moment brought its lessons. A naval officer on active service indeed found himself engaged on strange duties. It was well after dark before Hornblower called a halt to the labours of his men, and it was before dawn that he roused them up to work again. It was still early in the morning that the last of the grain sacks was stowed away and Hornblower had to face the operation of swaying up the cattle from the lighter. After their night down there, with little water and less food, they were in no mood to be trifled with, but it was easier at first while they were crowded together. A bellyband was slipped round the nearest, the tackle hooked on, and the animal was swayed up, lowered to the deck through an opening in the gangways, and herded into one of the stalls with ease. The seamen, shouting and waving their shirts, thought it was great fun, but they were not sure when the next one, released from its bellyband went on the rampage and chased them about the deck, threatening death with its horns, until it wandered into its stall where the bar could be promptly dropped to shut it in. Hornblower, looking at the sun rising rapidly in the east, did not think it fun at all.

And the emptier the lighter became, the more room the cattle had to rush about in it; to capture each one so as to put a bellyband on it was a desperate adventure. Nor were those half-wild bullocks soothed by the sight of their companions being successively hauled bellowing into the air over their heads. Before the day was half done Hornblower's men were as weary as if they had fought a battle, and there was not one of them who would not gladly have quitted this novel employment in exchange for some normal seamen's duty like going aloft to reef topsails on a stormy night. As soon as Hornblower had the notion of dividing the interior of the lighter up into sections with barricades of stout spars the work became easier, but it took time, and before it was done the cattle had already suffered a couple of casualties—weaker members of the herd crushed underfoot in the course of the wild rushes about the lighter.

And there was a distraction when a boat came out from the shore, with swarthy Moors at the oars and the Treasurer in the stern. Hornblower left Tapling to negotiate—apparently the Bey at least had not been so frightened of the plague as to forget to ask for his money. All Hornblower insisted upon was that the boat should keep well to leeward, and the money was floated off to it headed up in an empty rumpuncheon. Night found not more than half the cattle in the stalls on board, with Hornblower worrying about feeding and watering them, and snatching at hints diplomatically won from those members of his crew who had had bucolic experience. But the earliest dawn saw him driving his men to work again, and deriving a momentary satisfaction from the sight of Tapling having to leap for his life to the gangway out of reach of a maddened bullock which was charging about the deck and refusing to enter a stall. And by the time the last animal was safely packed in Hornblower was faced with another problem—that of dealing with what one of the men elegantly termed "mucking out". Fodder—water—mucking out; that deck-load of cattle seemed to promise enough work in itself to keep his eighteen men busy, without any thought of the needs of handling the ship.

But there were advantages about the men being kept busy, as Hornblower grimly decided; there had not been a single mention of plague since the work began. The anchorage where the *Caroline* lay was exposed to north-easterly winds, and it was necessary that he should take her out to sea before such a wind should blow. He mustered his men to divide them into watches; he was the only navigator, so that he had to appoint the coxswain and the under-coxswain, Jordan, as officers of the watch. Someone volunteered as cook, and Hornblower, running his eye over his assembled company, appointed Tapling as cook's mate. Tapling opened his mouth to protest, but there was that in Hornblower's expression which cut the protest short. There was no bos'n, no carpenter—no surgeon either, as Hornblower pointed out to himself gloomily. But on the other hand if the need for a doctor should arise it would, he hoped, be mercifully brief.

"Port watch, loose the jibs and main tops'l," ordered Hornblower. "Starboard watch, man the capstan."

So began that voyage of H.M. transport brig *Caroline* which became legendary (thanks to the highly coloured accounts retailed by the crew during innumerable dog-watches in later commissions) throughout the King's navy. The *Caroline* spent her three weeks of quarantine in homeless wanderings about the western Mediterranean. It was necessary that she should keep close up to the Straits, for fear lest the westerlies and the prevailing inward set of the current should take her out of reach of Gibraltar when the time came, so she beat about between the coasts of Spain and Africa trailing behind her a growing farmyard stench. The *Caroline* was a worn-out ship; with any sort of sea running she leaked like a sieve; and there were always hands at work on the pumps, either pumping her out or pumping sea water onto her deck to clean it or pumping up fresh water for the cattle.

Her top hamper made her almost unmanageable in a fresh breeze; her deck seams leaked, of course, when she worked, allowing a constant drip of unspeakable filth down below. The one consolation was in the supply of fresh meat—a commodity some of Hornblower's men had not tasted for three months. Hornblower recklessly sacrificed a bullock a day, for in that Mediterranean climate meat could not be kept sweet. So his men feasted on steaks and fresh tongues; there were plenty of men on board who had never in their whole lives before eaten a beef steak.

But fresh water was the trouble—it was a greater anxiety to Hornblower than even it was to the average ship's captain, for the cattle were always thirsty; twice Hornblower had to land a raiding party at dawn on the coast of Spain, seize a fishing village, and fill his water casks in the local stream.

It was a dangerous adventure, and the second landing revealed the danger, for while the *Caroline* was trying to claw off the land again a Spanish guarda-costa lugger came gliding round the point with all sail set. Maxwell saw her first, but Hornblower saw her before he could report her presence.

"Very well, Maxwell," said Hornblower, trying to sound composed.

He turned his glass upon her. She was no more than three miles off, a trifle to windward, and the *Caroline* was embayed, cut off by the land from all chance of escape. The lugger could go three feet to her two, while the *Caroline*'s clumsy superstructure prevented her from lying nearer than eight points to the wind. As Hornblower gazed, the accumulated irritation of the past seventeen days boiled over. He was furious with fate for having thrust this ridiculous mission on him. He hated the *Caroline* and her clumsiness and her stinks and her cargo. He raged against the destiny which had caught him in this hopeless position.

"Hell!" said Hornblower, actually stamping his feet on the upper gangway in his anger. "Hell *and* damnation!"

He was dancing with rage, he observed with some curiosity. But with his fighting madness at the boil there was no chance of his yielding without a struggle, and his mental convulsions resulted in his producing a scheme for action. How many men of a crew did a Spanish guarda-costa carry? Twenty? That would be an outside figure—those luggers were only intended to act against petty smugglers. And with surprise on his side there was still a chance, despite the four eight-pounders that the lugger carried.

"Pistols and cutlasses, men," he said. "Jordan, choose two men and show yourselves up here. But the rest of you keep under cover. Hide yourselves. Yes, Mr. Tapling, you may serve with us. See that you are armed."

No one would expect resistance from a laden cattle transport; the Spaniards would expect to find on board a crew of a dozen at most, and not a disciplined force of twenty. The problem lay in luring the lugger within reach.

"Full and by," called Hornblower down to the helmsman below. "Be ready to jump, men. Maxwell, if a man shows himself before my order shoot him with your own hand. You hear me? That's an order, and you disobey me at your peril."

"Aye aye, sir," said Maxwell.

The lugger was romping up towards them; even in that light air there was a white wave under her sharp bows. Hornblower glanced up to make sure that the *Caroline* was displaying no colours. That made his plan legal under the laws of war. The report of a gun and a puff of smoke came from the lugger as she fired across the *Caroline*'s bows.

"I'm going to heave to, Jordan," said Hornblower. "Main tops'l braces. Helm-a-lee."

The *Caroline* came to the wind and lay there wallowing, a

surrendered and helpless ship apparently, if ever there was one.

"Not a sound, men," said Hornblower.

The cattle bellowed mournfully. Here came the lugger, her crew plainly visible now. Hornblower could see an officer clinging to the main shrouds ready to board, but no one else seemed to have a care in the world. Everyone seemed to be looking up at the clumsy superstructure and laughing at the farmyard noises issuing from it.

"Wait, men, wait," said Hornblower.

The lugger was coming alongside when Hornblower suddenly realized, with a hot flood of blood under his skin, that he himself was unarmed. He had told his men to take pistols and cutlasses; he had advised Tapling to arm himself, and yet he had clean forgotten about his own need for weapons. But it was too late now to try to remedy that. Someone in the lugger hailed in Spanish, and Hornblower spread his hands in a show of incomprehension. Now they were alongside.

"Come on, men!" shouted Hornblower.

He ran across the superstructure and with a gulp he flung himself across the gap at the officer in the shrouds. He gulped again as he went through the air; he fell with all his weight on the unfortunate man, clasped him round the shoulders, and fell with him to the deck. There were shouts and yells behind him as the *Caroline* spewed up her crew into the lugger. A rush of feet, a clatter and a clash. Hornblower got to his feet empty handed. Maxwell was just striking down a man with his cutlass. Tapling was heading a rush forward into the bows, waving a cutlass and yelling like a madman. Then it was all over; the astonished Spaniards were unable to lift a hand in their own defence.

So it came about that on the twenty-second day of her quarantine the *Caroline* came into Gibraltar Bay with a captured guarda-costa lugger under her lee. A thick barnyard stench trailed with her, too, but at least, when Hornblower went on board the *Indefatigable* to make his report, he had a suitable reply ready for Mr. Midshipman Bracegirdle.

"Hullo, Noah, how are Shem and Ham?" asked Mr. Bracegirdle.

"Shem and Ham have taken a prize," said Hornblower. "I regret that Mr. Bracegirdle can't say the same."

But the Chief Commissary of the squadron, when Hornblower reported to him, had a comment to which even Hornblower was unable to make a reply.

"Do you mean to tell me, Mr. Hornblower," said the Chief Commissary, "that you allowed your men to eat fresh beef? A bullock a day for your eighteen men? There must have been plenty of ship's provisions on board. That was wanton extravagance, Mr. Hornblower, I'm surprised at you."

THE DUCHESS AND THE DEVIL

Acting-Lieutenant Hornblower was bringing the sloop *Le Reve*, prize of H.M.S. *Indefatigable*, to anchor in Gibraltar Bay. He was nervous; if anyone had asked him if he thought that all the telescopes in the Mediterranean Fleet were trained upon him he would have laughed at the fantastic suggestion, but he felt as if they were. Nobody ever gauged more cautiously the strength of the gentle following breeze, or estimated more anxiously the distances between the big anchored ships of the line, or calculated more carefully the space *Le Reve* would need to swing at her anchor. Jackson, his petty officer, was standing forward awaiting the order to take in the jib, and he acted quickly at Hornblower's hail.

"Helm-a-lee," said Hornblower next, and *Le Reve* rounded into the wind. "Brail up!"

Le Reve crept forward, her momentum diminishing as the wind took her way off her.

"Let go!"

The cable growled a protest as the anchor took it out through the hawsehole—that welcome splash of the anchor, telling of the journey's end. Hornblower watched carefully while *Le Reve* took up on her cable, and then relaxed a little. He had brought the prize safely in. The commodore—Captain Sir Edward Pellew of H.M.S. *Indefatigable*—had clearly not yet returned, so that it was Hornblower's duty to report to the port admiral.

"Get the boat hoisted out," he ordered, and then, remembering his humanitarian duty. "And you can let the prisoners up on deck."

They had been battened down below for the last forty-eight hours, because the fear of a recapture was the nightmare of every prizemaster. But here in the Bay with the Mediterranean fleet all round that danger was at an end. Two hands at the oars of the gig sent her skimming over the water, and in ten minutes Hornblower was reporting his arrival to the admiral.

"You say she shows a fair turn of speed?" said the latter, looking over at the prize.

"Yes, sir. And she's handy enough," said Hornblower.

"I'll purchase her into the service. Never enough despatch vessels," mused the Admiral.

Even with that hint it was a pleasant surprise to Hornblower when he received heavily sealed official orders and, opening them, read that "you are hereby requested and required" to take H.M. sloop *Le Reve* under his command and to proceed "with the utmost expedition" to Plymouth as soon as the despatches destined for England should be put in his charge. It was an independent command; it was a chance of seeing England again (it was three years since Hornblower had last set foot on the English shore) and it was a high professional compliment. But there was another letter, delivered at the same moment which Hornblower read with less elation.

"Their Excellencies, Major-General Sir Hew and Lady Dalrymple, request the pleasure of Acting-Lieutenant Horatio Hornblower's company at dinner today, at three o'clock, at Government House."

It might be a pleasure to dine with the Governor of Gibraltar and his lady, but it was only a mixed pleasure at best for an acting-lieutenant with a single sea chest, faced with the need to dress himself suitably for such a function. Yet it was hardly possible for a young man to walk up to Government House from the landing slip without a thrill of excitement, especially as his friend Mr. Midshipman Bracegirdle, who came from a wealthy family and had a handsome allowance, had lent him a pair of the finest white stockings of China silk—Bracegirdle's calves were plump, and Hornblower's were skinny, but that difficulty had been artistically circumvented. Two small pads of oakum, some strips of sticking plaster from the surgeon's stores, and Hornblower now had a couple of legs of which no one need be ashamed. He could put his left leg forward to make his bow without any fear of wrinkles in his stockings, and sublimely conscious, as Bracegirdle said, of a leg of which any gentleman would be proud.

At Government House the usual polished and languid aide-de-camp took charge of Hornblower and led him forward. He made his bow to Sir Hew, a red-faced and fussy old gentleman, and to Lady Dalrymple, a red-faced and fussy old lady.

"Mr. Hornblower," said the latter, "I must present you—Your Grace, this is Mr. Hornblower, the new captain of *Le Reve*. Her Grace the Duchess of Wharfedale."

A duchess, no less! Hornblower poked forward his padded leg, pointed his toe, laid his hand on his heart and bowed with all the depth the tightness of his breeches allowed—he had still been growing when he bought them on joining the *Indefatigable*. Bold blue eyes, and a once beautiful middle-aged face.

"So this 'ere's the feller in question?" said the duchess. "Matilda, my dear, are you going to hentrust me to a hinfant in harms?"

The startling vulgarity of the accent took Hornblower's breath away. He had been ready for almost anything except that a superbly dressed duchess should speak in the accent of Seven Dials. He raised his eyes to stare, while forgetting to straighten himself up, standing with his chin poked forward and his hand still on his heart.

"You look like a gander on a green," said the duchess. "I hexpects you to 'iss hany moment."

She struck her own chin out and swung from side to side with her hands on her knees in a perfect imitation of a belligerent goose, apparently with so close a resemblance to Hornblower as well as to excite a roar of laughter from the other guests. Hornblower stood in blushing confusion.

"Don't be 'ard on the young feller," said the duchess, coming to his defence and patting him on the shoulder. " 'E's on'y young, an' thet's nothink to be ashamed of. Somethink to be prard of, for thet matter, to be trusted with a ship at thet hage."

It was lucky that the announcement of dinner came to save Hornblower from the further confusion into which this kindly remark had thrown him. Hornblower naturally found himself with the riff-raff, the ragtag and bobtail of the middle of the table along with the other junior officers—Sir Hew sat at one end with the duchess, while Lady Dalrymple sat with a commodore at the other. Moreover, there were not nearly as many women as men; that was only to be expected, as Gibraltar was, technically at least, a beleaguered fortress. So Hornblower had no woman on either side of him; at his right sat the young aide-de-camp who had first taken him in charge.

"Your health, Your Grace," said the commodore, looking down the length of the table and raising his glass.

"Thank'ee," replied the duchess. "Just in time to save my life. I was wonderin' 'oo'd come to my rescue."

She raised her brimming glass to her lips and when she put it down again it was empty.

"A jolly boon companion you are going to have," said the aide-de-camp to Hornblower.

"How is she going to be my companion?" asked Hornblower, quite bewildered.

The aide-de-camp looked at him pityingly.

"So you have not been informed?" he asked. "As always, the man most concerned is the last to know. When you sail with your despatches tomorrow you will have the honour of bearing Her Grace with you to England."

"God bless my soul," said Hornblower.

"Let's hope He does," said the aide-de-camp piously, nosing his wine. "Poor stuff this sweet Malaga is. Old Hare bought a job lot in '95, and every governor since then seems to think it's his duty to use it up."

"But who *is* she?" asked Hornblower.

"Her Grace the Duchess of Wharfedale," replied the aide-de-camp. "Did you not hear Lady Dalrymple's introduction?"

"But she doesn't talk like a duchess," protested Hornblower.

"No. The old duke was in his dotage when he married her. She was the innkeeper's widow, so her friends say. You can imagine, if you like, what her enemies say."

"But what is she doing here?" went on Hornblower.

"She is on her way back to England. She was at Florence when the French marched in, I understand. She reached Leghorn, and bribed a coaster to bring her here. She asked Sir Hew to find her a passage, and Sir Hew asked the Admiral—Sir Hew would ask anyone for anything on behalf of a duchess, even one said by her friends to be an innkeeper's widow."

"I see," said Hornblower.

There was a burst of merriment from the head of the table, and the duchess was prodding the governor's scarlet-coated ribs with the handle of her knife, as if to make sure he saw the joke.

"Maybe you will not lack for mirth on your homeward voyage," said the aide-de-camp.

Just then a smoking sirloin of beef was put down in front of Hornblower, and all his worries vanished before the necessity of carving it and remembering his manners. He took the carving knife and fork gingerly in his hands and glanced round at the company.

"May I help you to some of this beef, Your Grace? Madam? Sir? Well done or underdone, sir? A little of the brown fat?"

In the hot room the sweat ran down his face as he wrestled with the joint; he was fortunate that most of the guests desired helpings from the other removes so that he had little carving to do. He put a couple of haggled slices on his own plate as the simplest way of concealing the worst results of his own handiwork.

"Beef from Tetuan," sniffed the aide-de-camp. "Tough and stringy."

That was all very well for a governor's aide-de-camp—he could not guess how delicious was this food to a young naval officer fresh from beating about at sea in an overcrowded frigate. Even the thought of having to act as host to a duchess could not entirely spoil Hornblower's appetite. And the final dishes, the meringues and macaroons, the custards and the fruits, were ecstasy for a young man whose last pudding had been currant duff last Sunday.

"Those sweet things spoil a man's palate," said the aide-de-camp—much Hornblower cared.

They were drinking formal toasts now. Hornblower stood for the King and the royal family, and raised his glass for the duchess.

"And now for the enemy," said Sir Hew, "may their treasure galleons try to cross the Atlantic."

"A supplement to that, Sir Hew," said the commodore at the other end, "may the Dons make up their minds to leave Cadiz."

There was a growl almost like wild animals from round the table. Most of the naval officers present were from Jervis' Mediterranean squadron which had beaten about in the Atlantic for the past several months hoping to catch the Spaniards should they come out. Jervis had to detach his ships to Gibraltar two at a time to replenish their stores, and these officers were from the two ships of the line present at the moment in Gibraltar.

"Johnny Jervis would say amen to that," said Sir Hew. "A bumper to the Dons then, gentlemen, and may they come out from Cadiz."

The ladies left them then, gathered together by Lady Dalrymple, and as soon as it was decently possible Hornblower made his excuses and slipped away, determined not to be heavy with wine the night before he sailed in independent command.

Maybe the prospect of the coming on board of the duchess was a useful counter-irritant, and saved Hornblower from worrying too much about his first command. He was up before dawn—before even the brief Mediterranean twilight had begun—to see that his precious ship was in condition to face the sea, and the enemies who swarmed upon the sea. He had four popgun four-pounders to deal with those enemies, which meant that he was safe from no one; his was the weakest vessel at sea, for the smallest trading brig carried a more powerful armament. So that like all weak creatures his only safety lay in flight—Hornblower looked aloft in the half-light, where the sails would be set on which so much might depend. He went over the watch bill with his two watch-keeping officers, Midshipman Hunter and Master's Mate Winyatt, to make sure that every man of his crew of eleven knew his duty. Then all that remained was to put on his smartest seagoing uniform, try to eat breakfast, and wait for the duchess.

She came early, fortunately; Their Excellencies had had to rise at a most unpleasant hour to see her off. Mr. Hunter reported the approach of the governor's launch with suppressed excitement.

"Thank you, Mr. Hunter," said Hornblower coldly—that was what the service demanded, even though not so many weeks before they had been playing follow-my-leader through the *Indefatigable*'s rigging together.

The launch swirled alongside, and two neatly dressed seamen hooked on the ladder. *Le Reve* had such a small free-board that boarding her presented no problem even for ladies. The governor stepped on board to the twittering of the only two pipes *Le Reve* could muster, and Lady Dalrymple followed him. Then came the duchess, and the duchess's companion; the latter was a younger woman, as beautiful as the duchess must once have been. A couple of aides-de-camp followed, and by that time the minute deck of *Le Reve* was positively crowded, so that there was no room left to bring up the duchess's baggage.

"Let us show you your quarters, Your Grace," said the governor.

Lady Dalrymple squawked her sympathy at sight of the minute cabin which the two cots almost filled, and everyone's head, inevitably, bumped against the deck-beam above.

"We shall live through it," said the duchess stoically, "an' that's more than many a man makin' a little trip to Tyburn could say."

One of the aides-de-camp produced a last minute packet of despatches and demanded Hornblower's signature on the receipt; the last farewells were said, and Sir Hew and Lady Dalrymple went down the side again to the twittering of the pipes.

"Man the windlass!" bellowed Hornblower the moment the launch's crew bent to their oars.

A few seconds' lusty work brought *Le Reve* up to her anchor.

"Anchor's aweigh, sir," reported Winyatt.

"Jib halliards!" shouted Hornblower. "Mains'l halliards!"

Le Reve came round before the wind as her sails were set and her rudder took a grip on the water. Everyone was so busy catting the anchor and setting sail that it was Hornblower himself who dipped his colours in salute as *Le Reve* crept out beyond the mole before the gentle south-easter, and dipped her nose to the first of the big Atlantic rollers coming in through the Gut. Through the skylight beside him he heard a clatter and a wail, as something fell in the cabin with that first roll, but he could spare no attention for the woman below. He had the glass to his eye now, training it first on Algeciras and then upon Tarifa—some well-manned privateer or ship of war might easily dash out to snap up such a defenceless prey as *Le Reve*. He could not relax while the forenoon watch wore on. They rounded Cape Marroqui and he set a course for St. Vincent, and then the mountains of Southern Spain began to sink below the horizon. Cape Trafalgar was just visible on the starboard bow when at last he shut the telescope and began to wonder about dinner; it was pleasant to be captain of his own ship and to be able to order dinner when he choose. His aching legs told him he had been on his feet too long—eleven continuous hours; if the future brought him many independent commands he would wear himself out by this sort of behaviour.

Down below he relaxed gratefully on the locker, and sent the cook to knock at the duchess's cabin door to ask with his compliments if all was well; he heard the duchess's sharp voice saying that they needed nothing, not even dinner. Hornblower philosophically shrugged his shoulders and ate his dinner with a young man's appetite. He went on deck again as night closed in upon them; Winyatt had the watch.

"It's coming up thick, sir," he said.

So it was. The sun was invisible on the horizon, engulfed in watery mist. It was the price he had to pay for a fair wind, he knew; in the winter months in these latitudes there was always likely to be fog where the cool land breeze reached the Atlantic.

"It'll be thicker still by morning," he said gloomily, and revised his night orders, setting a course due west instead of west by north as he originally intended. He wanted to make certain of keeping clear of Cape St. Vincent in the event of fog.

That was one of those minute trifles which may affect a man's whole after life—Hornblower had plenty of time later to reflect on what might have happened had he not ordered that alteration of course. During the night he was often on deck, peering through the increasing mist, but at the time when the crisis came he was down below snatching a little sleep. What woke him was a seaman shaking his shoulder violently.

"Please, sir. Please, sir. Mr. Hunter sent me. Please, sir, won't you come on deck, he says, sir."

"I'll come," said Hornblower, blinking himself awake and rolling out of his cot.

The faintest beginnings of dawn were imparting some slight luminosity to the mist which was close about them. *Le Reve* was lurching over an ugly sea with barely enough wind behind her to give her steerage way. Hunter was standing with his back to the wheel in an attitude of tense anxiety.

"Listen!" he said, as Hornblower appeared.

He half-whispered the word, and in his excitement he omitted the "sir" which was due to his captain—and in his excitement Hornblower did not notice the omission. Hornblower listened. He heard the shipboard noises he could expect—the clattering of the blocks as *Le Reve* lurched, the sound of the sea at her bows. Then he heard other shipboard noises. There were other blocks clattering; the sea was breaking beneath other bows.

"There's a ship close alongside," said Hornblower.

"Yes, sir," said Hunter. "And after I sent below for you I heard an order given. And it was in Spanish—some foreign tongue, anyway."

The tenseness of fear was all about the little ship like the fog.

"Call all hands. Quietly," said Hornblower.

But as he gave the order he wondered if it would be any use. He could send his men to their stations, he could man and load his four-pounders, but if that ship out there in the fog was of any force greater than a merchant ship he was in deadly peril. Then he tried to comfort himself—perhaps the ship was some fat Spanish galleon bulging with treasure, and were he to board her boldly she would become his prize and make him rich for life.

"A 'appy Valentine's day to you," said a voice beside him, and he nearly jumped out of his skin with surprise. He had actually forgotten the presence of the duchess on board.

"Stop that row!" he whispered furiously at her, and she pulled up abruptly in astonishment. She was bundled up in a cloak and hood against the damp air, and no further detail could be seen of her in the darkness and fog.

"May I hask—" she began.

"Shut up!" whispered Hornblower.

A harsh voice could be heard through the fog, other voices repeating the order, whistles being blown, much noise and bustle.

"That's Spanish, sir, isn't it?" whispered Hunter.

"Spanish for certain. Calling the watch. Listen!"

The two double-strokes of a ship's bell came to them across the water. Four bells in the morning watch. And instantly from all round them a dozen other bells could be heard, as if echoing the first.

"We're in the middle of a fleet, by God!" whispered Hunter.

"Big ships, too, sir," supplemented Winyatt who had joined them with the calling of all hands. "I could hear half a dozen different pipes when they called the watch."

"The Dons are out, then," said Hunter.

And the course I set has taken us into the midst of them, thought Hornblower bitterly. The coincidence was maddening, heartbreaking. But he forbore to waste breath over it. He even suppressed the frantic gibe that rose to his lips at the memory of Sir Hew's toast about the Spaniards coming out from Cadiz.

"They're setting more sail," was what he said. "Dagos snug down at night, just like some fat Indiaman. They only set their t'gallants at daybreak."

All round them through the fog could be heard the whine of sheaves in blocks, the stamp-and-go of the men at the halliards, the sound of ropes thrown on decks, the chatter of a myriad voices.

"They make enough noise about it, blast 'em," said Hunter.

The tension under which he laboured was apparent as he stood straining to peer through the mist.

"Please God they're on a different course to us," said Winyatt, more sensibly. "Then we'll soon be through 'em."

"Not likely," said Hornblower.

Le Reve was running almost directly before what little wind there was; if the Spaniards were beating against it or had it on their beam they would be crossing her course at a considerable angle, so that the volume of sound from the nearest ship would have diminished or increased considerably in this time, and there was no indication of that whatever. It was far more likely that *Le Reve* had overhauled the Spanish fleet under its nightly short canvas and had sailed forward into the middle of it. It was a problem what to do next in that case, to shorten sail, or to heave to, and let the Spaniards get ahead of them again, or to clap on sail to pass through. But the passage of the minutes brought clear proof that fleet and sloop were on practically the same course, as otherwise they could hardly fail to pass some ship close. As long as the mist held they were safest as they were.

But that was hardly to be expected with the coming of day.

"Can't we alter course, sir?" asked Winyatt.

"Wait," said Hornblower.

In the faint growing light he had seen shreds of denser mist blowing past them—a clear indication that they could not hope for continuous fog. At that moment they ran out of a fog bank into a clear patch of water.

"There she is, by God!" said Hunter.

Both officers and seamen began to move about in sudden panic.

"Stand still, damn you!" rasped Hornblower, his nervous tension releasing itself in the fierce monosyllables.

Less than a cable's length away a three-decked ship of the line was standing along parallel to them on their starboard side. Ahead and on the port side could be seen the outlines, still shadowy, of other battleships. Nothing could save them if they drew attention to themselves; all that could be done was to keep going as if they had as much right there as the ships of the line. It was possible that in the happy-go-lucky Spanish navy the officer of the watch over there did not know that no sloop like *Le Reve* was attached to the fleet—or even possibly by a miracle there *might* be one. *Le Reve* was French built and French rigged, after all. Side by side *Le Reve* and the battleship sailed over the lumpy sea. They were within point-blank range of fifty big guns, when one well-aimed shot would sink them. Hunter was uttering filthy curses under his breath, but discipline had asserted itself; a telescope over there on the Spaniard's deck would not discover any suspicious bustle on board the sloop. Another shred of fog drifted past them, and then they were deep in a fresh fog bank.

"Thank God!" said Hunter, indifferent to the contrast between this present piety and his preceding blasphemy.

"Hands wear ship," said Hornblower. "Lay her on the port tack."

There was no need to tell the hands to do it quietly; they were as well aware of their danger as anyone. *Le Reve* silently rounded-to, the sheets were hauled in and coiled down without a sound; and the sloop, as close to the wind as she would lie, heeled to the small wind, meeting the lumpy waves with her port bow.

"We'll be crossing their course now," said Hornblower.

"Please God it'll be under their sterns and not their bows," said Winyatt.

There was the duchess still in her cloak and hood, standing right aft as much out of the way as possible.

"Don't you think Your Grace had better go below?" asked Hornblower, making use by a great effort of the formal form of address.

"Oh no, *please*," said the duchess. "I couldn't bear it." Hornblower shrugged his shoulders, and promptly forgot the duchess's presence again as a new anxiety struck him. He dived below and came up again with the two big sealed envelopes of despatches. He took a belaying pin from the rail and began very carefully to tie the envelopes to the pin with a bit of line.

"Please," said the duchess, "please, Mr. Hornblower, tell me what you are doing?"

"I want to make sure these will sink when I throw them overboard if we're captured," said Hornblower grimly.

"Then they'll be lost for good?"

"Better that than that the Spaniards should read 'em," said Hornblower with all the patience he could muster.

"I could look after them for you," said the duchess. "Indeed I could."

Hornblower looked keenly at her.

"No," he said, "they might search your baggage. Probably they would."

"Baggage!" said the duchess. "As if I'd put them in my baggage! I'll put them next my skin—they won't search *me* in any case. They'll never find 'em, not if I put 'em up my petticoats."

There was a brutal realism about those words that staggered Hornblower a little, but which also brought him to admit to himself that there was something in what the duchess was saying.

"If they capture us," said the duchess, "—I pray they won't, but if they do—they'll never keep me prisoner. You know that. They'll send me to Lisbon or put me aboard a King's ship as soon as they can. Then the despatches will be delivered eventually. Late, but better late than never."

"That's so," mused Hornblower.

"I'll guard them like my life," said the duchess. "I swear I'll never part from them. I'll tell no one I have them, not until I hand them to a King's officer."

She met Hornblower's eyes with transparent honesty in her expression.

"Fog's thinning, sir," said Winyatt.

"Quick!" said the duchess.

There was no time for further debate. Hornblower slipped the envelopes from their binding of rope and handed them over to her, and replaced the belaying pin in the rail.

"These damned French fashions," said the duchess. "I was right when I said I'd put these letters up my petticoats. There's no room in my bosom."

Certainly the upper part of her gown was not at all capacious; the waist was close up under the armpits and the rest of the dress hung down from there quite straight in utter defiance of anatomy.

"Give me a yard of that rope, quick!" said the duchess.

Winyatt cut her a length of the line with his knife and handed it to her. Already she was hauling at her petticoats; the appalled Hornblower saw a gleam of white thigh above her stocking tops before he tore his glance away. The fog was certainly thinning.

"You can look at me now," said the duchess; but her petticoats only just fell in time as Hornblower looked round again. "They're inside my shift, next my skin as I promised. With these Directory fashions no one wears stays any more. So I tied the rope round my waist outside my shift. One envelope is flat against my chest and the other against my back. Would you suspect anything?"

She turned round for Hornblower's inspection.

"No, nothing shows," he said. "I must thank Your Grace."

"There is a certain thickening," said the duchess, "but it does not matter what the Spaniards suspect as long as they do not suspect the truth."

Momentary cessation of the need for action brought some embarrassment to Hornblower. To discuss with a woman her shift and stays—or the absence of them—was a strange thing to do.

A watery sun, still nearly level, was breaking through the mist and shining in his eyes. The mainsail cast a watery shadow on the deck. With every second the sun was growing brighter.

"Here it comes," said Hunter.

The horizon ahead expanded rapidly, from a few yards to a hundred, from a hundred yards to half a mile. The sea was covered with ships. No less than six were in plain sight, four ships of the line and two big frigates, with the red-and-gold of Spain at their mastheads, and, what marked them even more obviously as Spaniards, huge wooden crosses hanging at their peaks.

"Wear ship again, Mr. Hunter," said Hornblower. "Back into the fog."

That was the one chance of safety. Those ships running down towards them were bound to ask questions, and they could not hope to avoid them all. *Le Reve* spun around on her heel, but the fog-bank from which she had emerged was already attenuated, sucked up by the thirsty sun. They could see a drifting stretch of it ahead, but it was lazily rolling away from them at the same time as it was dwindling. The heavy sound of a cannon shot reached their ears, and close on their starboard quarter a ball threw up a fountain of water before plunging into the side of a wave just ahead. Hornblower looked round just in time to see the last of the puff of smoke from the bows of the frigate astern pursuing them.

"Starboard two points," he said to the helmsman, trying to gauge at one and the same moment the frigate's course, the direction of the wind, the bearing of the other ships, and that of the thin last nucleus of that wisp of fog.

"Starboard two points," said the helmsman.

"Fore and main sheets!" said Hunter.

Another shot, far astern this time but laid true for line; Hornblower suddenly remembered the duchess.

"You must go below, Your Grace," he said curtly.

"Oh, no, no, no!" burst out the duchess with angry vehemence. "Please let me stay here. I can't go below to where that seasick maid of mine lies hoping to die. Not in that stinking box of a cabin."

There would be no safety in that cabin, Hornblower reflected—*Le Reve's* scantlings were too fragile to keep out any shot at all. Down below the water line in the hold the women might be safe, but they would have to lie flat on top of beef barrels.

"Sail ahead!" screamed the lookout.

The mist there was parting and the outline of a ship of the line was emerging from it, less than a mile away and on almost the same course as *Le Reve's*. Thud—thud from the frigate astern. Those gunshots by now would have warned the whole Spanish fleet that something unusual was happening. The battleship ahead would know that the little sloop was being pursued. A ball tore through the air close by, with its usual terrifying noise. The ship ahead was awaiting their coming; Hornblower saw her topsails slowly turning.

"Hands to the sheets!" said Hornblower. "Mr. Hunter, jibe her over."

Le Reve came round again, heading for the lessening gap on the port side. The frigate astern turned to intercept. More jets of smoke from her bows. With an appalling noise a shot passed within a few feet of Hornblower, so that the wind of it made him stagger. There was a hole in the mainsail.

"Your Grace," said Hornblower, "those aren't warning shots—"

It was the ship of the line which fired then, having succeeded in clearing away and manning some of her upper-deck guns. It was as if the end of the world had come. One shot hit *Le Reve's* hull, and they felt the deck heave under their feet as a result as if the little ship were disintegrating. But the mast was hit at the same moment, stays and shrouds parting, splinters raining all round. Mast, sails, boom, gaff and all went from above them over the side to windward. The wreckage dragged in the sea and turned the helpless wreck round with the last of her way. The little group aft stood momentarily dazed.

"Anybody hurt?" asked Hornblower, recovering himself.

"On'y a scratch, sir," said one voice.

It seemed a miracle that no one was killed.

"Carpenter's mate, sound the well," said Hornblower and then, re-collecting himself, "No, damn it. Belay that order. If the Dons can save the ship, let 'em try."

Already the ship of the line whose salvo had done the damage was filling her topsails again and bearing away from them, while the frigate which had pursued them was running down on them fast. A wailing figure came scrambling out of the after hatchway. It was the duchess's maid, so mad with terror that her seasickness was forgotten. The duchess put a protective arm round her and tried to comfort her.

"Your Grace had better look to your baggage," said Hornblower. "No doubt you'll be leaving us shortly for other quarters with the Dons. I hope you will be more comfortable."

He was trying desperately hard to speak in a matter-of-fact way, as if nothing out of the ordinary were happening, as if he were not soon to be a prisoner of the Spaniards; but the duchess saw the working of the usually firm mouth, and marked how the hands were tight clenched.

"How can I tell you how sorry I am about this?" asked the duchess, her voice soft with pity.

"That makes it the harder for me to bear," said Hornblower, and he even forced a smile.

The Spanish frigate was just rounding-to, a cable's length to windward.

"Please, sir," said Hunter.

"Well?"

"We can fight, sir. You give the word. Cold shot to drop in the boats when they try to board. We could beat 'em off once, perhaps."

Hornblower's tortured misery nearly made him snap out "Don't be a fool", but he checked himself. He contented himself with pointing to the frigate. Twenty guns were glaring at them at far less than point-blank range. The very boat the frigate was hoisting out would be manned by at least twice as many men as *Le Reve* carried—she was no bigger than many a pleasure yacht. It was not odds of ten to one, or a hundred to one, but odds of ten thousand to one.

"I understand, sir," said Hunter.

Now the Spanish frigate's boat was in the water, about to shove off.

"A private word with you, please, Mr. Hornblower," said the duchess suddenly.

Hunter and Winyatt heard what she said, and withdrew out of earshot.

"Yes, Your Grace?" said Hornblower.

The duchess stood there, still with her arm round her weeping maid, looking straight at him.

"I'm no more of a duchess than you are," she said.

"Good God!" said Hornblower. "Who—who are you, then?"

"Kitty Cobham."

The name meant a little to Hornblower, but only a little.

"You're too young for that name to have any memories for you, Mr. Hornblower, I see. It's five years since last I trod the boards."

That was it. Kitty Cobham the actress.

"I can't tell it all now," said the duchess—the Spanish boat was dancing over the waves towards them. "But when the French marched into Florence that was only the last of my misfortunes. I was penniless when I escaped from them. Who would lift a finger for a onetime actress— one who had been betrayed and deserted? What was I to do? But a duchess—that was another story. Old Dalrymple at Gibraltar could not do enough for the Duchess of Wharfedale."

"Why did you choose that title?" asked Hornblower in spite of himself.

"I knew of her," said the duchess with a shrug of the shoulders. "I knew her to be what I played her as. That was why I chose her—I always played character parts better than straight comedy. And not nearly so tedious in a long role."

"But my despatches!" said Hornblower in a sudden panic of realization. "Give them back, quick."

"If you wish me to," said the duchess. "But I can still be the duchess when the Spaniards come. They will still set me free as speedily as they can. I'll guard those despatches better than my life—I swear it, I swear it! In less than a month I'll deliver them, if you trust me."

Hornblower looked at the pleading eyes. She might be a spy, ingeniously trying to preserve the despatches from being thrown overboard before the Spaniards took possession. But no spy could have hoped that *Le Reve* would run into the midst of the Spanish fleet.

"I made use of the bottle, I know," said the duchess. "I drank. Yes, I did. But I stayed sober in Gibraltar, didn't I? And I won't touch a drop, not a drop, until I'm in England. I'll swear that, too. Please, sir —please. I beg of you. Let me do what I can for my country."

It was a strange decision for a man of nineteen to have to make— one who had never exchanged a word with an actress in his life before. A harsh voice overside told him that the Spanish boat was about to hook on.

"Keep them, then," said Hornblower. "Deliver them when you can."

He had not taken his eyes from her face. He was looking for a gleam of triumph in her expression. Had he seen anything of the sort he would have torn the despatches from her body at that moment. But all he saw was the natural look of pleasure, and it was then that he made up his mind to trust her—not before.

"Oh, thank you, sir," said the duchess.

The Spanish boat had hooked on now, and a Spanish lieutenant was awkwardly trying to climb aboard. He arrived on the deck on his hands and knees, and Hornblower stepped over to receive him as he got to his feet. Captor and captive exchanged bows. Hornblower could not understand what the Spaniard said, but obviously they were formal sentences that he was using. The Spaniard caught sight of the two women aft and halted in surprise; Hornblower hastily made the presentation in what he hoped was Spanish.

"Señor el tenente Espanol," he said. "Señora la Duquesa de Wharfedale."

The title clearly had its effect; the lieutenant bowed profoundly, and his bow was received with the most lofty aloofness by the duchess. Hornblower could be sure the despatches were safe. That was some alleviation of the misery of standing here on the deck of his water-logged little ship, a prisoner of the Spaniards. As he waited he heard, from far to leeward, roll upon roll of thunder coming up against the wind. No thunder could endure that long. What he could hear must be the broadsides of ships in action—of fleets in action. Somewhere over there by Cape St. Vincent the British fleet must have caught the Spaniards at last. Fiercer and fiercer sounded the roll of the artillery. There was excitement among the Spaniards who had scrambled onto the deck of *Le Reve*, while Hornblower stood bareheaded waiting to be taken into captivity.

Captivity was a dreadful thing. Once the numbness had worn off Hornblower came to realize what a dreadful thing it was. Not even the news of the dreadful battering which the Spanish navy had received at St. Vincent could relieve the misery and despair of being a prisoner. It was not the physical conditions—ten square feet of floor space per man in an empty sail loft at Ferrol along with other captive warrant officers—for they were no worse than what a junior officer often had to put up with at sea. It was the loss of freedom, the fact of being a captive, that was so dreadful.

There were four months of it before the first letter came through to Hornblower; the Spanish government, inefficient in all ways, had the worst postal system in Europe. But here was the letter, addressed and re-addressed, now safely in his hands after he had practically snatched it from a stupid Spanish non-commissioned officer who had been puzzling over the strange name. Hornblower did not know the handwriting, and when he broke the seal and opened the letter the salutation made him think for a moment that he had opened someone else's letter.

"Darling Boy" it began. Now who on earth would call him that? He read on in a dream.

"Darling Boy,

I hope it will give you happiness to hear that what you gave me has reached its destination. They told me, when I delivered it, that you are a prisoner, and my heart bleeds for you. And they told me too that they were pleased with you for what you had done. And one of those admirals is a shareholder in Drury Lane. Whoever would have thought of such a thing? But he smiled at me, and I smiled at him. I did not know he was a shareholder then, and I only smiled out of the kindness of my heart. And all that I told him about my dangers and perils with my precious burden were only histrionic exercises, I am afraid. Yet he believed me, and so struck was he by my smile and my adventures, that he demanded a part for me from Sherry, and behold, now I am playing second lead, usually a tragic mother, and receiving the acclaim of the groundlings. There are compensations in growing old, which I am discovering too. And I have not tasted wine since I saw you last, nor shall I ever again. As one more reward, my admiral promised me that he would forward this letter to you in the next cartel—an expression which no doubt means more to you than to me. I only hope that it reaches you in good time and brings you comfort in your affliction.

I pray nightly for you.

Ever your devoted friend,
Katharine Cobham."

Comfort in his affliction? A little, perhaps. There was some comfort in knowing that the despatches had been delivered; there was some comfort in a second-hand report that Their Lordships were pleased with him. There was comfort even in knowing that the duchess was re-established on the stage. But the sum total was nothing compared with his misery.

Here was a guard come to bring him to the commandant, and beside the commandant was the Irish renegade who served as interpreter. There were further papers on the commandant's desk—it looked as if the same cartel which had brought in Kitty Cobham's note had brought in letters for the commandant.

"Good afternoon, sir," said the commandant, always polite, offering a chair.

"Good afternoon, sir, and many thanks," said Hornblower. He was learning Spanish slowly and painfully.

"You have been promoted," said the Irishman in English.

"W-what?" said Hornblower.

"Promoted," said the Irishman. "Here is the letter—'The Spanish authorities are informed that on account of his meritorious service the acting-commission of Mr. Horatio Hornblower, midshipman and acting-lieutenant, has been confirmed. Their Lordships of the Admiralty express their confidence that Mr. Horatio Hornblower will be admitted immediately to the privileges of commissioned rank.' There you are, young man."

"My felicitations, sir," said the commandant.

"Many thanks, sir," said Hornblower.

The commandant was a kindly old gentleman with a pleasant smile for the awkward young man. He went on to say more, but Hornblower's Spanish was not equal to the technicalities he used, and Hornblower in despair looked at the interpreter.

"Now that you are a commissioned officer," said the latter, "you will be transferred to the quarters for captured officers."

"Thank you," said Hornblower.

"You will receive the half pay of your rank."

"Thank you."

"And your parole will be accepted. You will be at liberty to visit in the town and the neighbourhood for two hours each day on giving your parole."

"Thank you," said Hornblower.

Perhaps, during the long months which followed, it was some mitigation of his unhappiness that for two hours each day his parole gave him freedom; freedom to wander in the streets of the little town, to have a cup of chocolate or a glass of wine—providing he had any money—making polite and laborious conversation with Spanish soldiers or sailors or civilians. But it was better to spend his two hours wandering over the goat paths of the headland in the wind and the sun, in the companionship of the sea, which might alleviate the sick misery of captivity. There was slightly better food, slightly better quarters. And there was the knowledge that now he was a lieutenant, that he held the King's commission, that if ever, ever, the war should end and he should be set free he could starve on half pay—for with the end of the war there would be no employment for junior lieutenants. But he had earned his promotion. He had gained the approval of authority, that was something to think about on his solitary walks.

There came a day of south-westerly gales, with the wind shrieking in from across the Atlantic. Across three thousand miles of water it came, building up its strength unimpeded on its way, and heaping up the sea into racing mountain ridges which came crashing in upon the Spanish coast in thunder and spray. Hornblower stood on the headland above Ferrol harbour, holding his worn greatcoat about him as he leaned forward into the wind to keep his footing. So powerful was the wind that it was difficult to breathe while facing it. If he turned his back he could breathe more easily, but then the wind blew his wild hair forward over his eyes, almost inverted his greatcoat over his head, and furthermore forced him into little tottering steps down the slope towards Ferrol, whither he had no wish to return at present. For two hours he was alone and free, and those two hours were precious. He could breathe the Atlantic air, he could walk, he could do as he liked during that time. He could stare out to sea; it was not unusual to catch sight, from the headland, of some British ship of war which might be working slowly along the coast in the hope of snapping up a coasting vessel while keeping a watchful eye upon the Spanish naval activity. When such a ship went by during Hornblower's two hours of freedom, he would stand and gaze at it, as a man dying of thirst might gaze at a bucket of water held beyond his reach; he would note all the little details, the cut of the topsails and the style of the paint, while misery wrung his bowels. For this was the end of his second year as a prisoner of war. For twenty-two months, for twenty-two hours every day, he had been under lock and key, herded with five other junior lieutenants in a single room in the fortress of Ferrol. And today the wind roared by him, shouting in its outrageous freedom. He was facing into the wind; before him lay Corunna, its white houses resembling pieces of sugar scattered over the slopes. Between him and Corunna was all the open space of Corunna Bay, flogged white by the wind, and on his left hand was the narrow entrance to Ferrol Bay. On his right was the open Atlantic; from the foot of the low cliffs there the long wicked reef of the Dientes del Diablo—the Devil's Teeth—ran out to the northward, square across the path of the racing rollers driven by the wind. At half-minute intervals the rollers would crash against the reef with an impact that shook even the solid headland on which Hornblower stood, and each roller dissolved into spray which was instantly whirled away by the wind to reveal again the long black tusks of the rocks.

Hornblower was not alone on the headland; a few yards away from him a Spanish militia artilleryman on lookout duty gazed with watery eyes through a telescope with which he continually swept the seaward horizon. When at war with England it was necessary to be vigilant; a fleet might suddenly appear over the horizon, to land a little army to capture Ferrol, and burn the dockyard installations and the ships. No hope of that today, thought Hornblower—there could be no landing of troops on that raging lee shore.

But all the same the sentry was undoubtedly staring very fixedly through his telescope right to windward; the sentry wiped his streaming eyes with his coat sleeve and stared again. Hornblower peered in the same direction, unable to see what it was that had attracted the sentry's attention. The sentry muttered something to himself, and then turned and ran clumsily down to the little stone guardhouse where sheltered the rest of the militia detachment stationed there to man the guns of the battery on the headland. He returned with the sergeant of the guard, who took the telescope and peered out to windward in the direction pointed out by the sentry. The two of them jabbered in their barbarous Gallego dialect; in two years of steady application Hornblower had mastered Galician as well as Castilian, but in that howling gale he could not intercept a word. Then finally, just as the sergeant nodded in agreement, Hornblower saw with his naked eyes what they were discussing. A pale grey square on the horizon above the grey sea —a ship's topsail. She must be running before the gale making for the shelter of Corunna or Ferrol.

It was a rash thing for a ship to do, because it would be no easy matter for her to round-to into Corunna Bay and anchor, and it would be even harder for her to hit off the narrow entrance to the Ferrol inlet. A cautious captain would claw out to sea and heave-to with a generous amount of sea room until the wind moderated. These Spanish captains, said Hornblower to himself, with a shrug of his shoulders; but naturally they would always wish to make harbour as quickly as possible when the Royal Navy was sweeping the seas. But the sergeant and the sentry were more excited than the appearance of a single ship would seem to justify. Hornblower could contain himself no longer, and edged up to the chattering pair, mentally framing his sentences in the unfamiliar tongue.

"Please, gentlemen," he said, and then started again, shouting against the wind. "Please, gentlemen, what is it that you see?"

The sergeant gave him a glance, and then, reaching some undiscoverable decision, handed over the telescope—Hornblower could hardly restrain himself from snatching it from his hands. With the telescope to his eye he could see far better; he could see a ship-rigged vessel, under close-reefed topsails (and that was much more sail than it was wise to carry) hurtling wildly towards them. And then a moment later he saw the other square of grey. Another topsail. Another ship. The foretopmast was noticeably shorter than the maintopmast, and not only that, but the whole effect was familiar—she was a British ship of war, a British frigate, plunging along in hot pursuit of the other, which seemed most likely to be a Spanish privateer. It was a close chase; it would be a very near thing, whether the Spaniard would reach the protection of the shore batteries before the frigate overhauled her. He lowered the telescope to rest his eye, and instantly the sergeant snatched it from him. He had been watching the Englishman's face, and Hornblower's expression had told him what he wanted to know. Those two ships out there were behaving in such a way as to justify his rousing his officer and giving the alarm. Sergeant and sentry went running back to the guardhouse, and in a few moments the artillerymen were pouring out to man the batteries on the verge of the cliff. Soon enough came a mounted officer urging his horse up the path; a single glance through the telescope sufficed for him. He went clattering down to the battery and the next moment the boom of a gun from there alerted the rest of the defences. The flag of Spain rose up the flagstaff beside the battery, and Hornblower saw an answering flag rise up the flagstaff on San Anton where another battery guarded Corunna Bay. All the guns of the harbour defences were now manned, and there would be no mercy shown to any English ship that came in range.

Pursuer and pursued had covered quite half the distance already towards Corunna. They were hull-up over the horizon now to Hornblower on the headland, who could see them plunging madly over the grey sea—Hornblower momentarily expected to see them carry away their topmasts or their sails blow from the bolt-ropes. The frigate was half a mile astern still, and she would have to be much closer than that to have any hope of hitting with her guns in that sea. Here came the commandant and his staff, clattering on horseback up the path to see the climax of the drama; the commandant caught sight of Hornblower and doffed his hat with Spanish courtesy, while Hornblower, hatless tried to bow with equal courtesy. Hornblower walked over to him with an urgent request—he had to lay his hand on the Spaniard's saddle-bow and shout up into his face to be understood.

"My parole expires in ten minutes, sir," he yelled. "May I please extend it? May I please stay?"

"Yes, stay, señor," said the commandant generously.

Hornblower watched the chase, and at the same time observed closely the preparations for defence. He had given his parole, but no part of the gentlemanly code prevented him from taking note of all he could see. One day he might be free, and one day it might be useful to know all about the defences of Ferrol. Everyone else of the large group on the headland was watching the chase, and excitement rose higher as the ships came racing nearer. The English captain was keeping a hundred yards or more to seaward of the Spaniard, but he was quite unable to overhaul her—in fact it seemed to Hornblower as if the Spaniard was actually increasing his lead. But the English frigate being to seaward meant that escape in that direction was cut off. Any turn away from the land would reduce the Spaniard's lead to a negligible distance. If he did not get into Corunna Bay or Ferrol Inlet he was doomed.

Now he was level with the Corunna headland, and it was time to put his helm hard over and turn into the bay and hope that his anchors would hold in the lee of the headland. But with a wind of that violence hurtling against cliffs and headlands strange things can happen. A flaw of wind coming out of the bay must have caught her aback as she tried to round-to. Hornblower saw her stagger, saw her heel as the backlash died away and the gale caught her again. She was laid over almost on her beam-ends and as she righted herself Hornblower saw a momentary gap open up in her maintopsail. It was momentary because from the time the gap appeared the life of the topsail was momentary; the gap appeared and at once the sail vanished, blown into ribbons as soon as its continuity was impaired. With the loss of its balancing pressure the ship became unmanageable; the gale pressing against the foretopsail swung her round again before the wind like a weathervane. If there had been time to spare to set a fragment of sail farther aft she would have been saved, but in those enclosed waters there was no time to spare. At one moment she was about to round the Corunna headland; at the next she had lost the opportunity for ever.

There was still the chance that she might fetch the opening to the Ferrol inlet; the wind was nearly fair for her to do that—nearly. Hornblower on the Ferrol headland was thinking along with the Spanish captain down there on the heaving deck. He saw him try to steady the ship so as to head for the narrow entrance, notorious among seamen for its difficulty. He saw him get her on her course, and for a few seconds as she flew across the mouth of the bay it seemed as if the Spaniard would succeed, against all probability, in exactly hitting off the entrance to the inlet. Then the backlash hit her again. Had she been quick on the helm she might still have been safe, but with her sail pressure so outbalanced she was bound to be slow in her response to her rudder. The shrieking wind blew her bows round, and it was instantly obvious, too, that she was doomed, but the Spanish captain played the game out to the last. He would not pile his ship up against the foot of the low cliffs. He put his helm hard over; with the aid of the wind rebounding from the cliffs he made a gallant attempt to clear the Ferrol headland altogether and give himself a chance to claw out to sea.

A gallant attempt, but doomed to failure as soon as begun; he actually cleared the headland, but the wind blew his bows round again, and, bows first, the ship plunged right at the long jagged line of the Devil's Teeth. Hornblower, the commandant, and everyone, hurried across the headland to look down at the final act of the tragedy. With tremendous speed, driving straight before the wind, she raced at the reef. A roller picked her up as she neared it and seemed to increase her speed. Then she struck, and vanished from sight for a second as the roller burst into spray all about her. When the spray cleared she lay there transformed. Her three masts had all gone with the shock, and it was only a black hulk which emerged from the white foam. Her speed and the roller behind her had carried her almost over the reef—doubtless tearing her bottom out—and she hung by her stern, which stood out clear of the water, while her bows were just submerged in the comparatively still water in the lee of the reef.

There were men still alive on her. Hornblower could see them crouching for shelter under the break of her poop. Another Atlantic roller came surging up, and exploded on the Devil's Teeth, wrapping the wreck round with spray. But yet she emerged again, black against the creaming foam. She had cleared the reef sufficiently far to find shelter for most of her length in the lee of the thing that had destroyed her. Hornblower could see those living creatures crouching on her deck. They had a little longer to live—they might live five minutes, perhaps, if they were lucky. Five hours if they were not.

All round him the Spaniards were shouting maledictions. Women were weeping; some of the men were shaking their fists with rage at the British frigate, which, well satisfied with the destruction of her victim, had rounded-to in time and was now clawing out to sea again under storm canvas. It was horrible to see those poor devils down there die. If some larger wave than usual, bursting on the reef, did not lift the stern of the wreck clear so that she sank, she would still break up for the survivors to be whirled away with the fragments. And, if it took a long time for her to break up, the wretched men sheltering there would not be able to endure the constant beating of the cold spray upon them. Something should be done to save them, but no boat could round the headland and weather the Devil's Teeth to reach the wreck. That was so obvious as not to call for a second thought. But . . . Hornblower's thoughts began to race as he started to work on the alternatives. The commandant on his horse was speaking vehemently to a Spanish naval officer, clearly on the same subject, and the naval officer was spreading his hands and saying that any attempt would be hopeless. And yet . . . For two years Hornblower had been a prisoner; all his pent-up restlessness was seeking an outlet, and after two years of the misery of confinement he did not care whether he lived or died. He went up to the commandant and broke into the argument.

"Sir," he said, "let me try to save them. Perhaps from the little bay there. . . . Perhaps some of the fishermen would come with me."

The commandant looked at the officer and the officer shrugged his shoulders.

"What do you suggest, sir?" asked the commandant of Hornblower.

"We might carry a boat across the headland from the dockyard," said Hornblower, struggling to word his ideas in Spanish, "but we must be quick—quick!"

He pointed to the wreck, and force was added to his words by the sight of a roller bursting over the Devil's Teeth.

"How would you carry a boat?" asked the commandant.

To shout his plan in English against that wind would have been a strain; to do so in Spanish was beyond him.

"I can show you at the dockyard, sir," he yelled. "I cannot explain. But we must hurry!"

"You want to go to the dockyard, then?"

"Yes—oh yes."

"Mount behind me, sir," said the commandant.

Awkwardly Hornblower scrambled up to a seat astride the horse's haunches and clutched at the commandant's belt. He bumped frightfully as the animal wheeled round and trotted down the slope. All the idlers of the town and garrison ran beside them.

The dockyard at Ferrol was almost a phantom organization, withered away like a tree deprived of its roots, thanks to the British blockade. Situated as it was at the most distant corner of Spain, connected with the interior by only the roughest of roads, it relied on receiving its supplies by sea, and any such reliance was likely with British cruisers off the coast to be disappointed. The last visit of Spanish ships of war had stripped the place of almost all its stores, and many of the dockyard hands had been pressed as seamen at the same time. But all that Hornblower needed was there, as he knew, thanks to his careful observation. He slid off the horse's hindquarters—miraculously avoiding an instinctive kick from the irritated animal—and collected his thoughts. He pointed to a low dray—a mere platform on wheels—which was used for carrying beef barrels and brandy kegs to the pier.

"Horses," he said, and a dozen willing hands set to work harnessing a team.

Beside the jetty floated half a dozen boats. There was tackle and shears, all the apparatus necessary for swinging heavy weights about. To put slings under a boat and swing her up was the work of only a minute or two. These Spaniards might be dilatory and lazy as a rule, but inspire them with the need for instant action, catch their enthusiasm, present them with a novel plan, and they would work like madmen—and some of them were skilled workmen, too. Oars, mast and sail (not that they would need the sail), rudder, tiller and balers were all present. A group came running from a store shed with chocks for the boat, and the moment these were set up on the dray the dray was backed under the tackle and the boat lowered onto them.

"Empty barrels," said Hornblower. "Little ones—so."

A swarthy Galician fisherman grasped his intention at once, and amplified Hornblower's halting sentences with voluble explanation. A dozen empty water breakers, with their bungs driven well home, were brought, and the swarthy fisherman climbed on the dray and began to lash them under the thwarts. Properly secured, they would keep the boat afloat even were she filled to the gunwale with water.

"I want six men," shouted Hornblower, standing on the dray and looking round at the crowd. "Six fishermen who know little boats."

The swarthy fisherman lashing the breakers in the boat looked up from his task.

"I know whom we need, sir," he said.

He shouted a string of names, and half a dozen men came forward; burly, weather-beaten fellows, with the self-reliant look in their faces of men used to meeting difficulties. It was apparent that the swarthy Galician was their captain.

"Let us go, then," said Hornblower, but the Galician checked him.

Hornblower did not hear what he said, but some of the crowd nodded, turned away, and came hastening back staggering under a breaker of fresh water and a box that must contain biscuit. Hornblower was cross with himself for forgetting the possibility of their being blown out to sea. And the commandant, still sitting his horse and watching these preparations with a keen eye, took note of these stores too.

"Remembering, sir, that I have your parole," he said.

"You have my parole, sir," said Hornblower—for a few blessed moments he had actually forgotten that he was a prisoner.

The stores were safely put away into the sternsheets and the fishing-boat captain caught Hornblower's eye and got a nod from him.

"Let us go," he roared to the crowd.

The iron-shod hoofs clashed on the cobbles and the dray lurched forward, with men leading the horses, men swarming alongside, and Hornblower and the captain riding on the dray like triumphing generals in a procession. They went through the dockyard gate, along the level main street of the little town, and turned up a steep lane which climbed the ridge constituting the backbone of the headland. The enthusiasm of the crowd was still lively; when the horses slowed as they breasted the slope a hundred men pushed at the back, strained at the sides, tugged at the traces to run the dray up the hillside. At the crest the lane became a track, but the dray still lurched and rumbled along. From the track diverged an even worse track, winding its way sideways down the slope through arbutus and myrtle towards the sandy cove which Hornblower had first had in mind—on fine days he had seen fishermen working a seine net on that beach, and he himself had taken note of it as a suitable place for a landing party should the Royal Navy ever plan a descent against Ferrol.

The wind was blowing as wildly as ever; it shrieked round Hornblower's ears. The sea as it came in view was chaotic with wave-crests, and then as they turned a shoulder of the slope they could see the line of the Devil's Teeth running out from the shore up there to windward, and still hanging precariously from their jagged fangs was the wreck, black against the seething foam. Somebody raised a shout at the sight, everybody heaved at the dray, so that the horses actually broke into a trot and the dray leaped and bounced over the obstructions in its way.

"Slowly," roared Hornblower. "Slowly!"

If they were to break an axle or smash a wheel at this moment the attempt would end in ludicrous failure. The commandant on his horse enforced Hornblower's cries with loud orders of his own, and restrained the reckless enthusiasm of his people. More sedately the dray went on down the trail to the edge of the sandy beach. The wind picked up even the damp sand and flung it stinging into their faces, but only small waves broke here, for the beach was in a recess in the shoreline, the south-westerly wind was blowing a trifle off shore here, and up to windward the Devil's Teeth broke the force of the rollers as they raced along in a direction nearly parallel to the shoreline. The wheels plunged into the sand and the horses stopped at the water's edge. A score of willing hands unharnessed them and a hundred willing arms thrust the dray out into the water—all these things were easy with such vast manpower available. As the first wave broke over the floor of the dray the crew scrambled up and stood ready. There were rocks here, but mighty heaves by the militiamen and the dockyard workers waist-deep in water forced the dray over them. The boat almost floated off its chocks, and the crew forced it clear and scrambled aboard, the wind beginning to swing her immediately. They grabbed for their oars and put their backs into half a dozen fierce strokes which brought her under command; the Galician captain had already laid a steering oar in the notch in the stern, with no attempt at shipping rudder and tiller. As he braced himself to steer he glanced at Hornblower, who tacitly left the job to him.

Hornblower, bent against the wind, was standing in the sternsheets planning a route through the rocks which would lead them to the wreck. The shore and the friendly beach were gone now, incredibly far away, and the boat was struggling out through a welter of water with the wind howling round her. In those jumbled waves her motion was senseless and she lurched in every direction successively. It was well that the boatmen were used to rowing in broken water so that their oars kept the boat under way, giving the captain the means by which, tugging fiercely at the steering oar, he could guide her through that maniacal confusion. Hornblower, planning his course, was able to guide the captain by his gestures, so that the captain could devote all the necessary attention to keeping the boat from being suddenly capsized by an unexpected wave. The wind howled, and the boat heaved and pitched as she met each lumpy wave, but yard by yard they were struggling up to the wreck. If there was any order in the waves at all, they were swinging round the outer end of the Devil's Teeth, so that the boat had to be carefully steered, turning to meet the waves with her bows and then turning back to gain precarious yards against the wind. Hornblower spared a glance for the men at the oars; at every second they were exerting their utmost strength. There could never be a moment's respite—

tug and strain, tug and strain, until Hornblower wondered how human hearts and sinews could endure it.

But they were edging up towards the wreck. Hornblower, when the wind and spray allowed, could see the whole extent of her canted deck now. He could see human figures cowering under the break of the poop. He saw somebody there wave an arm to him. Next moment his attention was called away when a jagged monster suddenly leaped out of the sea twenty yards ahead. For a second he could not imagine what it was, and then it leaped clear again and he recognized it—the butt end of a broken mast. The mast was still anchored to the ship by a single surviving shroud attached to the upper end of the mast and to the ship, and the mast, drifting down to leeward, was jerking and leaping on the waves as though some sea god below the surface was threatening them with his wrath. Hornblower called the steersman's attention to the menace and received a nod in return; the steersman's shouted "Nombre de Dios" was whirled away in the wind. They kept clear of the mast, and as they pulled up along it Hornblower could form a clearer notion of the speed of their progress now that he had a stationary object to help his judgment. He could see the painful inches gained at each frantic tug on the oars, and could see how the boat stopped dead or even went astern when the wilder gusts hit her, the oar blades pulling ineffectively through the water. Every inch of gain was only won at the cost of an infinity of labour.

Now they were past the mast, close to the submerged bows of the ship, and close enough to the Devil's Teeth to be deluged with spray as each wave burst on the farther side of the reef. There were inches of water washing back and forth in the bottom of the boat, but there was neither time nor opportunity to bale it out. This was the trickiest part of the whole effort, to get close enough alongside the wreck to be able to take off the survivors without stoving in the boat; there were wicked fangs of rock all about the after end of the wreck, while forward, although the forecastle was above the surface at times the forward part of the waist was submerged. But the ship was canted a little over to port, towards them, which made the approach easier. When the water was at its lowest level, immediately before the next roller broke on the reef, Hornblower, standing up and craning his neck, could see no rocks beside the wreck in the middle part of the waist where the deck came down to water level. It was easy to direct the steersman towards that particular point, and then, as the boat moved in, to wave his arms and demand the attention of the little group under the break of the poop, and to point to the spot to which they were approaching. A wave burst upon the reef, broke over the stern of the wreck, and filled the boat almost full. She swung back and forth in the eddies, but the kegs kept her afloat and quick handling of the steering oar and lusty rowing kept her from being dashed against either the wreck or the rocks.

"Now!" shouted Hornblower—it did not matter that he spoke English at this decisive moment. The boat surged forward, while the survivors, releasing themselves from the lashings which had held them in their shelter, came slithering down the deck towards them. It was a little of a shock to see there were but four of them—twenty or thirty men must have been swept overboard when the ship hit the reef. The bows of the boat moved towards the wreck. At a shouted order from the steersman the oars fell still. One survivor braced himself and flung himself into the bows. A stroke of the oars, a tug at the steering oar, and the boat nosed forward again, and another survivor plunged into the boat. Then Hornblower, who had been watching the sea, saw the next breaker rear up over the reef. At his warning shout the boat backed away to safety—comparative safety—while the remaining survivors went scrambling back up the deck to the shelter of the poop. The wave burst and roared, the foam hissed and the spray rattled, and then they crept up to the wreck again. The third survivor poised himself for his leap, mistimed it, and fell into the sea, and no one ever saw him again. He was gone, sunk like a stone, crippled as he was with cold and exhaustion, but there was no time to spare for lamentation. The fourth survivor was waiting his chance and jumped at once, landing safely in the bows.

"Any more?" shouted Hornblower, and received a shake of the head in reply; they had saved three lives at the risk of eight.

"Let us go," said Hornblower, but the steersman needed no telling. Already he had allowed the wind to drift the boat away from the wreck, away from the rocks—away from the shore. An occasional strong pull at the oars sufficed to keep her bows to wind and wave. Hornblower looked down at the fainting survivors lying in the bottom of the boat with the water washing over them. He bent down and shook them into consciousness; he picked up the balers and forced them into their numb hands. They must keep active or die. It was astounding to find darkness closing about them, and it was urgent that they should decide on their next move immediately. The men at the oars were in no shape for any prolonged further rowing; if they tried to return to the sandy cove whence they had started they might be overtaken both by night and by exhaustion while still among the treacherous rocks off the shore there. Hornblower sat down beside the Galician captain, who laconically gave his views while vigilantly observing the waves racing down upon them.

"It is growing dark," said the captain, glancing round the sky. "Rocks. The men are tired."

"We had better not go back," said Hornblower.

"No."

"Then we must get out to sea."

Years of duty on blockade, of beating about off a lee shore, had in-grained into Hornblower the necessity for seeking sea-room.

"Yes," said the captain, and he added something which Hornblower, thanks to the wind and his unfamiliarity with the language, was un-able to catch. The captain roared the expression again, and accom-panied his words with a vivid bit of pantomime with the one hand he could spare from the steering oar.

"A sea anchor," decided Hornblower to himself. "Quite right."

He looked back at the vanishing shore, and gauged the direction of the wind. It seemed to be backing a little southerly; the coast here trended away from them. They could ride to a sea anchor through the hours of darkness and run no risk of being cast ashore as long as these conditions persisted.

"Good," said Hornblower aloud.

He imitated the other's bit of pantomime and the captain gave him a glance of approval. At a bellow from him the two men forward took in their oars and set to work at constructing a sea anchor—merely a pair of oars attached to a long painter paid out over the bows. With this gale blowing the pressure of the wind on the boat set up enough drag on the float to keep their bows to the sea. Hornblower watched as the sea anchor began to take hold of the water.

"Good," he said again.

"Good," said the captain, taking in his steering oar.

Hornblower realized only now that he had been long exposed to a winter gale while wet to the skin. He was numb with cold, and he was shivering uncontrollably. At his feet one of the three survivors of the wreck was lying helpless; the other two had succeeded in baling out most of the water and as a result of their exertions were conscious and alert. The men who had been rowing sat drooping with weariness on their thwarts. The Galician captain was already down in the bottom of the boat lifting the helpless man in his arms. It was a common impulse of them all to huddle down into the bottom of the boat, be-neath the thwarts, away from that shrieking wind.

So the night came down on them. Hornblower found himself wel-coming the contact of other human bodies; he felt an arm round him and he put his arm round someone else. Around them a little water still surged about on the floorboards; above them the wind still shrieked and howled. The boat stood first on her head and then on her tail as the waves passed under them, and at the moment of climbing each crest she gave a shuddering jerk as she snubbed herself to the sea anchor. Every few seconds a new spat of spray whirled into the boat upon their shrinking bodies; it did not seem long before the accumulation of spray in the bottom of the boat made it necessary for them to disentangle themselves, and set about, groping in the darkness, the task of baling the water out again. Then they could huddle down again under the thwarts.

It was when they pulled themselves together for the third baling that in the middle of his nightmare of cold and exhaustion Hornblower was conscious that the body across which his arm lay was unnaturally stiff; the man the captain had been trying to revive had died as he lay there between the captain and Hornblower. The captain dragged the body away into the sternsheets in the darkness, and the night went on, cold wind and cold spray, jerk, pitch, and roll, sit up and bale and cower down and shudder. It was hideous torment; Hornblower could not trust himself to believe his eyes when he saw the first signs that the darkness was lessening. And then the grey dawn came gradually over the grey sea, and they were free to wonder what to do next. But as the light increased the problem was solved for them, for one of the fishermen, raising himself up in the boat, gave a hoarse cry, and pointed to the northern horizon, and there, almost hull-up, was a ship, hove-to under storm canvas. The captain took one glance at her—his eyesight must have been marvellous—and identified her.

"The English frigate," he said.

She must have made nearly the same amount of leeway hove-to as the boat did riding to her sea anchor.

"Signal to her," said Hornblower, and no one raised any objections.

The only white object available was Hornblower's shirt, and he took it off, shuddering in the cold, and they tied it to an oar and raised the oar in the maststep. The captain saw Hornblower putting on his dripping coat over his bare ribs and in a single movement peeled off his thick blue jersey and offered it to him.

"Thank you, no," protested Hornblower, but the captain insisted; with a wide grin he pointed to the stiffened corpse lying in the sternsheets and announced he would replace the jersey with the dead man's clothing.

The argument was interrupted by a further cry from one of the fishermen. The frigate was coming to the wind; with treble-reefed fore and maintopsails she was heading for them under the impulse of the lessening gale. Hornblower saw her running down on them; a glance in the other direction showed him the Galician mountains, faint on the southern horizon—warmth, freedom and friendship on the one hand; solitude and captivity on the other. Under the lee of the frigate the boat bobbed and heaved fantastically; many inquisitive faces looked down on them. They were cold and cramped; the frigate dropped a boat and a couple of nimble seamen scrambled on board. A line was flung from the frigate, a whip lowered a breeches ring into the boat, and the English seamen helped the Spaniards one by one into the breeches and held them steady as they were swung up to the frigate's deck.

"I go last," said Hornblower when they turned to him. "I am a King's officer."

"Good Lor' lumme," said the seamen.

"Send the body up, too," said Hornblower. "It can be given decent burial."

The stiff corpse was grotesque as it swayed through the air. The Galician captain tried to dispute with Hornblower the honour of going last, but Hornblower would not be argued with. Then finally the seamen helped him put his legs into the breeches, and secured him with a line round his waist. Up he soared, swaying dizzily with the roll of the ship; then they drew him in to the deck, lowering and shortening, until half a dozen strong arms took his weight and laid him gently on the deck.

"There you are, my hearty, safe and sound," said a bearded seaman.

"I am a King's officer," said Hornblower. "Where's the officer of the watch?"

Wearing marvellous dry clothing, Hornblower found himself soon drinking hot rum-and-water in the cabin of Captain George Crome, of His Majesty's frigate *Syrtis*. Crome was a thin pale man with a depressed expression, but Hornblower knew of him as a first-rate officer.

"These Galicians make good seamen," said Crome. "I can't press them. But perhaps a few will volunteer sooner than go to a prison hulk."

"Sir," said Hornblower, and hesitated. It is ill for a junior lieutenant to argue with a post captain.

"Well?"

"Those men came to sea to save life. They are not liable to capture."

Crome's cold grey eyes became actively frosty—Hornblower was right about it being ill for a junior lieutenant to argue with a post captain.

"Are you telling me my duty, sir?" he asked.

"Good heavens no, sir," said Hornblower hastily. "It's a long time since I read the Admiralty Instructions and I expect my memory's at fault."

"Admiralty Instructions, eh?" said Crome, in a slightly different tone of voice.

"I expect I'm wrong, sir," said Hornblower, "but I seem to remember the same instruction applied to the other two—the survivors."

Even a post captain could only contravene Admiralty Instructions at his peril.

"I'll consider it," said Crome.

"I had the dead man sent on board, sir," went on Hornblower, "in the hope that perhaps you might give him proper burial. Those Galicians risked their lives to save him, sir, and I expect they'd be gratified."

"A Popish burial? I'll give orders to give 'em a free hand."

"Thank you, sir," said Hornblower.

"And now as regards yourself. You say you hold a commission as lieutenant. You can do duty in this ship until we meet the admiral again. Then he can decide. I haven't heard of the *Indefatigable* paying off, and legally you may still be borne on her books."

And that was when the devil came to tempt Hornblower, as he took another sip of hot rum-and-water. The joy of being in a King's ship again was so keen as to be almost painful. To taste salt beef and biscuit again, and never again to taste beans and garbanzos. To have a ship's deck under his feet, to talk English. To be free—to be free! There was precious little chance of ever falling again into Spanish hands. Hornblower remembered with agonising clarity the flat depression of captivity. All he had to do was not to say a word. He had only to keep silence for a day or two. But the devil did not tempt him long, only until he had taken his next sip of rum-and-water. Then he thrust the devil behind him and met Crome's eyes again.

"I'm sorry, sir," he said.

"What for?"

"I am here on parole. I gave my word before I left the beach."

"You did? That alters the case. You were within your rights, of course."

The giving of parole by captive British officers was so usual as to excite no comment.

"It was in the usual form, I suppose?" went on Crome. "That you would make no attempt to escape?"

"Yes, sir."

"Then what do you decide as a result?"

Of course Crome could not attempt to influence a gentleman's decision on a matter as personal as a parole.

"I must go back, sir," said Hornblower, "at the first opportunity."

He felt the sway of the ship, he looked round the homely cabin, and his heart was breaking.

"You can at least dine and sleep on board tonight," said Crome. "I'll not venture inshore again until the wind moderates. I'll send you to Corunna under a flag of truce when I can. And I'll see what the Instructions say about those prisoners."

It was a sunny morning when the sentry at Fort San Anton, in the harbour of Corunna, called his officer's attention to the fact that the British cruiser off the headland had hove-to out of gunshot and was lowering a boat. The sentry's responsibility ended there, and he could watch idly as his officer observed that the cutter, running smartly in under sail, was flying a white flag. She hove-to within musket shot, and it was a mild surprise to the sentry when in reply to the officer's hail someone rose up in the boat and replied in unmistakable Gallego dialect. Summoned alongside the landing slip, the cutter put ashore ten men and then headed out again to the frigate. Nine men were laughing and shouting; the tenth, the youngest, walked with a fixed expression on his face with never a sign of emotion—his expression did not change even when the others, with obvious affection, put their arms round his shoulders. No one ever troubled to explain to the sentry who the imperturbable young man was, and he was not very interested. After he had seen the group shipped off across Corunna Bay towards Ferrol he quite forgot the incident.

It was almost spring when a Spanish militia officer came into the barracks which served as a prison for officers in Ferrol.

"Señor Hornblower?" he asked—at least Hornblower, in the corner, knew that was what he was trying to say. He was used to the way Spaniards mutilated his name.

"Yes?" he said, rising.

"Would you please come with me? The commandant has sent me for you, sir."

The commandant was all smiles. He held a despatch in his hands.

"This, sir," he said, waving it at Hornblower, "is a personal order. It is countersigned by the Duke of Fuentesauco, Minister of Marine, but it is signed by the First Minister, Prince of the Peace and Duke of Alcudia."

"Yes, sir," said Hornblower.

He should have begun to hope at that moment, but there comes a time in a prisoner's life when he ceases to hope. He was more interested, even, in that strange title of Prince of the Peace which was now beginning to be heard in Spain.

"It says: 'We, Carlos Leonardo Luis Manuel de Godoy y Boégas, First Minister of His Most Catholic Majesty, Prince of the Peace, Duke of Alcudia and Grandee of the First Class, Count of Alcudia, Knight of the Most Sacred Order of the Golden Fleece, Knight of the Holy Order of Santiago, Knight of the Most Distinguished Order of Calatrava, Captain General of His Most Catholic Majesty's forces by Land and Sea, Colonel General of the Guardia de Corps, Admiral of the Two Oceans, General of the cavalry, of the infantry, and of the artillery'—in any event, sir, it is an order to me to take immediate steps to set you at liberty. I am to restore you under flag of truce to your fellow countrymen, in recognition of 'your courage and self-sacrifice in saving life at the peril of your own'."

"Thank you, sir," said Hornblower.

Lieutenant
Hornblower

I

Lieutenant William Bush came on board H.M.S. *Renown* as she lay at anchor in the Hamoaze and reported himself to the officer of the watch, who was a tall and rather gangling individual with hollow cheeks and a melancholy cast of countenance, whose uniform looked as if it had been put on in the dark and not readjusted since.

"Glad to have you aboard, sir," said the officer of the watch. "My name's Hornblower. The captain's ashore. First lieutenant went for'ard with the bosun ten minutes ago."

"Thank you," said Bush.

He looked keenly round him at the infinity of activities which were making the ship ready for a long period of service in distant waters.

"Hey there! You at the stay tackles! Handsomely! Handsomely! Belay!" Hornblower was bellowing this over Bush's shoulder. "Mr. Hobbs! Keep an eye on what your men are doing there!"

"Aye aye, sir," came a sulky reply.

"Mr. Hobbs! Lay aft here!"

A paunchy individual with a thick grey pigtail came rolling aft to where Hornblower stood with Bush at the gangway. He blinked up at Hornblower with the sun in his eyes; the sunlight lit up the sprouting grey beard on his tiers of chins.

"Mr. Hobbs!" said Hornblower. He spoke quietly, but there was an intensity of spirit underlying his words that surprised Bush. "That powder's got to come aboard before nightfall and you know it. So don't use that tone of voice when replying to an order. Answer cheerfully another time. How are you going to get the men to work if you sulk? Get for'ard and see to it."

Hornblower was leaning a little forward as he spoke; the hands which he clasped behind him served apparently to balance the jutting chin, but his attitude was negligent compared with the fierce intensity with which he spoke, even though he was speaking in an undertone inaudible to all except the three of them.

"Aye aye, sir," said Hobbs, turning to go forward again.

Bush was making a mental note that this Hornblower was a firebrand when he met his glance and saw to his surprise a ghost of a twinkle in its melancholy depths. In a flash of insight he realized that this fierce young lieutenant was not fierce at all, and that the intensity with which he spoke was entirely assumed—it was almost as if Hornblower had been exercising himself in a foreign language.

"If they once start sulking you can't do anything with 'em," explained Hornblower, "and Hobbs is the worst of 'em—acting-gunner, and no good. Lazy as they make 'em."

"I see," said Bush.

The duplicity—play acting—of the young lieutenant aroused a momentary suspicion in Bush's mind. A man who could assume an appearance of wrath and abandon it again with so much facility was not to be trusted. Then, with an inevitable reaction, the twinkle in the brown eyes called up a responsive twinkle in Bush's frank blue eyes, and he felt a friendly impulse towards Hornblower, but Bush was innately cautious and checked the impulse at once, for there was a long voyage ahead of them and plenty of time for a more considered judgment. Meanwhile he was conscious of a keen scrutiny, and he could see that a question was imminent—and even Bush could guess what it would be. The next moment proved him right.

"What's the date of your commission?" asked Hornblower.

"July '96," said Bush.

"Thank you," said Hornblower in a flat tone that conveyed so little information that Bush had to ask the question in his turn.

"What's the date of yours?"

"August '97," said Hornblower. "You're senior to me. You're senior to Smith, too—January '97."

"Are you the junior lieutenant, then?"

"Yes," said Hornblower.

His tone did not reveal any disappointment that the newcomer had proved to be senior to him, but Bush could guess at it. Bush knew by very recent experience what it was to be the junior lieutenant in a ship of the line.

"You'll be third," went on Hornblower. "Smith fourth, and I'm fifth."

"I'll be third?" mused Bush, more to himself than to anyone else.

Every lieutenant could at least dream, even lieutenants like Bush with no imagination at all. Promotion was at least theoretically possible; from the caterpillar stage of lieutenant one might progress to the butterfly stage of captain, sometimes even without a chrysalis period as commander. Lieutenants undoubtedly were promoted on occasions; most of them, as was to be expected, being men who had friends at Court, or in Parliament, or who had been fortunate enough to attract the attention of an admiral and then lucky enough to be under that admiral's command at the moment when a vacancy occurred. Most of the captains on the list owed their promotion to one or other of such causes.

But sometimes a lieutenant won his promotion through merit—through a combination of merit and good fortune, at least—and sometimes sheer blind chance brought it about. If a ship distinguished herself superlatively in some historic action the first lieutenant might be promoted (oddly enough, that promotion was considered a compliment to her captain) or if the captain should be killed in the action even a moderate success might result in a step for the senior surviving lieutenant who took his place. On the other hand some brilliant boat-action, some dashing exploit on shore, might win promotion for the lieutenant in command—the senior, of course. The chances were few enough in all conscience, but there were at least chances.

But of those few chances the great majority went to the senior lieutenant, to the first lieutenant; the chances of the junior lieutenant were doubly few. So that whenever a lieutenant dreamed of attaining the rank of captain, with its dignity and security and prize money, he soon found himself harking back to the consideration of his seniority as lieutenant. If this next commission of the *Renown's* took her away to some place where other lieutenants could not be sent on board by an admiral with favourites, there were only two lives between Bush and the position of first lieutenant with all its added chances of promotion. Naturally he thought about that; equally naturally he did not spare a thought for the fact that the man with whom he was conversing was divided by four lives from that same position.

"But still, it's the West Indies for us, anyway," said Hornblower philosophically. "Yellow fever. Ague. Hurricanes. Poisonous serpents. Bad water. Tropical heat. Putrid fever. And ten times more chances of action than with the Channel fleet."

"That's so," agreed Bush, appreciatively.

With only three and four years' seniority as lieutenants, respectively, the two young men (and with young men's confidence in their own immortality) could face the dangers of West Indian service with some complacence.

"Captain's coming off, sir," reported the midshipman of the watch hurriedly.

Hornblower whipped his telescope to eye and trained it on the approaching shore boat.

"Quite right," he said. "Run for'ard and tell Mr. Buckland. Bosun's mates! Sideboys! Lively, now!"

Captain Sawyer came up through the entry port, touched his hat to the quarterdeck, and looked suspiciously around him. The ship was in the condition of confusion to be expected when she was completing for foreign service, but that hardly justified the sidelong, shifty glances which Sawyer darted about him. He had a big face and a prominent hawk nose which he turned this way and that as he stood on the quarterdeck. He caught sight of Bush, who came forward and reported himself.

"You came aboard in my absence, did you?" asked Sawyer.

"Yes, sir," said Bush, a little surprised.

"Who told you I was on shore?"

"No one, sir."

"How did you guess it, then?"

"I didn't guess it, sir. I didn't know you were on shore until Mr. Hornblower told me."

"Mr. Hornblower? So you know each other already?"

"No, sir. I reported to him when I came on board."

"So that you could have a few private words without my knowledge?"

"No, sir."

Bush bit off the "of course not" which he was about to add. Brought up in a hard school, Bush had learned to utter no unnecessary words when dealing with a superior officer indulging in the touchiness superior officers might be expected to indulge in. Yet this particular touchiness seemed more unwarranted even than usual.

"I'll have you know I allow no one to conspire behind my back, Mr. —ah—Bush," said the captain.

"Aye aye, sir."

Bush met the captain's searching stare with the composure of innocence, but he was doing his best to keep his surprise out of his expression, too, and as he was no actor the struggle may have been evident.

"You wear your guilt on your face, Mr. Bush," said the captain. "I'll remember this."

With that he turned away and went below, and Bush, relaxing from his attitude of attention, turned to express his surprise to Hornblower. He was eager to ask questions about this extraordinary behaviour, but they died away on his lips when he saw that Hornblower's face was set in a wooden unresponsiveness. Puzzled and a little hurt, Bush was about to note Hornblower down as one of the captain's toadies—or as a madman as well—when he caught sight out of the tail of his eye of the captain's head reappearing above the deck. Sawyer must have swung round when at the foot of the companion and come up again simply for the purpose of catching his officers off their guard discussing him—and Hornblower knew more about his captain's habits than Bush did. Bush made an enormous effort to appear natural.

"Can I have a couple of hands to carry my sea-chest down?" he asked, hoping that the words did not sound nearly as stifled to the captain as they did to his own ears.

"Of course, Mr. Bush," said Hornblower, with a formidable formality. "See to it, if you please, Mr. James."

"Ha!" snorted the captain, and disappeared once more down the companion.

Hornblower flickered one eyebrow at Bush, but that was the only indication he gave, even then, of any recognition that the captain's actions were at all unusual, and Bush, as he followed his sea-chest down to his cabin, realized with dismay that this was a ship where no one ventured on any decisive expression of opinion. But the *Renown* was completing for sea, amid all the attendant bustle and confusion, and Bush was on board, legally one of her officers, and there was nothing he could do except reconcile himself philosophically to his fate. He would have to live through his commission, unless any of the possibilities catalogued by Hornblower in their first conversation should save him the trouble.

II

H.M.S. *Renown* was clawing her way southward under reefed topsails, a westerly wind laying her over as she thrashed along, heading for those latitudes where she would pick up the north-east trade wind and be able to run direct to her destination in the West Indies. The wind sang in the taut weather-rigging, and blustered round Bush's ears as he stood on the starboard side of the quarterdeck, balancing to the roll as the roaring wind sent one massive grey wave after another hurrying at the ship; the starboard bow received the wave first, beginning a leisurely climb, heaving the bowsprit up towards the sky, but before the pitch was in any way completed the ship began her roll, heaving slowly over, slowly, slowly, while the bowsprit rose still more steeply. And then as she still rolled the bows shook themselves free and began to slide down the far side of the wave, with the foam creaming round them; the bowsprit began the downward portion of its arc as the ship rose ponderously to an even heel again, and as she heeled a trifle into the wind with the send of the sea under her keel her stern rose while the last of the wave passed under it, her bows dipped, and she completed the corkscrew roll with the massive dignity to be expected of a ponderous fabric that carried five hundred tons of artillery on her decks. Pitch—roll—heave —roll; it was magnificent, rhythmic, majestic, and Bush, balancing on the deck with the practised ease of ten years' experience, would have felt almost happy if the freshening of the wind did not bring with it the approaching necessity for another reef, which meant, in accordance with the ship's standing orders, that the captain should be informed.

Yet there were some minutes of grace left him, during which he could stand balancing on the deck and allow his mind to wander free. Not that Bush was conscious of any need for meditation—he would have smiled at such a suggestion were anyone to make it to him. But the last few days had passed in a whirl, from the moment when his orders had arrived and he had said good-bye to his mother and sisters (he had had three weeks with them after the *Conqueror* had paid off) and hurried to Plymouth, counting the money he had left in his pockets to make sure he could pay the post-chaise charges. The *Renown* had been in all the flurry of completing for the West Indian station, and during the thirty-six hours that elapsed before she sailed Bush had hardly had time to sit down, let alone sleep—his first good night's rest had come while the *Renown* clawed her way across the bay. Yet almost from the moment of his first arrival on board he had been harassed by the fantastic moods of the captain, now madly suspicious and again stupidly easygoing. Bush was not a man sensitive to atmosphere—he was a sturdy soul philosophically prepared to do his duty in any of the difficult conditions to be expected at sea—but he could not help but be conscious of the tenseness and fear that pervaded life in the *Renown.* He knew that he felt dissatisfied and worried, but he did not know that these were his own forms of tenseness and fear. In three days at sea he had hardly come to know a thing about his colleagues: he could vaguely guess that Buckland, the first lieutenant, was capable and steady, and that Roberts, the second, was kindly and easygoing; Hornblower seemed active and intelligent, Smith a trifle weak; but these deductions were really guesses. The wardroom officers—the lieutenants and the master and the surgeon and the purser—seemed to be secretive and very much inclined to maintain a strict reserve about themselves. Within wide limits this was right and proper—Bush was no frivolous chatterer himself—but the silence was carried to excess when conversation was limited to half a dozen words, all strictly professional. There was much that Bush could have learned speedily about the ship and her crew if the other officers had been prepared to share with him the results of their experience and observations during the year they had been on board, but except for the single hint Bush had received from Hornblower when he came on board no one had uttered a word. If Bush had been given to Gothic flights of imagination he might have thought of himself as a ghost at sea with a company of ghosts, cut off from the world and from each other, ploughing across an endless sea to an unknown destination. As it was he could guess that the secretiveness of the wardroom was the result of the moods of the captain; and that brought him back abruptly to the thought that the wind was still freshening and a second reef was now necessary. He listened to the harping of the rigging, felt the heave of the deck under his feet, and shook his head regretfully. There was nothing for it.

"Mr. Wellard," he said to the volunteer beside him. "Go and tell the captain that I think another reef is necessary."

"Aye aye, sir."

It was only a few seconds before Wellard was back on deck again.

"Cap'n's coming himself, sir."

"Very good," said Bush.

He did not meet Wellard's eyes as he said the meaningless words; he did not want Wellard to see how he took the news, nor did he want to see any expression that Wellard's face might wear. Here came the captain, his shaggy long hair whipping in the wind and his hook nose turning this way and that as usual.

"You want to take in another reef, Mr. Bush?"

"Yes, sir," said Bush, and waited for the cutting remark that he expected. It was a pleasant surprise that none was forthcoming. The captain seemed almost genial.

"Very good, Mr. Bush. Call all hands."

The pipes shrilled along the decks.

"All hands! All hands! All hands to reef tops'ls. All hands!"

The men came pouring out; the cry of "All hands" brought out the officers from the wardroom and the cabins and the midshipmen's berths, hastening with their station-bills in their pockets to make sure that the reorganized crew were properly at their stations. The captain's orders pealed against the wind. Halliards and reef tackles were manned; the ship plunged and rolled over the grey sea under the grey sky so that a landsman might have wondered how a man could keep his footing on deck, far less venture aloft. Then in the midst of the evolution a young voice, soaring with excitement to a high treble, cut through the captain's orders.

" 'Vast hauling there! 'Vast hauling!"

There was a piercing urgency about the order, and obediently the men ceased to pull. Then the captain bellowed from the poop.

"Who's that countermanding my orders?"

"It's me, sir—Wellard."

The young volunteer faced aft and screamed into the wind to make himself heard. From his station aft Bush saw the captain advance to the poop rail; Bush could see he was shaking with rage, his big nose pointing forward as though seeking a victim.

"You'll be sorry, Mr. Wellard. Oh yes, you'll be sorry."

Hornblower now made his appearance at Wellard's side. He was green with seasickness, as he had been ever since the *Renown* left Plymouth Sound.

"There's a reef point caught in the reef tackle block, sir—weather side," he hailed, and Bush, shifting his position, could see that this was so; if the men had continued to haul on the tackle, damage to the sail might easily have followed.

"What d'you mean by coming between me and a man who disobeys me?" shouted the captain. "It's useless to try to screen him."

"This is my station, sir," replied Hornblower. "Mr. Wellard was doing his duty."

"Conspiracy!" replied the captain. "You two are in collusion!"

In the face of such an impossible statement Hornblower could only stand still, his white face turned towards the captain.

"You go below, Mr. Wellard," roared the captain, when it was apparent that no reply would be forthcoming, "and you too, Mr. Hornblower. I'll deal with you in a few minutes. You hear me? Go below! I'll teach you to conspire."

It was a direct order, and had to be obeyed. Hornblower and Wellard walked slowly aft; it was obvious that Hornblower was rigidly refraining from exchanging a glance with the midshipman, lest a fresh accusation of conspiracy should be hurled at him. They went below while the captain watched them. As they disappeared down the companion the captain raised his big nose again.

"Send a hand to clear that reef tackle!" he ordered, in a tone as nearly normal as the wind permitted. "Haul away!"

The topsails had their second reef, and the men began to lay in off the yards. The captain stood by the poop rail looking over the ship as normal as any man could be expected to be.

"Wind's coming aft," he said to Buckland. "Aloft there! Send a hand to bear those backstays abreast the top-brim. Hands to the weather-braces. After guard! Haul in the weather main brace! Haul together, men! Well with the foreyard! Well with the main yard! Belay every inch of that!"

The orders were given sensibly and sanely, and the hands stood waiting for the watch below to be dismissed.

"Bosun's mate! My compliments to Mr. Lomax and I'll be glad to see him on deck."

Mr. Lomax was the purser, and the officers on the quarterdeck could hardly refrain from exchanging glances; it was hard to imagine any reason why the purser should be wanted on deck at this moment.

"You sent for me, sir?" said the purser, arriving short of breath on the quarterdeck.

"Yes, Mr. Lomax. The hands have been hauling in the weather main brace."

"Yes, sir?"

"Now we'll splice it."

"Sir?"

"You heard me. We'll splice the main brace. A tot of rum to every man. Aye, and to every boy."

"Sir?"

"You heard me. A tot of rum, I said. Do I have to give my orders twice? A tot of rum for every man. I'll give you five minutes, Mr. Lomax, and not a second longer."

The captain pulled out his watch and looked at it significantly.

"Aye aye, sir," said Lomax, which was all he could say. Yet he still stood for a second or two, looking first at the captain and then at the watch, until the big nose began to lift in his direction and the shaggy eyebrows began to come together. Then he turned and fled; if the unbelievable order had to be obeyed five minutes would not be long in which to collect his party together, unlock the spirit room, and bring up the spirits. The conversation between captain and purser could hardly have been overheard by more than half a dozen persons, but every hand had witnessed it, and the men were looking at each other unbelievingly, some with grins on their faces which Bush longed to wipe off.

"Bosun's mate! Run and tell Mr. Lomax two minutes have gone. Mr. Buckland! I'll have the hands aft here, if you please."

The men came trooping along the waist; it may have been merely Bush's overwrought imagination that made him think their manner slack and careless. The captain came forward to the quarterdeck rail, his face beaming in smiles that contrasted wildly with his scowls of a moment before.

"I know where loyalty's to be found, men," he shouted, "I've seen it. I see it now. I see your loyal hearts. I watch your unremitting labours. I've noticed them as I notice everything that goes on in this ship. Everything, I say. The traitors meet their deserts and the loyal hearts their reward. Give a cheer, you men."

The cheer was given, halfheartedly in some cases, with overexuberance in others. Lomax made his appearance at the main hatchway, four men with him each carrying a two-gallon anker.

"Just in time, Mr. Lomax. It would have gone hard with you if you had been late. See to it that the issue is made with none of the unfairness that goes on in some ships. Mr. Booth! Lay aft here."

The bulky bosun came hurrying on his short legs.

"You have your rattan with you, I hope?"

"Aye aye, sir."

Booth displayed his long silver-mounted cane, ringed at every two inches by a pronounced joint. The dilatory among the crew knew that cane well and not only the dilatory—at moments of excitement Mr. Booth was likely to make play with it on all within reach.

"Pick the two sturdiest of your mates. Justice will be executed."

Now the captain was neither beaming nor scowling. There was a smile on his heavy lips, but it might be a smile without significance as it was not re-echoed in his eyes.

"Follow me," said the captain to Booth and his mates, and he left the deck once more to Bush, who now had leisure to contemplate ruefully the disorganization of the ship's routine and discipline occasioned by this strange whim.

When the spirits had been issued and drunk he could dismiss the watch below and set himself to drive the watch on deck to their duties again, slashing at their sulkiness and indifference with bitter words. And there was no pleasure now in standing on the heaving deck watching the corkscrew roll of the ship and the hurrying Atlantic waves, the trim of the sails and the handling of the wheel—Bush still was unaware that there was any pleasure to be found in these everyday matters, but he was vaguely aware that something had gone out of his life.

He saw Booth and his mates making their way forward again, and here came Wellard onto the quarterdeck.

"Reporting for duty, sir," he said.

The boy's face was white, set in a strained rigidity, and Bush, looking keenly at him, saw that there was a hint of moisture in his eyes. He was walking stiffly, too, holding himself inflexibly; pride might be holding back his shoulders and holding up his head, but there was some other reason for his not bending at the hips.

"Very good, Mr. Wellard," said Bush.

He remembered those knots on Booth's cane. He had known injustice often enough. Not only boys but grown men were beaten without cause on occasions, and Bush had nodded sagely when it happened, thinking that contact with injustice in a world that was essentially unjust was part of everyone's education. And grown men smiled to each other when boys were beaten, agreeing that it did all parties good; boys had been beaten since history began, and it would be a bad day for the world if ever, inconceivably, boys should cease to be beaten. This was all very true, and yet in spite of it Bush felt sorry for Wellard. Fortunately there was something waiting to be done which might suit Wellard's mood and condition.

"Those sandglasses need to be run against each other, Mr. Wellard," said Bush, nodding over to the binnacle. "Run the minute glass against the half-hour glass as soon as they turn it at seven bells."

"Aye aye, sir."

"Mark off each minute on the slate unless you want to lose your reckoning," added Bush.

"Aye aye, sir."

It would be something to keep Wellard's mind off his troubles without calling for physical effort, watching the sand run out of the minute glass and turning it quickly, marking the slate and watching again. Bush had his doubts about that half-hour glass and it would be convenient to have both checked. Wellard walked stiffly over to the binnacle and made preparation to begin his observations.

Now here was the captain coming back again, the big nose pointing to one side and the other. But now the mood had changed again; the activity, the restlessness, had evaporated. He was like a man who had dined well. As etiquette dictated, Bush moved away from the weather rail when the captain appeared and the captain proceeded to pace slowly up and down the weather side of the quarterdeck, his steps accommodating themselves by long habit to the heave and pitch of the ship. Wellard took one glance and then devoted his whole attention to the matter of the sandglasses; seven bells had just struck and the half-hour glass had just been turned. For a short time the captain paced up and down. When he halted he studied the weather to windward, felt the wind on his cheek, looked attentively at the dogvane and up at the topsails to make sure that the yards were correctly trimmed, and came over and looked into the binnacle to check the course the helmsman was steering. It was all perfectly normal behaviour; any captain in any ship would do the same when he came on deck. Wellard was aware of the nearness of his captain and tried to give no sign of disquiet; he turned the minute glass and made another mark on the slate.

"Mr. Wellard at work?" said the captain.

His voice was thick and a little indistinct, the tone quite different from the anxiety-sharpened voice with which he had previously spoken. Wellard, his eyes on the sandglasses, paused before replying. Bush could guess that he was wondering what would be the safest, as well as the correct, thing to say.

"Aye aye, sir."

In the navy no one could go far wong by saying that to a superior officer.

"Aye aye, sir," repeated the captain. "Mr. Wellard has learned better now perhaps than to conspire against his captain, against his lawful superior set in authority over him by the Act of His Most Gracious Majesty King George II?"

That was not an easy suggestion to answer. The last grains of sand were running out of the glass and Wellard waited for them; a "yes" or a "no" might be equally fatal.

"Mr. Wellard is sulky," said the captain. "Perhaps Mr. Wellard's mind is dwelling on what lies behind him. Behind him. 'By the waters of Babylon we sat down and wept.' But proud Mr. Wellard hardly wept. And he did not sit down at all. No, he would be careful not to sit down. The dishonourable part of him has paid the price of his dishonour. The grown man guilty of an honourable offence is flogged upon his back, but a boy, a nasty dirty-minded boy, is treated differently. Is not that so, Mr. Wellard?"

"Yes, sir," murmured Wellard. There was nothing else he could say, and an answer was necessary.

"Mr. Booth's cane was appropriate to the occasion. It did its work well. The malefactor bent over the gun could consider of his misdeeds."

Wellard inverted the glass again while the captain, apparently satisfied, took a couple of turns up and down the deck, to Bush's relief. But the captain checked himself in mid-stride beside Wellard and went on talking; his tone now was higher-pitched.

"So you chose to conspire against me?" he demanded. "You sought to hold me up to derision before the hands?"

"No, sir," said Wellard in sudden new alarm. "No, sir, indeed not, sir."

"You and that cub Hornblower. *Mister* Hornblower. You plotted and you planned, so that my lawful authority should be set at nought."

"No, sir!"

"It is only the hands who are faithful to me in this ship where everyone else conspires against me. And cunningly you seek to undermine my influence over them. To make me a figure of fun in their sight. Confess it!"

"No, sir. I didn't, sir."

"Why attempt to deny it? It is plain, it is logical. Who was it who planned to attach that reef point in the reef tackle block?"

"No one, sir. It—"

"Then who was it that countermanded my orders? Who was it who put me to shame before both watches, with all hands on deck? It was a deep-laid plot. It shows every sign of it."

The captain's hands were behind his back, and he stood easily balancing on the deck with the wind flapping his coat-tails and blowing his hair forward over his cheeks, but Bush could see he was shaking with rage again—if it was not fear. Wellard turned the minute glass again and made a fresh mark on the slate.

"So you hide your face because of the guilt that is written on it?" blared the captain suddenly. "You pretend to be busy so as to deceive me. Hypocrisy!"

"I gave Mr. Wellard orders to test the glasses against each other, sir," said Bush.

He was intervening reluctantly, but to intervene was less painful than to stand by as a witness. The captain looked at him as if this was his first appearance on deck.

"You, Mr. Bush? You're sadly deceived if you believe there is any good in this young fellow. Unless"—the captain's expression was one of sudden suspicious fear—"unless you are part and parcel of this infamous affair. But you are not, are you, Mr. Bush? Not you. I have always thought better of you, Mr. Bush."

The expression of fear changed to one of ingratiating good fellowship.

"Yes, sir," said Bush.

"With the world against me I have always counted on you, Mr. Bush," said the captain, darting restless glances from under his eyebrows. "So you will rejoice when this embodiment of evil meets his deserts. We'll get the truth out of him."

Bush had the feeling that if he were a man of instant quickness of thought and readiness of tongue he would take advantage of this new attitude of the captain's to free Wellard from his peril; by posing as the captain's devoted companion in trouble and at the same time laughing off the thought of danger from any conspiracy, he might modify the captain's fears. So he felt, but he had no confidence in himself.

"He knows nothing, sir," he said, and he forced himself to grin. "He doesn't know the bobstay from the spankerboom."

"You think so?" said the captain doubtfully, teetering on his heels with the roll of the ship. He seemed almost convinced, and then suddenly a new line of argument presented itself to him.

"No, Mr. Bush. You're too honest. I could see that the first moment I set eyes on you. You are ignorant of the depths of wickedness into which this world can sink. This lout has deceived you. Deceived you!"

The captain's voice rose again to a hoarse scream, and Wellard turned a white face towards Bush, lopsided with terror.

"Really, sir—" began Bush, still forcing a death's-head grin.

"No, no, no!" roared the captain. "Justice must be done! The truth must be brought to light! I'll have it out of him! Quartermaster! Quartermaster! Run for'ard and tell Mr. Booth to lay aft here. And his mates!"

The captain turned away and began to pace the deck as if to offer a safety valve to the pressure within him, but he turned back instantly.

"I'll have it out of him! Or he'll jump overboard! You hear me? Where's that bosun?"

"Mr. Wellard hasn't finished testing the glasses, sir," said Bush in one last feeble attempt to postpone the issue.

"Nor will he," said the captain.

Here came the bosun hurrying aft on his short legs, his two mates striding behind him.

"Mr. Booth!" said the captain; his mood had changed again and the mirthless smile was back on his lips. "Take that miscreant. Justice demands that he be dealt with further. Another dozen from your cane, properly applied. Another dozen, and he'll coo like a dove."

"Aye aye, sir," said the bosun, but he hesitated.

It was a momentary tableau: the captain with his flapping coat; the bosun looking appealingly at Bush and the burly bosun's mates standing like huge statues behind him; the helmsman apparently imperturbable while all this went on round him, handling the wheel and glancing up at the topsails; and the wretched boy beside the binnacle—all this under the grey sky, with the grey sea tossing about them and stretching as far as the pitiless horizon.

"Take him down to the maindeck, Mr. Booth," said the captain.

It was the utterly inevitable; behind the captain's words lay the authority of Parliament, the weight of ages-old tradition. There was nothing that could be done. Wellard's hands rested on the binnacle as though they would cling to it and as though he would have to be dragged away by force. But he dropped his hands to his sides and followed the bosun while the captain watched him, smiling.

It was a welcome distraction that came to Bush as the quartermaster reported, "Ten minutes before eight bells, sir."

"Very good. Pipe the watch below."

Hornblower made his appearance on the quarterdeck and made his way towards Bush.

"You're not my relief," said Bush.

"Yes I am. Captain's orders."

Hornblower spoke without any expression—Bush was used to the ship's officers by now being as guarded as that, and he knew why it was. But his curiosity made him ask the question.

"Why?"

"I'm on watch and watch," said Hornblower stolidly. "Until further orders."

He looked at the horizon as he spoke, showing no sign of emotion.

"Hard luck," said Bush, and for a moment felt a twinge of doubt as to whether he had not ventured too far in offering such an expression of sympathy. But no one was within earshot.

"No wardroom liquor for me," went on Hornblower, "until further orders either. Neither my own nor anyone else's."

For some officers that would be a worse punishment than being put on watch and watch—four hours on duty and four hours off day and night—but Bush did not know enough about Hornblower's habits to judge whether this was the case with him. He was about to say "hard luck" again, when at that moment a wild cry of pain reached their ears, cutting its way through the whistling wind. A moment later it was repeated, with even greater intensity. Hornblower was looking out at the horizon and his expression did not change. Bush watched his face and decided not to pay attention to the cries.

"Hard luck," he said.

"It might be worse," said Hornblower.

III

It was Sunday morning. The *Renown* had caught the north-east trades and was plunging across the Atlantic at her best speed, with studding sails set on both sides, the roaring trades driving her along with a steady pitch and heave, her bluff bows now and then raising a smother of spray that supported momentary rainbows. The rigging was piping loud and clear, the treble and the tenor to the baritone and bass of the noises of the ship's fabric as she pitched—a symphony of the sea. A few clouds of startling white dotted the blue of the sky, and the sun shone down from among them, revivifying and rejuvenating, reflected in dancing facets from the imperial blue of the sea.

The ship was a thing of exquisite beauty in an exquisite setting, and her bluff bows and her rows of guns added something else to the picture. She was a magnificent fighting machine, the mistress of the waves over which she was sailing in solitary grandeur. Her very solitude told the story; with the fleets of her enemies cooped up in port, blockaded by vigilant squadrons eager to come to grips with them, the *Renown* could sail the seas in utter confidence that she had nothing to fear. No furtive blockade-runner could equal her in strength; nowhere at sea was there a hostile squadron which could face her in battle. She could flout the hostile coasts; with the enemy blockaded and helpless she could bring her ponderous might to bear in a blow struck wherever she might choose. At this moment she was heading to strike such a blow, perhaps, despatched across the ocean at the word of the Lords of the Admiralty.

And drawn up in ranks on her maindeck was the ship's company, the men whose endless task it was to keep this fabric at the highest efficiency, to repair the constant inroads made upon her material by sea and weather and the mere passage of time. The snow-white decks, the bright paintwork, the exact and orderly arrangement of the lines and ropes and spars, were proofs of the diligence of their work; and when the time should come for the *Renown* to deliver the ultimate argument regarding the sovereignty of the seas, it would be they who would man the guns—the *Renown* might be a magnificent fighting machine, but she was so only by virtue of the frail humans who handled her. They, like the *Renown* herself, were only cogs in the greater machine which was the Royal Navy, and most of them, caught up in the time-honoured routine and discipline of the service, were content to be cogs, to wash decks and set up rigging, to point guns or to charge with cutlasses over hostile bulwarks, with little thought as to whether the ship's bows were headed north or south, whether it was Frenchman or Spaniard or Dutchman who received their charge. Today only the captain knew the mission upon which the Lords of the Admiralty—presumably in consultation with the Cabinet—had despatched the *Renown*. There had been the vague knowledge that she was headed for the West Indies, but whereabouts in that area, and what she was intended to do there was known only to one man in the seven hundred and forty on the *Renown's* decks.

Every possible man was drawn up on this Sunday morning on the maindeck, not merely the two watches, but every "idler" who had no place in the watches—the holders, who did their work so far below decks that for some of them it was literally true that they did not see the sun from one week's end to another, the cooper and his mates, the armourer and his mates, sail-maker and cook and stewards, all in their best clothes with the officers with their cocked hats and swords beside their divisions. Only the officer of the watch and his assistant warrant officer, the quartermasters at the wheel and the dozen hands necessary for lookouts and to handle the ship in a very sudden emergency were not included in the ranks that were drawn up in the waist at rigid attention, the lines swaying easily and simultaneously with the motion of the ship.

It was Sunday morning, and every hat was off, every head was bare as the ship's company listened to the words of the captain. But it was no church service; these bare-headed men were not worshipping their Maker. That could happen on three Sundays in every month, but on those Sundays there would not be quite such a strict inquisition throughout the ship to compel the attendance of every hand—and a tolerant Admiralty had lately decreed that Catholics and Jews and even Dissenters might be excused from attending church services. This was the fourth Sunday, when the worship of God was set aside in favour of a ceremonial more strict, more solemn, calling for the same clean shirts and bared heads, but not for the downcast eyes of the men in the ranks. Instead every man was looking to his front as he held his hat before him with the wind ruffling his hair; he was listening to laws as all-embracing as the Ten Commandments, to a code as rigid as Leviticus, because on the fourth Sunday of every month it was the captain's duty to read the Articles of War aloud to the ship's company, so that not even the illiterates could plead ignorance of them; a religious captain might squeeze in a brief church service as well, but the Articles of War had to be read.

The captain turned a page.

"Nineteenth Article," he read. "If any person in or belonging to the fleet shall make or endeavour to make any mutinous assembly upon any offence whatsoever, every person offending therein, and being convicted by the sentence of the court-martial, shall suffer death."

Bush, standing by his division, heard these words as he had heard them scores of times before. He had, in fact, heard them so often that he usually listened to them with inattention; the words of the previous eighteen Articles had flowed past him practically without his hearing them. But he heard this Nineteenth Article distinctly; it was possible that the captain read it with special emphasis, and in addition Bush, raising his eyes in the blessed sunshine, caught sight of Hornblower, the officer of the watch, standing at the quarterdeck rail listening as well. And there was that word "death". It struck Bush's ear with special emphasis, as emphatic and as final as the sound of a stone dropped into a well, which was strange, for the other articles which the captain had read had used the word freely—death for holding back from danger, death for sleeping while on duty.

The captain went on reading.

"And if any person shall utter any words of sedition or mutiny he shall suffer death. . . .

"And if any officer, mariner, or soldier shall behave himself with contempt to his superior officer . . ."

Those words had a fuller meaning for Bush now, with Hornblower looking down at him; he felt a strange stirring within him. He looked at the captain, unkempt and seedy in his appearance, and went back in his memory through the events of the past few days; if ever a man had shown himself unfit for duty it was the captain, but he was maintained in his position of unlimited power by these Articles of War which he was reading. Bush glanced up at Hornblower again; he felt that he knew for certain what Hornblower was thinking about as he stood there by the quarterdeck rail, and it was strange to feel this sympathy with the ungainly angular young lieutenant with whom he had had such little contact.

"And if any officer, mariner, or soldier or other person in the fleet," —the captain had reached the Twenty-Second Article now—"shall presume to quarrel with any of his superior officers, or shall disobey any lawful command, every such person shall suffer death."

Bush had not realized before how the Articles of War harped on this subject. He had served contentedly under discipline, and had always philosophically assured himself that injustice or mismanagement could be lived through. He could see now very special reasons why they should be. And as if to clinch the argument, the captain was now reading the final Article of War, the one which filled in every gap.

"All other crimes committed by any person or persons in the fleet which are not mentioned in this Act . . ."

Bush remembered that article; by its aid an officer could accomplish the ruin of an inferior who was clever enough to escape being pinned down by any of the others.

The captain read the final solemn words and looked up from the page. The big nose turned like a gun being trained round as he looked at each officer in turn; his face with its unshaven cheeks bore an expression of coarse triumph. It was as if he had gained by this reading of the Articles reassurance regarding his fears. He inflated his chest; he seemed to rise on tiptoe to make his concluding speech.

"I'll have you all know that these Articles apply to my officers as much as to anyone else."

Those were words which Bush could hardly believe he had heard. It was incredible that a captain could say such a thing in his crew's hearing. If ever a speech was subversive to discipline it was this one. But the captain merely went on with routine.

"Carry on, Mr. Buckland."

"Aye aye, sir." Buckland took a pace forward in the grip of routine himself.

"On hats!"

Officers and men covered their heads now that the ceremonial was completed.

"Division officers, dismiss your divisions!"

The musicians of the marine band had been waiting for this moment. The drum sergeant waved his baton and the drumsticks crashed down on the side drums in a long roll. Piercing and sweet the fifes joined in —"The Irish Washerwoman," jerky and inspiriting. Smack—smack —smack; the marine soldiers brought their ordered muskets up to their shoulders. Whiting, the captain of marines, shouted the orders which sent the scarlet lines marching and counter-marching in the sunshine over the limited area of the quarterdeck.

The captain had been standing by watching this orderly progress of the ship's routine. Now he raised his voice.

"Mr. Buckland!"

"Sir!"

The captain mounted a couple of steps of the quarterdeck ladder so that he might be clearly seen, and raised his voice so that as many as possible could hear his words.

"Rope-yarn Sunday today."

"Aye aye, sir."

"And double rum for these good men."

"Aye aye, sir."

Buckland did his best to keep the discontent out of his voice. Coming on top of the captain's previous speech this was almost too much. A rope-yarn Sunday meant that the men would spend the rest of the day in idleness. Double rum in that case most certainly meant fights and quarrels among the men. Bush, coming aft along the maindeck, was well aware of the disorder that was spreading among the crew, pampered by their captain. It was impossible to maintain discipline when every adverse report made by the officers was ignored by the captain. Bad characters and idlers were going unpunished; the willing hands were beginning to sulk, while the unruly ones were growing openly restless. "These good men," the captain had said. The men knew well enough how bad their record had been during the last week. If the captain called them "good men" after that, worse still could be expected next week. And besides all this the men most certainly knew about the captain's treatment of his lieutenants, of the brutal reprimands dealt out to them, the savage punishments. "Today's wardroom joint is tomorrow's lower-deck stew," said the proverb, meaning that whatever went on aft was soon being discussed in a garbled form forward; the men could not be expected to be obedient to officers whom they knew to be treated with contempt by the captain. Bush was worried as he mounted the quarterdeck.

The captain had gone in under the half-deck to his cabin; Buckland and Roberts were standing by the hammock nettings deep in conversation, and Bush joined them.

"These articles apply to my officers," said Buckland as he approached.

"Rope-yarn Sunday and double rum," added Roberts. "All for these good men."

Buckland shot a furtive glance round the deck before he spoke next. It was pitiful to see the first lieutenant of a ship of the line taking precautions lest what he should say should be overheard. But Hornblower and Wellard were on the other side of the wheel. On the poop the master was assembling the midshipmen's navigation class with their sextants to take their noon sights.

"He's mad," said Buckland in as low a voice as the northeast trade wind would allow.

"We all know that," said Roberts.

Bush said nothing. He was too cautious to commit himself at present.

"Clive won't lift a finger," said Buckland. "He's a ninny if there ever was one."

Clive was the surgeon.

"Have you asked him?" asked Roberts.

"I tried to. But he wouldn't say a word. He's afraid."

"Don't move from where you are standing, gentlemen," broke in a loud harsh voice; the well-remembered voice of the captain, speaking apparently from the level of the deck on which they stood. All three officers started in surprise.

"Every sign of guilt," blared the voice. "Bear witness to it, Mr. Hobbs."

They looked round them. The skylight of the captain's fore cabin was open a couple of inches, and through the gap the captain was looking at them; they could see his eyes and his nose. He was a tall man and by standing on anything low, a book or a footstool, he could look from under the skylight over the coaming. Rigid, the officers waited while another pair of eyes appeared under the skylight beside the captain's. They belonged to Hobbs, the acting-gunner.

"Wait there until I come to you, gentlemen," said the captain, with a sneer as he said the word "gentlemen". "Very good, Mr. Hobbs."

The two faces vanished from under the skylight, and the officers had hardly time to exchange despairing glances before the captain came striding up the ladder to them.

"A mutinous assembly, I believe," he said.

"No, sir," replied Buckland. Any word that was not a denial would be an admission of guilt, on a charge that could put a rope round his neck.

"Do you give me the lie on my own quarterdeck?" roared the captain. "I was right in suspecting my officers. Plotting. Whispering. Scheming. Planning. And now treating me with gross disrespect. I'll see that you regret this from this minute, Mr. Buckland."

"I intended no disrespect, sir," protested Buckland.

"You give me the lie again to my face! And you others stand by and abet him! You keep him in countenance! I thought better of you, Mr. Bush, until now."

Bush thought it wise to say nothing.

"Dumb insolence, eh?" said the captain. "Eager enough to talk when you think my eye isn't on you, all the same."

The captain glowered round the quarterdeck.

"And you, Mr. Hornblower," he said. "You did not see fit to report this assembly to me. Officer of the watch, indeed! And of course Wellard is in it too. That is only to be expected. But I fancy you will be in trouble with these gentlemen now, Mr. Wellard. You did not keep a sharp enough lookout for them. In fact you are in serious trouble now, Mr. Wellard, without a friend in the ship except for the gunner's daughter, whom you will be kissing again soon."

The captain stood towering on the quarterdeck with his gaze fixed on the unfortunate Wellard, who shrank visibly away from him. To kiss the gunner's daughter was to be bent over a gun and beaten.

"But later will still be sufficient time to deal with you, Mr. Wellard. The lieutenants first, as their lofty rank dictates."

The captain looked round at the lieutenants, fear and triumph strangely alternating in his expression.

"Mr. Hornblower is already on watch and watch," he said. "You others have enjoyed idleness in consequence, and Satan found mischief for your idle hands. Mr. Buckland does not keep a watch. The high and mighty and aspiring first lieutenant."

"Sir—" began Buckland, and then bit off the words which were about to follow. That word "aspiring" undoubtedly implied that he was scheming to gain command of the ship, but a court-martial would not read that meaning into it. Every officer was expected to be an aspiring officer and it would be no insult to say so.

"Sir!" jeered the captain. "Sir! So you have grace enough still to guard your tongue. Cunning, maybe. But you will not evade the consequences of your actions. Mr. Hornblower can stay on watch and watch. But these two gentlemen can report to you when every watch is called, and at two bells, at four bells, and at six bells in every watch. They are to be properly dressed when they report to you, and you are to be properly awake. Is that understood?"

Not one of the dumbfounded trio could speak for a moment.

"Answer me!"

"Aye aye, sir," said Buckland.

"Aye aye, sir," said Bush and Roberts as the captain turned his eyes on them.

"Let there be no slackness in the execution of my orders," said the captain. "I shall have means of knowing if I am obeyed or not."

"Aye aye, sir," said Buckland.

The captain's sentence had condemned him, Bush, and Roberts to be roused and awakened every hour, day and night.

IV

It was pitch dark down here, absolutely dark, not the tiniest glimmer of light at all. Out over the sea was the moonless night, and here it was three decks down, below the level of the sea's surface—through the oaken skin of the ship could be heard the rush of the water alongside, and the impact of the waves over which the ship rode; the fabric of the ship grumbled to itself with the alternating stresses of the pitch and the roll. Bush hung on to the steep ladder in the darkness and felt for foothold; finding it, he stepped off among the water barrels, and, crouching low, he began to make his way aft through the solid blackness. A rat squeaked and scurried past him, but rats were only to be expected down here in the hold, and Bush went on feeling his way aft unshaken. Out of the blackness before him, through the multitudinous murmurings of the ship, came a slight hiss, and Bush halted and hissed in reply. He was not self-conscious about these conspiratorial goings on. All precautions were necessary, for this was something very dangerous that he was doing.

"Bush!" whispered Buckland's voice.

"Yes."

"The others are here."

Ten minutes before, at two bells in the middle watch, Bush and Roberts had reported to Buckland in his cabin in obedience to the captain's order. A wink, a gesture, a whisper, and the appointment to meet here was made; it was an utterly fantastic state of affairs that the lieutenants of a King's ship should have to act in such a fashion for fear of spies and eavesdroppers, but it had been necessary. Then they had dispersed and by devious routes and different hatchways had made their way here. Hornblower, relieved by Smith on watch, had preceded them.

"We mustn't be here long," whispered Roberts.

Even by his whisper, even in the dark, one could guess at his nervousness. There could be no doubt about this being a mutinous assembly. They could all hang for what they were doing.

"Suppose we declare him unfit for command?" whispered Buckland. "Suppose we put him in irons?"

"We'd have to do it quick and sharp if we do it at all," whispered Hornblower. "He'll call on the hands and they might follow him. And then—"

There was no need for Hornblower to go on with that speech. Everyone who heard it formed a mental picture of corpses swaying at the yard-arms.

"Supposing we do it quick and sharp?" agreed Buckland. "Supposing we get him into irons?"

"Then we go on to Antigua," said Roberts.

"And a court-martial," said Bush, thinking as far ahead as that for the first time in this present crisis.

"Yes," whispered Buckland.

Into that flat monosyllable were packed various moods—inquiry and despair, desperation and doubt.

"That's the point," whispered Hornblower. "He'll give evidence. It'll sound different in court. We've been punished—watch and watch, no liquor. That could happen to anybody. It's no grounds for mutiny."

"But he's spoiling the hands."

"Double rum. Make and mend. I'll sound quite natural in court. It's not for us to criticize the captain's methods—so the court will think."

"But they'll see him."

"He's cunning. And he's no raving lunatic. He can talk—he can find reasons for everything. You've heard him. He'll be plausible."

"But he's held us up to contempt before the hands. He's set Hobbs to spy on us."

"That'll be a proof of how desperate his situation was, surrounded by us criminals. If we arrest him we're guilty until we've proved ourselves innocent. Any court's bound to be on the captain's side. Mutiny means hanging."

Hornblower was putting into words all the doubts that Bush felt in his bones and yet had been unable to express.

"That's right," whispered Bush.

"What about Wellard?" whispered Roberts. "Did you hear him scream the last time?"

"He's only a volunteer. Not even a midshipman. No friends. No family. What's the court going to say when they hear the captain had a boy beaten half a dozen times? They'll laugh. So would we if we didn't know. Do him good, we'd say, the same as it did the rest of us good."

A silence followed this statement of the obvious, broken in the end by Buckland whispering a succession of filthy oaths that could give small vent to his despair.

"He'll bring charges against us," whispered Roberts. "The minute we're in company with other ships. I know he will."

"Twenty-two years I've held my commission," said Buckland. "Now he'll break me. He'll break you as well."

There would be no chance at all for officers charged before a court-martial by their captain with behaving with contempt towards him in a manner subversive of discipline. Every single one of them knew that. It gave an edge to their despair. Charges pressed by the captain with the insane venom and cunning he had displayed up to now might not even end in dismissal from the service—they might lead to the prison and the rope.

"Ten more days before we make Antigua," said Roberts. "If this wind holds fair—and it will."

"But we don't know we're destined for Antigua," said Hornblower. "That's only our guess. It might be weeks—it might be months."

"God help us!" said Buckland.

A slight clatter farther aft along the hold—a noise different from the noises of the working of the ship—made them all start. Bush clenched his hairy fists. But they were reassured by a voice calling softly to them.

"Mr. Buckland—Mr. Hornblower—sir!"

"Wellard, by God!" said Roberts.

They could hear Wellard scrambling towards them.

"The captain, sir!" said Wellard. "He's coming!"

"Holy God!"

"Which way?" snapped Hornblower.

"By the steerage hatchway. I got to the cockpit and came down from there. He was sending Hobbs—"

"Get for'ard, you three," said Hornblower, cutting into the explanation. "Get for'ard and scatter when you're on deck. Quick!"

Nobody stopped to think that Hornblower was giving orders to officers immensely his senior. Every instant of time was of vital importance, and not to be wasted in indecision, or in silly blasphemy. That was apparent as soon as he spoke. Bush turned with the others and plunged forward in the darkness, barking his shins painfully as he fell over unseen obstructions. Bush heard Hornblower say "Come along, Wellard," as he parted from them in his mad flight with the others beside him.

The cable tier—the ladder—and then the extraordinary safety of the lower gundeck. After the utter blackness of the hold there was enough light here for him to see fairly distinctly. Buckland and Roberts continued to ascend to the maindeck; Bush turned to make his way aft. The watch below had been in their hammocks long enough to be sound asleep; here to the noises of the ship was added the blended snoring of the sleepers as the close-hung rows of hammocks swayed with the motion of the ship in such a coincidence of timing as to appear like solid masses. Far down between the rows a light was approaching. It was a horn lantern with a lighted purser's dip inside it, and Hobbs, the acting-gunner, was carrying it, and two seamen were following him as he hurried along. There was an exchange of glances as Bush met the party. A momentary hesitation on Hobbs' part betrayed the fact that he would have greatly liked to ask Bush what he was doing on the lower gundeck, but that was something no acting-warrant officer, even with the captain's favour behind him, could ask of a lieutenant. And there was annoyance in Hobbs' expression, too; obviously he was hurrying to secure all the exits from the hold, and was exasperated that Bush had escaped him. The seamen wore expressions of simple bewilderment at these goings on in the middle watch. Hobbs stood aside to let his superior pass, and Bush strode past him with no more than that one glance. It was extraordinary how much more confident he felt now that he was safely out of the hold and disassociated from any mutinous assembly. He decided to head for his cabin; it would not be long before four bells when by the captain's orders he had to report again to Buckland. The messenger sent by the officer of the watch to rouse him would find him lying on his cot. But as Bush went on and had progressed as far as the mainmast he arrived in the midst of a scene of bustle which he would most certainly have taken notice of if he had been innocent and which consequently he must (so he told himself) ask about now that he had seen it—he could not possibly walk by without a question or two. This was where the marines were berthed, and they were all of them out of their hammocks hastily equipping themselves —those who had their shirts and trousers on were putting on their cross-belts ready for action.

"What's all this?" demanded Bush, trying to make his voice sound as it would have sounded if he had no knowledge of anything irregular happening in the ship except this.

"Dunno, sir," said the private he addressed. "We was just told to turn out—muskets an' side arms and ball cartridge, sir."

A sergeant of marines looked out through the screen which divided the non-commissioned officers' bay from the rest of the deck.

"Captain's orders, sir," he said; and then with a roar at the men. "Come on! Slap it about, there!"

"Where's the captain, then?" asked Bush with all the innocence he could muster.

"Aft some'eres, sir. 'E sent for the corpril's guard same time as we was told to turn out."

Four marine privates and a corporal supplied the sentry who stood day and night outside the captain's cabin. A single order was all that was needed to turn out the guard and provide the captain with at least a nucleus of armed and disciplined men ready for action.

"Very well, Sergeant," said Bush, and he tried to look puzzled and to hurry naturally aft to find out what was going on. But he knew what fear was. He felt he would do anything rather than continue this walk to encounter whatever was awaiting him at the end of it. Whiting, the captain of marines, made his appearance, sleepy and unshaven, belting on his sword over his shirt.

"What in hell—?" he began, as he saw Bush.

"Don't ask *me*!" said Bush, striving after that natural appearance. So tense and desperate was he at that moment that his normally quiescent imagination was hard at work. He could imagine the prosecutor in the deceptive calm of a court-martial saying to Whiting, "Did Mr. Bush appear to be his usual self?" and it was frightfully necessary that Whiting should be able to answer, "Yes." Bush could even imagine the hairy touch of a rope round his neck. But next moment there was no more need for him to simulate surprise or ignorance. His reactions were genuine.

"Pass the word for the doctor," came the cry. "Pass the word, there." And here came Wellard, white-faced, hurrying.

"Pass the word for the doctor. Call Dr. Clive."

"Who's hurt, Wellard?" asked Bush.

"The c-captain, sir."

Wellard looked distraught and shaken, but now Hornblower made his appearance behind him. Hornblower was pale too, and breathing hard, but he seemed to have command of himself. The glance which he threw round him in the dim light of the lanterns passed over Bush without apparent recognition.

"Get Dr. Clive!" he snapped at one midshipman peering out from the midshipmen's berth; and then to another, "You, there. Run for the first lieutenant. Ask him to come below here. Run!"

Hornblower's glance took in Whiting and travelled forward to where the marines were snatching their muskets from the racks.

"Why are your men turning out, Captain Whiting?"

"Captain's orders."

"Then you can form them up. But I do not believe there is any emergency."

Only then did Hornblower's glance comprehend Bush.

"Oh, Mr. Bush. Will you take charge, sir, now that you're here? I've sent for the first lieutenant. The captain's hurt—badly hurt, I'm afraid, sir."

"But what's happened?" asked Bush.

"The captain's fallen down the hatchway, sir," said Hornblower.

In the dim light Hornblower's eyes stared straight into Bush's, but Bush could read no message in them. This after part of the lower gun-deck was crowded now, and Hornblower's definite statement, the first that had been made, raised a buzz of excitement. It was the sort of un-disciplined noise that most easily roused Bush's wrath, and, perhaps fortunately, it brought a natural reaction from him.

"Silence, there!" he roared. "Get about your business."

When Bush glowered round at the excited crowd it fell silent.

"With your permission I'll go below again, sir," said Hornblower. "I must see after the captain."

"Very well, Mr. Hornblower," said Bush; the stereotyped phrase had been uttered so often before that it escaped sounding stilted.

"Come with me, Mr. Wellard," said Hornblower, and turned away.

Several new arrivals made their appearance as he did so—Buckland, his face white and strained, Roberts at his shoulder, Clive in his shirt and trousers walking sleepily from his cabin. All of them started a little at the sight of the marines forming line on the cumbered deck, their musket barrels glinting in the feeble light of the lanterns.

"Would you come at once, sir?" asked Hornblower, turning back at sight of Buckland.

"I'll come," said Buckland.

"What in the name of God is going on?" asked Clive.

"The captain's hurt," said Hornblower curtly. "Come at once. You'll need a light."

"The captain?" Clive blinked himself wider awake. "Where is he?

Give me that lantern, you. Where are my mates? You, there, run and rouse my mates. They sling their hammocks in the sick bay."

So it was a procession of half a dozen that carried their lanterns down the ladder—the four lieutenants, Clive, and Wellard. While waiting at the head of the ladder Bush stole a side glance at Buckland; his face was working with anxiety. He would infinitely rather have been walking a shot-torn deck with grape flying round him. He rolled an inquiring eye at Bush, but with Clive within earshot Bush dared say no word—he knew no more than Buckland did, for that matter. There was no knowing what was awaiting them at the foot of the ladder— arrest, ruin, disgrace, perhaps death.

The faint light of a lantern revealed the scarlet tunic and white cross-belts of a marine, standing by the hatchway. He wore the chevrons of a corporal.

"Anything to report?" demanded Hornblower.

"No, sir. Nothink, sir."

"Captain's down there unconscious. There are two marines guarding him," said Hornblower to Clive, pointing down the hatchway, and Clive swung his bulk painfully onto the ladder and descended.

"Now, Corporal," said Hornblower, "tell the first lieutenant all you know about this."

The corporal stood stiffly at attention. With no fewer than four lieutenants eyeing him he was nervous, and he probably had a gloomy feeling based on his experience of the service that when there was trouble among the higher ranks it was likely to go ill with a mere corporal who was unfortunate enough to be involved, however innocently. He stood rigid, trying not to meet anybody's eye.

"Speak up, man," said Buckland, testily. He was nervous as well, but that was understandable in a first lieutenant whose captain had just met with a serious accident.

"I was corporal of the guard, sir. At two bells I relieved the sentry at the captain's door."

"Yes?"

"An'—an'—then I went to sleep again."

"Damn it," said Roberts. "Make your report."

"I was woke up, sir," went on the corporal, "by one of the gennel-men. Gunner, I think 'e is."

"Mr. Hobbs?"

"That may be 'is name, sir. 'E said, 'Cap'n's orders, and guard turn out.' So I turns out the guard, sir, an' there's the cap'n with Wade, the sentry I'd posted. 'E 'ad pistols in 'is 'ands, sir."

"Who—Wade?"

"No, sir, the cap'n, sir."

"What was his manner like?" demanded Hornblower.

"Well, sir—" the corporal did not want to offer any criticism of a captain, not even to a lieutenant.

"Belay that, then. Carry on."

"Cap'n says, sir, 'e says 'e says, sir, 'Follow me'; an' then 'e says to the gennelman 'e says, 'Do your duty, Mr. Hobbs.' So Mr. Hobbs, 'e goes one way, sir, an' we comes with the captain down 'ere, sir. 'There's mutiny brewing' says the cap'n, 'black bloody mutiny. We've got to catch the mutineers. Catch 'em red 'anded' says the cap'n."

The surgeon's head appeared in the hatchway.

"Give me another of those lanterns," he said.

"How's the captain?" demanded Buckland.

"Concussion and some fractures, I would say."

"Badly hurt?"

"No knowing yet. Where are my mates? Ah, there you are, Coleman. Splints and bandages, man, as quick as you can get 'em. And a carrying-plank and a canvas and lines. Run, man! You, Pierce, come on down and help me."

So the two surgeon's mates had hardly made their appearance than they were hurried away.

"Carry on, Corporal," said Buckland.

"I dunno what I said, sir."

"The captain brought you down here."

"Yessir. 'E 'ad 'is pistols in 'is 'ands, sir, like I said, sir. 'E sent one file for'ard 'Stop every bolt'ole' 'e says; an' 'e says, 'You, Corporal, take these two men down an' search.' 'E—'e was yellin', like. 'E 'ad 'is pistols in 'is 'ands."

The corporal looked anxiously at Buckland as he spoke.

"That's all right, Corporal," said Buckland. "Just tell the truth."

The knowledge that the captain was unconscious and perhaps badly hurt had reassured him, just as it had reassured Bush.

"So I took the other file down the ladder, sir," said the corporal. "I went first with the lantern, seein' as 'ow I didn't 'ave no musket with me. We got down to the foot of the ladder in among those cases down there, sir. The cap'n, 'e was yellin' down the hatchway. ''Urry,' he says. ''Urry. Don't let 'em escape. 'Urry.' So we started climbin' for'ard over the stores, sir."

The corporal hesitated as he approached the climax of his story. He might possibly have been seeking a crude dramatic effect, but more likely he was still afraid of being entangled in circumstances that might damage him despite his innocence.

"What happened then?" demanded Buckland.

"Well, sir—"

Coleman reappeared at this moment, encumbered with various gear including a light six-foot plank he had been carrying on his shoulder.

He looked to Buckland for permission to carry on, received a nod, laid the plank on the deck along with the canvas and lines, and disappeared with the rest down the ladder.

"Well?" said Buckland to the corporal.

"I dunno what 'appened, sir."

"Tell us what you know."

"I 'eard a yell, sir. An' a crash. I 'adn't 'ardly gone ten yards, sir. So I came back with the lantern."

"What did you find?"

"It was the cap'n, sir. Layin' there at the foot of the ladder. Like 'e was dead, sir. 'E'd fallen down the 'atchway, sir."

"What did you do?"

"I tried to turn 'im over, sir. 'Is face was all bloody-like. 'E was stunned, sir. I thought 'e might be dead but I could feel 'is 'eart."

"Yes?"

"I didn't know what I ought to do, sir. I didn't know nothink about this 'ere meeting, sir."

"But what *did* you do, in the end?"

"I left my two men with the cap'n, sir, an' I come up to give the alarm. I didn't know who to trust, sir."

There was irony in this situation—the corporal frightened lest he should be taken to task about a petty question as to whether he should have sent a messenger or come himself, while the four lieutenants eyeing him were in danger of hanging.

"Well?"

"I saw Mr. Hornblower, sir." The relief in the corporal's voice echoed the relief he must have felt at finding someone to take over his enormous responsibility. " 'E was with young Mr. Wellard, I think 'is name is. Mr. Hornblower, 'e told me to stand guard 'ere, sir, after I told 'im about the cap'n."

"It sounds as if you did right, Corporal," said Buckland, judicially.

"Thank 'ee, sir. Thank 'ee, sir."

Coleman came climbing up the ladder, and with another glance at Buckland for permission passed the gear he had left down to someone else under the hatchway. Then he descended again. Bush was looking at the corporal who, now his tale was told, was self-consciously awkward again under the concentrated gaze of four lieutenants.

"Now, Corporal," said Hornblower, speaking unexpectedly and with deliberation. "You have no idea how the captain came to fall down the hatchway?"

"No, sir. Indeed I haven't, sir."

Hornblower shot one single glance at his colleagues, one and no more. The corporal's words and Hornblower's glance were vastly reassuring.

"He was excited, you say? Come on, man, speak up."

"Well, yessir." The corporal remembered his earlier unguarded statement, and then in a sudden flood of loquacity he went on. " 'E was yellin' after us down the hatchway, sir. I expect 'e was leanin' over. 'E must 'ave been leanin' when the ship pitched, sir. 'E could catch 'is foot on the coamin' and fall 'ead first, sir."

"That's what must have happened," said Hornblower.

Clive came climbing up the ladder and stepped stiffly over the coaming.

"I'm going to sway him up now," he said. He looked at the four lieutenants and then put his hand in the bosom of his shirt and took out a pistol. "This was lying at the captain's side."

"I'll take charge of that," said Buckland.

"There ought to be another one down there, judging by what we've just heard," said Roberts, speaking for the first time. He spoke overloudly, too; excitement had worked on him, and his manner might appear suspicious to anyone with anything to suspect. Bush felt a twinge of annoyance and fear.

"I'll have 'em look for it after we've got the captain up," said Clive. He leaned over the hatchway and called down, "Come on up."

Coleman appeared first, climbing the ladder with a pair of lines in his hand, and after him a marine, clinging awkwardly to the ladder with one arm while the other supported a burden below him.

"Handsomely, handsomely, now," said Clive.

Coleman and the marine, emerging, drew the end of the plank up after them; swathed mummy-like in the canvas and bound to the plank was the body of the captain. That was the best way in which to mount ladders carrying a man with broken bones. Pierce, the other surgeon's mate, came climbing up next, holding the foot of the plank steady. The lieutenants clustered round to give a hand as the plank was hoisted over the coaming. In the light of the lanterns Bush could see the captain's face above the canvas. It was still and expressionless, what there was to be seen of it, for a white bandage concealed one eye and the nose. One temple was still stained with the traces of blood which the doctor had not entirely wiped away.

"Take him to his cabin," said Buckland.

That was the definite order. This was an important moment. The captain being incapacitated, it was the first lieutenant's duty to take command, and those five words indicated that he had done so. In command, he could even give orders for dealing with the captain. But although this was a momentous step, it was one of routine; Buckland had assumed temporary command of the ship, during the captain's absences, a score of times before. Routine had carried him through this present crisis; the habits of thirty years of service in the navy, as midshipman and lieutenant, had enabled him to carry himself with his usual bearing towards his juniors, to act normally even though he did not know what dreadful fate awaited him at any moment in the immediate future.

And yet Bush, turning his eyes on him now that he had assumed command, was not too sure about the permanence of the effect of habit. Buckland was clearly a little shaken. That might be attributed to the natural reaction of an officer with responsibility thrust upon him in such startling circumstances. So an unsuspicious person—someone without knowledge of the hidden facts—might conclude. But Bush, with fear in his heart, wondering and despairing about what the captain would do when he recovered consciousness, could see that Buckland shared his fear. Chains—a court-martial—the hangman's rope; thoughts of these were unmanning Buckland. And the lives, certainly the whole futures, of the officers in the ship might depend on Buckland's actions.

"Pardon, sir," said Hornblower.

"Yes?" said Buckland; and then with an effort, "Yes, Mr. Hornblower?"

"Might I take the corporal's statement in writing now, while the facts are clear in his memory?"

"Very good, Mr. Hornblower."

"Thank you, sir," said Hornblower. There was nothing to be read in his expression at all, nothing except a respectful attention to duty. He turned to the corporal. "Report to me in my berth after you have reposted the sentry."

"Yessir."

The doctor and his party had already carried the captain away. Buckland was making no effort to move from the spot. It was as if he was paralysed.

"There's the matter of the captain's other pistol, sir," said Hornblower, respectfully as ever.

"Oh yes." Buckland looked round him.

"Here's Wellard, sir."

"Oh yes. He'll do."

"Mr. Wellard," said Hornblower, "go down with a lantern and see if you can find the other pistol. Bring it to the first lieutenant on the quarterdeck."

"Aye aye, sir."

Wellard had recovered from most of his agitation; he had not taken his eyes from Hornblower for some time. Now he picked up the lantern and went down the ladder with it. What Hornblower had said about the quarterdeck penetrated into Buckland's mind, and he began to move off with the others following him. On the lower gundeck Captain Whiting saluted him.

"Any orders, sir?"

No doubt the word that the captain was incapacitated and that Buckland was in command had sped through the ship like wildfire. It took Buckland's numbed brain a second or two to function.

"No, captain," he said at length; and then, "Dismiss your men."

When they reached the quarterdeck the trade wind was still blowing briskly from over the starboard quarter, and the *Renown* was soaring along over the magic sea. Over their heads the great pyramids of sails were reaching up—up—up towards the uncounted stars; with the easy motion of the ship the mastheads were sweeping out great circles against the sky. On the port quarter a half-moon had just lifted itself out of the sea and hung, miraculously, above the horizon, sending a long glittering trail of silver towards the ship. The dark figures of the men on deck stood out plainly against the whitened planks.

Smith was officer of the watch. He came eagerly up to them as they came up the companionway. For the last hour and more he had been pacing about in a fever, hearing the noise and bustle down below, hearing the rumours which had coursed through the ship, and yet unable to leave his post to find out what was really going on.

"What's happened, sir?" he asked.

Smith had not been in the secret of the meeting of the other lieutenants. He had been less victimized by the captain, too. But he could not help being aware of the prevailing discontent; he must know that the captain was insane. Yet Buckland was not prepared for this question. He had not thought about it and had no particular reply. In the end it was Hornblower who answered.

"The captain fell down the hold," he said; his tone was even and with no particular stress. "They've just carried him to his cabin unconscious."

"But how in God's name did he come to fall down the hold?" asked the bewildered Smith.

"He was looking for mutineers," said Hornblower, in that same even tone.

"I see," said Smith. "But—"

There he checked himself. That even tone of Hornblower's had warned him that this was a delicate subject; if he pursued it the question of the captain's sanity would arise, and he would be committed to an opinion on it. He did not want to ask any more questions in that case.

"Six bells, sir," reported the quartermaster to him.

"Very good," said Smith, automatically.

"I must take the marine corporal's deposition, sir," said Hornblower. "I come on watch at eight bells."

If Buckland were in command he could put an end to the ridiculous order that Hornblower should stand watch and watch, and that Bush and Roberts should report to him hourly. There was a moment's awkward pause. No one knew how long the captain would remain unconscious, nor in what condition he would regain consciousness. Wellard came running up to the quarterdeck.

"Here's the other pistol, sir," he said, handing it to Buckland, who took it, at the same time drawing its fellow from his pocket; he stood rather helplessly with them in his hands.

"Shall I relieve you of those, sir?" asked Hornblower, taking them. "And Wellard might be of help to me with the marine's deposition. Can I take him with me, sir?"

"Yes," said Buckland.

Hornblower turned to go below, followed by Wellard.

"Oh, Mr. Hornblower—" said Buckland.

"Sir?"

"Nothing," said Buckland, the inflection in his voice revealing the indecision under which he laboured.

"Pardon, sir, but I should take some rest if I were you," said Hornblower, standing at the head of the companionway. "You've had a tiring night."

Bush was in agreement with Hornblower; not that he cared at all whether Buckland had had a tiring night or not, but because if Buckland were to retire to his cabin there would be no chance of his betraying himself—and his associates—by an unguarded speech. Then it dawned upon Bush that this was just what Hornblower had in mind. And at the same time he was aware of regret at Hornblower's leaving them, and knew that Buckland felt the same regret. Hornblower was level-headed, thinking fast whatever danger menaced him. It was his example which had given a natural appearance to the behaviour of all of them since the alarm down below. Perhaps Hornblower had a secret unshared with them; perhaps he knew more than they did about how the captain came to fall down the hold—Bush was puzzled and anxious about that—but if such was the case Hornblower had given no sign of it.

"When in God's name is that damned doctor going to report?" said Buckland, to no one in particular.

"Why don't you turn in, sir, until he does?" said Bush.

"I will." Buckland hesitated before he went on speaking. "You gentlemen had best continue to report to me every hour as the captain ordered."

"Aye aye, sir," said Bush and Roberts.

That meant, as Bush realized, that Buckland would take no chances; the captain must hear, when he should recover consciousness, that his orders had been carried out. Bush was anxious—desperate—as he went below to try to snatch half an hour's rest before he would next have to report. He could not hope to sleep. Through the slight partition that divided his cabin from the next he could hear a drone of voices as Hornblower took down the marine corporal's statement in writing.

V

Breakfast was being served in the wardroom. It was a more silent and less cheerful meal even than breakfast there usually was. The master, the purser, the captain of marines, had said their conventional "good mornings" and had sat down to eat without further conversation. They had heard—as had everyone in the ship—that the captain was recovering consciousness.

Through the scuttles in the side of the ship came two long shafts of sunlight, illuminating the crowded little place, and swinging back and forward across the wardroom with the easy motion of the ship; the fresh, delightful air of the northeast trades came in through the hooked-open door. The coffee was hot; the biscuit, only three weeks on board, could not have been more than a month or two in store before that, because it had hardly any weevils in it. The wardroom cook had intelligently taken advantage of the good weather to fry the remains of last night's salt pork with some of the ship's dwindling store of onions. A breakfast of fried slivers of salt pork with onions, hot coffee and good biscuit, fresh air and sunshine and fair weather; the wardroom should have been a cheerful place. Instead there was brooding anxiety, apprehension, tense uneasiness. Bush looked across the table at Hornblower, drawn and pale and weary; there were many things Bush wanted to say to him but they had to remain unsaid, at least at present, while the shadow of the captain's madness darkened the sunlit ship.

Buckland came walking into the wardroom with the surgeon following him, and everyone looked up questioningly—practically everyone stood up to hear the news.

"He's conscious," said Buckland, and looked round at Clive for him to elaborate on that statement.

"Weak," said Clive.

Bush looked round at Hornblower hoping that he would ask the questions that Bush wanted asked. Hornblower's face was set in a mask without expression. His glance was fixed penetratingly on Clive, but he did not open his mouth. It was Lomax, the purser, who asked the question in the end.

"Is he sensible?"

"Well—" said Clive, glancing sidelong at Buckland. Clearly the last thing Clive wanted to do was to commit himself definitely regarding the captain's sanity. "He's too weak at present to be sensible."

Lomax fortunately was inquisitive enough and bull-headed enough not to be deterred by Clive's reluctance.

"What about this concussion?" he asked. "What's it done to him?"

"The skull is intact," said Clive. "There are extensive scalp lacerations. The nose is broken. The clavicle—that's the collar-bone—and a couple of ribs. He must have fallen headfirst down the hatchway, as might be expected if he tripped over the coaming."

"But how on earth did he come to do that?" asked Lomax.

"He has not said," answered Clive. "I think he does not remember."

"What?"

"That is a usual state of affairs," said Clive. "One might almost call it symptomatic. After a severe concussion the patient usually displays a lapse of memory, extending back to many hours before the injury."

Bush stole a glance at Hornblower again. His face was still expressionless, and Bush tried to follow his example, both in betraying no emotion and in leaving the questioning to others. And yet this was great, glorious, magnificent news which could not be too much elaborated on for Bush's taste.

"Where does he think he is?" went on Lomax.

"Oh, he knows he's in this ship," said Clive, cautiously.

Now Buckland turned upon Clive; Buckland was hollow-cheeked, unshaven, weary, but he had seen the captain in his berth, and he was in consequence a little more ready to force the issue.

"In your opinion is the captain fit for duty?" he demanded.

"Well—" said Clive again.

"Well?"

"Temporarily, perhaps not."

That was an unsatisfactory answer, but Buckland seemed to have exhausted all his resolution in extracting it. Hornblower raised a masklike face and stared straight at Clive.

"You mean he is incapable at present of commanding this ship?"

The other officers murmured their concurrence in this demand for a quite definite statement, and Clive, looking round at the determined faces, had to yield.

"At present, yes."

"Then we all know where we stand," said Lomax, and there was satisfaction in his voice which was echoed by everyone in the wardroom except Clive and Buckland.

To deprive a captain of his command was a business of terrible, desperate importance. King and Parliament had combined to give Captain Sawyer command of the *Renown*, and to reverse their appointment savoured of treason, and anyone even remotely connected with the transaction might be tainted for the rest of his life with the unsavoury odour of insubordination and rebellion. Even the most junior master's mate in later years applying for some new appointment might be remembered as having been in the *Renown* when Sawyer was removed from his command and might have his application refused in consequence. It was necessary that there should be the appearance of the utmost legality in an affair which, under the strictest interpretation, could never be entirely legal.

"I have here Corporal Greenwood's statement, sir," said Hornblower, "signed with his mark and attested by Mr. Wellard and myself."

"Thank you," said Buckland, taking the paper; there was some slight hesitation in Buckland's gesture as though the document were a firecracker likely to go off unexpectedly. But only Bush, who was looking for it, could have noticed the hesitation. It was only a few hours since Buckland had been a fugitive in peril of his life, creeping through the bowels of the ship trying to avoid detection, and the names of Wellard and Greenwood, reminding him of this, were a shock to his ears. And like a demon conjured up by the saying of his name, Wellard appeared at that moment at the wardroom door.

"Mr. Roberts sent me down to ask for orders, sir," he said.

Roberts had the watch, and must be fretting with worry about what was going on below decks. Buckland stood in indecision.

"Both watches are on deck, sir," said Hornblower, deferentially.

Buckland looked an inquiry at him.

"You could tell this news to the hands, sir," went on Hornblower.

He was making a suggestion, unasked, to his superior officer, and so courting a snub. But his manner indicated the deepest respect, and nothing besides but eagerness to save his superior all possible trouble.

"Thank you," said Buckland.

Anyone could read in his face the struggle that was going on within him; he was still shrinking from committing himself too deeply—as if he was not already committed!—and he was shrinking from the prospect of making a speech to the assembled hands, even while he realized the necessity of doing so. And the necessity grew greater the more he thought about it—rumours must be flying about the lower deck, where the crew, already unsettled by the captain's behaviour, must be growing more restive still in the prevailing uncertainty. A hard, definite statement must be made to them; it was vitally necessary. Yet the greater the necessity the greater the responsibility that Buckland bore, and he wavered obviously between these two frightening forces.

"All hands, sir?" prompted Hornblower, very softly.

"Yes," said Buckland, desperately taking the plunge.

"Very well, Mr. Wellard," said Hornblower.

Bush caught the look that Hornblower threw to Wellard with the words. There was a significance in it which might be interpreted as of a nature only to be expected when one junior officer was telling another to do something quickly before a senior could change his mind—that was how an uninitiated person would naturally interpret it—but to Bush, clairvoyant with fatigue and worry, there was some other significance in that glance. Wellard was pale and weak with fatigue and worry too; he was being reassured. Possibly he was being told that a secret was still safe.

"Aye aye, sir," said Wellard, and departed.

The pipes twittered through the ship.

"All hands! All hands!" roared the bosun's mates. "All hands fall in abaft the mainmast! All hands!"

Buckland went nervously up on deck, but he acquitted himself well enough at the moment of trial. In a harsh expressionless voice he told the assembled hands that the accident to the captain, which they all must have heard about, had rendered him incapable at present of continuing in command.

"But we'll all go on doing our duty," said Buckland, staring down at the level plain of upturned faces.

Bush, looking with him, picked out the grey head and paunchy figure of Hobbs, the acting-gunner, the captain's toady and informer. Things would be different for Mr. Hobbs in future—at least as long as the captain's disability endured. That was the point; as long as the captain's disability endured. Bush looked down at Hobbs and wondered how much he knew, how much he guessed—how much he would swear to at a court-martial. He tried to read the future in the fat old man's face, but his clairvoyance failed him. He could guess nothing.

When the hands were dismissed there was a moment of bustle and confusion, as the watches resumed their duties and the idlers streamed off below. It was there, in the noise and confusion of a crowd, that momentary privacy and freedom from observation could best be found. Bush intercepted Hornblower by the mizzen-mast bitts and could ask the question that he had been wanting to ask for hours; the question on which so much depended.

"How did it happen?" asked Bush.

The bosun's mates were bellowing orders; the hands were scurrying hither and thither; all round the two of them was orderly confusion, a mass of people intent on their own business, while they stood face to face, isolated, with the beneficent sunshine streaming down on them, lighting up the set face which Hornblower turned towards his questioner.

"How did *what* happen, Mr. Bush?" said Hornblower.

"How did the captain fall down the hatchway?"

As soon as he had said the words Bush glanced back over his shoulder in sudden fright lest he should have been overheard. These might be hanging words. When he looked back Hornblower's face was quite expressionless.

"I think he must have overbalanced," he said, evenly, looking straight into Bush's eyes; and then he went on. "If you will excuse me, sir, I have some duties to attend to."

Later in the day every wardroom officer was introduced in turn to the captain's cabin to see with his own eyes what sort of wreck lay there. Bush saw only a feeble invalid, lying in the half-light of the cabin, the face almost covered with bandages, the fingers of one hand moving minutely, the other hand concealed in a sling.

"He's under an opiate," explained Clive in the wardroom. "I had to administer a heavy dose to enable me to try and set the fractured nose."

"I expect it was spread all over his face," said Lomax brutally. "It was big enough."

"The fracture was very extensive and comminuted," agreed Clive.

There were screams the next morning from the captain's cabin, screams of terror as well as of pain, and Clive and his mates emerged eventually sweating and worried. Clive went instantly to report confidentially to Buckland, but everyone in the ship had heard those screams or had been told about them by men who had; the surgeon's mates, questioned eagerly in the gunroom by the other warrant officers, could not maintain the monumental discretion that Clive aimed at in the wardroom. The wretched invalid was undoubtedly insane; he had fallen into a paroxysm of terror when they had attempted to examine the fractured nose, flinging himself about with a madman's strength so that, fearing damage to the other broken bones, they had had to swathe him in canvas as in a strait-jacket, leaving only his left arm out. Laudanum and an extensive bleeding had reduced him to insensibility in the end, but later in the day when Bush saw him he was conscious again, a weeping, pitiful object, shrinking in fear from every face that he saw, persecuted by shadows, sobbing—it was a dreadful thing to see that burly man sobbing like a child—over his troubles, and trying to hide his face from a world which to his tortured mind held no friendship at all and only grim enmity.

"It frequently happens," said Clive pontifically—the longer the captain's illness lasted the more freely he would discuss it—"that an injury, a fall, or a burn, or a fracture, will completely unbalance a mind that previously was a little unstable."

"A little unstable!" said Lomax. "Did he turn out the marines in the middle watch to hunt for mutineers in the hold? Ask Mr. Hornblower here, ask Mr. Bush, if they thought he was a little unstable. He had Hornblower doing watch and watch, and Bush and Roberts and Buckland himself out of bed every hour day and night. He was as mad as a hatter even then."

It was extraordinary how freely tongues wagged now in the ship, now that there was no fear of reports being made to the captain.

"At least we can make seamen out of the crew now," said Carberry, the master, with a satisfaction in his voice that was echoed round the wardroom. Sail drill and gun drill, tautened discipline and hard work, were pulling together a crew that had fast been disintegrating. It was what Buckland obviously delighted in, what he had been itching to do from the moment they had left the Eddystone behind, and exercising the crew helped to lift his mind out of the other troubles that beset it.

For now there was a new responsibility, that all the wardroom discussed freely in Buckland's absence—Buckland was already fenced in by the solitude that surrounds the captain of a ship of war. This was Buckland's sole responsibility, and the wardroom could watch Buckland wrestling with it, as they would watch a prizefighter in the ring; there even were bets laid on the result, as to whether or not Buckland would take the final plunge, whether or not he would take the ultimate step that would proclaim himself as in command of the *Renown* and the captain as incurable.

Locked in the captain's desk were the captain's papers, and among those papers were the secret orders addressed to him by the Lords of the Admiralty. No other eyes than the captain's had seen those orders as yet; not a soul in the ship could make any guess at their contents. They might be merely routine orders, directing the *Renown* perhaps to join Admiral Bickerton's squadron; but also they might reveal some vital diplomatic secret of the kind that no mere lieutenant could be entrusted with. On the one hand Buckland could continue to head for Antigua, and there he could turn over his responsibilities to whoever was the senior officer. There might be some junior captain who could be transferred to the *Renown*; to read the orders and carry off the ship on whatever mission was allotted her. On the other hand Buckland could read the orders now; they might deal with some matter of the greatest urgency. Antigua was a convenient landfall for ships to make from England, but from a military point of view it was not so desirable, being considerably to leeward of most of the points of strategic importance.

If Buckland took the ship down to Antigua and then she had to beat back to windward he might be sharply rapped on the knuckles by My Lords of the Admiralty; yet if he read the secret orders on that account he might be reprimanded for his presumption. The wardroom could guess at his predicament and each individual officer could congratulate himself upon not being personally involved while wondering what Buckland would do about it.

Bush and Hornblower stood side by side on the poop, feet wide apart on the heaving deck, as they steadied themselves and looked through their sextants at the horizon. Through the darkened glass Bush could see the image of the sun reflected from the mirror. With infinite pains he moved the arm round, bringing the image down closer and closer to the horizon. The pitch of the ship over the long blue rollers troubled him, but he persevered, decided in the end that the image of the sun was just sitting on the horizon, and clamped the sextant. Then he could read and record the measurement. As a concession to new-fangled prejudices, he decided to follow Hornblower's example and observe the altitude also from the opposite point of the horizon. He swung round and did so, and as he recorded his reading he tried to remember what he had to do about half the difference between the two readings. And the index error, and the "dip". He looked round to find that Hornblower had already finished his observation and was standing waiting for him.

"That's the greatest altitude I've ever measured," remarked Hornblower. "I've never been as far south as this before. What's your result?"

They compared readings.

"That's accurate enough," said Hornblower. "What's the difficulty?"

"Oh, I can shoot the sun," said Bush. "No trouble about that. It's the calculations that bother me—those damned corrections."

Hornblower raised an eyebrow for a moment. He was accustomed to taking his own observations each noon and making his own calculations of the ship's position, in order to keep himself in practice. He was aware of the mechanical difficulty of taking an accurate observation in a moving ship, but—although he knew of plenty of other instances—he still could not believe that any man could really find the subsequent mathematics difficult. They were so simple to him that when Bush had asked him if he could join him in their noontime exercise for the sake of improving himself he had taken it for granted that it was only the mechanics of using a sextant that troubled Bush. But he politely concealed his surprise.

"They're easy enough," he said, and then he added "sir." A wise officer, too, did not make too much display of his superior ability when speaking to his senior. He phrased his next speech carefully.

"If you were to come below with me, sir, you could check through my calculations."

Bush listened in patience to Hornblower's explanations. They made the problem perfectly clear for the moment—it was by a hurried last-minute reading up that Bush had been able to pass his examination for lieutenant, although it was seamanship and not navigation that got him through—but Bush knew by bitter experience that tomorrow it would be hazy again.

"Now we can plot the position," said Hornblower, bending over the chart.

Bush watched as Hornblower's capable fingers worked the parallel rulers across the chart; Hornblower had long bony hands with something of beauty about them, and it was actually fascinating to watch them doing work at which they were so supremely competent. The powerful fingers picked up the pencil and ruled a line.

"There's the point of interception," said Hornblower. "Now we can check against the dead reckoning."

Even Bush could follow the simple steps necessary to plot the ship's course by dead reckoning since noon yesterday. The pencil in the steady fingers made a tiny x on the chart.

"We're still being set to the s'uth'ard, you see," said Hornblower. "We're not far enough east yet for the Gulf Stream to set us to the nor'ard."

"Didn't you say you'd never navigated these waters before?" asked Bush.

"Yes."

"Then how—? Oh, I suppose you've been studying."

To Bush it was as strange that a man should read up beforehand and be prepared for conditions hitherto unknown as it was strange to Hornblower that a man should find trouble in mathematics.

"At any rate, there we are," said Hornblower, tapping the chart with the pencil.

"Yes," said Bush.

They both looked at the chart with the same thought in mind.

"What d'ye think Number One'll do?" asked Bush.

Buckland might be legally in command of the ship, but it was too early yet to speak of him as the captain—"the captain" was still that weeping figure swathed in canvas on the cot in the cabin.

"Can't tell," answered Hornblower, "but he makes up his mind now or never. We lose ground to loo'ard every day from now, you see."

"What'd *you* do?" Bush was curious about this junior lieutenant who had shown himself ready of resources and so guarded in speech.

"I'd read those orders," said Hornblower instantly. "I'd rather be in trouble for having done something than for not having done anything."

"I wonder," said Bush. On the other hand a definite action could be made the subject of a court-martial charge far more easily than the omission to do something; Bush felt this, but he had not the facility with words to express it easily.

"Those orders may detach us on independent service," went on Hornblower. "God, what a chance for Buckland!"

"Yes," said Bush.

The eagerness in Hornblower's expression was obvious. If ever a man yearned for an independent command and the consequent opportunity to distinguish himself it was Hornblower. Bush wondered faintly if he himself was as anxious to have the responsibility of the command of a ship of the line in troubled waters. He looked at Hornblower with an interest which he knew to be constantly increasing. Hornblower was a man always ready to adopt the bold course, a man who infinitely preferred action to inaction; widely read in his profession and yet a practical seaman, as Bush had already had plenty of opportunity to observe. A student yet a man of action; a fiery spirit and yet discreet —Bush remembered how tactfully he had acted during the crisis following the captain's injury and how dexterously he had handled Buckland.

And—and—what was the truth about the injury to the captain? Bush darted a more searching glance than ever at Hornblower as he followed up that train of thought. Bush's mind did not consciously frame the words "motive" and "opportunity" to itself—it was not that type of mind—but it felt its way along an obscure path of reasoning which might well have been signposted with those words. He wanted to ask again the question he had asked once before, but to do so would not merely invite but would merit a rebuff. Hornblower was established in a strong position and Bush could be sure that he would never abandon it through indiscretion or impatience. Bush looked at the lean eager face, at the long fingers drumming on the chart. It was not right or fit or proper that he should feel any admiration or even respect for Hornblower, who was not merely his junior in age by a couple of years— that did not matter—but was his junior as a lieutenant. The dates on their respective commissions really did matter; a junior was someone for whom it should be impossible to feel respect by the traditions of the service. Anything else would be unnatural, might even savour of the equalitarian French ideas which they were engaged in fighting. The thought of himself as infected with Red Revolutionary notions made Bush actually uneasy, and yet as he stirred uncomfortably in his chair he could not wholly discard those notions.

"I'll put these things away," said Hornblower, rising from his chair. "I'm exercising my lower-deck guns' crews after the hands have had their dinner. And I have the first dogwatch after that."

VI

The lower-deck guns had been secured, and the sweating crews came pouring up on deck. Now that the *Renown* was as far south as 30 deg. north latitude the lower gundeck, even with the ports open for artillery exercise, was a warm place, and hauling those guns in and running them out was warm work. Hornblower had kept the crews hard at it, one hundred and eighty men, who afterwards came pouring up into the sunshine and the fresh air of the trade wind to receive the good-humoured chaff of the rest of the crew who had not been working so hard but who knew perfectly well that their turn would come soon.

The guns' crews wiped their steaming foreheads and flung jests—jagged and unpolished like the flints in the soil from which they had sprung—back at their tormentors. It was exhilarating to an officer to see the high spirits of the men and to be aware of the good temper that prevailed; in the three days that had elapsed since the change in command the whole atmosphere of the ship had improved. Suspicion and fear had vanished; after a brief sulkiness the hands had found that exercise and regular work were stimulating and satisfactory.

Hornblower came aft, the sweat running down him, and touched his hat to Roberts, who was officer of the watch, where he stood chatting with Bush at the break of the poop. It was an unusual request that Hornblower made, and Roberts and Bush stared at him with surprise.

"But what about the deck, Mr. Hornblower?" asked Roberts.

"A hand can swab it off in two minutes, sir," replied Hornblower, wiping his face and looking at the blue sea overside with a longing that was obvious to the most casual glance. "I have fifteen minutes before I relieve you, sir—plenty of time."

"Oh, very well, Mr. Hornblower."

"Thank you, sir," said Hornblower, and he turned eagerly away with another touch of his hat, while Roberts and Bush exchanged glances which were as much amused as puzzled. They watched Hornblower give his orders.

"Captain of the waist! Captain of the waist, there!"

"Sir?"

"Get the wash-deck pump rigged at once."

"Rig the wash-deck pump, sir?"

231

"Yes. Four men for the handles. One for the hose. Jump to it, now. I'll be with you in two minutes."

"Aye aye, sir."

The captain of the waist set about obeying the strange order after a glance at the receding figure. Hornblower was as good as his word; it was only two minutes before he returned, but now he was naked except for a towel draped sketchily round him. This was all very strange.

"Give away," he said to the men at the pump handles.

They were dubious about all this, but they obeyed the order, and in alternate pairs they threw their weight upon the handles. Up—down, up—down; clank—clank. The seaman holding the hose felt it stir in his hands as the water from far overside came surging up along it; and next moment a clear stream of water came gushing out of it.

"Turn it on me," said Hornblower, casting his towel aside and standing naked in the sunshine. The hoseman hesitated.

"Hurry up, now!"

As dubiously as ever the hoseman obeyed orders, turning the jet upon his officer, who rotated first this way and then that as it splashed upon him; an amused crowd was gathering to watch.

"Pump, you sons of seacooks!" said Hornblower; and obediently the men at the pump handles, now grinning broadly, threw all their weight on the handles, with such enthusiasm that their feet left the deck as they hauled down upon them and the clear water came hurtling out through the hose with considerable force. Hornblower twirled round and round under the stinging impact, his face screwed up in painful ecstasy.

Buckland had been standing aft at the taffrail, lost in thought and gazing down at the ship's wake, but the clanking of the pump attracted his attention and he strolled forward to join Roberts and Bush and to look at the strange spectacle.

"Hornblower has some odd fancies," he remarked, but he smiled as he said it—a rather pathetic smile, for his face bore the marks of the anxieties he was going through.

"He seems to be enjoying himself, sir," said Bush.

Bush, looking at Hornblower revolving under the sparkling stream, was conscious of a prickling under his shirt in his heavy uniform coat, and actually had the feeling that it might be pleasurable to indulge in that sort of shower bath, however injurious it might be to the health.

" 'Vast pumping!" yelled Hornblower. "Avast, there!"

The hands at the pumps ceased their labours, and the jet from the hose died away to a trickle, to nothing.

"Captain of the waist! Secure the pump. Get the deck swabbed."

"Aye aye, sir."

Hornblower grabbed his towel and came trotting back along the maindeck. He looked up at the group of officers with a grin which revealed his exhilaration and high spirits.

"Dunno if it's good for discipline," commented Roberts, as Hornblower disappeared; and then, with a tardy flash of insight, "I suppose it's all right."

"I suppose so," said Buckland. "Let's hope he doesn't get himself a fever, checking the perspiration like that."

"He showed no sign of one, sir," said Bush; lingering in Bush's mind's eye was the picture of Hornblower's grin. It blended with his memory of Hornblower's eager expression when they were discussing what Buckland had best do in the dilemma in which he found himself.

"Ten minutes to eight bells, sir," reported the quartermaster.

"Very well," said Roberts.

The wet patch on the deck was now almost dry; a faint steam rose from it as the sun, still fierce at four o'clock in the afternoon, beat on it.

"Call the watch," said Roberts.

Hornblower came running up to the quarterdeck with his telescope; he must have pulled on his clothes with the orderly rapidity that marked all his actions. He touched his hat to the quarterdeck and stood by to relieve Roberts.

"You feel refreshed after your bath?" asked Buckland.

"Yes, sir, thank you."

Bush looked at the pair of them, the elderly, worried first lieutenant and the young fifth lieutenant, the older man pathetically envying the youngster's youth. Bush was learning something about personalities. He would never be able to reduce the results of his observations to a tabular system, and it would never occur to him to do so, but he could learn without doing so; his experience and observations would blend with his native wit to govern his judgments, even if he were too self-conscious to philosophize over them. He was aware that naval officers (he knew almost nothing of mankind on land) could be divided into active individuals and passive individuals, into those eager for responsibility and action and into those content to wait until action was forced on them. Before that he had learned the simpler lesson that officers could be divided into the efficient and the blunderers, and also into the intelligent and the stupid—this last division was nearly the same as the one immediately preceding, but not quite. There were the officers who could be counted on to act quickly and correctly in an emergency, and those who could not—again the dividing line did not quite coincide with the preceding. And there were officers with discretion and officers with none, patient officers and impatient ones, officers with strong nerves and officers with weak nerves. In certain cases Bush's estimates had to contend with his prejudices—he was liable to be suspicious of brains and of originality of thought and of eagerness for activity, especially because in the absence of some of the other desirable qualities these things might be actual nuisances. The final and most striking difference Bush had observed during ten years of continuous warfare was that between the leaders and the led, but that again was a difference of which Bush was conscious without being able to express it in words, and especially not in words as succinct or as definite as these; but he was actually aware of the difference even though he was not able to bring himself to define it.

But he had that difference at the back of his mind, all the same, as he looked at Buckland and Hornblower chatting together on the quarterdeck. The afternoon watch had ended, and the first dogwatch had begun, with Hornblower as officer of the watch. It was the traditional moment for relaxation; the heat of the day had passed, and the hands collected forward, some of them to gaze down at the dolphins leaping round the bows, while the officers who had been dozing during the afternoon in their cabins came up to the quarterdeck for air and paced up and down in little groups deep in conversation.

A ship of war manned for active service was the most crowded place in the world—more crowded than the most rundown tenement in Seven Dials—but long and hard experience had taught the inhabitants how to live even in those difficult conditions. Forward there were groups of men yarning, men skylarking; there were solitary men who had each preempted a square yard of deck for himself and sat, cross-legged, with tools and materials about them, doing scrimshaw work—delicate carvings on bone—or embroidery or whittling at models oblivious to the tumult about them. Similarly aft on the crowded quarterdeck the groups of officers strolled and chatted, avoiding the other groups without conscious effort.

It was in accordance with the traditions of the service that these groups left the windward side of the quarterdeck to Buckland as long as he was on deck; and Buckland seemed to be making a long stay this afternoon. He was deep in conversation with Hornblower, the two of them pacing up and down beside the quarterdeck carronades, eight yards forward, eight yards back again; long ago the navy had discovered that when the walking distance was so limited conversation must not be interrupted by the necessarily frequent turns. Every pair of officers turned inwards as they reached the limits of their walk, facing each other momentarily and continuing the conversation without a break, and walking with their hands clasped behind them as a result of the training they had all received as midshipmen not to put their hands in their pockets.

So walked Buckland and Hornblower, and curious glances were cast at them by the others, for even on this golden evening, with the blue-enamel sea overside and the sun sinking to starboard with the promise of a magnificent sunset, everyone was conscious that in the cabin just below their feet lay a wretched insane man, half-swathed in a strait-jacket; and Buckland had to make up his mind how to deal with him. Up and down, up and down walked Buckland and Hornblower. Hornblower seemed to be as deferential as ever, and Buckland seemed to be asking questions; but some of the replies he received must have been unexpected, for more than once Buckland stopped in the middle of a turn and stood facing Hornblower, apparently repeating his question, while Hornblower seemed to be standing his ground both literally and figuratively, sturdy and yet respectful, as Buckland stood with the sun illuminating his haggard features.

Perhaps it had been a fortunate chance that had made Hornblower decide to take a bath under the wash-deck pump—this conversation had its beginnings in that incident.

"Is that a council of war?" said Smith to Bush, looking across at the pair.

"Not likely," said Bush.

A first lieutenant would not deliberately ask the advice or even the opinion of one so junior. Yet—yet—it might be possible, starting with idle conversation about different matters.

"Don't tell me they're discussing Catholic Emancipation," said Lomax.

It was just possible, Bush realized guiltily, that they were discussing something else—that question as to how the captain had come to fall down the hatchway. Bush found himself automatically looking round the deck for Wellard when that thought occurred to him. Wellard was skylarking in the main rigging with the midshipmen and master's mates as if he had not a care in the world. But it could not be that question which Buckland and Hornblower were discussing. Their attitudes seemed to indicate that theories and not facts were the subject of the debate.

"Anyway, they've settled it," said Smith.

Hornblower was touching his hat to Buckland, and Buckland was turning to go below again. Several curious pairs of eyes looked across at Hornblower now that he was left solitary, and as he became conscious of their regard he strolled over to them.

"Affairs of state?" asked Lomax, asking the question which everyone wanted asked.

Hornblower met his gaze with a level glance.

"No," he said, and smiled.

"It certainly looked like matters of importance," said Smith.

"That depends on the definition," answered Hornblower.

He was still smiling, and his smile gave no clue at all regarding his thoughts. It would be rude to press him further; it was possible that he and Buckland had been discussing some private business. Nobody looking at him could guess.

"Come off those hammocks, there!" bellowed Hornblower; the skylarking midshipmen were not breaking one of the rules of the ship, but it was a convenient moment to divert the conversation.

Three bells rang out; the first dogwatch was threequarters completed.

"Mr. Roberts, sir!" suddenly called the sentry at the smokers' slow match by the hatchway. "Passing the word for Mr. Roberts!"

Roberts turned from the group.

"Who's passing the word for me?" he asked, although with the captain ill there could only be one man in the ship who could pass the word for the second lieutenant.

"Mr. Buckland, sir. Mr. Buckland passing the word for Mr. Roberts."

"Very well," said Roberts, hurrying down the companion.

The others exchanged glances. This might be the moment of decision. Yet on the other hand it might be only a routine matter. Hornblower took advantage of the distraction to turn away from the group and continue his walk on the weather side of the ship; he walked with his chin nearly down on his breast, his drooping head balanced by the hands behind his back. Bush thought he looked weary.

Now there came a fresh cry from below, repeated by the sentry at the hatchway.

"Mr. Clive! Passing the word for Mr. Clive. Mr. Buckland passing the word for Mr. Clive!"

"Oh-ho!" said Lomax in significant tones, as the surgeon hurried down.

"Something happens," said Carberry, the master.

Time went on without either the second lieutenant or the surgeon reappearing. Smith, under his arm the telescope that was the badge of his temporary office, touched his hat to Hornblower and prepared to relieve him as officer of the watch as the second dogwatch was called. In the east the sky was turning dark, and the sun was setting over the starboard quarter in a magnificent display of red and gold; from the ship towards the sun the surface of the sea was gilded and glittering, but close overside it was the richest purple. A flying fish broke the surface and went skimming along, leaving a transient, momentary furrow behind it like a groove in enamel.

"Look at that!" exclaimed Hornblower to Bush.

"A flying fish," said Bush, indifferently.

"Yes! There's another!"

Hornblower leaned over to get a better view.

"You'll see plenty of them before this voyage is over," said Bush.

"But I've never seen one before."

The play of expression on Hornblower's face was curious. One moment he was full of eager interest; the next he assumed an appearance of stolid indifference as a man might pull on a glove. His service at sea so far, varied though it might be, had been confined to European waters; years of dangerous activity on the French and Spanish coasts in a frigate, two years in the *Renown* in the Channel fleet, and he had been eagerly looking forward to the novelties he would encounter in tropical waters. But he was talking to a man to whom these things were no novelty, and who evinced no excitement at the sight of the first flying fish of the voyage. Hornblower was not going to be outdone in stolidity and self-control; if the wonders of the deep failed to move Bush they were not going to evoke any childish excitement in Hornblower, at least any apparent excitement if Hornblower could suppress it. He was a veteran, and he was not going to appear like a raw hand.

Bush looked up to see Roberts and Clive ascending the companionway in the gathering night, and turned eagerly towards them. Officers came from every part of the quarterdeck to hear what they had to say.

"Well, sir?" asked Lomax.

"He's done it," said Roberts.

"He's read the secret orders, sir?" asked Smith.

"As far as I know, yes."

"Oh!"

There was a pause before someone asked the inevitable silly question.

"What did they say?"

"They are secret orders," said Roberts, and now there was a touch of pomposity in his voice—it might be to compensate for his lack of knowledge, or it might be because Roberts was now growing more aware of the dignity of his position as second in command. "If Mr. Buckland had taken me into his confidence I still could not tell you."

"True enough," said Carberry.

"What did the captain do?" asked Lomax.

"Poor devil," said Clive. With all attention turned to him Clive grew expansive. "We might be fiends from the pit! You should have seen him cower away when we came in. Those morbid terrors grow more acute."

Clive awaited a request for further information, and even though none was forthcoming he went on with his story.

"We had to find the key to his desk. You would have thought we were going to cut his throat, judging by the way he wept and tried to hide. All the sorrows of the world—all the terrors of hell torment that wretched man."

"But you found the key?" persisted Lomax.

"We found it. And we opened his desk."

"And then?"

"Mr. Buckland found the orders. The usual linen envelope with the Admiralty seal. The envelope had been already opened."

"Naturally," said Lomax. "Well?"

"And now, I suppose," said Clive, conscious of the anti-climax, "I suppose he's reading them."

"And we are none the wiser."

There was a disappointed pause.

"Bless my soul!" said Carberry. "We've been at war since '93. Nearly ten years of it. D'ye still expect to know what lies in store for you? The West Indies today—Halifax tomorrow. We obey orders. Helm-a-lee—let go and haul. A bellyful of grape or champagne in a captured flagship. Who cares? We draw our four shillings a day, rain or shine."

"Mr. Carberry!" came the word from below. "Mr. Buckland passing the word for Mr. Carberry."

"Bless my soul!" said Carberry again.

"Now you can earn your four shillings a day," said Lomax.

The remark was addressed to his disappearing back, for Carberry was already hastening below.

"A change of course," said Smith. "I'll wager a week's pay on it."

"No takers," said Roberts.

It was the most likely new development of all, for Carberry, the master, was the officer charged with the navigation of the ship.

Already it was almost full night, dark enough to make the features of the speakers indistinct, although over to the westward there was still a red path on the horizon, and a faint red trail over the black water towards the ship. The binnacle lights had been lit and the brighter stars were already visible in the dark sky, with the mastheads seeming to brush past them, with the motion of the ship, infinitely far over their heads. The ship's bell rang out, but the group showed no tendency to disperse. And then interest quickened. Here were Buckland and Carberry returning, ascending the companionway; the group drew on one side to clear them a passage.

"Officer of the watch!" said Buckland.

"Sir!" said Smith, coming forward in the darkness.

"We're altering course two points. Steer southwest."

"Aye aye, sir. Course southwest. Mr. Abbott, pipe the hands to the braces."

The *Renown* came round on her new course, with her sails trimmed to the wind which was now no more than a point on her port quarter. Carberry walked over to the binnacle and looked into it to make sure the helmsman was exactly obeying his orders.

"Another pull on the weather forebrace, there!" yelled Smith. "Belay!"

The bustle of the change of course died away.

"Course sou'west, sir," reported Smith.

"Very good, Mr. Smith," said Buckland, by the rail.

"Pardon, sir," said Roberts, greatly daring, addressing him as he loomed in the darkness. "Can you tell us our mission, sir?"

"Not our mission. That is still secret, Mr. Roberts."

"Very good, sir."

"But I'll tell you where we're bound. Mr. Carberry knows already."

"Where, sir?"

"Santo Domingo. Scotchman's Bay."

There was a pause while this information was being digested.

"Santa Domingo," said someone, meditatively.

"Hispaniola," said Carberry, explanatorily.

"Hayti," said Hornblower.

"Santo Domingo—Hayti—Hispaniola," said Carberry. "Three names for the same island."

"Hayti!" exclaimed Roberts, some chord in his memory suddenly touched. "That's where the blacks are in rebellion."

"Yes," agreed Buckland.

Anyone could guess that Buckland was trying to say that word in as noncommittal a tone as possible; it might be because there was a difficult diplomatic situation with regard to the blacks, and it might be because fear of the captain was still a living force in the ship.

VII

Lieutenant Buckland, in acting command of H.M.S. *Renown*, of seventy-four guns, was on the quarterdeck of his ship peering through his telescope at the low mountains of Santo Domingo. The ship was rolling in a fashion unnatural and disturbing, for the long Atlantic swell, driven by the northeast trades, was passing under her keel while she lay hove-to to the final puffs of the land breeze which had blown since midnight and was now dying away as the fierce sun heated the island again. The *Renown* was actually wallowing, rolling her lower deck gunports under, first on one side and then on the other, for what little breeze there was was along the swell and did nothing to stiffen her as she lay with her mizzen topsail backed. She would lie right over on one side, until the gun tackles creaked with the strain of holding the guns in position, until it was hard to keep a foothold on the steep-sloping deck; she would lie there for a few harrowing seconds, and then slowly right herself, making no pause at all at the moment when she was upright and her deck horizontal, and continue, with a clattering of blocks and a rattle of gear in a sickening swoop until she was as far over in the opposite direction, gun tackles creaking and unwary men slipping and sliding, and lie there unresponsive until the swell had rolled under her and she repeated her behaviour.

"For God's sake," said Hornblower, hanging on to a belaying pin in the mizzen fife rail to save himself from sliding down the deck into the scuppers, "can't he make up his mind?"

There was something in Hornblower's stare that made Bush look at him more closely.

"Seasick?" he asked, with curiosity.

"Who wouldn't be?" replied Hornblower. "How she rolls!"

Bush's cast-iron stomach had never given him the least qualm, but he was aware that less fortunate men suffered from seasickness even after weeks at sea, especially when subjected to a different kind of motion. This funereal rolling was nothing like the free action of the *Renown* under sail.

"Buckland has to see how the land lies," he said in an effort to cheer Hornblower up.

"How much more does he want to see?" grumbled Hornblower. "There's the Spanish colours flying on the fort up there. Everyone on shore knows now that a ship of the line is prowling about, and the Dons won't have to be very clever to guess that we're not here on a yachting trip. Now they've all the time they need to be ready to receive us."

"But what else could he do?"

"He could have come in in the dark with the sea breeze. Landing parties ready. Put them ashore at dawn. Storm the place before they knew there was any danger. Oh, God!"

The final exclamation had nothing to do with what went before. It was wrenched out of Hornblower by the commotion of his stomach. Despite his deep tan there was a sickly green colour in his cheeks.

"Hard luck," said Bush.

Buckland still stood trying to keep his telescope trained on the coast despite the rolling of the ship. This was Scotchman's Bay—the Bahia de Escocesa, as the Spanish charts had it. To the westward lay a shelving beach; the big rollers here broke far out and ran in creamy white up to the water's edge with diminishing force, but to the eastward the shore line rose in a line of tree-covered hills standing bluffly with their feet in blue water; the rollers burst against them in sheets of spray that climbed far up the cliffs before falling back in a smother of white. For thirty miles those hills ran beside the sea, almost due east and west;

they constituted the Samaná peninsula, terminating in Samaná Point. According to the charts the peninsula was no more than ten miles wide; behind them, round Samaná Point, lay Samaná Bay, opening into the Mona Passage and a most convenient anchorage for privateers and small ships of war which could lie there, under the protection of the fort on the Samaná peninsula, ready to slip out and harass the West Indian convoys making use of the Mona Passage. The *Renown* had been given orders to clear out this raiders' lair before going down to leeward to Jamaica—everyone in the ship could guess that—but now that Buckland confronted the problem he was not at all sure how to solve it. His indecision was apparent to all the curious lookers-on who clustered on the *Renown*'s deck.

The main topsail suddenly flapped like thunder, and the ship began to turn slowly head to sea; the land breeze was expiring, and the trade winds, blowing eternally across the Atlantic, were resuming their dominion. Buckland shut his telescope with relief. At least that was an excuse for postponing action.

"Mr. Roberts!"

"Sir!"

"Lay her on the port tack. Full and by!"

"Aye aye, sir."

The after guard came running to the mizzen braces, and the ship slowly paid off. Gradually the topsails caught the wind, and she began to lie over, gathering way as she did so. She met the next roller with her port bow, thrusting boldly into it in a burst of spray. The tautened weather-rigging began to sing a more cheerful note, blending with the music of her passage through the water. She was a live thing again, instead of rolling like a corpse in the trough. The roaring trade wind pressed her over, and she went surging along, rising and swooping as if with pleasure, leaving a creamy wake behind her on the blue water while the sea roared under the bows.

"Better?" asked Bush of Hornblower.

"Better in one way," was the reply. Hornblower looked over at the distant hills of Santo Domingo. "I could wish we were going into action and not running away to think about it."

"What a fire-eater!" said Bush.

"A fire-eater? Me? Nothing like that—quite the opposite. I wish—oh, I wish for too much, I suppose."

There was no explaining some people, thought Bush, philosophically. He was content to bask in the sunshine now that its heat was tempered by the ship's passage through the wind. If action and danger lay in the future he could await it in stolid tranquillity; and he certainly could congratulate himself that he did not have to carry Buckland's responsibility of carrying a ship of the line and seven hundred and twenty men into action. The prospect of action at least took one's mind off the horrid fact that confined below lay an insane captain.

At dinner in the wardroom he looked over at Hornblower, fidgety and nervous. Buckland had announced his intention of taking the bull by the horns the next morning, of rounding Samaná Point and forcing his way straight up the bay. It would not take many broadsides from the *Renown* to destroy any shipping that lay there at anchor. Bush thoroughly approved of the scheme. Wipe out the privateers, burn them, sink them, and then it would be time to decide what, if anything, should be done next. At the meeting in the wardroom, when Buckland asked if any officer had any questions, Smith had asked sensibly about the tides, and Carberry had given him the information; Roberts had asked a question or two about the situation on the south shore of the bay; but Hornblower at the foot of the table had kept his mouth shut, although looking with eager attention at each speaker in turn.

During the dogwatches Hornblower had paced the deck by himself, head bent in meditation; Bush noticed the fingers of the hands behind his back twisting and twining nervously, and he experienced a momentary doubt. Was it possible that this energetic young officer was lacking in physical courage? That phrase was not Bush's own—he had heard it used maliciously somewhere or other years ago. It was better to use it now than to tell himself outright that he suspected Hornblower might be a coward. Bush was not a man of large tolerance; if a man were a coward he wanted no more to do with him.

Half-way through next morning the pipes shrilled along the decks; the drums of the marines beat a rousing roll.

"Clear the decks for action! Hands to quarters! Clear for action!"

Bush came down to the lower gundeck, which was his station for action; under his command was the whole deck and the seventeen twenty-four-pounders of the starboard battery, while Hornblower commanded under him those of the port side. The hands were already knocking down the screens and removing obstructions. A little group of the surgeon's crew came along the deck; they were carrying a straitjacketed figure bound to a plank. Despite the jacket and the lashings it writhed feebly and wept pitifully—the captain being carried down to the safety of the cable tier while his cabin was cleared for action. A hand or two in the bustle found time to shake their heads over the unhappy figure, but Bush checked them soon enough. He wanted to be able to report the lower gundeck cleared for action with creditable speed.

Hornblower made his appearance, touched his hat to Bush, and stood by to supervise his guns. Most of this lower deck was in twilight, for the stout shafts of sunlight that came down the hatchways did little to illuminate the farther parts of the deck with its sombre red paint. Half a dozen ship's boys came along, each one carrying a bucket of sand, which they scattered in handfuls over the deck. Bush kept a sharp eye on them, because the guns' crews depended on that sand for firm foothold. The water buckets beside each gun were filled; they served a dual purpose, to dampen the swabs that cleaned out the guns and for immediate use against fire. Round the mainmast stood a ring of extra fire buckets; in tubs at either side of the ship smouldered the slow matches from which the gun captains could rekindle their linstocks when necessary. Fire and water. The marine sentries came clumping along the deck in their scarlet coats and white crossbelts, the tops of their shakos brushing the deck beams over their heads. Corporal Greenwood posted one at each hatchway, bayonet fixed and musket loaded. Their duty was to see that no unauthorized person ran down to take shelter in the safety of that part of the ship comfortably below waterline. Mr. Hobbs, the acting-gunner, with his mates and helpers made a momentary appearance on their way down to the magazine. They were all wearing list slippers to obviate any chance of setting off loose powder which would be bound to be strewn about down there in the heat of action.

Soon the powder boys came running up, each with a charge for the guns. The breechings of the guns were cast off and the crews stood by the tackles, waiting for the word to open the ports and run out the guns. Bush darted his glance along both sides. The gun captains were all at their posts. Ten men stood by every gun on the starboard side, five by every gun on the port side—maximum and minimum crews for twenty-four-pounders. It was Bush's responsibility to see to it that whichever battery came into action the guns were properly manned. If both sides had to be worked at once he had to make a fair division, and when the casualties began and guns were put out of service he had to redistribute the crews. The petty officers and warrant officers were reporting their subdivisions ready for action, and Bush turned to the midshipman beside him whose duty was to carry messages.

"Mr. Abbott, report the lower deck cleared for action. Ask if the guns should be run out."

"Aye aye, sir."

A moment before the ship had been full of noise and bustle, and now everything down here was still and quiet save for the creaking of the timbers; the ship was rising and swooping rhythmically over the sea —Bush as he stood by the mainmast was automatically swaying with the ship's motion. Young Abbott came running down the ladder again.

"Mr. Buckland's compliments, sir, and don't run the guns out yet."

"Very good."

Hornblower was standing farther aft, in line with the ringbolts of the train tackles; he had looked round to hear what message Abbott bore, and now he turned back again. He stood with his feet apart, and

Bush saw him put one hand into the other, behind his back, and clasp it firmly. There was a rigidity about the set of his shoulders and in the way he held his head that might be significant of anything, eagerness for action or the reverse. A gun captain addressed a remark to Hornblower, and Bush watched him turn to answer it. Even in the half-light of the lower deck Bush could see there were signs of strain in his expression, and that smile might be forced. Oh well, decided Bush, as charitably as he could, men often looked like that before going into action.

Silently the ship sailed on; even Bush had his ears cocked, trying to hear what was going on above him so as to draw deductions about the situation. Faintly down the hatchway came the call of a seaman.

"No bottom, sir. No bottom with this line."

So there was a man in the chains taking casts with the lead, and they must be drawing near the land; everyone down on the lower deck drew the same conclusion and started to remark about it to his neighbour.

"Silence, there!" snapped Bush.

Another cry from the leadsman, and then a bellowed order. Instantly the lower deck seemed to be filled solid with noise. The maindeck guns were being run out; in the confined space below every sound was multiplied and reverberated by the ship's timbers so that the gun-tracks rolling across the planking made a noise like thunder. Everyone looked to Bush for orders, but he stood steady; he had received none. Now a midshipman appeared descending the ladder.

"Mr. Buckland's compliments, sir, and please to run your guns out."

He had squealed his message without ever setting foot on deck, and everyone had heard it. There was an instant buzz round the deck, and excitable people began to reach for the gunports to open them.

"Still!" bellowed Bush. Guiltily all movement ceased.

"Up ports!"

The twilight of the lower deck changed to daylight as the ports opened; little rectangles of sunshine swayed about on the deck on the port side, broadening and narrowing with the motion of the ship.

"Run out!"

With the ports open the noise was not so great; the crews flung their weight on the tackles and the trucks roared as the guns thrust their muzzles out. Bush stepped to the nearest gun and stooped to peer out through the open port. There were the green hills of the island at extreme gunshot distance; here the cliffs were not nearly so abrupt, and there was a jungle-covered shelf at their feet.

"Hands wear ship!"

Bush could recognize Roberts' voice hailing from the quarterdeck. The deck under his feet steadied to the horizontal, and the distant hills seemed to swing with the vessel. The masts creaked as the yards came round. That must be Samaná Point which they were rounding. The motion of the ship had changed far more than would be the result of mere alteration of course. She was not only on an even keel but she was in quiet water, gliding along into the bay. Bush squatted down on his heels by the muzzle of a gun and peered at the shore. This was the south side of the peninsula at which he was looking, presenting a coastline toward the bay nearly as steep as the one on the seaward side. There was the fort on the crest and the Spanish flag waving over it. The excited midshipman came scuttling down the ladder like a squirrel.

"Sir! Sir! Will you try a ranging shot at the batteries when your guns bear?"

Bush ran a cold eye over him.

"Whose orders?" he asked.

"M—Mr. Buckland's, sir."

"Then say so. Very well. My respects to Mr. Buckland, and it will be a long time before my guns are within range."

"Aye aye, sir."

There was smoke rising from the fort, and not powder smoke either. Bush realized with something like a quiver of apprehension that probably it was smoke from a furnace for heating shot; soon the fort would be hurling red-hot shot at them, and Bush could see no chance of retaliation; he would never be able to elevate his guns sufficiently to reach the fort, while the fort, from its commanding position on the crest, could reach the ship easily enough. He straightened himself up and walked over to the port side to where Hornblower, in a similar attitude, was peering out beside a gun.

"There's a point running out here," said Hornblower. "See the shallows there? The channel must bend round them. And there's a battery on the point—look at the smoke. They're heating shot."

"I daresay," said Bush.

Soon they would be under a sharp crossfire. He hoped they would not be subjected to it for too long. He could hear orders being shouted on deck, and the masts creaked as the yards came round; they were working the *Renown* round the bend.

"The fort's opened fire, sir," reported the master's mate in charge of the forward guns on the starboard side.

"Very well, Mr. Purvis." He crossed over and looked out. "Did you see where the shot fell?"

"No, sir."

"They're firing on this side, too, sir," reported Hornblower.

"Very well."

Bush saw the fort spurting white cannon smoke. Then straight in the line between his eye and the fort, fifty yards from the side of the ship, a pillar of water rose up from the golden surface, and within the same instant of time something crashed into the side of the ship just above Bush's head. A ricochet had bounded from the surface and had lodged somewhere in the eighteen inches of oak that constituted the ship's side. Then followed a devil's tattoo of crashes; a well-aimed salvo was striking home.

"I might just reach the battery on this side now, sir," said Hornblower.

"Then try what you can do."

Now here was Buckland himself, hailing fretfully down the hatchway.

"Can't you open fire yet, Mr. Bush?"

"This minute, sir."

Hornblower was standing by the centre twenty-four-pounder. The gun captain slid the rolling handspike under the gun carriage, and heaved with all his weight. Two men at each side tackle tugged under his direction to point the gun true. With the elevating coign quite free from the breech the gun was at its highest angle of elevation. The gun captain flipped up the iron apron over the touchhole, saw that the hole was filled with powder, and with a shout of "Stand clear" he thrust his smouldering linstock into it. The gun bellowed loud in the confined space; some of the smoke came drifting back through the port.

"Just below, sir," reported Hornblower, standing at the next port. "When the guns are hot they'll reach it."

"Carry on, then."

"Open fire, first division!" yelled Hornblower.

The four foremost guns crashed out almost together.

"Second division!"

Bush could feel the deck heaving under him with the shock of the discharge and the recoil. Smoke came billowing back into the confined space, acrid, bitter; and the din was paralysing.

"Try again, men!" yelled Hornblower. "Division captains, see that you point true!"

There was a frightful crash close beside Bush and something screamed past him to crash into the deck beam near his head. Something flying through an open gunport had struck a gun on its reinforced breech. Two men had fallen close beside it, one lying still and the other twisting and turning in agony. Bush was about to give an order regarding them when his attention was drawn to something more important. There was a deep gash in the deck beam by his head and from the depths of the gash smoke was curling. It was a red-hot shot that had struck the breech of the gun and had apparently flown into fragments. A large part—the largest part—had sunk deep into the beam and already the wood was smouldering.

"Fire buckets here!" roared Bush.

Ten pounds of red-hot glowing metal lodged in the dry timbers of the ship could start a blaze in a few seconds. At the same time there was a rush of feet overhead, the sound of gear being moved about, and then the clank-clank of pumps. So on the maindeck they were fighting fires too. Hornblower's guns were thundering on the port side, the gun-trucks roaring over the planking. Hell was unchained, and the smoke of hell was eddying about him.

The masts creaked again with the swing of the yards; despite everything the ship had to be sailed up the tortuous channel. He peered out through a port, but his eye told him, as he forced himself to gauge the distance calmly, that the fort on the crest was still beyond range. No sense in wasting ammunition. He straightened himself and looked round the murky deck. There was something strange in the feel of the ship under his feet. He teetered on his toes to put his wild suspicions to the test. There was the slightest perceptible slope to the deck—a strange rigidity and permanence about it. Oh my God! Hornblower was looking round at him and making an urgent gesture downwards to confirm the awful thought. The *Renown* was aground. She must have run so smoothly and slowly up a mudbank as to lose her speed without any jerk perceptible. But she must have put her bows far up on the bank for the slope of the deck to be noticeable. There were more rending crashes as other shots from the shore struck home, a fresh hurrying and bustle as the fire parties ran to deal with the danger. Hard aground, and doomed to be slowly shot to pieces by those cursed forts, if the shots did not set them on fire to roast alive on the mudbank. Hornblower was beside him, his watch in his hand.

"Tide's still rising," he said. "It's an hour before high water. But I'm afraid we're pretty hard aground."

Bush could only look at him and swear, pouring out filth from his mouth as the only means of relieving his overwrought feelings.

"Steady there, Duff!" yelled Hornblower, looking away from him at a gun's crew gathered round their gun. "Swab that out properly! D'ye want your hands blown off when you load?"

By the time Hornblower looked round at Bush again the latter had regained his self-control.

"An hour to high water, you say?" he asked.

"Yes, sir. According to Carberry's calculations."

"God help us!"

"My shot's just reaching the battery on that point, sir. If I can keep the embrasures swept I'll slow their rate of fire even if I don't silence them."

Another crash as a shot struck home, and another.

"But the one across the channel's out of range."

"Yes," said Hornblower.

The powder boys were running through all the bustle with fresh charges for the guns. And here was the messenger-midshipman thread-ing his way through them.

"Mr. Bush, sir! Will you please report to Mr. Buckland, sir? And we're aground, under fire, sir."

"Shut your mouth. I leave you in charge here, Mr. Hornblower."

"Aye aye, sir."

The sunlight on the quarterdeck was blinding. Buckland was stand-ing hatless at the rail, trying to control the working of his features. There was a roar and a spluttering of steam as someone turned the jet of a hose on a fiery fragment lodged in the bulkhead. Dead men in the scuppers; wounded being carried off. A shot, or the splinters it had sent flying, must have killed the man at the wheel so that the ship, tem-porarily out of control, had run aground.

"We have to kedge off," said Buckland.

"Aye aye, sir."

That meant putting out an anchor and heaving in on the cable with the capstan to haul the ship off the mud by main force. Bush looked round him to confirm what he had gathered regarding the ship's posi-tion from his restricted view below. Her bows were on the mud; she would have to be hauled off stern fist. A shot howled close overhead, and Bush had to exert his self-control not to jump.

"You'll have to get a cable out aft through a stern port."

"Aye aye, sir."

"Roberts'll take the stream anchor off in the launch."

"Aye aye, sir."

The fact that Buckland omitted the formal "Mister" was significant of the strain he was undergoing and of the emergency of the occasion.

"I'll take the men from my guns, sir," said Bush.

"Very good."

Now was the time for discipline and training to assert themselves; the *Renown* was fortunate in having a crew more than half composed of seasoned men drilled in the blockade of Brest. At Plymouth she had only been filled up with pressed men. What had merely been a drill, an evolution, when the *Renown* was one of the Channel Fleet, was now an operation on which the life of the ship depended, not something to be done perfunctorily in competition with the rest of the squadron. Bush gathered his guns' crews around him and set about the task of rousing out a cable and getting it aft to a port, while overhead Roberts' men were manning stay tackles and yard tackles to sway out the launch.

Down below the heat between the decks was greater even than above with the sun glaring down. The smoke from Hornblower's guns was eddying thick under the beams; Hornblower was holding his hat in his hand and wiping his streaming face with his handkerchief. He nodded as Bush appeared; there was no need for Bush to explain the duty on which he was engaged. With the guns still thundering and the smoke still eddying, powder boys still running with fresh charges and fire parties bustling with their buckets, Bush's men roused out the cable. The hundred fathoms of it weighed a trifle over a couple of tons; clear heads and skilled supervision were necessary to get the unwieldy cable laid out aft, but Bush was at his best doing work which called for single-minded attention to a single duty. He had it clear and faked down along the deck by the time the cutter was under the stern to receive the end, and then he watched the vast thing gradually snake out through the after port without a hitch. The launch came into his line of vision as he stood looking out, with the vast weight of the stream anchor dangling astern; it was a relief to know that the tricky business of getting the anchor into her had been successfully carried out. The second cutter carried the spring cable from the hawse-hole. Roberts was in command; Bush heard him hail the cutter as the three boats drew off astern. There was a sudden jet of water among the boats; one or other, if not both, of the batteries ashore had shifted targets; a shot now into the launch would be a disaster, and one into a cutter would be a serious setback.

"Pardon, sir," said Hornblower's voice beside him, and Bush turned back from looking out over the glittering water.

"Well?"

"I could take some of the foremost guns and run 'em aft," said Hornblower. "Shifting the weight would help."

"So it would," agreed Bush; Hornblower's face was streaked and grimy with his exertions, as Bush noted while he considered if he had sufficient authority to give the order on his own responsibility. "Better get Buckland's permission. Ask him in my name if you like."

"Aye aye, sir."

These lower-deck twenty-four-pounders weighed more than two tons each; the transfer of some from forward aft would be an important factor in getting the bows off the mudbank. Bush took another glance through the port. James, the midshipman in the first cutter, was turning to look back to check that the cable was out in exact line with the length of the ship. There would be a serious loss of tractive effort if there was an angle in the cable from anchor to capstan. Launch and cutter were coming together in preparation for dropping the anchor. All round them the water suddenly boiled to a salvo from the shore; the skipping jets of the ricochets showed that it was the fort on the hill that was firing at them—and making good practice for that extreme range. The sun caught an axe blade as it turned in the air in the stern-sheets of the launch; Bush saw the momentary flash. They were letting the anchor drop from where it hung from the gallows in the stern. Thank God.

Hornblower's guns were still bellowing out, making the ship tremble with their recoil, and at the same time a splintering crash over his head told him that the other battery was still firing on the ship and still scoring hits. Everything was still going on at once; Hornblower had a gang of men at work dragging aft the foremost twenty-four-pounder on the starboard side—a ticklish job with the rolling hand-spike under the transom of the carriage. The trucks squealed horribly as the men struggled to turn the cumbersome thing and thread their way along the crowded deck. But Bush could spare Hornblower no more than a glance as he hurried up to the maindeck to see for himself what was happening at the capstan.

The men were already taking their places at the capstan bars under the supervision of Smith and Booth; the maindeck guns were being stripped of the last of their crews to supply enough hands. Naked to the waist, the men were spitting on their hands and testing their foothold —there was no need to tell them how serious the situation was; no need for Booth's knotted rattan.

"Heave away!" hailed Buckland from the quarterdeck.

"Heave away!" yelled Booth. "Heave, and wake the dead!"

The men flung their weight on the bars and the capstan came round, the pawls clanking rapidly as the capstan took up the slack. The boys with the nippers at the messenger had to hurry to keep pace. Then the intervals between the clanking of the pawls became longer as the capstan turned more slowly. More slowly; clank—clank—clank. Now the strain was coming; the bitts creaked as the cable tightened. Clank—clank. That was a new cable, and it could be expected to stretch a trifle.

The sudden howl of a shot—what wanton fate had directed it there of all places in the ship? Flying splinters and prostrate men; the shot had ploughed through the whole crowded mass. Red blood was pouring out, vivid in the sunshine; in understandable confusion the men drew away from the bloody wrecks.

"Stand to your posts!" yelled Smith. "You, boys! Get those men out of the way. Another capstan bar here! Smartly now!"

The ball which had wrought such fearful havoc had not spent all its force on human flesh; it had gone on to shatter the checkpiece of a gun carriage and then to lodge in the ship's side. Nor had human blood quenched it; smoke was rising on the instant from where it rested. Bush himself seized a fire bucket and dashed its contents on the glowing ball; steam blended with the smoke and the water spat and sputtered. No single fire bucket could quench twenty-four pounds of red-hot iron, but a fire party came running up to flood the smouldering menace.

The dead and the wounded had been dragged away and the men were at the capstan bars again.

"Heave!" shouted Booth. Clank—clank—clank. Slowly and more

slowly still turned the capstan. Then it came to a dead stop while the bitts groaned under the strain.

"Heave! Heave!"

Clank! Then reluctantly, and after a long interval, clank! Then no more. The merciless sun beat down upon the men's straining backs; their horny feet sought for a grip against the cleats on the deck as they shoved and thrust against the bars. Bush went below again, leaving them straining away; he could, and did, send plenty of men up from the lower gundeck to treble-bank the capstan bars. There were men still hard at work in the smoky twilight hauling the last possible gun aft, but Hornblower was back among his guns supervising the pointing. Bush set his foot on the cable. It was not like a rope, but like a wooden spar, as rigid and unyielding. Then through the sole of his shoe Bush felt the slightest tremor, the very slightest; the men at the capstan were putting their reinforced strength against the bars. The clank of one more pawl gained reverberated along the ship's timbers; the cable shuddered a trifle more violently and then stiffened into total rigidity again. It did not creep over an eighth of an inch under Bush's foot, although he knew that at the capstan a hundred and fifty men were straining their hearts out at the bars. One of Hornblower's guns went off; Bush felt the jar of the recoil through the cable. Faintly down the hatchways came the shouts of encouragement from Smith and Booth at the capstan, but not an inch of gain could be noted at the cable. Hornblower came and touched his hat to Bush.

"D'you notice any movement when I fire a gun, sir?" As he asked the question he turned and waved to the captain of a midship gun which was loaded and run out. The gun captain brought the linstock down on the touchhole, and the gun roared out and came recoiling back through the smoke. Bush's foot on the cable recorded the effect.

"Only the jar—no—yes." Inspiration came to Bush. To the question he asked Bush already knew the answer Hornblower would give. "What are you thinking of?"

"I could fire all my guns at once. That might break the suction, sir."

So it might, indeed. The *Renown* was lying on mud, which was clutching her in a firm grip. If she could be severely shaken while the hawser was maintained at full tension the grip might be broken.

"I think it's worth trying, by God," said Bush.

"Very good, sir. I'll have my guns loaded and ready in three minutes, sir." Hornblower turned to his battery and funnelled his hands round his mouth. "Cease fire! Cease fire, all!"

"I'll tell 'em at the capstan," said Bush.

"Very good, sir." Hornblower went on giving his orders. "Load and double-shot your guns. Prime and run out."

That was the last that Bush heard for the moment as he went up on the maindeck and made his suggestion to Smith, who nodded in instant agreement.

" 'Vast heaving!" shouted Smith, and the sweating men at the bars eased their weary backs.

An explanation was necessary to Buckland on the quarterdeck; he saw the force of the argument. The unfortunate man, who was watching the failure of his first venture in independent command, and whose ship was in such deadly peril, was gripping at the rail and wringing it with his two hands as if he would twist it like a corkscrew. In the midst of all this there was a piece of desperately important news that Smith had to give.

"Roberts is dead," he said, out of the side of his mouth.

"No!"

"He's dead. A shot cut him in two in the launch."

"Good God!"

It was to Bush's credit that he felt sorrow at the death of Roberts before his mind recorded the fact that he was now first lieutenant of a ship of the line. But there was no time now to think of either sorrow or rejoicing, not with the *Renown* aground and under fire. Bush hailed down the hatchway.

"Below, there! Mr. Hornblower!"

"Sir!"

"Are your guns ready?"

"Another minute, sir."

"Better take the strain," said Bush to Smith; and then, louder, down the hatchway, "Await my order, Mr. Hornblower."

"Aye aye, sir."

The men settled themselves at the capstan bars again, braced their feet, and heaved.

"Heave!" shouted Booth. "Heave!"

The men might be pushing at the side of a church, so little movement did they get from the bars after the first inch.

"Heave!"

Bush left them and ran below. He set his foot on the rigid cable and nodded to Hornblower. The fifteen guns—two had been dragged aft from the port side—were run out and ready, the crews awaiting orders.

"Captains, take your linstocks!" shouted Hornblower. "all you others, stand clear! Now, I shall give you the words 'one, two, three'. At 'three' you touch your linstocks down. Understand?"

There was a buzz of agreement.

"All ready? All linstocks glowing?" The gun captains swung them about to get them as bright as possible. "Then one—two—three!"

Down came the linstocks on the touchholes, and almost simultaneously the guns roared out; even with the inevitable variation in the amounts of powder in the touchholes there was not a second between the first and the last of the fifteen explosions. Bush, his foot on the cable, felt the ship heave with the recoil—double-shotting the guns had increased the effect. The smoke came eddying into the sweltering heat, but Bush had no attention to give to it. The cable moved under his foot with the heave of the ship. Surely it was moving along. It was! He had to shift the position of his foot. The clank of a newly-gained pawl on the windlass could be heard by everyone. Clank—clank. Someone in the smoke started to cheer and others took it up.

"Silence!" bellowed Hornblower.

Clank—clank—clank. Reluctant sounds; but the ship was moving. The cable was coming in slowly, like a mortally wounded monster. If only they could keep her on the move! Clank—clank—clank. The interval between the sounds was growing shorter—even Bush had to admit that to himself. The cable was coming in faster—faster.

"Take charge here, Mr. Hornblower," said Bush, and sprang for the maindeck. If the ship were free there would be urgent matters for the first lieutenant to attend to. The capstan pawls seemed almost to be playing a merry tune, so rapidly did they sound as the capstan turned.

Undoubtedly there was much to be attended to on deck. There were decisions which must be made at once. Bush touched his hat to Buckland.

"Any orders, sir?"

Buckland turned unhappy eyes on him.

"We've lost the flood," he said.

This must be the highest moment of the tide; if they were to touch ground again, kedging off would not be so simple an operation.

"Yes, sir," said Bush.

The decision could only lie with Buckland; no one else could share the responsibility. But it was terribly hard for a man to have to admit defeat in his very first command. Buckland looked as if for inspiration round the bay, where the red-and-gold flags of Spain flew above the banked-up powder smoke of the batteries—no inspiration could be found there.

"We can only get out with the land breeze," said Buckland.

"Yes, sir."

There was almost no longer for the land breeze to blow, either, thought Bush; Buckland knew it as well as he did. A shot from the fort on the hill struck into the main chains at that moment, with a jarring crash and a shower of splinters. They heard the call for the fire party, and with that Buckland reached the bitter decision.

"Heave in on the spring cable," he ordered. "Get her round head to sea."

"Aye aye, sir."

Retreat—defeat; that was what that order meant. But defeat had to be faced; even with that order given there was much that had to be done to work the ship out of the imminent danger in which she lay. Bush turned to give the orders.

" 'Vast heaving at the capstan, there!"

The clanking ceased and the *Renown* rode free in the muddy, churned-up waters of the bay. To retreat she would have to turn tail, reverse herself in that confined space, and work her way out to sea. Fortunately the means were immediately available: by heaving in on the bow cable which had so far lain idle between hawsehole and anchor the ship could be brought short round.

"Cast off the stern cable messenger!"

The orders came quickly and easily; it was a routine piece of seamanship, even though it had to be carried out under the fire of red-hot shot. There were the boats still manned and afloat to drag the battered vessel out of harm's way if the precarious breeze should die away. Round came the *Renown*'s bows under the pull of the bow cable as the capstan set to work upon it. Even though the wind was dying away to a sweltering calm movement was obvious—but the shock of defeat and the contemplation of that accursed artillery! While the capstan was dragging the ship up to her anchor the necessity for keeping the ship on the move occurred to Bush. He touched his hat to Buckland again.

"Shall I warp her down the bay, sir?"

Buckland had been standing by the binnacle staring vacantly at the fort. It was not a question of physical cowardice—that was obvious—but the shock of defeat and the contemplation of the future had made the man temporarily incapable of logical thought. But Bush's question prodded him back into dealing with the current situation.

"Yes," said Buckland, and Bush turned away, happy to have something useful to do which he well knew how to do.

Another anchor had to be cockbilled at the port bow, another cable roused out. A hail to James, in command of the boats since Roberts' death, told him of the new evolution and called him under the bows for the anchor to be lowered down to the launch—the trickiest part of the whole business. Then the launch's crew bent to their oars and towed ahead, their boat crank with the ponderous weight that it bore dangling aft and with the cable paying out astern of it. Yard by yard, to the monotonous turning of the capstan, the *Renown* crept up to her first anchor, and when that cable was straight up and down the flutter of a signal warned James, now far ahead in the launch, to drop the anchor his boat carried and return for the stream anchor which was about to be hauled up. The stern cable, now of no more use, had to be unhitched and got in, the effort of the capstan transferred from one cable to the other, while the two cutters were given lines by which they could contribute their tiny effort to the general result, towing the ponderous ship and giving her the smallest conceivable amount of motion which yet was valuable when it was a matter of such urgency to withdraw the ship out of range.

Down below Hornblower was at work dragging forward the guns he had previously dragged aft; the rumble and squeal of the trucks over the planking was audible through the ship over the monotonous clanking of the capstan. Overhead blazed the pitiless sun, softening the pitch in the seams, while yard after painful yard, cable's length after cable's length, the ship crept on down the bay out of range of the red-hot shot, over the glittering still water; down the bay of Samaná until at last they were out of range, and could pause while the men drank a niggardly half-pint of warm odorous water before turning back to their labours. To bury the dead, to repair the damages, and to digest the realization of defeat. Maybe to wonder if the captain's malign influence still persisted, mad and helpless though he was.

VIII

When the tropic night closed down upon the battered *Renown*, as she stood off the land under easy sail, just enough to stiffen her to ride easily over the Atlantic rollers that the trade wind, reinforced by the sea breeze, sent hurrying under her bows, Buckland sat anxiously discussing the situation with his new first lieutenant. Despite the breeze, the little cabin was like an oven; the two lanterns which hung from the deck beams to illuminate the chart on the table seemed to heat the room unbearably. Bush felt the perspiration prickling under his uniform, and his stock constricted his thick neck so that every now and again he put two fingers into it and tugged, without relief. It would have been the simplest matter in the world to take off his heavy uniform coat and unhook his stock, but it never crossed his mind that he should do so. Bodily discomfort was something that one bore without complaint in a hard world; habit and pride both helped.

"Then you think we should bear up for Jamaica?" asked Buckland.

"I wouldn't go as far as to advise it, sir," replied Bush, cautiously.

The responsibility was Buckland's, entirely Buckland's, by the law of the navy, and Bush was a little irked at Buckland's trying to share it.

"But what else can we do?" asked Buckland. "What do you suggest?"

Bush remembered the plan of campaign Hornblower had sketched out to him, but he did not put it instantly forward; he had not weighed it sufficiently in his mind—he did not even know if he thought it practicable. Instead he temporized.

"If we head for Jamaica it'll be with our tail between our legs, sir," he said.

"That's perfectly true," agreed Buckland, with a helpless gesture. "There's the captain—"

"Yes," said Bush. "There's the captain."

If the *Renown* were to report to the admiral at Kingston with a resounding success to her record there might not be too diligent an inquiry into past events; but if she came limping in, defeated, battered, it would be far more likely that inquiry might be made into the reasons why her captain had been put under restraint, why Buckland had read the secret orders, why he had taken upon himself the responsibility of making the attack upon Samaná.

"It was young Hornblower who said the same thing to me," complained Buckland pettishly. "I wish I'd never listened to him."

"What did you ask him, sir?" asked Bush.

"Oh, I can't say that I asked him anything," replied Buckland, pettishly again. "We were yarning together on the quarterdeck one evening. It was his watch."

"I remember, sir," prompted Bush.

"We talked. The infernal little whippersnapper said just what you were saying—I don't remember how it started. But then it was a question of going to Antigua. Hornblower said that it would be better if we had the chance to achieve something before we faced an inquiry about the captain. He said it was my opportunity. So it was, I suppose. My great chance. But with Hornblower talking you'd think I was going to be posted captain tomorrow. And now—"

Buckland's gesture indicated how much chance he thought he had of ever being posted captain now.

Bush thought about the report Buckland would have to make: nine killed and twenty wounded; the *Renown*'s attack ignominiously beaten off; Samaná Bay as safe a refuge for privateers as ever. He was glad he was not Buckland, but at the same time he realized that there was grave danger of his being tarred with the same brush. He was first lieutenant now, he was one of the officers who had acquiesced, if nothing more, in the displacement of Sawyer from command, and it would take a victory to invest him with any virtue at all in the eyes of his superiors.

"Damn it," said Buckland in pathetic self-defence, "we did our best. Anyone could run aground in that channel. It wasn't our fault that the helmsman was killed. Nothing could get up the bay under that crossfire."

"Hornblower was suggesting a landing on the seaward side. In Scotchman's Bay, sir." Bush was speaking as cautiously as he could.

"Another of Hornblower's suggestions?" said Buckland.

"I think that's what he had in mind from the start, sir. A landing and a surprise attack."

Probably it was because the attempt had failed, but Bush now could see the unreason of taking a wooden ship into a situation where redhot cannon balls could be fired into her.

"What do *you* think?"

"Well, sir—"

Bush was not sure enough about what he thought to be able to express himself with any clarity. But if they had failed once they might as well fail twice; as well be hanged for a sheep as for a lamb. Bush was a sturdy soul; it went against his grain to yield in face of difficulties, and he was irritated at the thought of a tame retreat after a single repulse. The difficulty was to devise an alternative plan of campaign. He tried to say all these things to Buckland, and was sufficiently carried away to be incautious.

"I see," said Buckland. In the light of the swaying lamps the play of the shadows on his face accentuated the struggle in his expression. He came to a sudden decision. "Let's hear what he has to say."

"Aye aye, sir. Smith has the watch. Hornblower has the middle— I expect he has turned in until he's called."

Buckland was as weary as anyone in the ship—wearier than most, it seemed likely. The thought of Hornblower stretched at ease in his cot while his superiors sat up fretting wrought Buckland up to a pitch of decision that he might not otherwise have reached, determining him to act at once instead of waiting till the morrow.

"Pass the word for him," he ordered.

Hornblower came into the cabin with commendable promptitude, his hair tousled and his clothes obviously hastily thrown on. He threw a nervous glance round the cabin as he entered; obviously he suffered from not unreasonable doubts as to why he had been summoned thus into the presence of his superiors.

"What plan is this I've been hearing about?" asked Buckland. "You had some suggestion for storming the fort, I understand, Mr. Hornblower."

Hornblower did not answer immediately; he was marshalling his arguments and reconsidering his first plan in the light of the new situation—Bush could see that it was hardly fair that Hornblower should be called upon to state his plan now that the *Renown* had made one attempt and had failed after sacrificing the initial advantage of surprise. But Bush could see that he was reordering his ideas.

"I thought a landing might have more chance, sir," he said. "But that was before the Dons knew there was a ship of the line in the neighbourhood."

"And now you don't think so?"

Buckland's tone was a mixture of relief and disappointment—relief that he might not have to reach any further decisions, and disappointment that some easy way of gaining success was not being put forward. But Hornblower had had time now to sort out his ideas, and to think about times and distances. That showed in his face.

"I think something might well be tried, sir, as long as it was tried at once."

"At once?" This was night, the crew were weary, and Buckland's tone showed surprise at the suggestion of immediate activity. "You don't mean tonight?"

"Tonight might be the best time, sir. The Dons have seen us driven off with our tail between our legs—excuse me, sir, but that's how it'll look to them, at least. The last they saw of us was beating out of Samaná Bay at sunset. They'll be pleased with themselves. You know how they are, sir. An attack at dawn from another quarter, overland, would be the last thing they'd expect."

That sounded like sense to Bush, and he made a small approving noise, the most he would venture towards making a contribution to the debate.

"How would you make this attack, Mr. Hornblower?" asked Buckland.

Hornblower had his ideas in order now; the weariness disappeared and there was a glow of enthusiasm in his face.

"The wind's fair for Scotchman's Bay, sir. We could be back there in less than two hours—before midnight. By the time we arrive we can have the landing party told off and prepared. A hundred seamen and the marines. There's a good landing beach there—we saw it yesterday. The country inland must be marshy, before the hills of the peninsula start again, but we can land on the peninsula side of the marsh. I marked the place yesterday, sir."

"Well?"

Hornblower swallowed the realization that it was possible for a man not to be able to continue from that point with a single leap of his imagination.

"The landing party can make their way up to the crest without difficulty, sir. There's no question of losing their way—the sea one side and Samaná Bay on the other. They can move forward along the crest. At dawn they can rush the fort. What with the marsh and the cliffs the Dons'll keep a poor lookout on that side, I fancy, sir."

"You make it sound very easy, Mr. Hornblower. But—a hundred and eighty men?"

"Enough, I think, sir."

"What makes you think so?"

"There were six guns firing at us from the fort, sir. Ninety men at most—sixty more likely. Ammunition party; men to heat the furnaces. A hundred and fifty men altogether; perhaps as few as a hundred."

"But why should that be all they had?"

"The Dons have nothing to fear on that side of the island. They're holding out against the blacks, and the French, maybe, and the English in Jamaica. There's nothing to tempt the blacks to attack 'em across the marshes. It's south of Samaná Bay that the danger lies. The Don'll have every man that can carry a musket on that side. That's where the cities are. That's where this fellow Toussaint, or whatever his name is, will be threatening 'em, sir."

The last word of this long speech came as a fortunate afterthought; Hornblower clearly was restraining himself from pointing out the obvious too didactically to his superior officer. And Bush could see Buckland squirm in discomfort at this casual mention of blacks and French. Those secret orders—which Bush had not been allowed to read—must lay down some drastic instructions regarding the complicated political situation in Santo Domingo, where the revolted slaves, the French, and the Spaniards (nominal allies though these last might be, elsewhere in the world) all contended for the mastery.

"We'll leave the blacks and the French out of this," said Buckland, confirming Bush's suspicions.

"Yes, sir. But the Dons won't," said Hornblower, not very abashed. "They're more afraid of the blacks than of us at present."

"So you think this attack might succeed?" asked Buckland, desperately changing the subject.

"I think it might, sir. But time's getting on."

Buckland sat looking at his two juniors in painful indecision, and Bush felt full sympathy for him. A second bloody repulse—possibly something even worse, the cutting off and capitulation of the entire landing party—would be Buckland's certain ruin.

"With the fort in our hands, sir," said Hornblower, "we can deal with the privateers up the bay. They could never use it as an anchorage again."

"That's true," agreed Buckland. It would be a neat and economical fulfilment of his orders; it would restore his credit.

The timbers of the ship creaked rhythmically as the *Renown* rode over the waves. The trade wind came blowing into the cabin, relieving it of some of its stuffiness, breathing cooler air on Bush's sweaty face.

"Damn it," said Buckland with sudden reckless decision, "let's do it."

"Very good sir," said Hornblower.

Bush had to restrain himself from saying something that would express his pleasure; Hornblower had used a neutral tone—too obvious pushing of Buckland along the path of action might have a reverse effect and goad him into reversing his decision even now.

And although this decision had been reached there was another one, almost equally important, which had to be reached at once.

"Who will be in command?" asked Buckland. It could only be a rhetorical question; nobody except Buckland could possibly supply the answer, and to Bush and Hornblower this was obvious. They could only wait.

"It'd be poor Roberts' duty if he had lived," said Buckland, and then he turned to look at Bush.

"Mr. Bush, you will take command."

"Aye aye, sir."

Bush got up from his chair and stood with his head bowed uneasily under the deck timbers above.

"Who do you want to take with you?"

Hornblower had been on his feet during the whole interview; now he shifted his weight self-consciously from one foot to the other.

"Do you require me any more, sir?" he said to Buckland.

Bush could not tell by looking at him what emotions were at work in him; he had the pose merely of a respectful, attentive officer. Bush thought about Smith, the remaining lieutenant in the ship. He thought about Whiting, the captain of marines, who would certainly have to take part in the landing. There were midshipmen and master's mates to be used as subordinate officers. He was going to be responsible for a risky and desperate operation of war—now it was his own credit, as well as Buckland's, that was at stake. Whom did he want at his side at this, one of the most important moments in his career? Another lieutenant, if he asked for one, would be second in command, might expect to have a voice in the decisions to be made.

"Do we need Mr. Hornblower any more, Mr. Bush?" asked Buckland.

Hornblower would be an active subordinate in command. A restless one, would be another way of expressing it. He would be apt to criticize, in thought at least. Bush did not think he cared to exercise command with Hornblower listening to his every order. This whole internal debate of Bush's did not take definite shape, with formal arguments pro and con; it was rather a conflict of prejudices and instincts, the result of years of experience, which Bush could never have expressed in words. He decided he needed neither Hornblower nor Smith at the moment before he looked again at Hornblower's face. Hornblower was trying to remain impassive; but Bush could see, with sympathetic insight, how desperately anxious he was to be invited to join in the expedition. Any officer would want to go, of course, would yearn to be given an opportunity to distinguish himself, but actuating Hornblower was some motive more urgent than this. Hornblower's hands were at his sides, in the "attention" position, but Bush noticed how the long fingers tapped against his thighs, restrained themselves, and then tapped again uncontrollably. It was not cool judgment that finally brought Bush to his decision, but something quite otherwise. It might be called kindliness; it might be called affection. He had grown fond of this volatile, versatile young man, and he had no doubts now as to his physical courage.

"I'd like Mr. Hornblower to come with me, sir," he said: it seemed almost without his volition that the words came from his mouth; a softhearted elder brother might have said much the same thing, burdening himself with the presence of a much younger brother out of kindness of heart when contemplating some pleasant day's activities.

And as he spoke he received a glance in return from Hornblower that stifled at birth any regrets he may have felt at allowing his sentiments to influence his judgment. There was so much of relief, so much of gratitude, in the way Hornblower looked at him that Bush experienced a kindly glow of magnanimity; he felt a bigger and better man for what he had done. Naturally he did not for a moment see anything incongruous about Hornblower's being grateful for a decision that would put him in peril of his life.

"Very well, Mr. Bush," said Buckland; typically, he wavered for a space after agreeing. "That will leave me with only one lieutenant."

"Carberry could take watch, sir," replied Bush. "And there are several among the master's mates who are good watch-keeping officers."

It was as natural for Bush to argue down opposition once he had committed himself as it might be for a fish to snap at a lure.

"Very well," said Buckland again, almost with a sigh. "And what is it that's troubling you, Mr. Hornblower?"

"Nothing, sir."

"There was something you wanted to say. Out with it."

"Nothing important, sir. It can wait. But I was wondering about altering course, sir. We can head for Scotchman's Bay now and waste no time."

"I suppose we can." Buckland knew as well as any officer in the navy that the whims of wind and weather were unpredictable, and that action upon any decision at sea should in consequence never be delayed, but he was likely to forget it unless he were prodded. "Oh, very well. We'd better get her before the wind, then. What's the course?"

After the bustle of wearing the ship round had died away Buckland led the way back to his cabin and threw himself wearily into his chair again. He put on a whimsical air to conceal the anxiety which was now consuming him afresh.

"We've satisfied Mr. Hornblower for a moment," he said. "Now let's hear what you need, Mr. Bush."

The discussion regarding the proposed expedition proceeded along normal lines; the men to be employed, the equipment that was to be issued to them, the rendezvous that had to be arranged for next morning. Hornblower kept himself studiously in the background as these points were settled.

"Any suggestions, Mr. Hornblower?" asked Bush at length. Politeness, if not policy as well, dictated the question.

"Only one, sir. We might have with us some boat grapnels with lines attached. If we have to scale the walls they might be useful."

"That's so," agreed Bush. "Remember to see that they're issued."

"Aye aye, sir."

"Do you need a messenger, Mr. Hornblower?" asked Buckland.

"It might be better if I had one, sir."

"Anyone in particular?"

"I'd prefer to have Wellard, sir, if you've no objection. He's cool-headed and thinks quickly."

"Very well." Buckland looked hard at Hornblower at the mention of Wellard's name, but said nothing more on the subject for the moment.

"Anything else? No? Mr. Bush? All settled?"

"Yes, sir," said Bush.

Buckland drummed with his fingers on the table. The recent alteration of course had not been the decisive move; it did not commit him to anything. But the next order would. If the hands were roused out, arms issued to them, instructions given for a landing, he could hardly draw back. Another attempt; maybe another failure; maybe a disaster. It was not in his power to command success, while it was certainly in his power to obviate failure by simply not risking it. He looked up and met the gaze of his two subordinates turned on him remorselessly. No, it was too late now—he had been mistaken when he thought he could draw back. He could not.

"Then it only remains to issue the orders," he said. "Will you see to it, if you please?"

"Aye aye, sir," said Bush.

He and Hornblower were about to leave the cabin when Buckland asked the question he had wanted to ask for so long. It necessitated an abrupt change of subject, even though the curiosity that inspired the question had been reawakened by Hornblower's mention of Wellard. But Buckland, full of the virtuous glow of having reached a decision, felt emboldened to ask the question; it was a moment of exaltation in any case, and confidences were possible.

"By the way, Mr. Hornblower," he said, and Hornblower halted beside the door, "how did the captain come to fall down the hatchway?"

Bush saw the expressionless mask take the place of the eager look on Hornblower's face. The answer took a moment or two to come.

"I think he must have overbalanced, sir," said Hornblower, with the utmost respect and a complete absence of feeling in his voice. "The ship was lively that night, you remember, sir."

"I suppose she was," said Buckland; disappointment and perplexity were audible in his tone. He stared at Hornblower, but there was nothing to be gleaned from that face. "Oh, very well then. Carry on."

"Aye aye, sir."

IX

The sea breeze had died away with the cooling of the land, and it was that breathless time of night when air pressures over island and ocean were evenly balanced. Not many miles out at sea the trade winds could blow, as they blew eternally, but here on the beach a humid calm prevailed. The long swell of the Atlantic broke momentarily at the first hint of shallows far out, but lived on, like some once vigorous man now feeble after an illness, to burst rhythmically in foam on the beach to the westward; here, where the limestone cliffs of the Samaná peninsula began, there was a sheltered corner where a small watercourse had worn a wide gully in the cliff, at the most easterly end of the wide beach. And sea and surf and beach seemed to be afire; in the dark night the phosphorescence of the water was vividly bright, heaving up with the surf, running up the beach with the breakers, and lighting up the oar blades as the launches pulled to shore. The boats seemed to be floating on fire which derived new life from their passage; each launch left a wake of fire behind it, with a vivid streak on either side where the oar blades had bitten into the water.

Both landing and ascent were easy at the foot of the gully; the launches nuzzled their bows into the sand and the landing party had only to climb out, thigh-deep in the water—thigh-deep in liquid fire —holding their weapons and cartridge boxes high to make sure they were not wetted. Even the experienced seamen in the party were impressed by the brightness of the phosphorescence; the raw hands were excited by it enough to raise a bubbling chatter which called for a sharp order to repress it. Bush was one of the earliest to climb out of his launch; he splashed ashore and stood on the unaccustomed solidity of the beach while the others followed him; the water streamed down out of his soggy trouser legs.

A dark figure appeared before him, coming from the direction of the other launch.

"My party is all ashore, sir," it reported.

"Very good, Mr. Hornblower."

"I'll start up the gully with the advanced guard then, sir?"

"Yes, Mr. Hornblower. Carry out your orders."

Bush was tense and excited, as far as his stoical training and phlegmatic temperament would allow him to be; he would have liked to plunge into action at once, but the careful scheme worked out in consultation with Hornblower did not allow it. He stood aside while his own party was being formed up and Hornblower called the other division to order.

"Starbowlines! Follow me closely. Every man is to keep in touch with the man ahead of him. Remember your muskets aren't loaded—it's no use snapping them if we meet an enemy. Cold steel for that. If any one of you is fool enough to load and fire he'll get four dozen at the gangway tomorrow. That I promise you. Woolton!"

"Sir!"

"Bring up the rear. Now follow me, you men, starting from the right of the line."

Hornblower's party filed off into the darkness. Already the marines were coming ashore, their scarlet tunics black against the phosphorescence. The white crossbelts were faintly visible side by side in a rigid two-deep line as they formed up, the non-commissioned officers snapping low-voiced orders at them. With his left hand still resting on his sword hilt Bush checked once more with his right hand that his pistols were in his belt and his cartridges in his pocket. A shadowy figure halted before him with a military click of the heels.

"All present and correct, sir. Ready to march off!," said Whiting's voice.

"Thank you. We may as well start. Mr. Abbott!"

"Sir!"

"You have your orders. I'm leaving with the marine detachment now. Follow us."

"Aye aye, sir."

It was a long hard climb up the gully; the sand soon was replaced by rock, flat ledges of limestone, but even among the limestone there was a sturdy vegetation, fostered by the tropical rains which fell profusely on this northern face. Only in the bed of the watercourse itself, dry now with all the water having seeped into the limestone, was there a clear passage, if clear it could be called, for it was jagged and irregular, with steep ledges up which Bush had to heave himself.

In a few minutes he was streaming with sweat, but he climbed on stubbornly. Behind him the marines followed clumsily, boots clashing, weapons and equipment clinking, so that anyone might think the noise would be heard a mile away. Someone slipped and swore.

"Keep a still tongue in yer 'ead!" snapped a corporal.

"Silence!" snarled Whiting over his shoulder.

Onward and upward; here and there the vegetation was lofty enough to cut off the faint light from the stars, and Bush had to grope his way along over the rock, his breath coming with difficulty, powerfully built man though he was. Fireflies showed here and there as he climbed; it was years since he had seen fireflies last, but he paid no attention to them now. They excited irrepressible comment among the marines following him, though; Bush felt a bitter rage against the uncontrolled louts who were imperilling everything—their own lives as well as the success of the expedition—by their silly comments.

"I'll deal with 'em, sir," said Whiting, and dropped back to let the column overtake him.

Higher up a squeaky voice, moderated as best its owner knew how, greeted him from the darkness ahead.

"Mr. Bush, sir?"

"Yes."

"This is Wellard, sir. Mr. Hornblower sent me back here to act as guide. There's grassland beginning just above here."

"Very well," said Bush.

He halted for a space, wiping his streaming face with his coat sleeve, while the column closed up behind him. It was not much farther to climb when he moved on again; Wellard led him past a clump of shadowy trees, and, sure enough, Bush felt grass under his feet, and he could walk more freely, uphill still, but only a gentle slope compared with the gully. There was a low challenge ahead of them.

"Friend," said Wellard. "This is Mr. Bush here."

"Glad to see you, sir," said another voice—Hornblower's.

Hornblower detached himself from the darkness and came forward to make his report.

"My party is formed up just ahead, sir. I've sent Saddler and two reliable men on as scouts."

"Very good," said Bush, and meant it.

The marine sergeant was reporting to Whiting.

"All present, sir, 'cept for Chapman, sir. 'E's sprained 'is ankle, or 'e says 'e 'as, sir. Left 'im be'ind back there, sir."

"Let your men rest, Captain Whiting," said Bush.

Life in the confines of a ship of the line was no sort of training for climbing cliffs in the tropics, especially as the day before had been exhausting. The marines lay down, some of them with groans of relief which drew the unmistakable reproof of savage kicks from the sergeant's toe.

"We're on the crest here, sir," said Hornblower. "You can see over into the bay from that side there."

"Three miles from the fort, d'ye think?"

Bush did not mean to ask a question, for he was in command, but Hornblower was so ready with his report that Bush could not help doing so.

"Perhaps. Less than four, anyway, sir. Dawn in four hours from now, and the moon rises in half an-hour."

"Yes."

"There's some sort of track or path along the crest, sir, as you'd expect. It should lead to the fort."

"Yes."

Hornblower was a good subordinate, clearly. Bush realized now that there would naturally be a track along the crest of the peninsula—that would be the obvious thing—but the probability had not occurred to him until that moment.

"If you will permit me, sir," went on Hornblower, "I'll leave James in command of my party and push on ahead with Saddler and Wellard and see how the land lies."

"Very good, Mr. Hornblower."

Yet no sooner had Hornblower left than Bush felt a vague irritation. It seemed that Hornblower was taking too much on himself. Bush was not a man who would tolerate any infringement upon his authority. However, Bush was distracted from this train of thought by the arrival of the second division of seamen, who came sweating and gasping up to join the main body. With the memory of his own weariness when he arrived still fresh in his mind Bush allowed them a rest period before he should push on with his united force. Even in the darkness a cloud of insects had discovered the sweating force, and a host of them sang round Bush's ears and bit him viciously at every opportunity. The crew of the *Renown* had been long at sea and were tender and desirable in consequence. Bush slapped at himself and swore, and every man in his command did the same.

"Mr. Bush, sir?"

It was Hornblower back again.

"Yes?"

"It's a definite trail, sir. It crosses a gully just ahead, but it's not a serious obstacle."

"Thank you, Mr. Hornblower. We'll move forward. Start with your division, if you please."

"Aye aye, sir."

The advance began. The domed limestone top of the peninsula was covered with long grass, interspersed with occasional trees. Off the track walking was a little difficult on account of the toughness and irregularity of the bunches of high grass, but on the track it was comparatively easy. The men could move along it in something like a solid body, well closed up. Their eyes, thoroughly accustomed to the darkness, could see in the starlight enough to enable them to pick their way. The gully that Hornblower had reported was only a shallow depression with easily sloping sides and presented no difficulty.

Bush plodded on at the head of the marines with Whiting at his side, the darkness all about him like a warm blanket. There was a kind of dreamlike quality about the march, induced perhaps by the fact that Bush had not slept for twenty-four hours and was stupid with the fatigues he had undergone during that period. The path was ascending gently—naturally, of course, since it was rising to the highest part of the peninsula where the fort was sited.

"Ah!" said Whiting suddenly.

The path had wandered to the right, away from the sea and towards the bay, and now they had crossed the backbone of the peninsula and opened up the view over the bay. On their right they could see clear down the bay to the sea, and there it was not quite dark, for above the horizon a little moonlight was struggling through the clouds that lay at the lower edge of the sky.

"Mr. Bush, sir?"

This was Wellard, his voice more under command this time.

"Here I am."

"Mr. Hornblower sent me back again, sir. There's another gully ahead, crossing the path. An' we've come across some cattle, sir. Asleep on the hill. We disturbed 'em, and they're wandering about."

"Thank you, I understand," said Bush.

Bush had the lowest opinion of the ordinary man and the subordinary man who constituted the great bulk of his command. He knew perfectly well that if they were to blunder into cattle along this path they would think they were meeting the enemy. There would be excitement and noise, even if there was no shooting.

"Tell Mr. Hornblower I am going to halt for fifteen minutes."

"Aye aye, sir."

A rest and opportunity to close up the column were desirable for the weary men in any case, as long as there was time to spare. And during the rest the men could be personally and individually warned about the possibility of encountering cattle. Bush knew that merely to pass the word back down the column would be unsatisfactory, actually unsafe, with these tired and slow-witted men. He gave the order and the column came to a halt, of course with sleepy men bumping into the men in front of them with a clatter and a murmur that the whispered curses of the petty officers with difficulty suppressed. While the warning was being circulated among the men lying in the grass another trouble was reported to Bush by a petty officer.

"Seaman Black, sir. 'E's drunk."

"Drunk?"

" 'E must 'ave 'ad sperrits in 'is canteen, sir. You can smell it on 'is breff. Dunno 'ow 'e got it, sir."

With a hundred and eighty seamen and marines under his command one man at least was likely to be drunk. The ability of the British sailor to get hold of liquor and his readiness to over-indulge in it were part of his physical make-up, like his ears or his eyes.

"Where is he now?"

" 'E made a noise, sir, so I clipped 'im on the ear'ole an' 'e's quiet now, sir."

There was much left untold in that brief sentence, as Bush could guess, but he had no reason to make further inquiry while he thought of what to do.

"Choose a steady seaman and leave him with Black when we go on."

"Aye aye, sir."

So the landing party was the weaker now by the loss of the services not only of the drunken Black but of the man who must be left behind to keep him out of mischief. But it was lucky that there were not more stragglers than there had been up to now.

As the column moved forward again Hornblower's unmistakable gangling figure showed up ahead, silhouetted against the faint moonlight. He fell into step beside Bush and made his report.

"I've sighted the fort, sir."

"You have?"

"Yes, sir. A mile ahead from here, or thereabouts, there's another gully. The fort's beyond that. You can see it against the moon. Maybe half a mile beyond, maybe less. I've left Wellard and Saddler at the gully with orders to halt the advance there."

"Thank you."

Bush plodded on over the uneven surface. Now despite his fatigue he was growing tense again, as the tiger having scented his prey braces his muscles for the spring. Bush was a fighting man, and the thought of action close ahead acted as a stimulant to him. Two hours to sunrise; time and to spare.

"Half a mile from the gully to the fort?" he asked.

"Less than that, I should say, sir."

"Very well. I'll halt there and wait for daylight."

"Yes, sir. May I go on to join my division?"

"You may, Mr. Hornblower."

Bush and Whiting were holding down the pace of the march to a slow methodical step, adapted to the capacity of the slowest and clumsiest man in the column; Bush at this moment was checking himself from lengthening his stride under the spur of the prospect of action. Hornblower went plunging ahead; Bush could see his awkward gait but found himself approving of his subordinate's overflowing energy. He began to discuss with Whiting plans for the final assault.

There was a petty officer waiting for them at the approach to the gully. Bush passed the word back for the column to be ready to halt, and then halted it. He went forward to reconnoitre; with Whiting and Hornblower beside him he stared forward at the square silhouette of the fort against the sky. It even seemed possible to see the dark line of the flagpole. Now his tenseness was eased; the scowl that had been on his face in the last stages of the advance had softened into an expression of good humour, which was wasted in the circumstances.

The arrangements were quickly made, the orders whispered back and forth, the final warnings given. It was the most dangerous moment so far, as the men had to be moved up into the gully and deployed ready for a rush. One whisper from Whiting called for more than a moment's cogitation from Bush.

"Shall I give permission for the men to load, sir?"

"No," answered Bush at length. "Cold steel."

It would be too much of a risk to allow all those muskets to be loaded in the dark. There would not only be the noise of the ramrods, but there was also the danger of some fool pulling a trigger. Hornblower went off to the left, Whiting with his marines to the right, and Bush lay down in the midst of his division in the centre. His legs ached with their unaccustomed exercise, and as he lay his head was inclined to swim with fatigue and lack of sleep. He roused himself and sat up so as to bring himself under control again. Except for his weariness he did not find the waiting period troublesome to him; years of life at sea with its uncounted eventless watches, and years of war with its endless periods of boredom, had inured him to waiting. Some of the seamen actually slept as they lay in the rocky gully; more than once Bush heard snores begin, abruptly cut off by the nudges of the snorers' neighbours.

Now there, at last, right ahead, beyond the fort—was the sky a little paler? Or was it merely that the moon had climbed above the cloud? All round about save there the sky was like purple velvet, still spangled with stars. But there—there—undoubtedly there was a pallor in the sky which had not been there before. Bush stirred and felt again at the uncomfortable pistols in his belt. They were at half-cock; he must remember to pull the hammers back. On the horizon there was a suspicion, the merest suggestion, of a redness mingled with the purple of the sky.

"Pass the word down the line," said Bush. "Prepare to attack."

He waited for the word to pass, but in less time than was possible for it to have reached the ends of the line there were sounds and disturbances in the gully. The damned fools who were always to be found in any body of men had started to rise as soon as the word had reached them, probably without even bothering to pass the word on themselves. But the example would be infectious, at least; beginning at the wings, and coming back to the centre where Bush was, a double ripple of men rising to their feet went along the line. Bush rose too. He drew his sword, balanced it in his hand, and when he was satisfied with his grip he drew a pistol with his left hand and pulled back the hammer. Over on the right there was a sudden clatter of metal; the marines were fixing their bayonets. Bush could see the faces now of the men to right and to left of him.

"Forward!" he said, and the line came surging up out of the gully. "Steady, there!"

He said the last words almost loudly; sooner or later the hotheads in the line would start to run, and later would be better than sooner. He wanted his men to reach the fort in a single wave, not in a succession of breathless individuals. Out on the left he heard Hornblower's voice saying "Steady," as well. The noise of the advance must reach the fort now, must attract the attention even of sleepy, careless Spanish sentries. Soon a sentry would call for his sergeant, the sergeant would come to see, would hesitate a moment, and then give the alarm. The fort bulked square in front of Bush, still shadowy black against the newly red sky; he simply could not restrain himself from quickening his step, and the line came hurrying forward along with him. Then someone raised a shout, and then the other hotheads shouted, and the whole line started to run, Bush running with them.

Like magic, they were at the edge of the ditch, a six-foot scarp, almost vertical, cut in the limestone.

"Come on!" shouted Bush.

Even with his sword and his pistol in his hands he was able to precipitate himself down the scarp, turning his back to the fort and clinging to the edge with his elbows before allowing himself to drop. The bottom of the dry ditch was slippery and irregular, but he plunged across it to the opposite scarp. Yelling men clustered along it, hauling themselves up.

"Give me a hoist!" shouted Bush to the men on either side of him, and they put their shoulders to his thighs and almost threw him up bodily. He found himself on his face, lying on the narrow shelf above the ditch at the foot of the ramparts. A few yards along a seaman was already trying to fling his grapnel up to the top. It came thundering down, missing Bush by no more than a yard, but the seaman without a glance at him snatched it back, poised himself again, and flung the grapnel up the ramparts. It caught, and the seaman, setting his feet against the ramparts and grasping the line with his hands, began to climb like a madman. Before he was half-way up another seaman had grabbed the line and started to scale the ramparts after him, and a yelling crowd of excited men gathered round contending for the next place. Farther along the foot of the ramparts another grapnel had caught and another crowd of yelling men were gathered about the line. Now there was musketry fire; a good many loud reports, and a whiff of powder smoke came to Bush's nostrils in sharp contrast with the pure night air that he had been breathing.

Round on the other face of the fort on his right the marines would be trying to burst in through the embrasures of the guns; Bush turned to his left to see what could be done there. Almost instantly he found his reward; here was the sally port into the fort—a wide wooden door bound with iron, sheltered in the angle of the small projecting bastion at the corner of the fort. Two idiots of seamen were firing their muskets up at the heads that were beginning to show above—not a thought for the door. The average seaman was not fit to be trusted with a musket. Bush raised his voice so that it pealed like a trumpet above the din.

"Axemen here! Axemen! Axemen!"

There were still plenty of men down in the ditch who had not yet had time to scale the scarp; one of them, waving an axe, plunged through the crowd and began to climb up. But Silk, the immensely powerful bosun's mate who commanded a section of seamen in Bush's division, came running along the shelf and grabbed the axe. He began to hew at the door, with tremendous methodical blows, gathering his body together and then flinging the axehead into the wood with all the strength in his body. Another axeman arrived, elbowed Bush aside, and started to hack at the door as well, but he was neither as accomplished nor as powerful. The thunder of their blows resounded in the angle. The iron-barred wicket in the door opened, with a gleam of steel beyond the bars. Bush pointed his pistol and fired. Silk's axe drove clean through the door, and he wrenched the blade free; then, changing his aim, he began to swing the axe in a horizontal arc at the middle part of the door. Three mighty blows and he paused to direct the other axeman where to strike. Silk struck again and again; then he put down the axe, set his fingers in the jagged hole that had opened, his foot against the door and with one frightful muscle-tearing effort he rent away a whole section of the door. There was a beam across the gap he had opened; Silk's axe crashed onto it and through it, and again. With a hoarse shout Silk plunged, axe in hand, through the jagged hole.

"Come along, men!" yelled Bush, at the top of his lungs, and plunged through after him.

This was the open courtyard of the fort. Bush stumbled over a dead man and looked up to see a group of men before him, in their shirts, or naked; coffee-coloured faces with long disordered moustaches; men with cutlasses and pistols. Silk flung himself upon them like a maniac, the axe swinging. A Spaniard fell under the axe; Bush saw a severed finger fall to the ground as the axe crashed through the Spaniard's ineffectual guard. Pistols banged and smoke eddied about as Bush rushed forward too. There were other men swarming after him. Bush's sword clashed against a cutlass and then the group turned and fled. Bush swung with his sword at a naked shoulder fleeing before him, and saw a red wound open in the flesh and heard the man scream. The man he was pursuing vanished somewhere, like a wraith, and Bush, hurrying on to find other enemies, met a red-coated marine, hatless, his hair wild and his eyes blazing, yelling like a fiend. Bush actually had to parry the bayonet-thrust the marine made at him.

"Steady, you fool!" shouted Bush, only conscious after the words had passed his lips that they were spoken at the top of his voice.

There was a hint of recognition in the marine's mad eyes, and he turned aside, his bayonet at the charge, and rushed on. There were other marines in the background; they must have made their way in through the embrasures. They were all yelling, all drunk with fighting. And here was another rush of seamen, swarming down from the ramparts they had scaled. On the far side there were wooden buildings; his men were swarming round them and shots and screams were echoing from them. Those must be the barracks and storehouses, and the garrison must have fled there for shelter from the fury of the stormers.

Whiting appeared, his scarlet tunic filthy, his sword dangling from his wrist. His eyes were bleary and cloudy.

"Call 'em off," said Bush, grasping at his own sanity with a desperate effort.

It took Whiting a moment to recognize him and to understand the order.

"Yes, sir," he said.

A fresh flood of seamen came pouring into view beyond the buildings; Hornblower's division had found its way into the fort on the far side, evidently. Bush looked round him and called to a group of his own men who appeared at that moment.

"Follow me," he said, and pushed on.

A ramp with an easy slope led up the side of the ramparts. A dead man lay there, half-way up, but Bush gave the corpse no more attention than it deserved. At the top was the main battery, six huge guns pointing through the embrasures. And beyond was the sky, all bloody-red with the dawn. A third of the way up to the zenith reached the significant colour, but even while Bush halted to look at it a golden gleam of sun showed through the clouds on the horizon, and the red began to fade perceptibly; blue sky and white clouds and blazing golden sun took its place. That was the measure of the time the assault had taken; only the few minutes from earliest dawn to tropical sunrise. Bush stood and grasped this astonishing fact—it could have been late afternoon as far as his own sensations went.

Here from the gun platform the whole view of the bay opened up. There was the opposite shore; the shallows where the *Renown* had grounded (was it only yesterday?), the rolling country lifting immediately into the hills of that side, with the sharply defined shape of the other battery at the foot of the point. To the left the peninsula dropped sharply in a series of jagged headlands, stretching like fingers out into the blue, blue ocean; farther round still was the sapphire surface of Scotchman's Bay, and there, with her backed mizzen topsail catching brilliantly the rising sun, lay the *Renown*. At that distance she looked like a lovely toy; Bush caught his breath at the sight of her, not because of the beauty of the scene but with relief. The sight of the ship, and the associated memories which the sight called up in his mind, brought his sanity flooding back; there were a thousand things to be done now.

Hornblower appeared up the other ramp; he looked like a scarecrow with his disordered clothes. He held sword in one hand and pistol in the other, just as did Bush. Beside him Wellard swung a cutlass singularly large for him, and at his heels were a score or more of seamen still under discipline, their muskets, with bayonets fixed, held before them ready for action.

"Morning, sir," said Hornblower. His battered cocked hat was still on his head for him to touch it, and he made a move to do so, checking himself at the realization that his sword was in his hand.

"Good morning," said Bush, automatically.

"Congratulations, sir," said Hornblower. His face was white, and the smile on his lips was like the grin of a corpse. His beard sprouted over his lips and chin.

"Thank you," said Bush.

Hornblower pushed his pistol into his belt and then sheathed his sword.

"I've taken possession of all that side, sir," he went on, with a gesture behind him. "Shall I carry on?"

"Yes, carry on, Mr. Hornblower."

"Aye aye, sir."

This time Hornblower could touch his hat. He gave a rapid order posting a petty officer and men over the guns.

"You see, sir," said Hornblower, pointing, "a few got away."

Bush looked down the precipitous hillside that fell to the bay and could see a few figures down there.

"Not enough to trouble us," he said; his mind was just beginning to work smoothly now.

"No, sir. I've forty prisoners under guard at the main gate. I can see Whiting's collecting the rest. I'll go on now, sir, if I may."

"Very well, Mr. Hornblower."

Somebody at least had kept a clear head during the fury of the assault. Bush went on down the farther ramp. A petty officer and a couple of seamen stood there on guard; they came to attention as Bush appeared.

"What are you doing?" he asked.

"This yere's the magazine, zur," said the petty officer—Ambrose, captain of the foretop, who had never lost the broad Devon acquired in his childhood, despite his years in the navy. "We'm guarding of it."

"Mr. Hornblower's orders?"

"Iss, zur."

A forlorn party of prisoners were squatting by the main gate. Hornblower had reported the presence of them. But there were guards he had said nothing about: a sentry at the well; guards at the gate; Woolton, the steadiest petty officer of them all, at a long wooden building beside the gate, and six men with him.

"What's your duty?" demanded Bush.

"Guarding the provision store, sir. There's liquor here."

"Very well."

If the madmen who had made the assault—that marine, for instance, whose bayonet-thrust Bush had parried—had got at the liquor there would be no controlling them at all.

Abbott, the midshipman in subordinate command of Bush's own dedivision, came hurrying up.

"What the hell d'ye think you've been doing?" demanded Bush, testily. "I've been without you since the attack began."

"Sorry, sir," apologized Abbott. Of course he had been carried away by the fury of the attack, but that was no excuse; certainly no excuse when one remembered young Wellard still at Hornblower's side and attending to his duties.

"Get ready to make the signal to the ship," ordered Bush. "You ought to have been ready to do that five minutes ago. Clear three guns. Who was it who was carrying the flag? Find him and bend it on over the Spanish colours. Jump to it, damn you."

Victory might be sweet, but it had no effect on Bush's temper, now that the reaction had set in. Bush had had no sleep and no breakfast, and even though perhaps only ten minutes had elapsed since the fort had been captured, his conscience nagged at him regarding those ten minutes; there were many things he ought to have done in that time.

It was a relief to turn away from the contemplation of his

own shortcomings and to settle with Whiting regarding the safeguarding of the prisoners. They had all been fetched out of the barrack buildings by now; a hundred half-naked men, and at least a score of women, their hair streaming down their backs and their scanty clothing clutched about them. At a more peaceful moment Bush would have had an eye for those women, but as it was he merely felt irritated at the thought of an additional complication to deal with, and his eyes only took note of them as such.

Among the men there was a small sprinkling of Negroes and mulattoes, but most of them were Spaniards. Nearly all the dead men who lay here and there were fully clothed, in white uniforms with blue facings—they were the sentinels and the main guard who had paid the penalty for their lack of watchfulness.

"Who was in command?" asked Bush of Whiting.

"Can't tell, sir."

"Well, ask them, then."

Bush had command of no language at all save his own, and apparently neither had Whiting, judging by his unhappy glance.

"Please, sir—" This was Pierce, surgeon's mate, trying to attract his attention. "Can I have a party to help carry the wounded into the shade?"

Before Bush could answer him Abbott was hailing from the gun platform.

"Guns clear, sir. May I draw powder charges from the magazines?"

And then before Bush could give permission here was young Wellard, trying to elbow Pierce on one side so as to command Bush's attention.

"Please, sir. Please, sir. Mr. Hornblower's respects, sir, an' could you please come up to the tower there, sir. Mr. Hornblower says it's urgent, sir."

Bush felt at that moment as if one more distraction would break his heart.

X

At each corner of the fort there was a small bastion built out, to give flanking fire along the walls, and on top of the southwest bastion stood a little watch-tower which carried the flagstaff. Bush and Hornblower stood on the tower, the broad Atlantic behind them and before them the long gulf of the bay of Samaná. Over their heads waved two flags:

the White Ensign above, the red and gold of Spain below. Out in the *Renown* they might not be able to make out the colours, but they would certainly see the two flags. And when having heard the three signal guns boom out they trained their telescopes on the fort for they must have seen the flags slowly flutter down and rise again, dip and rise again. Three guns; two flags twice dipped. That was the signal that the fort was in English hands, and the *Renown* had seen it, for she had braced up her mizzen topsail and begun the long beat back along the coast of the peninsula.

Bush and Hornblower had with them the one telescope which a hasty search through the fort had brought to light; when one of them had it to his eye the other could hardly restrain his twitching fingers from snatching at it. At the moment Bush was looking through it, training it on the farther shore of the bay, and Hornblower was stabbing with an index finger at what he had been looking at a moment before.

"You see, sir?" he asked. "Farther up the bay than the battery. There's the town—Savaná, it's called. And beyond that there's the shipping. They'll up anchor any minute now."

"I see 'em," said Bush, the glass still at his eye. "Four small craft. No sail hoisted—hard to tell what they are."

"Easy enough to guess, though, sir."

"Yes, I suppose so," said Bush.

There would be no need for big men of war here, immediately adjacent to the Mona Passage. Half the Caribbean trade came up through here, passing within thirty miles of the bay of Samaná. Fast, handy craft, with a couple of long guns each and a large crew, could dash out and snap up prizes and retire to the protection of the bay, where the crossed fire of the batteries could be relied on to keep out enemies, as the events of yesterday had proved. The raiders would hardly have to spend a night at sea.

"They'll know by now we've got this fort," said Hornblower. "They'll guess that *Renown* will be coming round after 'em. They can sweep, and tow, and kedge. They'll be out of the bay before you can say Jack Robinson. And from Engano Point it's a fair wind for Martinique."

"Very likely," agreed Bush.

With a simultaneous thought they turned to look at the *Renown*. With her stern to them, her sails braced sharp on the starboard tack, she was making her way out to sea; it would be a long beat before she could go about in the certainty of being able to weather Cape Samaná. She looked lovely enough out there, with her white sails against the rich blue, but it would be hours before she could work round to stop the bolt hole. Bush turned back and considered the sheltered waters of the bay.

"Better man the guns and make ready for 'em," he said.

"Yes, sir," said Hornblower. He hesitated. "We won't have 'em under fire for long. They'll be shallow draught. They can hug the point over there closer than *Renown* could."

"But it won't take much to sink 'em, either," said Bush. "Oh, I see what you're after."

"Red-hot shot might make all the difference, sir," said Hornblower.

"Repay 'em in their own coin," said Bush, with a grin of satisfaction. Yesterday the *Renown* had endured the hellish fire of red-hot shot. To Bush the thought of roasting a few Dagoes was quite charming.

"That's right, sir," said Hornblower.

He was not grinning like Bush. There was a frown on his face; he was oppressed with the thought that the privateers might escape to continue their depredations elsewhere, and any means to reduce their chances should be used.

"But can you do it?" asked Bush suddenly. "D'ye know how to heat shot?"

"I'll find out, sir."

"I'll wager no man of ours knows how."

Shot could only be heated in a battery on land; a sea-going ship, constructed of inflammable material, could not run the risk of going into action with a flaming furnace inside her. The French, in the early days of the Revolutionary War, had made some disastrous experiments in the hope of finding a means of countering England's naval superiority, but after a few ships had set themselves on fire they had given up the attempt. Seagoing men now left the use of the heated weapon to shore-based garrison artillery.

"I'll try and find out for myself, sir," said Hornblower. "There's the furnace down there and all the gear."

Hornblower stood in the sunshine, already far too hot to be comfortable. His face was pale, dirty, and bearded, and in his expression eagerness and weariness were oddly at war.

"Have you had any breakfast yet?" asked Bush.

"No, sir." Hornblower looked straight at him. "Neither have you, sir."

"No," grinned Bush.

He had not been able to spare a moment for anything like that, with the whole defence of the fort to be organized. But he could bear fatigue and hunger and thirst, and he doubted if Hornblower could.

"I'll get a drink of water at the well, sir," said Hornblower.

As he said the words, and the full import came to him, a change in his expression was quite obvious. He ran the tip of his tongue over his lips; Bush could see that the lips were cracked and parched and that the tongue could do nothing to relieve them. The man had drunk nothing since he had landed twelve hours ago—twelve hours of desperate exertion in a tropical climate.

"See that you do, Mr. Hornblower," said Bush. "That's an order."

"Aye aye, sir."

Bush found the telescope leaving his hand and passing into Hornblower's.

"May I have another look, sir, before I go down? By George, I thought as much. That two-master's warping out, sir. Less than an hour before she's within range. I'll get the guns manned, sir. Take a look for yourself, sir."

He went darting down the stone stairs of the tower, having given back the telescope, but half-way down he paused.

"Don't forget your breakfast, sir," he said, his face upturned to Bush. "You've plenty of time for that."

Bush's glance through the telescope confirmed what Hornblower had said. At least one of the vessels up the bay was beginning to move. He turned and swept the rest of the land and water with a precautionary glance before handing the telescope to Abbott, who during all this conversation had been standing by, silent in the presence of his betters.

"Keep a sharp lookout," said Bush.

Down in the body of the fort Hornblower was already issuing rapid orders, and the men, roused to activity, were on the move. On the gun platform they were casting loose the remaining guns, and as Bush descended from the platform he saw Hornblower organizing other working parties, snapping out orders with quick gestures. At the sight of Bush he turned guiltily and walked over to the well. A marine was winding up the bucket, and Hornblower seized it. He raised the bucket to his lips, leaning back to balance the weight; and he drank and drank, water slopping in quantities over his chest as he drank, water pouring over his face, until the bucket was empty, and then he put it down with a grin at Bush, his face still dripping water. The very sight of him was enough to make Bush, who had already had one drink from the well, feel consumed with thirst all over again.

By the time Bush had drunk there was the usual group of people clamouring for his attention, for orders and information, and by the time he had dealt with them there was smoke rising from the furnace in the corner of the courtyard, and a loud crackling from inside it. Bush walked over. A seaman, kneeling, was plying a pair of bellows; two other men were bringing wood from the pile against the ramparts. When the furnace door was opened the blast of heat that rose into Bush's face was enough to make him step back. Hornblower turned up with his hurried pace.

"How's the shot, Saddler?" he asked.

The petty officer picked up some rags, and, with them to shield his hands, laid hold of two long handles that projected from the far side of the furnace, balancing two projecting from the near side. When he drew them out it became apparent that all four handles were part of a large iron grating, the centre of which rested inside the furnace above the blazing fuel. Lying on the grating were rows of shot, still black in the sunshine. Saddler shifted his quid, gathered his saliva, and spat expertly on the nearest one. The spittle boiled off, but not with violence.

"Not very hot yet, sir," said Saddler.

"Us'll fry they devils," said the man with the bellows, unexpectedly; he looked up, as he crouched on his knees, with ecstasy in his face at the thought of burning his enemies alive.

Hornblower paid him no attention.

"Here, you bearer men," he said, "let's see what you can do."

Hornblower had been followed by a file of men, every pair carrying a piece of apparatus formed of two iron bars joined with iron cross-pieces. The first pair approached. Saddler took a pair of tongs and gingerly worked a hot shot onto the bearer.

"Move on, you two," ordered Hornblower. "Next!"

When a shot lay on every bearer Hornblower led his men away.

"Now let's see you roll those into the guns," he said.

Bush followed, consumed with curiosity. The procession moved up the ramp to the gun platform, where now crews had been told off to every gun; the guns were run back with the muzzles well clear of the embrasures. Tubs of water stood by each pair of guns.

"Now, you rammers," said Hornblower, "are your dry wads in? Then in with your wet wads."

From the tubs the seamen brought out round flat discs of fibre, dripping with water.

"Two to a gun," said Hornblower.

The wet wads were thrust into the muzzles of the guns and then were forced down the bores with the club-ended ramrods.

"Ram 'em home," said Hornblower. "Now, bearers."

It was not such an easy thing to do, to put the ends of the bearing-stretchers at the muzzles of the guns and then to tilt so as to induce the hot shot to roll down into the bore.

"The Don must've exercised with these guns better than we'd give 'em credit for," said Hornblower to Bush, "judging by the practice they made yesterday. Rammers!"

The ramrods thrust the shot home against the charges; there was a sharp sizzling noise as each hot shot rested against the wet wads.

"Run up!"

The guns' crews seized the tackles and heaved, and the ponderous guns rolled slowly forward to point their muzzles out through the embrasures.

"Aim for the point over there and fire!"

With handspikes under the rear axles the guns were traversed at the orders of the captains; the priming tubes were already in the touchholes and each gun was fired as it bore. The sound of the explosions was very different here on the stone platform from when guns were fired in the confined spaces of a wooden ship. The slight wind blew the smoke sideways.

"Pretty fair!" said Hornblower, shading his eyes to watch the fall of the shot; and, turning to Bush, "That'll puzzle those gentlemen over there. They'll wonder what in the world we're firing at."

"How long," asked Bush, who had watched the whole process with a fascinated yet horrified interest, "before a hot shot burns through those wads and sets off the gun itself?"

"That is one of the things I do not know, sir," answered Hornblower with a grin. "It would not surprise me if we found out during the course of today."

"I dare say," said Bush; but Hornblower had swung round and was confronting a seaman who had come running up to the platform.

"What d'ye think you're doing?"

"Bringing a fresh charge, sir," said the man, surprised, indicating with a gesture the cartridge-container he carried.

"Then get back and wait for the order. Get back, all of you."

The ammunition carriers shrank back before his evident anger.

"Swab out!" ordered Hornblower to the guns' crews, and as the wetted sponges were thrust into the muzzles he turned to Bush again. "We can't be too careful, sir. We don't want any chance of live charges and red-hot shot coming together on this platform."

"Certainly not," agreed Bush.

He was both pleased and irritated that Hornblower should have dealt so efficiently with the organization of the battery.

"Fresh charges!" yelled Hornblower, and the ammunition carriers he had previously sent back came trotting up the ramp again. "These are English cartridges, sir, I'll wager."

"Why do you say that?"

"West-Country serge, stitched and choked exactly like ours, sir. Out of English prizes, I fancy."

It was most probable; the Spanish forces which held this end of the island against the insurgents most likely depended on renewing their stores from English ships captured in the Mona Passage. Well, with good fortune they would take no more prizes—the implication, forcing itself on Bush's mind despite his many preoccupations, made him stir uneasily as he stood by the guns with his hands clasped behind him and the sun beating down on his face. The Dons would be in a bad way with their source of supplies cut off. They would not be able to hold out long against the rebellious blacks that hemmed them in here in the eastern end of Santo Domingo.

"Ram those wads handsomely, there, Cray," said Hornblower. "No powder in that bore, or we'll have 'Cray D.D.' in the ship's books."

There was a laugh at that—"D.D." in the ship's books meant "discharged, dead"—but Bush was not paying attention. He had scrambled up the parapet and was staring out at the bay.

"They're standing down the bay," he said. "Stand by, Mr. Hornblower."

"Aye aye, sir."

Bush strained his sight to look at the four vessels creeping down the fairway. As he watched he saw the first one hoisting sail on both masts. Apparently she was taking advantage of a flaw of wind, blowing flukily in the confined and heated waters, to gain some of the desperately necessary distance towards the sea and safety.

"Mr. Abbott, bring down that glass!" shouted Hornblower.

As Abbott descended the steps Hornblower addressed a further comment to Bush.

"If they're making a bolt for it the moment they know we've got the fort it means they're not feeling too secure over there, sir."

"I suppose not."

"You might have expected 'em to try to recapture the fort one way or another. They could land a force up the peninsula and come down to attack us. I wonder why they're not trying that, sir? Why do they just unstick and run?"

"They're only Dagoes," said Bush. He refused to speculate further about the enemy's motives while action was imminent, and he grabbed the glass from Abbott's hands.

Through the telescope details were far plainer. Two large schooners with several guns a-side; a big lugger, and a vessel whose rig they still could not determine, as she was the farthest away and, with no sail set, was towing behind her boats out from the anchorage.

"It'll be long range, Mr. Hornblower," said Bush.

"Yes, sir. But they hit us with these same guns yesterday."

"Make sure of your aim. They won't be long under fire."

"Aye aye, sir."

The vessels were not coming down together. If they had done so they might stand a better chance, as the fort would only be able to fire on one at a time. But the panic feeling of every man for himself must have started them off as soon as each one separately could get under way— and perhaps the deep channel was too narrow for vessels in company. Now the leading schooner had taken in her sail again; the wind here, what there was of it, was foul for her when she turned to port along the channel. She had two boats out quickly enough to tow her; Bush's telescope could reveal every detail.

"Some time yet before she's in range, sir," said Hornblower. "I'll take a look at the furnace, with your permission."

"I'll come too," said Bush.

At the furnace the bellows were still being worked and the heat was tremendous—but it was far hotter when Saddler drew out the grating that carried the heated shot. Even in the sunshine they could see the glow of the spheres; as the heat rose from them the atmosphere above them wavered so that everything below was vague and distorted. It could be a scene in Hell. Saddler spat on the nearest cannon ball and the saliva leaped with an instant hiss from the smooth surface of the sphere, falling from it without contact to dance and leap on the grating under it until with a final hiss it vanished entirely. A second attempt by Saddler brought the same result.

"Hot enough, sir?" asked Saddler.

"Yes," said Hornblower.

Bush had often enough as a midshipman taken a smoothing-iron forward to the galley to heat it when there had been particular need to iron a shirt or a neckcloth; he remembered how he had made the same test of the temperature of the iron. It was a proof that the iron was dangerously hot to use when the spittle refused to make contact with it, but the shot was far hotter than that, infinitely hotter.

Saddler thrust the grating back into the furnace and wiped his streaming face with the rags that had shielded his hands.

"Stand by, you bearer men," said Hornblower. "You'll be busy enough soon."

With a glance at Bush for permission he was off again, back to the battery, hurrying with awkward galvanic strides. Bush followed more slowly; he was weary with all his exertions, and it crossed his mind as he watched Hornblower hurrying up the ramp that Hornblower had probably been more active than he and was not blessed with nearly as powerful a physique. By the time he came up to him Hornblower was watching the leading schooner again.

"Her scantling'll be weak," said Hornblower. "These twenty-four-pounders'll go clean through her most of the time, even at long range."

"Plunging shot," said Bush. "Maybe they'll go out through her bottom."

"Maybe so," said Hornblower, and then added "sir."

Even after all his years of service he was liable to forget that important monosyllable when he was thinking deeply.

"She's setting sail again!" said Bush. "They've got her head round."

"And the tows have cast off," added Hornblower. "Not long now."

He looked down the line of guns, all charged and primed, the quoins withdrawn so that they were at their highest elevation, the muzzles pointing upward as though awaiting the shot to be rolled into them. The schooner was moving perceptibly down the channel towards them. Hornblower turned and walked down the row; behind his back one hand was twisting impatiently within the other; he came back and turned again, walking jerkily down the row—he seemed incapable of standing still, but when he caught Bush's eye on him he halted guiltily, forcing himself, with an obvious effort, to stand still like his superior officer. The schooner crept on, a full half-mile ahead of the next vessel.

"You might try a ranging shot," said Bush at length.

"Aye aye, sir," said Hornblower with instant agreement, like a river bursting through a broken dam. It seemed as if he had been compelling himself to wait until Bush should speak.

"Furnace, there!" hailed Hornblower. "Saddler! Send up one shot."

The bearers came plodding up the ramp, carrying carefully between them the glowing cannon ball. The bright redness of it was quite obvious—even the heat that it gave off was distinctly perceptible. The wet wads were rammed down the bore of the nearest gun, the shot bearer was hoisted up level with its muzzle, and, coaxed into motion with wad-hook and rammer, the fiery shot was rolled in. There was an instant hissing and spluttering of steam as the ball came into contact with the wet wads; Bush wondered again how long it would be before the wads were burned through and the charge set off; the recoil would make it decidedly uncomfortable for anyone who happened to be aiming the gun at that moment.

"Run up!" Hornblower was giving the orders. The gun's crew heaved at the tackles and the gun rumbled forward.

Hornblower took his place behind the gun and, squatting down, he squinted along it.

"Trail right!" Tackles and handspikes heaved the gun around. "A touch more! Steady! No, a touch left. Steady!"

Somewhat to Bush's relief Hornblower straightened himself and came from behind the gun. He leaped onto the parapet with his usual uncontrollable vigour and shaded his eyes; Bush at one side kept his telescope trained on the schooner.

"Fire!" said Hornblower.

The momentary hiss of the priming was drowned in the instant bellow of the gun. Bush saw the black line of the shot's path across the blue of the sky, reaching upward during the time it might take to draw a breath, sinking downward again; a strange sort of line, an inch long if he had to say its length, constantly renewing itself in front and constantly disappearing at its back end, and pointing straight at the schooner. It was still pointing at her, just above her—to that extent did the speed of the shot outpace the recording of retina and brain—when

Bush saw the splash, right in line with the schooner's bows. He took his eye from the telescope as the splash disappeared, to find Hornblower looking at him.

"A cable's length short," he said, and Hornblower nodded agreement.

"We can open fire then, sir?" asked Hornblower.

"Yes, carry on, Mr. Hornblower."

The words were hardly out of his mouth before Hornblower was hailing again.

"Furnace, there! Five more shot!"

It took Bush a moment or two to see the point of that order. But clearly it was inadvisable to have hot shot and powder charges brought up on the platform at the same time; the gun that had been fired would have to remain unloaded until the other five had fired as well. Hornblower came down and stood at Bush's side again.

"I couldn't understand yesterday why they always fired salvos at us, sir," he said, "that reduced the rate of fire to the speed of the slowest gun. But I see now."

"So do I," said Bush.

"All your wet wads in?" demanded Hornblower of the guns' crews. "Certain? Carry on, then."

The shot were coaxed into the muzzles of the guns; they hissed and spluttered against the wads.

"Run up. Now take your aim. Make sure of it, captains."

The hissing and spluttering continued as the guns were trained.

"Fire when your gun bears!"

Hornblower was up on the parapet again; Bush could see perfectly well through the embrasure of the idle gun. The five guns all fired within a second or two of each other; through Bush's telescope the sky was streaked by the passage of their shot.

"Sponge out!" said Hornblower; and then, louder, "Six charges!" He came down to Bush.

"One splash pretty close," said Bush.

"Two very short," said Hornblower, "and one far out on the right. I know who fired that one and I'll deal with him."

"One splash I didn't see," said Bush.

"Nor did I, sir. Clean over, perhaps. But possibly a hit."

The men with the charges came running up to the platform, and the eager crews seized them and rammed them home and the dry wads on top of the charges.

"Six shot!" shouted Hornblower to Saddler; and then, to the gun captains, "Prime. Put in your wet wads."

"She's altered course," said Bush. "The range can't have changed much."

"No, sir. Load and run up! Excuse me, sir."

He went hurrying off to take his stand by the left-hand gun, which presumably was the one which had been incorrectly laid previously.

"Take your aim carefully," he called from his new position. "Fire when you're sure."

Bush saw him squat behind the left-hand gun, but he himself applied his attention to observing the results of the shooting.

The cycle repeated itself; the guns roared, the men came running with fresh charges, the red-hot shot were brought up. The guns were fired again before Hornblower came back to Bush's side.

"You're hitting, I think," said Bush. He turned back to look again through his glass. "I think—by God, yes! Smoke! Smoke!"

A faint black cloud was just visible between the schooner's masts. It thinned again, and Bush could not be perfectly sure. The nearest gun bellowed out, and a chance flaw of wind blew the powder smoke about them as they stood together, blotting out their view of the schooner.

"Confound it all!" said Bush, moving about restlessly in search of a better viewpoint.

The other guns went off almost simultaneously and added to the smoke.

"Bring up fresh charges!" yelled Hornblower, with the smoke eddying round him. "See that you swab those guns out properly."

The smoke eddied away, revealing the schooner, apparently unharmed, still creeping along the bay, and Bush cursed in his disappointment.

"The range is shortening and the guns are hot now," said Hornblower; and then, louder, "Gun captains! Get your quoins in!"

He hurried off to supervise the adjustment of the guns' elevation, and it was some seconds before he hailed again for hot shot to be brought up. In that time Bush noticed that the schooner's boats, which had been pulling in company with the schooner, were turning to run alongside her. That could mean that the schooner's captain was now sure that the flaws of wind would be sufficient to carry her round the point and safely to the mouth of the bay. The guns went off again in an irregular salvo, and Bush saw a trio of splashes rise from the water's surface close on the near side of the schooner.

"Fresh charges!" yelled Hornblower.

And then Bush saw the schooner swing round, presenting her stern to the battery and heading straight for the shallows of the further shore.

"What in hell—" said Bush to himself.

Then he saw a sudden fountain of black smoke appear spouting from the schooner's deck, and while this sight was rejoicing him he saw the schooner's booms swing over as she took the ground. She was afire and had been deliberately run ashore. The smoke was dense about her hull, and while he held her in his telescope he saw her big white mainsail above the smoke suddenly disintegrate and disappear—the flames had caught it and whisked it away into nothing. He took the telescope from his eye and looked round for Hornblower, who was standing on the parapet again. Powder and smoke had grimed his face, already dark with the growth of his beard, and his teeth showed strangely white as he grinned. The gunners were cheering, and the cheering was being echoed by the rest of the landing party in the fort.

Hornblower was gesticulating to make the gunners cease their noise so that he could be heard down in the fort as he countermanded his call for more shot.

"Belay that order, Saddler! Take those shot back, bearer men!"

He jumped down and approached Bush.

"That's done it," said the latter.

"The first one, anyway."

A great jet of smoke came from the burning wreck, reaching up and up from between her masts; the mainmast fell as they watched, and as it fell the report of the explosion came to their ears across the water; the fire had reached the schooner's powder store, and when the smoke cleared a little they could see that she now lay on the shore in two halves, blown asunder in the middle. The foremast still stood for a moment on the forward half, but it fell as they watched it; bows and stern were blazing fiercely, while the boats with the crew rowed away across the shallows.

"A nasty sight," said Hornblower.

But Bush could see nothing unpleasant about the sight of an enemy burning. He was exulting. "With half his men in the boats he didn't have enough hands to spare to fight the fires when we hit him," he said.

"Maybe a shot went through her deck and lodged in her hold," said Hornblower.

The tone of his voice made Bush look quickly at him, for he was speaking thickly and harshly like a drunken man; but he could not be drunk, although the dirty hairy face and blood-shot eyes might well have suggested it. The man was fatigued. Then the dull expression on Hornblower's face was replaced once more by a look of animation, and when he spoke his voice was natural again.

"Here comes the next," he said. "She must be nearly in range."

The second schooner, also with her boats in attendance, was coming down the channel, her sails set. Hornblower turned back to the guns.

"D'you see the next ship to aim at?" he called; and received a fierce roar of agreement, before he turned round to hail Saddler. "Bring up those shot, bearer men."

The procession of bearers with the glowing shot came up the ramp again—frightfully hot shot; the heat as each one went by—twenty-four pounds of white-hot iron—was like the passage of a wave. The routine of rolling the fiendish things into the gun muzzles proceeded. There were some loud remarks from the men at the guns, and one of the shot fell with a thump on the stone floor of the battery, and lay there glowing. Two other guns were still not loaded.

"What's wrong there?" demanded Hornblower.

"Please, sir—"

Hornblower was already striding over to see for himself. From the muzzle of one of the three loaded guns there was a curl of steam; in all three there was a wild hissing as the hot shot rested on the wet wads.

"Run up, train, and fire," ordered Hornblower. "Now what's the matter with you others? Roll that thing out of the way."

"Shot won't fit, sir," said more than one voice as someone with a wad-hook awkwardly rolled the fallen shot up against the parapet. The bearers of the other two stood by, sweating. Anything Hornblower could say in reply was drowned for the moment by the roar of one of the guns—the men were still at the tackles, and the gun had gone off on its own volition as they ran it up. A man sat crying out with pain, for the carriage had recoiled over his foot and blood was already pouring from it onto the stone floor. The captains of the other two loaded guns made no pretence at training and aiming. The moment their guns were run up they shouted "Stand clear!" and fired.

"Carry him down to Mr. Pierce," said Hornblower, indicating the injured man. "Now let's see about these shot."

Hornblower returned to Bush with a rueful look on his face, embarrassed and self-conscious.

"What's the trouble?" asked Bush.

"Those shot are too hot," explained Hornblower. "Damn it, I didn't think of that. They're half melted in the furnace and gone out of shape so that they won't fit the bore. What a fool I was not to think of that."

As his superior officer, Bush did not admit that he had not thought of it either. He said nothing.

"And the ones that hadn't gone out of shape were too hot anyway," went on Hornblower. "I'm the damndest fool God ever made. Mad as a hatter. Did you see how that gun went off? The men'll be scared now and won't lay their guns properly—too anxious to fire it off before the recoil catches them. God, I'm a careless son of a swab."

"Easy, easy," said Bush, a prey to conflicting emotions.

Hornblower pounding his left hand with his right fist as he upbraided himself was a comic sight; Bush could not help laughing at him. And Bush knew perfectly well that Hornblower had done excellently so far, really excellently, to have mastered at a moment's notice so much of the technique of using red-hot shot. Moreover, it must be confessed that Bush had experienced, during this expedition, more than one moment of pique at Hornblower's invariable bold assumption of responsibility; and the pique may even have been roused by a stronger motive, jealousy at Hornblower's good management—an unworthy motive, which Bush would disclaim with shocked surprise if he became aware of it. Yet it made the sight of Hornblower's present discomfiture all the more amusing at the moment.

"Don't take on so," said Bush with a grin.

"But it makes me wild to be such a—"

Hornblower cut the sentence off short. Bush could actually see him calling up his self-control and mastering himself, could see his annoyance at having been self-revelatory, could see the mask of the stoical and experienced fighting man put back into place to conceal the furious passions within.

"Would you take charge here, sir?" he said; it might be another person speaking. "I'll go and take a look at the furnace, if I may. They'll have to go easy with those bellows."

"Very good, Mr. Hornblower. Send the ammunition up and I'll direct the fire on the schooner."

"Aye aye, sir. I'll send up the last shot to go into the furnace. They won't be too hot yet, sir."

Hornblower went darting down the ramp while Bush moved behind the guns to direct the fire. The fresh charges came up and were rammed home, the wet wads went in on top of the dry wads, and then the bearers began to arrive with the shot.

"Steady, all of you," said Bush. "Those won't be as hot as the last batch. Take your aim carefully."

But when Bush climbed onto the parapet and trained his telescope on the second schooner he could see that the schooner was changing her mind. She had brailed up her foresail and taken in her jibs; her boats were lying at an angle to her course, and were struggling, beetle-like, off her bows. They were pulling her round—she was going back up the bay and deciding not to run the gauntlet of the red-hot shot. There was the smouldering wreck of her consort to frighten her.

"She's turning tail!" said Bush loudly. "Hit her while you can, you men."

He saw the shot curving in the air, he saw the splashes in the water; he remembered how yesterday he had seen a ricochet shot from these very guns rebound from the water and strike the *Renown*'s massive side —one of the splashes was dead true for line, and might well indicate a hit.

"Fresh charges!" he bellowed, turning to make himself heard down at the magazine. "Sponge out!"

But by the time the charges were in the guns the schooner had got her head right round, had reset her foresail, and was creeping back up the bay. Judging by the splashes of the last salvo she would be out of range before the next could be fired.

"Mr. Hornblower!"

"Sir!"

" 'Vast sending any shot."

"Aye aye, sir."

When Hornblower came up again to the battery Bush pointed to the retreating schooner.

"He thought better of it, did he?" commented Hornblower. "Yes, and those other two have anchored, I should say."

His fingers were twitching for the one telescope again, and Bush handed it over.

"The other two aren't moving either," said Hornblower, and then he swung round and trained the telescope down the bay towards the sea. "*Renown*'s gone about. She's caught the wind. Six miles? Seven miles? She'll be rounding the point in an hour."

It was Bush's turn to grab for the telescope. There was no mistaking the trim of those topsails. From the *Renown* he transferred his attention to the opposite shore of the bay. There was the other battery with the Spanish flag above it—the flag was now drooping, now flapping lazily in the light wind prevailing over the shore. He could make out no sign of activity whatever, and there was some finality in his gesture as he closed the telescope and looked at his second in command.

"Everything's quiet," he said. "Nothing to be done until *Renown* comes down."

"That is so," agreed Hornblower.

It was interesting to watch Hornblower's animation ebb away. Intense weariness was obvious in his face the moment he was off his guard.

"We can feed the men," said Bush. "And I'd like to have a look at the wounded. Those damned prisoners have to be sorted out—Whiting's got 'em all herded in the casemate, men and women, captains and drum boys. God knows what provisions there are here. We've got to see about that. Then we can set a watch, dismiss the watch below, and some of us can get some rest."

"So we can," said Hornblower; reminded of the necessary activities that still remained, he resumed his stolid expression. "Shall I go down and start attending to it, sir?"

XI

The sun at noontime was glaring down into the fort of Samaná. Within the walls the heat was pitilessly reflected inwards to a murderous concentration, so that even the corners which had shade were dreadfully hot. The sea breeze had not yet begun to blow, and from the flagstaff the White Ensign drooped spiritlessly, half covering the Spanish colours that drooped below it. Yet discipline still prevailed. On every bastion the lookouts stood in the blazing sun to guard against surprise. The marine sentries, with regular and measured step, were "walking their posts of duty in a smart and soldierly manner" in accordance with regulations, muskets sloped, scarlet tunics buttoned to the neck, crossbelts exactly in position. When one of them reached the end of his beat he would halt with a click of his heels, bring down his musket to the "order" position in three smart movements, and then, pushing his right hand forward and his left foot out, stand "at ease" until the heat and the flies drove him into motion again, when his heels would come together, the musket rise to his shoulder, and he would walk his beat once more. In the battery the guns' crew dozed on the unrelenting stone, the lucky men in the shade cast by the guns, the others in the narrow strip of shade at the foot of the parapet; but two men sat and kept themselves awake and every few minutes saw to it that the slow matches smouldering in the tubs were still alight, available to supply fire instantly if the guns had to be worked, whether to fire on ships in the bay or to beat off an attack by land. Out beyond Samaná Point H.M.S. *Renown* lay awaiting the first puffs of the sea breeze to come up the bay and get into touch with her landing party.

Beside the main storehouse Lieutenant Bush sat on a bench and tried to stay awake, cursing the heat, cursing his own kindness of heart that had led him to allow his junior officers to rest first while he assumed the responsibilities of officer on duty, envying the marines who lay asleep and snoring all about him. From time to time he stretched his legs, which were stiff and painful after all his exertions. He mopped his forehead and thought about loosening his neckcloth.

Round the corner came a hurried messenger.

"Mr. Bush, sir. Please, sir, there's a boat puttin' off from the battery across the bay."

Bush rolled a stupefied eye at the messenger.

"Heading which way?"

"Straight towards us, sir. She's got a flag—a white flag, it looks like."

290

"I'll come and see. No peace for the wicked," said Bush, and he pulled himself to his feet, with all his joints complaining, and walked stiffly over to the ramp and up to the battery.

The petty officer of the watch was waiting there with the telescope, having descended from the lookout tower to meet him. Bush took the glass and looked through it. A six-oared boat, black against the blue of the bay was pulling straight towards him, as the messenger had said. From the staff in the bow hung a flag, which might be white; there was no wind to extend it. But in the boat there were no more than ten people all told, so that there could be no immediate danger to the fort in any case. It was a long row across the glittering bay. Bush watched the boat heading steadily for the fort. The low cliffs which descended to meet the water on this side of the Samaná peninsula sank in an easy gradient here in the neighbourhood of the fort; diagonally down the gradient ran a path to the landing stage, which could be swept—as Bush had already noted—by the fire of the last two guns at the right-hand end of the battery. But there was no need to man those guns, for this could not be an attack. And in confirmation a puff of wind blew out the flag in the boat. It was white.

Undeviating, the boat pulled for the landing stage and came alongside it. There was a flash of bright metal from the boat, and then in the heated air the notes of a trumpet call, high and clear, rose to strike against the ears of the garrison. Then two men climbed out of the boat onto the landing stage. They wore uniforms of blue and white, one of them with a sword at his side while the other carried the twinkling trumpet, which he set to his lips and blew again. Piercingly and sweet, the call echoed along the cliffs; the birds which had been drowsing in the heat came fluttering out with plaintive cries, disturbed as much by the trumpet call as they had been by the thunder of the artillery in the morning. The officer wearing the sword unrolled a white flag, and then he and the trumpeter set themselves to climb the steep path to the fort. This was a parley in accordance with the established etiquette of war. The pealing notes of the trumpet were proof that no surprise was intended: the white flag attested the pacific intentions of the bearer.

As Bush watched the slow ascent he meditated on what powers he had to conduct a negotiation with the enemy, and he thought dubiously about the difficulties that would be imposed on any negotiation by differences of language.

"Turn out the guard," he said to the petty officer; and then to the messenger, "My compliments to Mr. Hornblower, and ask him to come here as soon as he can."

The trumpet echoed up the path again; many of the sleepers in the fort were stirring at the sound, and it was a proof of the fatigue of the others that they went on sleeping. Down in the courtyard the tramp of feet and the sound of curt orders told how the marine guard was forming up. The white flag was almost at the edge of the ditch; the bearer halted, looking up at the parapets, while the trumpeter blew a last final call, the wild notes of the fanfare calling the last of the sleepers in the garrison to wakefulness.

"I'm here, sir," reported Hornblower.

The hat to which he raised his hand was lopsided, and he was like a scarecrow in his battered uniform. His face was clean, but it bore a plentiful growth of beard.

"Can you speak Spanish enough to deal with him?" asked Bush, indicating the Spanish officer with a jerk of his thumb.

"Well, sir—yes."

The last word was in a sense spoken against Hornblower's will. He would have liked to temporize, and then he had given the definite answer which any military situation demanded.

"Let's hear you, then."

"Aye aye, sir."

Hornblower stepped up on the parapet; the Spanish officer, looking up from the edge of the ditch, took off his hat at sight of him and bowed courteously; Hornblower did the same. There was a brief exchange of apparently polite phrases before Hornblower turned back to Bush.

"Are you going to admit him to the fort, sir?" he asked. "He says he has many negotiations to carry out."

"No," said Bush, without hesitation. "I don't want him spying round here."

Bush was not too sure about what the Spaniard could discover, but he was suspicious and cautious by temperament.

"Very good, sir."

"You'll have to go out to him, Mr. Hornblower. I'll cover you from here with the marines."

"Aye aye, sir."

With another exchange of courtesies Hornblower came down from the parapet and went down one ramp while the marine guard summoned by Bush marched up the other one. Bush, standing in an embrasure, saw the look on the Spaniard's face as the shakos and scarlet tunics and levelled muskets of the marines appeared in the other embrasures. Directly afterwards Hornblower appeared round the angle of the fort, having crossed the ditch by the narrow causeway from the main gate. Bush watched while once more hats were removed and Hornblower and the Spaniard exchanged bows, bobbing and scraping in a ludicrous Continental fashion. The Spaniard produced a paper, which he offered with a bow for Hornblower to read—his credentials, presumably. Hornblower glanced at them and handed them back. A gesture towards Bush on the parapet indicated his own credentials.

Then Bush could see the Spaniard asking eager questions, and Hornblower answering them. He could tell by the way Hornblower was nodding his head that he was answering in the affirmative, and he felt dubious for a moment as to whether Hornblower might not be exceeding his authority. Yet the mere fact that he had to depend on someone else to conduct the negotiations did not irritate him; the thought that he himself might speak Spanish was utterly alien to him, and he was as reconciled to depending on an interpreter as he was to depending on cables to hoist anchors or on winds to carry him to his destination.

He watched the negotiations proceeding; observing closely he was aware when the subject under discussion changed. There was a moment when Hornblower pointed down the bay, and the Spaniard, turning, looked at the *Renown* just approaching the point. He looked long and searchingly before turning back to continue the discussion. He was a tall man, very thin, his coffee-coloured face divided by a thin black moustache. The sun beat down on the pair of them—the trumpeter had withdrawn out of earshot—for some time before Hornblower turned and looked up at Bush.

"I'll come in to report, sir, if I may," he hailed.

"Very well, Mr. Hornblower."

Bush went down to the courtyard to meet him. Hornblower touched his hat and waited to be asked before he began his report.

"He's Colonel Ortega," said Hornblower in reply to the "Well?" that Bush addressed to him. "His credentials are from Villanueva, the Captain-General, who must be just across the bay, sir."

"What does he want?" asked Bush, trying to assimilate this first rather indigestible piece of information.

"It was the prisoners he wanted to know about first, sir," said Hornblower, "the women especially."

"And you told him they weren't hurt?"

"Yes, sir. He was very anxious about them. I told him I would ask your permission for him to take the women back with him."

"I see," said Bush.

"I thought it would make matters easier here, sir. And he had a good deal that he wanted to say, and I thought that if I appeared agreeable he would speak more freely."

"Yes," said Bush.

"Then he wanted to know about the other prisoners, sir. The men. He wanted to know if any had been killed, and when I said yes he asked which ones. I couldn't tell him that, sir—I didn't know. But I said I was sure you would supply him with a list; he said most of them had wives over there"—Hornblower pointed across the bay—"who were all anxious."

"I'll do that," said Bush.

"I thought he might take away the wounded as well as the women, sir. It would free our hands a little, and we can't give them proper treatment here."

"I must give that some thought first," said Bush.

"For that matter, sir, it might be possible to rid ourselves of all the prisoners. I fancy it would not be difficult to exact a promise from him in exchange that they would not serve again while *Renown* was in these waters."

"Sounds fishy to me," said Bush; he distrusted all foreigners.

"I think he'd keep his word, sir. He's a Spanish gentleman. Then we wouldn't have to guard them, or feed them, sir. And when we evacuate this place what are we going to do with them? Pack 'em on board *Renown*?"

A hundred prisoners in *Renown* would be an infernal nuisance, drinking twenty gallons of fresh water a day and having to be watched and guarded all the time. But Bush did not like to be rushed into making decisions, and he was not too sure that he cared to have Hornblower treating as obvious the points that he only arrived at after consideration.

"I'll have to think about that, too," said Bush.

"There was another thing that he only hinted at, sir. He wouldn't make any definite proposal, and I thought it better not to ask him."

"What was it?"

Hornblower paused before answering, and that in itself was a warning to Bush that something complicated was in the air.

"It's much more important than just a matter of prisoners, sir."

"Well?"

"It might be possible to arrange for a capitulation, sir."

"What do you mean by that?"

"A surrender, sir. An evacuation of all this end of the island by the Dons."

"My God!"

That was a startling suggestion. Bush's mind plodded along the paths it opened up. It would be an event of international importance; it might be a tremendous victory. Not just a paragraph in the *Gazette*, but a whole page. Perhaps rewards, distinction—even possibly promotion. And with that Bush's mind suddenly drew back in panic, as if the path it had been following ended in a precipice. The more important the event, the more closely it would be scrutinized, the more violent would be the criticism of those who disapproved. Here in Santo Domingo there was a complicated political situation; Bush knew it to be so, although he had never attempted to find out much about it, and certainly never to analyse it. He knew vaguely that French and Spanish interests clashed in the island, and that the Negro rebellion, now almost successful, was in opposition to both. He even knew, still more vaguely, that there was an anti-slavery movement in Parliament which persistently called attention to the state of affairs here. The thought of Parliament, of the Cabinet, of the King himself scrutinizing his reports actually terrified Bush. The possible rewards that he had thought about shrank to nothing in comparison with the danger he ran. If he were to enter into a negotiation that embarrassed the government he would be offered up for instant sacrifice—not a hand would be raised to help a penniless and friendless lieutenant. He remembered Buckland's frightened manner when this question had been barely hinted at; the secret orders must be drastic in this regard.

"Don't lift a finger about that," said Bush. "Don't say a word."

"Aye aye, sir. Then if he brings the subject up I'm not to listen to him?"

"Well—" That might imply flinching away from duty. "It's a matter for Buckland to deal with, if anyone."

"Yes, sir. I could suggest something, sir."

"And what's that?" Bush did not know whether to be irritated or pleased that Hornblower had one more suggestion to make. But he doubted his own ability to bargain or negotiate; he knew himself to be lacking in chicane and dissimulation.

"If you made an agreement about the prisoners, sir, it would take some time to carry out. There'd be the question of the parole. I could argue about the wording of it. Then it would take some time to ferry the prisoners over. You could insist that only one boat was at the landing stage at a time—that's an obvious precaution to take. It would give time for *Renown* to work up into the bay. She can anchor down there just out of range of the other battery, sir. Then the hole'll be stopped, and at the same time we'll still be in touch with the Dons so that Mr. Buckland can take charge of the negotiations if he wishes to."

"There's something in that notion," said Bush. Certainly it would relieve him of responsibility, and it was pleasant to think of spinning out time until the *Renown* was back, ready to add her ponderous weight in the struggle.

"So you authorize me to negotiate for the return of the prisoners on parole, sir?" asked Hornblower.

"Yes," said Bush, coming to a sudden decision. "But nothing else, mark you, Mr. Hornblower. Not if you value your commission."

"Aye aye, sir. And a temporary suspension of hostilities while they are being handed over, sir?"

"Yes," said Bush, reluctantly. It was a matter necessarily arising out of the previous one, but it had a suspicious sound to it, now that Hornblower had suggested the possibility of further negotiations.

So the day proceeded to wear into afternoon. A full hour was con-

sumed in haggling over the wording of the parole under which the captured soldiers were to be released. It was two o'clock before agreement
was reached, and later than that before Bush, standing by the main gate,
watched the women troop out through it, carrying their bundles of be-
longings. The boat could not possibly carry them all; two trips had
to be made with them before the male prisoners, starting with the
wounded, could begin. To rejoice Bush's heart the *Renown* appeared
at last round the point; with the sea breeze beginning to blow she came
nobly up the bay.

And here came Hornblower again, clearly so weary that he could
hardly drag one foot after another, to touch his hat to Bush.

"*Renown* knows nothing about the suspension of hostilities, sir," he
said. "She'll see the boat crossing full of Spanish soldiers, an' she'll
open fire as sure as a gun."

"How are we to let her know?"

"I've been discussing it with Ortega, sir. He'll lend us a boat and
we can send a message down to her."

"I suppose we can."

Sleeplessness and exhaustion had given an edge to Bush's temper.
This final suggestion, when Bush came to consider it, with his mind
slowed by fatigue, was the last straw.

"You're taking altogether too much on yourself, Mr. Hornblower,"
he said. "Damn it, I'm in command here."

"Yes, sir," said Hornblower, standing at attention, while Bush gazed
at him and tried to reassemble his thoughts after this spate of ill temper. There was no denying that *Renown* had to be informed; if she were
to open fire it would be in direct violation of an agreement solemnly
entered into, and to which he himself was a party.

"Oh, hell and damnation!" said Bush. "Have it your own way, then.
Who are you going to send?"

"I could go myself, sir. Then I could tell Mr. Buckland everything
necessary."

"You mean about—about—" Bush actually did not like to mention
the dangerous subject.

"About the chance of further negotiations, sir," said Hornblower
stolidly. "He has to know sooner or later. And while Ortega's still
here—"

The implications were obvious enough, and the suggestion was sensible.

"All right. You'd better go, I suppose. And mark my words, Mr.
Hornblower, you're to make it quite clear that I've authorized no nego-
tiations of the sort you have in mind. Not a word. I've no responsibility.
You understand?"

"Aye aye, sir."

XII

Three officers sat in what had been the commanding officer's room in Fort Samaná; in fact, seeing that Bush was now the commanding officer there, it could still be called the commanding officer's room. A bed with a mosquito net over it stood in one corner; at the other side of the room Buckland, Bush, and Hornblower sat in leather chairs. A lamp hanging from a beam overhead filled the room with its acrid smell, and lit up their sweating faces. It was hotter and stuffier even than it was in the ship, but at least here in the fort there was no brooding knowledge of a mad captain the other side of the bulkhead.

"I don't doubt for one moment," said Hornblower, "that when Villanueva sent Ortega here to open negotiations about the prisoners he also told him to put out a feeler regarding this evacuation."

"You can't be sure of that," said Buckland.

"Well, sir, put yourself in Ortega's position. Would you say a word about a subject of that importance if you weren't authorized to? If you weren't expressly ordered to, sir?"

"No, I wouldn't," said Buckland.

No one could doubt that who knew Buckland, and for himself it was the most convincing argument.

"Then Villanueva had capitulation in mind as soon as he knew that we had captured this fort and that *Renown* would be able to anchor in the bay. You can see that must be so, sir."

"I suppose so," said Buckland, reluctantly.

"And if he's prepared to negotiate for a capitulation he must either be a poltroon or in serious danger, sir."

"Well—"

"It doesn't matter which is true, sir, whether his danger is real or imaginary, from the point of view of bargaining with him."

"You talk like a sea lawyer," said Buckland. He was being forced by logic into taking a momentous decision, and he did not want to be, so that in his struggles against it he used one of the worst terms of opprobrium in his vocabulary.

"I'm sorry, sir," said Hornblower. "I meant no disrespect. I let my tongue run away with me. Of course it's for you to decide where your duty lies, sir."

Bush could see that the word "duty" had a stiffening effect on Buckland.

"Well, then, what d'you think lies behind all this?" asked Buckland. That might be intended as a temporizing question, but it gave Hornblower permission to go on stating his views.

"Villanueva's been holding this end of the island against the insurgents for months now, sir. We don't know how much territory he holds, but we can guess that it's not much—only as far as the crest of those mountains across the bay, probably. Powder—lead—flints—shoes—he's probably in need of all of them."

"Judging by the prisoners we took, that's true, sir," interjected Bush. It would be hard to ascertain the motives that led him to make this contribution to the discussion; perhaps he was only interested in the truth for its own sake.

"Maybe it is," said Buckland.

"Now you've arrived, sir, and he's cut off from the sea. He doesn't know how long we can stay here. He doesn't know what your orders are."

Hornblower did not know either, commented Bush to himself, and Buckland stirred restlessly at the allusion.

"Never mind that," he said.

"He sees himself cut off, and his supplies dwindling. If this goes on he'll have to surrender. He would rather start negotiations now, while he can still hold out, while he has something to bargain with, than wait until the last moment and have to surrender unconditionally, sir."

"I see," said Buckland.

"And he'd rather surrender to us than to the blacks, sir," concluded Hornblower.

"Yes indeed," said Bush. Everyone had heard a little about the horrors of the servile rebellion which for eight years had deluged this land with blood and scorched it with fire. The three men were silent for a space as they thought about the implications of Hornblower's last remark.

"Oh, very well then," said Buckland at length. "Let's hear what this fellow has to say."

"Shall I bring him in here, sir? He's been waiting long enough. I can blindfold him."

"Do what you like," said Buckland with resignation.

A closer view, when the handkerchief had been removed, revealed Colonel Ortega as a younger man than he might have been thought at a distance. He was very slender, and he wore his threadbare uniform with some pretence at elegance. A muscle in his left cheek twitched continually. Buckland and Bush rose slowly to their feet to acknowledge the introductions Hornblower made.

"Colonel Ortega says he speaks no English," said Hornblower.

There was only the slightest extra stress on the word "says", and only the slightest lingering in the glance that Hornblower shot at his two superiors as he said it, but it conveyed a warning.

"Well, ask him what he wants," said Buckland.

The conversation in Spanish was formal; obviously all the opening remarks were cautious fencing as each speaker felt for the weaknesses in the other's position and sought to conceal his own. But even Bush was aware of the moment when the vague sentences ended and definite proposals began. Ortega was bearing himself as a man conferring a favour; Hornblower like someone who did not care whether a favour was conferred or not. In the end he turned to Buckland and spoke in English.

"He has terms for a capitulation pat enough," he said.

"Well?"

"Please don't let him guess what you think, sir. But he suggests a free passage for the garrison. Ships—men—civilians. Passports for the ships while on passage to a Spanish possession—Cuba or Puerto Rico, in other words, sir. In exchange he'll hand over everything intact. Military stores. The battery across the bay. Everything."

"But—" Buckland struggled wildly to keep himself from revealing his feelings.

"I haven't said anything to him worth mentioning, so far, sir," said Hornblower.

Ortega had been watching the byplay keenly enough, and now he spoke again to Hornblower, with his shoulders back and his head high. There was passion in his voice, but what was more at odds with the dignity of his bearing was a peculiar gesture with which he accentuated one of his remarks—a jerk of the hand which called up the picture of someone vomiting.

"He says otherwise he'll fight to the last," interposed Hornblower. "He says Spanish soldiers can be relied upon to die to the last man sooner than submit to dishonour. He says we can do no more to them than we've done already—that we've reached the end of our tether, in other words, sir. And that we daren't stay longer in the island to starve him out because of the yellow fever—the *vomito negro,* sir."

In the whirl of excitement of the last few days Bush had forgotten all about the possibility of yellow fever. He found that he was looking concerned at the mention of it, and he hurriedly tried to assume an appearance of indifference. A glance at Buckland showed his face going through exactly the same transitions.

"I see," said Buckland.

It was an appalling thought. If yellow fever were to strike it might within a week leave the *Renown* without enough men to work her sails.

Ortega broke into passionate speech again, and Hornblower translated.

"He says his troops have lived here all their lives. They won't get yellow jack as easily as our men, and many of them have already had it. He has had it himself, he says, sir."

Bush remembered the emphasis with which Ortega had tapped his breast.

"And the blacks believe us to be their enemies, because of what happened in Dominica, sir, so he says. He could make an alliance with them against us. They could send an army against us here in the fort tomorrow, then. But please don't look as if you believe him, sir."

"Damn it to hell," said Buckland, exasperated. Bush wondered vaguely what it was that had happened in Dominica. History—even contemporary history—was not one of his strong points.

Again Ortega spoke.

"He says that's his last word, sir. An honourable proposal and he won't abate a jot, so he says. You could send him away now that you've heard it all and say that you'll give him an answer in the morning."

"Very well."

There were ceremonious speeches still to be made. Ortega's bows were so polite that Buckland and Bush were constrained, though reluctantly, to stand and endeavour to return them. Hornblower tied the handkerchief round Ortega's eyes again and led him out.

"What do you think about it?" said Buckland to Bush.

"I'd like to think it over, sir," replied Bush.

Hornblower came in again while they were still considering the matter. He glanced at them both before addressing himself to Buckland.

"Will you be needing me again tonight, sir?"

"Oh, damn it, you'd better stay. You know more about these Dagoes than we do. What do you think about it?"

"He made some good arguments, sir."

"I thought so too," said Buckland with apparent relief.

"Can't we turn the thumbscrews on them somehow, sir?" asked Bush.

Even if he could not make suggestions himself, he was too cautious to agree readily to a bargain offered by a foreigner, even such a tempting one as this.

"We can bring the ship up the bay," said Buckland. "But the channel's tricky. You saw that yesterday."

Good God! it was still only yesterday that the *Renown* had tried to make her way in under the fire of red-hot shot. Buckland had had a day of comparative peace, so that the mention of yesterday did not appear as strange to him.

"We'll still be under the fire of the battery across the bay, even though we hold this one," said Buckland.

"We ought to be able to run past it, sir," protested Bush. "We can keep over to this side."

"And if we do run past? They've warped their ships right up the bay again. They draw six feet less of water than we do—and if they've got any sense they'll lighten 'em so as to warp 'em farther over the shallows. Nice fools we'll look if we come in an' then find 'em out of range, an' have to run out again under fire. That might stiffen 'em so that they wouldn't agree to the terms that fellow just offered."

Buckland was in a state of actual alarm at the thought of reporting two fruitless repulses.

"I can see that," said Bush, depressed.

"If we agree," said Buckland, warming to his subject, "the blacks'll take over all this end of the island. This bay can't be used by privateers then. The blacks'll have no ships, and couldn't man 'em if they had. We'll have executed our orders. Don't you agree, Mr. Hornblower?"

Bush transferred his gaze. Hornblower had looked weary in the morning, and he had had almost no rest during the day. His face was drawn and his eyes were rimmed with red.

"We might still be able to—to put the thumbscrews on 'em, sir," he said.

"How?"

"It'd be risky to take *Renown* into the upper end of the bay. But we might get at 'em from the peninsula here, all the same, sir, if you'd give the orders."

"God bless my soul!" said Bush, the exclamation jerked out of him.

"What orders?" asked Buckland.

"If we could mount a gun on the upper end of the peninsula we'd have the far end of the bay under fire, sir. We wouldn't need hot shot —we'd have all day to knock 'em to pieces however much they shifted their anchorage."

"So we would, by George," said Buckland. There was animation in his face. "Could you get one of these guns along there?"

"I've been thinking about it, sir, an' I'm afraid we couldn't. Not quickly, at least. Twenty-four-pounders. Two an' a half tons each. Garrison carriages. We've no horses. We couldn't move 'em with a hundred men over those gullies, four miles or more."

"Then what the hell's the use of talking about it?" demanded Buckland.

"We don't have to drag a gun from here, sir," said Hornblower. "We could use one from the ship. One of those long nine-pounders we've got mounted as bow chasers. Those long guns have a range pretty nearly as good as these twenty-fours, sir."

"But how do we get it there?"

Bush had a glimmering of the answer even before Hornblower replied.

"Send it round in the launch, sir, with tackle and cables, near to where we landed yesterday. The cliff's steep there. And there are big trees to attach the cables to. We could sway the gun up easy enough. Those nine-pounders only weigh a ton."

"I know that," said Buckland, sharply.

It was one thing to make unexpected suggestions, but it was quite another to tell a veteran officer facts with which he was well acquainted.

"Yes, of course, sir. But with a nine-pounder at the top of the cliff it wouldn't be so difficult to move it across the neck of land until we had the upper bay under our fire. We wouldn't have to cross any gullies. Half a mile—uphill, but not too steep, sir—and it would be done."

"And what d'you think would happen then?"

"We'd have those ships under fire, sir. Only a nine-pounder, I know, but they're not built to take punishment. We could batter 'em into wrecks in twelve hours' steady fire. Less than that, perhaps. An' I suppose we could heat the shot if we wanted to, but we wouldn't have to. All we'd have to do would be to open fire, I think, sir."

"Why?"

"The Dons wouldn't risk those ships, sir. Ortega spoke very big about making an alliance with the blacks, but that was only talking big, sir. Give the blacks a chance an' they'll cut every white throat they can. An' I don't blame 'em—excuse me, sir."

"Well?"

"Those ships are the Dons' only way of escape. If they see they're going to be destroyed they'll be frightened. It would mean surrendering to the blacks—that or being killed to the last man. And woman, sir. They'd rather surrender to us."

"So they would, by jingo," said Bush.

"They'd climb down, d'ye think?"

"Yes—I mean I think so, sir. You could name your own terms, then. Unconditional surrender for the soldiers."

"It's what we said at the start," said Bush. "They'd rather surrender to us than to the blacks, if they have to."

"You could allow some conditions to salve their pride, sir," said Hornblower. "Agree that the women are to be conveyed to Cuba or Puerto Rico if they wish. But nothing important. Those ships would be our prizes, sir."

"Prizes, by George!" said Buckland.

Prizes meant prize money, and as commanding officer he would have the lion's share of it. Not only that—and perhaps the money was the smallest consideration—but prizes escorted triumphantly into port were much more impressive than ships sunk out of sight of the eyes of authority. And unconditional surrender had a ring of finality about it, proof that the victory gained could not be more complete.

"What do you say, Mr. Bush?" asked Buckland.

"I think it might be worth trying, sir," said Bush.

He was fatalistic now about Hornblower. Exasperation over his activity and ingenuity had died of surfeit. There was something of resignation about Bush's attitude, but there was something of admiration too. Bush was a generous soul, and there was not a mean motive in him. Hornblower's careful handling of his superior had not been lost on him, and Bush was decently envious of the tact that had been necessary. Bush realistically admitted to himself that even though he had fretted at the prospect of agreeing to Ortega's terms he had not been able to think of a way to modify them, while Hornblower had. Hornblower was a very brilliant young officer, Bush decided; he himself made no pretence at brilliance, and now he had taken the last step and had overcome his suspicions of brilliance. He made himself abandon his caution and commit himself to a definite opinion.

"I think Mr. Hornblower deserves every credit," he said.

"Of course," said Buckland—but the slight hint of surprise in his voice seemed to indicate that he did not really believe it; and he changed the subject without pursuing it further. "We'll start tomorrow—I'll get both launches out as soon as the hands've had breakfast. By noon —now what's the matter with you, Mr. Hornblower?"

"Well, sir—"

"Come on. Out with it."

"Ortega comes back tomorrow morning to hear our terms again, sir. I suppose he'll get up at dawn or not long after. He'll have a bite of breakfast. Then he'll have a few words with Villanueva. Then he'll row across the bay. He might be here at eight bells. Later than that, probably, a little—"

"Who cares when Ortega has his breakfast? What's all this rigmarole for?"

"Ortega gets here at two bells in the forenoon. If he finds we haven't wasted a minute; if I can tell him that you've rejected his terms absolutely, sir, and not only that, if we can show him the gun mounted, and say we'll open fire in an hour if they don't surrender without conditions, he'll be much more impressed."

"That's true, sir," said Bush.

"Otherwise it won't be so easy, sir. You'll either have to temporize again while the gun's being got into position, or you'll have to use threats. I'll have to say to him *if* you don't agree then we'll start hoisting a gun up. In either case you'll be allowing him time, sir. He might think of some other way out of it. The weather might turn dirty—there might even be a hurricane get up. But if he's sure we'll stand no nonsense, sir—"

"That's the way to treat 'em," said Bush.

"But even if we start at dawn—" said Buckland, and having progressed so far in his speech he realized the alternative. "You mean we can get to work now?"

"We have all night before us, sir. You could have the launches hoisted out and the gun swayed down into one of them. Slings and cables and some sort of carrying cradle prepared. Hands told off—"

"And start at dawn!"

"At dawn the boats can be round the peninsula waiting for daylight, sir. You could send some hands with a hundred fathoms of line up from the ship to here. They can start off along the path before daylight. That'd save time."

"So it would, by George!" said Bush; he had no trouble in visualizing the problems of seamanship involved in hoisting a gun up the face of a cliff.

"We're shorthanded already in the ship," said Buckland. "I'll have to turn up both watches."

"That won't hurt 'em, sir," said Bush. He had already been two nights without sleep and was now contemplating a third.

"Who shall I send? I'll want a responsible officer in charge. A good seaman at that."

"I'll go if you like, sir," said Hornblower.

"No. You'll have to be here to deal with Ortega. If I send Smith I'll have no lieutenant left on board."

"Maybe you could send me, sir," said Bush. "That is, if you were to leave Mr. Hornblower in command here."

"Um—" said Buckland. "Oh well, I don't see anything else to do. Can I trust you, Mr. Hornblower?"

"I'll do my best, sir."

"Let me see—" said Buckland.

"I could go back to the ship with you in your gig, sir," said Bush. "Then there'd be no time wasted."

This prodding of a senior officer into action was something new to Bush, but he was learning the art fast. The fact that the three of them had not long ago been fellow conspirators made it easier; and once the ice was broken, as soon as Buckland had once admitted his juniors to give him counsel and advice, it became easier with repetition.

"Yes, I suppose you'd better," said Buckland, and Bush promptly rose to his feet, so that Buckland could hardly help doing the same.

Bush ran his eye over Hornblower's battered form.

"Now look you here, Mr. Hornblower," he said. "You take some sleep. You need it."

"I relieve Whiting as officer on duty at midnight, sir," said Hornblower, "and I have to go the rounds."

"Maybe that's true. You'll still have two hours before midnight. Turn in until then. And have Whiting relieve you at eight bells again."

"Aye aye, sir."

At the very thought of abandoning himself to the sleep for which he yearned Hornblower swayed with fatigue.

"You could make that an order, sir," suggested Bush to Buckland.

"What's that? Oh yes, get a rest while you can, Mr. Hornblower."

"Aye aye, sir."

Bush picked his way down the steep path to the landing stage at Buckland's heels, and took his seat beside him in the stern sheets of the gig.

"I can't make that fellow Hornblower out," said Buckland a little peevishly on one occasion as they rowed back to the anchored *Renown*.

"He's a good officer, sir," answered Bush, but he spoke a little absently. Already in his mind he was tackling the problem of hoisting a long nine-pounder up a cliff, and he was sorting out mentally the necessary equipment, and planning the necessary orders. Two heavy anchors —not merely boat grapnels—to anchor the buoy solidly. The thwarts of the launch had better be shored up to bear the weight of the gun. Travelling blocks. Slings—for the final hoist it might be safer to suspend the gun by its cascabel and trunnions.

Bush was not of the mental type that takes pleasure in theoretical exercises. To plan a campaign; to put himself mentally in the position of the enemy and think along alien lines; to devise unexpected expedients; all this was beyond his capacity. But to deal with a definite concrete problem, a simple matter of ropes and tackles and breaking strains, pure seamanship—he had a lifetime of experience to reinforce his natural bent in that direction.

XIII

"Take the strain," said Bush, standing on the cliff's edge and looking far, far down to where the launch floated moored to the buoy and with an anchor astern to keep her steady. Black against the Atlantic blue two ropes came down from over his head, curving slightly but almost vertical, down to the buoy. A poet might have seen something dramatic and beautiful in those spider lines cleaving the air, but Bush merely saw a couple of ropes, and the white flag down in the launch signalling that all was clear for hoisting. The blocks creaked as the men pulled in on the slack.

"Now, handsomely," said Bush. This work was too important to be delegated to Mr. Midshipman James, standing beside him. "Hoist away. Handsomely."

The creaking took on a different tone as the weight came on the blocks. The curves of the ropes altered, appeared almost deformed, as the gun began to rise from its cradle on the thwarts. The shallow, lovely catenaries changed to a harsher, more angular figure. Bush had his telescope to his eye and could see the gun stir and move, and slowly —that was what Bush meant by "handsomely" in the language of the sea—it began to upend itself, to dangle from the traveller, to rise clear of the launch; hanging, just as Bush had visualized it, from the slings through its cascabel and round its trunnions. It was safe enough—if those slings were to give way or to slip, the gun would crash through the bottom of the launch. The line about its muzzle restrained it from swinging too violently.

"Hoist away," said Bush again, and the traveller began to mount the rope with the gun pendant below it. This was the next ticklish moment, when the pull came most transversely. But everything held fast.

"Hoist away."

Now the gun was mounting up the rope. Beyond the launch's stern it dipped, with the stretching of the cable and the straightening of the curve, until its muzzle was almost in the sea. But the hoisting proceeded steadily, and it rose clear of the water, up, up, up. The sheaves hummed rhythmically in the blocks as the hands hove on the line. The sun shone on the men from its level position in the glowing east, stretching out their shadows and those of the trees to incredible lengths over the irregular plateau.

"Easy, there!" said Bush. "Belay!"

The gun had reached the cliff edge.

"Move that cat's cradle over this way a couple of feet. Now, sway in. Lower. Good. Cast off those lines."

The gun lay, eight feet of dull bronze, upon the cat's cradle that had been spread to receive it. This was a small area of stout rope-netting, from which diverged, knotted thickly to the central portion, a score or more of individual lines, each laid out separately on the ground.

"We'll get that on its way first. Take a line, each of you marines."

The thirty red-coated marines that Hornblower had sent along from the fort moved up to the cat's cradle. Their non-commissioned officers pushed them into position, and Bush checked to see that each man was there.

"Take hold."

It was better to go to a little trouble and see that everything was correctly balanced at the start rather than risk that the unwieldy lump of metal should roll off the cat's cradle and should have to be laboriously manoeuvred back into position.

"Now, all of you together when I give the word. Lift!"

The gun rose a foot from the ground as every man exerted himself.

"March! Belay that, Sergeant."

The sergeant had begun to call the step, but on this irregular ground with every man supporting eighty pounds of weight it was better that they should not try to keep step.

"Halt! Lower!"

The gun had moved twenty yards towards the position Bush had selected for it.

"Carry on, Sergeant. Keep 'em moving. Not too fast."

Marines were only dumb animals, not even machines, and were liable to tire. It was better to be conservative with their strength. But while they laboured at carrying the gun the necessary half-mile up to the crest the seamen could work at hauling up the rest of the stores from launches. Nothing would be as difficult as the gun. The gun carriage was a featherweight by comparison; even the nets, each holding twenty nine-pound cannon balls, were easy to handle. Rammers, sponges, and wad-hooks, two of each in case of accidents; wads; and now the powder charges. With only two and a half pounds of powder in each they seemed tiny compared with the eight-pound charges Bush had grown accustomed to on the lower gundeck. Last of all came the heavy timbers destined to form a smooth floor upon which the gun could be worked. They were awkward things to carry, but with each timber on the shoulders of four men they could be carried up the gentle slope fast enough, overtaking the unfortunate marines, who, streaming with sweat, were lifting and carrying, lifting and carrying, on their way up.

Bush stood for a moment at the cliff edge checking over the stores with James' assistance. Linstocks and slow match; primers and quills; barricoes of water; handspikes, hammers, and nails; everything necessary, he decided—not merely his professional reputation but his self-respect depended on his having omitted nothing. He waved his flag, and received an answer from the launches. The second launch cast off her mooring line, and then, hauling up her anchor, she went off with her consort to pull back round Samaná Point to rejoin *Renown*—in the ship they would be most desperately shorthanded until the launches' crews should come on board again. From the trees to which it was secured, over Bush's head, the rope hung down to the buoy, neglected unless it should be needed again; Bush hardly spared it a glance. Now he was free to walk up to the crest and prepare for action; a glance at the sun assured him that it was less than three hours since sunrise even now.

He organized the final carrying party and started up to the crest. When he reached it the bay opened below him. He put his glass to his eye: the three vessels were lying at anchor within easy cannon shot of where he stood, and when he swung the glass to his left he could just make out, far, far away, the two specks which were the flags flying over the fort—the swell of the land hid the body of the building from his sight. He closed the glass and applied himself to the selection of a level piece of ground on which to lay the timbers for the platform. Already the men with the lightest loads were around him, chattering and pointing excitedly until with a growl he silenced them.

The hammers thumped upon the nails as the crosspieces were nailed into position on the timbers. No sooner had they ceased than the gun carriage was swung up onto it by the lusty efforts of half a dozen men. They attached the tackles and saw to it that the gun-trucks ran easily before chocking them. The marines came staggering up, sweating and gasping under their monstrous burden. Now was the moment for the trickiest piece of work in the morning's programme. Bush distributed his steadiest men round the carrying ropes, a reliable petty officer on either side to watch that accurate balance was maintained.

"Lift and carry."

The gun lay beside the carriage on the platform.

"Lift. Lift. Higher. Not high enough. Lift, you men!"

There were gasps and grunts as the men struggled to raise the gun.

"Keep her at that! Back away, starboard side! Go with 'em, port side. Lift! Bring the bows round now. Steady!"

The gun in its cat's cradle hung precariously over the carriage as Bush lined it up.

"Now, back towards me! Steady! Lower! Slowly, damn you! Steady! For'ard a little! Now lower again!"

The gun sank down towards its position on the carriage. It rested there, the trunnions not quite in their holes, the breech not quite in position on the bed.

"Hold it! Berry! Chapman! Handspikes under those trunnions! Ease her along!"

With something of a jar the ton of metal subsided into its place on the carriage, trunnions home into their holes and breech settled upon the bed. A couple of hands set to work untying the knots that would free the cat's cradle from under the gun, but Berry, gunner's mate, had already snapped the capsquares down upon the trunnions, and the gun was now a gun, a vital fighting weapon and not an inanimate ingot of metal. The shot were being piled at the edge of the platform.

"Lay those charges out back there!" said Bush, pointing.

No one in his senses allowed unprotected explosives nearer a gun than was necessary. Berry was kneeling on the platform, bent over the flint and steel with which he was working to catch a spark upon the tinder with which to ignite the slow match. Bush wiped away the sweat that streamed over his face and neck; even though he had not taken actual physical part in the carrying and heaving he felt the effect of his exertions. He looked at the sun again to judge the time; this was no moment for resting upon his labours.

"Gun's crew fall in!" he ordered. "Load and run up!"

He applied his eye to the telescope.

"Aim for the schooner," he said. "Take a careful aim."

The gun-trucks squealed as the handspikes trained the gun round.

"Gun laid, sir," reported the gun captain.

"Then fire!"

The gun banged out sharp and clear, a higher-pitched report than the deafening thunderous roar of the massive twenty-four-pounders. That report would resound round the bay. Even if the shot missed its mark this time, the men down in those ships would know that the next, or the next, would strike. Looking up at the high shore through hastily trained telescopes they would see the powder smoke slowly drifting along the verge of the cliff, and would recognize their doom. Over on the southern shore Villanueva would have his attention called to it, and would know that escape was finally cut off for the men under his command and the women under his protection. Yet all the same, Bush, gazing through the telescope, could mark no fall of the shot.

"Load and fire again. Make sure of your aim."

While they loaded Bush turned his telescope upon the flags over the fort, until the gun captain's cry told him that loading was completed. The gun banged out, and Bush thought he saw the fleeting black line of the course of the shot.

"You're firing over her. Put the quoins in and reduce the elevation. Try again!"

He looked again at the flags. They were very slowly descending, down out of his sight. Now they rose once more, very slowly, fluttered for a moment at the head of the flagstaff, and sank again. The next time they rose they remained steady. That was the preconcerted signal. Dipping the colours twice meant that the gun had been heard in the fort and all was well. It was Bush's duty now to complete ten rounds of firing, slowly. Bush watched each round carefully; it seemed likely that the schooner was being hit. Those flying nine-pound balls of iron were crashing through the frail upper works, smashing and destroying, casting up showers of splinters.

At the eighth round something screamed through the air like a banshee two yards over Bush's head, a whirling irregular scream which died away abruptly behind his back.

"What the hell was that?" demanded Bush.

"The gun's unbushed, sir," said Berry.

"God—" Bush poured out a torrent of blasphemy, uncontrolled, almost hysterical. This was the climax of days and nights of strain and labour, the bitterest blow that could be imagined, with success almost within their grasp and now snatched away. He swore frightfully, and then came back to his senses; it would not be good for the men to know that their officer was as disappointed as Bush knew himself to be. His curses died away when he restrained himself, and he walked forward to look at the gun.

The damage was plain. The touchhole in the breech of a gun, especially a bronze gun, was always a weak point. At each round some small part of the explosion vented itself through the hole, the blast of hot gas and unconsumed powder grains eroding the edges of the hole, enlarging it until the loss of force became severe enough to impair the efficiency of the gun. Then the gun had to be "bushed"; a tapering plug, with a hole pierced through its length and a flange round its base, had to be forced into the touchhole from the inside of the gun, small end first. The hole in the plug served as the new touchhole, and the explosions of the gun served to drive the plug more and more thoroughly home, until the plug itself began to erode and to weaken, forcing itself up through the touchhole while the flange burned away in the fierce heat of the explosions until at last it would blow itself clean out, as it had done now.

Bush looked at the huge hole in the breech, a full inch wide; if the gun were to be fired in that condition half the powder charge would blow out through it. The range would be halved at best, and every subsequent round would enlarge the hole further.

"D'ye have a new vent-fitting?" he demanded.

"Well, sir—" Berry began to go slowly through his pockets, rummaging through their manifold contents while gazing absently at the sky and while Bush fumed with impatience. "Yes, sir."

Berry produced, seemingly at the eleventh hour, the cast-iron plug that meant so much.

"Lucky for you," said Bush, grimly. "Get it fitted and don't waste any more time."

"Aye aye, sir. I'll have to file it to size, sir. Then I'll have to put it in place."

"Start working and stop talking. Mr. James!"

"Sir!"

"Run to the fort." Bush took a few steps away from the gun as he spoke, so as to get out of earshot of the men. "Tell Mr. Hornblower that the gun's unbushed. It'll be an hour before we can open fire again. Tell him I'll fire three shots when the gun's ready, and ask him to acknowledge them as before."

"Aye aye, sir."

At the last moment Bush remembered something.

"Mr. James! Don't make your report in anyone's hearing. Don't let that Spanish fellow, what's-his-name, hear about this. Not if you want to be kind to your backside."

"Aye aye, sir."

"Run!"

That would be a very long hot run for Mr. James; Bush watched him go and then turned back to the gun. Berry had selected a file from his roll of tools and was sitting on the rear step of the gun scraping away at the plug. Bush sat on the edge of the platform; the irritation at the disablement of the gun was overlaid by his satisfaction with himself as a diplomat. He was pleased at having remembered to warn James against letting Ortega into the secret. The men were chattering and beginning to skylark about; a few minutes more and they would be scattering all over the peninsula. Bush lifted his head and barked at them.

"Silence, there! Sergeant!"

"Sir?"

"Post four sentries. Give 'em beats on all four sides. No one to pass that line on any account whatever."

"Yessir."

"Let the rest of your men sit down. You gun's crew! Sit there and don't chatter like Portuguese bumboat men."

The sun was very hot, and the rasp-rasp-rasp of Berry's file was, if anything, soothing. Bush had hardly ceased speaking when fatigue and sleepiness demanded their due; his eyes closed and his chin sank on his breast. In one second he was asleep; in three he was awake again, with the world whirling round him as he recovered himself from falling over. He blinked at the unreal world; the blink prolonged itself into sleep, and again he caught himself up on the point of keeling over. Bush felt that he would give anything at all, in this world or the next, to sink quietly on to his side and allow sleep to overwhelm him. He fought down the temptation; he was the only officer present and there might be an instant emergency. Straightening his back, he glowered at the world, and then even with his back straight he went to sleep again. There was only one thing to do. He rose to his feet, with his weary joints protesting, and began to pace up and down beside the gun platform, up and down in the sunshine, with the sweat pouring off him, while the gun's crew quickly subsided into the sleep he envied them—they lay like pigs in a sty, at all angles—and while Berry's file went whit-whit-whit on the vent-fitting. The minutes dragged by and the sun mounted higher and higher. Berry paused in his work to gauge the fitting against the touchhole, and then went on filing; he paused again to clean his file, and each time Bush looked sharply at him, only to be disappointed, and to go back to thinking how much he wanted to go to sleep.

"I have it to size now, sir," said Berry at last.

"Then fit it, damn you," said Bush. "You gun's crew, wake up, there! Rise and shine! Wake up, there!"

While Bush kicked the snoring men awake Berry had produced a length of twine from his pocket. With a slowness that Bush found maddening he proceeded to tie one end into a loop and then drop the loop in through the touchhole. Then he took the wad-hook, and, walking round to the muzzle of the gun and squatting down, he proceeded to push the hook up the eight-foot length of the bore and tried to catch the loop on it. Over and over again he twisted the hook and withdrew it a little with no corresponding reaction on the part of the twine hanging from the touchhole, but at last he made his catch. As he brought the hook out the twine slid down into the hole, and when the wad-hook was withdrawn from the muzzle the loop was hanging on it. Still with intense deliberation Berry calmly proceeded to undo the loop and pass the end of the twine through the hole in the vent-fitting, and then secure the end to a little toggle which he also took from his pocket. He dropped the vent-fitting into the muzzle and walked round to the breech again, and pulled in on the twine, the vent-fitting rattling down the bore until it leaped up to its position under the touchhole with a sharp tap that every ear heard. Even so it was only after some minutes of fumbling and adjustment that Berry had the vent-fitting placed to his satisfaction with its small end in the hole, and he gestured to the gun captain to hold it steady with the twine. Now he took the rammer and thrust it with infinite care up the muzzle, feeling sensitively with it and pressing down upon the handle when he had it exactly placed. Another gesture from Berry, and a seaman brought a hammer and struck down upon the handle which Berry held firm. At each blow the vent-fitting showed more clearly down in the touchhole, rising an eighth of an inch at a time until it was firmly jammed.

"Ready?" asked Bush as Berry waved the seaman away.

"Not quite, sir."

Berry withdrew the rammer and walked slowly round to the breech again. He looked down at the vent-fitting with his head first on one side and then on the other, like a terrier at a rat-hole. He seemed to be satisfied, and yet he walked back again to the muzzle and took up the wad-hook. Bush glared round the horizon to ease his impatience; over towards where the fort lay a tiny figure was visible coming towards them. Bush clapped a telescope to his eye. It was a white-trousered individual, now running, now walking, and apparently waving his arm as though to attract attention. It might be Wellard; Bush was nearly sure it was. Meanwhile Berry had caught the twine again with the wad-hook and drawn it out again. He cut the toggle free from the twine with a stroke of his sheath knife and dropped it in his pocket, and then, once more as if he had all the time in the world, he returned to the breech and wound up his twine.

"Two rounds with one-third charges ought to do it now, sir," he announced. "That'll seat—"

"It can wait a few minutes longer," said Bush, interrupting him with a short-tempered delight in showing this self-satisfied skilled worker that his decisions need not all be treated like gospel.

Wellard was in clear sight of them all now, running and walking and stumbling over the irregular surface. He reached the gun gasping for breath, sweat running down his face.

"Please, sir—" he began. Bush was about to blare at him for his disrespectful approach but Wellard anticipated him. He twitched his coat into position, settled his absurd little hat on his head, and stepped forward with all the stiff precision his gasping lungs would allow.

"Mr. Hornblower's respects, sir," he said, raising his hand to his hat brim.

"Well, Mr. Wellard?"

"Please will you not reopen fire, sir."

Wellard's chest was heaving, and that was all he could say between two gasps. The sweat running down into his eyes made him blink, but he manfully stood to attention ignoring it.

"And why not, pray, Mr. Wellard?"

Even Bush could guess at the answer, but asked the question because the child deserved to be taken seriously.

"The Dons have agreed to a capitulation, sir."

"Good! Those ships there?"

"They'll be our prizes, sir."

"Hurray!" yelled Berry, his arms in the air.

Five hundred pounds for Buckland, five shillings for Berry, but prize money was something to cheer about in any case. And this was a victory, the destruction of a nest of privateers, the capture of a Spanish regiment, security for convoys going through the Mona Passage. It had only needed the mounting of the gun to search the anchorage to bring the Dons to their senses.

"Very good, Mr. Wellard, thank you," said Bush.

So Wellard could step back and wipe the sweat out of his eyes, and Bush could wonder what item in the terms of the capitulation would be likely to rob him of his next night's rest.

XIV

Bush stood on the quarterdeck of the *Renown* at Buckland's side with his telescope trained on the fort.

"The party's leaving there now, sir," he said; and then, after an interval, "The boat's putting off from the landing stage."

The *Renown* swung at her anchor in the mouth of the Gulf of Samaná and close beside her rode her three prizes. All four ships were jammed with the prisoners who had surrendered themselves, and sails were ready to loose the moment the *Renown* should give the signal.

"The boat's well clear now," said Bush. "I wonder—ah!"

The fort on the crest had burst into a great fountain of smoke, within which could be made out flying fragments of masonry. A moment later came the crash of the explosion. Two tons of gunpowder, ignited by the slow match left burning by the demolition party, did the work. Ramparts and bastions, tower and platform, all were dashed into ruins. Already at the foot of the steep slope to the water lay what was left of the guns, trunnions blasted off, muzzles split, and touchholes spiked; the insurgents when they came to take over the place would have no means to re-establish the defences of the bay—the other battery on the point across the water had already been blown up.

"It looks as if the damage is complete enough, sir," said Bush.

"Yes," said Buckland, his eye to his telescope observing the ruins as they began to show through the smoke and dust. "We'll get under way as soon as the boat's hoisted in, if you please."

"Aye aye, sir," said Bush.

With the boat lowered onto its chocks the hands went to the capstan and hauled the ship laboriously up to her anchor; the sails were loosed as the anchor rose clear. The main topsail aback gave her a trifle of sternway, and then, with the wheel hard over and hands at the headsail sheets, she came round. The topsails, braced up, caught the wind as the quartermaster at the wheel spun the spokes over hastily, and now she was under full command, moving easily through the water, heeling a little to the wind, the sea swinging under her cutwater, heading out close-hauled to weather Engano Point. Somebody forward began to cheer, and in a moment the entire crew was yelling lustily as the *Renown* left the scene of her victory. The prizes were getting under way at the same time, and the prize crews on board echoed the cheering. Bush's telescope could pick out Hornblower on the deck of *La Gaditana*, the big ship-rigged prize, waving his hat to the *Renown*.

"I'll see that everything is secure below, sir," said Bush.

There were marine sentries beside the midshipmen's berth, bayonets fixed and muskets loaded. From within, as Bush listened, there was a wild babble of voices. Fifty women were cramped into that space, and almost as many children. That was bad, but it was necessary to confine them while the ship got under way. Later on they could be allowed on deck, in batches perhaps, for air and exercise. The hatchways in the lower gundeck were closed by gratings, and every hatchway was guarded by a sentry. Up through the gratings rose the smell of humanity; there were four hundred Spanish soldiers confined down there in conditions not much better than prevailed in a slave ship. It was only since dawn that they had been down there, and already there was this stench. For the men, as for the women, there would have to be arrangements made to allow them to take the air in batches. It meant endless trouble and precaution; Bush had already gone to considerable trouble to organize a system by which the prisoners should be supplied with food and drink. But every water butt was full, two boat-loads of yams had been brought on board from the shore, and, given the steady breeze that could be expected, the run to Kingston would be completed in less than a week. Then their troubles would be ended and the prisoners handed over to the military authorities—probably the prisoners would be as relieved as Bush would be.

On deck again Bush looked over at the green hills of Santo Domingo out on the starboard beam as, close-hauled, the *Renown* coasted along them; on that side too, under her lee as his orders had dictated, Hornblower had the three prizes under easy sail. Even with this brisk seven-knot breeze blowing and the *Renown* with all sail set those three vessels had the heels of her if they cared to show them; privateers depended both for catching their prey and evading their enemies on the ability to work fast to the windward, and Hornblower could soon have left the *Renown* far behind if he were not under orders to keep within sight and to leeward so that the *Renown* could run down to him and protect him if an enemy should appear. The prize crews were small enough in all conscience, and just as in the *Renown* Hornblower had all the prisoners he could guard battened down below.

Bush touched his hat to Buckland as the latter came on to the quarterdeck.

"I'll start bringing the prisoners up if I may, sir," he said.

"Do as you think proper, if you please, Mr. Bush."

The quarterdeck for the women, the maindeck for the men. It was hard to make them understand that they had to take turns; those of the women who were brought on deck seemed to fancy that they were going to be permanently separated from those kept below, and there was lamentation and expostulation which accorded ill with the dignified routine which should be observed on the quarterdeck of a ship of the line. And the children knew no discipline whatever, and ran shrieking about in all directions while harassed seamen tried to bring them back to their mothers. And other seamen had to be detailed to bring the prisoners their food and water. Bush, tackling each aggravating problem as it arose, began to think that life as first lieutenant in a ship of the line (which he had once believed to be a paradise too wonderful for him to aspire to) was not worth the living.

There were thirty officers crammed into the steerage, from the elegant Villanueva down to the second mate of the *Gaditana*; they were almost as much trouble to Bush as all the other prisoners combined, for they took the air on the poop, from which point of vantage they endeavoured to hold conversations with their wives on the quarterdeck, while they had to be fed from the wardroom stores, which were rapidly depleted by the large Spanish appetites. Bush found himself looking forward more and more eagerly to their arrival at Kingston, and he had neither time nor inclination to brood over what might be their reception there, which was probably just as well, for while he could hope for commendation for the part he had played in the attack on Santo Domingo he could also fear the result of an inquiry into the circumstances which had deprived Captain Sawyer of his command.

Day by day the wind held fair; day by day the *Renown* surged along over the blue Caribbean with the prizes to leeward on the port bow; the prisoners, even the women, began to recover from their seasickness, and feeding them and guarding them became more and more matters of routine making less demand on everyone. They sighted Cape Beata to the northward and could haul their port tacks on board and lay a course direct for Kingston, but save for that they hardly had to handle a sail, for the wind blew steady and the hourly heaving of the log recorded eight knots with almost monotonous regularity. The sun rose splendidly behind them each morning; and each evening the bowsprit pointed into a flaming sunset. In the daytime the sun blazed down upon the ship save for the brief intervals when sharp rainstorms blotted out sun and sea; at night the ship rose and swooped with the following sea under a canopy of stars.

It was a dark lovely night when Bush completed his evening rounds and went in to report to Buckland. The sentries were posted; the watch below was asleep with all lights out; the watch on deck had taken in the royals as a precaution against a rain squall striking the ship without warning in the darkness; the course was east by north and Mr. Carberry had the watch, and the convoy was in sight a mile on the port bow. The guard over the captain in his cabin was at his post. All this Bush recounted to Buckland in the time-honoured fashion of the navy, and Buckland listened to it with the navy's time-honoured patience.

"Thank you, Mr. Bush."

"Thank you, sir. Good night, sir."

"Good night, Mr. Bush."

Bush's cabin opened on the half-deck; it was hot and stuffy with the heat in the tropics, but Bush did not care. He had six clear hours in which to sleep, seeing that he was going to take the morning watch, and he was not the man to waste any of that. He threw off his outer clothes, and standing in his shirt he cast a final look round his cabin before putting out the light. Shoes and trousers were on the sea-chest ready to be put on at a moment's notice in the event of an emergency. Sword and pistols were in their beckets against the bulkhead. All was well. The messenger who would come to call him would bring a lamp, so, using his hand to deflect his breath, he blew out the light. Then he dropped upon the cot, lying on his back with his arms and legs spread wide so as to allow the sweat every chance to evaporate, and he closed his eyes. Thanks to his blessed stolidity of temperament he was soon asleep. At midnight he awoke long enough to hear the watch called, and tell himself blissfully that there was no need to awake and he had not sweated enough to make his position on the cot uncomfortable.

Later he awoke again, and looked up into the darkness with uncomprehending eyes as his ears told him all was not well. There were loud cries, there was a rush of feet overhead. Perhaps a fluky rain squall had taken the ship aback. But those were the wrong noises. Were some of those cries cries of pain? Was that the scream of a woman? Were those infernal women squabbling with each other again? Now there was another rush of feet, and wild shouting, which brought Bush off his cot in a flash. He tore open his cabin door, and as he did so he heard the bang of a musket which left him in no doubt as to what was happening. He turned back and grabbed for sword and pistol, and by the time he was outside his cabin door again the ship was full of a yelling tumult. It was as if the hatchways were the entrances to Hell, and pouring up through them were the infernal powers, screaming with triumph in the dimly lit recesses of the ship.

As he emerged the sentry under the lantern fired his musket, lantern and musket flash illuminating a wave of humanity pouring upon the sentry and instantly submerging him; Bush caught a glimpse of a woman leading the wave, a handsome mulatto woman, wife to one of the privateer officers, now screaming with open mouth and staring eyes as she led the rush. Bush levelled his pistol and fired, but they were up to him in an instant. He backed into his narrow doorway. Hands grabbed his sword blade, and he tore it through their grip; he struck wildly with his empty pistol, he kicked out with his bare feet to free

himself from the hands that grabbed at him. Thrusting overhand with
his sword he stabbed again and again into the mass of bodies pressing
against him. Twice his head struck against the deck beams above but
he did not feel the blows. Then the flood had washed past him. There
were shouts and screams and blows farther along, but he himself had
been passed by, saved by the groaning men who wallowed at his feet
—his bare feet slipping in the hot blood that poured over them.

His first thought was for Buckland, but a single glance aft assured
him that by himself he stood no chance of being of any aid to him, and
in that case his post was on the quarterdeck, and he ran out, sword in
hand, to make his way there. At the foot of the companion ladder there
was another whirl of yelling Spaniards; above there were shouts and
cries as the after guard fought it out. Forward there was other fighting
going on; the stars were shining on white-shirted groups that fought
and struggled with savage desperation. Unknown to himself he was
yelling with the rest; a band of men turned upon him as he approached,
and he felt the heavy blow of a belaying pin against his sword blade.
But Bush inflamed with fighting madness was an enemy to be feared;
his immense strength was allied to a lightfooted quickness. He struck
and parried, leaping over the cumbered deck. He knew nothing, and
during those mad minutes he thought of nothing save to fight against
these enemies, to reconquer the ship by the strength of his single arm.
Then he regained some of his sanity at the moment when he struck
down one of the group against whom he was fighting. He must rally the
crew, set an example, concentrate his men into a cohesive body. He
raised his voice in a bellow.

"Renowns! Renowns! Here, Renowns! Come on!"

There was a fresh swirl in the mad confusion on the maindeck. There
was a searing pain across his shoulder-blade; instinctively he turned
and his left hand seized a throat and he had a moment in which to
brace himself and exert all his strength, with a wrench and a heave flinging the man on to the deck.

"Renowns!" he yelled again.

There was a rush of feet as a body of men rallied round him.

"Come on!"

But the charge that he led was met by a wall of men advancing forward against him from aft. Bush and his little group were swept back,
across the deck, jammed against the bulwarks. Somebody shouted
something in Spanish in front of him, and there was an eddy in the
ring; then a musket flashed and banged. The flash lit up the swarthy
faces that ringed them round, lit up the bayonet on the muzzle of the
musket, and the man beside Bush gave a sharp cry and fell to the deck;
Bush could feel him flapping and struggling against his feet. Someone
at least had a firearm—taken from an arms rack or from a marine—

and had managed to reload it. They would be shot to pieces where they stood, if they were to stand.

"Come on!" yelled Bush again, and sprang forward.

But the disheartened little group behind him did not stir, and Bush gave back from the rigid ring. Another musket flashed and banged, and another man fell. Someone raised his voice and called to them in Spanish. Bush could not understand the words, but he could guess it was a demand for surrender.

"I'll see you damned first!" he said.

He was almost weeping with rage. The thought of his magnificent ship falling into alien hands was appalling now that the realization of the possibility arose in his mind. A ship of the line captured and carried off into some Cuban port—what would England say? What would the navy say? He did not want to live to find out. He was a desperate man who wanted to die.

This time it was with no intelligible appeal to his men that he sprang forward, but with a wild animal cry; he was insane with fury, a fighting lunatic and with a lunatic's strength. He burst through the ring of his enemies, slashing and smiting, but he was the only one who succeeded; he was out on to the clear deck while the struggle went on behind him.

But the madness ebbed away. He found himself leaning—hiding himself, it might almost be said—beside one of the maindeck eighteen-pounders, forgotten for the moment, his sword still in his hand, trying with a slow brain to take stock of his situation. Mental pictures moved slowly across his mind's eye. He could not doubt that some members of the ship's company had risked the ship for the sake of their lust. There had been no bargaining; none of the women had sold themselves in exchange for a betrayal. But he could guess that the women had seemed complacent, that some of the guards had neglected their duty to take advantage of such an opportunity. Then there would be a slow seepage of prisoners out of confinement, probably the officers from out of the midshipmen's berth, and then the sudden well-planned uprising. A torrent of prisoners pouring up, the sentries overwhelmed, the arms seized; the watch below, asleep in their hammocks and incapable of resistance, driven like sheep in a mass forward, herded into a crowd against the bulkhead and restrained there by an armed party while other parties secured the officers aft, and, surging on to the maindeck, captured or slew every man there. All about the ship now there must still be little groups of seamen and marines still free like himself, but weaponless and demoralized; with the coming of daylight the Spaniards would reorganize themselves and would hunt through the ship and destroy any further resistance piecemeal, group by group. It was unbelievable that such a thing could have happened, and yet it had. Four hundred disciplined and desperate men, reckless of their lives and guided by brave officers, might achieve much.

There were orders—Spanish orders—being shouted about the deck now. The ship had come up into the wind all aback when the quartermaster at the wheel had been overwhelmed, and she was wallowing in the trough of the waves, now coming up, now falling off again, with the canvas overhead all flapping and thundering. There were Spanish sea officers—those of the prizes—on board. They would be able to bring the ship under control in a few minutes. Even with a crew of landsmen they would be able to brace the yards, man the wheel, and set a course close-hauled up the Jamaica Channel. Beyond, only a long day's run, lay Santiago. Now there was the faintest, tiniest light in the sky. Morning—the awful morning—was about to break. Bush took a fresh grip of his sword hilt; his head was swimming and he passed his forearm over his face to wipe away the cobwebs that seemed to be gathering over his eyes.

And then, pale but silhouetted against the sky on the other side of the ship, he saw the topsail of another vessel moving slowly forward along the ship's side; masts, yards, rigging; another topsail slowly turning. There were wild shouts and yells from the *Renown*, a grinding crash as the two ships came together. An agonizing pause, like the moment before a roller breaks upon the shore. And then up over the bulwarks of the *Renown* appeared the heads and shoulders of men; the shakos of marines, the cold glitter of bayonets and cutlasses. There was Hornblower, hatless, swinging his leg over and leaping down to the deck, sword in hand, the others leaping with him on either hand. Weak and faint as he was, Bush still could think clearly enough to realize that Hornblower must have collected the prize crews from all three vessels before running alongside in the *Gaditana*; by Bush's calculation he could have brought thirty seamen and thirty marines to this attack. But while one part of Bush's brain could think with this clarity and logic the other part of it seemed to be hampered and clogged so that what went on before his eyes moved with nightmare slowness. It might have been a slow-order drill, as the boarding party climbed down on the deck. Everything was changed and unreal. The shouts of the Spaniards might have been the shrill cries of little children at play. Bush saw the muskets levelled and fired, but the irregular volley sounded in his ears no louder than popguns. The charge was sweeping the deck; Bush tried to spring forward to join with it but his legs strangely would not move. He found himself lying on the deck and his arms had no strength when he tried to lift himself up.

He saw the ferocious bloody battle that was waged, a fight as wild and as irregular as the one that had preceded it, when little groups of men seemed to appear from nowhere and fling themselves into the struggle, sometimes on this side and sometimes on that. Now came another surge of men, nearly naked seamen with Silk at their head; Silk was swinging the rammer of a gun, a vast unwieldy weapon with which he struck out right and left at the Spaniards who broke before them. Another swirl and eddy in the fight; a Spanish soldier trying to run, limping, with a wounded thigh, and a British seaman with a boarding pike in pursuit, stabbing the wretched man under the ribs and leaving him moving feebly in the blood that poured from him.

Now the maindeck was clear save for the corpses that lay heaped upon it, although below decks he could hear the fight going on, shots and screams and crashes. It all seemed to die away. This weakness was not exactly pleasant. To allow himself to put his head down on his arm and forget his responsibilities might seem tempting, but just over the horizon of his conscious mind there were hideous nightmare things waiting to spring out on him, of which he was frightened, but it made him weaker still to struggle against them. But his head was down on his arm, and it was a tremendous effort to lift it again; later it was a worse effort still, but he tried to force himself to make it, to rise and deal with all the things that must be done. Now there was a hard voice speaking, painful to his ears.

"This 'ere's Mr. Bush, sir. 'Ere 'e is!"

Hands were lifting his head. The sunshine was agonizing as it poured into his eyes, and he closed his eyelids tight to keep it out.

"Bush! Bush!" That was Hornblower's voice, pleading and tender. "Bush, please, speak to me."

Two gentle hands were holding his face between them. Bush could just separate his eyelids sufficiently to see Hornblower bending over him, but to speak called for more strength than he possessed. He could only shake his head a little, smiling because of the sense of comfort and security conveyed by Hornblower's hands.

XV

"Mr. Hornblower's respects, sir," said the messenger, putting his head inside Bush's cabin after knocking on the door. "The admiral's flag is flying off Mosquito Point, an' we're just goin' to fire the salute, sir."

"Very good," said Bush.

Lying on his cot he had followed in his mind's eye all that had been going on in the ship. She was on the port tack at the moment and had clewed up all sail save topsails and jib. They must be inside Gun Key, then. He heard Hornblower's voice hailing.

"Lee braces, there! Hands wear ship."

He heard the grumble of the tiller ropes as the wheel was put over; they must be rounding Port Royal point. The *Renown* rose to a level keel—she had been heeling very slightly—and then lay over to port, so little that, lying on his cot, Bush could hardly feel it. Then came the bang of the first saluting gun. Despite the kindly warning that Hornblower had sent down Bush was taken sufficiently by surprise to start a little at the sound. He was as weak and nervous as a kitten, he told himself. At five-second intervals the salute went on, while Bush resettled himself in bed. Movement was not very easy, even allowing for his weakness, on account of all the stitches that closed the numerous cuts and gashes on his body. He was sewn together like a crazy quilt; and any movement was painful.

The ship fell oddly quiet again when the salute was over—he was nearly sure it had been fifteen guns; Lambert presumably had been promoted to vice-admiral. They must be gliding northward up Port Royal bay; Bush tried to remember how Salt Pond Hill looked, and the mountains in the background—what were they called? Liguanea, or something like that—he could never tackle these Dago names. They called it the Long Mountain behind Rock Fort.

"Tops'l sheets!" came Hornblower's voice from above. "Tops'l clew lines."

The ship must be gliding slowly to her anchorage.

"Helm-a-lee!"

Turning into the wind would take her way off her.

"Silence, there in the waist!"

Bush could imagine how the hands would be excited and chattering at coming into harbour—the old hands would be telling the new ones about the grog shops and the unholy entertainments that Kingston, just up the channel, provided for seamen.

"Let go!"

That rumble and vibration; no sailor, not even one as matter-of-fact as Bush, could hear the sound of the cable roaring through the hawsehole without a certain amount of emotion. And this was a moment of very mixed and violent emotions. This was no homecoming; it might be the end of an incident, but it would be most certainly the beginning of a new series of incidents. The immediate future held the likelihood of calamity. Not the risk of death or wounds; Bush would have welcomed that as an alternative to the ordeal that lay ahead. Even in his weak state he could still feel the tension mount in his body as his mind tried to foresee the future. He would like to move about, at least fidget and wriggle if he could not walk, in an endeavour to ease that tension, but he could not even fidget while fifty-three stitches held together the half-closed gashes on his body. There would most certainly be an inquiry into the doings on board H.M.S. *Renown,* and there was a possibility of a court-martial—of a whole series of courts-martial—as a result.

Captain Sawyer was dead. Someone among the Spaniards, drunk with blood lust, at the time when the prisoners had tried to retake the ship, had struck down the wretched lunatic when they had burst into the cabin where he was confined. Hell had no fire hot enough for the man—or woman—who could do such a thing, even though it might be looked upon as a merciful release for the poor soul which had cowered before imagined terrors for so long. It was a strange irony that at the moment a merciless hand had cut the madman's throat some among the free prisoners had spared Buckland, had taken him prisoner as he lay in his cot and bound him with his bedding so that he lay helpless while the battle for his ship was being fought out to its bloody end. Buckland would have much to explain to a court of inquiry.

Bush heard the pipes of the bosun's mates and strained his ears to hear the orders given.

"Gig's crew away! Hands to lower the gig!"

Buckland would of course be going off at once to report to the admiral, and just as Bush came to that conclusion Buckland came into the cabin. Naturally he was dressed with the utmost care, in spotless white trousers and his best uniform coat. He was smoothly shaved, and the formal regularity of his neckcloth was the best proof of the anxious attention he had given to it. He carried his cocked hat in his hand as he stooped under the deck beams, and his sword hung from his hip. But he could not speak immediately; he could only stand and stare at Bush. Usually his cheeks were somewhat pudgy, but this morning they were hollow with care; the staring eyes were glassy, and the lips were twitching. A man on his way to the gallows might look like that.

"You're going to make your report, sir?" asked Bush, after waiting for his superior to speak first.

"Yes," said Buckland.

Beside his cocked hat he held in his hand the sealed reports over which he had been labouring. Bush had been called in to help him compose the first, the anxious one regarding the displacement of Captain Sawyer from command; and his own personal report was embodied in the second one, redolent with conscious virtue, telling of the capitulation of the Spanish forces in Santo Domingo. But the third, with its account of the uprising of the prisoners on board, and its confession that Buckland had been taken prisoner asleep in bed, had been written without Bush's help.

"I wish to God I was dead," said Buckland.

"Don't say that, sir," said Bush, as cheerfully as his own apprehensions and his weak state would allow.

"I wish I was," repeated Buckland.

"Your gig's alongside, sir," said Hornblower's voice. "And the prizes are just anchoring astern of us."

Buckland turned his dead-fish eyes towards him; Hornblower was not quite as neat in appearance, but he had clearly gone to some pains with his uniform.

"Thank you," said Buckland; and then, after a pause, he asked his question explosively: "Tell me, Mr. Hornblower—this is the last chance —how did the captain come to fall down the hatchway?"

"I am quite unable to tell you, sir," said Hornblower.

There was no hint whatever to be gleaned from his expressionless face or from the words he used.

"Now, Mr. Hornblower," said Buckland, nervously tapping the reports in his hand. "I'm treating you well. You'll find I've given you all the praise I could in these reports. I've given you full credit for what you did at Santo Domingo, and for boarding the ship when the prisoners rose. Full credit, Mr. Hornblower. Won't you—won't you—?"

"I really cannot add anything to what you already know, sir," said Hornblower.

"But what am I going to say when they start asking me?" asked Buckland.

"Just say the truth, sir, that the captain was found under the hatchway and that no inquiry could establish any other indication than that he fell by accident."

"I wish I knew," said Buckland.

"You know all that will ever be known, sir. Your pardon, sir"— Hornblower extended his hand and picked a thread of oakum from off Buckland's lapel before he went on speaking—"the admiral will be overjoyed at hearing that we've wiped out the Dons at Samaná, sir. He's probably been worrying himself grey-haired over convoys in the Mona Passage. And we've brought three prizes in. He'll have his oneeighth of their value. You can't believe he'll resent that, can you, sir?"

"I suppose not," said Buckland.

"He'll have seen the prizes coming in with us—everyone in the flagship's looking at them now and wondering about them. He'll be expecting good news. He'll be in no mood to ask questions this morning, sir. Except perhaps to ask you if you'll take Madeira or sherry."

For the life of him Bush could not guess whether Hornblower's smile was natural or not, but he was a witness of the infusion of new spirits into Buckland.

"But later on—" said Buckland.

"Later on's another day, sir. We can be sure of one thing, though —admirals don't like to be kept waiting, sir."

"I suppose I'd better go," said Buckland.

Hornblower returned to Bush's cabin after having supervised the departure of the gig. This time his smile was clearly not forced; it played whimsically about the corners of his mouth.

"I don't see anything to laugh at," said Bush.

He tried to ease his position under the sheet that covered him. Now that the ship was stationary and the nearby land interfered with the free course of the wind the ship was much warmer already; the sun was shining down mercilessly, almost vertically over the deck that lay hardly more than a yard above Bush's upturned face.

"You're quite right, sir," said Hornblower, stooping over him and adjusting the sheet. "There's nothing to laugh at."

"Then take that damned grin off your face," said Bush, petulantly. Excitement and the heat were working on his weakness to make his head swim again.

"Aye aye, sir. Is there anything else I can do?"

"No," said Bush.

"Very good, sir. I'll attend to my other duties, then."

Alone in his cabin Bush rather regretted Hornblower's absence. As far as his weakness would permit, he would have liked to discuss the immediate future; he lay and thought about it, muzzy-mindedly, while the sweat soaked the bandages that swathed him. But there could be no logical order in his thoughts. He swore feebly to himself. Listening, he tried to guess what was going on in the ship with hardly more success than when he had tried to guess the future. He closed his eyes to sleep, and he opened them again when he started wondering about how Buckland was progressing in his interview with Admiral Lambert.

A lob-lolly boy—sick-berth attendant—came in with a tray that bore a jug and a glass. He poured out a glassful of liquid and with an arm supporting Bush's neck he held it to Bush's lips. At the touch of the cool liquid, and as its refreshing scent reached his nose, Bush suddenly realized he was horribly thirsty, and he drank eagerly, draining the glass.

"What's that?" he asked.

"Lemonade, sir, with Mr. Hornblower's respects."

"Mr. Hornblower?"

"Yes, sir. There's a bumboat alongside an' Mr. Hornblower bought some lemons an' told me to squeeze 'em for you."

"My thanks to Mr. Hornblower."

"Aye aye, sir. Another glass, sir?"

"Yes."

That was better. Later on there were a whole succession of noises which he found hard to explain to himself: the tramp of booted feet on the deck, shouted orders, oars and more oars rowing alongside. Then there were steps outside his cabin door and Clive, the surgeon, entered, ushering in a stranger, a skinny, white-haired man with twinkling blue eyes.

"I'm Sankey, surgeon of the naval hospital ashore," he announced. "I've come to take you where you'll be more comfortable."

"I don't want to leave the ship," said Bush.

"In the service," said Sankey with professional cheerfulness, "you should have learned that it is the rule always to have to do what you don't want to do."

He turned back the sheet and contemplated Bush's bandaged form.

"Pardon this liberty," he said, still hatefully cheerful, "but I have to sign a receipt for you—I trust you've never signed a receipt for ship's stores without examining into their condition, Lieutenant."

"Damn you to hell!" said Bush.

"A nasty temper," said Sankey with a glance at Clive. "I fear you have not prescribed a sufficiency of opening medicine."

He laid hands on Bush, and with Clive's assistance dexterously twitched him over so that he lay face downward.

"The Dagoes seem to have done a crude job of carving you, sir," went on Sankey, addressing Bush's defenceless back. "Nine wounds, I understand."

"And fifty-three stitches," added Clive.

"That will look well in the *Gazette*," said Sankey with a giggle; and proceeded to extemporize a quotation: "Lieutenant—ah—Bush received no fewer than nine wounds in the course of his heroic defence, but I am happy to state that he is rapidly recovering from them."

Bush tried to turn his head so as to snarl out an appropriate reply, but his neck was one of the sorest parts of him and he could only growl unintelligibly, and he was not turned on to his back again until his growls had died down.

"And now we'll whisk our little cupid away," said Sankey. "Come in, you stretcher men."

Carried out on to the maindeck Bush found the sunlight blinding, and Sankey stooped to draw the sheet over his eyes.

"Belay that!" said Bush, as he realized his intention, and there was enough of the old bellow in his voice to cause Sankey to pause. "I want to see!"

The explanation of the trampling and bustle on the deck was plain now. Across the waist was drawn up a guard of one of the West Indian regiments, bayonets fixed and every man at attention. The Spanish prisoners were being brought up through the hatchways for despatch to the shore in the lighters alongside. Bush recognized Ortega, limping along with a man on either side to support him; one trouser leg had been cut off and his thigh was bandaged, and the bandage and the other trouser leg were black with dried blood.

"A cut-throat crew, to be sure," said Sankey. "And now, if you have feasted your eyes on them long enough, we can sway you down into the boat."

Hornblower came hurrying down from the quarterdeck and went down on his knee beside the stretcher.

"Are you all right, sir?" he asked anxiously.

"Yes, thank'ee," said Bush.

"I'll have your gear packed and sent ashore after you, sir."

"Thank you."

"Careful with those slings," snapped Hornblower, as the tackles were being attached to the stretcher.

"Sir! Sir!" Midshipman James was dancing about at Hornblower's elbow, anxious for his attention. "Boat's heading for us with a captain aboard."

That was news demanding instant consideration.

"Good-bye, sir," said Hornblower. "Best of luck, sir. See you soon."

He turned away and Bush felt no ill will at this brief farewell, for a captain coming on board had to be received with the correct compliments. Moreover, Bush himself was desperately anxious to know the business that brought this captain on board.

"Hoist away!" ordered Sankey.

"Avast!" said Bush; and in reply to Sankey's look of inquiry, "Let's wait a minute."

"I have no objection myself to knowing what's going on," said Sankey.

The calls of the bosun's mates shrilled along the deck. The sideboys came running; the military guard wheeled to face the entry port; the marines formed up beside them. Up through the entry port came the captain, his gold lace flaming in the sunshine. Hornblower touched his hat.

"You are Mr. Hornblower, at present the senior lieutenant on board this ship?"

"Yes, sir. Lieutenant Horatio Hornblower, at your service."

"My name is Cogshill," said the captain, and he produced a paper which he proceeded to unfold and read aloud. "Orders from Sir Richard Lambert, Vice Admiral of the Blue, Knight of the Bath, Commanding His Majesty's ships and vessels on the Jamaica station, to Captain James Edward Cogshill, of His Majesty's ship *Buckler*. You are hereby requested and required to repair immediately on board of His Majesty's ship *Renown* now lying in Port Royal bay and to take command pro tempore of the aforesaid ship *Renown*."

Cogshill folded his paper again. The assumption of command, even temporarily, of a king's ship was a solemn act, only to be performed with the correct ceremonial. No orders that Cogshill might give on board would be legal until he had read aloud the authority by which he gave them. Now he had "read himself in", and now he held the enormous powers of a captain on board—he could make and unmake warrant officers, he could order imprisonment or the lash, by virtue of the delegation of power from the King in Council down through the Lords of the Admiralty and Sir Richard Lambert.

"Welcome on board, sir," said Hornblower, touching his hat again.

"Very interesting," said Sankey, when Bush had been swayed down into the hospital boat alongside and Sankey had taken his seat beside the stretcher. "Take charge, coxs'n. I knew Cogshill was a favourite of the admiral's. Promotion to a ship of the line from a twenty-eight-gun frigate is a long step for our friend James Edward. Sir Richard has wasted no time."

"The orders said it was only—only temporary," said Bush, not quite able to bring out the words "pro tempore" with any aplomb.

"Time enough to make out the permanent orders in due form," said Sankey. "It is from this moment that Cogshill's pay is increased from ten shillings to two pounds a day."

The Negro oarsmen of the hospital boat were bending to their work, sending the launch skimming over the glittering water, and Sankey turned his head to look at the squadron lying at anchor in the distance —a three-decker and a couple of frigates.

"That's the *Buckler*," he said, pointing. "Lucky for Cogshill his ship was in here at this moment. There'll be plenty of promotion in the admiral's gift now. You lost two lieutenants in the *Renown*?"

"Yes," said Bush. Roberts had been cut in two by a shot from Samaná during the first attack, and Smith had been killed at the post of duty defending the quarterdeck when the prisoners rose.

"A captain and two lieutenants," said Sankey meditatively. "Sawyer had been insane for some time, I understand?"

"Yes."

"And yet they killed him?"

"Yes."

"A chapter of accidents. It might have been better for your first lieutenant if he had met the same fate."

Bush did not make any reply to that remark, even though the same thought had occurred to him. Buckland had been taken prisoner in his bed, and he would never be able to live that down.

"I think," said Sankey, judicially, "he will never be able to look for promotion. Unfortunate for him, seeing that he could otherwise have expected it as a result of your successes in Santo Domingo, on which so far I have not congratulated you, sir. My felicitations."

"Thank you," said Bush.

"A resounding success. Now it will be interesting to see what use Sir Richard—may his name be ever revered—will make of all these vacancies. Cogshill to the *Renown*. That seems certain. Then a commander must be promoted to the *Buckler*. The ineffable joy of post rank! There are four commanders on this station—I wonder which of them will enter through the pearly gates? You have been on this station before, I believe, sir?"

"Not for three years," said Bush.

"Then you can hardly be expected to be up to date regarding the relative standing of the officers here in Sir Richard's esteem. Then a lieutenant will be made commander. No doubt about who that will be."

Sankey spared Bush a glance, and Bush asked the question which was expected of him.

"Who?"

"Dutton. First lieutenant of the flagship. Are you acquainted with him?"

"I think so. Lanky fellow with a scar on his cheek?"

"Yes. Sir Richard believes that the sun rises and sets on him. And I believe that Lieutenant Dutton—Commander as he soon will be—is of the same opinion."

Bush had no comment to make, and he would not have made one if he had. Surgeon Sankey was quite obviously a scatter-brained old gossip, and quite capable of repeating any remarks made to him. He merely nodded—as much of a nod as his sore neck and his recumbent position allowed—and waited for Sankey to continue his monologue.

"So Dutton will be a commander. That'll mean vacancies for three lieutenants. Sir Richard will be able to gladden the hearts of three of his friends by promoting their sons from midshipmen. Assuming, that is to say, that Sir Richard has as many as three friends."

"Oars! Bowman!" said the coxswain of the launch; they were rounding the tip of the jetty. The boat ran gently alongside and was secured; Sankey climbed out and supervised the lifting of the stretcher. With steady steps the Negro bearers began to carry the stretcher up the road towards the hospital, while the heat of the island closed round Bush like the warm water in a bath.

"Let me see," said Sankey, falling into step beside the stretcher. "We had just promoted three midshipmen to lieutenant. So among the warrant ranks there will be three vacancies. But let me see—I fancy you had casualties in the *Renown*?"

"Plenty," said Bush.

Midshipmen and master's mates had given their lives in defence of their ship.

"Of course. That was only to be expected. So there will be many more than three vacancies. So the hearts of the supernumeraries, of the volunteers, of all those unfortunates serving without pay in the hope of eventual preferment, will be gladdened by numerous appointments. From the limbo of nothingness to the inferno of warrant rank. The path of glory—I do not have to asperse your knowledge of literature by reminding you of what the poet said."

Bush had no idea what the poet said, but he was not going to admit it.

"And now we are arrived," said Sankey. "I will attend you to your cabin."

Inside the building the darkness left Bush almost blind for a space after the dazzling sunshine. There were white-washed corridors; there was a long twilit ward divided by screens into minute rooms. He suddenly realized that he was quite exhausted, that all he wanted to do was to close his eyes and rest. The final lifting of him from the stretcher to the bed and the settling of him there seemed almost more than he could bear. He had no attention to spare for Sankey's final chatter. When the mosquito net was at last drawn round his bed and he was left alone he felt as if he were at the summit of a long sleek green wave, down which he went gliding, gliding, endlessly gliding. It was almost a pleasant sensation, but not quite.

When he reached the foot of the wave he had to struggle up it again, recovering his strength, through a night and a day and another night, and during that time he came to learn about the life in the hospital—the sounds, the groans that came from other patients behind other screens, the not-quite-muffled howls of lunatic patients at the far end of the whitewashed corridor; morning and evening rounds; by the end of his second day there he had begun to listen with appetite for the noises that presaged the bringing in of his meals.

"You are a fortunate man," remarked Sankey, examining his stitched-up body. "These are all incised wounds. Not a single deep puncture. It's contrary to all my professional experience. Usually the Dagoes can be relied upon to use their knives in a more effective manner. Just look at this cut here."

The cut in question ran from Bush's shoulder to his spine, so that Sankey could not literally mean what he had just said.

"Eight inches long at least," went on Sankey. "Yet not more than two inches deep, even though, as I suspect, the scapula is notched. Four inches with the point would have been far more effective. This other cut here seems to be the only one that indicates any ambition to plumb the arterial depths. Clearly the man who wielded the knife here intended to stab. But it was a stab from above downwards, and the jagged beginning of it shows how the point was turned by the ribs down which the knife slid, severing a few fibres of latissimus dorsi but tailing off at the end into a mere superficial laceration. The effort of a tyro. Turn over, please. Remember, Mr. Bush, if ever you use a knife, to give an upward inclination to the point. The human ribs lie open to welcome an upward thrust; before a downward thrust they overlap and forbid all entrance, and the descending knife, as in this case, bounds in vain from one rib to the next, knocking for admission at each in turn and being refused."

"I'm glad of that," said Bush. "Ouch!"

"And every cut is healing well," said Sankey. "No sign of mortification."

Bush suddenly realized that Sankey was moving his nose about close to his body; it was by its smell that gangrene first became apparent.

"A good clean cut," said Sankey, "rapidly sutured and bound up in its own blood, can be expected to heal by first intention more often than not. Many times more often than not. And these are mostly clean cuts, haggled, as I said, only a little here and there. Bend this knee if you please. Your honourable scars, Mr. Bush, will in the course of a few years become almost unnoticeable. Thin lines of white whose crisscross pattern will be hardly a blemish on your classic torso."

"Good," said Bush; he was not quite sure what his torso was, but he was not going to ask Sankey to explain all these anatomical terms.

This morning Sankey had hardly left him before he returned with a visitor.

"Captain Cogshill to inspect you," he said. "Here he is, sir."

Cogshill looked down at Bush upon the bed.

"Doctor Sankey gives me the good news that you are recovering rapidly," he said.

"I think I am, sir."

"The admiral has ordered a court of inquiry, and I am nominated a member of the court. Naturally your evidence will be required, Mr. Bush, and it is my duty to ascertain how soon you will be able to give it."

Bush felt a little wave of apprehension ripple over him. A court of inquiry was only a shade less terrifying than the court-martial to which it might lead. Even with a conscience absolutely clear Bush would rather—far rather—handle a ship on a lee shore in a gale than face questions and have to give answers, submit his motives to analysis and misconstruction, and struggle against the entanglements of legal forms. But it was medicine that had to be swallowed, and the sensible thing was to hold his nose and gulp it down however nauseating.

"I'm ready at any time, sir."

"Tomorrow I shall take out the sutures, sir," interposed Sankey. "You will observe that Mr. Bush is still weak. He was entirely exsanguinated by his wounds."

"What do you mean by that?"

"I mean he was drained of his blood. And the ordeal of taking out the sutures—"

"The stitches, do you mean?"

"The stitches, sir. The ordeal of removing them may momentarily retard Mr. Bush's recovery of his strength. But if the court will indulge him with a chair when he gives his evidence—"

"That can certainly be granted."

"Then in three days from now he can answer any necessary questions."

"Next Friday, then?"

"Yes, sir. That is the earliest. I could wish it would be later."

"To assemble a court on this station," explained Cogshill with his cold courtesy, "is not easy, when every ship is away on necessary duty so much of the time. Next Friday will be convenient."

"Yes, sir," said Sankey.

It was some sort of gratification to Bush, who had endured so much of Sankey's chatter, to see him almost subdued in his manner when addressing someone as eminent as a captain.

"Very well, then," said Cogshill. He bowed to Bush. "I wish you the quickest of recoveries."

"Thank you, sir," said Bush.

Even lying on his back he could not check the instinctive attempt to return the bow, but his wounds hurt him when he started to double up in the middle and prevented him from appearing ridiculous. With Cogshill gone Bush had time to worry about the future; the fear of it haunted him a little even while he ate his dinner, but the lob-lolly boy who came to take away the remains ushered in another visitor, the sight of whom drove away the black thoughts. It was Hornblower, standing at the door with a basket in his hand, and Bush's face lit up at the sight of him.

"How are you, sir?" asked Hornblower.

They shook hands, each reflecting the pleasure of the other's greeting.

"All the better for seeing you," said Bush, and meant it.

"This is my first chance of coming ashore," said Hornblower. "You can guess that I've been kept busy."

Bush could guess easily enough; it was no trouble to him to visualize all the duties that had been heaped on Hornblower, the necessity to complete *Renown* again with powder and shot, food and water, to clean up the ship after the prisoners had been removed, to eradicate the traces of the recent fighting, to attend to the formalities connected with the disposal of the prizes, the wounded, the sick, and the effects of the dead. And Bush was eager to hear the details, as a housewife might be when illness had removed her from the supervision of her household. He plied Hornblower with questions, and the technical discussion that ensued prevented Hornblower for some time from indicating the basket he had brought.

"Pawpaws," he said. "Mangoes. A pineapple. That's only the second pineapple I've ever seen."

"Thank you. Very kind of you," said Bush. But it was utterly beyond possibility that he could give the least hint of the feeling that the gift evoked in him, that after lying lonely for these days in the hospital he should find that someone cared about him—that in any case someone should give him so much as a thought. The words he spoke were limping and quite inadequate, and only a sensitive and sympathetic mind could guess at the feelings which the words concealed rather than expressed. But he was saved from further embarrassment by Hornblower abruptly introducing a new subject.

"The admiral's taking the *Gaditana* into the navy," he announced.

"Is he, by George!"

"Yes. Eighteen guns—six-pounders and nines. She'll rate as a sloop of war."

"So he'll have to promote a commander for her."

"Yes."

"By George!" said Bush again.

Some lucky lieutenant would get that important step. It might have been Buckland—it still might be, if no weight were given to the consideration that he had been captured asleep in bed.

"Lambert's renaming her the *Retribution*," said Hornblower.

"Not a bad name, either."

"No."

There was silence for a moment; each of them was reliving, from his own point of view, those awful minutes while the *Renown* was being recaptured, while the Spaniards who tried to fight it out were slaughtered without mercy.

"You know about the court of inquiry, I suppose?" asked Bush; it was a logical step from his last train of thought.

"Yes. How did you know about it?"

"Cogshill's just been in here to warn me that I'll have to give evidence."

"I see."

There followed silence more pregnant than the last as they thought about the ordeal ahead. Hornblower deliberately broke it.

"I was going to tell you," he said, "that I had to reeve new tiller

lines in *Renown*. Both of them were frayed—there's too much wear there.
I think they're led round too sharp an angle."

That provoked a technical discussion which Hornblower encouraged until it was time for him to leave.

XVI

The court of inquiry was not nearly as awe-inspiring as a court-martial.
There was no gun fired, no court-martial flag hoisted; the captains
who constituted the board wore their everyday uniforms, and the witnesses were not required to give their evidence under oath; Bush had
forgotten about this last fact until he was called into the court.

"Please take a seat, Mr. Bush," said the president. "I understand you
are still weak from your wounds."

Bush hobbled across to the chair indicated and was just able to reach
it in time to sit down. The great cabin of the *Renown*—here, where
Captain Sawyer had lain quivering and weeping with fear—was
sweltering hot. The president had the logbook and journal in front of
him, and he held in his hand what Bush recognized to be his own report
regarding the attack on Samaná, which he had addressed to Buckland.

"This report of yours does you credit, Mr. Bush," said the president.
"It appears that you stormed this fort with no more than six casualties,
although it was constructed with a ditch, parapets, and ramparts in
regular style, and defended by a garrison of seventy men, and armed
with twenty-four-pounders."

"We took them by surprise, sir," said Bush.

"It is that which is to your credit."

The surprise of the garrison of Samaná could not have been greater
than Bush's own surprise at this reception; he was expecting something
far more unpleasant and inquisitorial. A glance across at Buckland,
who had been called in before him, was not quite so reassuring; Buckland was pale and unhappy. But there was something he must say before
the thought of Buckland should distract him.

"The credit should be given to Lieutenant Hornblower, sir," he said.
"It was his plan."

"So you very handsomely say in your report. I may as well say at
once that it is the opinion of this court that all the circumstances regarding the attack on Samaná and the subsequent capitulation are in accordance with the best traditions of the service."

"Thank you, sir."

"Now we come to the next matter. The attempt of the prisoners to capture the *Renown*. You were by this time acting as first lieutenant of the ship, Mr. Bush?"

"Yes, sir."

Step by step Bush was taken through the events of that night. He was responsible under Buckland for the arrangements made for guarding and feeding the prisoners. There were fifty women, wives of the prisoners, under guard in the midshipmen's berth. Yes, it was difficult to supervise them as closely as the men. Yes, he had gone his rounds after pipedown. Yes, he had heard a disturbance. And so on.

"And you were found lying among the dead, unconscious from your wounds?"

"Yes, sir."

"Thank you, Mr. Bush."

A fresh-faced young captain at the end of the table asked a question.

"And all this time Captain Sawyer was confined to his cabin, until he was murdered?"

The president interposed.

"Captain Hibbert, Mr. Buckland has already enlightened us regarding Captain Sawyer's indisposition."

There was annoyance in the glance that the president of the court turned upon Captain Hibbert, and light suddenly dawned upon Bush. Sawyer had a wife, children, friends, who would not desire that any attention should be called to the fact that he had died insane. The president of the court was probably acting under explicit orders to hush that part of the business up. He would welcome questions about it no more than Bush himself would, now that Sawyer was dead in his country's cause. Buckland could not have been very closely examined about it, either. His unhappy look must be due to having to describe his inglorious part in the attempt on the *Renown*.

"I don't expect any of you gentlemen wish to ask Mr. Bush any more questions?" asked the president of the court in such a way that questions could not possibly have been asked. "Call Lieutenant Hornblower."

Hornblower made his bow to the court; he was wearing that impassive expression which Bush knew by now to conceal an internal turbulence. He was asked as few questions on Samaná as Bush had been.

"It has been suggested," said the president, "that this attack on the fort, and the hoisting up of the gun to search the bay, were on your initiative?"

"I can't think why that suggestion was made, sir. Mr. Buckland bore the entire responsibility."

"I won't press you further about that, Mr. Hornblower, then. I think we all understand. Now, let us hear about your recapture of the *Renown*. What first attracted your attention?"

It called for steady questioning to get the story out of Hornblower. He had heard a couple of musket shots, which had worried him, and then he saw the *Renown* come up into the wind, which made him certain something was seriously wrong. So he had collected his prize crews together and laid the *Renown* on board.

"Were you not afraid of losing the prizes, Mr. Hornblower?"

"Better to lose the prizes than the ship, sir. Besides—"

"Besides what, Mr. Hornblower?"

"I had every sheet and halliard cut in the prizes before we left them, sir. It took them some time to reeve new ones, so it was easy to recapture them."

"You seem to have thought of everything, Mr. Hornblower," said the president, and there was a buzz of approval through the court. "And you seem to have made a very prompt counter-attack on the *Renown*. You did not wait to ascertain the extent of the danger? Yet for all you knew the attempt to take the ship might have already failed."

"In that case no harm was done except the disabling of the rigging of the prizes, sir. But if the ship had actually fallen into the hands of the prisoners it was essential that an attack should be directed on her before any defence could be organized."

"We understand. Thank you, Mr. Hornblower."

The inquiry was nearly over. Carberry was still too ill with his wounds to be able to give evidence; Whiting of the marines was dead. The court conferred only a moment before announcing its findings.

"It is the opinion of this court," announced the president, "that strict inquiry should be made among the Spanish prisoners to determine who it was that murdered Captain Sawyer, and that the murderer, if still alive, should be brought to justice. And as the result of our examination of the surviving officers of H.M.S. *Renown* it is our opinion that no further action is necessary."

That meant there would be no court-martial. Bush found himself grinning with relief as he sought to meet Hornblower's eye, but when he succeeded his smile met with a cold reception. Bush tried to shut off his smile and look like a man of such clear conscience that it was no relief to be told that he would not be court-martialled. And a glance at Buckland changed his elation to a feeling of pity. The man was desperately unhappy; his professional ambitions had come to an abrupt end. After the capitulation of Samaná he must have cherished hope, for with that considerable achievement to his credit, and his captain unfit for service, there was every possibility that he would receive the vital promotion to commander at least, possibly even to captain. The fact that he had been surprised in bed meant an end to all that. He would always be remembered for it, and the fact would remain in people's minds when the circumstances were forgotten. He was doomed to remain an ageing lieutenant.

Bush remembered guiltily that it was only by good fortune that he himself had awakened in time. His wounds might be painful, but they had served an invaluable purpose in diverting attention from his own responsibility; he had fought until he had fallen unconscious, and perhaps that was to his credit, but Buckland would have done the same had the opportunity been granted him. But Buckland was damned, while he himself had come through the ordeal at least no worse off than he had been before. Bush felt the illogicality of it all, although he would have been hard pressed if he had to put it into words. And in any case logical thinking on the subject of reputation and promotion was not easy, because during all these years Bush had become more and more imbued with the knowledge that the service was a hard and ungrateful one, in which fortune was even more capricious than in other walks of life. Good luck came and went in the navy as unpredictably as death chose its victims when a broadside swept a crowded deck. Bush was fatalistic and resigned about that, and it was not a state of mind conducive to penetrating thought.

"Ah, Mr. Bush," said Captain Cogshill, "it's a pleasure to see you on your feet. I hope you will remain on board to dine with me. I hope to secure the presence of the other lieutenants."

"With much pleasure, sir," said Bush. Every lieutenant said that in reply to his captain's invitation.

"In fifteen minutes' time, then? Excellent."

The captains who had constituted the court of inquiry were leaving the ship, in strict order of seniority, and the calls of the bosun's mates echoed along the deck as each one left, a careless hand to a hat brim in acknowledgment of the compliments bestowed. Down from the entry port went each in turn, gold lace, epaulettes, and all, these blessed individuals who had achieved the ultimate beatitude of post rank, and the smart gigs pulled away towards the anchored ships.

"You're dining on board, sir?" said Hornblower to Bush.

"Yes."

On the deck of their own ship the "sir" came quite naturally, as naturally as it had been dropped when Hornblower had been visiting his friend in the hospital ashore. Hornblower turned to touch his hat to Buckland.

"May I leave the deck to Hart, sir? I'm invited to dine in the cabin."

"Very well, Mr. Hornblower." Buckland forced a smile. "We'll have two new lieutenants soon, and you'll cease to be the junior."

"I shan't be sorry, sir."

These men who had been through so much together were grasping eagerly at trivialities to keep the conversation going for fear lest more serious matters should lift their ugly heads.

"Time for us to go along," said Buckland.

Captain Cogshill was a courtly host. There were flowers in the great cabin now; they must have been kept hidden away in his sleeping cabin while the inquiry was being held so as not to detract from the formality of the proceedings. And the cabin windows were wide open, and a wind scoop brought into the cabin what little air was moving.

"That is a land-crab salad before you, Mr. Hornblower. Coconut-fed land crab. Some prefer it to dairy-fed pork. Perhaps you will serve it to those who would care for some?"

The steward brought in a vast smoking joint which he put on the table.

"A saddle of fresh lamb," said the captain. "Sheep do badly in these islands and I fear this may not be fit to eat. But perhaps you will at least try it. Mr. Buckland, will you carve? You see, gentlemen, I still have some real potatoes left—one grows weary of yams. Mr. Hornblower, will you take wine?"

"With pleasure, sir."

"And Mr. Bush—to your speedy recovery, sir."

Bush drained his glass thirstily. Sankey had warned him, when he left the hospital, that over indulgence in spirituous liquors might result in inflammation of his wounds, but there was pleasure in pouring the wine down his throat and feeling the grateful warmth it brought to his stomach. The dinner proceeded.

"You gentlemen who have served on this station before must be acquainted with this," said the captain, contemplating a steaming dish that had been laid before him. "A West Indian pepper pot—not as good as one finds in Trinidad, I fear. Mr. Hornblower, will you make your first essay? Come in!"

The last words were in response to a knock on the cabin door. A smartly dressed midshipman entered. His beautiful uniform, his elegant bearing, marked him as one of that class of naval officer in receipt of a comfortable allowance from home, or even of substantial means of his own. Some sprig of the nobility, doubtless, serving his legal time until favouritism and interest should whisk him up the ladder of promotion.

"I'm sent by the admiral, sir," he announced.

Of course. Bush, his perceptions comfortably sensitized with wine, could see at once that with those clothes and that manner he must be on the admiral's staff.

"And what's your message?" asked Cogshill.

"The admiral's compliments, sir, and he'd like Mr. Hornblower's presence on board the flagship as soon as is convenient."

"And dinner not half-way finished," commented Cogshill, looking at Hornblower. But an admiral's request for something as soon as convenient meant immediately, convenient or not. Very likely it was a matter of no importance, either.

"I'd better leave, sir, if I may," said Hornblower. He glanced at Buckland. "May I have a boat, sir?"

"Pardon me, sir," interposed the midshipman. "The admiral said that the boat which brought me would serve to convey you to the flagship."

"That settles it," said Cogshill. "You'd better go, Mr. Hornblower. We'll save some of this pepper pot for you against your return."

"Thank you, sir," said Hornblower, rising.

As soon as he had left, the captain asked the inevitable question.

"What in the world does the admiral want with Hornblower?"

He looked round the table and received no verbal reply. There was a strained look on Buckland's face, however, as Bush saw. It seemed as if in his misery Buckland was clairvoyant.

"Well, we'll know in time," said Cogshill. "The wine's beside you, Mr. Buckland. Don't let it stagnate."

Dinner went on. The pepper pot rasped on Bush's palate and inflamed his stomach, making the wine doubly grateful when he drank it. When the cheese was removed, and the cloth with it, the steward brought in fruit and nuts in silver dishes.

"Port," said Captain Cogshill. " '79. A good year. About this brandy I know little, as one might expect in these times."

Brandy could only come from France, smuggled, presumably, and as a result of trading with the enemy.

"But here," went on the captain, "is some excellent Dutch geneva —I bought it at the prize sale after we took St. Eustatius. And here is another Dutch liquor—it comes from Curaçao, and if the orange flavour is not too sickly for your palates you might find it pleasant. Swedish schnapps, fiery but excellent, I fancy—that was after we captured Saba. The wise man does not mix grain and grape, so they say, but I understand schnapps is made from potatoes, and so does not come under the ban. Mr. Buckland?"

"Schnapps for me," said Buckland a little thickly.

"Mr. Bush?"

"I'll drink along with you, sir."

That was the easiest way of deciding.

"Then let us make it brandy. Gentlemen, may Boney grow bonier than ever."

They drank the toast, and the brandy went down to warm Bush's interior to a really comfortable pitch. He was feeling happy and relaxed, and two toasts later he was feeling better than he had felt since the *Renown* left Plymouth.

"Come in!" said the captain.

The door opened slowly, and Hornblower stood framed in the opening. There was the old look of strain in his face; Bush could see it even though Hornblower's figure seemed to waver a little before his eyes—the way objects appeared over the rack of red-hot cannon balls at Samaná—and although Hornblower's countenance seemed to be a little fuzzy round the edges.

"Come in, come in, man," said the captain. "The toasts are just beginning. Sit in your old place. Brandy for heroes, as Johnson said in his wisdom. Mr. Bush!"

"V-victorious war. O-ceans of gore. P-prizes galore. B-b-beauty ashore. Hic," said Bush, inordinately proud of himself that he had remembered that toast and had it ready when called upon.

"Drink fair, Mr. Hornblower," said the captain, "we have a start of you already. A stern chase is a long chase."

Hornblower put his glass to his lips again.

"Mr. Buckland!"

"Jollity and—jollity and—jollity and—and—and—mirth," said Buckland, managing to get the last word out at last. His face was as red as a beetroot and seemed to Bush's heated imagination to fill the entire cabin like the setting sun; most amusing.

"You've come back from the admiral, Mr. Hornblower," said the captain with sudden recollection.

"Yes, sir."

The curt reply seemed out of place in the general atmosphere of goodwill; Bush was distinctly conscious of it, and of the pause which followed.

"Is all well?" asked the captain at length, apologetic about prying into someone else's business and yet led to do so by the silence.

"Yes, sir." Hornblower was turning his glass round and round on the table between long nervous fingers, every finger a foot long, it seemed to Bush. "He has made me commander of *Retribution*."

The words were spoken quietly, but they had the impact of pistol shots in the silence of the room.

"God bless my soul!" said the captain. "Then that's our new toast. To the new commander, and a cheer for him too!"

Bush cheered lustily and downed his brandy.

"Good old Hornblower!" he said. "Good old Hornblower!"

To him it was really excellent news; he leaned over and patted Hornblower's shoulder. He knew his face was one big smile, and he put his head on one side and his shoulder on the table so that Hornblower should get the full benefit of it.

Buckland put his glass down on the table with a sharp tap.

"Damn you!" he said. "Damn you! Damn you to Hell!"

"Easy there!" said the captain hastily. "Let's fill the glasses. A brimmer there, Mr. Buckland. Now, our country! Noble England! Queen of the waves!"

Buckland's anger was drowned in the fresh flood of liquor, yet later in the session his sorrows overcame him and he sat at the table weeping quietly, with the tears running down his cheeks; but Bush was too happy to allow Buckland's misery to affect him. He always remembered that afternoon as one of the most successful dinners he had ever attended. He could also remember Hornblower's smile at the end of dinner.

"We can't send you back to the hospital today," said Hornblower. "You'd better sleep in your own cot tonight. Let me take you there."

That was very agreeable. Bush put both arms round Hornblower's shoulders and walked with dragging feet. It did not matter that his feet dragged and his legs would not function while he had this support; Hornblower was the best man in the world and Bush could announce it by singing "For He's a Jolly Good Fellow" while lurching along the alleyway. And Hornblower lowered him onto the heaving cot and grinned down at him as he clung to the edges of the cot; Bush was a little astonished that the ship should sway like this while at anchor.

XVII

That was how Hornblower came to leave the *Renown*. The coveted promotion was in his grasp, and he was busy enough commissioning the *Retribution*, making her ready for sea, and organizing the scratch crew which was drafted into her. Bush saw something of him during this time, and could congratulate him soberly on the epaulette which, worn on the left shoulder, marked him as a commander, one of those gilded individuals for whom bosuns' mates piped the side and who could look forward with confidence to eventual promotion to captain. Bush called him "sir", and even when he said it for the first time the expression did not seem unnatural.

Bush had learned something during the past few weeks which his service during the years had not called to his attention. Those years had been passed at sea, among the perils of the sea, amid the ever-changing conditions of wind and weather, deep water and shoal. In the ships of the line in which he had served there had only been minutes of battle for every week at sea, and he had gradually become fixed in the idea that seamanship was the one requisite for a naval officer. To be master of the countless details of managing a wooden sailing ship; not only to be able to handle her under sail, but to be conversant with all the petty but important trifles regarding cordage and cables, pumps and salt pork, dry rot and the Articles of War; that was what was necessary: But he knew now of other qualities equally necessary: a bold and yet thoughtful initiative, moral as well as physical courage, tactful handling both of superiors and of subordinates, ingenuity and quickness of thought. A fighting navy needed to fight, and needed fighting men to lead it.

Yet even though this realization reconciled him to Hornblower's promotion, there was irony in the fact that he was plunged back immediately into petty detail of the most undignified sort. For now he had to wage war on the insect world and not on mankind; the Spanish prisoners in the six days they had been on board had infested the ship with all the parasites they had brought with them. Fleas, lice, and bedbugs swarmed everywhere, and in the congenial environment of a wooden ship in the tropics full of men they flourished exceedingly. Heads had to be cropped and bedding baked; and in a desperate attempt to wall in the bedbugs woodwork had to be repainted—a success of a day or two flattered only to deceive, for after each interval the pests showed up again. Even the cockroaches and the rats that had always been in the ship seemed to multiply and become omnipresent.

It was perhaps an unfortunate coincidence that the height of his exasperation with this state of affairs coincided with the payment of prize money for the captures at Samaná. A hundred pounds to spend, a couple of days' leave granted by Captain Cogshill, and Hornblower at a loose end at the same time—those two days were a lurid period, during which Hornblower and Bush contrived to spend each of them a hundred pounds in the dubious delights of Kingston. Two wild days and two wild nights, and then Bush went back on board the *Renown*, shaken and limp, only too glad to get out to sea and recover. And when he returned from his first cruise under Cogshill's command Hornblower came to say goodbye.

"I'm sailing with the land breeze tomorrow morning," he said.

"Whither bound, sir?"

"England," said Hornblower.

Bush could not restrain a whistle at the news. There were men in the squadron who had not seen England for ten years.

"I'll be back again," said Hornblower. "A convoy to the Downs. Despatches for the Commissioners. Pick up the replies and a convoy out again. The usual round."

For a sloop of war it was indeed the usual round. The *Retribution* with her eighteen guns and disciplined crew could fight almost any privateer afloat; with her speed and handiness she could cover a convoy more effectively than the ship of the line or even the frigates that accompanied the larger convoys to give solid protection.

"You'll get your commission confirmed, sir," said Bush, with a glance at Hornblower's epaulette.

"I hope so," said Hornblower.

Confirmation of a commission bestowed by a commander-in-chief on a foreign station was a mere formality.

"That is," said Hornblower, "if they don't make peace."

"No chance of that, sir," said Bush; and it was clear from Hornblower's grin that he, too, thought there was no possibility of peace either, despite the hints in the two-months-old newspapers that came out from England to the effect that negotiations were possible. With Bonaparte in supreme power in France, restless, ambitious, and unscrupulous, and with none of the points settled that were in dispute between the two countries, no fighting man could believe that the negotiations could result even in an armistice, and certainly not in a permanent peace.

"Good luck in any case, sir," said Bush, and there was no mere formality about those words.

They shook hands and parted; it says much for Bush's feelings towards Hornblower that in the grey dawn next morning he rolled out of his cot and went up on deck to watch the *Retribution*, ghost-like under her topsails, and with the lead going in the chains, steal out round the point, wafted along by the land breeze. Bush watched her go; life in the service meant many partings. Meanwhile there was war to be waged against bedbugs.

Eleven weeks later the squadron was in the Mona Passage, beating against the trade winds. Lambert had brought them out here with the usual double objective of every admiral, to exercise his ships and to see an important convoy through the most dangerous part of its voyage. The hills of Santo Domingo were out of sight at the moment over the westerly horizon, but Mona was in sight ahead, table-topped and, from this point of view, an unrelieved oblong in outline; over on the port bow lay Mona's little sister Monita, exhibiting a strong family resemblance.

The lookout frigate ahead sent up a signal.

"You're too slow, Mr. Truscott," bellowed Bush at the signal midshipman, as was right and proper.

"Sail in sight, bearing northeast," read the signal midshipman, glass to eye.

That might be anything, from the advanced guard of a French squadron broken out from Brest to a wandering trader.

The signal came down and was almost instantly replaced.

"Friendly sail in sight bearing northeast," read Truscott.

A squall came down and blotted out the horizon. The *Renown* had to pay off momentarily before its impact. The rain rattled on the deck as the ship lay over, and then the wind abruptly moderated, the sun came out again, and the squall was past. Bush busied himself with the task of regaining station, of laying the *Renown* her exact two cables' length astern of her next ahead. She was last in the line of three, and the flagship was the first. Now the strange sail was well over the horizon. She was a sloop of war as the telescope showed at once; Bush thought for a moment that she might be the *Retribution,* returned after a very quick double passage, but it only took a second glance to make sure she was not. Truscott read her number and referred to the list.

"*Clara,* sloop of war: Captain Ford," he announced.

The *Clara* had sailed for England with despatches three weeks before the *Retribution,* Bush knew.

"*Clara* to Flag," went on Truscott. "Have despatches."

She was nearing fast. Up the flagship's halliards soared a string of black balls which broke into flags at the top.

"All ships," read Truscott, with excitement evident in his voice, for this meant that the *Renown* would have orders to obey. "Heave-to."

"Main tops'l braces!" yelled Bush. "Mr. Abbott! My respects to the captain and the squadron's heaving-to."

The squadron came to the wind and lay heaving easily over the rollers. Bush watched the *Clara*'s boat dancing over the waves towards the flagship.

"Keep the hands at the braces, Mr. Bush," said Captain Cogshill. "I expect we'll fill again as soon as the despatches are delivered."

But Cogshill was wrong. Bush watched through his glass the officer from the *Clara* go up the flagship's side, but the minutes passed and the flagship still lay hove-to, the squadron still pitched on the waves. Now a new string of black balls went up the flagship's halliards.

"All ships," read Truscott. "Captains repair on board the flagship."

"Gig's crew away!" roared Bush.

It must be important, or at least unusual, news for the admiral to wish to communicate it to the captains immediately and in person. Bush walked the quarterdeck with Buckland while they waited. The French fleet might be out; the North Alliance might be growing restive again. The King's illness might have returned. It might be anything; they could be only certain that it was not nothing. The minutes passed and lengthened into half-hours; it could hardly be bad news—if it were, Lambert would not be wasting precious time like this, with the whole squadron going off slowly to leeward. Then at last the wind brought to their ears, over the blue water, the high-pitched sound of the pipes of the bosun's mates in the flagship. Bush clapped his glass to his eye.

"First one's coming off," he said.

Gig after gig left the flagship's side, and now they could see the *Renown*'s gig with her captain in the sternsheets. Buckland went to meet him as he came up the side. Cogshill touched his hat; he was looking a little dazed.

"It's peace," he said.

The wind brought them the sound of cheering from the flagship—the announcement must have been made to the ship's company on board, and it was the sound of that cheering that gave any reality at all to the news the captain brought.

"Peace, sir?" asked Buckland.

"Yes, peace. Preliminaries are signed. The ambassadors meet in France next month to settle the terms, but it's peace. All hostilities are at an end—they are to cease in every part of the world on arrival of this news."

"Peace!" said Bush.

For nine years the world had been convulsed with war; ships had burned, the men had bled, from Manila to Panama, west about and east about. It was hard to believe that he was living now in a world where men did not fire cannons at each other on sight. Cogshill's next remark had a bearing on this last thought.

"National ships of the French, Batavian, and Italian Republics will be saluted with the honours due to foreign ships of war," he said.

Buckland whistled at that, as well he might. It meant that England had recognized the existence of the red republics against which she had fought for so long. Yesterday it had been almost treason to speak the word "republic". Now a captain could use it casually in an official statement.

"And what happens to us, sir?" asked Buckland.

"That's what we must wait to hear," said Cogshill. "But the navy is to be reduced to peacetime establishment. That means that nine ships out of ten will be paid off."

"Holy Moses!" said Bush.

Now the next ship ahead was cheering, the sound coming shrilly through the air.

"Call the hands," said Cogshill. "They must be told."

The ship's company of the *Renown* rejoiced to hear the news. They cheered as wildly as did the crews of the other ships. For them it meant the approaching end of savage discipline and incredible hardship. Freedom, liberty, a return to their homes. Bush looked down at the sea of ecstatic faces and wondered what the news implied for him. Freedom and liberty, possibly; but they meant life on a lieutenant's half pay. That was something he had never experienced; in his earliest youth he had entered the navy as a midshipman—the peacetime navy which he could hardly remember—and during the nine years of the war he had only known two short intervals of leave. He was not too sure that he cared for the novel prospects that the future held out to him.

He glanced up at the flagship and turned to bellow at the signal midshipman.

"Mr. Truscott! Don't you see that signal? Attend to your duties, or it will be the worse for you, peace or no peace."

The wretched Truscott put his glass to his eye.

"All ships," he read. "Form line on the larboard tack."

Bush glanced at the captain for permission to proceed.

"Hands to the braces, there!" yelled Bush. "Fill that main tops'l. Smarter than that, you lubbers! Full and by, quartermaster. Mr. Cope, haven't you eyes in your head? Take another pull at that weatherbrace! God bless my soul! Easy there! Belay!"

"All ships," read Truscott with his telescope, as the *Renown* gathered way and settled in the wake of her next ahead. "Tack in succession."

"Stand by to go about!" yelled Bush.

He noted the progress of the next ahead, and then spared time to rate the watch for its dilatoriness in going to its stations for tacking ship.

"You slow-footed slobs! I'll have some of you dancing at the gratings before long!"

The next ahead had tacked by now, and the *Renown* was advancing into the white water she had left behind.

"Ready about!" shouted Bush. "Headsail sheets! Helm-a-lee!"

The *Renown* came ponderously about and filled on the starboard tack.

"Course sou'west by west," said Truscott, reading the next signal.

Southwest by west. The admiral must be heading back for Port Royal. He could guess that was the first step towards the reduction of the fleet to its peacetime establishment. The sun was warm and delightful, and the *Renown*, steadying before the wind, was roaring along over the blue Caribbean. She was keeping her station well; there was no need to shiver the mizzen topsail yet. This was a good life. He could not make himself believe that it was coming to an end. He tried to think of a winter's day in England, with nothing to do. No ship to handle. Half pay—his sisters had half his pay as it was, which would mean there would be nothing for him, as well as nothing to do. A cold winter's day. No, he simply could not imagine it, and he left off trying.

XVIII

It was a cold winter's day in Portsmouth; a black frost, and there was a penetrating east wind blowing down the street as Bush came out of the dockyard gates. He turned up the collar of his pea-jacket over his muffler and crammed his hands into his pockets, and he bowed his head into the wind as he strode forward into it, his eyes watering, his nose running, while that east wind seemed to find its way between his ribs, making the scars that covered them ache anew. He would not allow himself to look up at the Keppel's Head as he went past it. In there, he knew, there would be warmth and good company. The fortunate officers with prize money to spend; the incredibly fortunate officers who had found themselves appointments in the peacetime navy—they would be in there yarning and taking wine with each other. He could not afford wine. He thought longingly for a moment about a tankard of beer, but he rejected the idea immediately, although the temptation was strong. He had a month's half pay in his pocket—he was on his way back from the Clerk of the Cheque from whom he had drawn it—but that had to last four and a half weeks and he knew he could not afford it.

He had tried of course for a billet in the merchant service, as mate, but that was as hopeless a prospect at present as obtaining an appointment as lieutenant. Having started life as a midshipman and spent all his adult life in the fighting service he did not know enough about bills of lading or cargo stowage. The merchant service looked on the navy with genial contempt, and said the latter always had a hundred men available to do a job the merchantman had to do with six. And with every ship that was paid off a fresh batch of master's mates, trained for the merchant service and pressed from it, sought jobs in their old profession, heightening the competition every month.

Someone came out from a side street just in front of him and turned into the wind ahead of him—a naval officer. That gangling walk; those shoulders bent into the wind; he could not help but recognize Hornblower.

"Sir! Sir!" he called, and Hornblower turned.

There was a momentary irritation in his expression but it vanished the moment he recognized Bush.

"It's good to see you," he said, his hand held out.

"Good to see *you*, sir," said Bush.

"Don't call me 'sir'," said Hornblower.

"No, sir? What—why—?"

Hornblower had no greatcoat on; and his left shoulder was bare of the epaulette he should have worn as a commander. Bush's eyes went to it automatically. He could see the old pin-holes in the material which showed where the epaulette had once been fastened.

"I'm not a commander," said Hornblower. "They didn't confirm my appointment."

"Good God!"

Hornblower's face was unnaturally white—Bush was accustomed to seeing it deeply tanned—and his cheeks were hollow, but his expression was set in the old unrevealing cast that Bush remembered so well.

"Preliminaries of peace were signed the day I took *Retribution* into Plymouth," said Hornblower.

"What infernal luck!" said Bush.

Lieutenants waited all their lives for the fortunate combination of circumstances that might bring them promotion, and most of them waited in vain. It was more than likely now Hornblower would wait in vain for the rest of his life.

"Have you applied for an appointment as lieutenant?" asked Bush.

"Yes. And I suppose you have?" replied Hornblower.

"Yes."

There was no need to say more than that on that subject. The peacetime navy employed one-tenth of the lieutenants who were employed in wartime; to receive an appointment one had to be of vast seniority or else have powerful friends.

"I spent a month in London," said Hornblower. "There was always a crowd round the Admiralty and the Navy Office."

"I expect so," said Bush.

The wind came shrieking round the corner.

"God, but it's cold!" said Bush.

His mind toyed with the thought of various ways to continue the conversation in shelter. If they went to the Keppel's Head now it would mean paying for two pints of beer, and Hornblower would have to pay for the same.

"I'm going into the Long Rooms just here," said Hornblower. "Come in with me—or are you busy?"

"No, I'm not busy," said Bush, doubtfully "but—"

"Oh, it's all right," said Hornblower. "Come on."

There was reassurance in the confident way in which Hornblower spoke about the Long Rooms. Bush only knew of them by reputation. They were frequented by officers of the navy and the army with money to spare. Bush had heard much about the high stakes that were indulged in at play there, and about the elegance of the refreshments offered by the proprietor. If Hornblower could speak thus casually about the Long Rooms he could not be as desperately hard up as he seemed to be. They crossed the street and Hornblower held open the door and ushered him through. It was a long oak-panelled room; the gloom of the outer day was made cheerful here by the light of candles, and a magnificent fire flamed on the hearth. In the centre several card tables with chairs round them stood ready for play; the ends of the room were furnished as comfortable lounges. A servant in a green baize apron was making the room tidy, and came to take their hats and Bush's coat as they entered.

"Good morning, sir," he said.

"Good morning, Jenkins," said Hornblower.

He walked with unconcealed haste over to the fire and stood before it warming himself. Bush saw that his teeth were chattering.

"A bad day to be out without your pea-jacket," he said.

"Yes," said Hornblower.

He clipped that affirmative a little short, so that in a minute degree it failed to be an indifferent, flat agreement. It was that which caused Bush to realize that it was not eccentricity or absent-mindedness that had brought Hornblower out into a black frost without his greatcoat. Bush looked at Hornblower sharply, and he might even have asked a tactless question if he had not been forestalled by the opening of an inner door beside them. A short, plump, but exceedingly elegant gentleman came in; he was dressed in the height of fashion, save that he wore his hair long, tied back and with powder in the style of the last generation. This made his age hard to guess. He looked at the pair of them with keen dark eyes.

"Good morning, Marquis," said Hornblower. "It is a pleasure to present—M. le Marquis de Sainte-Croix—Lieutenant Bush."

The Marquis bowed gracefully, and Bush endeavoured to imitate him. But for all that graceful bow, Bush was quite aware of the considering eyes running over him. A lieutenant looking over a likely hand, or a farmer looking at a pig at a fair, might have worn the same expression. Bush guessed that the Marquis was making a mental estimate as to how much Bush might be good for at the card tables, and suddenly became acutely conscious of his shabby uniform. Apparently the Marquis reached the same conclusion as Bush did, but he began a conversation nevertheless.

"A bitter wind," he said.

"Yes," said Bush.

"It will be rough in the Channel," went on the Marquis, politely raising a professional topic.

"Indeed it will," agreed Bush.

"And no ships will come in from the westward."

"You can be sure of that."

The Marquis spoke excellent English. He turned to Hornblower.

"Have you seen Mr. Truelove lately?" he asked.

"No," said Hornblower. "But I met Mr. Wilson."

Truelove and Wilson were names familiar to Bush; they were the most famous prize agents in England—a quarter of the navy at least employed that firm to dispose of their captures for them. The Marquis turned back to Bush.

"I hope you have been fortunate in the matter of prize money, Mr. Bush?" he said.

"No such luck," said Bush. His hundred pounds had gone in a two days' debauch at Kingston.

"The sums they handle are fabulous, nothing less than fabulous. I understand the ship's company of the *Caradoc* will share seventy thousand pounds when they come in."

"Very likely," said Bush. He had heard of the captures the *Caradoc* had made in the Bay of Biscay.

"But while this wind persists they must wait before enjoying their good fortune, poor fellows. They were not paid off on the conclusion of peace, but were ordered to Malta to assist in relieving the garrison. Now they are expected back daily."

For an immigrant civilian the Marquis displayed a laudable interest in the affairs of the service. And he was consistently polite, as his next speech showed.

"I trust you will consider yourself at home here, Mr. Bush," he said. "Now I hope you will pardon me, as I have much business to attend to."

He withdrew through the curtained door, leaving Bush and Hornblower looking at each other.

"A queer customer," said Bush.

"Not so queer when you come to know him," said Hornblower.

The fire had warmed him by now, and there was a little colour in his cheeks.

"What do you *do* here?" asked Bush, curiosity finally overcoming his politeness.

"I play whist," said Hornblower.

"Whist?"

All that Bush knew about whist was that it was a slow game favoured by intellectuals. When Bush gambled he preferred something with a greater element of chance and which did not make any demand on his thoughts.

"A good many men from the services drop in here for whist," said Hornblower. "I'm always glad to make a fourth."

"But I'd heard—"

Bush had heard of all sorts of other games being played in the Long Rooms: hazard, vingt-et-un, even roulette.

"The games for high stakes are played in there," said Hornblower, pointing to the curtain door. "I stay here."

"Wise man," said Bush. But he was quite sure there was some further information that was being withheld from him. And he was not actuated by simple curiosity. The affection and interest that he felt towards Hornblower drove him into further questioning.

"Do you win?" he asked.

"Frequently," said Hornblower. "Enough to live."

"But you have your half pay?" went on Bush.

Hornblower yielded in face of this persistence.

"No," he said. "I'm not entitled."

"Not entitled?" Bush's voice rose a semitone. "But you're a permanent lieutenant."

"Yes. But I was a temporary commander. I drew three months' full pay for that rank before the Admiralty refused to confirm."

"And then they put you under stoppages?"

"Yes. Until I've repaid the excess." Hornblower smiled; a nearly natural smile. "I've lived through two months of it. Only five more and I'll be back on half pay."

"Holy Peter!" said Bush.

Half pay was bad enough; it meant a life of constant care and economy, but one could live. Hornblower had nothing at all. Bush knew now why Hornblower had no greatcoat. He felt a sudden wave of anger. A recollection rose in his mind, as clear to his inward eye as this pleasant room was to his outward one. He remembered Hornblower swinging himself down, sword in hand, on to the deck of the *Renown*, plunging into a battle against odds which could only result in either death or victory. Hornblower, who had planned and worked endlessly to ensure success and then had flung his life upon the board as a final stake; and today Hornblower was standing with chattering teeth trying to warm himself beside a fire by the charity of a frog-eating gambling-hall keeper with the look of a dancing master.

"It's a hellish outrage," said Bush, and then he made his offer. He offered his money, even though he knew as he offered it that it meant most certainly that he would go hungry, and that his sisters, if not exactly hungry, would hardly have enough to eat. But Hornblower shook his head.

"Thank you," he said. "I'll never forget that. But I can't accept it. You know that I couldn't. But I'll never cease to be grateful to you. I'm grateful in another way, too. You've brightened the world for me by saying that."

Even in the face of Hornblower's refusal Bush repeated his offer, and tried to press it, but Hornblower was firm in his refusal. Perhaps it was because Bush looked so downcast that Hornblower gave him some further information in the hope of cheering him up.

"Things aren't as bad as they seem," he said. "You don't understand that I'm in receipt of regular pay—a permanent salarium from our friend the Marquis."

"I didn't know that," said Bush.

"Half a guinea a week," explained Hornblower. "Ten shillings and sixpence every Saturday morning, rain or shine."

"And what do you have to do for it?" Bush's half pay was more than twice that sum.

"I only have to play whist," explained Hornblower. "Only that. From twelve midday until two in the morning I'm here to play whist with any three that need a fourth."

"I see," said Bush.

"The Marquis in his generosity also makes me free of these rooms. I have no subscription to pay. No table money. And I can keep my winnings."

"And pay your losses?"

Hornblower shrugged.

"Naturally. But the losses do not come as often as one might think. The reason's simple enough. The whist players who find it hard to obtain partners, and who are cold-shouldered by the others, are naturally the bad players. Strangely anxious to play, even so. And when the Marquis happens to be in here and Major Jones and Admiral Smith and Mr. Robinson are seeking a fourth while everyone seems strangely preoccupied he catches my eye—the sort of reproving look a wife might throw at a husband talking too loud at a dinner party—and I rise to my feet and offer to be the fourth. It is odd they are flattered to play with Hornblower, as often it costs them money."

"I see," said Bush again, and he remembered Hornblower standing by the furnace in Fort Samaná organizing the firing of red-hot shot at the Spanish privateers.

"The life is not entirely one of beer and skittles, naturally," went on Hornblower; with the dam once broken he could not restrain his loquacity. "After the fourth hour or so it becomes irksome to play with bad players. When I go to Hell I don't doubt that my punishment will be always to partner players who pay no attention to my discards. But then on the other hand I frequently play a rubber or two with the good players. There are moments when I would rather lose to a good player than win from a bad one."

"That's just the point," said Bush, harking back to an old theme. "How about the losses?"

Bush's experiences of gambling had mostly been of losses, and in this hard-headed moment he could remember the times when he had been weak.

"I can deal with them," said Hornblower. He touched his breast pocket. "I keep ten pounds here. My *corps de réserve*, you understand. I can always endure a run of losses in consequence. Should that reserve be depleted, then sacrifices have to be made to build it up again."

The sacrifices being skipped meals, thought Bush grimly. He looked so woebegone that Hornblower offered further comfort.

"But five more months," he said, "and I'll be on half pay again. And before that—who knows? Some captain may take me off the beach."

"That's true," said Bush.

It was true insofar as the possibility existed. Sometimes ships were recommissioned. A captain might be in need of a lieutenant; a captain might invite Hornblower to fill the vacancy. But every captain was besieged by friends seeking appointments, and in any event the Admiralty was also besieged by lieutenants of great seniority—or lieutenants with powerful friends—and captains were most likely to listen to recommendations of high authority.

The door opened and a group of men came in.

"It's high time for customers to arrive," said Hornblower, with a grin at Bush. "Stay and meet my friends."

The red coats of the army, the blue coats of the navy, the bottle-green and snuff-coloured coats of civilians; Bush and Hornblower made room for them before the fire after the introductions were made, and the coat-tails were parted as their wearers lined up before the flames. But the exclamations about the cold, and the polite conversation, died away rapidly.

"Whist?" asked one of the newcomers tentatively.

"Not for me. Not for us," said another, the leader of the red-coats. "The Twenty-Ninth Foot has other fish to fry. We've a permanent engagement with our friend the Marquis in the next room. Come on, Major, let's see if we can call a main right this time."

"Then will you make a four, Mr. Hornblower? How about your friend Mr. Bush?"

"I don't play," said Bush.

"With pleasure," said Hornblower. "You will excuse me, Mr. Bush, I know. There is the new number of the *Naval Chronicle* on the table there. There's a *Gazette* letter on the last page which might perhaps hold your interest for a while. And there is another item you might think important, too."

Bush could guess what the letter was even before he picked the periodical up, but when he found the place there was the same feeling of pleased shock to see his name in print there, as keen as the first time he saw it: "I have the honour to be, etc., WM. BUSH."

The *Naval Chronicle* in these days of peace found it hard, apparently, to obtain sufficient matter to fill its pages, and gave much space to the reprinting of these despatches. "Copy of a letter from Vice-Admiral Sir Richard Lambert to Evan Nepean, Esq., Secretary to the Lords Commissioners of the Admiralty." That was only Lambert's covering letter enclosing the reports. Here was the first one—it was with a strange internal sensation that he remembered helping Buckland with the writing of it, as the *Renown* ran westerly along the coast of Santo Domingo the day before the prisoners broke out. It was Buckland's report on the fighting at Samaná. To Bush the most important line was "in the handsomest manner—under the direction of Lieutenant William Bush, the senior officer, whose report I enclose". And here was his very own literary work, as enclosed by Buckland.

H.M.S. Renown, *off Santo Domingo. January 9th, 1802*
SIR,
    I have the honour to inform you . . .

Bush relived those days of a year ago as he reread his own words; those words which he had composed with so much labour even though he had referred, during the writing of them, to other reports written by other men so as to get the phrasing right.

    . . . I cannot end this report without a reference to the gallant conduct and most helpful suggestions of Lieutenant Horatio Hornblower, who was my second in command on this occasion, and to whom in great part the success of the expedition is due.

There was Hornblower now, playing cards with a post captain and two contractors.

Bush turned back through the pages of the *Naval Chronicle*. Here was the Plymouth letter, a daily account of the doings in the port during the last month.

"Orders came down this day for the following ships to be paid off. . . ." "Came in from Gibraltar *La Diana*, 44, and the *Tamar*, 38, to be paid off as soon as they go up the harbour and to be laid up." "Sailed the *Caesar*, 80, for Portsmouth, to be paid off." And here was an item just as significant, or even more so: "Yesterday there was a large sale of serviceable stores landed from different men of war." The navy was growing smaller every day and with every ship that was paid off another batch of lieutenants would be looking for billets. And here was an item—"This afternoon a fishing boat turning out of atwater jibed and overset, by which accident two industrious fishermen with large families were drowned." This was the *Naval Chronicle*, whose pages had once bulged with the news of the Nile and of Camperdown; now it told of accidents to industrious fishermen. Bush was too interested in his own concerns to feel any sympathy towards their large families.

There was another drowning as a final item; a name—a combination of names—caught Bush's attention so that he read the paragraph with a quickened pulse.

> Last night the jolly boat of His Majesty's cutter *Rapid,* in the Revenue service, while returning in the fog from delivering a message on shore, was swept by the ebb tide athwart the hawse of a merchantman anchored off Fisher's Nose, and capsized. Two seamen and Mr. Henry Wellard, Midshipman, were drowned. Mr. Wellard was a most promising young man recently appointed to the *Rapid,* having served as a volunteer in His Majesty's ship *Renown.*

Bush read the passage and pondered over it. He thought it important to the extent that he read the remainder of the *Naval Chronicle* without taking in any of it; and it was with surprise that he realized he would have to leave quickly in order to catch the carrier's waggon back to Chichester.

A good many people were coming into the Rooms now; the door was continually opening to admit them. Some of them were naval officers with whom he had a nodding acquaintance. All of them made straight for the fire for warmth before beginning to play. And Hornblower was on his feet now; apparently the rubber was finished, and Bush took the opportunity to catch his eye and give an indication that he wished to leave. Hornblower came over to him. It was with regret that they shook hands.

"When do we meet again?" asked Hornblower.

"I come in each month to draw my half pay," said Bush. "I usually spend the night because of the carrier's waggon. Perhaps we could dine—?"

"You can always find me here," said Hornblower. "But—do you have a regular place to stay?"

"I stay where it's convenient," replied Bush.

They both of them knew that meant that he stayed where it was cheap.

"I lodge in Highbury Street. I'll write the address down." Hornblower turned to a desk in the corner and wrote on a sheet of paper which he handed to Bush. "Would you care to share my room when next you come? My landlady is a sharp one. No doubt she will make a charge for a cot for you, but even so—"

"It'll save money," said Bush, putting the paper in his pocket; his grin as he spoke masked the sentiment in his next words. "And I'll see more of you."

"By George, yes," said Hornblower. Words were not adequate.

Jenkins had come sidling up and was holding Bush's greatcoat for him to put on. There was that in Jenkins' manner which told Bush that gentlemen when helped into their coats at the Long Rooms presented Jenkins with a shilling. Bush decided at first that he would be eternally damned before he parted with a shilling, and then he changed his mind. Maybe Hornblower would give Jenkins a shilling if he did not. He felt in his pocket and handed the coin over.

"Thank you, sir," said Jenkins.

With Jenkins out of earshot again Bush lingered, wondering how to frame his question.

"That was hard luck on young Wellard," he said, tentatively.

"Yes," said Hornblower.

"D'you think," went on Bush, plunging desperately, "he had anything to do with the captain's falling down the hatchway?"

"I couldn't give an opinion," answered Hornblower. "I didn't know enough about it."

"But—" began Bush, and checked himself again; he knew by the look on Hornblower's face that it was no use asking further questions.

The Marquis had come into the room and was looking round in unobtrusive inspection. Bush saw him take note of the several men who were not playing, and of Hornblower standing in idle gossip by the door. Bush saw the meaning glance which he directed at Hornblower, and fell into sudden panic.

"Good-bye," he said, hastily.

The black northeast wind that greeted him in the street was no more cruel than the rest of the world.

XIX

It was a short, hard-faced woman who opened the door in reply to Bush's knock, and she looked at Bush even harder when he asked for Lieutenant Hornblower.

"Top of the house," she said, at last, and left Bush to find his way up.

There could be no doubt about Hornblower's pleasure at seeing him. His face was lit with a smile and he drew Bush into the room while shaking his hand. It was an attic, with a steeply sloping ceiling; it contained a bed and a night table and a single wooden chair, but, as far as Bush's cursory glance could discover, nothing else at all.

"And how is it with you?" asked Bush, seating himself in the proffered chair, while Hornblower sat on the bed.

"Well enough," replied Hornblower—but was there, or was there not, a guilty pause before that answer? In any case the pause was covered up by the quick counter-question. "And with you?"

"So-so," said Bush.

They talked indifferently for a space, with Hornblower asking questions about the Chichester cottage that Bush lived in with his sisters.

"We must see about your bed for tonight," said Hornblower at the first pause. "I'll go down and give Mrs. Mason a hail."

"I'd better come too," said Bush.

Mrs. Mason lived in a hard world, quite obviously; she turned the proposition over in her mind for several seconds before she agreed to it.

"A shilling for the bed," she said. "Can't wash the sheets for less than that with soap as it is."

"Very good," said Bush.

He saw Mrs. Mason's hand held out, and he put the shilling into it; no one could be in any doubt about Mrs. Mason's determination to be paid in advance by any friend of Hornblower's. Hornblower had dived for his pocket when he caught sight of the gesture, but Bush was too quick for him.

"And you'll be talking till all hours," said Mrs. Mason. "Mind you don't disturb my other gentlemen. And douse the light while you talk, too, or you'll be burning a shilling's worth of tallow."

"Of course," said Hornblower.

"Maria! Maria!" called Mrs. Mason.

A young woman—no, a woman not quite young—came up the stairs from the depths of the house at the call.

"Yes, Mother?"

Maria listened to Mrs. Mason's instructions for making up a truckle bed in Mr. Hornblower's room.

"Yes, Mother," she said.

"Not teaching today, Maria?" asked Hornblower pleasantly.

"No, sir." The smile that lit her plain face showed her keen pleasure at being addressed.

"Oak-Apple Day? No, not yet. It's not the King's Birthday. Then why this holiday?"

"Mumps, sir," said Maria. "They all have mumps, except Johnnie Bristow."

"That agrees with everything I've heard about Johnnie Bristow," said Hornblower.

"Yes, sir," said Maria. She smiled again, clearly pleased not only that Hornblower should jest with her but also because he remembered what she had told him about the school.

Back in the attic again Hornblower and Bush resumed their conversation, this time on a more serious plane. The state of Europe occupied their attention.

"This man Bonaparte," said Bush. "He's a restless cove."

"That's the right word for him," agreed Hornblower.

"Isn't he satisfied? Back in '96 when I was in the old *Superb* in the Mediterranean—that was when I was commissioned lieutenant—he was just a general. I can remember hearing his name for the first time, when we were blockading Toulon. Then he went to Egypt. Now he's First Consul—isn't that what he calls himself?"

"Yes. But he's Napoleon now, not Bonaparte any more. First Consul for life."

"Funny sort of name. Not what I'd choose for myself."

"Lieutenant Napoleon Bush," said Hornblower. "It wouldn't sound well."

They laughed together at the ridiculous combination.

"The *Morning Chronicle* says he's going a step farther," went on Hornblower. "There's talk that he's going to call himself Emperor."

"Emperor!"

Even Bush could catch the connotations of that title, with its claims to univeral pre-eminence.

"I suppose he's mad?" asked Bush.

"If he is, he's the most dangerous madman in Europe."

"I don't trust him over this Malta business. I don't trust him an inch," said Bush, emphatically. "You mark my words, we'll have to fight him again in the end. Teach him a lesson he won't forget. It'll come sooner or later—we can't go on like this."

"I think you're quite right," said Hornblower. "And sooner rather than later."

"Then—" said Bush.

He could not talk and think at the same time, not when his thoughts were as tumultuous as the ones this conclusion called up; war with France meant the re-expansion of the navy; the threat of invasion and the needs of convoy would mean the commissioning of every small craft that could float and carry a gun. It would mean the end of half pay for him; it would mean walking a deck again and handling a ship under sail. And it would mean hardship again, danger, anxiety, monotony —all the concomitants of war. These thoughts rushed into his brain with so much velocity, and in such a continuous stream, that they made a sort of whirlpool of his mind, in which the good and the bad circled after each other, each in turn chasing the other out of his attention.

"War's a foul business," said Hornblower, solemnly. "Remember the things you've seen."

"I suppose you're right," said Bush; there was no need to particularize. But it was an unexpected remark, all the same. Hornblower grinned and relieved the tension.

"Well," he said, "Boney can call himself Emperor if he likes. I have to earn my half guinea at the Long Rooms."

Bush was about to take this opportunity to ask Hornblower how he was profiting there, but he was interrupted by a rumble outside the door and a knock.

"Here comes your bed," said Hornblower, walking over to open the door.

Maria came trundling the thing in. She smiled at them.

"Over here or over there?" she asked.

Hornblower looked at Bush.

"It doesn't matter," said Bush.

"I'll put it against the wall, then."

"Let me help," said Hornblower.

"Oh no, sir. Please sir, I can do it."

The attention fluttered her—and Bush could see that with her sturdy figure she was in no need of help. To cover her confusion she began to thump at the bedding, putting the pillows into the pillowslips.

"I trust you have already had the mumps, Maria?" said Hornblower.

"Oh yes, sir. I had them as a child, on both sides."

The exercise and her agitation between them had brought the colour into her cheeks. With blunt but capable hands she spread the sheet. Then she paused as another implication of Hornblower's inquiry occurred to her.

"You've no need to worry, sir. I shan't give them to you if you haven't had them."

"I wasn't thinking about that," said Hornblower.

"Oh, sir," said Maria, twitching the sheet into mathematical smoothness. She spread the blankets before she looked up again. "Are you going out directly, sir?"

"Yes. I ought to have left already."

"Let me take that coat of yours for a minute, sir. I can sponge it and freshen it up."

"Oh, I wouldn't have you go to that trouble, Maria."

"It wouldn't be any trouble, sir. Of course not. Please let me, sir. It looks—"

"It looks the worse for wear," said Hornblower, glancing down at it. "There's no cure for old age that's yet been discovered."

"Please let me take it, sir. There's some spirits of hartshorn downstairs. It will make quite a difference. Really it will."

"But—"

"Oh, please, sir."

Hornblower reluctantly put up his hand and undid a button.

"I'll only be a minute with it," said Maria, hastening to him. Her hands were extended to the other buttons, but a sweep of Hornblower's quick nervous fingers had anticipated her. He pulled off his coat and she took it out of his hands.

"You've mended that shirt yourself," she said, accusingly.

"Yes, I have."

Hornblower was a little embarrassed at the revelation of the worn garment. Maria studied the patch.

"I would have done that for you if you'd asked me, sir."

"And a good deal better, no doubt."

"Oh, I wasn't saying that, sir. But it isn't fit that you should patch your own shirts."

"Whose should I patch, then?"

Maria giggled.

"You're too quick with your tongue for me," she said. "Now, just wait here and talk to the lieutenant while I sponge this."

She darted out of the room and they heard her footsteps hurrying down the stairs, while Hornblower looked half-ruefully at Bush.

"There's a strange pleasure," he said, "in knowing that there's a human being who cares whether I'm alive or dead. Why that should give pleasure is a question to be debated by the philosophic mind."

"I suppose so," said Bush.

He had sisters who devoted all their attention to him whenever it was possible, and he was used to it. At home he took their ministrations for granted. He heard the church clock strike the half-hour, and it recalled his thoughts to the further business of the day.

"You're going to the Long Rooms now?" he asked.

"Yes. And you, I suppose, want to go to the dockyard? The monthly visit to the Clerk of the Cheque?"

"Yes."

"We can walk together as far as the Rooms, if you care to. As soon as our friend Maria returns my coat to me."

"That's what I was thinking," said Bush.

It was not long before Maria came knocking at the door again.

"It's done," she said, holding out the coat. "It's nice and fresh now.

But something seemed to have gone out of her. She seemed a little frightened, a little apprehensive.

"What's the matter, Maria?" asked Hornblower, quick to feel the change of attitude.

"Nothing. Of course there's nothing the matter with me," said Maria, defensively, and then she changed the subject. "Put your coat on now, or you'll be late."

Walking along Highbury Street Bush asked the question he had had in mind for some time, regarding whether Hornblower had ex-

perienced good fortune lately at the Rooms. Hornblower looked at him
oddly.

"Not as good as it might be," he said.

"Bad?"

"Bad enough. My opponents' aces lie behind my kings, ready for
instant regicide. And my opponents' kings lie behind my aces, so that
when they venture out from the security of the hand they survive all
perils and take the trick. In the long run the chances right themselves
mathematically. But the periods when they are unbalanced in the wrong
direction can be distressing."

"I see," said Bush, although he was not too sure that he did; but one
thing he did know, and that was that Hornblower had been losing. And
he knew Hornblower well enough by now to know that when he talked
in an airy fashion as he was doing now he was more anxious than he
cared to admit.

They had reached the Long Rooms, and paused at the door.

"You'll call in for me on your way back?" asked Hornblower.
"There's an eating house in Broad Street with a fourpenny ordinary.
Sixpence with pudding. Would you care to try it?"

"Yes, indeed. Thank you. Good luck," said Bush, and he paused
before continuing. "Be careful."

"I shall be careful," said Hornblower, and went in through the
door.

The weather was in marked contrast with what had prevailed during
Bush's last visit. Then there had been a black frost and an east wind;
today there was a hint of spring in the air. As Bush walked along the
Hard the harbour entrance revealed itself to him on his left, its muddy
water sparkling in the clear light. A flush-decked sloop was coming
out with the ebb, the gentle puffs of wind from the northwest just giving her steerage way. Despatches for Halifax, perhaps. Money to pay
the Gibraltar garrison. Or maybe a reinforcement for the revenue cutters
that were finding so much difficulty in dealing with the peacetime wave
of smuggling. Whatever it was, there were fortunate officers on board,
with an appointment, with three years' employment ahead of them,
with a deck under their feet and a wardroom in which to dine. Lucky
devils. Bush acknowledged the salute of the porter at the gate and went
into the yard.

He emerged into the late afternoon and made his way back to the
Long Rooms. Hornblower was at a table near the corner and looked up
to smile at him, the candlelight illuminating his face. Bush found himself the latest *Naval Chronicle* and settled himself to read it. Beside
him a group of army and navy officers argued in low tones regarding
the difficulties of living in the same world as Bonaparte. Malta and
Genoa, Santo Domingo and Miquelet, came up in the conversation.

There was a murmur of agreement.

"Mark my words," said one of them, thumping his hand with his fist, "we'll be at war with him again soon enough."

"It'll be war to the knife," supplemented another. "If once he drives us to extremity, we shall never rest until Mr. Napoleon Bonaparte is hanging to the nearest tree."

The others agreed to that with a fierce roar, like wild beasts.

"Gentlemen," said one of the players at Hornblower's table, looking round over his shoulder. "Could you find it convenient to continue your discussion at the far end of the room? This end is dedicated to the most scientific and difficult of all games."

The words were uttered in a pleasant high tenor, but it was obvious that the speaker had every expectation of being instantly obeyed.

"Very good, my lord," said one of the naval officers.

That made Bush look more closely, and he recognized the speaker, although it was six years since he had seen him last. It was Admiral Lord Parry, who had been made a lord after Camperdown; now he was one of the commissioners of the navy, one of the people who could make or break a naval officer. The mop of snow-white curls that ringed the bald spot on the top of his head, his smooth old-man's face, his mild speech, accorded ill with the nickname of "Old Bloody bones" which had been given him by the lower-deck far back in the American War. Hornblower was moving in very high society. Bush watched Lord Parry extend a skinny white hand and cut the cards to Hornblower. It was obvious from his colouring that Parry, like Hornblower, had not been to sea for a long time. Hornblower dealt and the game proceeded in its paralysing stillness; the cards made hardly a sound as they fell on the green cloth, and each trick was picked up and laid down almost silently, with only the slightest click. The line of tricks in front of Parry grew like a snake, silent as a snake gliding over a rock, like a snake it closed on itself and then lengthened again, and then the hand was finished and the cards swept together.

"Small slam," said Parry as the players attended to their markers, and that was all that was said. The two tiny words sounded as clearly and as briefly in the silence as two bells in the middle watch. Hornblower cut the cards and the next deal began in the same mystic silence. Bush could not see the fascination of it. He would prefer a game in which he could roar at his losses and exult over his winnings; and preferably one in which the turn of a single card, and not of the whole fifty-two, would decide who had won and who had lost. No, he was wrong. There was undoubtedly a fascination about it, a poisonous fascination. Opium? No. This silent game was like the quiet interplay of duelling swords as compared with the crash of cutlass blades, and it was as deadly. A small-sword through the lungs killed as effectively as—more effectively than—the sweep of a cutlass.

"A short rubber," commented Parry; the silence was over, and the cards lay in disorder on the table.

"Yes, my lord," said Hornblower.

Bush, taking note of everything with the keen observation of anxiety, saw Hornblower put his hand to his breast pocket—the pocket that he had indicated as holding his reserve—and take out a little fold of one-pound notes. When he had made his payment Bush could see that what he returned to his pocket was only a single note.

"You encountered the worst of good fortune," said Parry, pocketing his winnings. "On the two occasions when you dealt, the trump that you turned up proved to be the only one that you held. I cannot remember another occasion when the dealer has held a singleton trump twice running."

"In a long enough period of play, my lord," said Hornblower, "every possible combination of cards can be expected."

He spoke with a polite indifference that for a moment almost gave Bush heart to believe his losses were not serious, until he remembered the single note that had been put back into Hornblower's breast pocket.

"But it is rare to see such a run of ill luck," said Parry. "And yet you play an excellent game, Mr.—Mr.—please forgive me, but your name escaped me at the moment of introduction."

"Hornblower," said Hornblower.

"Ah, yes, of course. For some reason the name is familiar to me.

Bush glanced quickly at Hornblower. There never was such a perfect moment for reminding a Lord Commissioner about the fact that his promotion to commander had not been confirmed.

"When I was a midshipman, my lord," said Hornblower, "I was sea-sick while at anchor in Spithead on board the *Justinian*. I believe the story is told."

"That doesn't seem to be the connection I remember," answered Parry. "But we have been diverted from what I was going to say. I was about to express regret that I cannot give you your immediate revenge, although I should be most glad to have the opportunity of studying your play of the cards again."

"You are very kind, my lord," said Hornblower, and Bush writhed —he had been writhing ever since Hornblower had given the go-by to that golden opportunity. This last speech had a flavour of amused bitterness that Bush feared would be evident to the admiral. But fortunately Parry did not know Hornblower as well as Bush did.

"Most unfortunately," said Parry, "I am due to dine with Admiral Lambert."

This time the coincidence startled Hornblower into being human.

"Admiral Lambert, my lord?"

"Yes. You know him?"

"I had the honour of serving under him on the Jamaica station. This is Mr. Bush, who commanded the storming party from the *Renown* that compelled the capitulation of Santo Domingo."

"Glad to see you, Mr. Bush," said Parry, and it was only just evident that if he was glad he was not overjoyed. A commissioner might well find embarrassment at an encounter with an unemployed lieutenant with a distinguished record. Parry lost no time in turning back to Hornblower.

"It was in my mind," he said, "to try to persuade Admiral Lambert to return here with me after dinner so that I could offer you your revenge. Would we find you here if we did?"

"I am most honoured, my lord," said Hornblower with a bow, but Bush noted the uncontrollable flutter of his fingers towards his almost empty breast pocket.

"Then would you be kind enough to accept a semi-engagement? On account of Admiral Lambert I can make no promise, except that I will do my best to persuade him."

"I'm dining with Mr. Bush, my lord. But I would be the last to stand in the way."

"Then we may take it as being settled as near as may be?"

"Yes, my lord."

Parry withdrew then, ushered out by his flag lieutenant who had been one of the whist four, with all the dignity and pomp that might be expected of a peer, an admiral, and a commissioner, and he left Hornblower grinning at Bush.

"D'you think it's time for us to dine too?" he asked.

"I think so," said Bush.

The eating house in Broad Street was run, as might almost have been expected, by a wooden-legged sailor. He had a pert son to assist him, who stood by when they sat at a scrubbed oaken table on oak benches, their feet in the sawdust, and ordered their dinner.

"Ale?" asked the boy.

"No. No ale," said Hornblower.

The pert boy's manner gave some indication of what he thought about gentlemen of the navy who ate the fourpenny ordinary and drank nothing with it. He dumped the loaded plates in front of them: boiled mutton—not very much mutton—potatoes and carrots and parsnips and barley and a dab of pease pudding, all swimming in pale gravy.

"It keeps away hunger," said Hornblower.

It might indeed do that, but apparently Hornblower had not kept hunger away lately. He began to eat his food with elaborate unconcern, but with each mouthful his appetite increased and his restraint decreased. In an extraordinarily short time his plate was empty; he mopped it clean with his bread and ate the bread. Bush was not a slow eater, but he was taken a little aback when he looked up and saw that Hornblower had finished every mouthful while his own plate was still half full. Hornblower laughed nervously.

"Eating alone gives one bad habits," he said—and the best proof of his embarrassment was the lameness of his explanation.

He was aware of that, as soon as he had spoken, and he tried to carry it off by leaning back on his bench in a superior fashion; and to show how much at ease he was he thrust his hands into the side pockets of his coat. As he did so his whole expression changed. He lost some of the little colour there was in his cheeks. There was utter consternation in his expression—there was even fear. Bush took instant alarm; he thought Hornblower must have had a seizure, and it was only after that first thought that he connected Hornblower's changed appearance with his gesture of putting his hands in his pockets. But a man who had found a snake in his pocket would hardly wear that look of horror.

"What's the matter?" asked Bush. "What in God's name—?"

Hornblower slowly drew his right hand out of his pocket. He kept it closed for a moment round what it held, and then he opened it, slowly, reluctantly, like a man fearful of his destiny. Harmless enough; it was a silver coin—a half-crown.

"That's nothing to take on about," said Bush, quite puzzled. "I wouldn't even mind finding a half-crown in my pocket."

"But—but—" stammered Hornblower, and Bush began to realize some of the implications.

"It wasn't there this morning," said Hornblower, and then he smiled the old bitter smile. "I know too well what money I have in my pockets."

"I suppose you do," agreed Bush; but even now, with his mind going back through the events of the morning, and making the obvious deductions, he could not understand quite why Hornblower should be so worried. "That wench put it there?"

"Yes. Maria." said Hornblower. "It must have been her. That's why she took my coat to sponge it."

"She's a good soul," said Bush.

"Oh God!" said Hornblower. "But I can't—I can't—"

"Why not?" asked Bush, and he really thought that question unanswerable.

"No," said Hornblower. "It's—it's—I wish she hadn't done it. The poor girl—"

" 'Poor girl' be blowed!" said Bush. "She's only trying to do you a good turn."

Hornblower looked at him for a long time without speaking, and then he made a little hopeless gesture, as though despairing of ever making Bush see the matter from his point of view.

"You can look like that if you like," said Bush, steadily, determined to stick to his guns, "but there's no need to act as if the French had landed just because a girl slips half a crown into your pocket."

"But don't you see—" began Hornblower, and then he finally abandoned all attempt at explanation. Under Bush's puzzled gaze he mastered himself. The unhappiness left his face, and he assumed his old inscrutable look—it was as if he had shut down the vizor of a helmet over his face.

"Very well," he said. "We'll make the most of it, by God!"

Then he rapped on the table.

"Boy!"

"Yessir."

"We'll have a pint of wine. Let someone run and fetch it at once. A pint of wine—port wine."

"Yessir."

"And what's the pudding today?"

"Currant duff, sir."

"Good. We'll have some. Both of us. And let's have a saucer of jam to spread on it."

"Yessir."

"And we'll need cheese before our wine. Is there any cheese in the house, or must you send out for some?"

"There's some in the house, sir."

"Then put it on the table."

"Yessir."

Now was it not, thought Bush, exactly what might be expected of Hornblower that he should push away the half of his huge slice of currant duff unfinished? And he only had a nibble of cheese, hardly enough to clear his palate. He raised his glass, and Bush followed his example.

"To a lovely lady," said Hornblower.

They drank, and now there was an irresponsible twinkle in Hornblower's eyes that worried Bush even while he told himself that he was tired of Hornblower's tantrums. He decided to change the subject, and he prided himself on the tactful way in which he did so.

"To a fortunate evening," he said, raising his glass in his turn.

"A timely toast," said Hornblower.

"You can afford to play?" asked Bush.

"Naturally."

"You can stand another run of bad luck?"

"I can afford to lose one rubber," answered Hornblower.

"Oh."

"But on the other hand if I win the first I can afford to lose the next two. And if I win the first and second I can afford to lose the next three. And so on."

"Oh."

That did not sound too hopeful; and Hornblower's gleaming eyes looking at him from his wooden countenance were positively disturbing. Bush shifted uneasily in his seat and changed the conversation again.

"They're putting the *Hastings* into commission again," he said. "Had you heard?"

"Yes. Peacetime establishment—three lieutenants, and all three selected two months back."

"I was afraid that was so."

"But our chance will come," said Hornblower. "Here's to it."

"D'you think Parry will bring Lambert to the Long Rooms?" asked Bush when he took the glass from his lips.

"I have no doubt about it," said Hornblower.

Now he was restless again.

"I must be back there soon," he said. "Parry might hurry Lambert through his dinner."

"My guess is that he would," said Bush, preparing to rise.

"There's no necessity for you to come back with me if you don't care to," said Hornblower. "You might find it wearisome to sit idle there."

"I wouldn't miss it for worlds," said Bush.

XX

The Long Rooms were full with the evening crowd. At nearly every table in the outer room there were earnest parties playing serious games, while through the curtained door that opened into the inner room came a continuous murmur that indicated that play in there was exciting and noisy. But for Bush standing restlessly by the fire, occasionally exchanging absent-minded remarks with the people who came and went, there was only one point of interest, and that was the candle-lit table near the wall where Hornblower was playing in very exalted society. His companions were the two admirals and a colonel of infantry, the latter a bulky man with a face almost as red as his coat, whom Parry had brought with him along with Admiral Lambert. The flag lieutenant who had previously partnered Parry was now relegated to the role of onlooker, and stood beside Bush, and occasionally made incomprehensible remarks about the play. The Marquis had looked in more than once. Bush had observed his glance to rest upon the table

with something of approval. No matter if there were others who wanted
to play; no matter if the rules of the room gave any visitor the right
to join a table at the conclusion of a rubber; a party that included two
flag officers and a field officer could do as it pleased.

Hornblower had won the first rubber to Bush's enormous relief, although actually he had not been able to follow the details of the play
and the score well enough to know that such was the case until the cards
were swept up and payments made. He saw Hornblower tuck away some
money into that breast pocket.

"It would be pleasant," said Admiral Parry, "if we could restore
the old currency, would it not? If the country could dispense with these
dirty notes and go back again to our good old golden guineas?"

"Indeed it would," said the colonel.

"The longshore sharks," said Lambert, "meet every ship that comes
in from abroad. Twenty-three and sixpence they offer for every guinea,
so you can be sure they are worth more than that."

Parry took something from his pocket and laid it on the table.

"Boney has restored the French currency, you see," he said. "They
call this a napoleon, now that he is First Consul for life. A twenty-franc
piece—a louis d'or, as we used to say."

"Napoleon, First Consul," said the colonel, looking at the coin with
curiosity, and then he turned it over. "French Republic."

"The 'republic' is mere hypocrisy, of course," said Parry. "There
never was a worse tyranny since the days of Nero."

"We'll show him up," said Lambert.

"Amen to that," said Parry, and then he put the coin away again.
"But we are delaying the business of the evening. I fear that is my fault.
Let us cut again. Ah, I partner you this time, Colonel. Would you care
to sit opposite me? I omitted to thank you, Mr. Hornblower, for your
excellent partnership."

"You are too kind, my lord," said Hornblower, taking the chair at
the admiral's right.

The next rubber began and progressed silently to its close.

"I am glad to see that the cards have decided to be kind to you, Mr.
Hornblower," said Parry, "even though our honours have reduced your
winnings. Fifteen shillings, I believe?"

"Thank you," said Hornblower, taking the money.

Bush remembered what Hornblower had said about being able to
afford to lose three rubbers if he won the first two.

"Damned small stakes in my opinion, my lord," said the colonel.
"Must we play as low as this?"

"That is for the company to decide," replied Parry. "I myself have
no objection. Half a crown instead of a shilling? Let us ask Mr. Hornblower."

Bush turned to look at Hornblower with renewed anxiety.

"As you will, my lord," said Hornblower, with the most elaborate indifference.

"Sir Richard?"

"I don't mind at all," said Lambert.

"Half a crown a trick, then," said Parry. "Waiter, fresh cards, if you please."

Bush had hurriedly to revise his estimate of the amount of losses Hornblower could endure. With the stakes nearly trebled it would be bad if he lost a single rubber.

"You and I again, Mr. Hornblower," said Parry, observing the cut. "You wish to retain your present seat?"

"I am indifferent, my lord."

"I am not," said Parry. "Nor am I yet so old as to decline to change my seat in accordance with the run of the cards. Our philosophers have not yet decided that it is a mere vulgar superstition."

He heaved himself out of his chair and moved opposite Hornblower, and play began again, with Bush watching more anxiously even than at the start. He watched each side in turn take the odd trick, and then three times running he saw Hornblower lay the majority of tricks in front of him. During the next couple of hands he lost count of the score, but finally he was relieved to see only two tricks before the colonel when the rubber ended.

"Excellent," said Parry, "a profitable rubber, Mr. Hornblower. I'm glad you decided to trump my knave of hearts. It must have been a difficult decision for you, but it was undoubtedly the right one."

"It deprived me of a lead I could well have used," said Lambert. "The opposition was indeed formidable, Colonel."

"Yes," agreed the colonel, not quite as good-temperedly. "And twice I held hands with neither an ace nor a king, which helped the opposition to be formidable. Can you give me change, Mr. Hornblower?"

There was a five pound note among the money that the colonel handed over to Hornblower, and it went into the breast pocket of his coat.

"At least, Colonel," said Parry, when they cut again, "you have Mr. Hornblower as your partner this time."

As the rubber proceeded Bush was aware that the flag-lieutenant beside him was watching with greater and greater interest.

"By the odd trick, by George!" said he when the last cards were played.

"That was a close shave, partner," said the colonel, his good humour clearly restored. "I hoped you held that queen, but I couldn't be sure."

"Fortune was with us, sir," said Hornblower.

The flag lieutenant glanced at Bush; it seemed as if the flag lieutenant was of opinion that the colonel should have been in no doubt, from the previous play, that Hornblower held the queen. Now that Bush's attention was drawn to it, he decided that Hornblower must have thought just the same—the slightest inflection in his voice implied it—but was sensibly not saying so.

"I lose a rubber at five pounds ten and win one at fifteen shillings," said the colonel, receiving his winnings from Lambert. "Who'd like to increase the stakes again?"

To the credit of the two admirals they both glanced at Hornblower without replying.

"As you gentlemen wish," said Hornblower.

"In that case I'm quite agreeable," said Parry.

"Five shillings a trick then," said the colonel. "That makes the game worth playing."

"The game is always worth playing," protested Parry.

"Of course, my lord," said the colonel, but without suggesting that they should revert to the previous stakes.

Now the stakes were really serious; by Bush's calculation a really disastrous rubber might cost Hornblower twenty pounds, and his further calculation told him that Hornblower could hardly have more than twenty pounds tucked away in his breast pocket. It was a relief to him when Hornblower and Lambert won the next rubber easily.

"This is a most enjoyable evening," said Lambert, and he smiled with a glance down at the fistful of the colonel's money he was holding; "nor am I referring to any monetary gains."

"Instructive as well as amusing," said Parry, paying out to Hornblower.

Play proceeded, silently as ever, the silence only broken by the brief interchanges of remarks between rubbers. Now that he could afford it, fortunately, Hornblower lost a rubber, but it was a cheap one, and he immediately won another profitable one. His gains mounted steadily with hardly a setback. It was growing late, and Bush was feeling weary, but the players showed few signs of fatigue, and the flag lieutenant stayed on with the limitless patience he must have acquired during his present appointment, philosophic and fatalistic since he could not possibly do anything to accelerate his admiral's decision to go to bed. The other players drifted away from the room; later still the curtained door opened and the gamblers from the inner room came streaming out, some noisy, some silent, and the Marquis made his appearance, silent and unruffled, to watch the final rubbers with unobtrusive interest, seeing to it that the candles were snuffed and fresh ones brought, and new cards ready on demand. It was Parry who first glanced at the clock.

"Half-past three," he said. "Perhaps you gentlemen—?"

"Too late to go to bed now, my lord," said the colonel. "Sir Richard and I have to be up early, as you know."

"My orders are all given," said Lambert.

"So are mine," said the colonel.

Bush was stupid with long late hours spent in a stuffy atmosphere, but he thought he noticed an admonitory glance from Parry, directed at the two speakers. He wondered idly what orders Lambert and the colonel would have given, and still more idly why they should be orders that Parry did not wish to be mentioned. There seemed to be just the slightest trace of hurry, just the slightest hint of a desire to change the subject, in Parry's manner when he spoke.

"Very well, then, we can play another rubber, if Mr. Hornblower has no objection?"

"None at all, my lord."

Hornblower was imperturbable; if he had noticed anything remarkable about the recent interchange he gave no sign of it. Probably he was weary, though—Bush was led to suspect that by his very imperturbability. Bush knew by now that Hornblower worked as hard to conceal his human weaknesses as some men worked to conceal ignoble birth.

Hornblower had the colonel as partner, and no one could be in the room without being aware that this final rubber was being played in an atmosphere of even fiercer competition than its predecessors. Not a word was spoken between the hands; the score was marked, the tricks swept up, the other pack proffered and cut in deadly silence. Each hand was desperately close, too. In nearly every case it was only a single trick that divided the victors and the vanquished, so that the rubber dragged on and on with painful slowness. Then a hand finished amid a climax of tension. The flag lieutenant and the Marquis had kept count of the score, and when Lambert took the last trick they uttered audible sighs, and the colonel was so moved that he broke the silence at last.

"Neck and neck, by God!" he said. "This next hand must settle it."

But he was properly rebuked by the stony silence with which his remark was received. Parry merely took the cards from the colonel's right side and passed them over to Hornblower to cut. Then Parry dealt, and turned up the king of diamonds as trump, and the colonel led. Trick succeeded trick. For a space, after losing a single trick, Lambert and Parry carried all before them. Six tricks lay before Parry, and only one before Hornblower. The colonel's remark about being neck and neck was fresh in Bush's ears. One more trick out of the next six would give the rubber to the two admirals. Five to one was long odds, and Bush uncomfortably resigned himself to his friend losing this final rubber. Then the colonel took a trick and the game was still alive. Hornblower took the next trick, so that there was still hope. Hornblower led the ace of diamonds, and before it could be played to he laid down his other three cards to claim the rest of the tricks; the queen and knave of diamonds lay conspicuously on the table.

"Rubber!" exclaimed the colonel, "we've won it, partner! I thought all was lost."

Parry was ruefully contemplating his fallen king.

"I agree that you had to lead your ace, Mr. Hornblower," he said, "but I would be enchanted to know why you were so certain that my king was unguarded. There were two other diamonds unaccounted for. Would it be asking too much of you to reveal the secret?"

Hornblower raised his eyebrows in some slight surprise at a question whose answer was so obvious.

"You were marked with the king, my lord," he said, "but it was the rest of your hand which was significant, for you were also marked with holding three clubs. With only four cards in your hand the king could not be guarded."

"A perfect explanation," said Parry; "it only goes to confirm me in my conviction that you are an excellent whist player. Mr. Hornblower."

"Thank you, my lord."

Parry's quizzical smile had a great deal of friendship in it. If Hornblower's previous behaviour had not already won Parry's regard, this last coup certainly had.

"I'll bear your name in mind, Mr. Hornblower," he said. "Sir Richard has already told me the reason why it was familiar to me. It was regrettable that the policy of immediate economy imposed on the Admiralty by the Cabinet should have resulted in your commission as commander not being confirmed."

"I thought I was the only one who regretted it, my lord."

Bush winced again when he heard the words; this was the time for Hornblower to ingratiate himself with those in authority, not to offend them with unconcealed bitterness. This meeting with Parry was a stroke of good fortune that any half-pay naval officer would give two fingers for. Bush was reassured, however, by a glance at the speakers. Hornblower was smiling with infectious lightheartedness, and Parry was smiling back at him. Either the implied bitterness had escaped Parry's notice or it had only existed in Bush's mind.

"I was actually forgetting that I owe you a further thirty-five shillings," said Parry, with a start of recollection. "Forgive me. There, I think that settles my monied indebtedness; I am still in your debt for a valuable experience."

It was a thick wad of money that Hornblower put back in his pocket.

"I trust you will keep a sharp lookout for footpads on your way back, Mr. Hornblower," said Parry with a glance.

"Mr. Bush will be walking home with me, my lord. It would be a valiant footpad that would face him."

"No need to worry about footpads tonight," interposed the colonel. "Not tonight."

The colonel wore a significant grin; the others displayed a momentary disapproval of what apparently was an indiscretion, but the disapproval faded out again when the colonel waved a hand at the clock.

"Our orders go into force at four, my lord," said Lambert.

"And now it is half-past. Excellent."

The flag lieutenant came in at that moment; he had slipped out when the last card was played.

"The carriage is at the door, my lord," he said.

"Thank you. I wish you gentlemen a good evening, then."

They all walked to the door together; there was the carriage in the street, and the two admirals, the colonel, and the flag lieutenant mounted into it. Hornblower and Bush watched it drive away.

"Now what the devil are those orders that come into force at four?" asked Bush. The earliest dawn was showing over the rooftops.

"God knows," said Hornblower.

They headed for the corner of Highbury Street.

"How much did you win?"

"It was over forty pounds—it must be about forty-five pounds," said Hornblower.

"A good night's work."

"Yes. The chances usually right themselves in time." There was something flat and listless in Hornblower's tone as he spoke. He took several more strides before he burst out into speech again with a vigour that was in odd contrast. "I wish to God it had happened last week. Yesterday, even."

"But why?"

"That girl. That poor girl."

"God bless my soul!" said Bush. He had forgotten all about the fact that Maria had slipped half a crown into Hornblower's pocket and he was surprised that Hornblower had not forgotten as well. "Why trouble your head about her?"

"I don't know," said Hornblower, and then he took two more strides. "But I do."

Bush had no time to meditate over this curious avowal, for he heard a sound that made him grasp Hornblower's elbow with sudden excitement.

"Listen!"

Ahead of them, along the silent street, a heavy military tread could be heard. It was approaching. The faint light shone on white crossbelts and brass buttons. It was a military patrol, muskets at the slope, a sergeant marching beside it, his chevrons and his half-pike revealing his rank.

"Now, what the deuce—?" said Bush.

"Halt!" said the sergeant to his men; and then to the other two, "May I ask you two gentlemen who you are?"

"We are naval officers," said Bush.

The lantern the sergeant carried was not really necessary to reveal them. The sergeant came to attention.

"Thank you, sir," he said.

"What are you doing with this patrol, Sergeant?" asked Bush.

"I have my orders, sir," replied the sergeant. "Begging your pardon, sir. By the left, quick—march!"

The patrol strode forward, and the sergeant clapped his hand to his half-pike in salute as he passed on.

"What in the name of all that's holy?" wondered Bush. "Boney can't have made a surprise landing. Every bell would be ringing if that were so. You'd think the press gang was out, a real hot press. But it can't be."

"Look there!" said Hornblower.

Another party of men was marching along the street, but not in red coats, not with the military stiffness of the soldiers. Checked shirts and blue trousers; a midshipman marching at the head, white patches on his collar and his dirk at his side.

"The press gang for certain!" exclaimed Bush. "Look at the bludgeons!"

Every seaman carried a club in his hand.

"Midshipman!" said Hornblower, sharply. "What's all this?"

The midshipman halted at the tone of command and the sight of the uniforms.

"Orders, sir," he began, and then, realizing that with the growing daylight he need no longer preserve secrecy, especially to naval men, he went on. "Press gang, sir. We've orders to press every seaman we find. The patrols are out on every road."

"So I believe. But what's the press for?"

"Dunno, sir. Orders, sir."

That was sufficient answer, maybe.

"Very good. Carry on."

"The press, by jingo!" said Bush. "Something's happening."

"I expect you're right," said Hornblower.

They had turned into Highbury Street now, and were making their way along to Mrs. Mason's house.

"There's the first results," said Hornblower.

They stood on the doorstep to watch them go by, a hundred men at least, escorted along by a score of seamen with staves, a midshipman in command. Some of the pressed men were bewildered and silent; some were talking volubly—the noise they were making was rousing the street. Every man among them had at least one hand in a trouser pocket; those who were not gesticulating had both hands in their pockets.

"It's like old times," said Bush with a grin. "They've cut their waistbands."

With their waistbands cut it was necessary for them to keep a hand in a trouser pocket, as otherwise their trousers would fall down. No one could run away when handicapped in this fashion.

"A likely looking lot of prime seamen," said Bush, running a professional eye over them.

"Hard luck on them, all the same," said Hornblower.

"Hard luck?" said Bush in surprise.

Was the ox unlucky when it was turned into beef? Or for that matter was the guinea unlucky when it changed hands? This was life; for a merchant seaman to find himself a sailor of the King was as natural a thing as for his hair to turn grey if he should live so long. And the only way to secure him was to surprise him in the night, rouse him out of bed, snatch him from the grog shop and the brothel, converting him in a single second from a free man earning his livelihood in his own way into a pressed man who could not take a step on shore of his own free will without risking being flogged round the fleet. Bush could no more sympathize with the pressed man than he could sympathize with the night being replaced by day.

Hornblower was still looking at the press gang and the recruits.

"It may be war," he said, slowly.

"War!" said Bush.

"We'll know when the mail comes in," said Hornblower. "Parry could have told us last night, I fancy."

"But—war!" said Bush.

The crowd went on down the street towards the dockyard, its noise dwindling with the increasing distance, and Hornblower turned towards the street door, taking the ponderous key out of his pocket. When they entered the house they saw Maria standing at the foot of the staircase, a candlestick with an unlighted candle in her hand. She wore a long coat over her nightclothes; she had put on her mob-cap hastily, for a couple of curling papers showed under its edge.

"You're safe!" she said.

"Of course we're safe, Maria," said Hornblower. "What do you think could happen to us?"

"There was all that noise in the street," said Maria. "I looked out. Was it the press gang?"

"That's just what it was," said Bush.

"Is it—is it war?"

"That's what it may be."

"Oh!" Maria's face revealed her distress. "Oh!"

Her eyes searched their faces.

"No need to worry, Miss Maria," said Bush. "It'll be many a long year before Boney brings his flat-bottoms up Spithead."

"It's not that," said Maria. Now she was looking only at Hornblower. In a flash she had forgotten Bush's existence.

"You'll be going away!" she said.

"I shall have my duty to do if I am called upon, Maria," said Hornblower.

Now a grim figure appeared climbing the stairs from the basement —Mrs. Mason; she had no mob-cap on so that her curl papers were all visible.

"You'll disturb my other gentlemen with all this noise," she said.

"Mother, they think it's going to be war," said Maria.

"And not a bad thing perhaps if it means some people will pay what they owe."

"I'll do that this minute," said Hornblower hotly. "What's my reckoning, Mrs. Mason?"

"Oh, please, please—" said Maria interposing.

"You just shut your mouth, Miss," snapped Mrs. Mason. "It's only because of you that I've let this young spark run on."

"Mother!"

" 'I'll pay my reckoning,' he says, like a lord. And not a shirt in his chest. His chest'd be at the pawnbroker's too if I hadn't nobbled it."

"I said I'd pay my reckoning and I mean it, Mrs. Mason," said Hornblower with enormous dignity.

"Let's see the colour of your money, then," stipulated Mrs. Mason, not in the least convinced. "Twenty-seven and six."

Hornblower brought a fistful of silver out of his trouser pocket. But there was not enough there, and he had to extract a note from his breast pocket, revealing as he did so that there were many more.

"So!" said Mrs. Mason. She looked down at the money in her hand as if it were fairy gold, and opposing emotions waged war in her expression.

"I think I might give you a week's warning, too," said Hornblower, harshly.

"Oh no!" said Maria.

"That's a nice room you have upstairs," said Mrs. Mason. "You wouldn't be leaving me just on account of a few words."

"Don't leave us, Mr. Hornblower," said Maria.

If ever there was a man completely at a loss it was Hornblower. After a glance at him Bush found it hard not to grin. The man who could keep a cool head when playing for high stakes with admirals—the man who fired the broadside that shook the *Renown* off the mud when under the fire of red-hot shot—was helpless when confronted by a couple of women. It would be a picturesque gesture to pay his reckoning—if necessary to pay an extra week's rent in lieu of warning—and to shake the dust of the place from his feet. But on the other hand he had been allowed credit here, and it would be a poor return for that consideration to leave the moment he could pay. But to stay on in a house that knew his secrets was an irksome prospect too. The dignified Hornblower who was ashamed of ever appearing human would hardly feel at home among people who knew that he had been human enough to be in debt. Bush was aware of all these problems as they confronted Hornblower, of the kindly feelings and the embittered ones. And Bush could be fond of him even while he laughed at him, and could respect him even while he knew of his weaknesses.

"When did you gennelmen have supper?" asked Mrs. Mason.

"I don't think we did," answered Hornblower, with a side glance at Bush.

"You must be hungry, then, if you was up all night. Let me cook you a nice breakfast. A couple of thick chops for each of you. Now how about that?"

"By George!" said Hornblower.

"You go on up," said Mrs. Mason. "I'll send the girl up with hot water an' you can shave. Then when you come down there'll be a nice breakfast ready for you. Maria, run and make the fire up."

Up in the attic Hornblower looked whimsically at Bush.

"That bed you paid a shilling for is still virgin," he said. "You haven't had a wink of sleep all night and it's my fault. Please forgive me."

"It's not the first night I haven't slept," said Bush. He had not slept on the night they stormed Samaná; many were the occasions in foul weather when he had kept the deck for twenty-four hours continuously. And after a month of living with his sisters in the Chichester cottage, of nothing to do except to weed the garden, of trying to sleep for twelve hours a night for that very reason, the variety of excitement he had gone through had been actually pleasant. He sat down on the bed while Hornblower paced the floor.

"You'll have plenty more if it's war," Hornblower said; and Bush shrugged his shoulders.

A thump on the door announced the arrival of the maid of all work of the house, a can of hot water in each hand. Her ragged dress was too large for her—handed down presumably from Mrs. Mason or from Maria—and her hair was tousled, but she, too, turned wide eyes on Hornblower as she brought in the hot water. Those wide eyes were too big for her skinny face, and they followed Hornblower as he moved about the room, and never had a glance for Bush. It was plain that Hornblower was as much the hero of this fourteen-year-old foundling as he was of Maria.

"Thank you, Susie," said Hornblower; and Susie dropped an angular curtsey before she scuttled from the room with one last glance round the door as she left.

Hornblower waved a hand at the wash-hand stand and the hot water.

"You first," said Bush.

Hornblower peeled off his coat and his shirt and addressed himself to the business of shaving. The razor blade rasped on his bristly cheeks; he turned his face this way and that so as to apply the edge. Neither of them felt any need for conversation, and it was practically in silence that Hornblower washed himself, poured the wash water into the slop pail, and stood aside for Bush to shave himself.

"Make the most of it," said Hornblower. "A pint of fresh water twice a week for shaving'll be all you'll get if you have your wish."

"Who cares?" said Bush.

He shaved, restropped his razor with care, and put it back into his roll of toilet articles. The scars that seamed his ribs gleamed pale as he moved. When he had finished dressing he glanced at Hornblower.

"Chops," said Hornblower. "Thick chops. Come on."

There were several places laid at the table in the dining-room opening out of the hall, but nobody else was present; apparently it was not the breakfast hour of Mrs. Mason's other gentlemen.

"Only a minute, sir," said Susie, showing up in the doorway for a moment before hurrying down into the kitchen.

She came staggering back laden with a tray; Hornblower pushed back his chair and was about to help her, but she checked him with a scandalized squeak and managed to put the tray safely on the side table without accident.

"I can serve you, sir," she said.

She scuttled back and forward between the two tables like the boys running with the nippers when the cable was being hove in. Coffee-pot and toast, butter and jam, sugar and milk, cruet and hot plates and finally a wide dish which she laid before Hornblower; she took off the cover and there was a noble dish of chops whose delightful scent, hitherto pent up, filled the room.

"Ah!" said Hornblower, taking up a spoon and fork to serve. "Have you had your breakfast, Susie?"

"Me, sir? No, sir. Not yet sir."

Hornblower paused, spoon and fork in hand, looking from the chops to Susie and back again. Then he put down the spoon and thrust his right hand into his trouser pocket.

"There's no way in which you can have one of these chops?" he said.

"Me, sir? Of course not, sir."

"Now here's half a crown."

"Half a crown, sir!"

That was more than a day's wages for a labourer.

"I want a promise from you, Susie."

"Sir—sir—!"

Susie's hands were behind her.

"Take this, and promise me that the first chance that comes your way, the moment Mrs. Mason lets you out, you'll buy yourself something to eat. Fill that wretched little belly of yours. Faggots and pease pudding, pig's trotters, all the things you like. Promise me."

"But sir—"

Half a crown, the prospect of unlimited food, were things that could not be real.

"Oh, take it," said Hornblower testily.

"Yes, sir."

Susie clasped the coin in her skinny hand.

"Don't forget I have your promise."

"Yes, sir, please sir, thank you, sir."

"Now put it away and clear out quick."

"Yes, sir."

She fled out of the room and Hornblower began once more to serve the chops.

"I'll be able to enjoy my breakfast now," said Hornblower self-consciously.

"No doubt," said Bush; he buttered himself a piece of toast, dabbed mustard on his plate—to eat mustard with mutton marked him as a sailor, but he did it without a thought. With good food in front of him there was no need for thought, and he ate in silence. It was only when Hornblower spoke again that Bush realized that Hornblower had been construing the silence as accusatory of something.

"Half a crown," said Hornblower, defensively, "may mean many things to many people. Yesterday—"

"You're quite right," said Bush, filling in the gap as politeness dictated, and then he looked up and realized that it was not because he had no more to say that Hornblower had left the sentence uncompleted.

Maria was standing framed in the dining-room door; her bonnet, gloves, and shawl indicated that she was about to go out, presumably to early marketing since the school where she taught was temporarily closed.

"I—I looked in to see that you had everything you wanted," she said. The hesitation in her speech seemed to indicate that she had heard Hornblower's last words, but it was not certain.

"Thank you. Delightful," mumbled Hornblower.

"Please don't get up," said Maria, hastily and with a hint of hostility, as Hornblower and Bush began to rise. Her eyes were .wet.

A knocking on the street door relieved the tension, and Maria fled to answer it. From the dining-room they heard a masculine voice, and Maria reappeared, a corporal of marines towering behind her dumpy form.

"Lieutenant Hornblower?" he asked.

"That's me."

"From the admiral, sir."

The corporal held out a letter and a folded newspaper. There was a maddening delay while a pencil was found for Hornblower to sign the receipt. Then the corporal took his leave with a clicking of heels and Hornblower stood with the letter in one hand and the newspaper in the other.

"Oh, open it—please open it," said Maria.

Hornblower tore the wafer and unfolded the sheet. He read the note, and then reread it, nodding his head as if the note confirmed some preconceived theory.

"You see that sometimes it is profitable to play whist," he said, "in more ways than one."

He handed the note over to Bush; his smile was a little lopsided.

SIR [read Bush]

It is with pleasure that I take this opportunity of informing you in advance of any official notification that your promotion to Commander is now confirmed and that you will be shortly appointed to the Command of a Sloop of War.

"By God, sir!" said Bush. "Congratulations. For the second time, sir. It's only what you deserve, as I said before."

"Thank you," said Hornblower. "Finish it."

The arrival at this moment of the Mail Coach with the London newspapers [said the second paragraph] enables me to send you the information regarding the changed situation without being unnecessarily prolix in this letter. You will gather from what you read in the accompanying copy of the *Sun* the reasons why conditions of military secrecy should prevail during our very pleasant evening so that I need not apologize for not having enlightened you, while I remain,

Your obedient servant,

PARRY

By the time Bush had finished the letter Hornblower had opened the newspaper at the relevant passage, which he pointed out to Bush.

Message from HIS MAJESTY

House of Commons, March 8, 1803

The CHANCELLOR OF THE EXCHEQUER brought down the following message from HIS MAJESTY:

"His Majesty thinks it necessary to acquaint the House of Commons, that, as very considerable military preparations are carrying on in the ports of France and Holland, he has judged it expedient to adopt additional measures of precaution for the security of his dominions.

GEORGE R."

That was all Bush needed to read. Boney's fleet of flat-bottomed boats, and his army of invasion mustered along the Channel coast, were being met by the appropriate and necessary countermove. Last night's press-gang measures, planned and carried out with a secrecy for which Bush could feel nothing except wholehearted approval (he had led too many press gangs not to know how completely seamen made themselves scarce at the first hint of a press) would provide the crews for the ships necessary to secure England's safety. There were ships in plenty, laid up in every harbour in England; and officers—Bush knew very well how many officers were available. With the fleet manned and at sea England could laugh at the treacherous attack Boney had planned.

"They've done the right thing for once, by God!" said Bush, slapping the newspaper.

"But what is it?" asked Maria.

She had been standing silent, watching the two men, her glance shifting from one to the other in an endeavour to read their expressions. Bush remembered that she had winced at his outburst of congratulation.

"It'll be war next week," said Hornblower. "Boney won't endure a bold answer."

"Oh," said Maria. "But you—what about you?"

"I'm made commander," said Hornblower. "I'm going to be appointed to a sloop of war."

"Oh," said Maria again.

There was a second or two of agonized effort at self-control, and then she broke down. Her head drooped farther and farther, until she put her gloved hands to her face, turning away from the two men so that they only saw her shoulders with the shawl across them, shaking with sobs.

"Maria," said Hornblower gently. "Please, Maria, please don't."

Maria turned and presented a slobbered face to him, unevenly framed in the bonnet which had been pushed askew.

"I'll n-n-never see you again," sobbed Maria. "I've been so happy with the m-m-mumps at school, I thought I'd m-m-make your bed and do your room. And n-now this happens!"

"But, Maria," said Hornblower—his hands flapped helplessly—"I've my duty to do."

"I wish I was d-dead! Indeed I wish I was dead!" said Maria, and the tears poured down her cheeks to drip upon her shawl; they streamed from eyes which had a fixed look of despair, while the wide mouth was shapeless.

This was something Bush could not endure. He liked pretty, saucy women. What he was looking at now jarred on him unbearably—perhaps it rasped his aesthetic sensibility, unlikely though it might seem that Bush should have such a thing. Perhaps he was merely irritated by the spectacle of uncontrolled hysteria, but if that was the case he was irritated beyond all bearing. He felt that if he had to put up with Maria's water-works for another minute he would break a blood vessel.

"Let's get out of here," he said to Hornblower.

In reply he received a look of surprise. It had not occurred to Hornblower that he might run away from a situation for which his temperament necessarily made him feel responsible. Bush knew perfectly well that, given time, Maria would recover. He knew that women who wished themselves dead one day could be as lively as crickets the next day after another man had chucked them under the chin. In any case he did not see why he and Hornblower should concern themselves about something which was entirely Maria's fault.

"Oh!" said Maria; she stumbled forward and supported herself with her hands upon the table with its cooling coffee-pot and its congealing half-consumed chops. She lifted her head and wailed again.

"Oh, for God's sake—" said Bush in disgust. He turned to Hornblower. "Come along."

By the time Bush was on the staircase he realized that Hornblower had not followed him, would not follow him. And Bush did not go back to fetch him. Even though Bush was not the man to desert a comrade in peril; even though he would gladly take his place in a boat launching out through the most dreadful surf to rescue men in danger; even though he would stand shoulder to shoulder with Hornblower and be hewn to pieces with him by an overwhelming enemy; for all this he would not go back to save Hornblower. If Hornblower was going to be foolish Bush felt he could not stop him. And he salved his conscience by telling himself that perhaps Hornblower would not be foolish.

Up in the attic Bush set about rolling up his nightshirt with his toilet things. The methodical checking over of his razor and comb and brushes, seeing that nothing was left behind, soothed his irritated nerves. The prospect of immediate employment and immediate action revealed itself to him in all its delightful certainty, breaking through the evaporating clouds of his irritation. He began to hum to himself tunelessly. It would be sensible to call in again at the dockyard—he might even look in at the Keppel's Head to discuss the morning's amazing news; both courses would be advisable if he wanted to secure for himself quickly a new appointment. Hat in hand he tucked his neat package under his arm and cast a final glance round the room to make sure that he had left nothing, and he was still humming as he closed the attic door behind him. On the staircase, about to step down into the hall, he stood for a moment with one foot suspended, not in doubt as to whether he should go into the dining-room, but arranging in his mind what he should say when he went in.

Maria had dried her tears. She was standing there smiling, although her bonnet was still askew. Hornblower was smiling too; it might be with relief that Maria had left off weeping. He looked round at Bush's entrance, and his face revealed surprise at the sight of Bush's hat and bundle.

"I'm getting under way," said Bush. "I have to thank you for your hospitality, sir."

"But—" said Hornblower, "you don't have to go just yet."

There was that "sir" again in Bush's speech. They had been through so much together, and they knew so much about each other. Now war was coming again, and Hornblower was Bush's superior officer. Bush explained what he wanted to do before taking the carrier's cart back to Chichester, and Hornblower nodded.

"Pack your chest," he said. "It won't be long before you need it."

Bush cleared his throat in preparation for the formal words he was going to use.

"I didn't express my congratulations properly," he said portentously. "I wanted to say that I don't believe the Admiralty could have made a better choice out of the whole list of lieutenants when they selected you for promotion, sir."

"You're too kind," said Hornblower.

"I'm sure Mr. Bush is quite right," said Maria.

She gazed up at Hornblower with adoration shining in her face, and he looked down at her with infinite kindness. And already there was something a little proprietorial about the adoration, and perhaps there was something wistful about the kindness.

Hornblower and the 'Hotspur'

I

'Repeat after me,' said the parson. ' "I, Horatio, take thee, Maria Ellen—" '

The thought came up in Hornblower's mind that these were the last few seconds in which he could withdraw from doing something which he knew to be ill-considered. Maria was not the right woman to be his wife, even admitting that he was suitable material for marriage in any case. If he had a grain of sense, he would break off this ceremony even at this last moment, he would announce that he had changed his mind, and he would turn away from the altar and from the parson and from Maria, and he would leave the church a free man.

'To have and to hold—' he was still, like an automaton, repeating the parson's words. And there was Maria beside him, in the white that so little became her. She was melting with happiness. She was consumed with love for him, however misplaced it might be. He could not, he simply could not, deal her a blow so cruel. He was conscious of the trembling of her body beside him. That was not fear, for she had utter and complete trust in him. He could no more bring himself to shatter that trust than he could have refused to command the *Hotspur*.

'And thereto I plight thee my troth,' repeated Hornblower. That settled it, he thought. Those must be the final deciding words that made the ceremony legally binding. He had made a promise and now there was no going back on it. There was a comfort in the odd thought that he had really been committed from a week back, when Maria had come into his arms sobbing out her love for him, and he had been too soft-hearted to laugh at her and too – too weak? too honest? – to take advantage of her with the intention of betraying her. From the moment that he had listened to her, from the moment that he had returned her kisses, gently, all these later results, the bridal dress, this ceremony in the church of St Thomas à Becket – and the vague future of cloying affection – had been inevitable.

Bush was ready with the ring, and Hornblower slipped it over Maria's finger, and the final words were said.

'I now pronounce that they are man and wife,' said the parson, and he went on with the blessing, and then a blank five seconds followed, until Maria broke the silence.

'Oh, Horry,' she said, and she laid her hand on his arm.

Hornblower forced himself to smile down at her, concealing the newly discovered fact that he disliked being called 'Horry' even more than he disliked being called Horatio.

'The happiest day of my life,' he said; if a thing had to be done it might as well be done thoroughly, so that in the same spirit he continued. 'In my life so far.'

It was actually painful to note the unbounded happiness of the smile that answered this gallant speech. Maria put her other hand up to him, and he realised she expected to be kissed, then and there, in front of the altar. It hardly seemed a proper thing to do, in a sacred edifice – in his ignorance he feared lest he should affront the devout – but once more there was no drawing back, and he stooped and kissed the soft lips that she proffered.

'Your signatures are required in the register,' prompted the parson, and led the way to the vestry.

They wrote their names.

'Now I can kiss my son-in-law,' announced Mrs Mason loudly, and Hornblower found himself clasped by two powerful arms and soundly kissed on the cheek. He supposed it was inevitable that a man should feel a distaste for his mother-in-law.

But here was Bush to disengage him, with outstretched hand and unusual smile, offering felicitations and best wishes.

'Many thanks,' said Hornblower, and added, 'Many thanks for many services.'

Bush was positively embarrassed, and tried to brush away Hornblower's gratitude with the same gestures as he would have used to brush away flies. He had been a tower of strength in this wedding, just as he had been in the preparation of the *Hotspur* for sea.

'I'll see you again at the breakfast, sir,' he said, and with that he withdrew from the vestry, leaving behind him an awkward gap.

'I was counting on Mr Bush's arm for support down the aisle,' said Mrs Mason, sharply.

It certainly was not like Bush to leave everyone in the lurch like this; it was in marked contrast with his behaviour during the last few whirlwind days.

'We can bear each other company, Mrs Mason,' said the parson's wife. 'Mr Clive can follow us.'

'You are very kind, Mrs Clive,' said Mrs Mason, although there was nothing in her tone to indicate that she meant what she said. 'Then the happy pair can start now. Maria, take the captain's arm.'

Mrs Mason marshalled the tiny procession in businesslike fashion.

Hornblower felt Maria's hand slipped under his arm, felt the light pressure she could not help giving to it, and – he could not be cruel enough to ignore it – he pressed her hand in return, between his ribs and his elbow, to be rewarded by another smile. A small shove from behind by Mrs Mason started him back in the church, to be greeted by a roar from the organ. Half a crown for the organist and a shilling for the blower was what that music had cost Mrs Mason; there might be better uses for the money. The thought occupied Hornblower's mind for several seconds, and was naturally succeeded by the inevitable wonderment as to how anyone could possibly find enjoyment in these distasteful noises. He and Maria were well down the aisle before he came back to reality.

'The sailors are all gone,' said Maria with a break in her voice. 'There's almost no one in the church.'

Truth to tell, there were only two or three people in the pews, and these obviously the most casual idlers. All the few guests had trooped into the vestry for the signing, and the fifty seamen whom Bush had brought from *Hotspur* – all those who could be trusted not to desert – had vanished already. Hornblower felt a vague disappointment that Bush had failed again to rise to the situation.

'Why should we care?' he asked, groping wildly for words of comfort for Maria. 'Why should any shadow fall on our wedding day?'

It was strangely painful to see and to feel Maria's instant response, and her faltering step changed to a brave stride as they marched down the empty church. There was bright sunshine awaiting them at the west door, he could see; and he thought of something else a tender bridegroom might say.

'Happy is the bride the sun shines on.'

They came out of the dim light into the bright sun, and the transition was moral as well as physical, for Bush had not disappointed them; he had not been found wanting after all. Hornblower heard a sharp word and a ragged clash of steel, and there were the fifty seamen in a double rank stretching away from the door, making an arch of their drawn cutlasses for the couple to walk beneath.

'Oh, how nice!' said Maria, in childish delight; furthermore the array of seamen at the church door had attracted a crowd of spectators, all craning forward to see the captain and his bride. Hornblower darted a professional glance first down one line of seamen and then down the other. They were all dressed in the new blue and white checked shirts with which he had stocked the slop chest of the *Hotspur*; their white duck trousers were mostly well worn but well washed, and long enough and baggy enough to conceal the probable deficiencies of their shoes. It was a good turnout.

Beyond the avenue of cutlasses stood a horseless post-chaise, with
Bush standing behind it. Wondering a little, Hornblower led Maria
towards it; Bush gallantly handed Maria up into the front seat and
Hornblower climbed up beside her, finding time now to take his
cocked hat from under his arm and clap it on his head. He had heard
the cutlasses rasp back into their sheaths; now the guard of honour
came pattering forward in a disciplined rush. There were pipe-
clayed drag ropes where the traces should have been, and the fifty
men seized their coils, twenty-five to a coil, and ran them out. Bush
craned up towards Hornblower.

'Let the brake off, if you please, sir. That handle there, sir.'

Hornblower obeyed, and Bush turned away and let loose a subdued
bellow. The seamen took the strain in half a dozen quickening steps
and then broke into a trot, the post-chaise rattling over the cobbles,
while the crowd waved their hats and cheered.

'I never thought I could be so happy – Horry – darling,' said Maria.
The men at the drag ropes, with the usual exuberance of the seaman on land, swung round the corner into the High Street and headed
at the double towards the George, and with the turn Maria was flung
against him and clasped him in delicious fear. As they drew up it
was obvious that there was a danger of the chaise rolling forward into
the seamen, and Hornblower had to think fast and reach for the
brake lever, hurriedly casting himself free from Maria's arm. Then
he sat for a moment, wondering what to do next. On this occasion
there should be a group to welcome them, the host of the inn and
his wife, the boots, the ostler, the drawer, and the maids, but as it
was there was no one. He had to leap down from the chaise un-
assisted and single handed help Maria down.

'Thank you, men,' he said to the parting seamen, who acknowledged his thanks with a knuckling of foreheads and halting words.

Bush was in sight now round the corner, hurrying towards them;
Hornblower could safely leave Bush in charge while he led Maria into
the inn with a sad lack of ceremony.

But here was the host at last, bustling up with a napkin over his
arm and his wife at his heels.

'Welcome, sir, welcome, madam. This way, sir, madam.' He flung
open the door into the coffee-room to reveal the wedding breakfast
laid on a snowy cloth. 'The Admiral arrived only five minutes ago,
sir, so you must excuse us, sir.'

'Which Admiral?'

'The Honourable Admiral Sir William Cornwallis, sir, commanding the Channel Fleet. 'Is coachman says war's certain, sir.'

Hornblower had been convinced of this ever since, nine days ago,
he had read the King's message to Parliament, and witnessed the

activities of the press gangs, and had been notified of his appointment to the command of the *Hotspur* – and (he remembered) had found himself betrothed to Maria. Bonaparte's unscrupulous behaviour on the Continent meant—

'A glass of wine, madam? A glass of wine, sir?'

Hornblower was conscious of Maria's enquiring glance when the innkeeper asked this question. She would not venture to answer until she had ascertained what her new husband thought.

'We'll wait for the rest of the company,' said Hornblower. 'Ah—'

A heavy step on the threshold announced Bush's arrival.

'They'll all be here in two minutes,' said Bush.

'Very good of you to arrange about the carriage and the seamen, Mr Bush,' said Hornblower, and he thought that moment of something else that a kind and thoughtful husband would say. He slipped his hand under Maria's arm and added – 'Mrs Hornblower says you made her very happy.'

A delighted giggle from Maria told him that he had given pleasure by this unexpected use of her new name, as he expected.

'Mrs Hornblower, I give you joy,' said Bush, solemnly, and then to Hornblower, 'By your leave, sir, I'll return to the ship.'

'Now, Mr Bush?' asked Maria.

'I fear I must, ma'am,' replied Bush, turning back at once to Hornblower. 'I'll take the hands back with me, sir. There's always the chance that the lighters with the stores may come off.'

'I'm afraid you're right, Mr Bush,' said Hornblower. 'Keep me informed, if you please.'

'Aye aye, sir,' said Bush, and with that he was gone.

Here came the others, pouring in, and any trace of awkwardness about the party disappeared as Mrs Mason marshalled the guests and set the wedding breakfast into its stride. Corks popped and preliminary toasts were drunk. There was the cake to be cut, and Mrs Mason insisted that Maria should make the first cut with Hornblower's sword; Mrs Mason was sure that in this Maria would be following the example of naval brides in good society in London. Hornblower was not so sure; he had lived for ten years under a strict convention that cold steel should never be drawn under a roof or a deck. But his timid objections were swept away, and Maria, the sword in both hands, cut the cake amid general applause. Hornblower could hardly restrain his impatience to take the thing back from her, and he quickly wiped the sugar icing from the blade, wondering grimly what the assembled company would think if they knew he had once wiped human blood from it. He was still engaged on this work when he became aware of the innkeeper whispering hoarsely at his side.

'Begging your pardon, sir. Begging your pardon.'

'Well?'

'The Admiral's compliments, sir, and he would be glad to see you when you find it convenient.'

Hornblower stood sword in hand, staring at him in momentary uncomprehension.

'The Admiral, sir. 'E's in the first floor front, what we always calls the Admiral's Room.'

'You mean Sir William, of course?'

'Yes, sir.'

'Very well. My respects to the Admiral and – No, I'll go up at once. Thank you.'

'Thank'ee, sir. Begging your pardon again.'

Hornblower shot his sword back into its sheath and looked round at the company. They were watching the maid bustling round handing slices of wedding cake and had no eyes for him at present. He settled his sword at his side, twitched at his neck-cloth, and unobtrusively left the room, picking up his hat as he did so.

When he knocked at the door of the first floor front a deep voice that he well remembered said, 'Come in.' It was so large a room that the four-poster bed at the far end was inconspicuous; so was the secretary seated at the desk by the window. Cornwallis was standing in the middle, apparently engaged in dictation until this interruption.

'Ah, it's Hornblower. Good morning.'

'Good morning, sir.'

'The last time we met was over that unfortunate business with the Irish rebel. We had to hang him, I remember.'

'Yes, sir.'

Cornwallis, 'Billy Blue,' had not changed perceptibly during those four years. He was still the bulky man with the composed manner, obviously ready to deal with any emergency.

'Please sit down. A glass of wine?'

'No, thank you, sir.'

'I expected that, seeing the ceremony you've just come from. My apologies for interrupting your wedding, but you must blame Boney, not me.'

'Of course, sir.' Hornblower felt that a more eloquent speech would have been in place here, but he could not think of one.

'I'll detain you for as short a time as possible. You know I've been appointed to the command of the Channel Fleet?'

'Yes, sir.'

'You know that *Hotspur* is under my command?'

'I expected that, but I didn't know, sir.'

'The Admiralty letter to that effect came down in my coach. You'll find it awaiting you on board.'

'Yes, sir.'

'Is *Hotspur* ready to sail?'

'No, sir.' The truth and no excuses. Nothing else would do.

'How long?'

'Two days, sir. More if there's delay with the ordnance stores.'

Cornwallis was looking at him very sharply indeed, but Hornblower returned glance for glance. He had nothing with which to reproach himself; nine days ago *Hotspur* was still laid up in ordinary.

'She's been docked and breamed?'

'Yes, sir.'

'She's manned?'

'Yes, sir. A good crew – the cream of the press.'

'Rigging set up?'

'Yes, sir.'

'Yards crossed?'

'Yes, sir.'

'Officers appointed?'

'Yes, sir. A lieutenant and four master's mates.'

'You'll need three months' provisions and water.'

'I can stow a hundred and eleven days at full rations, sir. The cooperage is delivering the water-butts at noon. I'll have it all stowed by nightfall, sir.'

'Have you warped her out?'

'Yes, sir. She's at anchor now in Spithead.'

'You've done well,' said Cornwallis.

Hornblower tried not to betray his relief at that speech; from Cornwallis that was more than approval – it was hearty praise.

'Thank you, sir.'

'So what do you need now?'

'Bos'n's stores, sir. Cordage, canvas, spare spars.'

'Not easy to get the dockyard to part with those at this moment. I'll have a word with them. And then the ordnance stores, you say?'

'Yes, sir. Ordnance are waiting for a shipment of nine-pounder shot. None to be had here at the moment.'

Ten minutes ago Hornblower had been thinking of words to please Maria. Now he was selecting words for an honest report to Cornwallis.

'I'll deal with that, too,' said Cornwallis. 'You can be certain of sailing the day after tomorrow if the wind serves.'

'Yes, sir.'

'Now for your orders. You'll get them in writing in the course of the day, but I'd better tell you now, while you can ask questions. War's coming. It hasn't been declared yet, but Boney may anticipate us.'

'Yes, sir.'

'I'm going to blockade Brest as soon as I can get the fleet to sea, and you're to go ahead of us.'

'Yes, sir.'

'You're not to do anything to precipitate war. You're not to provide Boney with an excuse.'

'No, sir.'

'When war's declared you can of course take the appropriate action. Until then you have merely to observe. Keep your eye on Brest. Look in as far as you can without provoking fire. Count the ships of war – the number and rate of ships with their yards crossed, ships still in ordinary, ships in the roads, ships preparing for sea.'

'Yes, sir.'

'Boney sent the best of his ships and crews to the West Indies last year. He'll have more trouble manning his fleet even than we have. I'll want your report as soon as I arrive on the station. What's the *Hotspur's* draught?'

'She'll draw thirteen feet aft when she's complete with stores, sir.'

'You'll be able to use the Goulet pretty freely, then. I don't have to tell you not to run her aground.'

'No, sir.'

'But remember this. You'll find it hard to perform your duty unless you risk your ship. There's folly and there's foolhardiness on one side, and there's daring and calculation on the other. Make the right choice and I'll see you through any trouble that may ensue.'

Cornwallis's wide blue eyes looked straight into Hornblower's brown ones. Hornblower was deeply interested in what Cornwallis had just said, and equally interested in what he had left unsaid. Cornwallis had made a promise of sympathetic support, but he had refrained from uttering the threat which was the obvious corollary. This was no rhetorical device, no facile trick of leadership – it was a simple expression of Cornwallis's natural state of mind. He was a man who preferred to lead rather than to drive; most interesting.

Hornblower realised with a start that for several seconds he had been staring his commander-in-chief out of countenance while following up this train of thought; it was not the most tactful behaviour, perhaps.

'I understand, sir,' he said, and Cornwallis rose from his chair.

'We'll meet again at sea. Remember to do nothing to provoke war before war is declared,' he said, with a smile – and the smile revealed the man of action. Hornblower could read him as someone to whom the prospect of action was stimulating and desirable, and who would never seek reasons or excuses for postponing decisions.

Cornwallis suddenly withheld his proffered hand.

'By Jove!' he exclaimed. 'I was forgetting. This is your wedding day.'

'Yes, sir.'

'You were only married this morning?'

'An hour ago, sir.'

'And I've taken you away from your wedding breakfast.'

'Yes, sir.' It would be cheap rhetoric to add anything trite like 'For King and Country,' or even 'Duty comes first.'

'Your good lady will hardly be pleased.'

Nor would his mother-in-law, more especially, thought Hornblower, but again it would not be tactful to say so.

'I'll try to make amends, sir,' he contented himself with saying.

'It's I who should make amends,' replied Cornwallis. 'Perhaps I could join the festivities and drink the bride's health?'

'That would be most kind of you, sir,' said Hornblower.

If anything could reconcile Mrs Mason to his breach of manners, it would be the presence of Admiral the Hon. Sir William Cornwallis, K.B., at the breakfast table.

'I'll come, then, if you're certain I shan't be unwelcome. Hachett, find my sword. Where's my hat?'

So that when Hornblower appeared again through the door of the coffee-room Mrs Mason's instant and bitter reproaches died away on her lips, the moment she saw that Hornblower was ushering in an important guest. She saw the glittering epaulettes, and the red ribbon and the star which Cornwallis had most tactfully put on in honour of the occasion. Hornblower made the introductions.

'Long life and much happiness,' said Cornwallis, bowing over Maria's hand, 'to the wife of one of the most promising officers in the King's service.'

Maria could only bob, overwhelmed with embarrassment in this glittering presence.

'Enchanted to make your acquaintance, Sir William,' said Mrs Mason.

And the parson and his wife, and the few neighbours of Mrs Mason's who were the only other guests, were enormously gratified at being in the same room as – let alone being personally addressed by – the son of an Earl, a Knight of the Bath, and a Commander-in-Chief combined in one person.

'A glass of wine, sir?' asked Hornblower.

'With pleasure.'

Cornwallis took the glass in his hand and looked round. It was significant that it was Mrs Mason whom he addressed.

'Has the health of the happy couple been drunk yet?'

'No, sir,' answered Mrs Mason, in a perfect ecstasy.

'Then may I do so? Ladies, gentlemen. I ask you all to stand and join me on this happy occasion. May they never know sorrow. May they always enjoy health and prosperity. May the wife always find comfort in the knowledge that the husband is doing his duty for King and Country, and may the husband be supported in his duty by the loyalty of the wife. And let us hope that in time to come there will be a whole string of young gentlemen who will wear the King's uniform after their father's example, and a whole string of young ladies to be mothers of further young gentlemen. I give you the health of the bride and groom.'

The health was drunk amid acclamation, with all eyes turned on the blushing Maria, and then from her all eyes turned on Hornblower. He rose; he had realised, before Cornwallis had reached the midpoint of his speech, that the Admiral was using words he had used scores of times before, at scores of weddings of his officers. Hornblower, keyed up on the occasion, met Cornwallis's eyes and grinned. He would give as good as he got; he would reply with a speech exactly similar to the scores that Cornwallis had listened to.

'Sir William, ladies and gentlemen, I can only thank you in the name of' – Hornblower reached down and took Maria's hand – 'my wife and myself.'

As the laughter died away – Hornblower had well known that the company would laugh at his mention of Maria as his wife, although he himself did not think it a subject for laughter – Cornwallis looked at his watch, and Hornblower hastened to thank him for his presence and to escort him to the door. Beyond the threshold Corwallis turned and thumped him on the chest with his large hand.

'I'll add another line to my orders for you,' he said; Hornblower was acutely aware that Cornwallis's friendly smile was accompanied by a searching glance.

'Yes, sir?'

'I'll add my written permission for you to sleep out of your ship for tonight and tomorrow night.'

Hornblower opened his mouth to reply, but no words came; for once in his life his readiness of wit had deserted him. His mind was so busy re-assessing the situation that it had nothing to spare for his organ of speech.

'I *thought* you might have forgotten,' said Cornwallis, grinning. '*Hotspur's* part of the Channel Fleet now. Her captain is forbidden by law to sleep anywhere except on board without the permission of the Commander-in-Chief. Well, you have it.'

'Thank you, sir,' said Hornblower, at last able to articulate.

'Maybe you won't sleep ashore again for a couple of years. Maybe more than that, if Boney fights it out.'

'I certainly think he'll fight, sir.'

'In that case you and I will meet again off Ushant in three weeks' time. So now good-bye, once more.'

For some time after Cornwallis had left Hornblower stood by the half-closed door of the coffee-room in deep thought, shifting his weight from one foot to the other, which was the nearest he could get to pacing up and down. War was coming; he had always been certain of that, because Bonaparte would never retreat from the position he had taken up. But until this moment Hornblower had thought recklessly that he would not be ordered to sea until war was declared, in two or three weeks' time, after the final negotiations had broken down. He had been utterly wrong in this surmise, and he was angry with himself on that account. The facts that he had a good crew – the first harvest of the press – that his ship could be quickly made ready for sea, that she was small and of no account in the balance of power, even that she was of light draught and therefore well adapted to the mission Cornwallis had allotted her, should have warned him that he would be packed off to sea at the earliest possible moment. He should have foreseen all this and he had not.

That was the first point, the first pill to swallow. Next he had to find out why his judgement had been so faulty. He knew the answer instantly, but – and he despised himself for this even more – he flinched from expressing it. But here it was. He had allowed his judgement to be clouded on account of Maria. He had shrunk from hurting her, and in consequence he had refused to allow his mind to make calculations about the future. He had gone recklessly forward in the wild hope that some stroke of good fortune would save him from having to deal her this blow.

He pulled himself up abruptly at this point. Good fortune? Nonsense. He was in command of his own ship, and was being set in the forefront of the battle. This was his golden chance to distinguish himself. That was his good fortune – it would have been maddening bad luck to have been left in harbour. Hornblower could feel the well-remembered thrill of excitement at the thought of seeing action again, of risking reputation – and life – in doing his duty, in gaining glory, and in (what was really the point) justifying himself in his own eyes. Now he was sane again; he could see things in their proper proportion. He was a naval officer first, and a married man only second, and a bad second at that. But – but – that did not make things any easier. He would still have to tear himself free from Maria's arms.

Nor could he stay here outside the coffee-room any longer. He must go back, despite his mental turmoil. He turned and re-entered the room, closing the door behind him.

'It will look well in the *Naval Chronicle*,' said Mrs Mason, 'that the Commander-in-Chief proposed the health of the happy pair. Now, Horatio, some of your guests have empty plates.'

Hornblower was still trying to be a good host when he saw across the room the worried face of the innkeeper again; it called for a second glance to see what had caused him to come in. He was ushering in Hornblower's new coxswain, Hewitt, a very short man who escaped observation across the room. Hewitt made up in breadth a good deal of what he lacked in height, and he sported a magnificent pair of glossy black side-whiskers in the style which was newly fashionable on the lower-deck. He came rolling across the room, his straw hat in his hand, and, knuckling his forehead, gave Horatio a note. The address was in Bush's handwriting and in the correct phrasing, although now a little old-fashioned – Horatio Hornblower, Esq., Master and Commander. Silence fell on the assembled company – a little rudely, Hornblower thought – as he read the few lines.

H.M. Sloop *Hotspur*
April 2nd, 1803
Sir,

I hear from the dockyard that the first of the lighters is ready to come alongside. Extra pay is not yet authorized for dockyard hands, so that work will cease at nightfall. I respectfully submit that I can supervise the embarkation of the stores if you should find it inconvenient to return on board.

Your obdt servant,
Wm Bush.

'Is the boat at the Hard?' demanded Hornblower.

'Yes, sir.'

'Very well. I'll be there in five minutes.'

'Aye aye, sir.'

'Oh, Horry,' said Maria, with a hint of reproach in her voice. No, it was disappointment, not reproach.

'My dear—' said Hornblower. It occurred to him that he might now quote 'I could not love thee, dear, so much—' but he instantly discarded the idea; it would not be at all suitable at this moment, with this wife.

'You're going to the ship again,' said Maria.

'Yes.'

He could not stay away from the ship while there was work to be done. Today, by driving the hands, they could get half the stores on board at least. Tomorrow they could finish, and if Ordnance responded to the prodding of the Admiral, they could get the powder and shot on board as well. Then they could sail at dawn the day after tomorrow.

'I'll be back again this evening,' he said. He forced himself to smile, to look concerned, to forget that he was on the threshold of adventure, that before him lay a career of possible distinction.

'Nothing shall keep me from you, dear,' he said.

He clapped his hands on her shoulders and gave her a smacking kiss that drew applause from the others; that was the way to re-introduce a note of comedy into the proceedings, and, under cover of the laughter, he made his exit. As he hastened down to the Hard two subjects for thought intertwined in his mind, like the serpents of the medical caduceus – the tender love that Maria wished to lavish upon him, and the fact that the day after tomorrow he would be at sea, in command.

II

Someone must have been knocking at the bedroom door for some time; Hornblower had been conscious of it but was too stupid with sleep to think more about it. But now the door opened with a clank of the latch, and Maria, awakening with a start, clutched at him in sudden fright, and he was now fully awake. There was the faintest gleam of light through the thick bed curtains, a shuffling step on the oak floor of the bedroom, and a high-pitched female voice.

'Eight bells, sir. Eight bells.'

The curtains opened an inch to let in a ray of brighter light still, and Maria's grip tightened, but they came together again as Hornblower found his voice.

'Very well. I'm awake.'

'I'll light your candles for you,' piped the voice, and the shuffling step went round the room and the light through the curtains grew brighter.

'Where's the wind? What way's the wind?' asked Hornblower, now so far awake as to feel the quickening of his heartbeat and the tensing of his muscles as he realised what this morning meant to him.

'Now that I can't tell you, sir,' piped the voice. 'I'm not one who can box the compass, and there's no one else awake as yet.'

Hornblower snorted with annoyance at being kept in ignorance of this vital information, and without a thought reached to fling off the bedclothes so as to get up and find out for himself. But there was

Maria clasping him, and he knew that he could not leap out of bed in such a cavalier fashion. He had to go through the proper ritual and put up with the delay. He turned and kissed her, and she returned his kisses, eagerly and yet differently from on other occasions. He felt something wet on his cheek; it was a tear, but there was only that one single tear as Maria forced herself to exert self control. His rather perfunctory embrace changed in character.

'Darling, we're being parted,' whispered Maria. 'Darling, I know you must go. But – but – I can't think how I'm going to live without you. You're my whole life. You're . . .'

A great gust of tenderness welled up in Hornblower's breast, and there was compunction too, a pricking of conscience. Not the most perfect man on earth could merit this devotion. If Maria knew the truth about him she would turn away from him, her whole world shattered. The cruellest thing he could do would be to let her find out; he must never do that. Yet the thought of being loved so dearly set flowing deeper and deeper wells of tenderness in his breast and he kissed her cheeks and sought out the soft eager lips. Then the soft lips hardened, withdrew.

'No, angel, darling. No, I mustn't keep you. You would be angry with me – afterwards. Oh, my dear life, say good-bye to me now. Say that you love me – say that you'll always love me. Then say good-bye, and say that you'll think of me sometimes as I shall always think of you.'

Hornblower said the words, the right words, and in his tenderness he used the right tone. Maria kissed him once more, and then tore herself free and flung herself on to the far side of the bed face downward. Hornblower lay still, trying to harden his heart to rise, and Maria spoke again; her voice was half muffled by the pillow, but her forced change of mood was apparent even so.

'Your clean shirt's on the chair, dear, and your second best shoes are beside the fireplace.'

Hornblower swung himself out of bed and out through the curtains. The air of the bedroom was certainly fresher than that inside. The door latch clanked again and he had just time to whip his bedgown in front of him as the old chambermaid put her head in. She let out a high cackle of mirth at Hornblower's modesty.

'The ostler says light airs from the s'uth'ard, sir.'

'Thank you.'

The door closed behind her.

'Is that what you want, darling?' asked Maria, still behind the curtains. 'Light airs from the s'uth'ard – that means south, does it not?'

'Yes, it may serve,' said Hornblower, hurrying over to the wash basin and adjusting the candles so as to illuminate his face.

Light airs from the south now, at the end of March, were hardly likely to endure. They might back or they might veer, but would certainly strengthen with the coming of day. If *Hotspur* handled as well as he believed she would he could weather the Foreland and be ready for the next development, with plenty of sea room. But of course – as always in the Navy – he could not afford to waste any time. The razor was rasping over his cheeks, and as he peered into the mirror he was vaguely conscious of Maria's reflection behind his own as she moved about the room dressing herself. He poured cold water into the basin with which to wash himself, and felt refreshed, turning away with his usual rapidity of movement to put on his shirt.

'Oh, you dress so fast,' said Maria in consternation.

Hornblower heard her shoes clacking on the oaken floor; she was hurriedly putting on a fresh mob cap over her hair, and clearly she was dressing as quickly as she could, even at the cost of some informality.

'I must run down to see that your breakfast is ready,' she said, and was gone before he could protest.

He folded his neckcloth carefully, but with practised fingers, and slipped on his coat, glanced at his watch, put it in his pocket and then put on his shoes. He rolled his toilet things into his housewife and tied the tapes. Yesterday's shirt and his nightshirt and bedgown he stuffed in the canvas bag that awaited them, and the housewife on top. A glance round the room told him that he had omitted nothing, although he had to look more carefully than usual because there were articles belonging to Maria scattered here and there. Bubbling with excitement, he opened the window curtains and glanced outside; no sign of dawn as yet. Bag in hand, he went downstairs and into the coffee-room. This smelt of stale living, and was dimly lit by an oil lamp dangling from the ceiling. Maria looked in at him from the farther door.

'Here's your place, dear,' she said. 'Only a moment before breakfast.'

She held the back of the chair for him to be seated.

'I'll sit down after you,' said Hornblower; it went against the grain to have Maria waiting on him.

'Oh, no,' said Maria. 'I have your breakfast to attend to – only the old woman is up as yet.'

She coaxed him into the chair. Hornblower felt her kiss the top of his head, felt a momentary touch of her cheek against his, but before he could seize her, reaching behind him, she was gone. She left behind her the memory of something between a sniff and a sob;

the opening of the door into the kitchen admitted a smell of cooking, the sizzling of something in a pan, and a momentary burst of conversation between Maria and the old woman. Then in came Maria, her rapid steps indicating that the plate she held was too hot to be comfortable. She dropped it in front of him, a vast rump steak, still sizzling on the plate.

'There, dear,' she said, and busied herself with putting the rest of the meal within his reach, while Hornblower looked down at the steak with some dismay.

'I picked that out for you specially yesterday,' she announced proudly. 'I walked over to the butcher's while you were on the ship.'

Hornblower steeled himself not to wince at hearing a naval officer's wife speak about being 'on' a ship; he also had to steel himself to having steak for breakfast, when steak was by no means his favourite dish, and when he was so excited that he felt he could eat nothing. And dimly he could foresee a future – if ever he returned, if ever, inconceivably, he settled down in domestic life – when steak would be put before him on any special occasion. That thought was the last straw; he felt he could not eat a mouthful, and yet he could not hurt Maria's feelings.

'Where's yours?' he asked, temporising.

'Oh, I shan't be having any steak,' replied Maria. The tone of her voice proved that it was quite inconceivable to her that a wife should eat equally well as her husband. Hornblower raised his voice and turned his head.

'Hey, there!' he called. 'In the kitchen! Bring another plate – a hot one.'

'Oh, no, darling,' said Maria, all fluttered, but Hornblower was by now out of his chair and seating her at her own place.

'Now, sit there,' said Hornblower. 'No more words. I'll have no mutineers in my family. Ah!'

Here came the other plate. Hornblower cut the steak in two, and helped Maria to the larger half.

'But darling—'

'I said I'll have no truck with mutiny,' growled Hornblower parodying his own quarter-deck rasp.

'Oh, Horry, darling. You're good to me, far too good to me.' Momentarily Maria clapped hands and handkerchief to her face, and Hornblower feared she would break down finally, but then she put her hands in her lap and straightened her back, controlling her emotions in an act of the purest heroism. Hornblower felt his heart go out to her. He reached out and pressed the hand she gladly proffered him.

'Now let me see you eat a hearty breakfast,' he said; he was still using his mock-bullying tone, but the tenderness he felt was still evident. Maria took up her knife and fork and Hornblower did the same. He forced himself to eat a few mouthfuls, and so mangled the rest of his steak that it did not appear as if he had left too much. He took a pull at his pot of beer – he did not like drinking beer for breakfast, not even beer as small as this, but he realised that the old woman could not be expected to have access to the tea-caddy.

A rattling at the windows attracted their attention. The ostler was opening the shutters, and they could dimly see his face for a moment, but it was still quite dark outside. Hornblower looked at his watch; ten minutes to five, and he had ordered his boat to be at the Sally Port at five. Maria saw the gesture and looked over at him. There was a slight trembling of her lips, a slight moisture in her eyes, but she kept herself under control.

'I'll get my cloak,' she said quietly, and fled from the room. She was back in no time, her grey cloak round her, and her face shadowed in her hood; in her arms was Hornblower's heavy coat.

'You're leaving us now, sir?' piped the old woman coming into the coffee-room.

'Yes. Madam will settle the score when she returns,' said Hornblower; he fumbled out half a crown from his pocket and put it on the table.

'Thank you kindly, sir. And a good voyage, and prize money galore.' The sing-song tone reminded Hornblower that she must have seen naval officers by the hundreds leaving the George to go to sea – her memories must go back to Hawke and Boscawen.

He buttoned up his coat and took up his bag.

'I'll have the ostler come with us with a lantern to escort you back,' he said, consideringly.

'Oh, no please, darling. It's so short a way, and I know every step,' pleaded Maria, and there was enough truth in what she said for him not to insist.

They walked out into the keen cold air, having to adjust their eyes to the darkness even after the miserable light of the coffee-room. Hornblower realised that if he had been an Admiral, or even a distinguished Captain, he would never have been allowed to leave with so little ceremony; the innkeeper and his wife would certainly have risen and dressed to see him on his way. They turned the corner and started on the steep slope down to the Sally Port, and it was borne in anew on Hornblower that he was about to start out for the wars. His concern for Maria had actually distracted him from this thought, but now he found himself gulping with excitement.

'Dear,' said Maria. 'I have a little present for you.'

She was bringing something out from the pocket of her cloak and pressing it into his hand.

'It's only gloves, dear, but my love comes with them,' she went on. 'I could make nothing better for you in this little time. I would have liked to have embroidered something for you – I would have liked to give you something worthy of you. But I have been stitching at these every moment since – since—'

She could not go on, but once more she straightened her back and refused to break down.

'I'll be able to think of you every moment I wear them,' said Hornblower. He struggled into the gloves despite the handicap of the bag he was carrying; they were splendid thick woollen gloves, each with separate thumb and forefinger.

'They fit me to perfection. I thank you for the kind thought, dear.'

Now they were at the head of the steep slope down the Hard, and this horrible ordeal would soon be over.

'You have the seventeen pounds safely?' asked Hornblower – an unnecessary question.

'Yes, thank you, dearest. I fear it too much—'

'And you'll be able to draw my monthly half pay,' went on Hornblower harshly, to keep the emotion from his voice, and then, realising how harshly, he continued. 'It is time to say good-bye now, darling.'

He had forced himself to use the unaccustomed last word. The water level was far up the Hard; that meant, as he had known when he had given the orders, that the tide was at the flood. He would be able to take advantage of the ebb.

'Darling!' said Maria, turning to him and lifting up her face to him in its hood.

He kissed her; down at the water's edge there was the familiar rattle of oars on thwarts, and the sound of male voices, as his boat's crew perceived the two shadowy figures on the Hard. Maria heard those sounds as clearly as Hornblower did, and she quickly snatched away from him the cold lips she had raised to his.

'Good-bye, my angel.'

There was nothing else to say now, nothing else to do; this was the end of this brief experience. He turned his back on Maria; he turned his back on peace and on civilian married life and walked down towards war.

III

'Slack water now, sir,' announced Bush. 'First of the ebb in ten minutes. And anchor's hove short, sir.'

'Thank you, Mr Bush.' There was enough grey light in the sky now to see Bush's face as something more definite than a blur. At Bush's shoulder stood Prowse, the acting-master, senior master's mate with an acting-warrant. He was competing unobtrusively with Bush for Hornblower's attention. Prowse was charged, by Admiralty instructions, with 'navigating and conducting the ship from port to port under the direction of the captain.' But there was no reason at all why Hornblower should not give his other officers every opportunity to exercise their skill; on the contrary. And it was possible, even likely, that Prowse, with thirty years of sea duty behind him, would endeavour to take the direction of the ship out of the hands of a young and inexperienced captain.

'Mr Bush!' said Hornblower. 'Get the ship under way, if you please. Set a course to weather the Foreland.'

'Aye aye, sir.'

Hornblower watched Bush keenly, while doing his best not to appear to be doing so. Bush took a final glance round him, gauging the gentle wind and the likely course of the ebb.

'Stand by there, at the capstan,' he ordered. 'Loose the heads'ls. Hands aloft to loose the tops'ls.'

Hornblower could see in a flash that he could place implicit reliance on Bush's seamanship. He knew he should never have doubted it, but his memories were two years old and might have been blurred by the passage of time. Bush gave his orders in a well-timed sequence. With the anchor broken out *Hotspur* gathered momentary sternway. With the wheel hard over and the forecastle hands drawing at the headsail sheets she brought her head round. Bush sheeted home and ordered hands to the braces. In the sweetest possible way *Hotspur* caught the gentle wind, lying over hardly more than a degree or two. In a moment she was under way, slipping forward through the water, rudder balanced against sail-pressure, a living, lovely thing.

There was no need to drop any word of commendation to Bush regarding such a simple operation as getting under way. Hornblower could savour the pleasure of being afloat, as the hands raced to set the topgallant sails and then the courses. Then suddenly he remembered.

'Let me have that glass, please, Mr Prowse.'

He put the massive telescope to his eye and trained it out over the port quarter. It was still not yet full daylight, and there was the usual hint of haze, and *Hotspur* had left her anchorage half a mile or more astern. Yet he could just see it; a solitary, lonely speck of grey, on the water's edge, over there on the Hard. Perhaps – just possibly – there was a flicker of white; Maria might be waving her handkerchief, but he could not be sure. In fact he thought not. There was just the solitary grey speck. Hornblower looked again, and then he made himself lower the telescope; it was heavy, and his hands were trembling a trifle so that the image was blurred. It was the first time in all his life that he had put to sea leaving behind him someone who was interested in his fate.

'Thank you, Mr Prowse,' he said, harshly, handing back the telescope.

He knew he had to think about something different, that he must quickly find something else to occupy his thoughts; fortunately as captain of a ship just setting sail there was no lack of subjects.

'Now, Mr Prowse,' he said, glancing at the wake and at the trim of the sails. 'The wind's holding steady at the moment. I want a course for Ushant.'

'Ushant, sir?' Prowse had a long lugubrious face like a mule's, and he stood there digesting this piece of information without any change of expression.

'You heard what I said,' snapped Hornblower, in sudden irritation.

'Yes, sir,' answered Prowse, hastily. 'Ushant, sir. Aye aye, sir.'

There was of course, some excuse for his first reaction. Nobody in the ship save Hornblower knew the content of the orders which were taking *Hotspur* to sea; nobody knew to what point in the whole world she was destined to sail. The mention of Ushant narrowed down the field to some extent at least. The North Sea and the Baltic were ruled out. So were Ireland and the Irish Sea and the St Lawrence across the Atlantic. But it still might be the West Indies or the Cape of Good Hope or the Mediterranean; Ushant was a point of departure for all those.

'Mr Bush!' said Hornblower.

'Sir!'

'You may dismiss the watch below, and send the hands to breakfast when you think proper.'

'Aye aye, sir.'

'Who's the officer of the watch?'

'Cargill, sir.'

'He has charge of the deck, then.'

Hornblower looked about him. Everything was in order, and *Hotspur* was standing out for the Channel. But there was something odd, something different, something unusual. Then it dawned upon him.

For the first time in his life he was going to sea in time of peace He had served ten years as a naval officer without this experience Always before, whenever his ship emerged from harbour, she was in instant danger additional to the hazards of the sea. In every previous voyage any moment might bring an enemy up over the horizon; at an hour's notice ship and ship's company might be fighting for their lives. And the most dangerous time of all was when first putting to sea with a raw crew, with drill and organisation incomplete – it was a likely moment to meet an enemy, as well as the most inconvenient one.

Now here they were putting to sea without any of these worries. It was an extraordinary sensation, something new – something new, like leaving Maria behind. He tried to shake that thought from him; as a buoy slithered past the starboard quarter he tried to leave the thought with it. It was a relief to see Prowse approaching again, with a piece of paper in his hand as he glanced up to the commission pendant and then out to the horizon in an attempt to forecast the weather.

'Course is sou'west by west, half west, sir,' he said. 'When we tack we may just be able to make that good, close-hauled.'

'Thank you, Mr Prowse. You may mark it on the board.'

'Aye aye, sir,' Prowse was pleased at this mark of confidence. He naturally had no idea that Hornblower, revolving in his mind, yesterday afternoon, all the responsibilities he would be carrying on the morrow, had made the same calculation to reach the same result. The green hills of the Isle of Wight were momentarily touched by a watery and level sun.

'There's the buoy, sir,' said Prowse.

'Thank you. Mr Cargill! Tack the ship, if you please.'

'Aye aye, sir.'

Hornblower withdrew aft. He wanted not merely to observe how Cargill handled the ship, but also how *Hotspur* behaved. When war should come it was not a mere possibility, but a definite probability, that success or failure, freedom or captivity, might hinge on how *Hotspur* went about, how handy she was in stays.

Cargill was a man of thirty, red-faced and corpulent in advance of his years; he was obviously trying hard to forget that he was under the simultaneous scrutiny of the captain, the first lieutenant, and the sailing master, as he applied himself to the manoeuvre. He stood beside the wheel looking warily up at the sails and aft at the wake. Hornblower watched Cargill's right hand, down by his thigh, opening and shutting. That might be a symptom of nervousness or a mere habitual gesture of calculation. The watch on deck were all at their stations. So far the men were all unknown faces to Hornblower;

it would be profitable to devote some of his attention to the study of their reactions as well.

Cargill obviously braced himself for action and then gave his preliminary order to the wheel.

'Helm's a-lee!' he bellowed, but not a very effective bellow, for his voice cracked half-way.

'Headsail sheets!' That was hardly better. It would not have served in a gale of wind, although it carried forward in present conditions. Jib and fore-topsail began to shiver.

'Raise up tacks and sheets!'

Hotspur was coming round into the wind, rising to an even keel. She was coming round, coming round – now was she going to hang in stays?

'Haul, mains'l! Haul!'

This was the crucial moment. The hands knew their business; the port-side bowlines and braces were cast off smartly, and the hands tailed on to the starboard-side ones. Round came the yards, but the *Hotspur* refused to answer. She baulked. She hung right in the eye of the wind, and then fell off again two points to port, with every sail ashiver and every yard of way lost. She was in irons, helpless until further action should be taken.

'A fine thing if we were on a lee shore, sir,' growled Bush.

'Wait,' said Hornblower. Cargill was glancing round at him for orders, and that was disappointing. Hornblower would have preferred an officer who went stolidly on to retrieve the situation. 'Carry on, Mr Cargill.'

The hands were behaving well. There was no chatter, and they were standing by for further orders. Cargill was drumming on his right thigh with his fingers, but for his own sake he must find his way out of his troubles unaided. Hornblower saw the fingers clench, saw Cargill glance ahead and astern as he pulled himself together. *Hotspur* was slowly gathering stern-way as the wind pushed directly back on the sails. Cargill took the plunge, made the effort. A sharp order put the wheel hard-a-port, another order brought the yards ponderously round again. *Hotspur* hung reluctant for a moment, and then sulkily turned back on the starboard tack and gathered way as Cargill in the nick of time sent the wheel spinning back and took a pull on the braces. There was no lack of sea room, there was no dangerous lee shore to demand instant action, and Cargill could wait until every sail was drawing full again and *Hotspur* had plenty of way on her to enable the rudder to bite. Cargill even had the sense to allow her head to fall off another point so as to give plenty of momentum for his next attempt, although Hornblower noticed with a slight pang of regret that he hurried it a trifle more than he should have done. He should have waited perhaps two more minutes.

'Headsail sheets!' ordered Cargill again; his fingers started drumming on his thigh once more with the strain of waiting.

But Cargill's head was clear enough to give his orders in the correct sequence. Round came *Hotspur* into the wind again. Sheets and braces were handled smartly. There was a paralysing moment as she baulked again, hung as though she was determined once more to miss stays, but this time she had a trifle more momentum, and in the last possible second a fortunate combination of wind and wave pushed her bows round through the vital final degrees of swing. Round she came, at last.

'Full and bye!' said Cargill to the helmsman, the relief very evident in his voice. 'Fore tack, there! Sheets! Braces!'

With the operation completed he turned to face the criticism of his superiors; there was sweat trickling down his forehead. Hornblower could feel Bush beside him ready to rate him thoroughly; Bush believed sincerely that everyone was the better for a severe dressing-down in any circumstance, and he was usually right. But Hornblower had been watching *Hotspur's* behaviour closely.

'Carry on, Mr Cargill,' he said, and Cargill, relieved, turned away again, and Bush met Hornblower's glance with some slight surprise.

'The ship's trimmed too much by the head,' said Hornblower. 'That makes her unhandy in stays.'

'It might do so,' agreed Bush, doubtfully.

If the bow gripped the water more firmly than the stern *Hotspur* would act like a weather-vane, persisting in keeping her bow to the wind.

'We'll have to try it,' said Hornblower. 'She'll never do as she is. We'll have to trim her so that she draws six inches more aft. At least that. Now, what is there we can shift aft?'

'Well—' began Bush.

In his mind's eye he called up a picture of the interior of the *Hotspur*, with every cubic foot crammed with stores. It had been a Herculean feat to prepare her for sea; to find room for everything necessary had called for the utmost ingenuity. It seemed as if no other arrangement could be possible. Yet maybe—

'Perhaps—' went on Bush, and they were instantly deep in a highly technical discussion.

Prowse came up and touched his hat, to report that *Hotspur* was just able to make good the course for Ushant. Bush could hardly help but prick up his ears at the mention of the name; Prowse could hardly help but be drawn into the discussion regarding the alteration in the trim of the ship. They had to move aside to make room for the hourly casting of the log; the breeze flapped their coats round them. Here they were at sea; the nightmare days and nights of fitting out were over, and so were the – what was the right word? Delirious, perhaps – the delirious days of marriage. This was a normal life. Creative life, making a living organism out of *Hotspur*, working out improvements in material and in personnel.

Bush and Prowse were still discussing possible alteration in the ship's trim as Hornblower came back into his present world.

'There's a vacant port right aft on each side,' said Hornblower; a simple solution had presented itself to his mind, as so often happened when his thoughts had strayed to other subjects. 'We can bring two of the forward guns aft.'

Prowse and Bush paused while they considered the matter; Hornblower's rapid mind was already dealing with the mathematics of it. The ship's nine-pounders weighed twenty-six hundredweight each. Along with the gun carriages and the ready use shot which would have to be brought aft too there would be a total transfer of four tons. Hornblower's eye measured the distances, forward and aft of the centre of flotation, from forty feet before to thirty feet abaft. No, the leverage would be a little excessive, even though *Hotspur's* dead weight was over four hundred tons.

'Maybe she'd gripe a little, sir,' suggested Prowse, reaching the same conclusions two minutes later.

'Yes. We'll take the No. 3 guns. That should be exactly right.'

'And leave a gap, sir?' asked Bush in faint protest.

It certainly would, as conspicuous as a missing front tooth. It would break into the two ordered rows of cannon, conveying a make-shift appearance to the ship.

'I'd rather have an ugly ship afloat,' said Hornblower, 'than a good-looking one on the rocks of a lee shore.'

'Yes, sir,' said Bush, swallowing this near-heresy.

'As the stores are consumed we can put things to rights again,' added Hornblower soothingly. 'Perhaps you'll be good enough to attend to it now?'

'Aye aye, sir.' Bush turned his mind to the practical aspects of the problem of shifting cannon in a moving ship. 'I'll hoist 'em out of the carriages with the stay tackles and lower them on to a mat—'

'Quite right. I'm sure you can deal with it, Mr Bush.'

No one in his senses would try to move a gun in its carriage along a heeling deck – it would go surging about out of control in a moment. But out of its carriage, lying helpless on a mat, with its trunnions prohibiting any roll, it could be dragged about comparatively easily, and hoisted up into its carriage again after that had been moved into its new position. Bush had already passed the word for Mr Wise, the boatswain, to have the stay-tackles rigged.

'The quarter-bill will have to be changed,' said Hornblower incautiously as the thought struck him – the guns' crews would need to be re-allotted.

'Aye aye, sir,' said Bush. His sense of discipline was too acute to allow more than a hint of reproach to be apparent in his tone. As first lieutenant it was his business to remember these things without being reminded by his captain. Hornblower made amends as best he could.

'I'll leave it all in your charge, then, Mr Bush. Report to me when the guns are moved.'

'Aye aye, sir.'

Hornblower crossed the quarter-deck to go to his cabin, passing Cargill as he went; Cargill was keeping an eye on the hands rigging the stay-tackles.

'The ship will be more handy in stays when those guns are shifted, Mr Cargill,' said Hornblower. 'Then you'll have another opportunity to show how you can handle her.'

'Thank you, sir,' replied Cargill. He had clearly been brooding over his recent failure.

Hornblower walked along to his cabin; the moving cogs in the complex machine that was a ship always needed lubrication, and it was a captain's duty to see that it was provided. The sentry at his door came to attention as he passed in. He glanced round at the bare necessities there. His cot swung from the deck-beams; there was a single chair, a mirror on the bulkhead with a canvas basin on a frame below it. On the opposite bulkhead was clamped his desk, with his sea chest beneath it. A strip of canvas hanging from the deck-beams served as a wardrobe to screen the clothes hanging within. That was all; there was no room for anything else, but the fact that the cabin was so tiny was an advantage in one way. There were no guns mounted in it – it was right aft – and there would be no necessity when the ship cleared for action, to sweep all this away.

And this was luxury, this was affluence, this was the most superlative good fortune. Nine days ago – no, ten days, now – he had been a half-pay lieutenant, under stoppage of pay because the Peace of Amiens had resulted in his promotion not being confirmed. He had been doubtful where his next meal would be coming from. A single night had changed all this. He had won forty-five pounds at a sitting of whist from a group of senior officers, one of them a Lord of Admiralty. The King had sent a message to Parliament announcing the government's decision to set the Navy on a war footing again. And he had been appointed Commander and given the *Hotspur* to prepare for sea. He could be sure now of his next meal, even though it would be salt beef and biscuit. And – not so much as a coincidence, but rather as a sequel to all this – he had found himself betrothed to Maria and committed to an early marriage.

The fabric of the ship transmitted the sound of one of the nine-pounders being dragged aft; Bush was a fast worker. Bush had been a half-pay lieutenant too, ten days ago, and senior to Hornblower. It was with diffidence that Hornblower had asked him if he would care to serve as first lieutenant – as the only lieutenant allowed on the establishment of a sloop of war – of the *Hotspur*, under Hornblower's command. It had been astonishing, and extremely flattering, to see the delight in Bush's face at the invitation.

'I'd been hoping you'd ask me, sir,' said Bush. 'I couldn't really think you'd want me as a first lieutenant.'

'Nobody I'd like better,' Hornblower had replied.

At this moment he nearly lost his footing as *Hotspur* heaved up her bows, rolled, and then cocked up her stern in the typical motion of a ship close-hauled. She was out now from the lee of the Wight, meeting the full force of the Channel rollers. Fool that he was! He had almost forgotten about this; on the one or two occasions during the past ten days when the thought of sea-sickness had occurred to him he had blithely assumed that he had grown out of that weakness in eighteen months on land. He had not thought about it at all this morning, being too busy. Now with his first moment of idleness here it came. He had lost his sea-legs – a new roll sent him reeling – and he was going to be sick. He could feel a cold sweat on his skin and the first wave of nausea rising to his throat. There was time for a bitter jest – he had just been congratulating himself on knowing where his next meal was coming from, but now he could be more certain still about where his last meal was going to. Then the sickness struck, horribly.

Now he lay face downward across his cot. He heard the rumble of wheels, and cleared his thoughts sufficiently to make the deduction that, with the guns brought aft, Bush was bringing the gun-carriages aft as well. But he hardly cared. His stomach heaved again and he cared even less. He could think about nothing but his own misery. Now what was that? Someone pounding vigorously on the door, and he realised that the pounding had grown-up from an earlier gentle tapping that he had ignored.

'What is it?' he called, croaking.

'Message from the master, sir,' said an unknown voice. 'From Mr Prowse.'

He had to hear what it was. He dragged himself from his cot, and staggered over and dumped himself into his chair, hunching his shoulders over his desk so that his face could not be seen.

'Come in!' he called.

The opening of the door admitted considerably more of the noise that had been more and more insistently making itself heard.

'What is it?' repeated Hornblower, hoping that his attitude indicated deep concentration upon the paper-work of the ship.

'Message from Mr Prowse, sir,' said a voice that Hornblower could hardly place. 'Wind's freshening an' hauling forward. Course will have to be altered, sir.'

'Very well. I'll come.'

'Aye aye, sir.'

He certainly would have to come. He stood up, holding on to the desk with one hand while he adjusted his clothes with the other. He braced himself, and then he plunged out on to the quarter-deck. He had forgotten all these things; he had forgotten how fresh the wind blew at sea, how the rigging shrieked in a gust, how the deck heaved under unwary feet. As the stern rose he was hurried forward, struggling vainly to retain his dignity, and just managed to fetch up without disaster against the hammock netting. Prowse came up at once.

'Course is sou'west by south, now, sir,' he said. 'I had to let her fall off a couple of points. Wind's still backing westerly.'

'So I see,' said Hornblower. He looked at sky and sea, making himself think. 'How's the glass?'

'Hardly fallen at all, sir. But it's going to blow harder before nighfall, sir.'

'Perhaps you're right.'

Bush appeared at this moment, touching the hat that was now pulled down hard on to his head.

'The guns are shifted aft, sir. The lashings are bowsed up taut.'

'Thank you.'

Hornblower kept his hands on the hammock netting, and his gaze steadily forward, so that, by not turning either to Bush on one side or to Prowse on the other, the whiteness of his land-lubber's face might not be noticed. He struggled to picture the chart of the Channel that he had studied so carefully yesterday. There was the twenty-league gap between the Casquets and the Start; an incorrect decision now might keep them windbound for days inside it.

'We might just weather the Start on this course, sir,' prompted Prowse.

Unexpected nausea suddenly welled up in Hornblower, and he moved restlessly as he fought with it. He did not want Prowse to prompt him, and as he swung about he caught sight of Cargill standing by the wheel. It was still Cargill's watch – that was one more factor to bring Hornblower to a decision, along with Bush's report and Prowse's prompting.

'No,' he said. 'We'll put the ship about.'

'Aye aye, sir,' said Prowse, in reluctant agreement.

Hornblower looked towards Cargill, summoning him with a glance; he did not wish to leave the comforting support of the hammock netting.

'Mr Cargill,' said Hornblower. 'Let's see you tack the ship again, now that we've altered her trim.'

'Aye aye, sir,' answered Cargill. That was the only thing the poor devil could say in any case, in reply to a direct order. But he was clearly nervous. He went back to the wheel and took the speaking trumpet from its beckets – the freshening wind made that necessary.

'Hands 'bout ship!' he called, and the order was instantly underlined by the calls of the bos'n's mates and the bellowings of Mr Wise. The hands ran to their stations. Cargill stared round at wind and sea; Hornblower saw him swallow as he nerved himself. Then he gave the order to the wheel; this time it was the fingers of his left hand that drummed upon his thigh, for his right was occupied by the speaking-trumpet. *Hotspur* rose to an even keel while sheets and braces were being handled. She was turning – she was turning.

'Let go and haul!' yelled Cargill into the speaking-trumpet. Hornblower felt he would have waited three or four more seconds before giving that order, but he knew that he might be wrong; not only was sea-sickness dulling his judgement but, standing as he did, looking aft, he did not have the 'feel' of the ship. Events proved that Cargill did, or else was lucky, for *Hotspur* came on round without hesitation.

'Hard-a-lee!' snapped Cargill to the helmsman, and the wheel spun round in a blur of spokes, catching *Hotspur* at the moment when she was beginning to fall off. A straining group of men hauled out the fore-tack; others tailed on to the bowlines. *Hotspur* was on the new tack, having handled as sweetly, apparently, as anyone could ask.

Hornblower walked up to the wheel.

'Does she gripe?' he asked the quartermaster.

The quartermaster eased off the wheel a couple of spokes, squinting up at the leech of the main-topsail, and then brought her up to the wind again.

'Can't say that she does, sir,' he decided. 'Mebbe she does, a trifle. No, sir, I can't say that she gripes. Just a touch of weather helm's all she needs now, sir.'

'That's as it should be,' said Hornblower. Bush and Prowse had not spoken a word, and there was no need even for a glance to underline the situation, but a word to Cargill would not be out of place. 'You can go off watch feeling better pleased with yourself now, Mr Cargill.'

'Yes, sir, thank you, sir,' said Cargill.

Cargill's round red face split into a grin. *Hotspur* rose to a wave, lay over, and Hornblower, taken by surprise, staggered down the deck on to Cargill's broad chest. Luckily Cargill was a heavyweight and fast of footing; he took the shock without staggering – otherwise he and his captain might have gone reeling across the deck into the scuppers. Hornblower felt a burst of shame. He had no more sea-legs than the merest landlubber; his envy of Cargill and Bush and Prowse, standing firm and swaying easily with the send of the ship, amounted to positive dislike. And his stomach was about to betray him again. His dignity was in peril, and he summoned up all that was left of it, turning to Bush stiff-legged and stiff-necked.

'See that I am called when any alteration of course is necessary, if you please, Mr Bush,' he said.

'Aye aye, sir.'

The deck was heaving, but he knew it was not heaving as much as his distorted mind told him it was. He forced himself somehow to walk aft to his cabin; twice he had to stop and brace himself, and when *Hotspur* rose to a wave he was nearly made to run – certainly he had to walk faster than a captain should – past the sentry, and he fetched up against the door with some little violence. It was no comfort – in fact it added to his distress – to see that the sentry had a bucket on the deck beside him. He wrenched open the door, hung suspended for a moment as *Hotspur* completed her pitch, with her stern in the air, and then crashed down groaning on to his cot, his feet dragging on the deck as the cot swung.

IV

Hornblower sat at his desk in his cabin holding a package in his hand. Five minutes earlier he had unlocked his chest and taken this out; in five minutes more he would be entitled to open it – at least, that was what his dead reckoning indicated. It was a remarkably heavy package; it might be weighted with shot or scrap metal, except that Admiral Cornwallis was hardly likely to send shot or scrap metal to one of his captains. It was heavily sealed, in four places, and the seals were unbroken. Inked upon the canvas wrapper was the superscription:

'Instructions for Horatio Hornblower, Esq., Master and Commander, H.M. Sloop *Hotspur*. To be opened on passing the Sixth Degree of Longitude West of Greenwich.'

Sealed orders. Hornblower had heard about such things all his professional life, but this was his first contact with them. They had been sent on board the *Hotspur* on the afternoon of his wedding day, and he had signed for them. Now the ship was about to cross the sixth meridian; she had come down-Channel with remarkable ease; there had been only one single watch when she had not been able to make good her direct course. Putting her about in order to restore Cargill's self-confidence had been extraordinarily fortunate. The wind had hardly backed westerly at all, and only momentarily even then. *Hotspur* had escaped being embayed in Lyme Bay; she had neatly weathered the Casquets, and it all stemmed from that fortunate order. Hornblower was aware that Prowse was feeling a new respect for him as a navigator and a weather prophet. That was all to the good, and Hornblower had no intention of allowing Prowse to guess that the excellent passage was the result of a fortunate fluke, of a coincidence of circumstances.

Hornblower looked at his watch and raised his voice in a shout to the sentry at the door.

'Pass the word for Mr Bush.'

Hornblower could hear the sentry shouting, and the word being passed on along the quarter-deck. *Hotspur* rose in a long, long pitch with hardly any roll about it. She was meeting the long Atlantic swell now, changing her motion considerably, and all for the better, in Hornblower's opinion – and his sea-sickness was rapidly coming under control. Bush was taking a long time to respond to the call – he obviously was not on the quarter-deck, and the chances were he was taking a nap or was engaged on some other private business. Well, it would do him no harm and cause him no surprise to be summoned from it, for that was the way of the Navy.

At last came the knock on the door, and Bush entered.

'Sir?'

'Ah, Mr Bush,' said Hornblower pedantically. Bush was the closest friend he had, but this was a formal matter, to be carried through normally. 'Can you tell me the ship's position at this moment?'

'No, sir, not exactly, sir,' replied the puzzled Bush. 'Ushant bears ten leagues to the east'ard, I believe, sir.'

'At this moment,' said Hornblower, 'we are in longitude six degrees and some seconds west. Latitude 48° 40′, but we do not have to devote any thought to our latitude at present, oddly enough. It is our longitude that matters. Would you be so kind as to examine this packet?'

'Ah. I see, sir,' said Bush, having read the superscription.

'You observe that the seals are unbroken?'

'Yes, sir.'

'Then perhaps you will have the further kindness, when you leave this cabin, to make sure of the ship's longitude so that, should it become necessary, you can bear witness that I have carried out my orders?'

'Yes, sir, I will,' said Bush, and then, after a pause long enough for him to realise that Hornblower intended the interview to be at an end, 'Aye aye, sir.'

The temptation to tease Bush was a very strong one, Hornblower realised as Bush left the cabin. It was a temptation he must resist. It might be indulged to the extent of causing resentment; in any case, Bush was too easy a target – he was a sitting bird.

And thinking along those lines had actually delayed for several seconds the exciting moment of opening the orders. Hornblower took out his penknife and cut the stitching. Now the weight of the packet was explained. There were three rolls of coins – golden coins. Hornblower spilt them out on to his desk. There were fifty small ones, about the size of sixpences; twenty larger ones, and ten larger still. Examination revealed that the medium-sized ones were French twenty-franc pieces, exactly like one he had seen in Lord Parry's possession a week or two ago, with 'Napoleon First Consul' on one side and 'French Republic' on the other. The small ones were ten franc pieces, the larger ones forty francs. Altogether it made a considerable sum, over fifty pounds without allowing for the premium on gold in an England plagued by a depreciating paper currency.

And here were his supplementary instructions, explaining how he should employ the money. 'You are therefore required—' said the instructions after the preliminary sentences. Hornblower had to make contact with the fishermen of Brest; he had to ascertain if any of them would accept bribes; he had to glean from them all possible information regarding the French fleet in that port; finally he was informed that in case of war information of any kind, even newspapers, would be acceptable.

Hornblower read his instructions through twice; he referred again to the unsealed orders he had received at the same time; the ones that had sent him to sea. There was need for thought, and automatically he rose to his feet, only to sit down again, for there was no chance whatever of walking about in that cabin. He must postpone his walk for a moment. Maria had stitched neat linen bags in which to put his hair brushes – quite useless, of course, seeing that he always rolled his brushes in his housewife. He reached for one, and swept the money into it, put the bag and the orders back into his chest and was about to lock it when a further thought struck him, and he counted out ten ten-franc pieces and put them into his trouser pocket. Now, with his chest locked, he was free to go on deck.

Prowse and Bush were pacing the weather side of the quarter-deck in deep conversation; no doubt the news that their captain had opened his sealed orders would spread rapidly through the ship – and no one on board save Hornblower could be really sure that *Hotspur* was not about to set course for the Cape and India. It was a temptation to keep them all on tenterhooks, but Hornblower put the temptation aside. Besides, it would be to no purpose – after a day or two of hanging about outside Brest everyone would be able to guess *Hotspur's* mission. Prowse and Bush were hurriedly moving over to the lee side, leaving the weather side for their captain, but Hornblower halted them.

'Mr Bush! Mr Prowse! We are going to look into Brest and see what our friend Boney is up to.'

Those few words told the whole story to men who had served in the last war and who had beaten about in the stormy waters off the Brittany coast.

'Yes, sir,' said Bush, simply.

Together they looked into the binnacle, out to the horizon, up to the commission pendant. Simple enough to set a course; Bush and Prowse could do that easily, but it was not so simple to deal with problems of international relations, problems of neutrality, problems of espionage.

'Let's look at the chart, Mr Prowse. You can see that we'll have to keep well clear of Les Fillettes.'

The islands of the Little Girls, in the middle of the fairway into Brest; it was a queer name for rocks that would be sites for batteries of guns.

'Very well, Mr Prowse. You can square away and set course.'

There were light airs from the northwestward today, and it was the easiest matter in the world to stand down towards Brest; *Hotspur* was hardly rolling at all and was pitching only moderately. Hornblower was fast recovering his sea-legs and could trust himself to walk the deck, and could almost trust his stomach to retain its contents. There was a certain feeling of well-being that came with a remission from sea-sickness. The April air was keen and fresh, but not paralysingly cold; Hornblower's gloves and heavy coat were barely necessary. In fact Hornblower found it hard to concentrate on his problems; he was willing to postpone their consideration, and he halted his step and looked across at Bush with a smile that brought the latter over with hurried steps.

'I suppose you have plans for exercising the crew, Mr Bush?'

'Yes, sir.' Bush did not say, 'Of course, sir,' for he was too good a subordinate. But his eyes lit up, for there was nothing Bush enjoyed more than reefing topsails and unreefing them, sending down topgallant yards and sending them up again, rousting out cables and carrying them to a stern port in readiness to be used as a spring, and in fact rehearsing all the dozens – hundreds – of manoeuvres that weather or war might make necessary.

'Two hours of that will do for today, Mr Bush. I can only remember one short exercise at the guns?'

Tortured by sea-sickness while running down the Channel he could not be sure.

'Only one, sir.'

'Then after dinner we'll have an hour at the guns. One of these days we might use them.'

'We might, sir,' said Bush.

Bush could face with equanimity the prospects of a war that would engulf the whole world.

The pipes of the bos'n's mates called all hands, and very soon the exercises were well under way, the sweating sailors racing up and down the rigging tailing on to ropes under the urgings of the petty officers and amid a perfect cloud of profanity from Mr Wise. It was as well to drill the men, simply to keep them exercised, but there were no serious deficiencies to make up. *Hotspur* had benefited by being the very first ship to be manned after the press had been put into force. Of her hundred and fifty hands no fewer than a hundred were prime seamen, rated A.B. She had twenty ordinary seamen and only ten landsmen all told, and no more than twenty boys. It was an extraordinary proportion, one that would never be seen again as the manning of the fleet continued. Not only that, but more than half the men had seen service in men o' war before the Peace of Amiens. They were not only seamen, but Royal Navy seamen, who had hardly had time to make more than a single voyage in the merchant navy during the peace before being pressed again. Consequently most of them had had experience with ship's guns; twenty or thirty of them had actually seen action. The result was that when the gun exercise was ordered they went to their stations in business-like fashion. Bush turned to Hornblower and touched his hat awaiting the next order.

'Thank you, Mr Bush. Order "silence," if you please.'

The whistles pealed round the deck, and the ship fell deathly still.

'I shall now inspect, if you will be so kind as to accompany me, Mr Bush.'

'Aye aye, sir.'

Hornblower began by glowering down at the starboard-side quarter-deck carronade. Everything was in order there, and he walked down into the waist to inspect the starboard-side nine-pounders. At each he stopped to look over the equipment. Cartridge, crowbar, hand-spike. Sponge, quoin. He passed on from gun to gun.

'What's your station if the larboard guns are being worked?'

He had picked for questioning the youngest seaman visible, who moved uneasily from one foot to another finding himself addressed by the captain.

'Stand to attention, there!' bellowed Bush.

'What's your station?' repeated Hornblower, quietly.

'O – over there, sir. I handle the rammer, sir.'

'I'm glad you know. If you can remember your station when the captain and the first lieutenant are speaking to you I can trust you to remember it when round-shot are coming in through the side.'

Hornblower passed on; a captain could always be sure of raising a laugh if he made a joke. Then he halted again.

'What's this? Mr Cheeseman!'

'Sir.'

'You have an extra powder-horn here. There should be only one for every two guns.'

'Er – yessir. It's because—'

'I know the reason. A reason's no excuse, though, Mr Cheeseman. Mr Orrock! What powder-horns have you in your section? Yes, I see.'

Shifting No. 3 gun aft had deprived Orrock's section of a powder-horn and given and additional one to Cheeseman's.

'It's the business of you young gentlemen to see that the guns in your section are properly equipped. You don't have to wait for orders.'

Cheeseman and Orrock were two of the four 'young gentlemen' sent on board from the Naval College to be trained as midshipmen. Hornblower liked nothing he had seen as yet of any of them. But they were what he had to use as petty officers, and for his own sake he must train them into becoming useful lieutenants – his needs corresponded with his duty. He must make them and not break them.

'I'm sure I won't have to speak to you young gentlemen again,' he said. He was sure he would, but a promise was better than a threat. He walked on, completing the inspection of the guns on the starboard-side. He went up to the forecastle to look at the two carronades there, and then back down the main-deck guns of the port side. He stopped at the marine stationed at the forehatchway.

'What are your orders?'

The marine stood stiffly at attention, feet at an angle of forty-five degrees, musket close in at his side, forefinger of the left hand along the seam of his trousers, neck rigid in its stock, so that, as Hornblower was not directly in front of him, he stared over Hornblower's shoulder.

'To guard my post—' he began, and continued in a monotonous sing-song, repeating by rote the sentry's formula which he had probably uttered a thousand times before. The change in his tone was marked when he reached the final sentence added for this particular station – 'To allow no one to go below unless he is carrying an empty cartridge bucket.'

That was so that cowards could not take refuge below the water-line.

'What about men carrying wounded?'

The astonished marine found it hard to answer; he found it hard to think after years of drill.

'I have no orders about them, sir,' he said at last, actually allowing his eyes, though not his neck, to move.

Hornblower glanced at Bush.

'I'll speak to the sergeant of marines, sir,' said Bush.

'Who's on the quarter-bill to attend to the wounded?'

'Cooper and his mate, sir. Sailmaker and his mate. Four altogether, sir.'

Trust Bush to have all those details at his fingers' ends, even though Hornblower had found two small points to find fault with, for which Bush was ultimately responsible. No need to stress those matters with Bush – he was burning with silent shame.

Down the hatchway to the magazine. A candle glimmered faintly through the glass window of the light-room, throwing just enough light for powder boys to see what they were doing as they received loaded cartridges through the double serge curtains opening into the magazine; inside the magazine the gunner and his mate, wearing list slippers, were ready to pass out, and, if necessary, fill cartridges. Down the after hatchway to where the surgeon and his lob-lolly boy were ready to deal with the wounded. Hornblower knew that he himself might at some time be dragged in here with blood streaming from some shattered limb – it was a relief to ascend to the main-deck again.

'Mr Foreman,' – Foreman was another of the 'young gentlemen' – 'what are your orders regarding lanterns during a night action?'

'I am to wait until Mr Bush expressly orders them, sir.'

'And who do you send if you receive those orders?'

'Firth, sir.'

Foreman indicated a likely-looking young seaman at his elbow. But was there perhaps the slightest moment of hesitation about that reply? Hornblower turned on Firth.

'Where do you go?'

Firth's eyes flickered towards Foreman for a moment. That might be with embarrassment; but Foreman swayed a little on his feet, as if he were pointing with his shoulder, and one hand made a small sweeping gesture in front of his middle, as if he might be indicating Mr Wise's abdominal rotundity.

'For'rard, sir,' said Firth. 'The bos'n issues them. At the break of the fo'c'sle.'

'Very well,' said Hornblower.

He had no doubt that Foreman had quite forgotten to pass on Bush's orders regarding battle lanterns. But Foreman had been quick-witted enough to remedy the situation, and Firth had not merely been quick-witted but also loyal enough to back up his petty officer. It would be well to keep an eye on both those two, for various reasons. The break of the forecastle had been an inspired guess, as being adjacent to the bos'n's locker.

Hornblower walked up on to the quarter-deck again, Bush following him, and he cast a considering eye about him, taking in the last uninspected gun – the port-side quarter-deck carronade. He selected a position where the largest possible number of ears could catch his words.

'Mr Bush,' he said, 'we have a fine ship. If we work hard we'll have a fine crew too. If Boney needs a lesson we'll give it to him. You may continue with the exercises.'

'Aye aye, sir.'

The six marines on the quarter-deck, the helmsman, the carronades' crews, Mr Prowse and the rest of the afterguard had all heard him. He had felt it was not the time for a formal speech, but he could be sure his words would be relayed round the ship during the next dog watch. And he had chosen them carefully. That 'we' was meant as a rallying call. Meanwhile Bush was continuing with the exercise. 'Cast loose your guns. Level your guns. Take out your tompions,' and all the rest of it.

'We'll have them in shape soon enough, sir,' said Bush. 'Then we'll only have to get alongside the enemy.'

'Not necessarily alongside, Mr Bush. When we come to burn powder at the next exercise I want the men schooled in firing at long range.'

'Yes, sir. Of course,' agreed Bush.

But that was lip-service only on Bush's part. He had not really thought about the handling of *Hotspur* in battle – close action, where the guns could not miss, and only needed to be loaded and fired as rapidly as possible, was Bush's ideal. Very well for a ship of the line in a fleet action, but perhaps not so suitable for *Hotspur*. She was only a sloop of war, her timbers and her scantlings more fragile even than those of a frigate. Her twenty nine-pounders that gave her 'rate' – the four carronades not being counted – were 'long guns,' better adapted for work at a couple of cables' lengths than for close action when the enemy's guns stood no more chance of missing than hers did. She was the smallest thing with three masts and quarter-deck and forecastle in the Navy List. The odds were heavy that any enemy she might meet would be her superior in size, in weight of metal, in number of men – probably immeasurably her superior. Dash and courage might snatch a victory for her, but skill and forethought and good handling might be more certain. Hornblower felt the tremor of action course through him, accentuated by the vibrating rumble of the guns being run out.

'Land ho! Land ho!' yelled the look-out of the fore-topmast head. 'Land one point on the lee bow!'

That would be France, Ushant, the scene of their future exploits, perhaps where they would meet with disaster or death. Naturally there was a wave of excitement through the ship. Heads were raised and faces turned.

'Sponge your guns!' bellowed Bush through his speaking-trumpet. Bush could be relied on to maintain discipline and good order through any distraction. 'Load!'

It was hard for the men to go through the play-acting of gun drill in these circumstances; discipline on the one side, resentment, disillusionment on the other.

'Point your guns! Mr Cheeseman! The hand-spike man on No. 7 gun isn't attending to his duty. I want his name.'

Prowse was training a telescope forward; as the officer responsible for navigation that was his duty, but it was also his privilege.

'Run your guns in!'

Hornblower itched to follow Prowse's example, but he restrained himself; Prowse would keep him informed of anything vital. He allowed the drill to go on through one more mock broadside before he spoke.

'Mr Bush, you may secure the guns now, thank you.'

'Aye aye, sir.'

Prowse was offering his telescope.

'That's the light-tower on Ushant, sir,' he said.

Hornblower caught a wavering glimpse of the thing, a gaunt framework topped by a cresset, where the French government in time of peace maintained a light for the benefit of the ships – half the world's trade made a landfall off Ushant – that needed it.

'Thank you, Mr Prowse.' Hornblower visualised the chart again; recalled the plans he had made in the intervals of commissioning his ship, in the intervals of his honeymoon, in the intervals of seasickness, during the past crowded days. 'Wind's drawing westerly. But it'll be dark before we can make Cape Matthew. We'll stand to the s'uth'ard under easy sail until midnight. I want to be a league off the Black Stones an hour before dawn.'

'Aye aye, sir.'

Bush joined them from the business of securing the guns.

'Look at that, sir! There's a fortune passing us by.'

A large ship was hull-up to windward, her canvas reflecting the westering sun.

'French Indiaman,' commented Hornblower, turning his glass on her.

'A quarter of a million pounds, all told!' raved Bush. 'Maybe a hundred thousand for you, sir, if only war were declared. Doesn't that tease you, sir? She'll carry this wind all the way to Havre and she'll be safe.'

'There'll be others,' replied Hornblower soothingly.

'Not so many, sir. Trust Boney. He'll send warnings out the moment he's resolved on war, and every French flag'll take refuge in neutral ports. Madeira and the Azores, Cadiz and Ferrol, while we could make our fortunes!'

The possibilities of prize money bulked large in the thoughts of every naval officer.

'Maybe we will,' said Hornblower. He thought of Maria and his allotment of pay; even a few hundreds of pounds would make a huge difference.

'Maybe, sir,' said Bush, clearly discounting the possibility.

'And there's another side to the picture,' added Hornblower, pointing round the horizon.

There were half a dozen other sails all visible at this time, all British. They marked the enormous extent of British maritime commerce. They bore the wealth that could support navies, sustain allies, maintain manufactories of arms – to say nothing of the fact that they provided the basic training for seamen who later would man the ships of war which kept the seas open for them and closed them to England's enemies.

'They're only British, sir,' said Prowse, wonderingly. He had not the vision to see what Hornblower saw. Bush had to look hard at his captain before it dawned upon him.

The heaving of the log, with the changing of the watch, relieved Hornblower of the temptation to preach a sermon.

'What's the speed, Mr Young?'

'Three knots and a half, sir.'

'Thank you.' Hornblower turned back to Prowse. 'Keep her on her present course.'

'Aye aye, sir.'

Hornblower was training his telescope out over the port bow. There was a black dot rising and falling out there towards Molene Island. He kept it under observation.

'I think, Mr Prowse,' he said, his glass still at his eye, 'we might edge in a little more inshore. Say two points. I'd like to pass that fishing-boat close.'

'Aye aye, sir.'

She was one of the small craft employed in the pilchard fishery, very similar to those seen off the Cornish coast. She was engaged at the moment in hauling in her seine; as *Hotspur* approached more closely the telescope made plain the rhythmical movements of the four men.

'Up with the helm a little more, Mr Prowse, if you please. I'd like to pass her closer still.'

Now Hornblower could make out a little area of water beside the fishing-boat that was of a totally different colour. It had a metallic sheen quite unlike the rest of the grey sea; the fishing-boat had found a shoal of pilchards and her seine was now closing in on it.

'Mr Bush. Please try to read her name.'

They were fast closing on her; within a few moments Bush could make out the bold white letters on her stern.

'From Brest, sir. *Duke's Freers.*'

With that prompting Hornblower could read the name for himself, the *Deux Frères*, Brest.

'Back the maintops'l, Mr Young!' bellowed Hornblower to the officer of the watch, and then, turning back to Bush and Prowse, 'I want fish for my supper tonight.'

They looked at him in ill-concealed surprise.

'Pilchards, sir?'

'That's right.'

The seine was close in alongside the *Deux Frères*, and masses of silver fish were being heaved up into her. So intent were the fishermen on securing their catch that they had no knowledge of the silent approach of the *Hotspur*, and looked up in ludicrous astonishment at the lovely vessel towering over them in the sunset. They even displayed momentary panic, until they obviously realised that in time of peace a British ship of war would do them less harm than a French one might, a French one enforcing the *Inscription Maritime*.

Hornblower took the speaking-trumpet from its beckets. He was pulsing with excitement now, and he had to be firm with himself to keep calm. This might be the first step in the making of the history of the future; besides, he had not spoken French for a considerable time and he had to concentrate on what he was going to say.

'Good day, captain!' he yelled, and the fishermen, reassured, waved back to him in friendly fashion. 'Will you sell me some fish?'

Hurriedly they conferred, and then one of them replied.

'How much?'

'Oh, twenty pounds.'

Again they conferred.

'Very well.'

'Captain,' went on Hornblower, searching in his mind not only for the necessary French words but also for an approach to bring about the situation he desired. 'Finish your work. Then come aboard. We can drink a glass of rum to the friendship of nations.'

The beginning of that sentence was clumsy, he knew, but he could not translate 'Get in your catch;' but the prospect of British navy rum he knew would be alluring – and he was a little proud of *l'amitié des nations*. What was the French for 'dinghy?' *Chaloupe,* he fancied. He expanded on his invitation, and someone in the fishing-boat waved in assent before bending to the business of getting in the catch. With the last of it on board two of the four men scrambled into the dinghy that lay alongside the *Deux Frères;* it was nearly as big as the fishing-boat itself, as was to be expected when she had to lay out the seine. Two oars stoutly handled brought the dinghy rapidly towards *Hotspur*.

'I'll entertain the captain in my cabin,' said Hornblower. 'Mr Bush, see that the other man is taken forward and well looked after. See he has a drink.'

'Aye aye, sir.'

A line over the side brought up two big buckets of fish, and these were followed by two blue-jerseyed men who scrambled up easily enough despite their sea-boots.

'A great pleasure, captain,' said Hornblower in the waist to greet him. 'Please come with me.'

The captain looked curiously about him as he was led up to the quarter-deck and aft to the cabin. He sat down cautiously in the only chair while Hornblower perched on the cot. The blue jersey and trousers were spangled with fish scales – the cabin would smell of fish for a week. Hewitt brought rum and water, and Hornblower poured two generous glasses; the captain sipped appreciatively.

'Has your fishing been successful?' asked Hornblower, politely.

He listened while the captain told him, in his almost unintelligible Breton French, about the smallness of the profits to be earned in the pilchard fishery. The conversation drifted on. It was an easy transition from the pleasures of peace to the possibilities of war – two seamen could hardly meet without that prospect being discussed.

'I suppose they make great efforts to man the ships of war?'

The captain shrugged.

'Certainly.'

The shrug told much more than the word.

'It marches very slowly, I imagine,' said Hornblower, and the captain nodded.

'But of course the ships are ready to take the sea?'

Hornblower had no idea of how to say 'laid-up in ordinary' in French, and so he had to ask the question in the opposite sense.

'Oh, no,' said the captain. He went on to express his contempt for the French naval authorities. There was not a single ship of the line ready for service. Of course not.

'Let me refill your glass, captain,' said Hornblower. 'I suppose the frigates receive the first supplies of men?'

Such supplies as there were, perhaps. The Breton captain was not sure. Of course there was – Hornblower had more than a moment's difficulty at this point. Then he understood. The frigate *Loire* had been made ready for sea last week (it was the Breton pronunciation of that name which had most puzzled Hornblower) for service in Far Eastern waters, but with the usual idiocy of the naval command had now been stripped of most of her trained men to provide nuclei for the other ships. The Breton captain, whose capacity for rum was quite startling, did nothing to conceal either the smouldering Breton resentment against the atheist régime now ruling France or the contempt of a professional user of the sea for the blundering policies of the Republican Navy. Hornblower had only to nurse his glass and listen, his faculties at full stretch to catch all the implications of a conversation in a foreign language. When at last the captain rose to say good-bye there was a good deal of truth in what Hornblower said, haltingly, about his regrets at the termination of the visit.

'Yet perhaps even if war should come, captain, we may still meet again. As I expect you know, the Royal Navy of Great Britain does not make war on fishing vessels. I shall always be glad to buy some of your catch.'

The Frenchman was looking at him keenly now, perhaps because the subject of payment was arising. This was a most important moment, calling for accurate judgement. How much? What to say?

'Of course I must pay for today's supply,' said Hornblower, his hand in his pocket. He took out two ten-franc pieces and dropped them into the horny palm, and the captain could not restrain an expression of astonishment from appearing in his weather-beaten face. Astonishment, followed instantly by avarice, and then by suspicion, calculation, and finally by decision as the hand clenched and hurried the money into a trouser-pocket. Those emotions had played over the captain's face like the colours of a dying dolphin. Twenty francs in gold, for a couple of buckets of pilchards; most

likely the captain supported himself, his wife and children for a week
on twenty francs. Ten francs would be a week's wage for his hands.
This was important money; either the British captain did not know
the value of gold or—. At least there was the indubitable fact that the
French captain was twenty francs richer, and there was at least the
possibility of more gold where this came from.

'I hope we shall meet again, captain,' said Hornblower. 'As of
course you understand, out here at sea we are always glad to have
news of what is happening on land.'

The two Bretons went over the side with their two empty buckets,
leaving Bush ruefully contemplating the mess left on the deck.

'That can be swabbed up, Mr Bush,' said Hornblower. 'It will be
a good ending to a good day.'

V

The cabin was quite dark when Hornblower awoke; there was not
even the glimmering of light through the two stern windows. He lay
curled on his side only half conscious, and then a single sharp note
from the ship's bell recalled him to the world, and he turned over on
his back and stretched himself, half fretfully and half luxuriously
trying to put his thoughts into order. That must be one bell in the
morning watch, because one bell in the middle watch had sounded
as he was getting back into bed after being roused when the ship was
put about at midnight. He had had six hours of sleep, even after
making allowance for that break; there were great advantages about
being in command of a ship; the watch which had retired to bed at
that time had been up on deck again for half an hour already.

The cot on which he lay was swaying easily and slowly. *Hotspur*
must be under very easy sail indeed, and, as far as he could judge,
with a moderate wind on the starboard beam. That was as it should
be. He would soon have to get up – he turned on to his other side and
went to sleep again.

'Two bells, sir,' said Grimes, entering the cabin with a lighted
lamp. 'Two bells, sir. Bit of haze, and Mr Prowse says he'd like to
go about on the other tack.' Grimes was a weedy young seaman who
affirmed that he had acted as captain's steward in a West India
packet.

'Get me my coat,' said Hornblower.

It was cold in the misty dawn, with only a greatcoat on over his nightshirt. Hornblower found Maria's gloves in a pocket and pulled them on gratefully.

'Twelve fathoms, sir,' reported Prowse as the ship steadied on her new course with the lead going in the forechains.

'Very well.'

There was time to dress, there was time to have breakfast. There was time for – Hornblower felt a wave of temptation breaking round him. He wanted a cup of coffee. He wanted two or three cups of coffee, strong and scalding hot. Yet he had on board no more than two pounds of coffee. At seventeen shillings a pound that was all he had been able to afford to buy. The miraculous forty-five pounds had melted away which he had won at whist the night before the appearance of the King's message regarding the fleet. There had been his sea-going clothing and his sword to get out of pawn, his cabin furniture to buy, and he had had to leave seventeen pounds with Maria for her support until she could draw his allotment of pay. So there had been little enough left over for 'captain's stores'. He had not bought a sheep or a pig; not a single chicken. Mrs Mason had bought six dozen eggs for him – they were packed in shavings in a tub lashed to the deck in the chart room – and six pounds of heavily salted butter. There was a loaf of sugar and some pots of jam, and then the money had run out. He had no bacon, no potted meat. He had dined yesterday on pilchards – the fact that they had been bought with secret service money was some kind of sauce for them, but pilchards were unattractive fish. And of course there was the absurd prejudice of seamen regarding fish, creatures from their own element. They hated having their eternal round of salt beef and pork interrupted by a meal of fish – allowance must be made, of course, for the fact that the cooking of fish left behind a lingering scent, hard to eradicate from utensils sketchily washed in seawater. At this very moment, in the growing dawn, one of the lambs netted down in the boat chocked in the waist emitted a lingering baa-aaa as it woke. The wardroom officers had invested in four of the creatures while the *Hotspur* was commissioning, and any day now they would be dining on roast lamb – Hornblower determined to get himself invited to dinner in the ward-room that day. The thought reminded him that he was hungry; but that was quite minor compared with his yearning for coffee.

'Where's my servant?' he suddenly roared. 'Grimes! Grimes!'

'Sir?'

Grimes put his head round the chart-room door.

'I'm going to dress, and I'll want my breakfast. I'll have coffee.'

'Coffee, sir?'

'Yes.' Hornblower bit off the 'damn you' he nearly added. To swear at a man who could not swear back and whose only offence lay in being unoffending was not to his taste, just as some men could not shoot foxes. 'You don't know anything about coffee?'

'No, sir.'

'Get the oak box and bring it in to me.'

Hornblower explained about coffee to Grimes while working up a lather with a quarter of a pint of fresh-water.

'Count out twenty of those beans. Put them in an open jar – get that from the cook. Then you toast 'em over the galley fire. And be careful with 'em. Keep shaking 'em. They've got to be brown, not black. Toasted, not burnt. Understand?'

'Well, yes, sir.'

'Then you take 'em to the surgeon, with my compliments.'

'The surgeon? Yes, sir.' Grimes, seeing Hornblower's brows come together like thunderclouds, had the sense to suppress in the nick of time his astonishment at the entry of the surgeon's name into this conversation.

'He has a pestle and mortar to pound his jalap with. You pound those beans in that mortar. You break 'em up small. Small, mark you, but you don't make dust of 'em. Like large grain gunpowder, not mealed gunpowder. Understand?'

'Yes, sir. I suppose so, sir.'

'Next you – oh go and get that done and then report to me again.'

Grimes was clearly not a man to do things quickly. Hornblower had shaved and dressed and was pacing the quarter-deck, raging for his breakfast, before Grimes appeared again with a panful of dubious powder. Hornblower gave him brief instructions on how to make coffee with it, and Grimes listened doubtfully.

'Go and get it done. Oh, and Grimes!'

'Sir?'

'I'll have two eggs. Fried. Can you fry eggs?'

'Er – yes, sir.'

'Fry 'em so the yolk's nearly hard but not quite. And get out a crock of butter and a crock of jam.'

Hornblower was throwing discretion to the winds; he was determined on a good breakfast. And those winds to which he had thrown discretion suddenly asserted themselves. With hardly a warning puff there was a sudden gust which almost took *Hotspur* aback, and with it, while *Hotspur* paid off and recovered herself, there came driving rain, an April shower, icy cold. Hornblower shook off Grimes the first time he appeared to report that breakfast was ready, and only went off with him on his second appearance, after *Hotspur* was steady on her course again. With the weather clearing and daylight growing there was little time he could spare.

'I'll be on deck again in ten minutes, Mr Young,' he said.

The chart-room was a minute compartment beside his cabin – cabin, chart-room, and the captain's pantry and head occupied the whole space of the *Hotspur's* tiny poop. Hornblower squeezed himself into the chair at the little table.

'Sir,' said Grimes. 'You didn't come when breakfast was ready.'

Here were the eggs. The rim of the whites was black; the yolks were obviously hard.

'Very well,' growled Hornblower. He could not blame Grimes for that.

'Coffee, sir?' said Grimes. With the chart-room door shut he was wedged against it hardly able to move. He poured from a jug into a cup, and Hornblower sipped. It was only just hot enough to drink, which meant that it was not hot enough, and it was muddy.

'See that it's hotter than this another time,' said Hornblower. 'And you'll have to strain it better than this.'

'Yes, sir.' Grimes voice seemed to come from a great distance. The man could hardly whisper. 'Sir—'

Hornblower looked up at him; Grimes was cold with fright.

'What is it?'

'I kept these to show you, sir.' Grimes produced a pan containing a bloody and stinking mess. 'The first two eggs was bad, sir. I didn't want you to think—'

'Very well.' Grimes was afraid in case he should be accused of stealing them. 'Take the damned things away.'

Now was it not exactly like Mrs Mason to buy eggs for him of which half were bad? Hornblower ate his unpleasant eggs – even these two, although not exactly bad, were flavoured – while reconciling himself with the prospect of making up for it all with the jam. He spread a biscuit with the precious butter, and here was the jam. Blackcurrant! Of all the misguided purchases! Grimes, squeezing back into the chart-room, positively jumped as Hornblower let out the oath that had been seeking an outlet for several minutes.

'Sir?'

'I'm not speaking to you, damn you,' said Hornblower, his restraint at an end.

Hornblower was fond of jam, but of all the possible varieties he liked blackcurrant least. It was a poor last best. Well, it would have to do; he bit at the iron-hard biscuit.

'Don't knock at the door when you're serving a meal,' he said to Grimes.

'No, sir. I won't sir. Not any more, sir.'

Grimes's hand holding the coffeepot was shaking, and when Hornblower looked up he could see that his lips were trembling too. He was about to ask sharply what was the matter, but he suppressed the question as the answer became apparent to him. It was physical fear that was affecting Grimes. A word from Hornblower could have Grimes bound to a grating at the gangway, there to have the flesh flogged from the bones of his writhing body. There were captains in the navy who would give just that order when served with such a breakfast. There would never be a time when more things went wrong than this.

There was a knocking at the door.

'Come in!'

Grimes shrank against the bulkhead to avoid falling out through the door as it opened.

'Message from Mr Young, sir,' said Orrock. 'Wind's veering again.'

'I'll come,' said Hornblower.

Grimes cowered against the bulkhead as he pushed his way out; Hornblower emerged on to the quarter-deck. Six dozen eggs, and half of them bad. Two pounds of coffee – far less than a month's supply if he drank coffee every day. Blackcurrant jam, and not much even of that. Those were the thoughts coursing through his mind as he walked past the sentry, and then they were expunged by the blessed air from the sea, and the instant approach of professional problems.

Prowse was peering out to port through his telescope; it was almost full daylight, and the haze had dissipated with the rain.

'Black Stones broad on the port-beam, sir,' reported Prowse. 'You can see the breakers sometimes.'

'Excellent,' said Hornblower. At least his breakfast troubles had kept him from fretting during these final minutes before entering on to a decisive day. In fact he had actually to pause for several seconds to collect his thoughts before issuing the orders that would develop the plans already matured in his fevered mind.

'Do you have good eyesight, Mr Orrock?'

'Well, sir—'

'Have you or haven't you?'

'Well, yes, sir.'

'Then take a glass and get aloft. See what you can see of the shipping as we pass the entrance to the roadstead. Consult with the lookout.'

'Aye aye, sir.'

'Good morning, Mr Bush. Call the hands.'

'Aye aye, sir.'

Not for the first time Hornblower was reminded of the centurion in the New Testament who illustrated his authority by saying: 'I say to one, come, and he cometh, and to another, go, and he goeth.' The Royal Navy and the Roman Army were identical in discipline.

'Now, Mr Prowse. How far is the horizon now?'

'Two miles, sir. Perhaps three miles,' answered Prowse, looking round and collecting his thoughts after being taken by surprise by the question.

'Four miles, I should think,' said Hornblower.

'Maybe, sir,' admitted Prowse.

'Sun's rising. Air's clearing. It'll be ten miles soon. Wind's north of west. We'll go down to the Parquette.'

'Aye aye, sir.'

'Mr Bush, get the topgallants in, if you please. And the courses. Tops'ls and jib's all we need.'

'Aye aye, sir.'

That way they would attract less notice; also they would, by moving more slowly, have longer for observation as they crossed the passage that led into Brest.

'Sunset on a clear day,' said Hornblower to Prowse. 'Would be a better moment. Then we could look in with the sun behind us.'

'Yes, sir. You're right, sir,' answered Prowse. There was a gleam of appreciation in his melancholy face as he said this; he knew, of course, that the Goulet lay almost east and west, but he had not made any deductions or plans on that basis.

'But we're here. We have this chance. Wind and weather serve us now. It may be days before we have another opportunity.'

'Yes, sir,' said Prowse.

'Course east by south, Mr Prowse.'

'Aye aye, sir.'

Hotspur crept along. The day was cloudy but clear, and the horizon was extending every minute. There was the mainland of France, Pointe St Mathieu – Point Matthew – in plain view. From there the land trended away out of sight again.

'Land on the lee bow!' yelled Orrock from the foretopmast-head.

'That'll be the other headland, sir,' said Prowse.

'Toulinguet,' agreed Hornblower and then he corrected his pronunciation of 'Toolingwette.' For months or years to come he might be beating about this coast, and he wanted no chance of misunderstanding with any of his officers when he gave orders.

Between those two headlands the Atlantic broke in through the wild Breton coast and reached deep inland to form the roadstead of Brest.

'Can you make out the channel yet, Mr Orrock?' yelled Hornblower.

'Not yet, sir. At least, not very well.'

A ship of war – a King's ship – approaching a foreign coast was under a handicap on this sort of mission in peacetime. She could not enter into foreign territorial waters (except under stress of weather) without permission previously asked and obtained; she certainly could not trespass within the limits of a foreign naval base without occasioning a series of angry notes between the respective governments.

'We must keep out of long cannon shot of the shore,' said Hornblower.

'Yes, sir. Oh yes, of course, sir,' agreed Prowse.

The second more hearty agreement was called forth when Prowse realised the implications of what Hornblower was saying. Nations asserted sovereignty over all the waters that could be dominated by their artillery, even if there was no cannon mounted at any particular point. In fact international law was hardening into a convention fixing an arbitrary limit of three miles.

'Deck!' yelled Orrock. 'I can see masts now. Can just see 'em.'

'Count all you can see, very carefully, Mr Orrock.'

Orrock went on with his report. He had an experienced sailor beside him at the masthead, but Hornblower, listening, had no intention of trusting entirely to their observation, and Bush was fuming with impatience.

'Mr Bush,' said Hornblower. 'I'll be wearing ship in fifteen minutes. Would you be so kind as to take a glass to the mizzen topmast-head? You'll have a good chance of seeing all that Orrock's seeing. Please take notes.'

'Aye aye, sir,' said Bush.

He was at the mizzen shrouds in a moment. Soon he was running up the ratlines at a speed that would have been a credit to any young seaman.

'That makes twelve of the line, sir,' yelled Orrock. 'No topmasts hoisted. No yards crossed.'

The seaman beside him interrupted his report.

'Breakers on the lee bow!'

'That's the Parquette,' said Hornblower.

The Black Stones on the one side, the Parquette on the other, and, farther up, the Little Girls in the middle, marked off the passage into Brest. On a clear day like this, with a gentle wind, they were no menace, but lives by the hundred had been lost on them during storms. Prowse was pacing restlessly back and forward to the binnacle taking bearings. Hornblower was carefully gauging the direction of the wind. If the French squadron had no ship of the line ready for sea there was no need to take risks. A shift in the wind might soon find *Hotspur* embayed on a lee shore. He swept his glass round the wild coast that had grown up round his horizon.

'Very well, Mr Prowse. We'll wear ship now, while we can still weather the Parquette.'

'Aye aye, sir.'

Prowse's relief was obvious. His business was to keep the ship out of danger, and he clearly preferred a wide margin of safety. Hornblower looked round at the officer of the watch.

'Mr Poole! Wear the ship, if you please.'

The pipes shrilled and the orders were passed. Hands went to the braces as the helm was put up while Hornblower scanned the shore warily.

'Steady as you go!'

Hotspur settled sweetly on her new course. Hornblower was growing intimate with her ways, like a bridegroom learning about his bride. No, that was an unlucky simile, to be discarded instantly. He hoped that he and *Hotspur* were better suited to each other than he and Maria. And he must think about something else.

'Mr Bush! Mr Orrock! You will please come down when you are sure you will see nothing more useful.'

The ship was alive with a new atmosphere; Hornblower was sensitively aware of it as the hands went about their duties. Everyone on board was conscious that they were bearding Boney in his den, that they were boldly looking into the principal naval base of France, proclaiming the fact that England was ready to meet any challenge at sea. High adventure was looming up in the near future. Hornblower had the gratifying feeling that during these past days he had tempered a weapon ready for his hand, ship and ship's company ready for any exploit, like a swordsman knowing well the weight and balance of his sword before entering upon a duel.

Orrock appeared, touching his hat, and Hornblower listened to his report. It was fortunate that Bush in the mizzentop still had a view up the Goulet and had not descended; reports should be made independently, each officer out of the hearing of the other, but it would have been tactless to ask Bush to stand aside. Bush did not descend for several more minutes; he had methodically taken notes with paper and pencil, but Orrock could hardly be blamed for not having done so. The thirteen or fourteen ships of the line at anchor in the Roads were none of them ready for sea and three of them were missing at least one mast each. There were six frigates, three with their topmast sent up and one with her yards crossed and sails furled.

'That will be the *Loire*,' commented Hornblower to Bush.

'You know about her, sir?' asked Bush.

'I know she's there,' answered Hornblower. He would gladly have explained further, but Bush was going on with his report, and Hornblower was content to have something more added to his reputation for omniscience.

On the other hand, there was considerable activity in the roadstead. Bush had seen lighters and tenders moving about, and believed he had identified a sheer hulk, a vessel rigged solely for the purpose of putting new masts into large ships.

'Thank you, Mr Bush,' said Hornblower. 'That is excellent. We must look in like this every day if possible.'

'Yes, sir.'

Constant observation would increase their information in geometrical progression – ships changing anchorage, ships sending up topmasts, ships setting up their rigging. The changes would be more significant than anything that could be deduced from a single inspection.

'Now let's find some more fishing boats,' went on Hornblower.

'Yes, sir.'

Bush trained his glass out towards the Parquette, whose sullen black rocks, crowned by a navigation beacon, seemed to rise and fall as the Atlantic swell surged round them.

'There's one in the lee of the reef there, sir,' said Bush.

'What's he doing there?'

'Lobster pots, sir,' reported Bush. 'Getting in his catch, I should say, sir.'

'Indeed?'

Twice in his life Hornblower had eaten lobster, both occasions being during those bleak bitter days when under the compulsion of hunger and cold he had acted as a professional gambler in the Long Rooms. Wealthy men there had called for supper, and had tossed him an invitation. It was a shock to realise that it was only a fortnight ago that that horrible period in his life had ended.

'I think,' said Hornblower, slowly, 'I should like lobster for my supper tonight. Mr Poole! Let her edge down a little towards the reef. Mr Bush, I would be obliged if you would clear away the quarter-boat ready for launching.'

The contrast between these days and those was quite fantastic. These were golden April days; a strange limbo between peace and war. They were busy days, during which Hornblower had friendly chats with fishing boats' captains and dispensed gold pieces in exchange for a small portion of their catch. He could drill his crew and he could take advantage of those exercises to learn all he could about the behaviour of the *Hotspur*. He could peep up the Goulet and measure the preparation of the French fleet for sea. He could study this Gulf of Iroise – the approaches to Brest, in other words – with its tides and its currents. By observing the traffic there he could obtain an insight into the difficulties of the French naval authorities in Brest.

Brittany was a poor province, neither productive nor well populated, at the extremity of France, and by land the communications between

Brest and the rest of the country were more inferior. There were no navigable rivers, no canals. The enormously ponderous materials to equip a fleet could never be brought to Brest by road. The artillery for a first-rate weighed two hundred tons; guns and anchors and shot could only be brought by sea from the foundries in Belgium round to the ships in Brest. The mainmast of a first-rate was a hundred feet long and three feet thick; only ships could transport those, in fact only ships specially equipped.

To man the fleet that lay idle in Brest would call for twenty thousand men. The seamen – what seamen there were – would have to march hundreds of miles from the merchant ports of Le Havre and Marseille if they were not sent round by sea. Twenty thousand men needed food and clothing, and highly specialised food and clothing moreover. The flour to make biscuit, the cattle and pigs and the salt to salt them down, and the barrel-staves in which to store them – where were they to come from? And provisioning was no day-to-day, hand-to-mouth operation, either. Before going to sea the ships would need rations for a hundred days – two million rations to be accumulated over and above daily consumption. Coasting vessels by the hundred were needed – Hornblower observed a constant trickle of them heading into Brest, rounding Ushant from the north and the Pointe du Raz from the south. If war should come – when war should come – it would be the business of the Royal Navy to cut off this traffic. More particularly it would be the business of the light craft to do this – it would be *Hotspur's* business. The more he knew about all these conditions the better.

These were the thoughts that occupied Hornblower's mind as *Hotspur* stood in once more past the Parquette for a fresh look into Brest. The wind was south-easterly this afternoon, and *Hotspur* was running free – creeping along under topsails – with her look-outs posted at her mastheads in the fresh morning sunshine. From foremast and mizzenmast came two successive hails.

'Deck! There's a ship coming down the channel!'

'She's a frigate, sir!' That was Bush supplementing Cheeseman's report.

'Very well,' hailed Hornblower in return. Maybe the appearance of the frigate had nothing to do with his own evolutions in the Iroise, but the contrary was much more likely. He glanced round the ship; the hands were engaged in the routine of holystoning the decks, but he could effect a transformation in five minutes. He could clear for action or he could set all sail at a moment's notice.

'Steady as you go,' he growled at the quartermaster. 'Mr Cargill, we'll hoist our colours, if you please.'

'There she is, sir,' said Prowse. The glass showed a frigate's topgallant sails; she was reaching down the Goulet with a fair wind, on a course that would intersect *Hotspur's* some miles ahead.

'Mr Bush! I'd like you on deck, if you please, as soon as you have completed your observations.'

'Aye aye, sir.'

Hotspur stole quietly along; there was no purpose in hurriedly setting additional sail and pretending to be innocent – the French fleet must have heard from a dozen sources about her continued presence in the approaches.

'You're not going to trust 'em, sir?' This was from Bush, back on the quarter-deck and in a state of some anxiety; the anxiety was not displayed by any change in Bush's imperturbable manner, but by the very fact that he volunteered advice in this positive form.

Hornblower did not want to run away. He had the weather gauge, and in a moment he could set all sail and come to the wind and stand out to sea, but he did not want to. He could be quite sure that if he were to do so the frigate would follow his example and chase him, ignominiously, out into the Atlantic with his tail between his legs. A bold move would stimulate his crew, would impress the French and – this was the point – would subdue his own doubts about himself. This was a test. His instinct was to be cautious; but he told himself that his caution was probably an excuse for cowardice. His judgement told him that there was no need for caution; his fears told him that the French frigate was planning to lure him within range of her guns and then overwhelm him. He must act according to his judgement and he must abhor the counsel of his fears, but he wished his heart would not beat so feverishly, he wished his palms would not sweat nor his legs experience these pins-and-needles feelings. He wished Bush were not crowding him at the hammock netting, so that he might take a few paces up and down the quarter-deck, and then he told himself that he could not possibly at this moment pace up and down and reveal to the world that he was in a state of indecision.

Today coasters had been swarming out of Brest, taking advantage of the fair wind; if war had been declared they would have been doing nothing of the sort. He had spoken to three different fishing boats, and from none of them had he received a hint of war – they might all have been taking part in a conspiracy to lull him into a sense of security, but that was most unlikely. If news of war had reached Brest only an hour ago the frigate could never have prepared herself for sea and come down the Goulet in this time. And to support his judgement from the other direction was the thought that the French naval authorities, even if war was not declared, would act in just this way. Hearing of the audacious British sloop cruising outside they would find men enough for the frigate by stripping other ships of their skeleton crews and would send her out to scare the British ship away. He must not be scared away; this wind could easily persist for days, and if he once ran down to leeward it would be a long time before he could beat back and resume his observation of Brest.

The frigate was hull-up now; through his glass he could see her down to the waterline. She was big; there were her painted ports, twenty of them a side besides the guns on quarter-deck and fore-castle. Eighteen-pounders, probably; she had not merely twice as many guns as *Hotspur* but would discharge a weight of broadside four times as great. But her guns were not run out, and then Hornblower raised his glass to study her yards. He strained his eyes; this time he must not only trust his judgement but his eyesight. He was sure of what he saw. Fore-yard and fore-topsail-yard, main-yard and main-topsail-yard; they were not supported by chain slings. If the frigate were ready for action they would never have omitted that precaution. She could not be planning to fight; this could not be an ambush.

'Any orders, sir?' asked Bush.

Bush would have liked to clear for action, to open the ports and run out the guns. If anything could precipitate hostilities it would be that, and Hornblower remembered how his orders from Cornwallis, both written and oral, had stressed the necessity to do nothing that would bring on England the odium of starting a war.

'Yes,' said Hornblower in reply to Bush's question, but the relief that showed instantly in Bush's expression changed back into concern as he noted the gleam in Hornblower's eyes.

'We must render passing honours, Mr Bush,' said Hornblower. There was something madly stimulating in forcing himself to be coldly formal when internally he was boiling with excitement. That must be what went on inside one of Mr Watt's steam engines when the safety valve did not function.

'Aye aye, sir,' said Bush; the disciplined answer, the only answer when a superior officer spoke.

'Do you remember the procedure, Mr Bush?'

Never in his life had Hornblower rendered honours to a French ship of war; through his whole professional career until now sighting had meant fighting.

'Yes, sir.'

'Then be so good as to give the orders.'

'Aye aye, sir. All hands! All hands! Man the side! Mr Wise! See that the men keep order. Sergeant of marines! Parade your men on the quarter-deck! Smartly now. Drummer on the right. Bos'n's mates! Stand by to pipe on the beat of the drum.' Bush turned to Hornblower. 'We've no music, sir, except the drum and the pipes.'

'They won't expect more,' said Hornblower, his eye still at his glass. One sergeant, one corporal, twelve privates and a drummer were all the marines allotted to a sloop of war, but Hornblower was not devoting any further thought to the marines. His whole attention was concentrated on the French frigate. No doubt on the Frenchman's deck a dozen glasses were being trained on the *Hotspur*. As the bustle began on the *Hotspur's* deck he could see a corresponding bustle on the Frenchman's. They were manning the side, an enormous crowd of them. Carried by the water came the noise as four hundred excited Frenchmen took up their stations.

'Silence!' ordered Bush at that very moment. There was a certain strangeness about his voice as he continued, because he did not want his words to be overheard in the Frenchman, and so he was endeavouring to bellow *sotto voce*. 'Show the Frogs how a British crew behaves. Heads up, there, and keep still.'

Blue coats and white breeches; these were French soldiers forming up on the frigate's quarter-deck; Hornblower's glass detected the flash of steel as bayonets were fixed, and the gleam of brass from the musical instruments. The ships were closing steadily on their converging courses, with the frigate under her greater canvas drawing ahead of the sloop. Nearer and nearer. *Hotspur* was the visiting ship. Hornblower put away his telescope.

'Now,' he said.

'Drum!' ordered Bush.

The drummer beat a long roll.

'Present-arr-ums!' ordered the sergeant of marines, and in a much lower voice, 'One. Two. Three!'

The muskets of the marines and the half-pike of the sergeant came to the present in the beautiful movements of the prescribed drill. The pipes of the bos'n's mates twittered, long and agonisingly. Hornblower took off his hat and held it before his chest; the off-hand salute with hand to the brim was not for this occasion. He could see the French captain on his quarter-deck now, a bulky man, holding his hat over his head in the French fashion. On his breast gleamed a star, which must be this new-fangled Legion of Honour which Boney had instituted. Hornblower came back to reality; he had been the first to render the honours, and he must be the first to terminate them. He growled a word to Bush.

'Drum!' ordered Bush, and the long roll ended. With that the twittering of the pipes died away, a little more raggedly than Hornblower liked. On the French quarter-deck someone – the drum major, perhaps – raised a long staff hung with brass bells into the air and brought it down again with a thump. Instantly the drums rolled, half a dozen of them, a martial, thrilling sound, and then over the water came the sound of music, that incomprehensible blend of noises which Hornblower could never appreciate; the drum major's staff rose and fell rhythmically. At last the music stopped, with a final roll of the drums. Hornblower put on his hat, and the French captain did the same.

'Sl-o-o-ope arrums,' yelled the sergeant of marines.

'All hands! Dismiss!' yelled Bush, and then, reverting to his softer tone, 'Quietly, there! Silence!'

The hands were excited and prone to chatter with the order to dismiss – never in any of their lives, either, had they passed a French ship of war so close without guns firing. But Bush was determined to make the Frenchman believe that *Hotspur* was manned entirely by stoics. Wise with his rattan enforced the order, and the crew dispersed in an orderly mob, the good order only disturbed by a single quickly suppressed yelp as the rattan struck home on some rash posterior.

'She's the *Loire,* surely enough, sir,' said Bush. They could see the name entwined in gilded letters amid the scrollwork of the frigate's stern; Hornblower remembered that Bush still was in ignorance of his source of information. It was amusing to be thought omniscient, even without justification.

'And you were right, sir, not to run away from them,' went on Bush. Why was it so intolerable in this case to note the gleam of admiration in Bush's eyes? Bush did not know of the quickening heartbeats and the sweaty palms.

'It's given our fellows a close look at a Frenchman,' said Hornblower, uneasily.

'It certainly did that, sir,' agreed Bush. 'I never expected in all my life to hear that tune from a French frigate!'

'What tune?' asked Hornblower unguardedly, and was instantly furious with himself for this revelation of his weakness.

'God Save The King, sir,' answered Bush, simply. Luckily it never occurred to him that anyone could possibly fail to recognise the national anthem. 'If we'd had any music on board we'd have had to play their Marseillaise.'

'So we would,' said Hornblower; it was desperately necessary to change the subject. 'Look! He's getting in his topgallants. Quick! Time him! We'll see what sort of seamen they are.'

Now it was blowing a gale, a two-reef gale from the westward. The unbelievably fine weather of the past week had come to an end, and now the Atlantic was asserting itself in its usual fashion. Under her close-reefed topsails *Hotspur* was battling against it, close-hauled on the port-tack. She was presenting her port bow to the huge rollers that were advancing upon her, unimpeded in their passage over three thousand miles of water, from Canada to France. She would roll, lift, pitch, and then roll again. The tremendous pressure of the wind on her topsails steadied her to the extent that she hardly leaned over at all to windward; she would heel over to starboard, hang for a moment, and then come back to the vertical. But even with her roll restricted in this fashion, she was pitching extravagantly, and she was rising and falling bodily as each wave passed under her bottom, so that a man standing on her deck would feel the pressure of his feet on her planking increasing and diminishing as she ascended and dropped away again. The wind was shrieking in the rigging, and her fabric groaned as the varying strains worked on her, bending her lengthwise, upward in the centre first and then upward at the ends next. But that groaning was a reassuring sound; there were no sharp cracks or disorderly noises, and what could be heard was merely an indication that *Hotspur* was being flexible and sensible instead of being rigid and brittle.

Hornblower came out on to the quarter-deck. He was pallid with sea-sickness because the change of motion had found him out, but the attack had not been as severe as he had experienced during the run down-channel. He was muffled in his coat, and he had to support himself against the roll, for his sea-legs had not yet learned this advanced lesson. Bush appeared from the waist, followed by the boatswain; he touched his hat and then turned, with Wise beside him, to survey the ship in searching fashion.

'It's not until the first gale that you know what can carry away, sir,' said Bush.

Gear that seemed perfectly well secured would begin to show alarming tendencies to come adrift when submitted to the unpredictable strains of continued heavy weather, and Bush and Wise had just completed a long tour of inspection.

'Anything amiss?' asked Hornblower.

'Only trifles, sir, except for the stream anchor. That's secure again now.'

Bush had a grin on his face and his eyes were dancing; obviously he enjoyed this change of climate, this bustling of the wind, and the activity it called for. He rubbed his hands and breathed deep of the gale. Hornblower could console himself with the memory that there had been times when he had enjoyed dirty weather, and even the hope that there would be more, but as he felt at present, he bitterly told himself, it was a hollow memory and an empty hope.

Hornblower took his glass and looked about him. Momentarily the weather was fairly clear and the horizon at some distance. Far away on the starboard quarter the telescope picked up a flash of white; steadying himself as best he could he managed to catch it in the field again. That was the surf on Ar Men – curious Breton name, that – the most southerly and the most seaward of the rocks and reefs that littered the approaches to Brest. As he watched a fresh roller came in to catch the rock fully exposed. The surf burst upon it in a towering pillar of white water, reaching up as high as a first-rate's main-topsails, before the wind hurled it into nothingness again. Then a fresh squall hurtled down upon the ship bringing with it driving rain, so that the horizon closed in around them, and *Hotspur* became the centre of a tiny area of tossing grey sea, with the lowering clouds hardly clear of the mastheads.

She was as close in to that lee shore as Hornblower dared risk. A timid man would have gone out farther to sea at the first sign of bad weather, but then a timid man would be likely next to find himself with a shift of wind far away to leeward of the post he was supposed to be watching. Then whole days might pass before he could be back at his post – days when that wind would be fair for the French to do whatever they wanted, unobserved. It was as if there were a line drawn on the chart along with the parallels of longitude – rashness on the one side, boldness on the other, and Hornblower keeping to the very boundary of rashness. Now there was nothing further to do except – as always in the navy – to watch and wait. To battle with the gale with a wary eye noting every shift in the wind, to struggle northward on one tack and then to go about and struggle southward on the other, beating up and down outside Brest until he had a chance to risk a closer view again. So he had done all day yesterday, and so he would do for countless days to come should the threatening war break out. He went back into his cabin to conceal another flurry of sea-sickness.

Some time after the misery had in part subsided he was summoned by a thundering at the door.

'What is it?'

'Lookout's hailing from the masthead, sir. Mr Bush is calling him down.'

'I'll come.'

Hornblower emerged just in time to see the look-out transfer himself to the backstay and come sliding all the way down the deck.

'Mr Cargill,' said Bush. 'Send another hand aloft to take his place.' Bush turned to Hornblower.

'I couldn't hear what this man was saying, sir, thanks to the wind, so I called him down. Well, what d'you have to say?'

The look-out stood cap in hand, a little abashed at confronting the officers.

'Don't rightly know if it's important, sir, But during that last clear spell I caught a glimpse of the French frigate.'

'Where away?' demanded Hornblower; at the last moment before he spoke he had managed to modify his originally intended brusqueness. There was nothing to be gained and something to be lost by bullying this man.

'Two points on the lee bow, sir. She was hull-down but I could see her tops'ls, sir. I know 'em.'

Since the incident of the passing honours *Hotspur* had frequently sighted the *Loire* at various points in the Iroise channel – it had been a little like a game of hide-and-seek.

'What was her course?'

'She was close-hauled, sir, under double-reefed tops'ls, on the starboard-tack, sir.'

'You were quite right to report her. Get back to your post now. Keep that other man aloft with you.'

'Aye aye, sir.'

The man turned away and Hornblower gazed out to sea. Thick weather had closed round them again, and the horizon was close in. Was there anything odd about the *Loire's* coming out and braving the gale? She might well wish to drill her men in heavy weather. No; he had to be honest in his thinking, and that was a rather un-French notion. There was a very marked tendency in the French navy to conserve material in a miserly fashion.

Hornblower became aware that Bush was standing beside him waiting for him to speak.

'What do you think, Mr Bush?'

'I expect she anchored last night in Berthon Bay, sir.'

Bush was referring to Bertheaume Bay, just on the seaward side of the Goulet, where it was just possible to ride to a long cable with the wind anywhere to the north of west. And if she lay there she would be in touch with the shore. She could receive news and orders sent overland from Brest, ten miles away. She might have heard of a declaration of war. She might be hoping to take *Hotspur* by surprise, and he must act on that assumption. In that case the safest thing to do would be to put the ship about. Heading south on the starboard-tack he would have plenty of sea room, would be in no danger from a lee shore, and would be so far ahead of the *Loire* as to be able to laugh at pursuit. But – this was like Hamlet's soliloquy, at the point where Hamlet says 'There's the rub' – he would be far from his post when Cornwallis should arrive, absent perhaps for days. No, this was a case where he must risk his ship. *Hotspur* was only a trifle in the clash of two enormous navies. She was important to him personally, but the information she had gleaned was a hundred times more important than her fabric to Cornwallis.

'We'll hold our course, Mr Bush,' said Hornblower.

'She was two points on our lee bow, sir,' said Bush. 'We ought to be well to windward of her when we meet.'

Hornblower had already made that calculation; if the result had been different he would have put *Hotspur* about five minutes ago and would have been racing for safety.

'Clearing again a little, sir,' commented Bush, looking about him, and at that very moment the masthead yelled again.

'There she is, sir! One point before the starboard beam!'

'Very well!'

With the moderation of the squall it was just possible to carry on a conversation with the masthead from the deck.

'She's there all right, sir,' said Bush, training his glass.

As *Hotspur* lifted to a wave Hornblower saw her topsails, not very plainly. They were braced sharp round, presenting only their edge to his telescope. *Hotspur* was at least four miles to windward of her.

'Look! She's going about, sir!'

The topsails were broadening into oblongs; they wavered for a moment, and then settled down; they were braced round now parallel to the *Hotspur's* topsails; the two ships were now on the same tack.

'She went about the moment she was sure who we were, sir. She's still playing hide-and-seek with us.'

'Hide-and-seek? Mr Bush, I believe we are at war.'

It was hard to make that momentous statement in the quiet conversational tone that a man of iron nerve would employ; Hornblower did his best. Bush had no such inhibitions. He stared at Hornblower and whistled. But he could follow now the same lines of thought as Hornblower had already traced.

'I think you're right, sir.'

'Thank you, Mr Bush.' Hornblower said that spitefully, to his instant regret. It was not fair to make Bush pay for the tensions his captain had been experiencing; nor was it in accord with Hornblower's ideal of imperturbability to reveal that such tensions had existed. It was well that the next order to be given would most certainly distract Bush from any hurt he might feel.

'I think you had better send the hands to quarters, Mr Bush. Clear for action, but don't run out the guns.'

'Aye aye, sir!'

Bush's grin revealed his instant excitement. Now he was bellowing his orders. The pipes were twittering through the ship. The marine drummer came scrambling up from below. He was a child of no more than twelve, and his equipment was all higgledy-piggledy. He made not only a slap-dash gesture of coming to attention on the quarter-deck, he quite omitted the formal drill of raising the drum-sticks high before he began to beat the long roll, so anxious was he to begin.

Prowse approached; as acting-master his station in battle was on the quarter-deck beside his captain.

'She's broad on the starboard beam now, sir,' he said, looking over at the *Loire*. 'She took a long time to go about. That's what you'd expect.'

One of the factors that had entered into Hornblower's calculations was the fact that *Hotspur* would be quicker in stays than the *Loire*. Bush came up, touching his hat.

'Ship cleared for action, sir.'

'Thank you, Mr Bush.'

Now here was navy life epitomised in these few minutes. A moment of decision, of bustle, and excitement, and then – settle down to a long wait again. The two ships were thrashing along close-hauled, four miles apart. *Hotspur* almost dead to windward of the *Loire*. Those four miles, that direction of the wind, conferred immunity upon *Hotspur*. As long as she could preserve that distance she was safe. If she could not – if some accident occurred – then the *Loire's* forty eighteen-pounders would make short work of her. She could fight for honour, but with no hope of victory. Clearing for action was hardly more than a gesture; men would die, men would be horribly mutilated, but the result would be the same as if *Hotspur* had tamely surrendered.

'Who's at the wheel?' asked Prowse of nobody in particular, and he walked over to supervise the steering – perhaps his thoughts were running along those same lines.

The boatswain came rolling aft; as the warrant officer charged with the general supervision of sails and rigging he had no particular station in action, and was justified in moving about. But he was being very formal at the moment. He took off his hat to Bush, instead of merely touching it, and stood holding it, his pigtail thumping his shoulders in the gale. He must be asking permission to speak.

'Sir,' said Bush. 'Mr Wise is asking on behalf of the hands, sir. Are we at war?'

Yes? Or no?

'The Frogs know, and we don't – yet, Mr Wise.' There was no harm in a captain admitting ignorance when the reason for it should be perfectly clear as soon as the hands had time to consider the matter, as they would have. This might be the time to make a resplendent speech, but second thoughts assured Hornblower it was not. Yet Hornblower's instinct told him that the situation demanded something more than his last bald sentence.

'Any man in this ship who thinks there's a different way of doing his duty in peacetime is likely to have his back scratched, Mr Wise. Say that to the hands.'

That was sufficient for the occasion; Prowse was back again, squinting up at the rigging and gauging the behaviour of the ship.

'Do you think she could carry the main-topmast stays'l, sir?'

That was a question with many implications, but there was only one answer.

'No,' said Hornblower.

That staysail might probably give *Hotspur* a little more speed through the water. But it would lay her over very considerably, which along the additional area exposed to the wind would increase her leeway by an appreciable proportion. Hornblower had seen *Hotspur* in dry dock, knew the lines of the turn of her bilge, and could estimate the maximum angle at which she could retain her grip on the water. Those two factors would balance out, and there was a third one to turn the scale – any increase in the amount of canvas exposed would increase the chances of something carrying away. A disaster, petty or great, from the parting of a line to the loss of a topmast, would thrust *Hotspur* helplessly within range of the enemy's guns.

'If the wind moderates that's the first extra canvas I'll set,' went on Hornblower to modify the brusqueness of his refusal, and he added, 'Take note of how that ship bears from us.'

'I've done that, sir,' answered Prowse; a good mark to Prowse.

'Mr Bush! You may dismiss the watch below.'

'Aye aye, sir.'

This chase – this race – might continue for hours, even for days, and there was no purpose in fatiguing all hands prematurely. The gale developed a new gust within itself, hurling rain and spray across the deck; the *Loire* faded from sight again as he looked at her, while the *Hotspur* plunged and tossed like a toy boat as she battled against wind and wave.

'I wonder how many hands are sea-sick over there?' said Hornblower. He uttered that distasteful word in the same way that a man might tease a sore tooth.

'A good few, I dare say, sir,' answered Bush in a completely neutral tone.

'Call me when she's in sight again,' said Hornblower. 'Call me in any case of need, of course.'

He said these words with enormous dignity. Then it was an exhausting physical exercise to struggle aft again back into his cabin; his dizziness exaggerated the leaping of the deck under his feet, and the swing of his cot as he sank groaning across it. It was Bush himself who roused him later on.

'Weather's clearing, sir,' came Bush's voice through the cabin door, over the clamour of the storm.

'Very well. I'll come.'

A shadowy shape was already visible to starboard when he came out, and soon the *Loire* was revealed sharply as the air cleared. There she was, lying steeply over, yards braced up, her gun ports plain enough to be counted when she rose level again, spray bursting in clouds over her weather bow, and then, as she lay over again, a momentary glimpse, pinky-brown, of her copper bottom. Hornblower's eye told him something that Prowse and Bush put simultaneously into words.

'She's head-reaching on us!' said Bush.

'She's a full point for'rard of the beam now,' said Prowse.

The *Loire* was going faster through the water than *Hotspur*, gaining in the race to that extent. Everyone knew that French ship designers were cleverer than English ones; French ships were usually faster. But in this particular case it might mean tragedy. But there was worse news than this.

'I think, sir,' said Bush, slowly, as if each word caused him pain, 'she's weathering on us, too.'

Bush meant that the *Loire* was not yielding to the same extent as the *Hotspur* to the thrust of the wind down to leeward; relatively *Hotspur* was drifting down upon the *Loire,* closer to her guns. Hornblower, with a twinge of apprehension, knew that he was right. It would only be a question of time, if the present weather conditions persisted, before the *Loire* could open her ports and commence fire. So the simplest way of keeping out of trouble was denied him. If *Hotspur* had been the faster and the more weatherly of the two he could have maintained any distance he chose. His first line of defence was broken through.

'It's not to be wondered at,' he said. He tried to speak coldly, or nonchalantly, determined to maintain his dignity as captain. 'She's twice our size.'

Size was important when clawing to windward. The same waves

battered against small ships as against big ones, but they would push the small ships farther to leeward; moreover the keels of big ships reached down farther below the surface, farther below the turbulence, and maintained a better hold in the more tranquil water.

The three telescopes, as of one mind, trained out towards the *Loire*. 'She's luffing up a little,' said Bush.

Hornblower could see the *Loire's* topsails shiver momentarily. She was sacrificing some of her headway to gain a few yards to windward; having superior speed through the water she could afford to do so.

'Yes. We've drawn level with her again,' said Prowse.

That French captain knew his business. Mathematically, the best course to take when trying to close on a ship to windward was to keep the ship being chased right in the wind's eye, and that was where the *Hotspur* now found herself again, relative to the *Loire,* while the latter, resuming her former course, close-hauled, was twenty or thirty yards nearer to her in the direction of the wind. A gain of twenty or thirty yards, repeated often enough, and added to the steady gain resulting from being the more weatherly ship, would eventually close the gap.

The three telescopes came down from the three eyes, and Hornblower met the gaze of his two subordinates. They were looking to him to make the next move in this crisis.

'Call all hands, if you please, Mr Bush. I shall put the ship about.'

'Aye aye, sir.'

Here was a moment of danger. If *Hotspur* were mishandled she was lost. If she missed stays – as she once had done with Cargill handling her – she would lie dead in the water for minutes, sagging down to leeward with the *Loire* coming up fast upon her, while in this gale the sails might thrash themselves to ribbons leaving her more helpless still, even if nothing more vital carried away. The operation must be carried out to perfection. Cargill by coincidence was officer of the watch. He could be given the task. So might Bush, or Prowse. But Hornblower knew perfectly well that he could not tolerate the thought of anyone other than himself bearing the responsibility, whether in his own eyes or in those of the ship's company.

'I'm going to put the ship about, Mr Cargill,' he said, and that fixed the responsibility irrevocably.

He walked over the wheel, and stared round him. He felt the tension, he felt the beating of his heart, and noticed with momentary astonishment that this was pleasurable, that he was enjoying this moment of danger. Then he forced himself to forget everything except the handling of the ship. The hands were at their stations; every eye was on him. The gale shrieked past his ears as he planted his feet firmly and watched the approaching seas. This was the moment.

'Handsomely, now,' he growled to the hands at the wheel. 'Put your wheel down.'

There was a brief interval before *Hotspur* answered. Now her bow was turning.

'Helm's a-lee!' shouted Hornblower.

Headsail sheets and bowlines were handled, with Hornblower watching the behaviour of the ship like a tiger stalking its prey.

'Tacks and sheets!' and then turning back to the wheel. 'Now! Hard over!'

She was coming rapidly into the wind.

'Mains'l haul!' The hands were keyed up with the excitement of the moment. Bowlines and braces were cast off and the yards came ponderously round at the exact moment that *Hotspur* was pointing directly into the wind.

'Now! Meet her! Hard over!' snapped Hornblower to the wheel. *Hotspur* was turning fast, and still carrying so much way that the rudder could bite effectively, checking the swing before she could turn too far.

'Haul off all!'

The thing was done; *Hotspur* had gone from one tack to the other without the unnecessary loss of a second or a yard, thrashing along now with her starboard bow butting into the waves. But there was no time to feel relief or pleasure; Hornblower hurried to the port quarter to train his glass on the *Loire*. She was tacking naturally; the mathematics of the theory of the pursuit to windward demanded that the pursuer should tack at the same moment as the pursued. But she was bound to be a little late; her first inkling that *Hotspur* was about to tack would be when she saw her fore-topsail shiver, and even if *Loire* had all hands at their stations for going about the *Hotspur* would have two minutes' grace. And she was far slower in stays. Even now, when *Hotspur* was settled on the new tack with every inch of sail drawing, the *Loire's* fore-topsail was still shivering, her bows were still turning. The longer she took to go about the more distance she would lose in the race to windward.

'We've weathered on her, sir,' said Prowse, watching through his glass. 'Now we're head reaching on her.'

Hotspur had won back some of her precious lead, and Hornblower's second line of defence was proving at least stronger than his first.

'Take the bearing again,' ordered Hornblower.

Once settled on the new tack the *Loire's* natural advantages asserted themselves once more. She showed her extra speed and extra weatherliness; she drew up again from *Hotspur's* quarter to her beam; then she could luff up briefly and gain a little more to windward on the *Hotspur*. The minutes passed like seconds, an hour like a minute, as the *Hotspur* plunged along, with every man braced on the heeling deck and the wind shrieking.

'Time to go about again, sir?' asked Bush, tentatively and greatly daring, but the theoretically correct moment was passing.

'We'll wait a little longer,' said Hornblower. 'We'll wait for that squall.'

It was hurtling down wind upon them, and as it reached them the world was blotted out with driving rain. Hornblower turned from the hammock netting over which he was peering and climbed up the steep deck to the wheel. He took the speaking-trumpet.

'Stand by to go about.'

In the gusts that were blowing the crew could hardly hear what he said, but every eye was on him, everyone was alert, and, drilled as they were, they could not mistake his orders. It was a tricky business to tack while the squall prevailed, because the gusts were liable to veer a point or two, unpredictably. But the *Hotspur* was so handy – as long as the manoeuvre was well timed – that she had a good deal to spare for emergencies. The slight change in the wind's direction which threatened to take her aback was defeated because she still had sufficient steerage way and command to keep her swinging. The gust died away and the blinding chilly rain ceased while the hands were trimming all sharp, and the last of the squall drove off to leeward, still hiding the *Loire* from view.

'That's done him!' said Bush with satisfaction. He was revelling in the mental picture of the *Loire* still thrashing along on the one tack while the *Hotspur* was comfortably on the other and the gap between the two ships widening rapidly.

They watched the squall travelling over the foam-flecked grey water, shrieking towards France. Then in the thickness they saw a more solid nucleus take shape; they saw it grow sharper in outline.

'God—' exclaimed Bush; he was too disconcerted, too dumb-founded, to finish the oath. For there was *Loire* emerging from the squall, comfortably on the same tack as *Hotspur,* plunging along in her relentless pursuit with the distance in no way diminished.

'That's a trick we won't try a second time,' said Hornblower. He was forcing a smile, tight-lipped.

The French captain was no fool, evidently. He had observed the *Hotspur* delaying past the best moment for tacking, he had seen the squall engulfing her, and had anticipated her action. He must have tacked at the very same moment. In consequence he had lost little while tacking, and that little had been regained by the time the two ships were in sight of each other once more. Certainly he was a dangerous enemy. He must be one of the more able captains that the French navy possessed. There were several who had distinguished themselves in the last war; true, in consequence of the over-powering British naval strength, most of them had ended the war as prisoners, but the Peace of Amiens had set them free.

Hornblower turned away from Bush and Prowse and tried to pace the heeling deck, to think out all the implications. This was a dangerous situation, as dangerous as the worst he had envisaged. Inexorably wind and wave were forcing *Hotspur* closer to the *Loire*. Even as he tried to pace the deck he felt her shudder and lurch, out of the rhythm of her usual pitch and roll. That was the 'rogue wave,' generated by some unusual combination of wind and water, thumping against *Hotspur's* weather side like a battering ram. Every few seconds rogue waves made themselves felt, checking *Hotspur's* way and pushing her bodily to leeward; *Loire* was encountering exactly similar rogue waves, but with her greater size she was not so susceptible to their influence. They played their part along with the other forces of nature in closing the gap between the two ships.

Supposing he were compelled to fight a close action? No, he had gone through that before. He had a good ship and well-trained crew, but on this tossing sea that advantage would be largely discounted by the fact that the *Loire* provided a steadier gun platform. Odds of four to one in weight of metal were greater than it was advisable to risk. Momentarily Hornblower saw himself appearing in the written history of the future. He might have the distinction of being the first British captain in the present war to fall a victim to the French navy. What a distinction! Then even in the cold gale blowing round him he could feel the blood hot under his skin as he pictured the action. Horrors presented themselves in endless succession to the crack of doom like the kings in *Macbeth*. He thought of death. He thought of mutilation, of agony under the surgeon's knife, and of being wheeled about legless through a blank future. He thought of being a prisoner of war; he had experienced that already in Spain and only by a miracle he had achieved release. The last war had gone on for ten years; this one might do the same. Ten years in prison! Ten years during which his brother officers would be gaining fame, distinguishing themselves, making fortunes in prize money while he would fret himself to pieces in prison, emerging at the end a cranky eccentric, forgotten by all his world – forgotten even by Maria, he fancied. He would rather die, just as he would rather die than be mutilated; or so he thought (he told himself brutally) until the choice should be more imminently presented to him. Then he might well flinch, for he did not want to die. He tried to tell himself that he was not afraid of death, that he merely regretted the prospect of missing all the interesing and amusing things that life held in store for him, and then he found himself sneering at himself for not facing the horrid truth that he was afraid.

Then he shook himself out of this black mood. He was in danger, and this was no time for morbid introspection. It was resolution and ingenuity that he demanded of himself. He tried to make his face a mask to hide his recent feelings as he met the gaze of Bush and Prowse.

'Mr Prowse,' he said. 'Bring your journal. Let's look at the chart.'

The rough log recorded every change of course, every hourly measurement of speed, and by its aid they could calculate – or guess at – the present position of the ship starting from her last point of departure at Ar Men.

'We're making fully two points of leeway,' said Prowse despondently. His long face seemed to grow longer and longer as he looked down at Hornblower seated at the chart-table. Hornblower shook his head.

'Not more than a point and a half. And the tide's been making in our favour for the last two hours.'

'I hope you're right, sir,' said Prowse.

'If I'm not,' said Hornblower, working the parallel rulers, 'we'll have to make fresh plans.'

Despondency for the sake of despondency irritated Hornblower when displayed by other people; he knew too much about it.

'In another two hours,' said Prowse, 'The Frenchman'll have us under his guns.'

Hornblower looked fixedly at Prowse, and under that unwavering gaze Prowse was at length reminded of his omission, which he hastily remedied by belatedly adding the word 'sir.' Hornblower was not going to allow any deviation from discipline, not in any crisis whatever – he knew well enough how these things might develop in the future. Even if there might be no future. Having made his point there was no need to labour it.

'You can see we'll weather Ushant,' he said, looking down at the line he had pencilled on the chart.

'Maybe, sir,' said Prowse.

'Comfortably,' went on Hornblower.

'I wouldn't say exactly comfortably, sir,' demurred Prowse.

'The closer the better,' said Hornblower. 'But we can't dictate that. We daren't make an inch more of leeway.'

He had thought more than once about that possibility, of weathering Ushant so close that *Loire* would not be able to hold her course. Then *Hotspur* would free herself from pursuit like a whale scraping off a barnacle against a rock; an amusing and ingenious idea, but not practicable as long as the wind stayed steady.

'But even if we weather Ushant, sir,' persisted Prowse, 'I don't see how it will help us. We'll be within range by then, sir.'

Hornblower put down his pencil. He had been about to say 'Perhaps you'd advise saving trouble by hauling down our colours this minute, Mr Prowse,' but he remembered in time that such a mention of the possibility of surrender, even with a sarcastic intention, was contrary to the Articles of War. Instead he would penalise Prowse by revealing nothing of the plan he had in mind; and that would be just as well, in case the plan should fail and he should have to fall back on yet another line of defence.

'We'll see when the time comes,' he said, curtly, and rose from his chair. 'We're wanted on deck. By now it'll be time to go about again.'

On deck there was the wind blowing as hard as ever; there was the spray flying; there was the *Loire,* dead to leeward and luffing up to narrow the gap by a further important trifle. The hands were at work on the pumps; in these weather conditions the pumps had to be employed for half an hour every two hours to free the ship from the sea water which made its way on board through the straining seams.

'We'll tack the ship, Mr Poole, as soon as the pumps suck.'

'Aye aye, sir.'

Some way ahead lay Ushant and his plan to shake off the *Loire,* but before that he had to tack twice more at least, each time with its possibilities of making a mistake, of handing *Hotspur* and himself over to the enemy. He must not stumble over an obstacle at his feet through keeping his eyes on the horizon. He made himself perform the manoeuvre as neatly as ever, and made himself ignore any feeling of relief when it was completed.

'We gained a full cable's length on him that time, sir,' said Bush, after watching *Loire* steady herself on the starboard tack on *Hotspur's* beam.

'We may not always be so lucky,' said Hornblower. 'But we'll make this leg a short one and see.'

On the starboard tack he was heading away from his objective; when they went about on the port tack again he must hold on for a considerably longer time, but he must make it appear as though by inadvertence. If he could deceive Bush it would be an indication that he was deceiving the French captain.

The hands seemed to be actually enjoying this sailing contest. They were light-hearted, revelling in the business of cheating the wind and getting every inch of way out of the *Hotspur*. It must be quite obvious to them that *Loire* was gaining in the race, but they did not care;

they were laughing and joking as they looked across at her. They had no conception of the danger of the situation, or, rather, they made light of it. The luck of the British navy would save them, or the un-handiness of the French. Or the skill of their captain – without faith in him they would be far more frightened.

Time to go about again and beat towards Ushant. He resumed charge of the ship and turned her about. It was only after the turn was completed that he noted, with satisfaction, that he had forgotten his nervousness in the interest he was taking in the situation.

'We're closing fast, sir,' said Prowse, gloomy as ever. He had his sextant in his hand and had just finished measuring the angle sub-tended between the *Loire's* masthead and her waterline.

'I can see that for myself, thank you, Mr Prowse,' snapped Horn-blower. For that matter the eye was as trustworthy as any instrumental observation on that heaving sea.

'My duty, sir,' said Prowse.

'I'm glad to see you executing your duty, Mr Prowse,' said Horn-blower. The tone he used was the equivalent of saying, 'Damn your duty,' which would have also been contrary to the Articles of War.

Northward the *Hotspur* held her steady course. A squall engulfed her, blinding her, while the quartermasters juggled desperately at the wheel, allowing her, perforce, to pay off in the worst of the gusts, and putting down the wheel to keep her to the wind when the wind backed a point. The final gust went by, flapping Hornblower's coat-tails. It whipped the trouser-legs of the quartermasters at the wheel so that a momentary glance would make a stranger believe that, with their swaying arms and wavering legs, they were dancing some strange ritual dance. As ever, when the squall passed on, all eyes not dedicated to present duty turned to leeward to look for the *Loire*.

'Look at that!' yelled Bush. 'Look at that, sir! We've fooled him properly!'

Loire had gone about. There she was, just settling down on the starboard tack. The French captain had been too clever. He had decided that Hotspur would go about when concealed by the squall, and had moved to anticipate her. Hornblower watched the *Loire*. That French captain must be boiling with rage at having his too-great-cleverness revealed to his ship's company in this fashion. That might cloud his judgement later. It might make him over-anxious. Even so, he showed little sign of it from here. He had been about to haul his bowlines, but he reached a rapid and sensible decision. To tack again would necessitate standing on for sometime on his present course while his ship regained speed and manoeuvrability, so that instead he made use of the turning momentum she still possessed, put up his helm and completed the circle, wearing his ship round so that she momentarily presented her stern to the wind before arriving at last on her original tack again. It was a cool-headed piece of work, making the best of a bad job, but the *Loire* had lost a good deal of ground.

'Two full points abaft the beam,' said Prowse.

'And he's farther down to looard, too,' supplemented Bush.

The greatest gain, Hornblower decided, watching her, was that it made possible, and plausible, the long leg to the northward that his plan demanded. He could make a long beat on the port tack without the French captain seeing anything unusual in that.

'Keep her going, there!' he shouted to the wheel. 'Let her fall off a little! Steady as you go!'

The race was resumed, both ships plunging along, battling with the unremitting gale. Hornblower could see the wide angle from the vertical described by the *Loire*'s masts as she rolled; he could see her yards dipped towards the sea, and he could be sure that *Hotspur* was acting in the same way, rolling even a trifle more deeply, perhaps. So this very deck on which he stood was over at that fantastic angle too; he was proud of the fact that he was regaining his sea legs so rapidly. He could stand balanced, one knee straight and rigid, the other considerably bent, while he leaned over against the heel, and then he could straighten with the roll almost as steadily as Bush could. And his sea-sickness was better as well – no; a pity he had let that subject return to his mind, for he had to struggle with a qualm the moment it did so.

'Making a long leg like this gives him a chance, sir,' grumbled Prowse, juggling with telescope and sextant. 'He's drawing up on us fast.'

'We're doing our best,' answered Hornblower.

His glass could reveal many details of the *Loire* now, as he concentrated upon her to distract himself from his sea-sickness. Then, as he was about to lower the glass to ease his eye he saw something new. The gun ports along her weather side seemed to change their shape, and as he continued to look he saw, first from one gun-port and then from another and finally from the whole line, the muzzles of her guns come nosing their way out, as the invisible crews strained at the tackles to drag the ponderous weights up against the slope of the deck.

'She's running out her guns, sir,' said Bush, a little unnecessarily.

'Yes.'

There was no purpose in imitating her example yet. It would be the lee side guns that *Hotspur* would have to run out. They would increase her heel and render her by that much less weatherly. Lying over as she was she would probably take in water over the port-sills at the low point of her roll. Lastly, even at extreme elevation, they would nearly all the time be depressed by the heel below the horizontal, and would be useless, even with good timing on the part of the gun captains, against a target at any distance.

The look-outs at the fore-topmasthead were yelling something, and then one of them launched himself into the rigging and came running aft to the quarter-deck.

'Why don't you use the backstay like a seaman?' demanded Bush, but Hornblower checked him.

'What is it?'

'Land, sir,' spluttered the seaman. He was wet to the skin with water streaming from every angle, whisked away by the wind as it dripped.

'Where away?'

'On the lee bow, sir.'

'How many points?'

He thought for a moment.

'A good four, sir.'

Hornblower looked across at Prowse.

'That'll be Ushant, sir. We ought to weather it with plenty to spare.'

'I want to be sure of that. You'd better go aloft, Mr Prowse. Make the best estimate you can.'

'Ayé aye, sir.'

It would not do Prowse any harm to make the tiring and exacting journey to the masthead.

'He'll be opening fire soon, sir,' said Bush, referring to the Frenchman and not to Prowse's departing figure. 'Not much chance of replying as yet. On the other tack, maybe, sir.'

Bush was ready for a fight against any odds, and he was unaware that Hornblower had no intention of tacking again.

'We'll see when the time comes,' said Hornblower.

'He's opening fire now, sir.'

Hornblower whipped round, just in time to see a puff of smoke vanishing in the gale, and then others, all down the *Loire's* side, enduring hardly for a second before the wind overcame the force of the powder that impelled them. That was all. No sound of the broadside reached them against the wind, and there was not a sight of the fall of shot.

'Long range, sir,' said Bush.

'A chance for him to exercise his guns' crews,' said Hornblower.

His glass showed him the *Loire's* gun-muzzles disappearing back into the ship as the guns were run in again for reloading. There was a strange unreality about all this, about the silence of that broadside, about the fact that *Hotspur* was under fire, about the fact that he himself might be dead at any moment now as the result of a lucky hit.

'He's hoping for a lucky hit, I suppose, sir,' said Bush, echoing the very words of Hornblower's thoughts in a manner that made the situation all the more uncanny and unreal.

'Naturally.' Hornblower forced himself to say that word, and in this strange mood his voice, pitched against the gale, seemed to come from very far away.

If the Frenchman had no objection to a prodigious waste of powder and shot he might as well open fire at this range, at extreme cannon-shot, in the hope of inflicting enough damage on *Hotspur's* rigging to slow her down. Hornblower could think clearly enough, but it was as if he was looking on at someone else's adventure.

Now Prowse was returning to the quarter-deck.

'We'll weather the land by a good four miles, sir,' he said; the spray tossed up by the weather-bow had wetted him just as thoroughly as the seamen. He looked over at the *Loire*. 'Not a chance of our paying off, I suppose, sir.'

'Of course not,' said Hornblower. Long before such a plan could bear fruit he would be engaged in close action were he to drop down to leeward, in the hope of forcing the *Loire* to go about to avoid running ashore. 'How long before we're up to the land?'

'Less than an hour, sir. Maybe half. It ought to be in sight from the deck any minute.'

'Yes!' said Bush. 'There it is, sir!'

Over the lee bow Hornblower could see the black bold shoreline of Ushant. Now the three points of the triangle, Ushant, *Hotspur* and *Loire*, were all plain to him, and he could time his next move. He would have to hold on to his present course for some considerable time; he would have to brave further broadsides, whether he liked it or not – insane words those last, for no one could like being under fire. He trained his glass on the land, watching his ship's movement relative to it, and then as he looked away he saw something momentarily out of the corner of his eye. It took him a couple of seconds to deduce what it was he had seen; two splashes, separated by a hundred feet in space and by a tenth of a second in time. A cannon-ball had skipped from the top of one wave crest and plunged into the next.

'They're firing very deliberately, sir,' said Bush.

Hornblower's attention was directed to the *Loire* in time to see the next brief puff of smoke from her side; they saw nothing of the ball. Then came the next puff.

'I expect they have some marksman on board moving along from gun to gun,' said Hornblower.

If that were the case the marksman must wait each time for the right conditions of roll – a slow rate of firing, but, allowing for the length of time to reload and run up, not impossibly slower than firing broadsides.

'You can hear the guns now, sir. The sound's carried by the water.'

It was an ugly, flat, brief clap, following just after each puff of smoke.

'Mr Bush,' said Hornblower speaking slowly as he felt the excitement of the approaching crisis boiling up within him. 'You know your watch – and quarter-bills off by heart, I'm sure.'

'Yes, sir,' replied Bush, simply.

'I want—' Hornblower checked the position of *Loire* again. 'I want sufficient hands at the braces and bowlines to handle the ship properly. But I want crews sufficient for the guns of one side too.'

'Not very easy, sir.'

'Impossible?'

'Nearly, sir. I can do it, though.'

'Then I want you to arrange it. Station crews at the port-side guns, if you please.'

'Aye aye, sir. Port side.'

The repetition was in the usual navy style to ensure against misunderstanding; there was only the faintest questioning note in Bush's voice, for the port side was that turned away from the enemy.

'I want—' went on Hornblower, still slowly. 'I want the portside guns run out when we go about, Mr Bush. I'll give the order. Then I want them run in again like lightning and the ports closed. I'll give the order for that, too.'

'Aye aye, sir. Run 'em in again.'

'Then they're to cross to the starboard side and run those guns out ready to open fire. You understand, Mr Bush?'

'Y-yes, sir.'

Hornblower looked round at the *Loire* and at Ushant again.

'Very well, Mr Bush. Mr Cargill will need four hands for a special duty, but you can start stationing the rest.'

Now he was committed. If his calculations were incorrect he would appear a fool in the eyes of the whole ship's company. He would also be dead or a prisoner. But now he was keyed up, the fighting spirit boiling within him as it had done once when he boarded *Renown* to effect her recapture. There was a sudden shriek overhead, so startling that even Bush stopped short as he was moving forward. A line mysteriously parted in mid-air, the upper end blowing out horizontal in the wind, the lower end flying out to trail overside. A luckier shot than any so far had passed over the *Hotspur* twenty feet above her deck.

'Mr Wise!' yelled Hornblower into the speaking-trumpet. 'Get that halliard re-rove.'

'Aye aye, sir.'

The spirit of mischief asserted itself in Hornblower's mind along with his excitement, and he raised the trumpet again.

'And Mr Wise! If you think proper you can tell the hands we're at war!'

That raised the laugh that Hornblower anticipated, all over the ship, but there was no more time for frivolity.

'Pass the word for Mr Cargill.'

Cargill presented himself with a faint look of anxiety on his round face.

'You're not in trouble, Mr Cargill. I've selected you for a responsible duty.'

'Yes, sir?'

'Arrange with Mr Bush to give you four steady hands and take your station on the fo'c'sle at the jib halliard and jib sheet. I shall be going about very shortly, and then I shall change my mind and come back on my original tack. So now you can see what you have to do. The moment you get my signal run the jib up the stay and then flat it out to port. I want to be quite sure you understand?'

Several seconds went by while Cargill digested the plan before he answered 'Yes, sir.'

'I'm relying on you to keep us from being laid flat a-back, Mr Cargill. You'll have to use your own judgment after that. The moment the ship's turning and under command again run the jib down. You can do that?'

'Yes, sir.'

'Very well, carry on.'

Prowse was standing close by, straining to hear all this. His long face was longer than ever, it seemed.

'Is it the gale that's making your ears flap, Mr Prowse?' snapped Hornblower, in no mood to spare anyone; he regretted the words as soon as they were said, but now there was no time to compensate for them.

Loire was dead to leeward, and beyond her was Ushant. They had opened up the Bay of Lampoul on Ushant's seaward side, and now were beginning to close it again. The moment had come; no, better to wait another minute. The scream of a cannon-ball and a simultaneous crash. There was a gaping hole in the weather side bulwark; the shot had crossed the heeling deck and smashed its way through from within outwards. A seaman at the gun there was looking stupidly at his left arm where the blood was beginning to flow from a splinter wound.

'Stand by to go about!' yelled Hornblower.

Now for it. He had to fool the French captain, who had already proved he was no fool.

'Keep your glass on the Frenchman, Mr Prowse. Tell me just what he's doing. Quartermaster, a little lee helm. Just a little. Handsomely. Helm's a-lee!'

The fore-topsail shivered. Now every moment was precious, and yet he must delay so as to induce the Frenchman to commit himself.

'His helm's a-lee, sir! He's coming round.'

This would be the moment – actually it was just past the moment – when the Frenchman would expect him to tack to avoid the gunfire, and the Frenchman would try to tack as nearly simultaneously as possible.

'Now, quartermaster. Hard down. Tacks and sheets!'

Hotspur was coming to the wind. Despite the brief delay she was still well under command.

'Mr Bush!'

On the weather side they opened the gun-ports, and the straining gun crews dragged the guns up the slope. A rogue wave slapping against the side came in through the ports and flooded the deck knee deep in water; but the Frenchman must see those gun muzzles run out on the port side.

'He's coming about, sir!' reported Prowse. 'He's casting off the braces!'

He must make quite sure.

'Mainsail haul!'

This was the danger point.

'He's past the wind's eye, sir. His foretops'ls coming round.'

'Ava-a-ast!'

The surprised crew stopped dead as Hornblower screamed into the speaking-trumpet.

'Brace all back again! Jump to it! Quartermaster! Hard-a-port! Mr Cargill!'

Hornblower waved his hand, and the jib rushed up the stay. With its tremendous leverage on the bowsprit the jib, given a chance, would turn the ship back irresistibly. Cargill and his men were hauling it out to port by main force. There was just enough of an angle for the wind to act upon it in the right direction. Was there? Yes! *Hotspur* was swinging back again, gallantly ignoring her apparent mistreatment and the wave that she met bows-on which burst over her forecastle. She was swinging, more and more rapidly, Cargill and his men hauling down the jib that had played so great a part in the operation.

'Braces, there! She's coming before the wind. Stand by! Quartermaster, meet her as she swings. Mr Bush!'

The guns' crews flung themselves on the tackles and ran the guns in again. It was a pleasure to see Bush restraining their excitement and making certain that they were secure. The ports slammed shut and the crews raced over to the starboard side. He could see the *Loire* now that *Hotspur* had completed her turn, but Prowse was still reporting, as his order dictated.

'She's in irons, sir. She's all a-back.'

That was the very thing Hornblower had hoped for. He had believed it likely that he would be able to effect his escape to leeward, perhaps after an exchange of broadsides; this present situation had appeared possible but too good to materialise. The *Loire* was hanging helpless in the wind. Her captain had noted *Hotspur's* manoeuvre just too late. Instead of going round on the other tack, getting his ship under command, and then tacking once more in pursuit, he had tried to follow *Hotspur's* example and revert to his previous course. But with an unskilled crew and without a carefully prepared plan the improvisation had failed disastrously. While Hornblower watched he saw *Loire* yaw off the wind and then swing back again, refusing obstinately, like a frightened horse, to do the sensible thing. And *Hotspur*, dead before the wind, was rushing down upon her. Hornblower measured the dwindling gap with a calculating eye all the keener for his excited condition.

'We'll render passing honours, Mr Bush!' he yelled – no trumpet needed with the wind behind him. 'You gunners! Hold your fire until her mainmast comes into your sights. Quartermaster! Starboard a little. We'll pass her close.'

'Pistol shot' was the ideal range for firing a broadside according to old tradition, or even 'half pistol shot,' twenty yards or ten yards. *Hotspur* was passing *Loire* starboard side to starboard side but on the starboard side *Hotspur* had her guns run out, manned, and ready, while *Loire* presented to his gaze a line of blank ports – no wonder, with the ship in her present state of confusion.

They were level with her. No. 1 gun went off with a crash; Bush was standing beside it and gave the word, and apparently he intended to walk along the battery firing each gun in turn, but *Hotspur* with the wind behind her was going far too fast for him. The other guns went off in a straggling roll. Hornblower saw the splinters fly from the Frenchman's side, saw the holes battered in it. With the wind behind her *Hotspur* was hardly rolling at all; she was pitching, but any cool-headed gun captain could make sure of hitting his mark at fifteen yards. Hornblower saw a single gun-port open in *Loire's* side – they were trying to man the guns, minutes too late. Then he was level with the *Loire's* quarter-deck. He could see the bustling crowd there; for a moment he thought he distinguished the figure of the French captain, but at that moment the carronade beside him went off with a crash that took him by surprise so that he almost leaped from the deck.

'Canister on top of the round-shot, sir,' said the gun captain turning to him with a grin. 'That'll learn 'em.'

A hundred and fifty musket bullets in a round of canister would sweep the *Loire's* quarter-deck like a broom. The marines posted on the deck were all biting fresh cartridges and plying their ramrods – they must have been firing too, without Hornblower perceiving it. Bush was back beside him.

'Every shot told!' he spluttered. 'Every single shot, sir!'

It was amazing and interesting to see Bush so excited, but there was still no time for trifles. Hornblower looked back at the *Loire*, she was still in irons – that broadside must have thrown her crew into complete disorder again. And over there was Ushant, grim and black.

'Port two points,' he said to the men at the wheel. A sensible man would conserve all the sea room available.

'Shall we come to the wind and finish her off, sir?' asked Bush.

'No.'

That was the sensible decision, reached in spite of his fighting madness. Despite the advantage gained by firing an unanswered broadside *Hotspur* was far too weak to enter voluntarily into a duel with *Loire*. If *Loire* had lost a mast, if she had been disabled, he would have tried it. The ships were already a mile apart; in the time necessary to beat back to his enemy she would recover and be ready to receive him. There she was; now she had swung, she had come under control again. It simply would not do.

The crew were chattering like monkeys, and like monkeys they were dancing about the deck in their excitement. Hornblower took the speaking-trumpet to magnify his order.

'Silence!'

At his bellow the ship instantly fell silent, with every eye turned towards him. He was impervious to that, strangely. He paced across the quarter-deck and back again, judging the distance of Ushant, now receding over the starboard quarter, and of the *Loire*, now before the wind. He waited, almost reached his decision, and then waited again, before he gave his orders.

'Helm a-weather! Mr Prowse, back the maintops'l, if you please.'

They were in the very mouth of the English Channel now, with *Loire* to windward and with an infinite avenue of escape available to leeward. If *Loire* came down upon him he would lure her up-channel. In a stern chase and with night coming on he would be in little enough danger, and the *Loire* would be cutting herself off from safety with every prospect of encountering powerful units of the British Navy. So he waited, hove-to, on the faint chance that the Frenchman might not resist temptation. Then he saw her yards swing, saw her come about, on to the starboard tack. She was heading for home, heading to keep Brest under her lee. She was acting conservatively and sensibly. But to the world, to everyone in *Hotspur* – and to everyone in the *Loire*, for that matter – *Hotspur* was challenging her to action and she was running for safety with her tail between her legs. At the sight of her in flight the *Hotspur's* crew raised an undisciplined cheer; Hornblower took the speaking-trumpet again.

'Silence!'

The rasp in his voice came from fatigue and strain, for reaction was closing in upon him in the moment of victory. He had to stop and think, he had to prod his mind into activity before he could give his next orders. He hung the speaking-trumpet on its becket and turned to Bush; the two unplanned gestures took on a highly dramatic quality in the eyes of the ship's company, who were standing watching him and expecting some further speech.

'Mr Bush! You can dismiss the watch below, if you would be so kind.' Those last words were the result of a considerable effort.

'Aye aye, sir.'

'Secure the guns, and dismiss the men from quarters.'

'Aye aye, sir.'

'Mr Prowse!' Hornblower gauged by a glance at Ushant the precious distance they had lost to leeward. 'Put the ship on the port tack close-hauled, if you please.'

'Close-hauled on the port tack. Aye aye, sir.'

Strictly speaking, that was the last order he need give at this moment. He could abandon himself to his fatigue now, this very second. But a few words of explanation were at least desirable, if not quite necessary.

'We shall have to beat back. Call me when the watch is changed.' As he said those words he could form a mental picture of what they implied. He would be able to fall across his cot, take the weight off his weary legs, let the tensions drain out of him, abandon himself to his fatigue, close his aching eyes, revel in the thought that no further decisions would be demanded of him for an hour or two. Then he recalled himself in momentary surprise. Despite those visions he was still on the quarter-deck with all eyes on him. He knew what he had to say; he knew what was necessary – he had to make an exit, like some wretched actor leaving the stage as the curtain fell. On these simple seamen it would have an effect that would compensate them for their fatigue, that would be remembered and quoted months later, and would – this was the only reason for saying it – help to reconcile them to the endless discomforts of the blockade of Brest. He set his tired legs in motion towards his cabin, and paused at the spot where the greatest number of people could hear his words to repeat them later.

'We are going back to watch Brest again.' The melodramatic pause. '*Loire* or no *Loire*.'

VII

Hornblower was seated in the cramped chart-room eating his dinner. This salt beef must have come from the new cask, for there was an entirely different tang about it, not unpleasant. Presumably it had been pickled at some other victualling yard, with a different quality of salt. He dipped the tip of his knife into the mustard pot; that mustard was borrowed – begged – from the wardroom, and he felt guilty about it. The wardroom stores must be running short by now – but on the other hand he himself had sailed with no mustard at all, thanks to the distractions of getting married while commissioning his ship.

'Come in!' he growled in response to a knock.

It was Cummings, one of the 'young gentlemen,' First Class Volunteers, King's Letter Boys, with whom the ship was plagued in place of experienced midshipmen, thanks again to the haste with which she had been commissioned.

'Mr Poole sent me, sir. There's a new ship joining the Inshore Squadron.'

'Very well. I'll come.'

It was a lovely summer day. A few cumulus clouds supplied relief to the blue sky. *Hotspur* was hardly rocking at all as she lay hove-to, her mizzen topsail to the mast, for she was so far up in the approaches to Brest that the moderate easterly wind had little opportunity, since leaving the land, to raise a lop on the water. Hornblower swept his eye round as he emerged on the quarterdeck, landward at first, naturally. They lay right in the mouth of the Goulet, with a view straight up into the Outer Roads. On one side, was the Capuchins, on the other the Petit Minou, with *Hotspur* carefully stationed – as in the days of peace but for a more forceful reason – so that she was just out of cannon-shot of the batteries on those two points. Up the Goulet lay the reefs of the Little Girls, with their outlier, Pollux Reef, and beyond the Little Girls, in the outer roadstead, lay the French navy at anchor, forced to tolerate this constant invigilation because of the superior might of the Channel Fleet waiting outside, just over the horizon.

Hornblower naturally turned his gaze in that direction next. The main body was out of sight, so as to conceal its strength; even Hornblower did not know its present numbers correctly – some twelve ships of the line or so. But well in sight, only three miles out to sea, lay the Inshore Squadron, burly two-deckers lying placidly hove-to, ready at any minute to support *Hotspur* and the two frigates, *Doris* and *Naiad*, should the French decide to come out and drive off these insolent sentries. There had been three of these ships of the line; now, as Hornblower looked, a fourth was creeping in close-hauled to join them. Automatically Hornblower looked over again at the Petit Minou. As he expected, the semaphore arms of the telegraph on the cliffs at the point there were swinging jerkily, from vertical to horizontal and back again. The watchers there were signalling to the French fleet the news of the arrival of this fourth ship to join the inshore squadron; even the smallest activity was noted and reported, so that in clear weather the French admiral was informed within minutes. It was an intolerable nuisance – it helped to smooth the path of the coasters perennially trying to sneak into Brest through the passage of the Raz. Some action should be taken about that semaphore station.

Bush was rating Foreman, whom he was patiently – impatiently – training to be the signal officer of the *Hotspur*.

'Can't you get that number yet?' he demanded.

Foreman was training his telescope; he had not acquired the trick of keeping the other eye open, yet idle. In any case it was not easy to read the flags, with the wind blowing almost directly from one ship to the other.

'Seventy-nine, sir,' said Foreman at length.

'You've read it right for once,' marvelled Bush. 'Now let's see what you do next.'

Foreman snapped his fingers as he recalled his duties, and hastened to the signal book on the binnacle. The telescope slipped with a crash to the deck from under his arm as he tried to turn the pages, but he picked it up and managed to find the reference. He turned back to Bush, but a jerk of Bush's thumb diverted him to Hornblower.

'*Tonnant*, sir,' he said.

'Now, Mr Foreman, you know better than that. Make your report in proper form and as fully as you can.'

'*Tonnant*, sir. Eighty-four guns. Captain Pellew.' Hornblower's stony face and steady silence spurred Foreman into remembering the rest of what he should say. 'Joining the Inshore Squadron.'

'Thank you, Mr Foreman,' said Hornblower with the utmost formality, but Bush was already addressing Foreman again, his voice pitched as loudly as if Foreman were on the forecastle instead of three yards away.

'Mr Foreman! The *Tonnant's* signalling! Hurry up, now.'

Foreman scuttled back and raised his telescope.

'That's our number!' he said.

'So I saw five minutes ago. Read the signal.'

Foreman peered through the telescope, referring to the book, and checked his reference before looking up at the raging Bush.

' "Send boat," it says, sir.'

'Of course it does. You ought to know all routine signals by heart, Mr Foreman. You've had long enough. Sir, *Tonnant* signals us to send a boat.'

'Thank you, Mr Bush. Acknowledge, and clear away the quarter boat.'

'Aye aye, sir. Acknowledge!' A second later Bush was blaring again. 'Not that halliard, you careless – you careless young gentleman. *Tonnant* can't see the signal through the mizzen tops'l. Send it up to the main-tops'l yardarm.'

Bush looked over at Hornblower and spread his hands in resignation. Partly he was indicating that he was resigned to this duty of training ignorant young subordinates, but partly the dumb show conveyed some of the feelings aroused by having, in view of Hornblower's known preferences, to call Foreman a 'young gentleman' instead of using some much more forcible expression. Then he turned away to supervise Cummings as he hoisted out the quarter boat. There was everything to be said in favour of these young men being harassed and bullied as they went about their duties, although Hornblower did not subscribe to the popular notion that young men were actually the better for harassment and bullying. They would learn their duties all the quicker; and one of these days Foreman might easily find himself having to read and transmit signals amid the smoke and confusion and slaughter of a fleet action, while Cummings might be launching and manning a boat in desperate haste for a cutting out expedition.

Hornblower remembered his unfinished dinner.

'Call me when the boat returns, if you please, Mr Bush.'

This was the last of the blackcurrant jam; Hornblower, ruefully contemplating the sinking level in the final pot, admitted to himself that compulsorily he had actually acquired a taste for blackcurrant. The butter was all gone, the eggs used up, after forty days at sea. For the next seventy-one days, until the ship's provisions were all consumed he was likely to be living on seamen's fare, unrelieved salt beef and pork, dried peas, biscuit. Cheese twice a week and suet pudding on Sundays.

At any rate there was time for a nap before the boat returned. He could go to sleep peacefully – a precaution in case the exigencies of the service disturbed his night – thanks to the naval might of Britain, although five miles away there were twenty thousand enemies any one of whom would kill him on sight.

'Boat coming alongside, sir.'

'Very well,' answered Hornblower sleepily.

The boat was deeply laden, right down to her gunwales. The hands must have had a long stiff pull back to the *Hotspur*; it was the purest bad luck on them that they could run under sail to the *Tonnant* when lightly laden and then have to row all the way back deeply laden in the teeth of the gentle wind. From the boat as she approached there came a strange roaring noise, a kind of bellow.

'What the devil's that?' asked Bush of himself as he stood beside Hornblower on the gangway.

The boat was heaped high with sacks.

'There's fresh food, anyway,' said Hornblower.

'Reeve a whip at the main-yardarm!' bellowed Bush – odd how his bellow was echoed from the boat.

Foreman came up the side to report.

'Cabbages, potatoes, cheese, sir. And a bullock.'

'Fresh meat, by God!' said Bush.

With half a dozen hands tailing on to the whip at the yardarm the sacks came rapidly up to the deck; as the boat was cleared there lay revealed in the bottom a formless mass of rope netting; still bellowing. Slings were passed beneath it and soon it lay on deck; a miserable undersized bullock, lowing faintly. A terrified eye rolled at them through the netting that swathed it. Bush turned to Hornblower as Foreman completed his report.

'*Tonnant* brought twenty-four cattle out for the fleet from Plymouth, sir. This one's our share. If we butcher it tomorrow, sir, and let it hang for a day, you can have steak on Sunday, sir.'

'Yes,' said Hornblower.

'We can swab the blood off the deck while it's still fresh, sir. No need to worry about that. An' there'll be tripe, sir! Ox tongue!'

He could still see that terrified eye. He could wish that Bush was not so enthusiastic, because he felt quite the reverse. As his vivid imagination pictured the butchering he felt no desire at all for meat provided by such a process. He had to change the subject.

'Mr Foreman! Were there no messages from the fleet?'

Foreman started guiltily and plunged his hand into his side pocket to produce a bulky packet. He blanched as he saw the fury on Hornblower's face.

'Don't you ever do that again, Mr Foreman! Despatches before everything! You need a lesson and this is the time for it.'

'Shall I pass the word for Mr Wise, sir?' asked Bush.

The boatswain's rattan could make vigorous play over Foreman's recumbent form bent over the breech of a gun. Hornblower saw the sick fright in Foreman's face. The boy was as terrified as the bullock; he must have the horror of corporal punishment that occasionally was evident in the navy. It was a horror that Hornblower himself shared. He looked into the pleading desperate eyes for five long seconds to let the lesson sink in.

'No,' he said, at length. 'Mr Foreman would only remember that for a day. I'll see he gets reminded every day for a week. No spirits for Mr Foreman for seven days. And anyone in the midshipman's berth who tries to help him out will lose his ration for fourteen days. See to that, if you please, Mr Bush.'

'Aye aye, sir.'

Hornblower snatched the packet from Foreman's lifeless hand, and turned away with contempt in the gesture. No child of fifteen would be any the worse for being deprived of ardent spirits.

In the cabin he had to use his penknife to open the tarred canvas packet. The first thing to tumble out was a grape-shot; the navy had developed through the centuries a routine in these matters – the tarred canvas preserved he contents from salt water if it had to be transported by boat in stormy weather, and the grape-shot would sink it if there were danger of its falling into the hands of the enemy. There were three official letters and a mass of private ones; Hornblower opened the official ones in haste. The first was signed 'Wm Cornwallis, Vice Ad.' It was in the usual form, beginning with the statement of the new situation. Captain Sir Edward Pellew, K.B., in the *Tonnant*, had, as senior officer, received the command of the Inshore Squadron. 'You are therefore requested and required' to obey the orders of the said Captain Sir Edward Pellew, and to pay him the strictest attention, as issued with the authority of the Commander in Chief. The next was signed 'Ed. Pellew, Capt,' and was drily official in three lines, confirming the fact that Pellew now considered Hornblower and *Hotspur* as under his command. The third abandoned the formal 'Sir' which began the others.

'My dear Hornblower,

It is with the greatest of pleasure that I hear that you are serving under me, and what I have been told of your actions already in the present war confirms the opinion I formed when you were my best midshipman in the old *Indefatigable*. Please consider yourself at liberty to make any suggestions that may occur to you for the confounding of the French and the confusion of Bonaparte.

Your sincere friend,
Edward Pellew.'

Now that was a really flattering letter, warming and comforting.

Warming, indeed; as Hornblower sat with the letter in his hand he could feel the blood running faster through his veins. For that matter he could almost feel a stirring within his skull as the ideas began to form, as he thought about the signal station on Petit Minou, as the germs of plans began to sprout. They were taking shape; they were growing fast in the hot-house atmosphere of his mind. Quite unconsciously he began to rise from his chair; only by pacing briskly up and down the quarter-deck could he bring those plans to fruition and create an outlet for the pressure building up inside him. But he remembered the other letters in the packet; he must not fall into the same fault as Foreman. There were letters for him – one, two, six letters all in the same handwriting. It dawned upon him that they must be from Maria – odd that he did not recognise his own wife's handwriting. He was about to open them when he checked himself again. Not one of the other letters was addressed to him, but people in the ship were probably anxiously waiting for them.

'Pass the word for Mr Bush,' he bellowed; Bush, when he arrived, was handed the other letters without a word, nor did he stay for one, seeing that his captain was so deeply engaged in reading that he did not even look up.

Hornblower read, several times, that he was Maria's Dearest Husband. The first two letters told him how much she missed her Angel, how happy she had been during their two days of marriage, and how anxious she was that her Hero was not running into danger, and how necessary it was to change his socks if they should get wet. The third letter was dated from Plymouth. Maria had ascertained that the Channel Fleet was based there, and she had decided to move so as to be on the spot should the necessities of the Service send *Hotspur* back into port; also, as she admitted sentimentally, she would be nearer her Beloved. She had made the journey in the coasting hoy, committing herself (with many thoughts of her Precious) to the Briny Deep for the first time, and as she gazed at the distant land she had reached a better understanding of the feelings of her Valiant Sailor Husband. Now she was comfortably established in lodgings kept by a most respectable woman, widow of a boatswain.

The fourth letter began precipitately with the most delightful, the most momentous news for her Darling. Maria hardly knew how to express this to her most Loved, her most Adored Idol. Their marriage, already so Blissful, was now to be further Blessed, or at least she fancied so. Hornblower opened the fifth letter in haste, passing over the hurried postscript which said that Maria had just learned the news of her Intrepid Warrior adding to his Laurels by engaging with the *Loire*, and that she hoped he had not exposed himself more than was necessary to his Glory. He found the news confirmed. Maria was more sure than ever that she was destined to be so vastly fortunate in the future as to be the Mother of the Child of her Ideal. And the sixth letter repeated the confirmation. There might be a Christmas Baby, or a New Year's Child; Hornblower noted wryly that much more space in these later letters was devoted to the Blessed Increase than to her Longed-for but Distant Jewel. In any case Maria was consumed with hope that the Little Cherub, if a Boy, would be the Image of his Famous Father, or, if a Girl, that she should display his Sweetness of Disposition.

So that was the news. Hornblower sat with the six letters littered before him, his mind in just as much disorder. Perhaps to postpone realisation he dwelt at first on the thought of the two letters he had written – addressed to Southsea they would be a long time before they caught up with Maria – and their comparatively formal and perhaps chilling content. He would have to remedy that. He would have to write a letter full of affection and full of delight at the news, whether he were delighted or not – and at that point he could reach no decision. Plunged as he was into professional problems the episode of his marriage was suffused in his memory with unreal quality. The affair was so brief, and even at the time it had been so overlain by the business of getting to sea, that it had seemed strange to him that it should involve the lasting effects of marriage; and this news was an indication of more lasting and permanent effects still. He was going to be a father. For the life of him he could not tell if he were pleased or not. Certainly he was sorry for the child if he – or she – were destined to inherit his accursed unhappy temperament. The more the child should prove to be like him, whether in looks or in morals, the sorrier he would be. Yet was that quite true? Was there not something flattering, something gratifying, in the thought that his own characteristics might be perpetuated? It was hard to be honest with himself.

He could remember, with his mind now diverted from his present life, more clearly the details of his honeymoon. He could conjure up more exactly his memories of Maria's doting affection, of the whole-hearted way in which she gave herself to believe, that she could not give so much love without its being as hotly reciprocated. He must never let her guess at the quality of his feelings for her, because that would be a cruelty that he could not contemplate. He reached for pen and paper, returning to the commonplace world with his routine annoyance at having a left wing pen. Pens from the left wing of the goose were cheaper than right wing ones, because when held in position for writing they pointed towards the writer's eye and not conveniently out over his elbow as right wing ones did. But at least he had cut a good point and the ink had not yet grown muddy.

Grimly he applied himself to his task. Partly it was a literary exercise, an Essay on Unbounded Affection, and yet – and yet – he found himself smiling as he wrote; he felt tenderness within him, welling out perhaps along his arm and down his pen. He was even on the verge of admitting to himself that he was not entirely the cold-hearted and unscrupulous individual he believed himself to be.

Towards the close of the letter, as he searched for synonyms for 'wife' and 'child', his glance strayed back to the letters from Pellew, and he actually caught his breath, his thoughts reverting to his duty, to his plans for slaughter, to the harsh realities of the world he was living in. *Hotspur* was riding easily over the placid sea, but the very fact that she was lying hove-to meant that there was a fair wind out of Brest and that at any moment a shout from the top-mast-head would announce that the French Navy was on its way out to contest in thunder and smoke the mastery of the sea. And he had plans; even as he re-read the latest lines of his letter to Maria his vision was blurred by the insistence on his attention of his visualisation of the chart of the entrance to Brest. He had to take tight hold of himself to compel himself to finish the letter to Maria in the same strain as he had begun it. He made himself finish it, he made himself re-read it, he made himself fold it; a shout to the sentry brought in Grimes with a lighted dip with which to seal it, and when he had completed the tiresome process it was with eager relief that he laid the letter aside and reached for a fresh sheet of paper.

'H.M. Sloop *Hotspur,* at sea, the Petit Minou bearing north one league.
May 14th, 1803
Sir—'
This was an end of mellifluous phrasing, of blundering attempts to deal with a totally unfamiliar situation; no longer was he addressing (as if in a dream) the Dear Companion of our Lives Together in Happy Years to Come. Now he was applying himself to a task that he felt competent and eager to do, and for phrasing he had only to draw upon the harsh and unrelieved wording of a myriad official letters before this one. He wrote rapidly and with little pause for consideration, because fantastically his plans had reached complete maturity during his pre-occupation with Maria. The sheet was covered, turned and half covered again, and the plan was sketched out in full detail. He wrote the conclusion:
'Respectfully submitted by
Your ob'd't servant
Horatio Hornblower.'
He wrote the address:

'Captain Sir E. Pellew, K.B.
H.M.S. *Tonnant.*'

When the second letter was sealed he held the two of them in his hand; new life in the one, and death and misery in the other. That was a fanciful thought – of far more importance was the question as to whether Pellew would approve of his suggestions.

VIII

Hornblower lay stretched out on his cot waiting for the time to pass. He would have preferred to be asleep, but during the afternoon sleep had refused to come to him. It was better to go on lying here in any case, for he would need all his strength during the night to come, and if he followed his inclinations and went on deck he would not only tire himself but he would reveal his anxieties and tensions to his subordinates. So he lay as relaxed as he could manage, flat on his back with his hands behind his head; the sounds that he heard on deck told him of the progress of the ship's routine. Just over his head the tell-tale compass which he had had fitted to the deckbeams was literally carrying out its functions and telling the tale of *Hotspur's* small alterations of heading as she lay hove-to, and these could be correlated with the play of the beams of sunshine that came in through the stern windows. Those were now curtained, and the sunbeams came in around the curtains as they swayed gently with the ship's motion. Most captains curtained – and furnished – their cabins with gay chintz, or even, if wealthy, with damask, but these curtains were of canvas. They were of the finest, No. 8, sailcloth to be found in the ship and had only hung there for the last two days. Hornblower thought about this pleasantly, for they had been a present to him from the ward-room; Bush and Prowse, and the surgeon, Wallis, and the purser, Huffnell, had made the presentation after a mysterious request from Bush that they should be allowed to enter his cabin for a moment in his absence. Hornblower had returned to the cabin to find the deputation there and the cabin transformed. There were curtains and cushions – stuffed with oakum – and a coverlet, all gay with red and blue roses and green leaves painted on with ship's paint by some unknown artist in the ship's company. Hornblower had looked round in astonishment that made it impossible to conceal his pleasure. There was no time to glower or look stern, as nine captains out of ten would have done at such an unwarrantable liberty on the part of the ward-room. He could do no more than thank them in halting phrases; and the greatest pleasure only came after later consideration, when he faced the situation realistically. They had not done this as a joke, or in a silly attempt to win his favour. He had to believe the unbelievable, and accept the fact that they had done it because they liked him. That showed their poor judgement; gratification warred with guilt in his mind, yet the fact that they had dared to do such a thing was a strange but undeniable confirmation that the *Hotspur* was welding herself into a fighting entity.

Grimes knocked at the door and entered.

'They're calling the watch, sir,' he said.

'Thank you. I'll come.' The squeals of the pipes and the bellowings of the petty officers echoing through the ship made Grimes' words a little superfluous, but Hornblower had to act the part of a newly awakened man. He retied his neckcloth and pulled on his coat, slipped on his shoes and walked out on deck. Bush was there with paper and pencil in his hand.

'The semaphore's been signalling, sir,' he reported. 'Two long messages at fifteen minutes past four and four-thirty. Two short ones at – there they go again, sir.'

The long gaunt arms of the semaphore were jerkily swinging out and up and back again.

'Thank you, Mr Bush.' It was sufficient to know that the semaphore had been busy. Hornblower took the glass and trained it out to seaward. The Inshore Squadron was sharply silhouetted against the clear sky; the sun just down on the horizon, was still so bright that he could not look towards it at all, but the squadron was well to the northward of it.

'*Tonnants* signalling again, sir, but it's a ninety-one signal,' reported Foreman.

'Thank you.'

It had been agreed that all flag-signals from *Tonnant* preceded by the numerals ninety-one should be disregarded; *Tonnant* was only making them to deceive the French on Petit Minou into thinking some violent action was being planned by the inshore squadron.

'There goes *Naiad*, sir,' said Bush.

Under easy sail the frigate was creeping northward from her station to the south where she had been watching over Camaret Bay, heading to join the big ships and the *Doris*. The sun was now touching the sea; small variations in the water content of the nearly clear air were causing strange freaks of refraction, so that the reddening disc was slightly out of shape as it sank.

'They're heaving the long boat up out of its chocks, sir,' commented Bush.

'Yes.'

The sun was half-way down in the sea, the remaining half pulled by refraction into twice its normal length. There was still plenty of light for an observer with a good glass on Petit Minou – and undoubtedly there was one – to pick out the preparations going on on the *Doris's* deck and in the big ships. The sun had gone. Above where it had sunk a small sliver of cloud shone brilliantly gold and then turned to pink as he looked. Twilight was closing in on them.

'Send the hands to the braces, if you please, Mr Bush. Fill the main-tops'l and lay her on the starboard tack.'

'Starboard tack. Aye aye, sir.'

Hotspur crept northward through the growing night, following after *Doris*, heading towards the big ships and Point Matthew.

'There goes the semaphore again, sir.'

'Thank you.'

There was just light enough in the darkening sky to see the telegraphic arms silhouetted against it, as they spun round, signalling the latest move on the part of the British, this concentration towards the north – this relaxing of the hold of the British navy on the passages of the south.

'Only just keep her going,' said Hornblower to the quartermasters at the helm. 'Don't let the Frogs see what we're up to.'

'Aye aye, sir.'

Hornblower was feeling nervous; he did not want to leave the Toulinguet Passage too far behind him. He turned his glass towards the Inshore Squadron. Now there was a strip of red sky along the horizon behind it – the last light of day – and against it the sails of the ships of the line stood out in startling black. The red was fading rapidly, and above it Venus could be seen; Pellew over there was holding on to the last possible moment. Pellew was not only a man of iron nerve; he was a man who never underestimated his enemy. At last; the rectangles of the silhouetted topsails shortened, hesitated, and lengthened again.

'Inshore Squadron's hauled its wind, sir.'

'Thank you.'

Already the topsails were out of sight with the complete fading of the sky. Pellew had timed the move perfectly. A Frenchman on Petit Minou could not help but think that Pellew, looking towards the night-covered east, had thought that his ships were now invisible, and had come to the wind without realising that the move could still be seen by an observer looking towards the west. Hornblower stared round him. His eyes were aching, so that with his hands on the hammock netting he closed his eyes to rest them. Never had a minute seemed so long as that one. Then he opened them again. The light was all gone. Venus was shining where once the sun had shone. The figures about him were almost invisible. Now one or two of the brighter stars could be seen, and *Hotspur* must be lost to sight, to that unknown observer on Petit Minou. He gulped, braced himself, and plunged into action.

'Take in the tops'ls and topgallants!'

Hands rushed aloft. In the gentle night the vibration of the shrouds as fifty men ran up the ratlines could be distinctly heard.

'Now, Mr Bush, wear the ship, if you please. Course sou' by west.'

'Sou' by west, sir.'

Soon it was time for the next order.

'Send the topgallant masts down!'

This was the time when drill and practice revealed their value. In the dark night what had once been a mere toilsome exercise was performed without a hitch.

'Set the fore and main topmast stays'ls. Get the fores'l in.'

Hornblower walked over to the binnacle.

'How does she handle under this sail?'

There was a pause while the almost invisible figure at the wheel spun it tentatively this way and that. 'Well enough, sir.'

'Very well.'

Hornblower had altered the silhouette of the *Hotspur* as entirely as he could. With only her fore and aft sails and her main course set, and her topgallant masts sent down, even an experienced seaman on this dark night would have to look twice or thrice to recognise what he saw. Hornblower peered at the chart in the faint light of the binnacle. He concentrated on it, to find the effort unnecessary. For two days now he had been studying it and memorising this particular section; it was fixed in his mind and it seemed as if he would be able to visualise it to his dying day – which might be today. He looked up, to find, as he expected, that exposure to that faint light had temporarily made his eyes quite blind in the darkness. He would not do it again.

'Mr Prowse! You can keep your eye on the chart from now on when you think it necessary. Mr Bush! Choose the best two hands you know with the lead and send them aft to me.' When the two dark figures reported Hornblower gave them curt orders. 'Get into the main chains on each side. I don't want you to make a sound more than you can help. Don't make a cast unless I order it. Haul your lines in and then let 'em out to four fathoms. We're making three knots through the water, and when the flood starts we'll be making next to nothing over the ground. Keep your fingers on your lines and pass the word quietly about what you feel. I'll station hands to pass the word. Understand?'

'Aye aye, sir.'

Four bells struck to mark the end of the second dog watch.

'Mr Bush, that's the last time I want the bell to strike. Now you may clear for action. No, wait a moment, if you please. I want the guns loaded with two rounds of shot each and run out. Have the coigns in and the guns at extreme depression. And as soon as the men are at their quarters I don't want to hear another sound. Not a word, not a whisper. The man who drops a hand-spike on the deck will get two dozen. Not the slightest sound.'

'Aye aye, sir.'

'Very well, Mr Bush. Carry on.'

There was a roar and a rattle as the hands went to their quarters, as the gun-ports opened and the guns were run out. Then silence closed in upon the ship. Everything was ready, from the gunner down in the magazine to the look-out in the foretop, as the *Hotspur* reached silently down to the southward with the wind one point abaft the beam.

'One bell in the first watch, sir,' whispered Prowse, turning the sand-glass by the binnacle. An hour ago the flood tide had started to make. In another half-hour the clustered coasters to the southward, huddled under the shelter of the batteries at Camaret, would be casting off; no, they would be doing that at this moment, for there should be just enough water for them. They would be sweeping and kedging out, to run with the flood up the dangerous Toulinguet Passage, round the point and up the Goulet. They would hope to reach the Little Girls and safety, as the tide carried them into Brest Roads where the provisions and the cordage and the canvas with which they were laden were so eagerly awaited by the French fleet. To the north, back at the Petit Minou, Hornblower could imagine the bustle and the excitement. The movements of the Inshore Squadron must have been noted. Sharp eyes on the French shore had told anxious minds of the insufficiently concealed preparations for a concentration of force and a heavy blow. Four ships of the line and two big frigates could muster a landing force – even without drawing on the main fleet – of a thousand men or more. There were probably twice as many French infantry and artillery-men along the coast there, but, spread out along five miles, they were vulnerable to a sharp attack launched at an unexpected point on a dark night. There was a large accumulation of coasting vessels there as well, sheltering under the batteries on the far side of Cape Matthew. They had crept from battery to battery for hundreds of miles – spending weeks in doing so – and now were huddled in the little creeks and bays waiting for a chance to complete the last and most dangerous run into Brest. The menacing approach of the Inshore Squadron would make them nervous in case the British meditated some new attack, a cutting-out expedition, or fire-ships, or bomb-vessels, or even these new-fangled rockets. But at least this concentration of the British strength to the north left the south unwatched, as the signal station of Petit Minou would report. The coasters round Camaret – chasse-marees, tide-chasers – would be able to take advantage of the tide run through the horribly dangerous Toulinguet Passage up into the Goulet. Hornblower was hoping, in fact he was confident, that *Hotspur* had not been seen to turn back to stop this bolt hole. She drew six feet of water less than any frigate, hardly more than the big chasse-marees, and were she boldly handled her arrival among the rocks and shoals of Toulinguet would be totally unexpected.

'Two bells, sir,' whispered Prowse. This was the moment when the tide would be running at its fastest, a four knot tide, rising a full thirty feet, racing up through Toulinguet Passage and round the Council Rocks into the Goulet. The hands were behaving well; only twice had restless individuals started skylarking in the darkness, to be instantly suppressed by stern mutterings from the petty officers.

'Touching bottom to starboard, sir,' came a whisper from the gang-way, and instantly afterwards, 'Touching bottom to port.'

The hands at the leads had twenty-four feet of line out between the leads and the surface of the water, but with the ship moving gently in this fashion even the heavy leads trailed behind to some extent. There must be some sixteen feet only – five feet to spare.

'Pass the word. What bottom do you feel?'

In ten seconds the answer came back. 'Sandy bottom, sir.'

'That must be well off Council Rocks, sir,' whispered Prowse.

'Yes. Quartermaster, one point to starboard.'

Hornblower stared through the night-glass. There was the shadowy shore-line just visible. Yes, and there was a gleam of white, the gentlest of surfs breaking on Council Rocks. A whisper from the gangway.

'Rocky bottom now, sir, shoaling a little.'

'Very well.'

On the starboard bow he could see faint whiteness too. That was the surf on all the wild tangle of rocks and shoals outside the Passage – Corbin, Trepieds, and so on. The tiny night breeze was still holding steady.

'Pass the word. What bottom?'

The question awaited an answer for some time, as the chain of communication broke down and the answer had to be repeated. At last it came.

'Rocky bottom, sir. But we're hardly moving over the ground.'

So *Hotspur* was now stemming the rising tide, hanging suspended in the darkness, less than a yard of water under her keel, the tide rushing past her, the wind thrusting her into it. Hornblower worked out problems in his head.

'Quartermaster, two points to port.'

It called for nice calculation, for now *Hotspur* was braced sharp up – twice the staysails had flapped in warning – and there was leeway to be allowed for as *Hotspur* crept crabwise across the tide.

'Mr Bush, go for'rard to the port side main chains and come back to report.'

What a lovely night it was, with this balmy air sighing through the rigging, the stars shining and the gentle sound of the surf.

'We're moving over the ground, sir,' whispered Bush. 'Rocky bottom, and the port side lead's under the ship.'

Hotspur's crabwise motion would produce that effect.

'Three bells, sir,' reported Prowse.

There would be water enough now for the coasters to negotiate the shoals off Rougaste and to have entered into the channel. It could not be long now, for the tide flowed for no more than four and a half hours and the coasters could not afford to waste time – or so he had calculated when he had made his suggestion to Pellew, for this moonless night with the tide making at this particular moment. But it might of course all end in a ridiculous fiasco, even if *Hotspur* did not touch on one of the menacing rocks that beset her course.

'Look, sir! Look!' whispered Bush urgently. 'One point before the beam!'

Yes. A shadowy shape, a darker nucleus on the dark surface. More than that; the splash of a sweep at work. More than that; other dark shapes beyond. There had been fifty coasters, by the last intelligence, at Camaret, and the chances were they would try the run all together.

'Get down to the starboard battery, Mr Bush. Warn the guns' crews. Wait for my order, and then make every shot tell.'

'Aye aye, sir.'

Despite the precautions he had taken, *Hotspur* would be far more visible than the coasters; she should have been observed from them by now; except that the Frenchmen would be preoccupied with their problems of navigation. Ah! There was a yell from the nearest coaster, a whole series of hails and shouts and warnings.

'Open fire, Mr Bush!'

A red glare in the darkness, an ear-splitting bang, the smell of powder smoke. Another glare, another bang. Hornblower fumbled for the speaking-trumpet, ready to make himself heard through the firing. But Bush was behaving admirably, and the gunners were keeping their heads, with the guns going off singly as the captains made sure of their targets. With the guns depressed the two round-shot hurtling from each would sweep the smooth surface of the sea. Hornblower thought he could hear shrieks from the stricken coasters, but the guns were firing at only the briefest intervals. The gentle wind swept the smoke along the ship, clouds of it billowing in dark waves round Hornblower. He leaned out to keep clear of it. The din was continuous now, as guns fired, as the carriage-trucks rumbled over the deck, as gun-captains bellowed orders. The flash of a gun illuminated something close overside – a sinking coaster, deck level with the water. Her frail side must have been beaten in by half a dozen round-shot. A yell from the main chains cut through the din.

'Here's one of 'em coming aboard!'

Some desperate swimmer had reached the *Hotspur*; Hornblower could leave Bush to deal with prisoners of that sort. There were more dark shapes to starboard, more targets presenting themselves. The mass of the coasters was being hurried along by the three-knot tide which *Hotspur* was stemming by the aid of the wind. Tug at their sweeps as they might, the French crews could not possibly counter the tide. They could not turn back; to turn aside was possible – but on one side were the Council Rocks, on the other were Corbin and Trepids and the whole tangle of reefs round-about them. *Hotspur* was having experiences like those of Gulliver; she was a giant compared with these Lilliputian coasters after having been a dwarf in her encounter with the Brobdingnagian *Loire*.

Fine on the port bow Hornblower caught sight of half a dozen pinpoints of fire. That would be the battery on Toulinguet, two thousand yards away. At that range they were welcome to try their luck, firing at *Hotspur*'s gun flashes. *Hotspur*, still travelling slowly over the ground, was a moving target, and the French would be disturbed in their aim through fear of hitting the coasters. Night-firing in those conditions was a waste of powder and shot. Foreman was yelling, wild with excitement, to the crew of the quarter-deck carronade.

'She's aground! Drop it – dead 'un!'

Hornblower swung round to look; the coaster there was undoubtedly on the rocks and consequently not worth firing at. He mentally gave a mark of approval to Foreman, who despite his youth and his excitement was keeping his head, even though he made use of the vocabulary of the rat-killing pit.

'Four bells, sir,' reported Prowse amid the wild din. That was an abrupt reminder to Hornblower that he must keep his head, too. It was hard to think and to calculate, harder still to recall his visualisation of the chart, and yet he had to do so. He realised that *Hotspur* could have nothing to spare over on the landward side.

'Wear the ship – Mr Prowse,' he said; he remembered just too late to use the formal address completely naturally. 'Get her over on the port tack.'

'Aye aye, sir.'

Prowse seized the speaking-trumpet and somewhere in the darkness disciplined men hurried to sheets and braces. As *Hotspur* swung about another dark shape came down at her from the channel.

'*Je me rends! Je me rends!*' a voice was shouting from it.

Someone in that coaster was trying to surrender before *Hotspur's* broadside could blow her out of the water. She actually bumped against the side as the current took her round, and then she was free – her surrender had been premature, for now she was past *Hotspur* and vanishing in the farther darkness.

'Main chains, there,' yelled Hornblower. 'Take a cast of the lead.'

'Two fathoms!' came the answering cry. There was only six inches under *Hotspur's* keel, but now she was drawing away from the perils on one side and approaching those on the other.

'Man the port-side guns! Keep the lead going on the starboard!'

Hotspur was steady on her new course as another unhappy coaster loomed up. In the momentary stillness Hornblower could hear Bush's voice as he called the port-side guns' crews to attention, and then came the crash of the firing. The smoke billowed round, and through the clouds came the cry of the leadsman.

'By the mark three!'

The smoke and the lead told conflicting stories.

'And a half three!'

'Wind must be backing, Mr Prowse. Keep your eye on the binnacle.'

'Aye aye, sir. And it's five bells, sir.'

The tide was almost at its height; another factor to be remembered. At the port-side quarter-deck carronade the crew were slewing their weapon round to the limit of its arc, and Hornblower, looking over the quarter, could see a coaster escaping past *Hotspur's* stern. Two flashes from the dark shape, and a simultaneous crash under Hornblower's feet. That coaster had guns mounted, and was firing her pop-gun broadside, and at least one shot had told. A pop-gun broadside perhaps, but even a four-pounder could smash a hole in *Hotspur's* frail side. The carronade roared out in reply.

'Luff a little,' said Hornblower to the quartermasters; his mind was simultaneously recording the cries of the men at the leads. 'Mr Bush! Stand by with the port-side guns as we luff.'

Hotspur came to the wind; on the main-deck there were creakings and groanings as the guns' crews laboured with hand-spike and crowbar to train their weapons round.

'Take your aim!' shouted Bush, and after some pregnant seconds, 'Fire!'

The guns went off almost together, and Hornblower thought – although he was sure he was wrong – that he could hear instantly afterwards the crash of the shot upon the coasters' hulls. Certainly after that he heard shouts and cries from that direction while the smoke blinded him, but he had no time to spare for that. There was only half an hour of floodtide left. No more coasters could be coming along the channel, for if they did they would not be able to round the Council Rocks before the ebb set in. And it was full time to extricate *Hotspur* from the reefs and shoals that surrounded her. She needed what was left of the flood to carry her out, and even at half-tide she was likely to touch bottom and be left ignominiously stranded, helpless in daylight under the fire of the Toulinguet battery.

'Time to say good-bye,' he said to Prowse. He realised with a shock that he was on the edge of being lightheaded with strain and excitement, for otherwise he would not have said such a ridiculous thing. He must keep himself under control for a long while to come. It would be far more dangerous to touch bottom on a falling tide than on a rising one. He gulped and steadied himself, regaining his self-command at the cost of one more fierce effort.

'I'll handle the ship, Mr Prowse.' He raised the trumpet.

'Hands to the braces! Hands wear ship.'

A further order to the wheel brought the ship round on the other tack, with Prowse at the binnacle calling her heading. Now he had to thread his way out through the perils that encompassed her. The hands, completely carefree, were inclined to show their elation by noisy skylarking, but one single savage reproof from Bush silenced them, and *Hotspur* fell as quiet as a church as she crept out.

'Wind's backed three points since sunset, sir,' reported Prowse.

'Thank you.'

With the wind just abaft the beam *Hotspur* handled easily, but by this time instinct had to take the place of calculation. Hornblower had come in to the very limit of safety at high water over shallows hardly covered at high tide. He had to feel his way out, by the aid of the lead, by what could be seen of the shore and the shoals. The wheel spun over and back again as the ship nosed her way out. For a few perilous seconds she was sailing by the lee, but Hornblower was able to order the helm over again in the nick of time.

'Slack water now, sir,' reported Prowse.

'Thank you.'

Slack water, if any of the incalculable factors had not intervened. The wind had been slight but steady for several days from the south-eastward. He had to bear that in mind along with all the other factors.

'By the mark five!' called the leadsman.

'Thank God!' muttered Prowse.

For the first time *Hotspur* had nearly twenty feet of water under her keel, but there were still some outlying pinnacles of rock to menace her.

'Starboard a point,' ordered Hornblower.

'Deep six!'

'Mr Bush!' Hornblower must stay steady and calm. He must betray no relief, no human feelings, although within him the desire to laugh like an idiot welled up in combat with the frightful exhaustion he felt. 'Kindly secure the guns. Then you may dismiss the hands from general quarters.'

'Aye aye, sir.'

'I must thank you, Mr Prowse, for your very able assistance.'

'Me, sir?' Prowse went on in incoherent self-depreciation. Hornblower could imagine the lantern-jaws working in surprise, and he ignored the mumblings.

'You may heave the ship to, Mr Prowse. We don't want dawn to find us under the guns of Petit Minou.'

'No, sir, of course not, sir.'

All was well. *Hotspur* had gone in and come out again. The coasters from the south had received a lesson they would not forget for a long time. And now it was apparent that the night was not so dark; it was not a question of eyes becoming habituated to the darkness, but something more definite than that. Faces were now a blur of white, visible across the deck. Looking aft Hornblower could see the low hills of Quelern standing out in dark relief against a lighter sky, and while he watched a grain of silver became visible over their summits. He had actually forgotten until this moment that the moon was due to rise now; that had been one of the factors he had pointed out in his letter to Pellew. The gibbous moon rose above the hilltops and shone serenely down upon the Gulf. The topgallant masts were being sent up, topsails were being set, staysails got in.

'What's that noise?' asked Hornblower, referring to a dull thumping somewhere forward.

'Carpenter plugging a shot hole, sir,' explained Bush. 'That last coaster holed us just above the waterline on the starboard side right for'rard.'

'Anyone hurt?'

'No, sir.'

'Very well.'

His questions and his formal termination of the conversation were the result of one more effort of will.

'I can trust you not to lose your way now, Mr Bush,' he said. He could not help being jocular, although he knew it sounded a false note. The hands at the braces were backing the main-topsail, and *Hotspur* could lie hove-to in peace and quiet. 'You may set the ordinary watches, Mr Bush. And see that I am called at eight bells in the middle watch.'

'Aye aye, sir.'

There were four and a half hours of peace and quiet ahead of him. He yearned with all his weary mind and body for rest – for oblivion, rather than rest. An hour after dawn, at the latest, Pellew could expect him to send in his report on the events of the evening, and it would take an hour to compose it. And he must take the opportunity to write to Maria so that the letter could be sent to *Tonnant* along with the report and so have a chance to reach the outside world. It would take him longer to write to Maria than to Pellew. That reminded him of something else. He had to make one more effort.

'Oh, Mr Bush!'

'Sir?'

'I'll be sending a boat to *Tonnant* during the morning watch. If any officer – or if any of the men – wish to send letters that will be their opportunity.'

'Aye aye, sir. Thank you, sir.'

In his cabin he faced one further effort to pull off his shoes, but the arrival of Grimes saved him the trouble. Grimes took off his shoes, eased him out of his coat, unfastened his neckcloth. Hornblower allowed him to do it; he was too weary even to be self-conscious. For one moment he luxuriated in allowing his weary feet free play in his stockings, but then he fell spreadeagled on to his cot, half-prone, half on his side, his head on his arms, and Grimes covered him up and left him.

That was not the most sensible attitude to adopt, as he discovered when Grimes shook him awake. He ached in every joint, it seemed, while to dash cold sea water on his face did little enough to clear his head. He had to struggle out of the after-effects of a long period of strain as other men had to struggle out of the after effects of a drinking bout. But he had recovered sufficiently to move his left-handed pen when he sat down and began his report.

'Sir,

In obedience to your instructions, dated the 16th instant, I proceeded on the afternoon of the 18th . . .'

He had to leave the last paragraph until the coming of daylight should reveal what he should write in it, and he laid the letter aside and took another sheet. He had to bite the end of his pen before he could even write the salutation in this second letter, and when he had written 'My dear Wife' he had to bite it again before he could continue. It was something of a relief to have Grimes enter at last.

'Mr Bush's compliments, sir, and it's not far off daylight.'

That made it possible to conclude the letter.

'And now, my dearest—' Hornblower glanced at Maria's letter to select an endearment – 'Angel, my duty calls me once more on deck, so that I must end this letter with—' another reference – 'fondest love to my dear Wife, the loved Mother of the Child to be.

Your affectionate Husband,

Horatio.'

Daylight was coming up fast when he arrived on deck.

'Brace the maintops'l round, if you please, Mr Young. We'll stand to the s'uth'ard a little. Good morning, Mr Bush.'

'Good morning, sir.'

Bush was already trying to see to the southward through his telescope. Increasing light and diminishing distance brought rapid results.

'There they are, sir! God, sir – one, two, three – and there are two others over on the Council Rocks. And that looks like a wreck right in the fairway – that's one we sunk, I'll wager, sir.'

In the glittering dawn the half-tide revealed wrecks littering the shoals and the shore, black against the crystal light, the coasters which had paid the penalty of trying to run the blockade.

'They're all holed and waterlogged, sir,' said Bush. 'Not a hope of salvage.'

Hornblower was already composing in his mind the final paragraph of his report.

'I have reason to believe that not less than ten sail of coasters were sunk or forced to run aground during this encounter. This happy result . . .'

'That's a fortune lost, sir,' grumbled Bush. 'That's a tidy sum in prize money over on those rocks.'

No doubt, but in those decisive moments last night there could have been no question of capture. *Hotspur's* duty had been to destroy everything possible, and not to fill her captain's empty purse by sending boats to take possession, at the cost of allowing half the quarry to escape. Hornblower's reply was cut off short, as the smooth water on the starboard beam suddenly erupted in three successive jets of water. A cannon-ball had come skipping towards them over the surface, to make its final plunge a cable's length away. The sound of gunfire reached their ears at the same moment, and their instantly elevated telescopes revealed a cloud of smoke engulfing the Toulinguet battery.

'Fire away, Monseer le Frog,' said Bush. 'The damage is done.'

'We may as well make sure we're out of range,' said Hornblower. 'Put the ship about, if you please.'

He was trying as best he could to reproduce Bush's complete indifference under fire. He told himself that he was only being sensible, and not cowardly, in making certain that there was no chance of *Hotspur's* being hit by a salvo of twenty-four-pounders, but he was inclined to sneer at himself, all the same.

Yet there was one source of self-congratulation. He had held his tongue when the subject of prize money had come up in the conversation. He had been about to burst out condemning the whole system as pernicious, but he had managed to refrain. Bush thought him a queer character in any case, and if he had divulged his opinion of prize money – of the system by which it was earned and paid – Bush would have thought him more than merely eccentric. Bush would think him actually insane, and liberal-minded, revolutionary, subversive and dangerous as well.

IX

Hornblower stood ready to go down the side into the waiting boat. He made the formal, legal speech.

'Mr Bush, you will take command.'

'Aye aye, sir.'

Hornblower remembered to look about him as he prepared to make the descent. He glowered round at the sideboys in the white gloves that Bush had had made for this ceremonial purpose out of white twine by some seaman adept with a hook – 'crochet' was the French name for this process. He ran his eyes up and down the bos'n's mates as they piped his departing salute. Then he went over the side. The piping stopped at the same moment as his foot reached for the thwart – that was a measure of the height of *Hotspur's* free-board, for by the rules of ceremonial the honours ceased the moment the departing officer's head was at the level of the deck. Hornblower scrambled into the stern sheets, embarrassed by hat and gloves and sword and boat cloak, and he barked an order to Hewitt. The boat-hook released its hold and there was a moment of apparent disorder as the boat left the ship's side and four brawny arms at the halliards sent the balance-lug up the mast. There was a decided strangeness at sitting here on a level with the water, with the green waves close at hand; it was over eight weeks since Hornblower had last set foot outside the ship.

The boat settled on her course, running free because the wind had backed southerly several points, and Hornblower looked back at *Hotspur* lying hove-to. He ran a professional eye over her lines, noting, as an observer from the outside again, the relative heights of her masts, the distances at which they were stepped, the rake of the bowspit. He knew a great deal now about the behaviour of the ship under sail, but there was always more to learn. Not at this moment, though, for a stronger puff of wind laid the boat over and Hornblower felt suddenly uncertain both of his surroundings and himself. The little waves of which *Hotspur* took no notice were monstrous when encountered in a small boat, which, besides lying over, was now rising and swooping in a most unpleasant fashion. After the reassuring solidity of *Hotspur's* deck – after painfully accustoming himself to her motion – these new surroundings and these new antics were most unsettling, especially as Hornblower was excited and tense at the prospect before him. He swallowed hard, battling against the sea-sickness which had leaped out of ambush for him; to divert his mind he concentrated his attention upon the *Tonnant*, growing slowly nearer – much too slowly.

At her main topgallant masthead she sported the coveted broad pendant in place of the narrow one worn by other ships in commission. It was the sign of a captain with executive powers over other ships besides his own. Pellew was not only high up in the captains' list but clearly destined for important command as soon as he reached flag rank; there must be rear admirals in the Channel Fleet bitterly jealous of Pellew's tenure of the Inshore Command. A boat came along her starboard side, painted white picked out with red, and of a design unlike that of the workaday boats supplied by the Navy Office. Hornblower could see the matching red and white uniforms of the boat's crew; this must be some very dandy captain at last, paying a call – or more likely a flag officer. Hornblower saw a ribboned and epauletted figure go up the side, and across the water came the sound of the squealing of the pipes and the boomp-bump noise that to his ears indicated a band playing. Next moment the White Ensign broke out at the foretopmast-head. A vice-admiral of the White! That could be no other than Cornwallis himself.

Hornblower realised that this meeting to which he had been summoned by the curt signal 'All captains,' was something more than a sociable gathering. He looked down in distress at his shabby clothing, reminded as he did so to open his boat cloak and reveal the epaulette on his left shoulder – a shabby brassy thing, dating back to the time of his earlier, disallowed appointment as commander, two years ago. Hornblower distinctly saw the officer of the watch, in attendance at the gangway, turn from his telescope and give an order which sent four of the eight white-gloved side-boys there scurrying out of sight, so that a mere commander should not share the honours given a vice-admiral. The admiral's barge had sheered off and the *Hotspur*'s boat took its place, with Hornblower not too sea-sick and nervous to worry about the way it was handled, in case it did not reflect credit on his ship. The worry, however, was instantly overlaid by the necessity for concentration on the process of going up the side. This was a lofty two-decker, and although the considerable 'tumble-home' was of help it was a tricky business for the gangling Hornblower to mount with dignity encumbered as he was. Somehow he reached the deck, and somehow, despite his shyness and embarrassment, he remembered to touch his hat in salute to the guard that presented arms to him.

'Captain Hornblower?' enquired the officer of the watch. He knew him by the single epaulette on his left shoulder, the only commander in the Inshore Squadron, perhaps the only one in the Channel Fleet. 'This young gentleman will act as your guide.'

The deck of the *Tonnant* seemed incredibly spacious after the cramped deck of the *Hotspur*, for the *Tonnant* was no mere seventy-four. She was an eighty-four, with dimensions and scantlings worthy of a three-decker. She was a reminder of the era when the French built big ships in the hope of overpowering the British seventy-fours by brute force instead of by skill and discipline. How the venture had turned out was proved by the fact that *Tonnant* now flew the flag of England.

The great poop-cabins had been thrown into a single suite for Pellew, in the absence of a flag-officer permanently on board. It was incredibly luxurious. Once past the sentry the decks were actually carpeted – Wilton carpets in which the foot sank noiselessly. There was an anteroom with a steward in dazzling white ducks to take Hornblower's hat and gloves and cloak.

'Captain Hornblower, sir,' announced the young gentleman, throwing open the door.

The deck-beams above were six feet clear, over the carpet, and Pellew had grown so used to this that he advanced to shake hands with no stoop at all, in contrast with Hornblower, who instinctively crouched with his five-foot-eleven.

'Delighted to see you, Hornblower,' said Pellew. "Genuinely delighted. There is much to say to you, for letters are always inadequate. But I must make the introductions. The Admiral has already made your acquaintance, I think?'

Hornblower shook hands with Cornwallis, mumbling the same politenesses as he had already addressed to Pellew. Other introductions followed, names known to everyone who had read in the *Gazette* the accounts of naval victories; Grindall of the *Prince*,

Marsfield of the *Minotaur,* Lord Henry Paulet of the *Terrible,* and
half a dozen others. Hornblower felt dazzled, although he had just
come in from the bright outer world. In all this array there was one
other officer with a single epaulette, but he wore it on his right
shoulder, proof that he, too, had attained the glorious rank of post
captain, and had only to go on living to mount a second epaulette
on attaining three years' seniority, and – if long life was granted him
– eventually to attain the unspeakable heights of flag rank. He was
far higher above a commander than a commander was above a lowly
lieutenant.

Hornblower sat in the chair offered him, instinctively edging it
backward so as to make himself, the most junior, the infinitely junior
officer, as inconspicuous as possible. The cabin was finished in some
rich material – damask, Hornblower guessed – with a colour scheme
of nutmeg and blue unobtrusive and yet incredibly satisfying to the
eye. Daylight poured in through a vast stern window, to glint upon
the swaying silver lamps. There was a shelf of books, some in good
leather bindings, but Hornblower's sharp eye detected tattered copies
of the *Mariners' Guide* and the Admiralty publications for the coasts
of France. On the far side were two large masses so draped as to be
shapely and in keeping so that no uninitiated person could guess that
inside were two eighteen-pounder carronades.

'This must take you a full five minutes to clear for action, Sir
Edward,' said Cornwallis.

'Four minutes and ten seconds by stop-watch, sir,' answered Pellew,
'to strike everything below, including the bulkheads.'

Another steward, also in dazzling white ducks, entered at this
moment and spoke a few words in a low tone to Pellew, like a well-
trained butler in a ducal house, and Pellew rose to his feet.

'Dinner, gentlemen,' he announced. 'Permit me to lead the way.'

A door, thrown open in the midships bulkhead, revealed a dining-
room, an oblong table with white damask, glittering silver, sparkling
glasses, while more stewards in white ducks were ranged against the
bulkhead. There could be little doubt about precedence, when every
captain in the Royal Navy had, naturally, studied his place in the
captains' list ever since his promotion; Hornblower and the single-
epauletted captain were headed for the foot of the table when Pellew
halted the general sorting-out.

'At the Admiral's suggestion,' he announced, 'We are dispensing
with precedence today. You will find your names on cards at your
places.'

So now every one began a feverish hunt for their names; Hornblower found himself seated between Lord Henry Paulet and Hosier
of the *Fame,* and opposite him was Cornwallis himself.

'I made the suggestion to Sir Edward,' Cornwallis was saying as he leisurely took his seat, 'because otherwise we always find ourselves sitting next to our neighbours in the captains' list. In blockade service especially, variety is much to be sought after.'

He lowered himself into his chair, and when he had done so his juniors followed his example. Hornblower, cautiously on guard about his manners, still could not restrain his mischievous inner self from mentally adding a passage to the rules of naval ceremonial, to the lines of the rule about the officer's head reaching the level of the main-deck – 'when the Admiral's backside shall touch the seat of his chair—'.

'Pellew provides good dinners,' said Lord Henry, eagerly, scanning the dishes with which the stewards were now crowding the table. The largest dish was placed in front of him, and when the immense silver dish cover was whipped away a magnificent pie was revealed. The pastry top was built up into a castle, from the turret of which flew a paper Union Jack.

'Prodigious!' exclaimed Cornwallis. 'Sir Edward, what lies below the dungeons here?'

Pellew shook his head sadly. 'Only beef and kidneys, sir. Beef stewed to rags. Our ship's bullock this time, as ever, was too tough for ordinary mortals, and only stewing would reduce his steaks to digestibility. So I called in the aid of his kidneys for a beefsteak and kidney pie.'

'But what about the flour?'

'The Victualling Officer sent me a sack, sir. Unfortunately it had rested in bilge water, as could only be expected, but there was just enough at the top unspoiled for the pie-crust.'

Pellew's gesture, indicating the silver bread barges filled with ship's biscuit, hinted that in more fortunate circumstances they might have been filled with fresh rolls.

'I'm sure it's delicious,' said Cornwallis. 'Lord Henry, might I trouble you to serve me, if you can find it in your heart to destroy those magnificent battlements?'

Paulet set to work with carving knife and fork on the pie, while Hornblower pondered the phenomenon of the son of a Marquis helping the son of an Earl to a steak and kidney pie made from a ration bullock and spoiled flour.

'That's a ragout of pork beside you, Captain Hosier,' said Pellew. 'Or so my chef would call it. You may find it even saltier than usual, because of the bitter tears he shed into it. Captain Durham has the only live pig left in the Channel Fleet, and no gold of mine would coax it from him, so that my poor fellow had to make do with the contents of the brine tub.'

'He has succeeded perfectly with the pie, at least,' commented Cornwallis. 'He must be an artist.'

'I engaged him during the Peace,' said Pellew, 'and brought him with me on the outbreak of war. At quarters he points a gun on the starboard side lower-deck.'

'If his aim is as good as his cooking,' said Cornwallis, reaching for his glass which a steward had filled, 'then – confusion to the French!'

The toast was drunk with murmured acclaim.

'Fresh vegetables!' said Lord Henry ecstatically. 'Cauliflower!'

'Your quota is on the way to your ship at this moment, Hornblower,' said Cornwallis. 'We try not to forget you.'

'*Hotspur*'s like Uriah the Hittite,' said a saturnine captain at the end of the table whose name appeared to be Collins. 'In the forefront of the battle.'

Hornblower was grateful to Collins for that speech, because it brought home to him a truth, like a bright light, that he had not realised before; he would rather be on short commons in the forefront of the battle than back in the main body with plenty of vegetables.

'Young carrots!' went on Lord Henry, peering into each vegetable dish in turn. 'And what's this? I can't believe it!'

'Spring greens, Lord Henry,' said Pellew. 'We still have to wait for peas and beans.'

'Wonderful!'

'How do you get these chickens so fat, Sir Edward?' asked Grindall.

'A matter of feeding, merely. Another secret of my chef.'

'In the public interest you should disclose it, said Cornwallis. 'The life of a sea-sick chicken rarely conduces to putting on flesh.'

'Well, sir, since you ask. This ship has a complement of six hundred and fifty men. Every day thirteen fifty-pound bread bags are emptied. The secret lies in the treatment of those bags.'

'But how?' asked several voices.

'Tap them, shake them, before emptying. Not enough to make wasteful crumbs, but sharply enough. Then take out the biscuits quickly, and behold! At the bottom of each bag is a mass of weevils and maggots, scared out of their natural habitat and with no time allowed to seek shelter again. Believe me, gentlemen, there is nothing that fattens a chicken so well as a diet of rich biscuit-fed weevils. Hornblower, your plate's still empty. Help yourself, man.'

Hornblower had thought of helping himself to chicken, but somehow – and he grinned at himself internally – this last speech diverted him from doing so. The beefsteak pie was in great demand and had almost disappeared, and as a junior officer he knew better than to anticipate his seniors' second helpings. The ragout of pork, rich in onions, was at the far end of the table.

'I'll make a start on this, sir,' he said, indicating an untouched dish before him.

'Hornblower has a judgement that puts us all to shame,' said Pellew. 'That's a kickshaw in which my chef takes particular pride. To go with it you'll need these purée potatoes, Hornblower.'

It was a dish of brawn, from which Hornblower cut himself moderately generous slices, and it had dark flakes in it. There was no doubt that it was utterly delicious; Hornblower diving down into his general knowledge, came up with the conclusion that the black flakes must be truffle, of which he had heard but which he had never tasted. The purée potatoes, which he would have called mashed, were like no mashed potatoes he had ever sampled either on shipboard or in a sixpenny ordinary in England. They were seasoned subtly and yet to perfection – if angels ever ate mashed potatoes they would call on Pellew's chef to prepare them. With spring greens and carrots – for both of which he hungered inexpressibly – they made a plateful, along with the brawn, of sheer delight. He found himself eating like a wolf and pulled himself up short, but the glance that he stole round the table reassured him, for the others were eating like wolves too, to the detriment of conversation, with only a few murmured words to mingle with the clash of cutlery.

'Wine with you, sir.' 'Your health, Admiral.' 'Would you give the onions a fair wind, Grindall?' and so on.

'Won't you try the galantine, Lord Henry?' asked Pellew. 'Steward, a fresh plate for Lord Henry.'

That was how Hornblower learned the real name of the brawn he was eating. The ragout of pork drifted his way and he helped himself generously; the steward behind him changed his plate in the nick of time. He savoured the exquisite boiled onions that wallowed in the beatific sauce. Then like magic the table was cleared and fresh dishes made their appearance, a pudding rich with raisins and currants, jellies of two colours; much labour must have gone into boiling down the bullock's feet and into subsequent straining to make that brilliant gelatine.

'No flour for that duff,' said Pellew apologetically. 'The galley staff has done its best with biscuit crumbs.'

That best was as near perfection as mind could conceive; there was a sweet sauce with it, hinting of ginger, that made the most of the richness of the fruit. Hornblower found himself thinking that if ever he became a post captain, wealthy with prize money, he would have to devote endless thought to the organisation of his cabin stores. And Maria would not be of much help, he thought ruefully. He was still drifting along with thoughts of Maria when the table was swept clear again.

'Caerphilly, sir?' murmured a steward in his ear. 'Wensleydale? Red Cheshire?'

These were cheeses that were being offered him. He helped himself at random – one name meant no more to him than another – and went on to make an epoch-making discovery, that Wensleydale cheese and vintage port were a pair of heavenly twins, Castor and Pollux riding triumphantly as the climax of a glorious procession. Full of food and with two glasses of wine inside him – all he allowed himself – he felt vastly pleased with the discovery, rivalling those of Columbus and Cook. Almost simultaneously he made another discovery which amused him. The chased silver fingerbowls which were put on the table were very elegant; the last time he had seen anything like them was as a midshipman at a dinner at Government House in Gibraltar. In each floated a fragment of lemon peel, but the water in which the peel floated – as Hornblower discovered by a furtive taste as he dabbed his lips – was plain sea water. There was something comforting in that fact.

Cornwallis's blue eyes were fixed on him.

'Mr Vice, the King,' said Cornwallis.

Hornblower came back from pink hazes of beatitude. He had to take a grip of himself, as when he had tacked *Hotspur* with the *Loire* in pursuit; he had to await the right moment for the attention of the company. Then he rose to his feet and lifted his glass, carrying out the ages old ritual of the junior officer present.

'Gentlemen, the King,' he said.

'The King!' echoed everyone present, and some added phrases like 'God Bless him' and 'Long may he reign' before they sat down again.

'His Royal Highness the Duke of Clarence,' said Lord Henry in conversational tone, 'told me that during his time at sea he had knocked his head – he's a tall man, as you know – so often on so many deck beams while drinking his father's health that he seriously was considering requesting His Majesty's permission, as a special privilege, for the Royal Navy to drink the royal health while sitting down.'

At the other corner of the table Andrews, captain of the *Flora*, was going on with an interrupted conversation.

'Fifteen pounds a man,' he was saying. 'That's what my Jacks were paid on account of prize money, and we were in Cawsand Bay ready to sail. The women had left the ship, not a bumboat within call, and so my men – the ordinary seamen, mind you – still have fifteen pounds apiece in their pockets.'

'All the better when they get a chance to spend it,' said Marsfield.

Hornblower was making a rapid calculation. The *Flora* would have a crew of some three hundred men, who divided a quarter of the prize money between them. The captain had one quarter to himself, so that Andrews would have been paid – on account, not necessarily in full – some four thousand five hundred pounds as a result of some lucky cruise, probably without risk, probably without a life being lost, money for seizing French merchant ships intercepted at sea. Hornblower thought ruefully about Maria's latest letter, and about the uses to which he could put four thousand five hundred pounds.

'There'll be lively times in Plymouth when the Channel Fleet comes in,' said Andrews.

'That is something which I wish to explain to you gentlemen,' said Cornwallis, breaking in on the conversation. There was something flat and expressionless about his voice, and there was a kind of mask-like expression on his good-tempered face, so that all eyes turned on him.

'The Channel Fleet will not be coming in to Plymouth,' said Cornwallis. 'This is the time to make that plain.'

A silence ensued, during which Cornwallis was clearly waiting for a cue. The saturnine Collins supplied it.

'What about water, sir? Provisions?'

'They are going to be sent out to us.'

'Water, sir?'

'Yes. I have had four water-hoys constructed. They will bring us water. Victualling ships will bring us our food. Each new ship which joins us will bring us fresh food, vegetables and live cattle, all they can carry on deck. That will help against scurvy. I'm sending no ship back to replenish.'

'So we'll have to wait for the winter gales before we see Plymouth again, sir?'

'Not even then,' said Cornwallis. 'No ship, no captain, is to enter Plymouth without my express orders. Do I have to explain why, to experienced officers like you?'

The reasons were as obvious to Hornblower as to the others. The Channel Fleet might well have to run for shelter when southwesterly gales blew, and with a gale at southwest the French fleet could not escape from Brest. But Plymouth Sound was difficult; a wind from the eastward would delay the British fleet's exit, prolong it over several days, perhaps, during which time the wind would be fair for the French fleet to escape. There were plenty of other reasons, too. There was disease; every captain knew that ships grew healthier the longer they were at sea. There was desertion. There was the fact that discipline could be badly shaken by debauches on shore.

'But in a gale, sir?' asked someone. 'We could get blown right up-Channel.'

'No,' answered Cornwallis decisively. 'If we're blown off this station our rendezvous is Tor Bay. There we anchor.'

Confused murmurings showed how this information was being digested. Tor Bay was an exposed uncomfortable anchorage, barely sheltered from the west, but it had the obvious advantage that at the first shift of wind the fleet could put to sea, could be off Ushant again before the unwieldy French fleet could file out down the Goulet.

'So none of us will set foot on English soil again until the end of the war, sir?' said Collins.

Cornwallis's face was transfigured by a smile. 'We need never say that. All of you, any one of you, can go ashore . . .' the smile broadened as he paused, 'the moment I set foot ashore myself.'

That caused a laugh, perhaps a grudging laugh, but with an admiring echo. Hornblower, watching the scene keenly, suddenly came to a fresh realisation. Collins's questions and remarks had been very apt, very much to the point. Hornblower suspected that he had been listening to a prepared piece of dialogue, and his suspicions were strengthened by the recollection that Collins was First Captain under Cornwallis, somebody whom the French would call a Chief of Staff. Hornblower looked about him again. He could not help feeling admiration for Cornwallis, whose guileless behaviour concealed such unsuspected depths of subtlety. And it was a matter for self-congratulation that he had guessed the secret, he, the junior officer present, surrounded by all these captains of vast seniority, of distinguished records and of noble descent. He felt positively smug, a most unusual and gratifying feeling.

Smugness and vintage port combined to dull his awareness of all the implications at first, and then suddenly everything changed. The new thought sent him sliding down an Avernus of depression. It brought about an actual physical sensation in the pit of his stomach, like the one he felt when *Hotspur*, close hauled, topped a wave and went slithering and rolling down the farther side. Maria! He had written so cheerfully saying he would be seeing her soon. There were only fifty days' provisions and water left in *Hotspur*; fresh food would eke out the provisions, but little enough could be done (he had thought) regarding water. He had been confident that *Hotspur* would be making periodic calls at Plymouth for food and water and firewood. Now Maria would never have the comfort of his presence during her pregnancy. Nor would he himself (and the violence of this reaction surprised him) have the pleasure of seeing her during her pregnancy. And one more thing; he would have to write to her and tell her that he would not be keeping his promises, that there was no chance of their meeting. He would be causing her terrible pain, not only because her idol would be revealed to her as a man who could not, or perhaps even would not, keep his word.

He was recalled suddenly from these thoughts, from these mental pictures of Maria, by hearing his name spoken during the conversation round the table. Nearly every one present was looking at him, and he had to ferret hurriedly through his unconscious memory to recapture what had been said. Someone – it must have been Cornwallis himself – had said that the information he had gathered from the French coast had been satisfactory and illuminating. But for the life of him Hornblower could not recall what had next been said, and now here he was, with every eye on him, gazing round the table with a bewilderment that he tried to conceal behind an impassive countenance.

'We are all interested in your sources of information, Hornblower,' prompted Cornwallis, apparently repeating something already said.

Hornblower shook his head in decisive negation; that was his instant reaction, before he could analyse the situation, and before he could wrap up a blunt refusal in pretty words.

'No,' he said, to back up the shaking of his head.

There were all these people present; nothing would remain a secret if known to so large a group. The pilchard fishermen and lobster-pot men with whom he had been having furtive dealings and on whom he had been lavishing British gold – French gold, to be exact – would meet with short shrift if their activities became known to the French authorities. Not only would they die, but they would never be able to supply him with any further news. He was passionately anxious for his secrets to remain secrets, yet he was surrounded by all these senior officers any one of whom might have an influence on his career. Luckily he was already committed by the curt negative that had been surprised out of him – nothing could commit him more deeply than that, and that was thanks to Maria. He must not think about Maria, yet he must find some way of softening his abrupt refusal.

'It's more important than a formula for fattening chickens, sir,' he said, and then, with a bright further inspiration he shifted the responsibility. 'I would not like to disclose my operations without a direct order.'

His sensibilities, keyed to the highest pitch, detected sympathy in Cornwallis's reaction.

'I'm sure there's no need, Hornblower,' said Cornwallis, turning back to the others. Now, before he turned, was it true that the eyelid of his left eye, nearest to Hornblower, flickered a trifle? Was it? Hornblower could not be sure.

As the conversation reverted to a discussion of future operations Hornblower's sense, almost telepathic, became aware of something else in the past atmosphere which called up hot resentment in his mind. These fighting officers, these captains of ships of the line, were content to leave the dirty details of the gathering of intelligence to a junior, to someone hardly worthy of their lofty notice. They would not sully their aristocratic white hands; if the insignificant Commander of an insignificant sloop chose to do the work they would leave it to him in tolerant contempt.

Now the contempt was in no way one-sided. Fighting captains had their place in the scheme of things, but only an insignificant place, and anyone could be a fighting captain, even if he had to learn to swallow down the heart from his mouth and master the tensions that set his limbs a-tremble. Hornblower was experiencing symptoms not unlike these at this moment, when he was in no danger at all. Vintage port and a good dinner, thoughts of Maria and resentment against the captains, combined within him in a witches' brew that threatened to boil over. Luckily the bubbling mixture happened to distil off a succession of ideas, first one and then another. They linked themselves in a logical chain. Hornblower, along with his agitation, could feel the flush of blood under his skin that foretold the development of a plan, in the same way that the witch in Macbeth could tell the approach of something wicked by the pricking in her thumbs. Soon the plan was mature, complete, and Hornblower was left calm and clear-headed after his spiritual convulsion; it was like the clearness of head that follows the crisis of an attack of fever – possibly that was exactly what it was.

The plan called for a dark night, and for half-flood an hour before dawn; nature would supply those sooner or later, following her immutable laws. It called for some good fortune, and it would call for resolution and promptitude of action, but those were accessory ingredients in every plan. It included possibilities of disaster, but was there ever a plan that did not? It also called for the services of a man who spoke perfect French, and Hornblower, measuring his abilities with a cold eye, knew that he was not that man. The penniless noble French refugee who in Hornblower's boyhood had instructed him, with fair success, in French and Deportment (and, totally unsuccessfully, in Music and Dancing), had never managed to confer a good accent upon his tone-deaf pupil. His grammar and his construction were excellent, but no one would ever mistake him for a Frenchman.

Hornblower had reached every necessary decision by the time the party began to break up, and he made it his business to take his stand, casually, beside Collins at the moment the Admiral's barge was called.

'Is there anyone in the Channel Fleet who speaks perfect French, sir?' he asked.

'You speak French yourself,' replied Collins.

'Not well enough for what I have in mind, sir,' said Hornblower, more struck by the extent of Collins's knowledge than flattered. 'I might find a use for a man who speaks French exactly like a Frenchman.'

'There's Côtard,' said Collins, meditatively rubbing his chin. 'Lieutenant in the *Marlborough*. He's a Guernsey-man. Speaks French like a native – always spoke it as a child, I believe. What do you want him to do?'

'Admiral's barge coming alongside, sir,' reported a breathless messenger to Pellew.

'Hardly time to tell you now, sir,' said Hornblower. 'I can submit a plan to Sir Edward. But it'll be no use without someone speaking perfect French.'

The assembled company was now filing to the gangway; Collins, in accordance with naval etiquette, would have to go down the side into the barge ahead of Cornwallis.

'I'll detail Côtard from his ship on special service,' said Andrews hastily. 'I'll send him over to you and you can look him over.'

'Thank you, sir.'

Cornwallis was now thanking his host and saying good-bye to the other captains; Collins unobtrusively yet with remarkable rapidity contrived to do the same, and disappeared over the side. Cornwallis followed, with all the time honoured ceremonial of guard of honour and band and sideboys, while his flag was hauled down from the fortopmast head. After his departure barge after barge came alongside, each gaudy with new paint, with every crew tricked out in neat clothing paid for out of their captains' pockets, and captain after captain went down into them, in order of seniority, and shoved off to their respective ships.

Lastly came *Hotspur's* drab little quarter-boat, its crew dressed in the clothes issued to them in the slop-ship the day they were sent on board.

'Good-bye, sir,' said Hornblower, holding out his hand to Pellew.

Pellew had shaken so many hands, and had said so many good-byes, that Hornblower was anxious to cut this farewell as short as possible.

'Good-bye, Hornblower,' said Pellew, and Hornblower quickly stepped back, touching his hat. The pipes squealed until his head was below the level of the main-deck, and then he dropped perilously into the boat, hat, gloves, sword and all, all of them shabby.

X

'I'll take this opportunity, Mr Bush,' said Hornblower, 'of repeating what I said before. I'm sorry you're not being given your chance.'

'It can't be helped, sir. It's the way of the Service, replied the shadowy figure confronting Hornblower on the dark quarter-deck. The words were philosophical, but the tone was bitter. It was all part of the general logical madness of war, that Bush should feel bitter at not being allowed to risk his life, and that Hornblower, about to be doing so, should commiserate with Bush, speaking in flat formal tones as if he were not in the least excited – as if he were feeling no apprehension at all.

Hornblower knew himself well enough to be sure that if some miracle were to happen, if orders were to arrive forbidding him to take personal part in the coming raid, he would feel a wave of relief; delight as well as relief. But it was quite impossible, for the orders had definitely stated that 'the landing party will be under the command of Captain Horatio Hornblower of the *Hotspur*.' That sentence had been explained in advance in the preceding one . . . 'because Lieut Côtard is senior to Lieut Bush.' Côtard could not possibly have been transferred from one ship and given command of a landing party largely provided by another; nor could he be expected to serve under an officer junior to him, and the only way round the difficulty had been that Hornblower should command. Pellew, writing out those orders in the quiet of his magnificent cabin, had been like a Valkyrie in the Norse legends now attaining a strange popularity in England – he had been a Chooser of the Slain. Those scratches of his pen could well mean that Bush would live and Hornblower would die.

But there was another side to the picture. Hornblower had grudgingly to admit to himself that he would have been no more happy if Bush had been in command. The operation planned could only be successful if carried through with a certain verve and with an exactness of timing that Bush possibly could not provide. Absurdly, Hornblower was glad he was to command, and that was one demonstration in his mind of the defects of his temperament.

'You are sure about your orders until I return, Mr Bush?' he said. 'And in case I don't return?'

'Yes, sir.'

Hornblower had felt a cold wave up his spine while he spoke so casually about the possibility of his death. An hour from now he might be a disfigured stiffening corpse.

'Then I'll get myself ready,' he said, turning away with every appearance of nonchalance.

He had hardly reached his cabin when Grimes entered.

'Sir!' said Grimes, and Hornblower swung round and looked at him. Grimes was in his early twenties, skinny, highly strung, and excitable. Now his face was white – his duties as steward meant that he spent little time on deck in the sun – and his lips were working horribly.

'What's the matter?' demanded Hornblower curtly.

'Don't make me come with you, sir!' spluttered Grimes. 'You don't want me with you, sir, do you, sir?'

It was an astonishing moment. In all his years of service Hornblower had never met with any experience in the least similar, and he was taken aback. This was cowardice; it might even be construed as mutiny. Grimes had in the last five seconds made himself liable not merely to the cat but to the noose. Hornblower could only stand and stare, wordless.

'I'll be no use, sir,' said Grimes. 'I – I might scream!'

Now that was a very definite point. Hornblower, giving his orders for the raid, had nominated Grimes as his messenger and aide-de-camp. He had given no thought to the selection; he had been a very casual Chooser of the Slain. Now he was learning a lesson. A frightened man at his elbow, a man made clumsy by fear, could imperil the whole expedition. Yet the first words he could say echoed his earlier thoughts.

'I could hang you, by God!' he exclaimed.

'No, sir! No, sir! Please, sir—' Grimes was on the point of collapse; in another moment he would be down on his knees.

'Oh, for God's sake—' said Hornblower. He was conscious of contempt, not for the coward, but for the man who allowed his cowardice to show. And then he asked himself by what right he felt this contempt. And then he thought about the good of the Service, and then—. He had no time to waste in these trivial analyses.

'Very well,' he snapped. 'You can stay on board. Shut your mouth, you fool!'

Grimes was about to show gratitude, but Hornblower's words cut it off short.

'I'll take Hewitt out of the second boat. He can come with me. Pass the word for him.'

The minutes were fleeting by, as they always did with the final touches to put on to a planned scheme. Hornblower passed his belt through the loop on a cutlass sheath, and buckled it round him. A sword hanging on slings could be a hindrance, would strike against obstructions, and the cutlass was a handier weapon for what he contemplated. He gave a final thought to taking a pistol, and again rejected the idea. A pistol might be useful in certain circumstances, but it was a bulky encumbrance. Here was something more silent – a long sausage of stout canvas filled with sand, with a loop for the wrist. Hornblower settled it conveniently in his right hand pocket.

Hewitt reported, and had to be briefly told what was expected of him. The sidelong glance he gave to Grimes revealed much of what Hewitt thought, but there was no time for discussion; that matter would have to be sorted out later. Hewitt was shown the contents of the bundle originally allotted to Grimes – the flint and steel for use if the dark lantern were extinguished, the oily rags, the slow match, the quick match, the blue lights for instant intense combustion. Hewitt took solemn note of each item and weighed his sandbag in his hand.

'Very well. Come along,' said Hornblower.

'Sir!' said Grimes at that moment in a pleading tone, but Hornblower would not – indeed could not – spare time to hear any more.

On deck it was pitch dark, and Hornblower's eyes took long to adjust themselves.

Officer after officer reported all ready.

'You're sure of what you have to say, Mr Côtard?'

'Yes, sir.'

There was no hint of the excitable Frenchman about Côtard. He was as phlegmatic as any commanding officer could desire.

'Fifty-one rank and file present, sir,' reported the captain of marines.

Those marines, brought on board the night before, had lain huddled below decks all day, concealed from the telescopes on Petit Minou.

'Thank you, Captain Jones. You've made sure no musket is loaded?'

'Yes, sir.'

Until the alarm was given not a shot was to be fired. The work was to be done with the bayonet and the butt, and the sandbag – but the only way to be certain of that was to keep the muskets unloaded.

'First landing party all down in the fishing-boat, sir,' reported Bush.

'Thank you, Mr Bush. Very well, Mr Côtard, we may as well start.'

The lobster-boat, seized earlier in the night to the surprise of its crew, lay alongside. The crew were prisoners down below; their surprise was due to the breach of the traditional neutrality enjoyed during the long wars by fishing-boats. These men were all acquainted with Hornblower, had often sold him part of their catch in exchange for gold, yet they had hardly been reassured when they were told that their boat would be returned to them later. Now it lay alongside, and Côtard followed Hewitt, and Hornblower followed Côtard, down into it. Eight men were squatting in the bottom where the lobster-pots used to lie.

'Sanderson, Hewitt, Black, Downes take the oars. The rest of you get down below the gunnels. Mr Côtard, sit here against my knees, if you please.'

Hornblower waited until they had settled themselves. The black silhouette of the boat must appear no different in the dark night. Now came the moment.

'Shove off,' said Hornblower.

The oars dragged through the water, bit more effectively at the next stroke, pulled smoothly at the third, and they were leaving *Hotspur* behind them. They were setting off on an adventure, and Hornblower was only too conscious that it was his own fault. If he had not been bitten with this idea they might all be peacefully asleep on board; tomorrow men would be dead who but for him would still be alive.

He put the morbid thought to one side, and then immediately he had to do the same with thoughts about Grimes. Grimes could wait perfectly well until his return, and Hornblower would not trouble his mind about him until then. Yet even so, as Hornblower concentrated on steering the lobster-boat, there was a continual undercurrent of thought — like ship's noises during a discussion of plans — regarding how the crew on board would be treating Grimes, for Hewitt, before leaving the ship, would have certainly told the story to his cronies.

Hornblower, with his hand on the tiller, steered a steady course northward towards Petit Minou. A mile and a quarter to go, and it would never do if he missed the little jetty so that the expedition would end in a miserable fiasco. He had the faint outline of the steep hills on the northern shore of the Goulet to guide him; he knew them well enough now, after all these weeks of gazing at them, and the abrupt shoulder, where a little stream came down to the sea a quarter of a mile west of the semaphore, was his principal guide. He had to keep that notch open as the boat advanced, but after a few minutes he could actually make out the towering height of the semaphore itself, just visible against the dark sky, and then it was easy.

The oars groaned in the rowlocks, the blades splashing occasionally in the water; the gentle waves which raised them and lowered them seemed to be made of black glass. There was no need for a silent or invisible approach; on the contrary, the lobster-boat had to appear as if she were approaching on her lawful occasions. At the foot of the abrupt shore was a tiny half-tide jetty, and it was the habit of the lobster-boats to land there and put ashore a couple of men with the pick of the catch. Then, each with a basket on his head containing a dozen live lobsters, they would run along the track over the hills into Brest so as to be ready for the opening of the market, regardless of whether the boat was delayed by wind and tide or not. Hornblower, scouting at a safe distance in the jolly boat, had ascertained during a succession of nights such of the routine as he had not been able to pick up in conversation with the fishermen.

There it was. There was the jetty. Hornblower found his grip tightening on the tiller. Now came the loud voice of the sentry at the end of the jetty.

'Qui va là?'

Hornblower nudged Côtard with his knee, unnecessarily, for Côtard was ready with the answer.

'Camille,' he hailed, and continued in French, 'Lobster-boat. Captain Quillien.'

They were already alongside; the crucial moment on which everything depended. Black, the burly Captain of the Forecastle, knew what he had to do the moment opportunity offered. Côtard spoke from the depths of the boat.

'I have the lobster for your officer.'

Hornblower, standing up and reaching for the jetty, could just see the dark of the sentry looking down, but Black had already leaped up from the bows like a panther, Downes and Sanderson following him. Hornblower saw a swift movement of shadows, but there was not a sound – not a sound.

'All right, sir,' said Black.

Hornblower, with a line in his hand, managed to propel himself up the slippery side, arriving on the top on his hands and knees. Black was standing holding the inanimate body of the sentry in his arms. Sandbags were silent; a vicious blow from behind at the exposed back of the neck, a quick grab, and it was finished. The sentry had not even dropped his musket; he and it was safe in Black's monstrous arms.

Black lowered the body – senseless or dead, it did not matter which – on to the slimy stone flags of the jetty.

'If he makes a sound cut his throat,' said Hornblower.

This was all orderly and yet unreal, like a nightmare. Hornblower, turning to drop a clove-hitch with his line over a bollard, found his upper lip was still drawn up in a snarl like a wild beast's. Côtard was already beside him; Sanderson had already made the boat fast forward.

'Come on.'

The jetty was only a few yards long; at the far end, where the paths diverged up to the batteries, they would find the second sentry. From the boat they passed up a couple of empty baskets, and Black and Côtard held them on their heads and set off, Côtard in the middle, Hornblower on the left, and Black on the right where his right arm would be free to swing his sandbag. There was the sentry. He made

no formal challenge, greeting them in jocular fashion while Côtard
spoke again about the lobster which was the recognised though unofficial toll paid to the officer commanding the guard for the use of the
jetty. It was a perfectly ordinary encounter until Black dropped his
basket and swung with his sandbag and they all three leaped on the
sentry, Côtard with his hands on the sentry's throat, Hornblower
striking madly with his sandbag as well, desperately anxious to make
sure. It was over in an instant, and Hornblower looked round at the
dark and silent night with the sentry's body lying at his feet. He and
Black and Côtard were the thin point of the wedge that had pierced
the ring of the French defences. It was time for the wedge to be driven
home. Behind them were the half-dozen others who had crouched
in the lobster-boat, and following them up were the seventy marines
and seamen in the boats of the *Hotspur*.

They dragged the second sentry back to the jetty and left him with
the two boat-keepers. Now Hornblower had eight men at his back
as he set his face to the steep climb up the path, the path he had only
seen through a telescope from *Hotspur's* deck. Hewitt was behind
him; the smell of hot metal and fat in the still night air told him that
the dark lantern was still alight. The path was stony and slippery, and
Hornblower had to exert his self-control as he struggled up it. There
was no need for desperate haste, and although they were inside the
ring of sentries, in an area where civilians apparently passed fairly
freely, there was no need to scramble noisily and attract too much
attention.

Now the path became less steep. Now it was level, and here it inter-
sected another path at right angles.

'Halt!' grunted Hornblower to Hewitt, but he took another two
paces forward while Hewitt passed the word back; a sudden stop
would mean that the people behind would be cannoning into each other.

This was indeed the summit. Owing to the levelling-off of the
top this was an area unsearched by telescopes from the *Hotspur*; even
from the main topgallant masthead, with the ship far out in the Iroise,
they had not been able to view the ground here. The towering telegraph had been plainly in view, and at its foot just a hint of a roof,
but they had not been able to see what was at ground level here, nor
had Hornblower been able to obtain any hint in his conversations with
fishermen.

'Wait!' he whispered back, and stepped cautiously forward, his
hands extended in front of him. Instantly they came into contact with
a wooden paling, quite an ordinary fence and by no means a military
obstacle. And this was a gate, an ordinary gate with a wooden latch.
Obviously the semaphore station was not closely guarded – fence and
gate were only polite warnings to unauthorised intruders – and of

course there was no reason why they should be, here among the French coastal batteries.

'Hewitt! Côtard!'

They came up to him and all three strained their eyes in the darkness.

'Do you see anything?'

'Looks like a house,' whispered Côtard.

Something in two storeys. Windows in the lower one, and above that a sort of platform. The crew who worked the telegraph must live here. Hornblower cautiously fumbled with the latch of the gate, and it opened without resistance. Then a sudden noise almost in his ear tensed him rigid, to relax again. It was a cock crowing, and he could hear a fluttering of wings. The semaphore crew must keep chickens in coops here, and the cock was giving premature warning of day. No reason for further delay; Hornblower whispered his orders to his band whom he called up to the gate. Now was the time; and this was the moment when the parties of marines must be half-way up the climb to the battery. He was on the point of giving the final word whe nhe saw something else which stopped him dead, and Côtard grabbed his shoulder at the same moment. Two of the windows before him were showing a light, a tiny glimmer, which nevertheless to their dilated pupils made the whole cottage plain to their view.

'Come on!'

They dashed forward, Hornblower, Côtard, Hewitt, and the two men with axes in one group, the other four musket men scattering to surround the place. The path led straight to a door, again with a wooden latch, which Hornblower feverishly tried to work. But the door resisted; it was bolted on the inside, and at the rattling of the latch a startled cry made itself heard inside. A woman's voice! It was harsh and loud, but a woman's voice, undoubtedly. The axeman at Hornblower's shoulder heaved up his axe to beat in the door, but at the same moment the other axeman shattered a window and went leaping through followed by Côtard. The woman's voice rose to a scream; the bolt was drawn and the door swung open and Hornblower burst in.

A tallow dip lit the odd scene, and Hewitt opened the shutter of the dark lantern to illuminate it further, sweeping its beam in a semi-circle. There were large baulks of timber, each set at an angle of forty-five degrees, to act as struts for the mast. Where floor space remained stood cottage furniture, a table and chairs, a rush mat on the floor, a stove. Côtard stood in the centre with sword and pistol, and at the far side stood a screaming woman. She was hugely fat, with a tangle of black hair, and all she wore was a nightshirt that hardly came to her knees. There was an inner door from which emerged a bearded man with hairy legs showing below his shirt-tails. The woman still screamed, but Côtard spoke loudly in French, waving his pistol – empty presumably – and the noise ceased, not, perhaps, because of Côtard's threats but because of the woman's sheer curiosity regarding these dawn intruders. She stood goggling at them, making only the most perfunctory gestures to conceal her nakedness.

But decisions had to be made; those screams might have given the alarm and probably had done so. Against the thick bulk of the semaphore mast a ladder led up to a trap door. Overhead must be the apparatus for working the semaphore-arms. The bearded man in his shirt must be the telegraphist, a civilian perhaps, and he and his wife presumably lived beside their work. It must have been convenient for them that the construction of the working platform overhead made it easy to build these cottage rooms underneath.

Hornblower had come to burn the semaphore, and burn it he would, even if a civilian dwelling were involved. The rest of his party were crowding into the living-room, two of the musket men appearing from the bedroom into which they must have made their way by another window. Hornblower had to stop and think for a perceptible space. He had expected that at this moment he would be fighting French soldiers, but here he was already in complete possession and with a woman on his hands. But his wits returned to him and he was able to put his thoughts in order.

'Get out, you musket men,' he said. 'Get out to the fence and keep watch. Côtard, up that ladder. Bring down all the signal books you can find. Any papers there are. Quick – I'll give you two minutes. Here's the lantern. Black, get something for this woman. The clothes from the bed'll do, and then take these two out and guard 'em. Are you ready to burn this place, Hewitt?'

It flashed through his mind that the *Moniteur* in Paris could make a great deal of noise about ill-treatment of a woman by the licentious British sailors, but it would do that however careful he might be. Black hung a ragged quilt over the woman's shoulders and then hustled his charge out of the front door. Hewitt had to stop and think. He had never set about burning a house before, and clearly he did not adapt himself readily to new situations.

'That's the place,' snapped Hornblower, pointing to the foot of the telegraph mast. There were the great baulks of timber round the mast; Hornblower joined with Hewitt in pushing the furniture under them, and then hurried into the bedroom to do the same.

'Bring some rags here!' he called.

Côtard came scrambling down the ladder with one arm full of books.

'Now. Let's start the fire,' said Hornblower.

It was a strange thing to do, in cold blood.

'Try the stove,' suggested Côtard.

Hewitt unlatched the door of the stove, but it was too hot to touch after that. He set his back to the wall and braced his feet against the stove and shoved; the stove fell and rolled, scattering a few embers over the floor. But Hornblower had snatched up a handful of blue lights from Hewitt's bundle; the tallow dip was still burning and available to light the fuses. The first fuse spluttered and then the firework spouted flames. Sulphur and saltpetre with a sprinkling of gunpowder; blue lights were ideal for this purpose. He tossed the blazing thing on to the oily rags, lit another and threw it, lit another still.

This was like some scene in Hell. The uncanny blue gleam lit the room, but soon the haze of smoke made everything dim, and the fumes of the burning sulphur offended their nostrils as the fireworks hissed and roared, while Hornblower went on lighting fuses and thrusting the blue lights where they would be most effective in living-room and bedroom. Hewitt in an inspired moment tore the rush mat up from the floor and flung it over rising flames of the rags. Already the timber was crackling and throwing out showers of yellow sparks to compete with the blue glare and the thickening smoke.

'That'll burn!' said Côtard.

The flames from the blazing mat were playing on one of the sloping timbers, and engendering new flames which licked up the rough wooden surface. They stood and watched fascinated. On this rocky summit there could be no well, no spring, and it would be impossible to extinguish this fire once it was thoroughly started. The laths of the partition wall were alight in two places where Hornblower had thrust blue lights into the crannies; he saw the flames at one point suddenly leap two feet up the partition with a volley of loud reports and fresh showers of sparks.

'Come on!' he said.

Outside the air was keen and clear and they blinked their dazzled eyes and stumbled over inequalities at their feet, but there was a faint tiny light suffusing the air, the first glimmer of daylight. Hornblower saw the vague shape of the fat woman standing huddled in her quilt; she was sobbing in a strange way, making a loud gulping noise regularly at intervals of a couple of seconds or so. Somebody must have kicked over the chicken coop, because there seemed to be clucking chickens everywhere in the half-light. The interior of the cottage was all ablaze, and now there was light enough in the sky for Hornblower to see the immense mast of the telegraph against it, oddly shaped with its semaphore arms dangling. Eight stout cables radiated out from it, attached to pillars sunk in the rock. The cables braced the unwieldy mast against the rude winds of the Atlantic, and the pillars served also to support the tottering picket fence that surrounded the place. There was a pathetic attempt at a garden on small patches of soil that might well have been carried up by hand from the valley below; a few pansies, a patch of lavender, and two unhappy geraniums trodden down by some blunderer.

Yet the light was still only just apparent; the flames that were devouring the cottage were brighter. He saw illuminated smoke pouring from the side of the upper storey, and directly after that flames shot out from between the warping timbers.

'The devil of a collection of ropes and blocks and levers up there,' said Côtard. 'Not much of it left by this time.'

'No one'll put that out now. And we've heard nothing from the marines,' said Hornblower. 'Come along, you men.'

He had been prepared to fight a delaying action with his musket men if the enemy had appeared before the place was well alight. Now it was unnecessary, so well had everything gone. So well, indeed, that it called for a moment or two's delay to collect the men. These leisurely minutes had made all haste appear unnecessary as they filed out through the gate. There was a slight haze lying over the surface of the summer sea; the topsails of the *Hotspur* – main-topsail aback – were far more visible than her hull, a grey pearl in the pearly mist. The fat woman stood at the gate, all modesty gone with the quilt that had fallen from her shoulders, waving her arms and shrieking curses at them.

From the misty valley on their right as they faced the descent came the notes of a musical instrument, some trumpet or bugle.

'That's their reveille,' commented Côtard, sliding down the path on Hornblower's heels.

He had hardly spoken when the call was taken up by other bugles. A second or two later came the sound of a musket shot, and then more musket shots, and along with them the echoing roll of a drum, and then more drums beating the alarm.

'That's the marines,' said Côtard.

'Yes,' snapped Hornblower. 'Come on!'

Musketry meant a bad mark against the landing party that had gone up against the battery. Very likely there was a sentry there, and he should have been disposed of silently. But somehow the alarm had been given. The guard had turned out – say twenty men armed and equipped – and now the main body was being roused. That would be the artillery unit in their hutments below the ridge; not too effective, perhaps, fighting with musket and bayonet, but over the other side there was a battalion of infantry at this very moment being roused from sleep. Hornblower had given his order and broken into a run along the right-hand path towards the battery before these thoughts had formulated themselves quite so clearly. He was ready with his new plan before they topped the ridge.

'Halt!'

They assembled behind him.

'Load!'

Cartridges were bitten open; pans were primed, and charges poured down the barrels of muskets and pistols. The wadded cartridge papers were thrust into the muzzles, the bullets were spat in on top, and then the ramrods were plied to drive all home.

'Côtard, take the musket men out to the flank. You others, come with me.'

There was the great battery with its four thirty-two pounders looking through the embrasures of its curving parapet. Beyond it a skirmish line of marines, their uniforms showing scarlet in the growing light, were holding at bay a French force only outlined by musket flashes and puffs of smoke. The sudden arrival of Côtard and his men, an unknown force on their flank caused the momentary withdrawal of this French force.

In the centre of the inner face of the parapet Captain Jones in his red coat with four other men were struggling with a door; beside him was laid out a bundle similar to the one Hewitt carried, blue lights, reels of slow match and quick match. Beyond him lay two dead marines, one of them shot hideously in the face. Jones looked up as Hornblower arrived, but Hornblower wasted no time in discussion.

'Stand aside! Axemen!'

The door was of solid wood and reinforced with iron, but it was only intended to keep out thieving civilians; a sentry was supposed to guard it, and under the thundering of the axes, it gave way rapidly.

'The guns are all spiked,' said Jones.

That was only the smallest part of the business. An iron spike driven into the touch-hole of a gun would render it useless in the heat of the moment, but an armourer working with a drill would clear it in an hour's work. Hornblower was on the step of the parapet looking over the top; the French were rallying for a new attack. But an axe-handle was working as a lever through a gap driven in the door. Black had hold of the edge of a panel and with a wild effort tore it free. A dozen more blows, another wrench, and there was a way open through the door. A crouching man could make his way into the blackness inside.

'I'll go,' said Hornblower. He could not trust Jones or the marines. He could trust no one but himself. He seized the reel of quick match and squeezed through the shattered door. There were timbered steps under his feet, but he expected that and so did not fall down them. He crouched under the roof and felt his way down. There was a

landing and a turn, and then more steps, much darker, and then his
outstretched hands touched a hanging curtain of serge. He thrust this
aside and stepped cautiously beyond it. Here it was utterly black. He
was in the magazine. He was in the area where the ammunition party
would wear list slippers, because nailed shoes might cause a spark to
ignite the gun-powder. He felt cautiously about him; one hand
touched the harsh outline of a cask. Those were the powder-barrels –
his hand involuntarily withdrew itself, as though it had touched a
snake. No time for that sort of idiocy, he was surrounded by violent
death.

He drew his cutlass, snarling in the darkness with the intensity of
his emotion. Twice he stabbed into the wall of cartridges, and his
ears were rewarded by the whispering sound of a cascade of powder-
grains pouring out through the gashes he had made. He must have
a firm anchorage for the fuse; and he stooped and sank the blade of
the cutlass into another cartridge. He unravelled a length of quick
match and wound a bight firmly round the hilt, and he buried the
end in the pile of powder-grains on the floor; an unnecessarily careful
measure, perhaps, when a single spark would set off the explosion.
Unreeling the quick match behind him, carefully, very carefully, lest
he jerk the cutlass loose, he made his way out past the curtain again,
and up the steps, up into the growing light, round the corner.
The light through the broken door was dazzling, and he blinked
as he came out crouching through it, still unreeling the quick
match.

'Cut this!' he snapped, and Black whipped out his knife and sawed
through the quick match at the point indicated by Hornblower's hand.

Quick match burned faster than the eye could follow; the fifty feet
or so that extended down to the magazine would burn in less than a
second.

'Cut me a yard off that!' said Hornblower pointing to the slow
match.

Slow match was carefully tested. It burned in still air at exactly
thirty inches in one hour, one inch in two minutes. Hornblower had
no intention whatever of allowing an hour or more for the combustion
of this yard, however. He could hear the muskets banging; he could
hear drums echoing in the hills. He must keep calm.

'Cut off another foot and light it!'

While Black was executing this order Hornblower was tying quick
match to slow match, making sure they were closely joined. Yet he
still had to think of the general situation in addition to these vital
details.

'Hewitt!' he snapped, looking up from his work. 'Listen carefully.
Run to the lieutenant's party of marines over the ridge there. Tell him

we're going to fall back now, and he is to cover our retreat at the last slope above the boats. Understand?'

'Aye aye, sir.'

'Then run.'

Just as well that it was not Grimes who had to be entrusted with the mission. The fuses were knotted together now, and Hornblower looked round him.

'Bring that dead man over here!'

Black asked no questions, but dragged the corpse to the foot of the door. Hornblower had looked first for a stone, but a corpse would be better in every way. It was not yet stiff, and the arm lay limply across the quick match just above the knot, after Hornblower had passed all excess slack back through the shattered door. The dead man served to conceal the existence of the fuse. If the French arrived too early he would gain valuable seconds for the plan; the moment the fire reached the quick match it would flash under the dead man's arm and shoot on down to the powder. If to investigate the magazine they dragged the corpse out of the way, the weight of a fuse inside the door would whisk the knot inside and so gain seconds too – perhaps the burning end would tumble down the steps, perhaps right into the magazine.

'Captain Jones! Warn everybody to be ready to retreat. At once, please. Give me that burning fuse, Black.'

'Let me do that, sir.'

'Shut your mouth.'

Hornblower took the smouldering slow match and blew on it to quicken its life. Then he looked down at the length of slow match knotted to the quick match. He took special note of a point an inch and a half from the knot; there was a black spot there which served to mark the place. An inch and a half. Three minutes.

'Get up on the parapet, Black. Now. Yell for them to run. Yell!'

As Black began to bellow Hornblower pressed the smouldering end down upon the black spot. After two seconds he withdrew it; the slow match was alight and burning in two directions – in one, harmlessly towards the inoperative excess, and in the other towards the knot, the quick match an inch and a half away. Hornblower made sure it was burning, and then he scrambled to his feet and leaped up on the parapet.

The marines were trooping past him, with Côtard and his seamen bringing up the rear. A minute and a half – a minute, now, and the French were following them up, just out of musket range.

'Better hurry, Côtard. Come on!'

They broke into a dogtrot.

'Steady, there!' yelled Jones. He was concerned about panic among his men if they ran from the enemy instead of retreating steadily, but there was a time for everything. The marines began to run, with Jones yelling ineffectually and waving his sword.

'Come on, Jones,' said Hornblower as he passed him, but Jones was filled with fighting madness, and went on shouting defiance at the French, standing alone with his face to the enemy.

Then it happened. The earth moved back and forth under their feet so that they tripped and staggered, while a smashing, overwhelming explosion burst on their ears, and the sky went dark. Hornblower looked back. A column of smoke was still shooting upwards, higher and higher, and dark fragments were visible in it. Then the column spread out, mushrooming at the top. Something fell with a crash ten yards away, throwing up chips of stone which rattled round Hornblower's feet. Something came whistling through the air, something huge, curving down as it twirled. Selectively, inevitably, it fell, half a ton of rock, blown from where it roofed the magazine right on to Jones in his red coat, sliding along as if bestially determined to wipe out completely the pitiful thing it dragged beneath it. Hornblower and Côtard gazed at it in mesmerised horror as it came to rest six feet from their left hands.

It was the most difficult moment of all for Hornblower to keep his senses, or to regain them. He had to shake himself out of a daze.

'Come on.'

He still had to think clearly. They were at the final slope above the boats. The lieutenant's party of marines, sent out as a flank guard, had fallen back to this point and were drawn up here firing at a threatening crowd of Frenchmen. The French wore white facings on their blue uniforms – infantry men, not the artillery men who had opposed them round the battery. And beyond them was a long column of infantry, hurrying along, with a score of drums beating an exhilarating rhythm – the *pas de charge*.

'You men get down into the boats,' said Hornblower, addressing the rallying group of seamen and marines from the battery, and then he turned to the lieutenant.

'Captain Jones is dead. Make ready to run for it the moment those others reach the jetty.'

'Yes, sir.'

Behind Hornblower's back, turned as it was to the enemy, they heard a sharp sudden noise, like the impact of a carpenter's axe against wood. Hornblower swung round again. Côtard was staggering, his sword and the books and papers he had carried all this time fallen to the ground at his feet. Then Hornblower noticed his left arm, which was swaying in the air as if hanging by a thread. Then came the blood. A musket bullet had crashed into Côtard's upper armbone, shattering it. One of the axemen who had not yet left caught him as he was about to fall.

'Ah – ah – ah!' gasped Côtard, with the jarring of his shattered arm. He stared at Hornblower with bewildered eyes.

'Sorry you've been hit,' said Hornblower, and to the axeman, 'Get him down to the boat.'

Côtard was gesticulating towards the ground with his right hand, and Hornblower spoke to the other axeman.

'Pick those papers up and go down to the boat too.'

But Côtard was not satisfied.

'My sword! My sword!'

'I'll look after your sword,' said Hornblower. These absurd notions of honour were so deeply engrained that even in these conditions Côtard could not bear the thought of leaving his sword on the field of battle. Hornblower realised he had no cutlass as he picked up Côtard's sword. The axeman had gathered up the books and papers.

'Help Mr Côtard down,' said Hornblower, and added, as another thought struck him. 'Put a scarf round his arm above the wound and strain it tight. Understand?'

Côtard, supported by the other axeman was already tottering down the path. Movement meant agony. That heartrending 'ah – ah – ah!' came back to Hornblower's ears at every step Côtard took.

'Here they come!' said the marine lieutenant.

The skirmishing Frenchmen, emboldened by the near approach of their main body, were charging forward. A hurried glance told Hornblower that the others were all down on the jetty; the lobster-boat was actually pushing off, full of men.

'Tell your men to run for it,' he said, and the moment after they started he followed them.

It was a wild dash, slipping and sliding, down the path to the jetty, with the French yelling in pursuit. But here was the covering party, as Hornblower had ordered so carefully the day before; *Hotspur's* own thirteen marines, under their own sergeant. They had built a breastwork across the jetty, again as Hornblower had ordered when he had visualised this hurried retreat. It was lower than waist-high, hurriedly put together with rocks and fish-barrels full of stones. The hurrying mob poured over it, Hornblower, last of all, gathering himself together and leaping over it, arms and legs flying, to stumble on the far side and regain his footing by a miracle.

'*Hotspur's* marines! Line the barricade. Get into the boats, you others!'

Twelve marines knelt at the barricade; twelve muskets levelled themselves over it. At the sight of them the pursuing French hesitated, tried to halt.

'Aim low!' shouted the marine lieutenant hoarsely.

'Go back and get the men into the boats, Mr What's-your-name,' snapped Hornblower. 'Have the launch ready to cast off, while you shove off in the yawl and get away.'

The French were coming forward again; Hornblower looked back and saw the lieutenant drop off the jetty on the heels of the last marine.

'Now sergeant. Let 'em have it.'

'Fire!' said the sergeant.

That was a good volley, but there was not a moment to admire it.

'Come on!' yelled Hornblower. 'Over to the launch!'

With the weight of *Hotspur's* marines leaping into it the launch was drifting away by the time he was at the edge; there was a yard of black water for Hornblower to leap over, but his feet reached the gunnel and he pitched forward among the men clustered there; he luckily remembered to drop Côtard's sword so that he fell harmlessly into the bottom of the boat without wounding anyone. Oars and boat-hook thrust against the jetty and the launch surged away while Hornblower scrambled into the stern sheets. He almost stepped on Côtard's face; Côtard was lying apparently unconscious on the bottom boards.

Now the oars were grinding in the rowlocks. They were twenty yards away, thirty yards away, before the first Frenchmen came yelling along the jetty, to stand dancing with rage and excitement on the very edge of the masonry. For an invaluable second or two they even forgot the muskets in their hands. In the launch the huddled men raised their voices in a yell of derision that excited Hornblower's cold rage.

'Silence! Silence, all of you!'

The stillness that fell on the launch was more unpleasant than the noise. One or two muskets banged off on the jetty, and Hornblower, looking over his shoulder, saw a French soldier drop on one knee and take deliberate aim, saw him choose a target, saw the musket barrel fore-shorten until the muzzle was pointed directly at him. He was wildly contemplating throwing himself down into the bottom of the boat when the musket went off. He felt a violent jar through his body, and realised with relief that the bullet had buried itself in the solid oak transom of the launch against which he was sitting. He recovered his wits; looking forward he saw Hewitt trying to force his way aft to his side and he spoke to him as calmly as his excitement permitted.

'Hewitt! Get for'ard to the gun. It's loaded with grape. Fire when it bears.' Then he spoke to the oarsmen and to Cargill at the tiller. 'Hard-a-port. Starboard-side oars, back water.'

The launch turned her clumsy length.

'Port side, back water.'

The launch ceased to turn; she was pointed straight at the jetty, and Hewitt, having shoved the other men aside, was cold-bloodedly looking along the sights of the four-pounder carronade mounted in the bows, fiddling with the elevating coign. Then he leaned over to one side and pulled the lanyard. The whole boat jerked sternwards abruptly with the recoil, as though when under way she had struck a rock, and the smoke came back round them in a sullen pall.

'Give way, starboard side! Pull! Hard-a-starboard!' The boat turned ponderously. 'Give way, port side!'

Nine quarter-pound grapeshot-balls had swept through the group on the jetty; there were struggling figures, quiescent figures, lying there. Bonaparte had a quarter of a million soldiers under arms, but he had now lost some of them. It could not be called a drop out of the bucketful, but perhaps a molecule. Now they were out of musket shot, and Hornblower turned to Cargill in the stern sheets beside him.

'You managed your part of the business well enough. Mr Cargill.'

'Thank you, sir.'

Cargill had been appointed by Hornblower to land with the marines and to take charge of the boats and prepare them for the evacuation.

'But it might have been better if you'd sent the launch away first and kept the yawl back until the last. Then the launch could have lain off and covered the others with her gun.'

'I thought of that, sir. But I couldn't be sure until the last moment how many men would be coming down in the last group. I had to keep the launch for that.'

'Maybe you're right,' said Hornblower, grudgingly, and then, his sense of justice prevailing, 'In fact I'm sure you're right.'

'Thank you, sir,' said Cargill again, and, after a pause, 'I wish you had let me come with you, sir.'

Some people had queer tastes, thought Hornblower bitterly to himself, having regard to Côtard lying unconscious with a shattered arm at their feet, but he had to smooth down ruffled feelings in these touchy young men thirsting for honour and for the promotion that honour might bring.

'Use your wits, man,' he said, bracing himself once more to think logically. 'Someone had to be in charge on the jetty, and you were the best man for the job.'

'Thank you, sir,' said Cargill all over again, but still wistfully, and therefore still idiotically.

A sudden thought struck Hornblower, and he turned and stared back over his shoulder. He actually had to look twice, although he knew what he was looking for. The silhouette of the hills had changed. Then he saw a wisp of black smoke still rising from the summit. The semaphore was gone. The towering thing that had spied on their movements and had reported every disposition of the Inshore Squadron was no more. Trained British seamen and riggers and carpenters could not replace it – if they had such a job to do – in less than a week's work. Probably the French would take two weeks at least; his own estimate would be three.

And there was *Hotspur* waiting for them, main-topsail aback, as he had seen her half an hour ago; half an hour that seemed like a week. The lobster-boat and the yawl were already going round to her port side, and Cargill steered for her starboard side; in these calm waters and with such a gentle wind there was no need for the boats to be offered a lee.

'Oars!' said Cargill, and the launch ran alongside, and there was Bush looking down on them from close overhead. Hornblower seized the entering-ropes and swung himself up. It was his right as captain to go first, and it was also his duty. He cut Bush's congratulations short.

'Get the wounded out as quick as you can, Mr Bush. Send a stretcher down for Mr Côtard.'

'Is he wounded, sir?'

'Yes.' Hornblower had no desire to enter into unnecessary explanations. 'You'll have to lash him to it and then sway the stretcher up with a whip from the yardarm. His arm's in splinters.'

'Aye aye, sir.' Bush by now had realised that Hornblower was in no conversational mood.

'The surgeon's ready?'

'He's started work, sir.'

A wave of Bush's hand indicated a couple of wounded men who had come on board from the yawl and were being supported below.

'Very well.'

Hornblower headed for his cabin; no need to explain that he had his report to write; no need to make excuses. But as always after action he yearned for the solitude of his cabin even more than he yearned to sink down and forget his weariness. But at the second step he pulled up short. This was not a neat clean end to the venture. No peace for him at the moment, and he swore to himself under this final strain, using filthy black blasphemies such as he rarely employed.

He would have to deal with Grimes, and instantly. He must make up his mind about what he should do. Punish him? Punish a man for being a coward? That would be like punishing a man for having red hair. Hornblower stood first on one foot and then on the other, unable to pace, yet striving to goad his weary mind to further action. Punish Grimes for showing cowardice? That was more to the point. Not that it would do Grimes any good, but it would deter other men from showing cowardice. There were officers who would punish, not in the interests of discipline, but because they thought punishment should be inflicted in payment for crime, as sinners had to go to Hell. Hornblower would not credit himself with the divine authority some officers thought natural.

But he would have to act. He thought of the court martial. He would be the sole witness, but the court would know he was speaking the truth. His word would decide Grimes' fate, and then – the hangman's noose, or at the very least five hundred lashes, with Grimes screaming in pain until he should fall unconscious, to be nursed round for another day of torture, and another after that, until he was a gibbering idiot with neither mind nor strength left.

Hornblower hated the thought. But he remembered that the crew must have already guessed. Grimes must have already started his punishment, and yet the discipline of the *Hotspur* must be preserved. Hornblower would have to do his duty; he must pay one of the penalties for being a naval officer, just as he suffered sea-sickness – just as he risked his life. He would have Grimes put under arrest at once, and while Grimes was spending twenty-four hours in irons he could make up his mind to the final decision. He strode aft to his cabin, with all relief gone from the thought of relaxation.

Then he opened the door, and there was no problem left; only horror, further horror. Grimes hung there, from a rope threaded through the hook that supported the lamp. He was swaying with the gentle motion of the ship, his feet dragging on the deck so that even his knees were almost on the deck too. There was a blackened face and protruding tongue – actually there was no likeness to Grimes at all in the horrible thing hanging there. Grimes had not the courage to face the landing operation, but when the realisation had come to him, when the crew had displayed their feelings, he had yet had the determination to do this thing, to submit himself to this slow strangulation, falling with a small preliminary jerk from a cramped position crouching on the cot.

In all the crew of the *Hotspur* Grimes had been the one man who as captain's steward could find the necessary privacy to do this thing. He had foreseen the flogging or the hanging, he had suffered the scorn of his shipmates; there was bitter irony in the thought that the semaphore station which he had feared to attack had turned out to be defended by a helpless civilian and his wife.

Hotspur rolled gently on the swell, and as she rolled the lolling head and the dangling arms swayed in unison, and the feet scraped over the deck. Hornblower shook off the horror that had seized him, drove himself to be clear-headed once more despite his fatigue and his disgust. He went to the door of the cabin; it was excusable that no sentry had yet been reposted there, seeing that the *Hotspur's* marines had only just come on board.

'Pass the word for Mr Bush,' he said.

Within a minute Bush hurried in, to pull up short as soon as he saw the thing.

'I'll have that removed at once, if you please, Mr Bush. Put it over the side. Give it a burial, Christian burial, if you like.'

'Aye aye, sir.'

Bush shut his mouth after his formal statement of compliance. He could see that Hornblower was in even less a conversational mood in this cabin than he had been when on deck. Hornblower passed into the chart-room and squeezed himself into the chair, and sat still, his hands motionless on the table. Almost immediately he heard the arrival of the working party Bush had sent. He heard loud amazed voices, and something like a laugh, all instantly repressed when they realised that he was next door. The voices died to hoarse whispers. There was a clump or two, and then a dragging noise and he knew the thing was gone.

Then he got to his feet to carry out the resolution formed during his recent clarity of mind. He walked firmly into the cabin, a little like someone unwillingly going into a duel. He did not want to; he hated this place, but in a tiny ship like *Hotspur* he had nowhere else to go. He would have to grow used to it. He put aside the weak thought that he could move himself into one of the screened-off cabins in the 'tween decks, and send, for instance, the warrant officers up here. That would occasion endless inconvenience, and – even more important – endless comment as well. He had to use this place and the longer he contemplated the prospect the less inviting it would be. And he was so tired he could hardly stand. He approached the cot; a mental picture developed in his mind's eye of Grimes kneeling on it, rope round his neck, to pitch himself off. He forced himself coldly to accept that picture, as something in the past. This was the present, and he dropped on to the cot, shoes on his feet, cutlass-sheath at his side, sandbag in his pocket. Grimes was not present to help him with those.

XI

Hornblower had written the address, the date, and the word 'Sir' before he realised that the report would not be so easy to write. He was quite sure that this letter would appear in the Gazette, but he had been sure of that from the moment he had faced the writing of it. It would be a 'Gazette Letter,' one of the few, out of the many hundreds of reports coming into the Admiralty, selected for publication, and it would be his first appearance in print. He had told himself that he would simply write a standard straightforward report along the time-honoured lines, yet now he had to stop and think, although stage fright had nothing to do with it. The publication of this letter meant that it would be read by the whole world. It would be read by the whole Navy, which meant that his subordinates would read it, and he knew, only too well, how every careless word would be scanned and weighed by touchy individuals.

Much more important still; it would be read by all England, and that meant that Maria would read it. It would open a peephole into his life that so far she had never been able to look through. From the point of view of his standing with the Navy it might be desirable to let the dangers he had undergone be apparent, in a modest sort of way, but that would be in direct contradiction of the breezy lighthearted letter he intended to write to Maria. Maria was a shrewd little person, and he could not deceive her; to read the Gazette letter after his letter would excite her mistrust and apprehension at a moment when she was carrying what might well be the heir to the Hornblower name, with possibly the worst effects both on Maria and on the child.

He faced the choice, and it had to be in favour of Maria. He would make light of his difficulties and dangers, and even then he could still hope that the Navy would read between the lines that which Maria in her ignorance would not guess at. He re-dipped his pen, and bit the end in a momentary mental debate as to whether all the Gazette Letters he had read had been written in the face of similar difficulties, and decided that was probably true of the majority. Well, it had to be written. There was no avoiding it – for that matter there was no postponing it. The necessary preliminary words, 'In accordance with your orders' set him off, started the flow. He had to remember all that he had to put in. 'Mr William Bush, my first lieutenant, very handsomely volunteered his services, but I directed him to remain in command of the ship.' Later on it was no effort to write 'Lieut Charles Côtard, of HMS *Marlborough*, who had volunteered for the expedition, gave invaluable assistance as a result of his knowledge of the French language. I regret very much to have to inform you that he received a wound which necessitated amputation, and his life is still in danger.' Then there was something else he had to put in. 'Mr' – what was his first name? – 'Mr Alexander Cargill, Master's Mate, was allotted by me the duty of superintending the re-embarkation, which he carried out very much to my satisfaction.' The next passage would satisfy Maria. 'The Telegraph Station was seized by the party under my personal command without the slightest opposition, and was set on fire and completely destroyed after the confidential papers had been secured.' Intelligent naval officers would have a higher opinion of an operation carried through without loss of life than of one which cost a monstrous butcher's bill.

Now for the battery; he had to be careful about this. 'Captain Jones of the Royal Marines, having gallantly secured the battery, was unfortunately involved in the explosion of the magazine, and I much regret to have to report his death, while several other Royal Marines of his party are dead or missing.' One of them had been as useful dead as alive. Hornblower checked himself. He still could not bear to remember those minutes by the magazine door. He went on with his letter. 'Lieutenant Reid of the Royal Marines guarded the flank and covered the retreat with small loss. His conduct calls for my unreserved approbation.'

That was very true, and pleasant to write. So was the next passage. 'It is with much gratification that I can inform you that the battery is completely wrecked. The parapet is thrown down along with the guns, and the gun-carriages destroyed, as will be understood because not less than one ton of gunpowder was exploded in the battery.' There were four thirty-two pounders in that battery. A single charge for one of these guns was ten pounds of powder, and the magazine, sunk deep below the parapets, must have contained charges for fifty rounds per gun as a minimum. A crater had been left where once the parapet stood.

Not much more to write now. 'The retreat was effected in good order. I append the list of killed, wounded, and missing.' The rough list lay in front of him, and he proceeded to copy it out carefully; there were widows and bereaved parents who might derive consolation from the sight of those names in the Gazette. One seaman had been killed and several slightly wounded. He recorded their names and began a fresh paragraph. 'Royal Marines. Killed. Captain Henry Jones. Privates—' A thought struck him at this moment and he paused with his pen in the air. There was not only consolation in seeing a name in the Gazette; parents and widows could receive the back pay of the deceased and some small gratuity. He was still thinking when Bush came hurrying in the door.

'Cap'n, sir. I'd like to show you something from the deck.'

'Very well. I'll come.'

He paused for only a short while. There was a single name in the paragraph headed 'Seamen killed' – James Johnson, Ordinary Seaman. He added another name. 'John Grimes, Captain's Steward' and then he put down the pen and came out on deck.

'Look over there, sir,' said Bush, pointing eagerly ashore and proffering his telescope.

The landscape was still unfamiliar, with the semaphore gone and the battery – easily visible previously – replaced now by a mound of earth. But that was not what Bush was referring to. There was a considerable body of men on horseback riding along the slopes; through the telescope Hornblower could fancy he could detect plumes and gold lace.

'Those must be generals, sir,' said Bush excitedly, 'come out to see the damage. The commandant, and the governor, an' the chief engineer, an' all the rest of 'em. We're nearly in range now, sir. We could drop down without their noticing, run out the guns smartly, full elevation, and – we ought to hit a target that size with one shot in a broadside at least, sir.'

'I think we could,' agreed Hornblower. He looked up at the wind-vane and over at the shore. 'We could wear ship and—'

Bush waited for Hornblower to complete his speech, but the end never came.

'Shall I give the order, sir?'

There was another pause.

'No,' said Hornblower at last. 'Better not.'

Bush was too good a subordinate to protest, but his disappointment showed plainly enough, and it was necessary to soften the refusal with an explanation. They might kill a general, although the odds were that it would merely be an orderly dragoon. On the other hand they would be drawing most forcible attention to the present weakness of this portion of coast.

'Then they'll be bringing field batteries,' went on Hornblower. 'Only nine-pounders, but—'

'Yes, sir. They might be a nuisance,' said Bush in reluctant agreement. 'Do you have anything in mind, sir?'

'Not me. Him,' said Hornblower. All operations of the Inshore Squadron were Pellew's responsibility and should be to Pellew's credit. He pointed towards the Inshore Squadron where Pellew's broad pendant flew.

But the broad pendant was to fly there no longer. The boat that took Hornblower's report to the *Tonnant* returned not only with stores but with official despatches.

'Sir,' said Orrock, after handing them over, 'the Commodore sent a man with me from the *Tonnant* who carries a letter for you.'

'Where is he?'

He seemed a very ordinary sort of seaman, dressed in the standard clothes of the slop chest. His thick blond pigtail, as he stood hat in

hand, indicated that he had long been a seaman. Hornblower took
the letter and broke the seal.

'My dear Hornblower,

It is with infinite pain to myself that I have to confirm the news,
conveyed to you in the official despatches, that your latest report will
also be the last that I shall have the pleasure of reading. My flag has
come, and I shall hoist it as Rear-Admiral commanding the squadron
assembling for the blockade of Rochefort. Rear Admiral Wm. Parker
will take over the command of the Inshore Squadron and I have
recommended you to him in the strongest terms although your actions
speak even more strongly for you. But Commanding officers are likely
to have their favourites, men with whom they are personally
acquainted. We can hardly quarrel on this score, seeing that I have
indulged myself in a favourite whose initials are H. H.! Now let us
leave this subject for another even more personal.

I noted in your report that you have had the misfortune to lose
your steward, and I take the liberty to send you James Doughty as a
substitute. He was steward of the late Captain Stevens of the
Magnificent, and he has been persuaded to volunteer for the *Hotspur*.
I understand that he has had much practical experience in attending
to gentlemen's needs, and I hope you will find him suitable and that
he will look after you for many years. If during that time you are
reminded of me by his presence I shall be well satisfied.

                                   Your sincere friend,

                                               Ed. Pellew

Even with all his quickness of mind it took Hornblower a little
while to digest the manifold contents of his letter after reading it. It
was all bad news; bad news about the change of command, and just
as bad, although in a different way, that he was being saddled with a
gentleman's gentleman who would sneer at his domestic arrangements.
Yet if there was anything that a naval career taught anybody, it
was to be philosophic about drastic changes.

'Doughty?' said Hornblower.

'Sir.'

Doughty looked respectful, but there might be something quizzical
in his glance.

'You're going to be my servant. Do your duty and you have nothing
to fear.'

'Yes, sir. No, sir.'

'You've brought your dunnage?'

'Aye aye, sir.'

'The First Lieutenant will detail someone to show you where to
sling your hammock. You'll share a berth with my clerk.'

The captain's steward was the only ordinary seaman in the ship who did not have to sleep in the tiers.

'Aye aye, sir.'

'Then you can take up your duties.'

'Aye aye, sir.'

It was only a few minutes later that Hornblower, in his cabin, looked up to find a silent figure slipping in through the door; Doughty knew that as a personal servant he did not knock if the sentry told him the captain was alone.

'Have you had your dinner, sir?'

It took a moment to answer that question, at the end of a broken day following an entirely sleepless night. During that moment Doughty looked respectfully over Hornblower's left shoulder. His eyes were a startling blue.

'No, I haven't. You'd better see about something for me,' replied Hornblower.

'Yes, sir.'

The blue eyes looked round the cabin and found nothing.

'No. There are no cabin stores. You'll have to go to the galley. Mr Simmonds will find something for me.' The ship's cook, as a warrant officer, rated the 'Mr' in front of his name. 'No. Wait. There are two lobsters somewhere in this ship. You'll find 'em in a barrel of seawater somewhere on the booms. And that reminds me. Your predecessor has been dead for nearly twenty-four hours and that water hasn't been changed. You must do that. Go to the officer of the watch with my compliments and ask him to put the wash-deck pump to work on it. That'll keep one lobster alive while I have the other.'

'Yes, sir. Or you could have this one hot tonight and the other one cold tomorrow if I boil them both now, sir.'

'I could,' agreed Hornblower without committing himself.

'Mayonnaise,' said Doughty. 'Are there any eggs in this ship, sir? Any salad oil?'

'No there are not!' rasped Hornblower. 'There are no cabin stores whatever in this ship except those two damned lobsters.'

'Yes, sir. Then I'll serve this one with drawn butter and I'll see what I can do tomorrow, sir.'

'Do whatever you damned well like and don't trouble me,' said Hornblower.

He was working into a worse and worse temper. He not only had to storm batteries but he also had to remember about keeping lobsters alive. And Pellew was leaving the Brest fleet; the official orders he had just read gave details about salutes to the new flags tomorrow. And tomorrow this damned Doughty and his damned mayonnaise, whatever that was, would be pawing over his patched shirts.

'Yes, sir,' said Doughty, and disappeared as quietly as he had entered.

Hornblower went out on deck to pace off his bad temper. The first breath of the delightful evening air helped to soothe him; so too, did the hurried movement of everyone on the quarter-deck over to the lee side so as to leave the weather side to him. For him there was as much space as heart could desire – five long strides forward and aft – but all the other officers had now to take the air under crowded conditions. Let 'em. He had to write out his report to Pellew three times, the original draft, the fair-copy, and the copy in his confidential letter book. Some captains gave that work to their clerks, but Hornblower would not do so. Captain's clerks made a practice of exploiting their confidential position; there were officers in the ship who would be glad to hear what their captain said about them, and what the future plans might be. Martin would never have the chance. He could confine himself to muster-rolls and returns of stores and the other nuisances that plagued a captain's life.

Now Pellew was leaving them, and that was a disaster. Earlier today Hornblower had actually allowed his mind to dally with the notion that some day he might know the inexpressible joy of being 'made Post', of being promoted to Captain. That called for the strongest influence, in the Fleet and in the Admiralty. With Pellew's transfer he had lost a friend in the Fleet. With Parry's retirement he had lost a friend in the Admiralty – he did not know a single soul there. His promotion to Commander had been a fantastic stroke of luck. When *Hotspur* should be paid off there were three hundred ambitious young Commanders all with uncles and cousins and all anxious to take his place. He could find himself rotting on the beach on half-pay. With Maria. With Maria and the child. The reverse side of the penny was no more attractive than the front.

This was not the way to work off the gloom that threatened to engulf him. He had written Maria a letter to be proud of, reassuring, cheerful, and as loving as he had found it possible to make it. Over there was Venus, shining out in the evening sky. This sea air was stimulating, refreshing, delightful. Surely this was a better world than his drained nervous condition allowed him to believe. It took a full hour of pacing to convince him fully of this. At the end of that time the comfortably monotonous exercise had slowed down his overactive mind. He was healthily tired now, and the moment he thought about it he knew he was ravenously hungry. He had seen Doughty flitting about the deck more than once, for however lost in distraction Hornblower might be he nevertheless took instant note, consciously or subconsciously, of everything that went on in the ship. He was growing desperately impatient, and night had entirely closed in, when his pacing was intercepted.

'Your dinner's ready, sir.'

Doughty stood respectfully in front of him.

'Very well. I'll come.'

Hornblower sat himself down at the chart-room table, Doughty standing at his chair in the cramped space.

'One moment, sir, while I bring your dinner from the galley. May I pour you some cider, sir?'

'Pour me some . . . ?'

But Doughty was already pouring from jug to cup, and then he vanished. Hornblower tasted gingerly. There was no doubt about it, it was excellent cider, rough and yet refined, fruity and yet in no way sweet. After water months in cask it was heavenly. He only took two preliminary sips before his head went back and the whole cupful shot delightfully down his throat. He had not begun to debate this curious phenomenon when Doughty slipped into the chart-room again.

'The plate is hot, sir,' he said.

'What the devil's this?' asked Hornblower.

'Lobster cutlets, sir,' said Doughty, pouring more cider, and then, with a gesture not quite imperceptible, he indicated the wooden saucer he had laid on the table at the same time. 'Butter sauce, sir.'

Extraordinary. There were neat brown cutlets on his plate that bore no outward resemblance to lobster, but when Hornblower cautiously added sauce and tasted, the result was excellent. Minced lobster. And when Doughty took the cover off the cracked vegetable dish there was a dream of delight revealed. New potatoes, golden and lovely. He helped himself hurriedly and very nearly burned his mouth on them. Nothing could be quite as nice as the first new potatoes of the year.

'These came with the ship's vegetables, sir,' explained Doughty. 'I was in time to save them.'

Hornblower did not need to ask from what those new potatoes had been saved. He knew a good deal about Huffnell the purser, and he could guess at the appetite of the ward-room mess. Lobster cutlets and new potatoes and this pleasant butter sauce; he was enjoying his dinner, resolutely putting aside the knowledge that the ship's biscuit in the bread barge was weevily. He was used to weevils, which always showed up after the first month at sea, or earlier if the biscuit had been long in store. He told himself as he took another mouthful of lobster cutlet that he would not allow a weevil in his biscuit to be a fly in his ointment.

He took another pull at the cider before he remembered to ask where it came from.

'I pledged your credit for it, sir,' said Doughty. 'I took the liberty of doing so, to the extent of a quarter of a pound of tobacco.'

'Who had it?'

'Sir,' said Doughty, 'I promised not to say.'

'Oh, very well,' said Hornblower.

There was only one source for cider – the *Camilla,* the lobster-boat he had seized last night. Of course the Breton fishermen who manned it would have a keg on board, and somebody had looted it; Martin, his clerk, most likely.

'I hope you bought the whole keg,' said Hornblower.

'Only some of it, I am afraid, sir. All that remained.'

Out of a two-gallon keg of cider – Hornblower hoped it might be more – Martin could hardly have downed more than a gallon in twenty-four hours. And Doughty must have noted the presence of a keg in the berth he shared with Martin; Hornblower was quite sure that more pressure than the offer of a mere quarter of a pound of tobacco had been applied to make Martin part with the keg, but he did not care.

'Cheese, sir,' said Doughty; Hornblower had eaten everything else in sight.

And the cheese – the ration cheese supplied for the ship's company – was reasonably good, and the butter was fresh; a new firkin must have come in the boat and Doughty must somehow have got at it although the rancid previous assignment had not been used up. The cider jug was empty and Hornblower felt more comfortable than he had felt for days.

'I'll go to bed now,' he announced.

'Yes, sir.'

Doughty opened the chart-room door and Hornblower passed into his cabin. The lamp swayed from the deck beam. The patched night-shirt was laid out on the cot. Perhaps it was because he was full of cider that Hornblower did not resent Doughty's presence as he brushed his teeth and made ready for bed. Doughty was at hand to take his coat as he pulled it off; Doughty retrieved his trousers when he let them fall; Doughty hovered by as he dropped into bed and pulled the blankets over him.

'I'll brush this coat, sir. Here's your bed gown if you're called in the night, sir. Shall I put out the lamp, sir?'

'Yes.'

'Good night, sir.'

It was not until next morning that Hornblower remembered again that Grimes had hanged himself in this cabin. It was not until next morning that he remembered those minutes down in the magazine with the gunpowder. Doughty had already proved his worth.

XII

The salutes had been fired. Pellew's flag had been hoisted and then the *Tonnant* had sailed away to initiate the blockade of Rochefort. The *Dreadnought* had hoisted Admiral Parker's flag, and each flag had received thirteen guns from every ship. The French on their hillsides must have seen the smoke and heard the firing, and the naval officers among them must have deduced that one more rear-admiral had joined the Channel Fleet; and must have shaken their heads a little sadly at this further proof that the British Navy was increasing its lead over the French in the race to build up maritime strength.

Hornblower, peering up the Goulet, over the black shapes of the Little Girls, could count the vessels of war swinging to their anchors in Brest Roads. Eighteen ships of the line now, and seven frigates, but with sub-minimum crews and incomplete stores; no match for the fifteen superb ships of the line under Cornwallis who waited for them outside, growing daily in efficiency and in moral ascendancy. Nelson off Toulon and now Pellew off Rochefort similarly challenged inferior French squadrons, and under their protection the merchant fleets of Britain sailed the seas unmolested except by privateers – and the merchant fleet themselves, bunched in vast convoys, received constant close cover from further British squadrons of a total strength even exceeding that of the blockading fleets. Cordage and hemp, timber and iron and copper, turpentine and salt, cotton and nitre, could all flow freely to the British Isles and be as freely distributed round them, maintaining the ship yards in constant activity, whilst the French yards were doomed to idleness, to the gangrene that follows the cutting off of the circulation.

But the situation was nevertheless not without peril. Along the Channel Coast Bonaparte had two hundred thousand soldiers, the most formidable army in the world, and collecting in the Channel Ports, from St Malo to Ostend and beyond was a flotilla of seven thousand flat-bottomed boats. Admiral Keith with his frigates, backed by a few ships of the line, held the Channel secure against Bonaparte's threat; there was no chance of invasion as long as England held naval command of the Channel.

Yet in a sense that command was precarious. If the eighteen ships of the line in Brest Roads could escape, could round Ushant and come up-Channel with Cornwallis distracted in some fashion, Keith might be driven away, might be destroyed. Three days would be sufficient to put Bonaparte's army into the boats and across the Channel, and Bonaparte would be issuing decrees from Windsor Castle as he had already done from Milan and Brussels. Cornwallis and his squadron, *Hotspur* and her mightier colleagues, were what made this impossible; a moment of carelessness, a misjudged movement, and the tricolour might fly over the Tower of London.

Hornblower counted the ships in Brest Roads, and as he did so he was very conscious that this morning routine was the ultimate, most insolent expression of the power of England at sea. England had a heart, a brain, an arm, and he and *Hotspur* were the final sensitive fingertip of that long arm. Eighteen ships of the line at anchor, two of them three-deckers. Seven frigates. They were the ones he had observed yesterday. Nothing had contrived to slip out unnoticed during the night, by the passage of the Four or the Raz.

'Mr Foreman! Signal to the Flag, if you please. "Enemy at anchor. Situation unchanged."'

Foreman had made that signal several times before, but, while Hornblower watched him unobtrusively, he checked the numbers in the signal book. It was Foreman's business to know all the thousand arbitrary signals off by heart, but it was best, when time allowed, that he should corroborate what his memory told him. An error of a digit might send the warning that the enemy was coming out.

'Flag acknowledges, sir,' reported Foreman.

'Very well.'

Poole, as officer of the watch, made note of the incident in the rough log. The hands were washing down the deck, the sun was lifting over the horizon. It was a beautiful day, with every promise of being a day like any other.

'Seven bells, sir,' reported Prowse.

Only half an hour more of the ebb; time to withdraw from this lee shore before the flood set in.

'Mr Poole! Wear the ship, if you please. Course west by north.'

'Good morning, sir.'

'Good morning, Mr Bush.'

Bush knew better than to indulge in further conversation, besides, he could devote his attention to watching how smartly the hands braced the main-topsail round, and to how Poole handled the ship when the topsails filled. Hornblower swept the northern shore, seeking as ever for any signs of change. His attention was concentrated on the ridge beyond which Captain Jones had met his death, when Poole reported again.

'Wind's come westerly, sir. Can't make west by north.'

'Make it west nor'west,' replied Hornblower, his eye still to the telescope.

'Aye aye, sir. West nor'west, full and bye.' There was a hint of relief in Poole's voice; an officer is likely to be apprehensive when he has to tell his captain that the last order was impossible to execute.

Hornblower was aware that Bush had taken his stand beside him with his telescope trained in the same direction.

'A column of troops, sir,' said Bush.

'Yes.'

Hornblower had detected the head of the column crossing the ridge. He was watching now to see to what length the column would stretch. It continued interminably over the ridge, appearing through his glass like some caterpillar hurrying over the even rougher hillside. Ah! There was the explanation. Beside the caterpillar appeared a string of ants, hurrying even faster along the path. Field artillery – six guns and limbers with a wagon bringing up the rear. The head of the caterpillar was already over the farther ridge before the tail appeared over the nearer one. That was a column of infantry more than a mile long, five thousand men or more – a division of infantry with its attendant battery. It might be merely a portion of the garrison of Brest turning out for exercises and manoeuvres on the hillside, but its movements were somewhat more hurried and purposeful than would be expected in that case.

He swept his glass farther round the coast, and then checked it with a start and a gulp of excitement. There were the unmistakable lugsails of a French coaster coming round the bold headland of Point Matthew. There was another pair – a whole cluster. Could it possibly be that a group of coasters was trying to run the blockade into Brest in broad daylight in the teeth of *Hotspur*? Hardly likely. Now there was a bang – bang – bang of guns, presumably from the field battery, invisible over the farther ridge. Behind the coasters appeared a British frigate, and then another, showing up at the moment when the coasters began to go about; as the coasters tacked they revealed that they had no colours flying.

'Prizes, sir. And that's *Naiad* an' *Doris*,' said Bush.

The two British frigates must have swooped down during the night by the passage of the Four inshore of Ushant and cut out these coasters from the creeks of Le Conquet where they had been huddled for shelter. A neat piece of work, undoubtedly, but bringing them out had only been made possible by the destruction of the battery on the Petit Minou. The frigates tacked in the wake of the coasters, like shepherd dogs following a flock of sheep. They were escorting their prizes in triumph back to the Inshore Squadron, whence, presumably they would be dispatched to England for sale. Bush had taken his telescope from his eye and had turned his gaze full on Hornblower, while Prowse came up to join them.

'Six prizes, sir,' said Bush.

'A thousand pound each, those coasters run, sir,' said Prowse.

'More, if it's naval stores, and I expect it is. Six thousand pound. Seven thousand. An' no trouble selling 'em, sir.'

By the terms of the royal proclamation issued on the declaration of war, prizes taken by the Royal Navy became – as was traditional by now – the absolute property of the captors.

'And we weren't in sight, sir,' said Bush.

The proclamation also laid down the proviso that the value of the prizes, after a deduction for flag officers, should be shared among those ships in sight at the moment the colours came down or possession was secured.

'We couldn't expect to be,' said Hornblower. He was honestly implying that *Hotspur* was too preoccupied with her duty of watching the Goulet, but the others misinterpreted the speech.

'No, sir, not with—' Bush broke off what he was saying before he became guilty of mutiny. He had been about to continue 'not with Admiral Parker in command' but he had more sense than to say it, after Hornblower's meaning had become clear to him.

'One eighth'd be nigh on a thousand pounds,' said Prowse.

An eighth of the prizes was, by the proclamation, to be divided among the lieutenants and masters taking part in the capture of the ships. Hornblower was making a different calculation. The share of the captains was two-eighths; if *Hotspur* had been associated in the venture with *Naiad* and *Doris* he would have been richer by five hundred pounds.

'And it was us that opened the way for 'em, sir,' went on Prowse.

'It was you, sir, who—' Bush broke off his speech for the second time.

'That's the fortune of war,' said Hornblower, lightly. 'Or the misfortune of war.'

Hornblower was quite convinced that the whole system of prize money was vicious, and tended towards making the navy less effective in war. He told himself that this was sour grapes, that he would think differently if he had won great amounts of prize money, but that did not soften his present conviction.

'For'ard, there!' yelled Poole from beside the binnacle. 'Get the lead going in the main chains.'

The three senior officers beside the hammock nettings came back to the present world with a general start. Hornblower felt a chill wave of horror over his ribs as he realised his inexcusable carelessness. He had forgotten all about the course he had set. *Hotspur* was sailing tranquilly into peril, was in danger of running aground, and it was his fault, the result of his own inattention. He had no time for self-reproach at the present moment, all the same. He lifted his voice, trying to pitch it steadily.

'Thank you, Mr Poole,' he called. 'Belay that order. Put the ship on the other tack, if you please.'

Bush and Prowse were wearing guilty, hangdog looks. It had been their duty, it had been Prowse's particular duty, to warn him when *Hotspur* was running into navigational dangers. They would not meet his eye; they tried to assume a pose of exaggerated interest in Poole's handling of the ship as she went about. The yards creaked as she came round, the sails flapped and then drew again, the wind blew on their faces from a different angle.

'Hard-a-lee!' ordered Poole, completing the manoeuvre. 'Foretack! Haul the bowlines!'

Hotspur settled down on her new course, away from the dangerous shore to which she had approached too close, and all danger was averted.

'You see, gentlemen,' said Hornblower coldly, and he waited until he had the full attention of Bush and Prowse. 'You see, there are many disadvantages about the system of prize money. I am aware now of a new one, and I hope you are too. Thank you, that will do.'

He remained by the hammock netting as they slunk away; he was taking himself to task. It was his first moment of carelessness in a professional career of ten years. He had made mistakes through ignorance, through recklessness, but never carelessness before. If there had been a fool as officer of the watch just now utter ruin would have been possible. If *Hotspur* had gone aground, in clear weather and a gentle breeze, it would have been the end of everything for him. Court martial and dismissal from the service, and then . . . ? In his bitter self-contempt he told himself that he would not be capable even of begging his bread, to say nothing of Maria's. He might perhaps ship before the mast, and with his clumsiness and abstraction he would be the victim of the cat, of the boatswain's rattan. Death would be better. He shuddered with cold.

Now he turned his attention to Poole, standing impassive by the binnacle. What had been the motives that had impelled him to order the lead into use? Had it been mere precaution, or had it been a tactful way of calling his captain's attention to the situation of the ship? His present manner and bearing gave no hint of the answer. Hornblower had studied his officers carefully since *Hotspur* was commissioned; he was not aware of any depths of ingenuity or tact in Poole, but he freely admitted to himself that they might exist, unobserved. In any case, he must allow for them. He sauntered down the quarter-deck.

'Thank you, Mr Poole,' he said, slowly and very distinctly.

Poole touched his hat in reply, but his homely face did not change its expression. Hornblower walked on, nettled – amused – that his questions remained unanswered. It was a momentary relief from the torments of conscience which still plagued him.

The,lesson he had learned remained with him during that summer to trouble his conscience. Otherwise during those golden months the blockade of Brest might have been for *Hotspur* and Hornblower a yachting holiday with a certain macabre quality. Just as some lay theologians advanced the theory that in Hell sinners would be punished by being forced to repeat, in unutterable tedium and surfeit, the sins they had committed during life, so Hornblower spent those delightful months doing delightful things until he felt he could not do them any longer. Day after day, and night after night, through the finest summer in human memory, *Hotspur* cruised in the approaches to Brest. She pressed up to the Goulet with the last of the flood, and cannily withdrew in to safety with the last of the ebb. She counted the French fleet, she reported the result of her observations to Admiral Parker. She drifted, hove-to, over calm seas amid gentle breezes. With westerly winds she worked her way out to give the lee shore a wide berth; with easterly winds she beat back again to beard the impotent French in their safe harbour.

They were months of frightful peril for England, with the Grande Armee, two hundred thousand strong, poised within thirty miles of the Kentish beaches, but they were months of tranquillity for *Hotspur*, even with a score of hostile battleships in sight. There were occasional flurries when the coasters tried too boldly to enter or leave; there were occasional busy moments when squalls came down and topsails had to be reefed. There were encounters after dark with fishing vessels, conversations over a glass of rum with the Breton captains, purchases of crabs and lobsters and pilchards – and of the latest decree of the Inscription Maritime, or of a week-old copy of the *Moniteur*.

Hornblower's telescope revealed ant-like hordes of workmen re-building the blown-up batteries, and for a couple of weeks he watched the building of scaffolding and the erection of sheers on the Petit Minou, and, for three continuous days, as a result, the slow elevation to the vertical of the new mast of the semaphore station. The subsequent days added horizontal and vertical arms; before the summer was over those arms were whirling about reporting once more the movements of the blockading squadron.

Much good might that do the French, huddled in their anchored ships in the Roads. Inertia and a sense of inferiority would work their will on the unfortunate crews. The ships ready for sea might slowly increase in number; men might slowly be found for them, but every day the balance of fighting quality, of naval power, swung faster and faster over in favour of the British, constantly exercising at sea, and constantly reinforced by the seaborne tribute of the world.

There was a price to be paid; the dominion of the seas was not given free by destiny. The Channel Fleet paid in blood, in lives, as well as in the sacrifice of the freedom and leisure of every officer and man on board. There was a constant petty drain. Ordinary sickness took only small toll; among men in the prime of life isolated from the rest of the world illnesses were few, although it was noticeable that after the arrival of victualling ships from England epidemics of colds would sweep through the fleet, while rheumatism – the sailor's disease – was always present.

The losses were mainly due to other causes. There were men who, in a moment of carelessness or inattention, fell from the yards. There were the men who ruptured themselves, and they were many, for despite the ingenuity of blocks and tackles there were heavy weights to haul about by sheer manpower. There were crushed fingers and crushed feet when ponderous casks of salted provisions were lowered into boats from the storeships and hauled up on to the decks of the fighting ships. And frequently a lacerated limb would end – despite all the care of the surgeons – in gangrene, in amputation, and death. There were the careless men who, during target practice with the cannon, lost their arms by ramming a cartridge into an improperly sponged gun, or who did not remove themselves from the line of the recoil. Three times that year there were men who died in quarrels, when boredom changed to hysteria and knives were drawn; and on each of those occasions another life was lost, a life for a life, a hanging with the other ships clustered round and the crews lining the sides to learn what happened when a man lost his temper. And once the crews manned the sides to see what happened when a wretched young seaman paid the price for a crime worse even than murder – for raising his fist to his superior officer. Incidents of that sort were inevitable as the ships beat back and forth monotonously, over the eternal grey inhospitable sea.

It was as well for the *Hotspur* that she was under the command of a man to whom any form of idleness or monotony was supremely distasteful. The charts of the Iroise were notoriously inaccurate; *Hotspur* set herself to run line after line of soundings, to take series after series of careful triangulations from the headlands and hilltops. When the fleet ran short of silver sand, so necessary to keep the decks spotless white, it was *Hotspur* who supplied the deficiency, finding tiny lost beaches round the coast where a party could land – trespassing upon Bonaparte's vaunted dominion over Europe – to fill sacks with the precious commodity. There were fishing competitions, whereby the lower-deck's rooted objection to fish as an item of diet was almost overcome; a prize of a pound of tobacco for the biggest catch by an individual mess set all the messes to work on devising more novel fish-hooks and baits. There were experiments in ship-handling, when obsolescent and novel methods were tested, when by careful and accurate measurement with the log the effect of goose-winging the topsails was ascertained; or, it being assumed that the rudder was lost, the watch-keeping officers tried their hands at manoeuvring the ship by the sails alone.

Hornblower himself found mental exercise in working out observations, and by their aid it was possible to arrive at an accurate determination of longitude – a subject of debate since the days of the Carthaginians – at the cost of endless calculations. Hornblower was determined to perfect himself in this method, and his officers and young gentlemen bewailed the decision, for they, too, had to make lunar observations and work out the resulting sums. The longitude of the Little Girls was calculated on board the *Hotspur* a hundred times that summer, with nearly a hundred different results.

To Hornblower it was a satisfactory occupation, the more satisfactory as it became obvious that he was acquiring the necessary knack. He tried to acquire the same facility in another direction, without the same satisfaction, as he wrote his weekly letters to Maria. There was only a limited number of endearments, only a limited number of ways of saying that he missed her, that he hoped her pregnancy was progressing favourably. There was only the one way of excusing himself for not returning to England as he had promised to do, and Maria was inclined to be a little peevish in her letters regarding the exigencies of the service. When the water-hoys arrived periodically and the enormous labour had to be undertaken of transferring the already stale liquid into the *Hotspur* Hornblower always found himself thinking that getting those eighteen tons of water on board meant another month of writing letters to Maria.

XIII

Hotspur's bell struck two double strokes; it was six o'clock in the evening, and the first dog watch had come to an end in the gathering darkness.

'Sunset, sir,' said Bush.

'Yes,' agreed Hornblower.

'Six o'clock exactly. The equinox, sir.'

'Yes,' agreed Hornblower again; he knew perfectly well what was coming.

'We'll have a westerly gale, sir, or my name's not William Bush.'

'Very likely,' said Hornblower, who had been sniffing the air all day long.

Hornblower was a heretic in this matter. He did not believe that the mere changing from a day a minute longer than twelve hours to one a minute shorter made gales blow from out of the west. Gales happened to blow at this time because winter was setting in, but ninety-nine men out of a hundred firmly believed in a more direct, although more mysterious causation.

'Wind's freshening and sea's getting up a bit, sir,' went on Bush, inexorably.

'Yes.'

Hornblower fought down the temptation to declare that it was not because the sun happened to set at six o'clock, for he knew that if he expressed such an opinion it would be received with the tolerant and concealed disagreement accorded to the opinions of children and eccentrics and captains.

'We've water for twenty-eight days, sir. Twenty-four allowing for spillage and ullage.'

'Thirty-six, on short allowance,' corrected Hornblower.

'Yes, sir,' said Bush, with a world of significance in those two syllables.

'I'll give the order within the week,' said Hornblower.

No gale could be expected to blow for a month continuously, but a second gale might follow the first before the water-hoys could beat down from Plymouth to refill the casks. It was a tribute to the organisation set up by Cornwallis that during nearly six continuous months at sea *Hotspur* had not yet had to go on short allowance for water. Should it become necessary, it would be one more irksome worry brought about by the passage of time.

'Thank you, sir,' said Bush, touching his hat and going off about his business along the darkened reeling deck.

There were worries of all sorts. Yesterday morning Doughty had pointed out to Hornblower that there were holes appearing in the elbows of his uniform coat, and he only had two coats apart from full dress. Doughty had done a neat job of patching, but a search through the ship had not revealed any material of exactly the right weather-beaten shade. Furthermore the seats of nearly all his trousers were paper-thin, and Hornblower did not fancy himself in the baggy slop-chest trousers issued to the lower-deck; yet as that store was fast running out he had had to secure a pair for himself before they should all go. He was wearing his thick winter underclothing; three sets had appeared ample last April, but now he faced the prospect, in a gale, of frequent wettings to the skin with small chance of drying anything. He cursed himself and went off to try to make sure of some sleep in anticipation of a disturbed night. At least he had a good dinner inside him; Doughty had braised an oxtail, the most despised and rejected of all the portions of the weekly ration bullock, and had made of it a dish fit for a king. It might be his last good dinner for a long time if the gale lasted – winter affected land as well as sea, so that he could expect no other vegetables than potatoes and boiled cabbage until next spring.

His anticipation of a disturbed night proved correct. He had been awake for some time, feeling the lively motion of the *Hotspur* and trying to make up his mind to rise and dress or to shout for a light and try to read, when they came thundering on his door.

'Signal from the Flag, sir!'

'I'll come.'

Doughty was really the best of servants; he arrived at the same moment, with a storm lantern.

'You'll need your pea jacket, sir, and oilskins over it. Your sou'wester, sir. Better have your scarf, sir, to keep your pea jacket dry.'

A scarf round the neck absorbed spray that might otherwise drive in between sou'wester and oilskin coat and soak the pea jacket. Doughty tucked Hornblower into his clothes like a mother preparing her son for school, while they reeled and staggered on the leaping deck. Then Hornblower went out into the roaring darkness.

'A white rocket and two blue lights from the Flag, sir,' reported Young. 'That means "take offshore stations." '

'Thank you. What sail have we set?' Hornblower could guess the answer by the feel of the ship, but he wanted to be sure. It was too dark for his dazzled eyes to see as yet.

'Double reefed tops'ls and main course, sir.'

'Get that course in and lay her on the port tack.'

'Port tack. Aye aye, sir.'

The signal for offshore stations meant a general withdrawal of the Channel Fleet. The main body took stations seventy miles to seaward off Brest, safe from that frightful lee shore and with a clear run open to them for Tor Bay – avoiding Ushant on the one hand and the Start on the other – should the storm prove so bad as to make it impossible to keep the sea. The Inshore Squadron was to be thirty miles closer in. They were the most weatherly ships and could afford the additional risk in order to be close up to Brest should a sudden shift of wind enable the French to get out.

But there was not merely the question of the French coming out, but of other French ships coming in. Out in the Atlantic there were more than one small French squadron – Bonaparte's own brother was on board one of them, with his American wife – seeking urgently to regain a French port before food and water should be completely exhausted. So *Naiad* and *Doris* and *Hotspur* had to stay close in, to intercept and report. They could best encounter the dangers of the situation. And they could best be spared if they could not. So *Hotspur* had to take her station only twenty miles to the west of Ushant, where French ships running before the gale could be best expected to make their landfall.

Bush loomed up in the darkness, shouting over the gale.

'The equinox, just as I said, sir.'

'Yes.'

'It'll be worse before it's better, sir.'

'No doubt.'

Hotspur was close-hauled now, soaring, pitching, and rolling over the vast invisible waves that the gale was driving in upon her port bow. Hornblower felt resentfully that Bush was experiencing pleasure at this change of scene. A brisk gale and a struggle to windward was stimulating to Bush after long days of fair weather, while Hornblower struggled to keep his footing and felt a trifle doubtful about the behaviour of his stomach as a result of this sudden change.

The wind howled round them and the spray burst over the deck so that the black night was filled with noise. Hornblower held on to the hammock netting; the circus riders he had seen in his childhood, riding round the ring, standing upright on two horses with one foot on each, had no more difficult task than he had at present. And the circus riders were not smacked periodically in the face with bucketfuls of spray.

There were small variations in the violence of the wind. They could hardly be called gusts; Hornblower took note that they were increases in force without any corresponding decreases. Through the soles of his feet, through the palms of his hands, he was aware of a steady increase in *Hotspur's* heel and a steady stiffening in her reaction. She was showing too much canvas. With his mouth a yard from Young's ear he yelled his order.

'Four reefs in the tops'ls!'

'Aye aye, sir.'

The exaggerated noises of the night were complicated now with the shrilling of the pipes of the bos'n's mates; down in the waist the orders were bellowed at hurrying, staggering men.

'All hands reef tops'ls!'

The hands clawed their way to their stations; this was the moment when a thousand drills bore fruit, when men carried out in darkness and turmoil the duties that had been ingrained into them in easier conditions. Hornblower felt *Hotspur's* momentary relief as Young set the topsails a-shiver to ease the tension on them. Now the men were going aloft to perform circus feats compared with which his maintenance of his foothold was a trifle. No trapeze artist ever had to do his work in utter darkness on something as unpredictable as a footrope in a gale, or had to exhibit the trained strength of the seaman passing the ear-ring while hanging fifty feet above an implacable sea. Even the lion tamer, keeping a wary eye on his treacherous brutes, did not have to encounter the ferocious enmity of the soulless canvas that tried to tear the topmast men from their precarious footing.

A touch of the helm set the sails drawing again, and *Hotspur* lay over in her fierce struggle with the wind. Surely there was no better example of the triumph of man's ingenuity over the blind forces of nature than this, whereby a ship could wring advantage out of the actual attempt of the gale to push her to destruction. Hornblower clawed his way to the binnacle and studied the heading of the ship, working out mental problems of drift and leeway against the background of his mental picture of the trend of the land. Prowse was there, apparently doing the same thing.

'I should think we've made our offing, sir.' Prowse had to shout each syllable separately. Hornblower had to do the same when he replied.

'We'll hold on a little longer, while we can.'

Extraordinary how rapidly time went by in these circumstances. It could not be long now until daylight. And this storm was still working up; it was nearly twenty-four hours since Hornblower had detected the premonitory symptoms, and it had not yet reached its full strength. It was likely to blow hard for a considerable time, as much as three days more, possibly even longer than that. Even when it should abate the wind might stay westerly for some considerable further time, delaying the water-hoys and the victuallers in their passage from Plymouth, and when eventually they should come, *Hotspur* might well be up in her station off the Goulet.

'Mr Bush!' Hornblower had to reach out and touch Bush's shoulder to attract his attention in the wind. 'We'll reduce the water allowance from today. Two between three.'

'Aye aye, sir. Just as well, I think, sir.'

Bush gave little thought to hardship, either for the lower-deck or for himself. It was no question of giving up a luxury; to reduce the water ration meant an increase in hardship. The standard issue of a gallon a day a head was hardship, even though a usual one; a man could just manage to survive on it. Two thirds of a gallon a day was a horrible deprivation; after a few days thirst began to colour every thought. As if in mockery the pumps were going at this moment. The elasticity and springiness that kept *Hotspur* from breaking up under these strains meant also that the sea had greater opportunities of penetrating her fabric, working its way in through the straining seams both above and below the water line. It would accumulate in the bilge, one – two – three feet deep. While the storm blew most of the crew would have six hours' hard physical work a day – an hour each watch – pumping the water out.

Here was the grey dawn coming, and the wind was still increasing, and *Hotspur* could not battle against it any longer.

'Mr Cargill!' Cargill was now officer of the watch. 'We'll heave to. Put her under main-topmast stays'l.'

Hornblower had to shout the order at the top of his lungs before Cargill nodded that he understood.

'All hands! All hands!'

Some minutes of hard work effected a transformation. Without the immense leverage of the topsails *Hotspur* ceased to lie over quite so steeply; the more gentle influence of the main-topmast stay-sail kept her reasonably steady, and now the rudder desisted from its hitherto constant effort to force the little ship to battle into the wind. Now she rose and swooped more freely, more extravagantly yet with less strain. She was leaping wildly enough, and still shipping water over her weather bow, but her behaviour was quite different as she yielded to the wind instead of defying it at the risk of being torn apart.

Bush was offering him a telescope, and pointing to windward, where there was now a grey horizon dimly to be seen – a serrated horizon, jagged with the waves hurrying towards them. Hornblower braced himself to put two hands to the telescope. Sea and then sky raced past the object glass as *Hotspur* tossed over successive waves. It was hard to sweep the area indicated by Bush; that had to be done in fits and starts, but after a moment something flashed across the field, was recaptured – many hours of using a telescope had developed Hornblower's reflex skills – and soon could be submitted to intermittent yet close observation.

'*Naiad*, sir,' shouted Bush into his ear.

The frigate was several miles to windward, hove-to like *Hotspur*. She had one of those new storm-topsails spread, very shallow and without reefs. It might be of considerable advantage when lying-to, for even the reduction in height alone would be considerable, but when Hornblower turned his attention back to the *Hotspur* and observed her behaviour under her main-topmast stay-sail he felt no dissatisfaction. Politeness would have led him to comment on it when he handed back the glass, but politeness stood no chance against the labour of making conversation in the wind, and contented himself with a nod. But the sight of *Naiad* out there to windward was confirmation that *Hotspur* was on her station, and beyond her Hornblower had glimpses of the *Doris* reeling and tossing on the horizon. He had done all there was to be done at present. A sensible man would get his breakfast while he might, and a sensible man would resolutely ignore the slight question of stomach occasioned by this new and different motion of the ship. All he had to do now was to endure it.

There was a pleasant moment when he reached his cabin and Huffnell the purser came in to make his morning report, for then it appeared that at the first indication of trouble Bush and Huffnell between them had routed out Simmonds the cook and had set him to work cooking food.

'That's excellent, Mr Huffnell.'

'It was laid down in your standing orders, sir.'

So it was, Hornblower remembered. He had added that paragraph after reading Cornwallis's orders regarding stations to be assumed in westerly gales. Simmonds had boiled three hundred pounds of salt pork in *Hotspur's* cauldrons, as well as three hundred pounds of dried peas, before the weather had compelled the galley fires to be extinguished.

'Pretty nigh on cooked, anyway, sir,' said Huffnell.

So that for the next three days – four at a pinch – the hands would have something more to eat than dry biscuit. They would have cold parboiled pork and cold pease porridge; the latter was what the Man in the Moon burned his mouth on according to the nursery rhyme.

'Thank you, Mr Huffnell. It's unlikely that this gale will last more than four days.'

That was actually the length of time that gale lasted, the gale that ushered in the worst winter in human memory, following the best summer. For those four days *Hotspur* lay hove-to, pounded by the sea, flogged by the wind, while Hornblower made anxious calculations regarding leeway and drift; as the wind backed northerly his attention was diverted from Ushant to the north to the Isle de Sein to the south of the approaches to Brest. It was not until the fifth day that *Hotspur* was able to set three-reefed topsails and thrash her way back to station while Simmonds managed to start his galley fires again and to provide the crew – and Hornblower – with hot boiled beef as a change from cold boiled pork.

Even then that three-reefed gale maintained the long Atlantic rollers in all their original vastness, so that *Hotspur* soared over them and slithered unhappily down the far side, adding her own corkscrew motion as her weather-bow met the swells, her own special stagger when a rogue wave crashed into her, and the worse lurch when – infrequently – a higher wave than usual blanketed her sails so that she reeled into the sea instead of yielding, with a bursting of green water over her decks. But an hour's work at the pumps every watch kept the bilges clear, and by tacking every two hours *Hotspur* was able to beat painfully out to sea again – not more than half a mile's gain to windward on each tack – and recover the comparative safety of her original station before the next storm.

It was as if in payment for that fair weather summer that these gales blew, and perhaps that was not an altogether fanciful thought; to Hornblower's mind there might be some substance to the theory that prolonged local high pressure during the summer now meant that the pent-up dirty weather to the westward could exert more than its usual force. However that might be, the mere fresh gale that endured for four days after the first storm then worked up again into a tempest, blowing eternally from the westward with almost hurricane force; grey dreary days of lowering cloud, and wild black nights, with the wind howling unceasingly in the rigging until the ear was sated with the noise, until no price seemed too great to pay for five minutes of peace – and yet no price however great could buy even a second of peace. The creaking and the groaning of *Hotspur's* fabric blended with the noise of the wind, and the actual woodwork of the ship vibrated with the vibration of the rigging until it seemed as if body and mind, exhausted with the din and with the fatigues of mere movement, could not endure for another minute, and yet went on to endure for days.

The tempest died down to a fresh gale, to a point when the top-sails needed only a single reef, and then, unbelievably, worked up into a tempest again, the third in a month, during which all on board renewed the bruises that covered them as a result of being flung about by the motion of the ship. And it was during that tempest that Hornblower went through a spiritual crisis. It was not a mere question of calculation, it went far deeper than that, even though he did his best to appear quite imperturbable as Bush and Huffnell and Wallis the surgeon made their daily reports. He might have called them into a formal council of war; he might have covered himself by asking for their opinions in writing, to be produced in evidence should there be a court of inquiry, but that was not in his nature. Responsibility was the air he breathed; he could no more bring himself to evade it than he could hold his breath indefinitely.

It was the first day that reefed topsails could be set that he reached his decision.

'Mr Prowse, I'd be obliged if you would set a course to close *Naiad* so that she can read our signals.'

'Aye aye, sir.'

Hornblower, standing on the quarter-deck in the eternal, infernal wind, hated Prowse for darting that inquiring glance at him. Of course the ward-room had discussed his problem. Of course they knew of the shortage of drinking water; of course they knew that Wallis had discovered three cases of sore gums – the earliest symptoms of scurvy in a navy that had overcome scurvy except in special conditions. Of course they had wondered about when their captain would yield to circumstances. Perhaps they had made bets on the date. The problem, the decision, had been his and not theirs.

Hotspur clawed her way over the tossing sea to the point on *Naiad's* lee bow when the signal flags would blow out at right angles to the line of sight.

'Mr Foreman! Signal to *Naiad,* if you please. "Request permission to return to port." '

'Request permission to return to port. Aye aye, sir.'

Naiad was the only ship of the Inshore Squadron – of the Channel Fleet – in sight, and her captain was therefore senior officer on the station. Every captain was senior to the captain of the *Hotspur*.

'*Naiad* acknowledges, sir,' reported Foreman, and then, after ten seconds' wait, '*Naiad* to *Hotspur,* sir, "Interrogative." '

Somehow it might have been more politely put. Chambers of the *Naiad* might have signalled 'Kindly give reasons for request,' or something like that. But the single interrogative hoist was convenient and rapid. Hornblower framed his next signal equally tersely.

'*Hotspur* to *Naiad*. "Eight days water." '

Hornblower watched the reply soar up *Naiad's* signal halliards. It was not the affirmative; if it was permission, it was a qualified permission.

'*Naiad* to *Hotspur,* sir. "Remain four more days." '

'Thank you, Mr Foreman.'

Hornblower tried to keep all expression out of his voice and his face.

'I'll wager he has two months' water on board, sir,' said Bush, angrily.

'I hope he has, Mr Bush.'

They were seventy leagues from Tor Bay; two days' sailing with a fair wind. There was no margin for misfortune. If at the end of four days the wind should shift easterly, as was perfectly possible, they could not reach Tor Bay in a week or even more; the water-hoys might come down-channel, but might easily not find them at once, and then it was not unlikely that the sea would be too rough for boat work. There was an actual possibility that the crew of the *Hotspur* might die of thirst. It had not been easy for Hornblower to make his request; he had no desire to be thought one of those captains whose sole desire was to return to port, and he had waited to the last sensible moment. Chambers saw the problem differently, as a man well might do as regards the possible misfortune of other people. This was an easy way of demonstrating his resolution and firmness. An easy way, a comfortable way, a cheap way.

'Send this signal, if you please, Mr Foreman. "Thank you. Am returning to station. Good-bye.' Mr Prowse, we can bear away when that signal is acknowledged. Mr Bush, from today the water ration is reduced. One between two.'

Two quarts of water a day for all purposes – and such water – to men living on salted food, was far below the minimum for health. It meant sickness as well as discomfort, but the reduction also meant that the last drop of water would not be drunk until sixteen days had passed.

Captain Chambers had not foreseen the future weather, and perhaps he could not be blamed for that, seeing that on the fourth day after the exchange of signals the westerly wind worked up again, unbelievably, into the fourth tempest of that gale-ridden autumn. It was towards the end of the afternoon watch that Hornblower was called on deck again to give his permission for the reefed topsails to be got in and the storm stay-sail set once more. Significantly it was growing dark already; the days of the equinox when the sun set at six o'clock were long past, and, equally significantly, that roaring westerly gale now had a chilling quality about it. It was cold; not freezing, not icy, but cold, searchingly cold. Hornblower tried to pace the unstable deck in an endeavour to keep his circulation going; he grew warm, not because of his walking, but because the physical labour of keeping his feet was great enough for the purpose. *Hotspur* was leaping like a deer beneath him, and from down below, too, came the dreary sound of the pumps at work.

Six days' water on board now; twelve at half-rations. The gloom of the night was no more gloomy than his thoughts. It was five weeks since he had last been able to send a letter to Maria, and it was six weeks since he had last heard from her, six weeks of westerly gales and westerly tempests. Anything might have happened to her or to the child, and she would be thinking that anything might have happened to the *Hotspur* or to him.

A more irregular wave than usual, roaring out of the darkness, burst upon *Hotspur's* weather bow. Hornblower felt her sudden sluggishness, her inertia, beneath his feet. That wave must have flooded the waist to a depth of a yard or more, fifty or sixty tons of water piled up on her deck. She lay like something dead for a moment. Then she rolled, slightly at first, and then more freely; the sound of the cataracts of water pouring across could be clearly heard despite the gale. She freed herself as the water cascaded out through the overworked scuppers, and she came sluggishly back to life, to leap once more in her mad career from wave crest to trough. A blow like that could well be her death; some time she might not rise to it; some time her deck might be burst in. Another wave beat on her bow like the hammer of a mad giant, and another after that.

Next day was worse, the worst day that *Hotspur* had experienced in all these wild weeks. Some slight shift in the wind, or the increase in its strength, had worked up the waves to a pitch that was particularly unsuited to *Hotspur's* idiosyncrasies. The waist was flooded most of the time now, so that she laboured heavily without relief, each wave catching her before she could free herself. That meant that the pumps were at work three hours out of every four, so that even with petty officers and idlers and waisters and marines all doing their share, every hand was engaged on the toilsome labour for twelve hours a day.

Bush's glance was more direct even than usual when he came to make his report.

'We're still sighting *Naiad* now and then, sir, but not a chance of signals being read.'

This was the day when by Captain Chambers's orders they were free to run for harbour.

'Yes. I don't think we can bear away in this wind and sea.'

Bush's expression revealed a mental struggle. *Hotspur's* powers of resistance to the present battering were not unlimited, but on the other hand to turn tail and run would be an operation of extreme danger.

'Has Huffnell reported to you yet, sir?'

'Yes,' said Hornblower.

There were nine hundred-gallon casks of fresh water left down below, which had been standing in the bottom tier for a hundred days. And now one of them had proved to be contaminated with seawater and was hardly drinkable. The others might perhaps be even less so.

'Thank you, Mr Bush,' said Hornblower, terminating the interview. 'We'll remain hove-to for today at least.'

Surely a wind of this force must moderate soon, even though Hornblower had a premonition that it would not.

Nor did it. The slow dawn of the new day found *Hotspur* still labouring under the dark clouds, the waves still as wild, the wind still as insane. The time had come for the final decision, as Hornblower well knew as he came out on deck in his clammy clothes. He knew the dangers, and he had spent a large part of the night preparing his mind to deal with them.

'Mr Bush, we'll get before the wind.'

'Aye aye, sir.'

Before she could come before the wind she would have to present her vulnerable side to the waves. There would be seconds during which she could be rolled over on to her beam ends, beaten down under the waves, pounded into a wreck.

'Mr Cargill!'

This was going to be a moment far more dangerous than being chased by the *Loire*, and Cargill would have to be trusted to carry out a similar duty as on a tense occasion then. Face close to face, Hornblower shouted his instructions.

'Get for'ard. Make ready to show a bit of the fore-topmast stays'l. Haul it up when I wave my arm.'

'Aye aye, sir.'

'Get it in the moment I wave a second time.'

'Aye aye, sir.'

'Mr Bush! We shall need the for-tops'l.'

'Aye aye, sir.'

'Goose-wing it.'

'Aye aye, sir.'

'Stand by the sheets. Wait for me to wave my arm the second time.'

'The second time. Aye aye, sir.'

Hotspur's stern was nearly as vulnerable as her side. If she presented it to the waves while stationary she would be 'pooped' – a wave would burst over her and sweep her from stern to stem, a blow she would probably not survive. The fore-topsail would give her the necessary way, but spreading it before she was before the wind would lay her over on her beam ends. 'Goose-winging it' – pulling down the lower corners while leaving the centre portion still furled – would expose less canvas than the reefed sail; enough in that gale to carry her forward at the necessary speed.

Hornblower took his station beside the wheel, where he could be clearly seen from forward. He ran his eyes aloft to make sure that the preparations for goose-winging the fore-topsail were complete, and his gaze lingered for a while longer as he observed the motion of the spars relative to the wild sky. Then he transferred his attention to the sea on the weather side, to the immense rollers hurrying towards the ship. He watched the roll and the pitch; he gauged the strength of the howling wind which was trying to tear him from his footing. That wind was trying to stupefy him, to paralyse him, too. He had to keep the hard central core of himself alert and clear thinking while his outer body was numbed by the wind.

A rogue wave burst against the weather bow in a huge but fleeting pillar of spray, the green mass pounding aft along the waist, and Hornblower swallowed nervously while it seemed as if *Hotspur* would never recover. But she did, slowly and wearily, rolling off the load

from her deck. As she cleared herself the moment came, a moment
of regularity in the on-coming waves, with her bow just lifting to the
nearest one. He waved his arm, and saw the slender head of the fore-
topmast stay-sail rising up the stay, and the ship lay over wildly to
the pressure.

'Hard-a-port,' he yelled to the hands at the wheel.

The enormous leverage of the stay-sail, applied to the bow-sprit,
began to swing the *Hotspur* round like a weather vane; as she turned,
the wind thrusting more and more from aft gave her steerage way so
that the rudder could bite and accelerate the turn. She was down in
the trough of the wave but turning, still turning. He waved his arm
again. The clews of the fore-topsail showed themselves as the hands
hauled on the sheets, and *Hotspur* surged forward with the impact of
the wind upon the canvas. The wave was almost upon them, but it
disappeared out of the tail of Hornblower's eye as *Hotspur* presented
first her quarter and then her stern to it.

'Meet her! Midships!'

The tug of the sail on the foremast would put *Hotspur* right before
the wind without the use of the rudder; indeed the rudder would
only delay her acquiring all the way she could. Time enough to put
the rudder to work again when she was going at her fastest. Hornblower braced himself for the impact of the wave now following them
up. The seconds passed and then it came, but the stern had begun to
lift and the blow was deprived of its force. Only a minor mass of
water burst over the taffrail, to surge aft again as *Hotspur* lifted her
bows. Now they were racing along with the waves; now they were
travelling through the water ever so little faster. That was the most
desirable point of speed; there was no need to increase or decrease
even minutely the area of canvas exposed by the goose-winged fore-
topsail. The situation was safe and yet unutterably precarious,
balanced on a knife edge. The slightest yawing and *Hotspur* was lost.

'Keep her from falling off!' Hornblower yelled to the men at the
wheel, and the grizzled senior quartermaster, his wet grey ringlets
flapping over his cheeks from out of his sou'wester, nodded without
taking his eyes from the fore-topsail. Hornblower knew – with his
vivid imagination he could feel the actual sensation up his arms –
how uncertain and unsatisfactory was the feel of wheel and rudder
when running before a following sea, the momentary lack of response
to the turning spokes, the hesitation of the ship as a mounting wave
astern deprived the fore-topsail of some of the wind that filled it,
the uncontrolled slithering sensation as the ship went down a slope.
A moment's inattention – a moment's bad luck – could bring ruin.

Yet here they were momentarily safe before the wind, and running
for the Channel. Prowse was already staring into the binnacle and

noting the new course on the traverse board, and at a word from him Orrock and a seaman struggled aft to cast the log and determine the speed. And here came Bush, ascending to the quarter-deck, grinning over the success of the manoeuvre and with the exhilaration of the new state of affairs.

'Course nor'east by east, sir,' reported Prowse. 'Speed better than seven knots.'

Now there was a new set of problems to deal with. They were entering the Channel. There were shoals and headlands ahead of them; there were tides – the tricky tidal streams of the Channel – to be reckoned with. The very nature of the waves would change soon, with the effect upon the Atlantic rollers of the shallowing water and the narrowing Channel and the varying tides. There was the general problem of avoiding being blown all the way up Channel, and the particular one of trying to get into Tor Bay.

All this called for serious calculation and reference to tide tables, especially in face of the fact that running before the wind like this it would be impossible to take soundings.

'We ought to get a sight of Ushant on this course, sir,' yelled Prowse.

That would be a decided help, a solid base for future calculations, a new departure. A shouted word sent Orrock up to the fore-top-masthead with a telescope to supplement the look-out there, while Hornblower faced the first stage of the new series of problems – the question of whether he could bring himself to leave the deck – and the second stage – the question of whether he should invite Prowse to share his calculations. The answer to both was necessarily in the affirmative. Bush was a good seaman and could be trusted to keep a vigilant eye on the wheel and on the canvas; Prowse was a fair navigator and was by law co-responsible with Hornblower for the course to be set and so would have just cause for grievance if he was not consulted, however much Hornblower wished to be free of his company.

So it came about that Prowse was with Hornblower in the chart-room, struggling with the tide tables, when Foreman opened the door – his knocking not having been heard in the general din – and admitted all the noise of the ship in full volume.

'Message from Mr Bush, sir. Ushant in sight on the starboard beam, seven or eight miles, sir.'

'Thank you, Mr Foreman.'

That was a stroke of good fortune, the first they had had. Now they could plan the next struggle to bend the forces of nature to their will. It was a struggle indeed; for the men at the wheel a prolonged physical ordeal which made it necessary to relieve them every half-hour and for Hornblower a mental ordeal which was to keep him at full-strain for the next thirty hours. There was the tentative trying of the wheel, to see if it was possible to bring the wind a couple of points on her port quarter. Three times they made the attempt, to abandon it hastily as wind and wave rendered the ship unmanageable, but at the fourth try it became possible, with the shortening of the waves in their advance up-Channel and the turn of the tide over on the French coast. Now they tore through the water, speed undiminished despite the drag of the rudder as the helmsmen battled with the wheel that kicked and struggled as if it were alive and malignant under their hands, and while the whole strength of the crew handled the braces to trim the yard exactly to make certain there was no danger of sailing by the lee.

At least the danger of running *Hotspur* bodily under water was now eliminated. There was no chance of her putting her bows into the slack back of a dilatory wave and never lifting them again. To balance the leverage of the fore-topsail they hauled up the mizzen stay-sail, which brought relief to the helmsmen even though it laid *Hotspur* over until her starboard gun-ports were level with the water. It lasted for a frantic hour, and it seemed to Hornblower that he was holding his breath during all that time, and until it burst in the centre with a report like a twelve pounder, splitting into flying pendants of canvas that cracked in the wind like coach-whips as the helmsmen fought against the renewed tendency of *Hotspur* to turn away from the wind. Yet the temporary success justified replacing the sail with the mizzen topmast stay-sail, just a corner of it showing, and the head and the tack still secured by gaskets. It was a brand-new sail, and it managed to endure the strain, to compensate for the labour and difficulty of setting it.

The short dark day drew to an end, and now everything had to be done in roaring night, while lack of sleep intensified the numbness and fatigue and the stupidity induced by the unremitting wind. With his dulled sensitivity Hornblower's reaction was slow to the changed behaviour of *Hotspur* under his feet. The transition was gradual, in any case, but at last it became marked enough for him to notice it, his sense of touch substituting for his sense of sight to tell him that the waves were becoming shorter and steeper; this was the choppiness of the Channel and not the steady sweep of the Atlantic rollers.

Hotspur's motion was more rapid, and in a sense more violent; the waves broke over her bow more frequently though in smaller volume. Although still far below the surface the floor of the Channel was rising, from a hundred fathoms deep to forty fathoms, and there was the turn of the tide to be considered, even though this westerly tempest must have piled up the waters of the Channel far above mean level. And the Channel was narrower now; the rollers that had found ample passage between Ushant and Scilly were feeling the squeeze, and all these factors were evident in their behaviour. *Hotspur* was wet all the time now, and only continuous working of the pumps kept the water down below within bounds – pumps worked by weary men, thirsty men, hungry men, sleepy men, throwing their weight on the long handles each time with the feeling that they could not repeat the effort even once more.

At four in the morning Hornblower was conscious of a shift in the wind, and for a precious hour he was able to order a change of course until a sudden veering of the wind forced them back on the original course again, but he had gained, so his calculations told him, considerably to the northward; there was so much satisfaction in that that he put his forehead down on his forearms on the chart-room table and was surprised into sleep for several valuable minutes before a more extravagant leaping of the ship banged his head upon his arms and awakened him to make his way wearily out upon the quarter-deck again.

'Wish we could take a sounding, sir,' shouted Prowse.

'Yes.'

There was no sense in wasting strength in voicing wishes.

Yet now, even in the darkness, Hornblower could feel that the recent gain and the change in the character of the sea made it justifiable to heave to for a space. He could goad his mind to deal with the problem of drift and leeway; he could harden his heart to face the necessity of calling upon the exhausted topmen to make the effort to furl the goose-winged fore-topsail while he stood by, alert, to bring the ship to under the mizzen stay-sail; bring the helm over at the right moment so that she met the steep waves with her bow. Riding to the wind her motion was wilder and more extravagant than ever, but they managed to cast the deep sea lead, with the crew lined up round the ship, calling 'Watch! Watch!' as each man let his portion of line loose. Thirty-eight – thirty-seven – thirty-eight fathoms again; the three casts consumed an hour, with everyone wet to the skin and exhausted. It was a fragment more of the data necessary, while heaving-to eased the labour of the worn-out quartermasters and actually imposed so much less strain on the seams that the pumps steadily gained on the water below.

At the first watery light of dawn they set the goose-winged fore-topsail again while Hornblower faced the problem of getting *Hotspur* round with the wind over her quarter without laying her over on her beam ends. Then they were thrashing along in the old way, decks continually under water, rolling until every timber groaned, with Orrock freezing at the fore-topmast-head with his glass. It was noon before he sighted the land; half an hour later Bush returned to the quarter-deck from the ascent he made to confirm Orrock's findings. Bush was more weary than he would ever admit, his dirty hollow cheeks overgrown with a stubble of beard, but he could still show surprise and pleasure.

'Bolt Head, sir!' he yelled. 'Fine on the port bow. And I could just make out the Start.'

'Thank you.'

Even though it meant shouting, Bush wanted to express his feelings about this feat of navigation, but Hornblower had no time for that, nor the patience, nor, for that matter, the strength. There was the question of not being blown too far to leeward at this eleventh hour, of making preparations to come to an anchor in conditions that would certainly be difficult. There was the tide rip off the Start to be borne in mind, the necessity of rounding to as close under Berry Head as possible. There was the sudden inexpressible change in wind and sea as they came under the lee of the Start; the steep choppiness here seemed nothing compared with what *Hotspur* had been enduring five minutes before, and the land took the edge of the hurricane wind to reduce it to the mere force of a full gale that still kept *Hotspur* flying before it. There was the Newstone and the Blackstones – here as well as in the Iroise – and the final tricky moment of the approach to Berry Head.

'Ships of war at anchor, sir,' reported Bush, sweeping Tor Bay with his glass as they opened it up. 'That's *Dreadnought*. That's *Temeraire*. It's the Channel Fleet. My God! There's one aground in Torquay Roads. Two-decker – she must have dragged her anchors.'

'Yes. We'll back the best bower anchor before we let go, Mr Bush. We'll have to use the launch's carronade. You've time to see about that.'

'Aye aye, sir.'

Even in Tor Bay there was a full gale blowing; where a two-decker had dragged her anchors every precaution must be taken at whatever further cost in effort. The seven hundredweight of the boat carronade, attached to the anchor-cable fifty feet back from the one ton of the best bower, might just save that anchor from lifting and dragging. And so *Hotspur* came in under goose-winged fore-topsail and storm mizzen stay-sail, round Berry Head, under the eyes of the Channel Fleet, to claw her way in towards Brixham pier and to round-to with her weary men furling the fore-topsail and to drop her anchors while with a last effort they sent down the topmasts and Prowse and Hornblower took careful bearings to make sure she was not dragging. It was only then that there was leisure to spare to make her number to the flag-ship.

'Flag acknowledges, sir,' croaked Foreman.

'Very well.'

It was still possible to do something more without collapsing. 'Mr Foreman, kindly make this signal. "Need drinking water." '

XIV

Tor Bay was a tossing expanse of white horses. The land lessened the effect of the wind to some extent; the Channel waves were hampered in their entry by Berry Head, but all the same the wind blew violently and the waves racing up the Channel managed to wheel leftwards, much weakened, but now running across the wind, and with the tide to confuse the issue Tor Bay boiled like a cauldron. For forty hours after *Hotspur's* arrival the *Hibernia*, Cornwallis's big three-decker, flew the signal 715 with a negative beside it, and 715 with a negative meant that boats were not to be employed.

Not even the Brixham fishermen, renowned for their small boat work, could venture out into Tor Bay while it was in that mood, so that until the second morning at anchor the crew of the *Hotspur* supported an unhappy existence on two quarts of tainted water a day. And Hornblower was the unhappiest man on board, from causes both physical and mental. The little ship almost empty of stores was the plaything of wind and wave and tide; she surged about at her anchors like a restive horse. She swung and she snubbed herself steady with a jerk; she plunged and snubbed herself again. With her topmasts sent down she developed a shallow and rapid roll. It was a mixture of motions that would test the strongest stomach, and Hornblower's stomach was by no means the strongest, while there was the depressing association in his memory of his very first day in a ship of war, when he had made himself a laughing stock by being seasick in the old *Justinian* at anchor in Spithead.

He spent those forty hours vomiting his heart out, while to the black depression of sea-sickness was added the depression resulting from the knowledge that Maria was only thirty miles away in Plymouth, and by a good road. Cornwallis's representations had caused the government to cut that road, over the tail end of Dartmoor, so that the Channel Fleet in its rendezvous could readily be supplied from the great naval base. Half a day on a good horse and Hornblower could be holding Maria in his arms, he could be hearing news first-hand about the progress of the child, on whom (to his surprise) his thoughts were beginning to dwell increasingly. The hands spent their free moments on the forecastle, round the knightheads, gazing at Brixham and Brixham Pier; even in that wind with its deluges of rain there were women to be seen occasionally, women in skirts, at whom the crew stared like so many Tantaluses. After one good night's sleep, and with pumping only necessary now for half an hour in each watch, those men had time and energy so that their imaginations had free play. They could think about women, and they could think about liquor – most of them dreamed dreams of swilling themselves into swinish unconsciousness on Brixham's smuggled brandy, while Hornblower could only vomit and fret.

But he slept during the second half of the second night, when the wind not only moderated but backed two points northerly, altering the conditions in Tor Bay like magic, so that after he had assured himself at midnight that the anchors were still holding his fatigue took charge and he could sleep without moving for seven hours. He was still only half awake when Doughty came bursting in on him.

'Signal from the Flag, sir.'

There were strings of bunting flying from the halliards of the *Hibernia*; with the shift of wind they could be read easily enough from the quarter-deck of the *Hotspur*.

'There's our number there, sir,' said Foreman, glass at eye. 'It comes first.'

Cornwallis was giving orders for the victualling and re-watering of the fleet, establishing the order in which the ships were to be re-plenished, and that signal gave *Hotspur* priority over all the rest.

'We're lucky, sir,' commented Bush.

'Possibly,' agreed Hornblower. No doubt Cornwallis had been informed about *Hotspur's* appeal for drinking water, but he might have further plans, too.

'Look at that, sir,' said Bush. 'They waste no time.'

Two lighters, each propelled by eight sweeps, and with a six-oared yawl standing by, were creeping out round the end of Brixham Pier.

'I'll see about the fend-offs, sir,' said Bush, departing hastily.

These were the water-lighters, marvels of construction, each of them containing a series of vast cast-iron tanks. Hornblower had heard about them; they were of fifty tons' burthen each of them, and each of them carried ten thousand gallons of drinking water, while *Hotspur*, with every cask and hogshead brim full, could not quite store fifteen thousand.

So now began an orgy of fresh water, clear springwater which had not lain in the cast-iron tanks for more than a few days. With the lighters chafing uneasily alongside, a party from *Hotspur* went down to work the beautiful modern pumps which the lighters carried, forcing the water up through four superb canvas hoses passed in through the ports and then down below. The deck scuttle butt, so long empty, was swilled out and filled, to be instantly emptied by the crew and filled again; just possibly at that moment the hands would rather have fresh water than brandy.

It was glorious waste; down below the casks were swilled and scrubbed out with fresh water, and the swillings drained into the bilge whence the ship's pumps would later have to force it overboard at some cost of labour. Every man drank his fill and more; Hornblower gulped down glass after glass until he was full, yet half an hour later found him drinking again. He could feel himself expanding like a desert plant after rain.

'Look at this, sir,' said Bush, telescope in hand and gesturing towards Brixham.

The telescope revealed a busy crowd at work there, and there were cattle visible.

'Slaughtering,' said Bush. 'Fresh meat.'

Soon another lighter was creeping out to them; hanging from a frame down the midship line were sides of beef, carcasses of sheep and pigs.

'I won't mind a roast of mutton, sir,' said Bush.

Bullocks and sheep and swine had been driven over the moors to Brixham, and slaughtered and dressed on the waterfront immediately before shipping so that the meat would last fresh as long as possible.

'Four days' rations there, sir,' said Bush making a practised estimate. 'An' there's a live bullock an' four sheep an' four pigs. Excuse me, sir, and I'll post a guard at the side.

Most of the hands had money in their pockets and would spend it freely on liquor if they were given the chance, and the men in the victualling barges would sell to them unless the closest supervision were exercised. The water-lighters had finished their task and were casting off. It had been a brief orgy; from the moment that the hoses were taken in ship's routine would be re-established. One gallon of water per man per day for all purposes from now on.

The place of the watering barges was taken by the dry victualling barge, with bags of biscuit, sacks of dried peas, kegs of butter, cases of cheese, sacks of oatmeal, but conspicuous on top of all this were half a dozen nets full of fresh bread. Two hundred four-pound loaves – Hornblower could taste the crustiness of them in his watering mouth when he merely looked at them. A beneficent government, under the firm guidance of Cornwallis, was sending these luxuries aboard; the hardships of a life at sea were the result of natural circumstances quite as much as of ministerial ineptitude.

There was never a quiet moment all through that day. Here was Bush touching his hat again with a final demand on his attention.

'You've given no order about wives, sir.'

'Wives?'

'Wives, sir.'

There was an interrogative lift in Hornblower's voice as he said the word; there was a flat, complete absence of expression in Bush's. It was usual in His Majesty's Ship when they lay in harbour for women to be allowed on board, and one or two of them might well be wives. It was some small compensation for the system that forbade a man to set foot on shore lest he desert; but the women inevitably smuggled liquor on board, and the scenes of debauchery that ensued on the lower-deck were as shameless as in Nero's court. Disease and indiscipline were the natural result; it took days or weeks to shake the crew down again into an efficient team. Hornblower did not want his fine ship ruined but if *Hotspur* were to stay long at anchor in Tor Bay he could not deny what was traditionally a reasonable request. He simply could not deny it.

'I'll give my orders later this morning,' he said.

It was not difficult, some minutes later, to intercept Bush at a moment when a dozen of the hands were within earshot.

'Oh, Mr Bush!' Hornblower hoped his voice did not sound as stilted and theatrical as he feared. 'You've plenty of work to be done about the ship.'

'Yes, sir. There's a good deal of standing rigging I'd like set up again. And there's running rigging to be re-rove. And there's the paint work—'

'Very well, Mr Bush. When the ship's complete in all respects we'll allow the wives on board, but not until then. Not until then, Mr Bush. And if we have to sail before then it will be the fortune of war.'

'Aye aye, sir.'

Next came the letters; word must have reached the post office in Plymouth of the arrival of *Hotspur* in Tor Bay, and the letters had been sent across overland. Seven letters from Maria; Hornblower tore open the last first, to find that Maria was well and her pregnancy progressing favourably, and then he skimmed through the others, to find, as he expected, that she had rejoiced to read her Valiant Hero's Gazette letter although she was perturbed by the risks run by her Maritime Alexander, and although she was consumed with sorrow because the Needs of the Service had denied from her eyes the light of his Countenance. Hornblower was half-way through writing a reply when a midshipman came escorted to his cabin door with a note . . .

'HMS *Hibernia*
Tor Bay
Dear Captain Hornblower,

If you can be tempted out of your ship at three o'clock this afternoon to dine in the flagship it would give great pleasure to

Your ob't servant,

Wm. Cornwallis, Vice Ad.

P.S.—An affirmative signal hung out in the *Hotspur* is all the acknowledgement necessary.'

Hornblower went out on to the quarter-deck.

'Mr Foreman. Signal "*Hotspur* to Flag. Affirmative." '

'Just affirmative, sir?'

'You heard me.'

An invitation from the Commander-in-Chief was as much a royal command as if it had been signed George R. – even if the postscript did not dictate the reply.

Then there was the powder to be put on board, with all the care and precautions that operation demanded; *Hotspur* had fired away one ton of the five tons of gunpowder that her magazine could hold. The operation was completed when Prowse brought up one of the hands who manned the powder-barge.

'This fellow says he has a message for you, sir.'

This was a swarthy gipsy-faced fellow who met Hornblower's eye boldly with all the assurance to be expected of a man who carried in his pocket a protection against impressment.

'What is it?'

'Message for you from a lady, sir, and I was to have a shilling for delivering it to you.'

Hornblower looked him over keenly. There was only one lady who could be sending a message.

'Nonsense. That lady promised sixpence. Now didn't she?'

Hornblower knew that much about Maria despite his brief married life.

'Well, yes, sir.'

'Here's the shilling. What's the message?'

'The lady said look for her on Brixham Pier, sir.'

'Very well.'

Hornblower took the glass from its becket and walked forward. Busy though the ship was, there were nevertheless a few idlers round the knightheads who shrank away in panic at the remarkable sight of their captain here. He trained the glass; Brixham Pier, as might be expected, was crowded with people, and he searched for a long time without result, training the glass first on one woman and then on another. Was that Maria? She was the only woman wearing a bonnet and not a shawl. Of course it was Maria; momentarily he had forgotten that this was the end of the seventh month. She stood in the front row of the crowd; as Hornblower watched she raised an arm and fluttered a scarf. She could not see him, or at least she certainly could not recognise him at that distance without a telescope. She must have heard, along with the rest of Plymouth, of the arrival of *Hotspur* in Tor Bay; presumably she had made her way here via Totnes in the carrier's cart – a long and tedious journey.

She fluttered her scarf again, in the pathetic hope that he was looking at her. In that part of his mind which never ceased attending to the ship Hornblower became conscious of the pipes of the bos'n's mate – the pipes had been shrilling one call or another all day long.

'Quarter-boat away-ay-ay!'

Hornblower had never been so conscious of the slavery of the King's service. Here he was due to leave the ship to dine with the Commander-in-Chief, and the Navy had a tradition of punctuality that he could not flout. And there was Foreman, breathless from his run forward.

'Message from Mr Bush, sir. The boat's waiting.'

What was he to do? Ask Bush to write Maria a note and send it by a shore boat? No, he would have to risk being late – Maria could not bear to receive second-hand messages at this time of all times. A hurried scribble with the left-handed quill.

'My own darling,

So much pleasure in seeing you, but not a moment to spare yet. I will write to you at length.

Your devoted husband,

H.'

He used that initial in all his letters to her; he did not like his first name and he could not bring himself to sign 'Horry.' Damn it all, here was the half-finished letter, interrupted earlier that day and never completed. He thrust it aside and struggled to apply a wafer to the finished note. Seven months at sea had destroyed every vestige of gum and the wafer would not adhere. Doughty was hovering over him with sword and hat and cloak – Doughty was just as aware of the necessity for punctuality as he was. Hornblower gave the open note to Bush.

'Seal this, if you please, Mr Bush. And send it by shore boat to Mrs Hornblower on the pier. Yes, she's on the pier. By a shore boat, Mr Bush; no one from the ship's to set foot on land.'

Down the side and into the boat. Hornblower could imagine the explanatory murmur through the crowd on the pier, as Maria would learn from better informed bystanders what was going on.

'That's the captain going down into the boat.' She would feel a surge of excitement and happiness. The boat shoved off, the conditions of wind and current dictating that her bow was pointing right at the pier; that would be Maria's moment of highest hope. Then the boat swung round while the hands hauled at the halliards and the balance-lug rose up the mast. Next moment she was flying towards the flagship, flying away from Maria without a word or a sign, and Hornblower felt a great welling of pity and remorse within his breast.

Hewitt responded to the flagship's hail, turned the boat neatly into the wind, dropped the sail promptly, and with the last vestige of the boat's way ran her close enough to the starboard main-chains for the bowman to hook on. Hornblower judged his moment and went up the ship's side. As his head reached the level of the main-deck the pipes began to shrill in welcome. And through that noise Hornblower heard the three sharp double strokes of the ship's bell. Six bells in the afternoon watch; three o'clock, the time stated in his invitation.

The great stern cabin in the *Hibernia* was furnished in a more subdued fashion than Pellew had affected in the *Tonnant*, more Spartan and less lavish, but comfortable enough. Somewhat to Hornblower's surprise there were no other visitors; present in the cabin were only Cornwallis, and Collins, the sardonic Captain of the Fleet, and the flag lieutenant, whose name Hornblower vaguely heard as one of these new-fangled double barrelled names with a hyphen.

Hornblower was conscious of Cornwallis's blue eyes fixed upon him, examining him closely in a considering, appraising way that might have unsettled him in other conditions. But he was still a little preoccupied with his thoughts about Maria, on the one hand, while on the other seven months at sea, seven weeks of continuous storms, provided all necessary excuse for his shabby coat and his seaman's trousers. He could meet Cornwallis's glance without shyness. Indeed, the effect of Cornwallis's kindly but unsmiling expression was much modified because his wig was slightly awry; Cornwallis still affected a horsehair bobwig of the sort that was now being relegated by fashion to noblemen's coachmen, and today it had a rakish cant that dissipated all appearance of dignity.

Yet, wig or no wig, there was something in the air, some restraint, some tension, even though Cornwallis was a perfect host who did the honours of his table with an easy grace. The quality of the atmosphere was such that Hornblower hardly noticed the food that covered the table, and he felt acutely that the polite conversation was guarded and cautious. They discussed the recent weather; *Hibernia* had been in Tor Bay for several days, having run for shelter just in time to escape the last hurricane.

'How were your stores when you came in, Captain?' asked Collins.

Now here was another sort of atmosphere, something artificial. There was an odd quality about Collins's tone, accentuated by the formal 'Captain', particularly when addressed to a lowly Commander. Then Hornblower identified it. This was a stilted and prepared speech, exactly of the same nature as his recent speech to Bush regarding the admission of women to the ship. He could identify the tone, but he still could not account for it. But he had a commonplace answer, so commonplace that he made it in a commonplace way.

'I still had plenty, sir. Beef and pork for a month at least.'

There was a pause a shade longer than natural, as if the information was being digested, before Cornwallis asked the next question in a single word.

'Water?'

'That was different, sir. I'd never been able to fill my casks completely from the hoys. We were pretty low when we got in. That was why we ran for it.'

'How much did you have?'

'Two days at half-rations, sir. We'd been on half-rations for a week, and two-thirds rations for four weeks before that.'

'Oh,' said Collins, and in that instant the atmosphere changed.

'You left very little margin for error, Hornblower,' said Cornwallis, and now he was smiling, and now Hornblower in his innocence realised what had been going on. He had been suspected of coming in unnecessarily early, of being one of those captains who wearied of combating tempests. Those were the captains Cornwallis was anxious to weed out from the Channel Fleet, and Hornblower had been under consideration for weeding out.

'You should have come in at least four days earlier,' said Cornwallis.

'Well, sir—' Hornblower could have covered himself by quoting the orders of Chambers of the *Naiad*, but he saw no reason to, and he changed what he was going to say. 'It worked out all right in the end.'

'You'll be sending in your journals, of course, sir?' asked the flag lieutenant.

'Of course,' said Hornblower.

The ship's log would be documentary proof of his assertions, but the question was a tactless, almost an insulting, impugning of his veracity, and Cornwallis instantly displayed a hot-tempered impatience at this awkwardness on the part of his flag lieutenant.

'Captain Hornblower can do that all in his own good time,' he said. 'Now, wine with you, sir?'

It was extraordinary how pleasant the meeting had become; the change in the atmosphere was as noticable as the change in the lighting at this moment when the stewards brought in candles. The four of them were laughing and joking when Newton, captain of the ship, came in to make his report and for Hornblower to be presented to him.

'Wind's steady at west nor'west, sir,' said Newton.

'Thank you, captain.' Cornwallis rolled his blue eyes on Hornblower. 'Are you ready for sea?'

'Yes, sir.' There could be no other reply.

'The wind's bound to come easterly soon,' meditated Cornwallis. 'The Downs, Spithead, Plymouth Sound – all of them jammed with ships outward bound and waiting for a fair wind. But one point's all you need with *Hotspur*.'

'I could fetch Ushant with two tacks now, sir,' said Hornblower. There was Maria huddled in some lodging in Brixham at this moment, but he had to say it.

'M'm,' said Cornwallis, still in debate with himself. 'I'm not comfortable without you watching the Goulet, Hornblower. But I can let you have one more day at anchor.'

'Thank you, sir.'

'That is if the wind doesn't back any further.' Cornwallis reached a decision. 'Here are your orders. You sail at nightfall tomorrow. But if the wind backs one more point you hoist anchor instantly. That is, with the wind at nor'west by west.'

'Aye aye, sir.'

Hornblower knew how he liked his own officers to respond to his orders, and he matched his deportment with that mental model. Cornwallis went on, his eye still considering him.

'We took some reasonable claret out of a prize a month ago, I wonder if you would honour me by accepting a dozen, Hornblower?'

'With the greatest of pleasure, sir.'

'I'll have it put in your boat.'

Cornwallis turned to give the order to his steward, who apparently had something to say in return in a low voice; Hornblower heard Cornwallis reply, 'Yes, yes, of course,' before he turned back.

'Perhaps your steward would pass the word for my boat at the same time, sir?' said Hornblower, who was in no doubt that his visit had lasted long enough by Cornwallis's standards.

It was quite dark when Hornblower went down the side into the boat, to find at his feet the case that held the wine, and by now the wind was almost moderate. The dark surface of Tor Bay was spangled with the lights of ships, and there were the lights of Torquay and of Paignton and Brixham visible as well. Maria was somewhere there, probably uncomfortable, for these little places were probably full of naval officers' wives.

'Call me the moment the wind comes nor'west by west,' said Hornblower to Bush as soon as he reached the deck.

'Nor'west by west. Aye aye, sir. The hands managed to get liquor on board, sir.'

'Did you expect anything else?'

The British sailor would find liquor somehow at any contact with the shore; if he had no money he would give his clothes, his shoes, even his earrings in exchange.

'I had trouble with some of 'em, sir, especially after the beer issue.'

Beer was issued instead of rum whenever it could be supplied.

'You dealt with 'em?'

'Yes, sir.'

'Very well, Mr Bush.'

A couple of hands were bringing the case of wine in from the boat, under the supervision of Doughty, and when Hornblower entered his cabin he found the case lashed to the bulkhead, occupying practically the whole of the spare deck space, and Doughty bending over it, having prized it open with a hand-spike.

'The only place to put it, sir,' explained Doughty, apologetically.

That was probably true in two senses; with the ship crammed with stores, even with raw meat hung in every place convenient and inconvenient, there could hardly be any space to spare, and in addition wine would hardly be safe from the hands unless it were here where a sentry constantly stood guard. Doughty had a large parcel in his arms, which he had removed from the case.

'What's that?' demanded Hornblower; he had already observed that Doughty was a little disconcerted, so that when his servant hesitated he repeated the question more sharply still.

'It's just a parcel from the Admiral's steward, sir.'

'Show me.'

Hornblower expected to see bottles of brandy or some other smuggled goods.

'It's only cabin stores, sir.'

'Show me.'

'Just cabin stores, sir, as I said.' Doughty examined the contents while exhibiting them in a manner which proved he had not been certain of what he would find. 'This is sweet oil, sir, olive oil. And here are dried herbs. Marjoram, thyme, sage. And here's coffee — only half a pound, by the look of it. And pepper. And vinegar. And . . .'

'How the devil did you get these?'

'I wrote a note, sir, to the Admiral's steward, and sent it by your coxs'n. It isn't right that you shouldn't have these things, sir. Now I can cook for you properly.'

'Does the Admiral know?'

'I'd be surprised if he did, sir.'

There was an assured superior expression on Doughty's face as he said this, which suddenly revealed to Hornblower a world of which he had been ignorant until then. There might be Flag Officers and Captains, but under that glittering surface was an unseen circle of stewards, with its own secret rites and passwords, managing the private lives of their officers without reference to them.

'Sir!' This was Bush, entering the cabin with hurried step. 'Wind's nor'west by west, sir. Looks as if it'll back further still.'

It took a moment for Hornblower to re-orient his thoughts, to switch from stewards and dried herbs to ships and sailing orders. Then he was himself again, rapping his commands.

'Call all hands. Sway the topmasts up. Get the yards crossed. I want to be under way in twenty minutes. Fifteen minutes.'

'Aye aye, sir.'

The quiet of the ship was broken by the pipes and the curses of the petty officers, as they drove the hands to work. Heads bemused by beer and brandy cleared themselves with violent exercise and the fresh air of the chilly night breeze. Clumsy fingers clutched hoists and halliards. Men tripped and stumbled in the darkness and were kicked to their feet by petty officers goaded on by the master's mates goaded on in turn by Bush and Prowse. The vast cumbersome sausages that were the sails were dragged out from where they had been laid away on the booms.

'Ready to set sail, sir,' reported Bush.

'Very well. Send the hands to the capstan. Mr Foreman, what's the night signal for "Am getting under way." '

'One moment, sir.' Foreman had not learned the night signal book as thoroughly as he should have done in seven months. 'One blue light and one Bengal fire shown together, sir.'

'Very well. Make that ready. Mr Prowse, a course from the Start to Ushant, if you please.'

That would let the hands know what fate awaited them, if they did not guess already. Maria would know nothing at all until she looked out at Tor Bay tomorrow to find *Hotspur's* place empty. And all she had to comfort her was the curt note he had sent before dinner; cold comfort, that. He must not think of Maria, or of the child.

The capstan was clanking as they hove the ship up towards the best bower. They would have to deal with the extra weight of the boat carronade that backed that anchor; the additional labour was the price to be paid for the security of the past days. It was a clumsy, as well as a laborious operation.

'Shall I heave short on the small bower, sir?'

'Yes, if you please, Mr Bush. And you can get under way as soon as is convenient to you.'

'Aye aye, sir.'

'Make that signal, Mr Foreman.'

The quarter-deck was suddenly illuminated, the sinister blue light blending with the equally sinister crimson of the Bengal fire. The last splutterings had hardly died away before the answer came from the flagship, a blue light that winked three times as it was momentarily screened.

'Flagship acknowledges, sir!'

'Very well.'

And this was the end of his stay in harbour, of his visit to England. He had seen the last of Maria for months to come; she would be a mother when he saw her next.

'Sheet home!'

Hotspur was gathering way, turning on her heel with a fair wind to weather Berry Head. Hornblower's mind played with a score of inconsequential thoughts as he struggled to put aside his overwhelming melancholy. He remembered the brief private conversation that he had witnessed between Cornwallis and the steward. He was quite sure that the latter had been telling his Admiral about the parcel prepared for transmission to *Hotspur*. Doughty was not nearly as clever as he thought he was. That conclusion called up a weak smile as *Hotspur* breasted the waters of the Channel, with Berry Head looming up on her starboard beam.

XV

Now it was cold, horribly cold; the days were short and the nights were very, very long. Along with the cold weather came easterly winds – the one involved the other – and a reversal of the tactical situation. For although with the wind in the east *Hotspur* was relieved of the anxiety of being on a lee shore her responsibilities were proportionately increased. There was nothing academic now about noting the direction of the wind each hour; it was no mere navigational routine. Should the wind blow from any one of ten points of the compass out of thirty-two it would be possible even for the lubberly French to make their exit down the Goulet and enter the Atlantic. Should they make the attempt it was *Hotspur's* duty to pass an instant warning for the Channel Fleet to form line of battle if the French were rash enough to challenge action, and to cover every exit – by the Raz, by the Iroise, by the Four – if, as would be more likely, they attempted merely to escape.

Today the last of the flood did not make until two o'clock in the afternoon, a most inconvenient time, for it was not until then that *Hotspur* could venture in to make her daily reconnaissance at closest range. To do so earlier would be to risk that a failure of the wind, leaving her at the mercy of the tide, would sweep her helplessly up, within range of the batteries on Petit Minou and the Capuchins – the Toulinguet battery; and more assuredly fatal than the batteries would be the reefs, Pollux and the Little Girls.

Hornblower came out on deck with the earliest light – not very early on this almost the shortest day of the year – to check the position of the ship while Prowse took the bearings of the Petit Minou and the Grand Gouin.

'Merry Christmas, sir,' said Bush. It was typical of a military service that Bush should have to touch his hat while saying those words.

'Thank you. The same to you, Mr Bush.'

It was typical, also, that Hornblower should have been acutely aware that it was December 25th and yet should have forgotten that it was Christmas Day; tide tables made no reference to the festivals of the church.

'Any news of your good lady, sir?' asked Bush.

'Not yet,' answered Hornblower, with a smile that was only half-forced. 'The letter I had yesterday was dated the eighteenth, but there's nothing as yet.'

It was one more indication of the way the wind had been blowing, that he should have received a letter from Maria in six days; a victualler had brought it out with a fair wind. That also implied that it might be six weeks before his reply reached Maria, and in six weeks – in one week – everything would be changed, and the child would be born. A naval officer writing to his wife had to keep one eye on the wind-vane just as the Lords of the Admiralty had to do when drafting their orders for the movements of fleets. New Year's Day was the date Maria and the midwife had decided upon; at that time Maria would be reading the letters he wrote a month ago. He wished he had written more sympathetically, but nothing he could do could recall, alter, or supplement those letters.

All he could do would be to spend some of this morning composing a letter that might belatedly compensate for the deficiencies of its predecessors (and Hornblower realised with a stab of conscience that this was not the first time he had reached that decision) while it would be even more difficult than usual because it would have to be composed with an eye to all eventualities. All eventualities; Hornblower felt in that moment the misgivings of every prospective father.

He spent until eleven o'clock on these unsatisfactory literary exercises, and it was with guilty relief that he returned to the quarter-deck to take *Hotspur* up with the last of the tide with the well-remembered coasts closing in upon her on both sides. The weather was reasonably clear; not a sparkling Christmas Day, but with little enough haze at noon, when Hornblower gave the orders that hove *Hotspur* to, as close to Pollux Reef as he dared. The dull thud of a gun from Petit Minou coincided with his orders. The rebuilt battery there was firing its usual range-testing shot in the hope that this time he had come in too far. Did they recognise the ship that had done them so much damage? Presumably.

'Their morning salute, sir,' said Bush.

'Yes.'

Hornblower took the telescope into his gloved, yet frozen, hands and trained it up the Goulet as he always did. Often there was something new to observe. Today there was much.

'Four new ships at anchor, sir,' said Bush.

'I make it five. Isn't that a new one – the frigate in line with the church steeple?'

'Don't think so, sir. She's shifted anchorage. Only four new ones by my count.'

'You're right, Mr Bush.'

'Yards crossed, sir. And – sir, would you look at those tops'l yards?'

Hornblower was already looking.

'I can't be sure.'

'I think those are tops'ls furled over-all, sir.'

'It's possible.'

A sail furled over-all was much thinner and less noticeable, with the loose part gathered into the bunt about the mast, than one furled in the usual fashion.

'I'll go up to the masthead myself, sir. And young Foreman has good eyes. I'll take him with me.'

'Very well. No, wait a moment, Mr Bush. I'll go myself. Take charge of the ship, if you please. But you can send Foreman up.'

Hornblower's decision to go aloft was proof of the importance he attached to observation of the new ships. He was uncomfortably aware of his slowness and awkwardness, and it was only reluctantly that he exhibited them to his lightfooted and lighthearted subordinates. But there was something about those ships . . .

He was breathing heavily by the time he reached the fore-topmast-head, and it took several seconds to steady himself sufficiently to fix the ships in the field of the telescope, but he was much warmer. Foreman was there already, and the regular look-out shrank away out of the notice of his betters. Neither Foreman nor the look-out could be sure about those furled topsails.

They thought it likely, yet they would not commit themselves.

'D'you make out anything else about those ships, Mr Foreman?'

'Well, no, sir. I can't say that I do.'

'D'you think they're riding high?'

'Maybe, yes, sir.'

Two of the new arrivals were small two-deckers – sixty-fours, probably – and the lower tier of gun-ports in each case might be farther above the water line than one might expect. It was not a matter of measurement, all the same; it was more a matter of intuition, of good taste. Those hulls were just not quite right, although, Foreman, willing enough to oblige, clearly did not share his feelings.

Hornblower's glass swept the shores round the anchorage, questing for any further data. There were the rows of hutments that housed the troops. French soldiers were notoriously well able to look after themselves, to build themselves adequate shelter; the smoke of their cooking fires was clearly visible – today, of course they would be cooking their Christmas dinners. It was from here that had come the battalion that had chased him back to the boats the day he blew up the battery. Hornblower's glass checked itself, moved along and returned again. With the breeze that was blowing he could not be certain, but it seemed to him that from two rows of huts there was no smoke to be seen. It was all a little vague; he could not even estimate the number of troops those huts would house; two thousand men, five thousand men; and he was still doubtful about the absence of cooking smoke.

'Captain, sir!' Bush was hailing from the deck. 'The tide's turned.'

'Very well. I'll come down.'

He was abstracted and thoughtful when he reached the deck.

'Mr Bush, I'll be wanting fish for my dinner soon. Keep a special look-out for the *Duke's Freers*.'

He had to pronounce it that way to make sure Bush understood him. Two days later he found himself in his cabin drinking rum – pretending to drink rum – with the captain of the *Deux Frères*. He had bought himself half a dozen unidentifiable fish, which the captain strongly recommended as good eating. 'Carrelets,' the captain called them – Hornblower had a vague idea that they might be flounders. At any rate, he paid for them with a gold piece which the captain slipped without comment into the pockets of his scale-covered serge trousers.

Inevitably the conversation shifted to the sights to be seen up the Goulet, and from the general to the particular, centring on the new arrivals in the anchorage. The captain dismissed them with a gesture as unimportant.

'*Armé's en flûte*,' he said, casually.

En flûte! That told the story. That locked into place the pieces of the puzzle. Hornblower took an unguarded gulp at his glass of rum and water and fought down the consequent cough so as to display no special interest. A ship of war with her guns taken out was like a flute when her ports were opened – she had a row of empty holes down her side.

'Not to fight,' explained the captain. 'Only for stores, or troops, or what you will.'

For troops especially. Stores could best be carried in merchant ships designed for cargo, but ships of war were constructed to carry large numbers of men – their cooking arrangements and water storage facilities had been built in with that in mind. With only as many seamen on board as were necessary to work the ship there was room to spare for soldiers. Then the guns would be unnecessary, and at Brest they could be immediately employed in arming new ships. Removing the guns meant a vast increase in available deck space into which more troops could be crammed; the more there were the more strain on the cooking and watering arrangements, but on a short voyage they would not have long to suffer. A short voyage. Not the West Indies, nor Good Hope, and certainly not India. A forty-gun frigate armed *en flûte* might have as many as a thousand soldiers packed into her. Three thousand men, plus a few hundred more in the armed escorts. The smallness of the number ruled out England – not even Bonaparte, so improvident with human life, would throw away a force that size in an invasion of England where there was at least a small army and a large militia. There was only one possible target; Ireland, where a disaffected population meant a weak militia.

'They are no danger to me, then,' said Hornblower, hoping that the interval during which he had been making these deductions had not been so long as to be obvious.

'Not even to this little ship,' agreed the Breton captain with a smile.

It called for the exertion of all Hornblower's moral strength to continue the interview without allowing his agitation to show. He wanted to get instantly into action, but he dared not appear impatient; the Breton captain wanted another three-finger glass of rum and was unaware of any need for haste. Luckily Hornblower remembered an admonition from Doughty, who had impressed on him the desirability of buying cider as well as fish, and Hornblower introduced the new subject. Yes, agreed the captain, there was a keg of cider on board the *Deux Frères*, but he could not say how much was left, as they had tapped it already during the day. He would sell what was left.

Hornblower forced himself to bargain; he did not want the Breton captain to know that his recent piece of information was worth further gold. He suggested that the cider, of an unknown quantity, should be given him for nothing extra, and the captain with an avaricious gleam in his peasant's eye, indignantly refused. For some minutes the argument proceeded while the rum sank lower in the captain's glass.

'One franc, then,' offered Hornblower at last. 'Twenty sous.'

'Twenty sous and a glass of rum,' said the captain, and Hornblower had to reconcile himself to that much further delay, but it was worth it to retain the captain's respect and to allay the captain's suspicions.

So that it was with his head swimming with rum – a sensation he detested – that Hornblower sat down at last to write his urgent despatch, having seen his guest down the side. No mere signal could convey all that he wanted to say, and no signal would be secret enough, either. He had to choose his words as carefully as the rum would permit, as he stated his suspicions that the French might be planning an invasion of Ireland, and as he gave his reasons for those suspicions. He was satisfied at last, and wrote 'H. Hornblower, Commander,' at the foot of the letter. Then he turned over the sheet and wrote the address: 'Rear Admiral William Parker, Commanding the Inshore Squadron,' on the other side, and folded and sealed the letter. Parker was one of the extensive Parker clan; there were and had been admirals and captains innumerable with that name, none of them specially distinguished; perhaps his letter would alter that tradition.

He sent it off – a long and arduous trip for the boat, and waited impatiently for the acknowledgement.

'Sir,

Your letter of this date has been received and will be given my full attention.

Your ob'd serv't,
Wm. Parker.'

Hornblower read the few words in a flash; he had opened the letter on the quarter-deck without waiting to retire with it to his cabin, and he put it in his pocket hoping that his expression betrayed no disappointment.

'Mr Bush,' he said, 'We shall have to maintain a closer watch than ever over the Goulet, particularly at night and in thick weather.'

'Aye aye, sir.'

Probably Parker needed time to digest the information, and would later produce a plan; until that time it was Hornblower's duty to act without orders.

'I shall take the ship up to the Little Girls whenever I can do so unobserved.'

'The Little Girls? Aye aye, sir.'

It was a very sharp glance that Bush directed at him. No one in his senses – at least no one except under the strongest compulsion – would risk his ship near those navigational dangers in conditions of bad visibility. True; but the compulsions existed. Three thousand well-trained French soldiers landing in Ireland would set that distressful country in a flame from end to end, a wilder flame than had burned in 1798.

'We'll try it tonight,' said Hornblower.

'Aye aye, sir.'

The Little Girls lay squarely in the middle of the channel of the Goulet; on either side lay a fairway a scant quarter of a mile wide, and up and down those fairways raced the tide; it would only be during the ebb that the French would be likely to come down. No, that was not strictly true, for the French could stem the flood tide with a fair wind – with this chill easterly wind blowing. The Goulet had to be watched in all conditions of bad visibility and *Hotspur* had to do the watching.

XVI

'I beg your pardon, sir,' said Bush, lingering after delivering his afternoon report, and hesitating before taking the next step he had clearly decided upon.

'Yes, Mr Bush?'

'You know, sir, you're not looking as well as you should.'

'Indeed?'

'You've been doing too much, sir. Day and night.'

'That's a strange thing for a seaman to say, Mr Bush. And a King's officer.'

'It's true, all the same, sir. You haven't had an hour's sleep at a time for days. You're thinner than I've ever known you, sir.'

'Thank you, Mr Bush. I'm going to turn in now, as a matter of fact.'

'I'm glad of that, sir.'

'See that I'm called the moment the weather shows signs of thickening.'

'Aye aye, sir.'

'Can I trust you, Mr Bush?'

That brought a smile into what was too serious a conversation.

'You can, sir.'

'Thank you, Mr Bush.'

It was interesting after Bush's departure to look into the speckled chipped mirror and observe his thinness, the cheeks and temples fallen in, the sharp nose and the pointed chin. But this was not the real Hornblower. The real one was inside, unaffected – as yet, at least – by privation or strain. The real Hornblower looked out at him from the hollow eyes in the mirror with a twinkle of recognition, a twinkle that brightened, not with malice, but with something akin to that – a kind of cynical amusement – at the sight of Hornblower seeking proof of the weaknesses of the flesh. But time was too precious to waste; the weary body that the real Hornblower had to drag about demanded repose. And, as regards the weaknesses of the flesh, how delightful, how comforting it was to clasp to his stomach the hot-water bottle that Doughty had put into his cot, to feel warm and relaxed despite the clamminess of the bedclothes and the searching cold that pervaded the cabin.

'Sir,' said Doughty, coming into the cabin after what seemed to be one minute's interval but which, his watch told him, was two hours. 'Mr Prowse sent me. It's snowing, sir.'

'Very well. I'll come.'

How often had he said those words? Every time the weather had thickened he had taken *Hotspur* up the Goulet, enduring the strain of advancing blind up into frightful danger, watching wind and tide, making the most elaborate calculations, alert for any change in conditions, ready to dash out again at the first hint of improvement, not only to evade the fire of the batteries, but also to prevent the French from discovering the close watch that was being maintained over them.

'It's only just started to snow, sir,' Doughty was saying. 'But Mr Prowse says it's set in for the night.'

With Doughty's assistance Hornblower had bundled himself automatically into his deck clothing without noticing what he was doing. He went out into a changed world, where his feet trod a thin carpet of snow on the deck, and where Prowse loomed up in the darkness shimmering in the white coating of snow on his oilskins.

'Wind's nor' by east, sir, moderate. An hour of flood still to go.'

'Thank you. Turn the hands up and send them to quarters, if you please. They can sleep at the guns.'

'Aye aye, sir.'

'Five minutes from now I don't want to hear a sound.'

'Aye aye, sir.'

This was only regular routine. The less the distance one could see the readier the ship had to be to open fire should an enemy loom up close alongside. But there was no routine about his own duties; every time he took the ship up conditions were different, the wind blowing from a different compass point and the tide of a different age. This was the first time the wind had been so far round to the north. To-night he would have to shave the shallows off Petit Minou as close as he dared, and then, close-hauled, with the last of the flood behind him, *Hotspur* could just ascend the northern channel, with the Little Girls to starboard.

There was spirit left in the crew; there were jokes and cries of surprise when they emerged into the snow from the stinking warmth of the 'tween deck, but sharp orders suppressed every sound. *Hotspur* was deadly quiet, like a ghost ship when the yards had been trimmed and the helm orders given and she began to make her way through the impenetrable night, night more impenetrable than ever with the air full of snowflakes silently dropping down upon them.

A shuttered lantern at the taffrail for reading the log, although the log's indications were of minor importance, when speed over the ground could be so different – instinct and experience were more important. Two hands in the port-side main-chains with the lead. Hornblower on the weather side of the quarter-deck could hear quite a quiet call, even though there was a hand stationed to relay it if necessary. Five fathoms. Four fathoms. If his navigation were faulty they would strike before the next cast. Aground under the guns of Petit Minou, ruined and destroyed; Hornblower could not restrain himself from clenching his gloved hands and tightening his muscles. Six and a half fathoms. That was what he had calculated upon, but it was a relief, nevertheless – Hornblower felt a small contempt for himself at feeling relieved, at his lack of faith in his own judgement.

'Full and bye,' he ordered.

They were as close under Petit Minou as possible, a quarter of a mile from those well-known hills, but there was nothing visible at all. There might be a solid black wall a yard from Hornblower's eyes whichever way he turned them. Eleven fathoms; they were on the edge of the fairway now. The last of the flood, two days after the lowest neaps, and wind north by east; the current should be less than a knot and the eddy off Mengam non-existent.

'No bottom!'

More than twenty fathoms; that was right.

'A good night this for the Frogs, sir,' muttered Bush beside him; he had been waiting for this moment.

Certainly it was a good night for the French if they were determined to escape. They knew the times of ebb and flood as well as he did. They would see the snow. Comfortable time for them to up anchor and get under weigh, and make the passage of the Goulet with a fair wind and ebb tide. Impossible for them to escape by the Four with this wind; the Iroise was guarded – he hoped – by the Inshore Squadron, but on a night as black as this they might try it in preference to the difficult Raz du Sein.

Nineteen fathoms; he was above the Little Girls, and he could be confident of weathering Mengam. Nineteen fathoms.

'Should be slack water now, sir,' muttered Prowse, who had just looked at his watch in the light of the shaded binnacle.

They were above Mengam now; the lead should record a fairly steady nineteen fathoms for the next few minutes, and it was time that he should plan out the next move – the next move but one, rather. He conjured up the chart before his mental eye.

'Listen!' Bush's elbow dug into Hornblower's ribs with the urgency of the moment.

'Avast there at the lead!' said Hornblower. He spoke in a normal tone to make sure he was understood; with the wind blowing that way his voice would not carry far in the direction he was peering into.

There was the sound again; there were other noises. A long drawn monosyllable borne by the wind, and Hornblower's straining senses picked it up. It was a Frenchman calling 'Seize,' sixteen. French pilots still used the old-fashioned *toise* to measure depths, and the *toise* was slightly greater than the English fathom.

'Lights!' muttered Bush, his elbow at Hornblower's ribs again. There was a gleam here and there – the Frenchman had not darkened his ship nearly as effectively as the *Hotspur*. There was enough light to give some sort of indication. A ghost ship sweeping by within biscuit toss. The topsails were suddenly visible – there must be a thin coating of snow on the after surfaces whose gleaming white could reflect any light there was. And then—

'Three red lights in a row on the mizzen tops'l yard,' whispered Bush.

Visible enough now; shaded in front, presumably, with the light directed aft to guide following ships. Hornblower felt a surge of inspiration, of instant decision, plans for the moment, plans for the next five minutes, plans for the more distant future.

'Run!' he snapped at Bush. 'Get three lights hoisted the same way. Keep 'em shaded, ready to show.'

Bush was off at the last word, but the thoughts had to come more rapidly like lightning. *Hotspur* dared not tack; she must wear.

'Wear ship!' he snapped at Prowse – no time for the politenesses he usually employed.

As *Hotspur* swung round he saw the three separated red lights join together almost into one, and at the same moment he saw a blue glare; the French ship was altering course to proceed down the Goulet and was burning a blue light as an indication to the ships following to up helm in succession. Now he could see the second French ship, a second faint ghost – the blue light helped to reveal it.

Pellew in the old *Indefatigable*, when Hornblower was a prisoner in Ferrol, had once confused a French squadron escaping from Brest by imitating the French signals, but that had been in the comparatively open waters of the Iroise. It had been in Hornblower's mind to try similar tactics, but here in the narrow Goulet there was a possibility of more decisive action.

'Bring her to the wind on the starboard tack,' he snapped at Prowse, and *Hotspur* swung round further still, the invisible hands hauling at the invisible braces.

There was the second ship in the French line just completing her turn, with *Hotspur's* bows pointing almost straight at her.

'Starboard a little.' *Hotspur's* bows swung away. 'Meet her.'

He wanted to be as close alongside as he possibly could be without running foul of her.

'I've sent a good hand up with the lights, sir.' This was Bush reporting. 'Another two minutes and they'll be ready.'

'Get down to the guns,' snapped Hornblower, and then, with the need for silence at an end, he reached for the speaking-trumpet.

'Main-deck! Man the starboard guns! Run 'em out.'

How would the French squadron be composed? It would have an armed escort, not to fight its way through the Channel Fleet, but to protect the transports, after the escape, from stray British cruising frigates. There would be two big frigates, one in the van and one bringing up the rear, while the intermediate ships would be defenceless transports, frigates armed *en flûte*.

'Starboard! Steady!'

Yard arm to yard arm with the second ship in the line, going down the Goulet alongside her, ghost ships side by side in the falling snow. The rumble of gun-trucks had ceased.

'Fire!'

At ten guns, ten hands jerked at the lanyards, and *Hotspur's* side burst into flame, illuminating the sails and hull of the Frenchman with a bright glare; in the instantaneous glare of the gun-fire snowflakes were visible as if stationary in mid air.

'Fire away, you men!'

There were cries and shouts to be heard from the French ship, and then a French voice speaking almost in his ear – the French captain hailing him from thirty yards away with his speaking-trumpet pointed straight at him. It would be an expostulation, the French captain wondering why a French ship should be firing into him, here where no British ship could possibly be. The words were cut off abruptly by the bang and the flash of the first gun of the second broadside, the others following as the men loaded and fired as fast as they could. Each flash brought a momentary revelation of the French ship, a flickering, intermittent picture. Those nine-pounder balls were crashing into a ship crammed with men. At this very moment, as he stood there rigid on the deck, men were dying in agony by the score just over there, for no more reason than that they had been forced into the service of a continental tyrant. Surely the French would not be able to bear it. Surely they would flinch under this unexpected and unexplainable attack. Ah! She was turning away, although she had nowhere to turn to except the cliffs and shoals of the shore close over-side. There were the three red lights on her mizzen topsail yard. By accident or design she had put her helm down. He must make sure of her.

'Port a little.'

Hotspur swung to starboard, her guns blazing. Enough.

'Starboard a little. Steady as you go.'

Now the speaking-trumpet. 'Cease fire!'

The silence that followed was broken by the crash as the Frenchman struck the shore, the clatter of falling spars, the yells of despair. And in this darkness, after the glare of the guns, he was blinder than ever, and yet he must act as if he could see; he must waste no moment.

'Back the main tops'l! Stay by the braces!'

The rest of the French line must be coming down, willy-nilly; with the wind over their quarter and the ebb under their keels and rocks on either side of them they could do nothing else. He must think quicker than they; he still had the advantage of surprise – the French captain in the following ship would not yet have had time to collect his thoughts.

The Little Girls were under their lee; he must not delay another moment.

'Braces, there!'

Here she came, looming up, close, close, yells of panic from her forecastle.

'Hard-a-starboard!'

Hotspur had just enough way through the water to respond to her rudder; the two bows swung from each other, collision averted by a hair's breadth.

'Fire!'

The Frenchman's sails were all a-shiver; she was not under proper control, and with those nine-pounder balls sweeping her deck she would not recover quickly. *Hotspur* must not pass ahead of her; he still had a little time and a little room to spare.

'Main tops'l aback!'

This was a well-drilled crew; the ship was working like a machine. Even the powder-boys, climbing and descending the ladders in pitch darkness, were carrying out their duties with exactitude, keeping the guns supplied with powder, for the guns never ceased from firing, bellowing in deafening fashion and bathing the Frenchman with orange light while the smoke blew heavily away on the disengaged side.

He could not spare another moment with the main topsail aback. He must fill and draw ahead even if it meant disengagement.

'Braces, there!'

He had not noticed until now the infernal din of the quarter-deck carronades beside him; they were firing rapidly, sweeping the transport's deck with grape. In their flashes he saw the Frenchman's masts drawing aft as *Hotspur* regained her way. Then in the next flash he saw something else, another momentary picture – a ship's bowsprit crossing the Frenchman's deck from the disengaged side, and he heard a crash and the screams. The next Frenchman astern had run bows on into her colleague. The first rending crash was followed by others; he strode aft to try to see, but already the darkness had closed like a wall round his blinded eyes. He could only listen, but what he heard told him the story. The ship that rammed was swinging with the wind, her bowsprit tearing through shrouds and halliards until it snapped against the main-mast. Then the fore-topmast would fall, yards would fall. The two ships were locked together and helpless, with the Little Girls under their lee. Now he saw blue lights burning as they tried to deal with the hopeless situation; with the ships swinging the blue lights and the red lights on the yards were revolving round each other like some planetary system. There was no chance of escape for them; as wind and current carried him away he thought he heard the crash as they struck upon the Little Girls, but he could not be sure, and there was no time – of course there was no time – to think about it. At this stage of the ebb there was an eddy that set in upon Pollux Reef and he must allow for that. Then he would be out in the Iroise, whose waters he used to think so dangerous before he had ventured up the Goulet, and an unknown number of ships was coming down from Brest, forwarned now by all the firing and the tumult that an enemy was in their midst.

He took a hasty glance into the binnacle, gauged the force of the wind on his cheeks. The enemy – what there was left of them – would certainly, with this wind, run for the Raz du Sein, and would certainly give the Trepieds shoal a wide berth. He must post himself to intercept them; the next ship in the line must be close at hand in any case, but in a few seconds she would no longer be confined to the narrow channel of the Goulet. And what would the first frigate be doing, the one he had allowed to pass without attacking her?'

'Main chains, there! Get the lead going.'

He must keep up to windward as best he could.

'No bottom! No bottom with this line.'

He was clear of Pollux, then.

'Avast, there, with the lead.'

They stood on steadily on the starboard-tack; in the impenetrable darkness he could hear Prowse breathing heavily at his side and all else was silence round him. He would have to take another cast of the lead soon enough. What was that? Wind and water had brought a distinctive sound to his ears, a solemn noise, of a solid body falling into the water. It was the sound of a lead being cast – and then followed, at the appropriate interval, the high pitched cry of the leadsman. There was a ship just up there to windward, and now with the distance lessening and with his hearing concentrated in that direction he could hear other sounds, voices, the working of yards. He leaned over the rail and spoke quietly down into the waist.

'Stand by your guns.'

There she was, looming faintly on the starboard bow.

'Starboard two points. Meet her.'

They saw *Hotspur* at that same moment; from out of the darkness came the hail of a speaking-trumpet, but in the middle of a word Hornblower spoke down into the waist again.

'Fire!'

The guns went off so nearly together that he felt *Hotspur's* light fabric heel a little with the force of the recoil, and there again was the shape of a ship lit up by the glare of the broadside. He could not hope to force her on the shoals; there was too much sea-room for that. He took the speaking- trumpet.

'Elevate your guns! Aim for her spars!'

He could cripple her. The first gun of the new broadside went off immediately after he said the words – some fool had not paid attention. But the other guns fired after the interval necessary to withdraw the coigns, flash after flash, bang after bang. Again and again and again. Suddenly a flash revealed a change in the shape of the illuminated mizzen topsail, and at the same moment that mizzen topsail moved slowly back abaft the beam. The Frenchman had thrown all aback in a desperate attempt to escape this tormentor, risking being raked in the hope of passing under *Hotspur's* stern to get before the wind. He would wear the *Hotspur* round and bring her under the fire of the port broadside and chase her on to the Trepieds; the speaking-trumpet was at his lips when the darkness ahead erupted into a volcano of fire.

Chaos. Out of the black snow-filled night had come a broadside, raking the *Hotspur* from bow to stern. Along with the sound and the flash came the rending crash of splintered woodwork, the loud ringing noise as a cannon-ball hit the breech of a gun, the shriek of the flying splinters, and following on that came the screaming of a wounded man, cutting through the sudden new stillness.

One of the armed frigates of the escort – the leader of the line, most likely – had seen the firing and had been close enough to intervene. She had crossed *Hotspur's* bows to fire in a raking broadside.

'Hard-a-starboard!'

He could not tack, even if he were prepared to take the chance of missing stays with the rigging as much cut up as it must be, for he was not clear of the transport yet. He must wear, even though it meant being raked once more.

'Wear the ship!'

Hotspur was turning even as her last guns fired into the transport. Then came the second broadside from ahead, flaring out of the darkness, a fraction of a second between each successive shot, crashing into *Hotspur's* battered bows, while Hornblower stood, trying not to wince, thinking what he must do next. Was that the last shot? Now there was a new and rending crash forward, a succession of snapping noises, another thundering crash, and cries and shrieks from forward. That must be the foremast fallen. That must be the fore-topsail yard crashing on the deck.

'Helm doesn't answer, sir,' called the quartermaster at the wheel.

With the foremast down *Hotspur* would tend to fly up in the wind, even if the wreckage were not dragging alongside to act as a sea-anchor. He could feel the wind shifting on his cheek. Now *Hotspur* was helpless. Now she could be battered to destruction by an enemy twice her size, with four times her weight of metal, with scantlings twice as thick to keep out *Hotspur's* feeble shot. He would have to fight despairingly to the death. Unless . . . The enemy would be putting his helm a-starboard to rake *Hotspur* from astern, or he would be doing so as soon as he could make out in the darkness what had happened. Time would pass very fast and the wind was still blowing, thank God, and there was the transport close on his starboard side still. He spoke loudly into the speaking-trumpet.

'Silence! Silence!'

The bustle and clatter forward, where the hands had been struggling with the fallen spars, died away. Even the groaning wounded fell silent; that was discipline, and not the discipline of the cat o' nine tails. He could just hear the rumble of the French frigate's gun-trucks as they ran out the guns for the next broadside, and he could hear shouted orders. The French frigate was turning to deliver the *coup de grâce* as soon as she made certain of her target. Hornblower pointed the speaking-trumpet straight upwards as if addressing the sky, and he tried to keep his voice steady and quiet. He did not want the French frigate to hear.

'Mizzen topsail yard! Unmask those lights.'

That was a bad moment; the lights might have gone out, the lad stationed on the yard might be dead. He had to speak again.

'Show those lights!'

Discipline kept the hand up there from hailing back, but there they were – one, two, three red lights along the mizzen topsail yard. Even against the wind he heard a wild order being shouted from the French frigate, excitement, even panic in the voice. The French captain was ordering his guns not to fire. Perhaps he was thinking that some horrible mistake had already been made; perhaps in the bewildering darkness he was confusing *Hotspur* with her recent victim not so far off. At least he was holding fire; at least he was going off to leeward, and a hundred yards to leeward in that darkness was the equivalent of a mile in ordinary conditions.

'Mask those lights again!'

No need to give the Frenchman a mark for gunfire or an objective to which to beat back when he should clear up the situation. Now a voice spoke out of the darkness close to him.

'Bush reporting, sir. I've left the guns for the moment, if you give me leave, sir. Fore-tops'ls all across the starboard battery. Can't fire those guns in any case yet.'

'Very well, Mr Bush. What's the damage?'

'Foremast's gone six feet above the deck, sir. Everything went over the starboard side. Most of the shrouds must have held – it's all trailing alongside.'

'Then we'll get to work – in silence, Mr Bush. I want every stitch of canvas got in first, and then we'll deal with the wreckage.'

'Aye aye, sir.'

Stripping the ship of her canvas would make her far less visible to the enemy's eyes, and would reduce *Hotspur's* leeway while she rode to her strange sea anchor. Next moment it was the carpenter, up from below.

'We're making water very fast, sir. Two feet in the hold. My men are plugging one shot hole, aft by the magazine, but there must be another one for'ard in the cable tier. We'll need hands at the pumps, sir, an' I'd like half a dozen more in the cable tier.'

'Very well.'

So much to be done, in a nightmare atmosphere of unreality, and then came an explanation of some of the unreality. Six inches of snow lay on the decks, piled in deeper drifts against the vertical surfaces, silencing as well as impeding every movement. But most of the sense of unreality stemmed from simple exhaustion, nervous and physical, and the exhaustion had to be ignored while the work went on, trying to think clearly in the numbing darkness, with the knowledge that the Trepieds shoal lay close under their lee, on a falling tide. Getting up sail when the wreckage had been cleared away, and discovering by sheer seaman's instinct how to handle *Hotspur* under sail without her foremast, with only the feel of the wind on his cheeks and the wavering compass in the binnacle to guide him, and the shoals waiting for him if he miscalculated.

'I'd like you to set the sprit-sail, Mr Bush, if you please.'

'Aye aye, sir.'

A dangerous job for the hands that had to spread the sprit-sail under the bowsprit in the dark, with all the accustomed stays swept away by the loss of the foremast, but it had to be done to supply the necessary leverage forward to keep *Hotspur* from turning into the wind. Setting the ponderous main-course, because the main-topmast could not be trusted to carry sail. Then creeping westward, with the coming of the dawn and the cessation of the snowfall. Then it was light enough to see the disorder of the decks and the trampled snow – snow stained pink here and there, in wide areas. Then at last came the sight of the *Doris*, and help at hand; it might almost be called safety, except that later they would have to beat back against contrary winds and with a jury foremast and in a leaky ship, to Plymouth and refitting.

It was when they saw *Doris* hoisting out her boats, despatching additional manpower, that Bush could turn to Hornblower with a conventional remark. Bush was not aware of his own appearance, his powder-blackened face, his hollow cheeks and his sprouting beard, but even without that knowledge the setting was bizarre enough to appeal to Bush's crude sense of humour.

'A Happy New Year to you, sir,' said Bush, with a death's head grin.

It was New Year's Day. Then to the two men the same thought occurred simultaneously, and Bush's grin was replaced by something more serious.

'I hope your good lady . . .'

He was taken unawares, and could not find the formal words.

'Thank you, Mr Bush.'

It was on New Year's Day that the child was expected. Maria might be in labour at this moment while they stood there talking.

XVII

'Will you be having dinner on board, sir?' asked Doughty.

'No,' replied Hornblower. He hesitated before he launched into the next speech that had occurred to him, but he decided to continue. 'Tonight Horatio Hornblower dines with Horatio Hornblower.'

'Yes, sir.'

No joke ever fell as flat as that one. Perhaps – certainly – it was too much to expect Doughty to catch the classical allusion, but he might at least have smiled, because it was obvious that his captain had condescended so far as to be facetious.

'You'll need your oilskins, sir. It's raining heavily still,' said Doughty of the almost immovable countenance.

'Thank you.'

It seemed to have rained every single day since *Hotspur* had crawled into Plymouth Sound. Hornblower walked out from the dockyard with the rain rattling on his oilskins as if it were hail and not rain, and it continued all the time it took him to make his way to Driver's Alley. The landlady's little daughter opened the door to his knock, and as he walked up the stairs to his lodgings he heard the voice of the other Horatio Hornblower loudly proclaiming his sorrows. He opened the door and entered the small, hot stuffy room where Maria was standing with the baby over her shoulder, its long clothes hanging below her waist. Her face lit with pleasure when she saw him, and she could hardly wait for him to peel off his dripping oilskins before she came to his arms. Hornblower kissed her hot cheek and tried to look round the corner at little Horatio, but the baby only put his face into his mother's shoulder and wailed.

'He's been fractious today, dear,' said Maria, apologetically.

'Poor little fellow! And what about you, my dear?' Hornblower was careful to make Maria the centre of his thoughts whenever he was with her.

'I'm well enough now, dear. I can go up and down the stairs like a bird.'

'Excellent.'

Maria patted the baby's back.

'I wish he would be good. I want him to smile for his father.'

'Perhaps I could try?'

'Oh, no!'

Maria was quite shocked at the notion that a man should hold a crying baby, even his own, but it was a delightful kind of shock, all the same, and she yielded the baby to his proffered arms. Hornblower held his child – it was always a slight surprise to find how light that bundle of clothes was – and looked down at the rather amorphous features and the wet nose.

'There!' said Hornblower. The act of transfer had quieted little Horatio for a moment at least.

Maria stood bathed in happiness at the sight of her husband holding her son. And Hornblower's emotions were strangely mixed; one emotion was astonishment at finding pleasure in holding his child, for he found it hard to believe that he was capable of such sentiment. Maria held the back of the fireside armchair so that he could sit down in it, and then, greatly daring, kissed his hair.

'And how is the ship?' she asked, leaning over him.

'She's nearly ready for sea,' said Hornblower.

Hotspur had been in and out of dock, her bottom cleaned, her seams recaulked, her shot holes patched. Her new foremast had been put in, and the riggers had set up the standing rigging. She only had to renew her stores.

'Oh dear,' said Maria.

'Wind's steady in the west,' said Hornblower. Not that that would deter him from beating down Channel if he could once work *Hotspur* down the Sound – he could not think why he had held out this shred of hope to Maria.

Little Horatio began to wail again.

'Poor darling!' said Maria. 'Let me take him.'

'I can deal with him.'

'No. It – it isn't right.' It was all wrong, in Maria's mind, that a father should be afflicted by his child's tantrums. She thought of something else. 'You wished to see this, dear. Mother brought it in this afternoon from Lockhart's Library.'

She brought a magazine from the side table, and gave it in exchange for the baby, whom she clasped once more to her breast.

The magazine was the new number of the *Naval Chronicle,* and Maria with her free hand helped Hornblower to turn the pages.

'There!' Maria pointed to the relevant passage, on almost the last page. 'On January 1st last . . .' it began, it was the announcement of little Horatio's birth.

'The Lady of Captain Horatio Hornblower of the Royal Navy, of a son,' read Maria. 'That's me and little Horatio. I'm – I'm more grateful to you, dear, than I can ever tell you.'

'Nonsense,' replied Hornblower. That was just what he thought it was, but he made himself look up with a smile that took out any sting from what he said.

'They call you "Captain," ' went on Maria, with an interrogative in the remark.

'Yes,' agreed Hornblower. 'That's because—'

He embarked once more on the explanation of the profound difference between a Commander by rank (and a Captain only by courtesy) and a Post Captain. He had said it all before, more than once.

'I don't think it's right,' decided Maria.

'Very few things are right, my dear,' said Hornblower, a little absently. He was leafing through the other pages of the *Naval Chronicle,* working forward from the back page where he had started. Here was the Plymouth Report, and here was one of the things he was looking for.

'Came in HM Sloop *Hotspur* under jury rig, from the Channel Fleet. She proceeded at once into dock. Captain Horatio Hornblower landed at once with despatches.' Then came the Law Intelligence, and the Naval Courts Martial, and the Monthly Register of Naval Events, and the Naval Debates in the Imperial Parliament, and then, between the Debates and the Poetry, came the Gazette Letters. And here it was. First, in italics, came the introduction.

'*Copy of a letter from Vice-Admiral Sir William Cornwallis to Sir Evan Nepean, Bart., dated on board of HMS* Hibernia, *the 2nd instant.*'

Next came Cornwallis's letter.

'Sir,

I herewith transmit for their Lordships' information, copies of letters I have received from Captains Chambers of HMS *Naiad* and Hornblower of HM Sloop *Hotspur,* acquainting me of the capture of the French national frigate *Clorinde* and of the defeat of an attempt by the French to escape from Brest with a large body of Troops. The conduct of both these officers appears to me to be highly commendable. I enclose also a copy of a letter I have received from Captain Smith of HMS *Doris.*

I have the honour to be, with deepest respect,

Your ob'd't serv't,

Wm. Cornwallis.'

Chambers' report came next. *Naiad* had caught *Clorinde* near Molene and had fought her to a standstill, capturing her in forty minutes. Apparently the other French frigate which had come out with the transports had escaped by the Raz du Sein and had still not been caught.

Then at last came his own report. Hornblower felt the flush of excitement he had known before on reading his own words in print. He studied them afresh at this interval, and was grudgingly satisfied. They told, without elaboration, the bare facts of how three transports had been run ashore in the Goulet, and of how *Hotspur* while attacking a fourth had been in action with a French frigate and had lost her foremast. Not a word about saving Ireland from invasion; the merest half-sentence about the darkness and the snow and the navigational perils, but men who could understand would understand.

Smith's letter from the *Doris* was brief, too. After meeting *Hotspur* he had pushed in towards Brest and had found a French frigate, armed *en flûte*, aground on the Trepieds with shore boats taking off her troops. Under the fire of the French coastal batteries *Doris* had sent in her boats and had burned her.

'There's something more in the *Chronicle* that might interest you, dear,' said Hornblower. He proffered the magazine with his finger indicating his letter.

'Another letter from you, dear!' said Maria. 'How pleased you must be!'

She read the letter quickly.

'I haven't had time to read this before,' she said, looking up. 'Little Horatio was so fractious. And – and – I never understand all these letters, dear. I hope you are proud of what you did. I'm sure you are, of course.'

Luckily little Horatio set up a wail at that moment to save Hornblower from a specific answer to that speech. Maria pacified the baby and went on.

'The shopkeepers will know about this tomorrow and they'll all speak to me about it.'

The door opened to admit Mrs Mason, her pattens clattering on her feet, raindrops sparkling on her shawl. She and Hornblower exchanged 'good evenings' while she took off her outer clothing.

'Let me take that child,' said Mrs Mason to her daughter.

'Horry has another letter in the *Chronicle*,' countered Maria.

'Indeed?'

Mrs Mason sat down across the fire from Hornblower and studied the page with more care than Maria had done, but perhaps with no more understanding.

'The Admiral says your conduct was "very Commendable,"' she said, looking up.

'Yes.'

'Why doesn't he make you a real captain, "post," as you call it?'

'The decision doesn't lie with him,' said Hornblower. 'And I doubt if he would in any case.'

'Can't admirals make captains?'

'Not in home waters.'

The god-like power of promotion freely exercised on distant

stations was denied to commanders-in-chief where speedy reference to the Admiralty was possible.

'And what about prize money?'

'There's none for the *Hotspur*.'

'But this – this *Clorinde* was captured?'

'Yes, but we weren't in sight.'

'But you were fighting, weren't you?'

'Yes, Mrs Mason. But only ships in sight share in prize money. Except for the flag officers.'

'And aren't you a flag officer?'

'No. Flag officer means "Admiral," Mrs Mason.'

Mrs Mason sniffed.

'It all seems very strange. So you do not profit at all by this letter?'

'No, Mrs Mason.' At least not in the way Mrs Mason meant.

'It's about time you made some prize money. I hear all the time about the ships that have made thousands. Eight pounds a month for Maria, and her with a child.' Mrs Mason looked round at her daughter. 'Threepence a pound for neck of mutton! The cost of things is more than I can understand.'

'Yes, mother. Horry gives me all he can, I'm sure.'

As captain of a ship below the sixth rate Hornblower's pay was twelve pounds a month, and he still needed those new uniforms. Prices were rising with war-time demand, and the Admiralty, despite many promises, had not yet succeeded in obtaining an increase in pay for naval officers.

'Some captains make plenty,' said Mrs Mason.

It was prize money, and the possibility of gaining it, that kept the Navy quiet under the otherwise intolerable conditions. The great mutinies at Spithead and the Nore were less than ten years old. But Hornblower felt he would be drawn into a defence of the prize money system shortly if Mrs Mason persisted in talking as she did. Luckily the entrance of the landlady to lay the table for supper changed the subject of conversation. With another person in the room neither Mrs Mason nor Maria would discuss such a low subject as money, and they talked about indifferent matters instead. They sat down to dinner when the landlady brought in a steaming tureen.

'The pearl barley's at the bottom, Horatio,' said Mrs Mason, supervising him as he served the food.

'Yes, Mrs Mason.'

'And you'd better give Maria that other chop – that one's meant for you.'

'Yes, Mrs Mason.'

Hornblower had learned to keep a still tongue in his head under the goadings of tyranny when he was a lieutenant in the old *Renown* under Captain Sawyer's command, but he had well-nigh forgotten those lessons by now, and was having painfully to relearn them. He had married of his own free will – he could have said 'no' at the altar, he remembered – and now he had to make the best of a bad business. Quarrelling with his mother-in-law would not help. It was a pity that *Hotspur* had come in for docking at the moment when Mrs Mason had arrived to see her daughter through her confinement, but he need hardly fear a repetition of the coincidence during the days – the endless days – to come.

Stewed mutton and pearl barley and potatoes and cabbage. It might have been a very pleasant dinner, except that the atmosphere was unfavourable; in two senses. The room, with its sea-coal fire, was unbearably hot. Thanks to the rain no washing could be hung out of doors, and Hornblower doubted if in the vicinity of Driver's Alley washing could be hung out of doors unwatched in any case. So that on a clothes-horse on the other side of room hung little Horatio's clothing, and somehow nature arranged it that every stitch little Horatio wore had to be washed, as often as several times a day. Hanging on the horse were the long embroidered gowns, and the long flannel gowns with their scalloped borders, and the flannel shirts, and the binders, as well as the innumerable napkins that might have been expected to sacrifice themselves, like a rearguard, in the defence of the main body. Hornblower's wet oilskins and Mrs Mason's wet shawl added variant notes to the smells in the room, and Hornblower suspected that little Horatio, now in the cradle beside Maria's chair, added yet another.

Hornblower thought of the keen clean air of the Atlantic and felt his lungs would burst. He did his best with his dinner, but it was a poor best.

'You're not making a very good dinner, Horatio,' said Mrs Mason, peering suspiciously at his plate.

'I suppose I'm not very hungry.'

'Too much of Doughty's cooking, I expect,' said Mrs Mason.

Hornblower knew already, without a word spoken, that the women were jealous of Doughty and ill at ease in his presence. Doughty had served the rich and the great; Doughty knew of fancy ways of cooking; Doughty wanted money to bring the cabin stores of the *Hotspur* up to his own fastidious standards; Doughty (in the women's minds, at least) was probably supercilious about Driver's Alley and the family his captain had married into.

'I can't abide that Doughty,' said Maria – the word was spoken now.

'He's harmless enough, my dear,' said Hornblower.

'Harmless!' Mrs Mason said only that one word, but Demosthenes could not have put more vituperation into a whole Philippic; and yet, when the landlady came in to clear the table, Mrs Mason contrived to be at her loftiest.

As the landlady left the room Hornblower's instincts guided him into an action of which he was actually unconscious. He threw up the window and drew the icy evening air deep into his lungs.

'You'll give him his death!' said Maria's voice, and Hornblower swung round, surprised.

Maria had snatched up little Horatio from his cradle and stood clasping him to her bosom, a lioness defending her cub from the manifest and well-known perils of the night air.

'I beg your pardon, dear,' said Hornblower. 'I can't imagine what I was thinking of.'

He knew perfectly well that little babies should be kept in stuffy heated rooms, and he was full of genuine contrition regarding little Horatio. But as he turned back and pulled the window shut again his mind was dwelling on the Blackstones and the Little Girls, on bleak harsh days and dangerous nights, on a deck that he could call his own. He was ready to go to sea again.

XVIII

With the coming of spring a new liveliness developed in the blockade of Brest. In every French port during the winter there had been much building of flat-bottomed boats. The French army, two hundred thousand strong, was still poised on the Channel coast, waiting for its chance to invade, and it needed gun-boats by the thousand to ferry it over when that chance should come. But the invasion coast from Boulogne to Ostend could not supply one-tenth, one-hundredth of the vessels needed; these had to be built whenever there were facilities, and then had to be moved along the coast to the assembling area.

To Hornblower's mind Bonaparte – the Emperor Napoleon, as he was beginning to call himself – was displaying a certain confusion of ideas in adopting this course of action. Seamen and shipbuilding materials were scarce enough in France; it was absurd to waste them on invasion craft when invasion was impossible without a covering fleet, and when the French navy was too small to provide such a fleet. Lord St Vincent had raised an appreciative smile throughout the Royal Navy when he had said in the House of Lords regarding the French army, 'I do not say they cannot come. I only say they cannot come by sea.' The jest had called up a ludicrous picture in everyone's mind of Bonaparte trying to transport an invading army by Montgolfier balloons, and the impossibility of such an attempt underlined the impossibility of the French building up a fleet strong enough to command the Channel even long enough for the gun-boats to row across.

It was only by the time summer was far advanced that Hornblower fully understood Bonaparte's quandary. Bonaparte had to persist in this ridiculous venture, wasting the substance of his empire on ships and landing-craft even though a sensible man might well write off the whole project and devote his resources to some more profitable scheme. But to do so would be an admission that England was impregnable, could never be conquered, and such an admission would not only hearten his potential Continental enemies but would have a most unsettling effect on the French people themselves. He was simply compelled to continue along this road, to go on building his ships and his gun-boats to make the world believe there was a likelihood that England would soon be overthrown, leaving him dominant everywhere on earth, lord of the whole human race.

And there was always chance, even if it were not one chance in ten or one chance in a hundred, but one in a million. Some extraordinary, unpredictable combination of good fortune, of British mismanagement, of weather, and of political circumstances might give him the week he needed to get his army across. If the odds were enormous at least the stakes were fantastic. In itself that might appeal to a gambler like Bonaparte even without the force of circumstance to drive him on.

So the flat-bottomed boats were built at every little fishing-village along the coast of France, and they crept from their places of origin towards the great military camp of Boulogne, keeping to the shallows, moving by oar more than by sail, sheltering when necessary under the coastal batteries, each boat manned by fifty soldiers and a couple of seamen. And because Bonaparte was moving these craft, the Royal Navy felt bound to interfere with the movement as far as possible.

That was how it came about that *Hotspur* found herself momentarily detached from the Channel Fleet and forming a part of a small squadron under the orders of Chambers of the *Naiad* operating to the northward of Ushant, which was doing its best to prevent the passage of half a dozen gun-boats along the wild and rocky shore of Northern Brittany.

'Signal from the Commodore, sir,' reported Foreman.

Chambers spent a great deal of time signalling to his little squadron.

'Well?' asked Hornblower; Foreman was referring to his signal book.

'Take station within sight bearing east nor'east, sir.'

'Thank you, Mr Foreman. Acknowledge. Mr Bush, we'll square away.'

A pleasant day, with gentle winds from the south east, and occasional white clouds coursing over a blue sky. Overside the sea was green and clear, and two miles off on the beam was the coast with its white breakers; the chart showed strange names, Aber Wrack and Aber Benoit, which told of the relationship between the Breton tongue and Welsh. Hornblower divided his attention between the *Naiad* and the coast as *Hotspur* ran down before the wind, and he experienced something of the miser's feeling at some depletion of his gold. It might be necessary to go off like this to leeward, but every hour so spent might call for a day of beating back to windward. The decisive strategical point was outside Brest where lay the French ships of the line, not here where the little gun-boats were making their perilous passage.

'You may bring-to again, Mr Bush.'

'Aye aye, sir.'

They were now so far from *Naiad* that it would call for a sharp eye and a good glass to read her signals.

'We're the terrier at the rat hole, sir,' said Bush, coming back to Hornblower as soon as *Hotspur* had lain-to with her main-topsail to the mast.

'Exactly,' agreed Hornblower.

'Boats are cleared away ready to launch, sir.'

'Thank you.'

They might have to dash in to attack the gun-boats when they came creeping along just outside the surf.

'Commodore's signalling, sir,' reported Foreman again. 'Oh, it's for the lugger, sir.'

'There she goes!' said Bush.

The small armed lugger was moving in towards the shore.

'That's the ferret going down the hole, Mr Bush,' said Hornblower, unwontedly conversational.

'Yes, sir. There's a gun! There's another!'

They could hear the reports, borne on the wind, and could see the gusts of smoke.

'Is there a battery there, sir?'

'Maybe. Maybe the gun-boats are using their own cannon.'

Each gun-boat mounted one or two heavy guns in the bows, but they laboured under the disadvantage that half a dozen discharges racked the little vessels to pieces by the recoil. The theory behind those guns was that they were to be used for clearing beaches of defending troops where the invasion should take place and the gun-boats should be safely beached.

'Can't make out what's happening,' fumed Bush; a low headland cut off their view.

'Firing's heavy,' said Hornblower. 'Must be a battery there.'

He felt irritated; the Navy was expending lives and material on an objective quite valueless, in his opinion. He beat his gloved hands together in an effort to restore their warmth, for there was an appreciable chilliness in the wind.

'What's that?' exclaimed Bush, excitedly training his telescope. 'Look at that, sir! Dismasted, by God!'

Just visible round the point now was a shape that could not instantly be recognised. It was the lugger, drifting disabled and helpless. Everything about the situation indicated that she had run into a well-planned ambush.

'They're still firing at her, sir,' remarked Prowse. The telescope just revealed the splashes round her as cannon-balls plunged into the sea.

'We'll have to save her,' said Hornblower, trying to keep the annoyance out of his voice. 'Square away, if you please, Mr Prowse, and we'll run down.'

It was extremely irritating to have to go into danger like this, to redeem someone else's mismanagement of an expedition unjustified from the start.

'Mr Bush, get a cable out aft ready to tow.'

'Aye aye, sir.'

'Commodore's signalling, sir.' This was Foreman speaking. 'Our number. "Assist damaged vessel." '

'Acknowledge.'

Chambers had ordered that signal before he could see that *Hotspur* was already on the move.

Hornblower scanned the shore on this side of the headland. There was no gun-smoke on this side, no sign of any battery. With luck all he would have to do was to haul the lugger round the corner. Down in the waist the voices of Bush and Wise were urging a working party to their utmost efforts as they took the ponderous cable aft. Things were happening fast, as they always did at crises. A shot screamed overhead as Hornblower reached for the speaking-trumpet.

'*Grasshopper*! Stand by to take a line!'

Somebody in the disabled lugger waved a handkerchief in acknowledgement.

'Back the main-tops'l, Mr Prowse, and we'll go down to her.'

That was when the *Grasshopper* disintegrated, blew apart, in two loud explosions and a cloud of smoke. It happened right under Hornblower's eyes, as he leaned over with his speaking-trumpet; one second there was the intact hull of the lugger, with living men working on the wreckage, and the next the smoking explosions, the flying fragments, the billowing smoke. It must have been a shell from the shore; there were howitzers or mortars mounted there. Most likely a field howitzer battery, light and easily moved across country, which had been brought up to protect the gun-boats. A shell must have dropped into the lugger and burst in the magazine.

Hornblower had seen it all, and when the cloud of smoke dispersed the bow and stern did not disappear from sight. They were floating water-logged on the surface, and Hornblower could see a few living figures as well, clinging to the wreckage among the fragments.

'Lower the quarter-boat! Mr Young, go and pick up those men.'

This was worse than ever. Shell fire was a horrible menace to a wooden ship that could so easily be set into an inextinguishable blaze. It was utterly infuriating to be exposed to these perils for no profit. The quarter-boat was on its way back when the next shell screamed overhead. Hornblower recognised the difference in the sound from that of a round-shot; he should have done so earlier. A shell from a howitzer had a belt about it, a thickening in the centre which gave its flight, as it arched across the sky, the peculiarly malevolent note he had already heard.

It was the French army that was firing at them. To fight the French navy was the essence of *Hotspur's* duty, and of his own, but to expose precious ships and seamen to the attack of soldiers who cost almost nothing to a government that enforced conscription was bad business, and to expose them without a chance of firing back was sheer folly. Hornblower drummed on the hammock cloths over the netting in front of him with his gloved hands in a fury of bad temper, while Young rowed about the wreckage picking up the survivors. A glance ashore coincided with the appearance of a puff of white smoke. That was one of the howitzers at least – before the wind dispersed it he could clearly see the initial upward direction of the puff; howitzers found their best range at an angle of fifty degrees, and at the end of their trajectory the shells dropped at sixty degrees. This one was behind a low bank, or in some sort of ditch; his glass revealed an officer standing above it directing the operation of the gun at his feet.

Now came the shriek of the shell, not so far overhead; even the fountain of water that it threw up when it plunged into the sea was different in shape and duration from those flung up by round-shot from a cannon. Young brought the quarter-boat under the falls and hooked on; Bush had his men ready to tail away at the tackles, while Hornblower watched the operation and fumed at every second of delay. Most of the survivors picked up were wounded, some of them dreadfully. He would have to go and see they were properly attended to – he would have to pay a visit of courtesy – but not until *Hotspur* were safely out of this unnecessary peril.

'Very well, Mr Prowse. Bring her before the wind.'

The yards creaked round; the quartermaster spun the wheel round into firm resistance, and *Hotspur* slowly gathered way, to leave this hateful coast behind her. Next came a sudden succession of noises, all loud, all different, distinguishable even though not two seconds elapsed between the first and the last – the shriek of a shell, a crash of timber aloft, a deep note as the main-topmast backstay parted, a thud against the hammock nettings beside Hornblower, and then a thump three yards from his feet, and there on the deck death, sizzling death, was rolling towards him and as the ship heaved death changed its course with the canting of the deck in a blundering curve as the belt round the shell deflected its roll. Hornblower saw the tiny thread of smoke, the burning fuse one-eighth of an inch long. No time to think. He sprang at it as it wobbled on its belt, and with his gloved hand he extinguished the fuse, rubbing at it to make sure the spark was out, rubbing at it again unnecessarily before he straightened up. A marine was standing by and Hornblower gestured to him.

'Throw the damned thing overboard!' he ordered; the fact that he swore indicated his bad temper.

Then he looked round. Every soul on that crowded little quarterdeck was rigid, posed in unnatural attitudes, as if some Gorgon's head had turned them all into stone, and then with his voice and his gesture they all came back to life again, to move and relax – it was as if time had momentarily stood still for everyone except himself. His bad temper was fanned by the delay, and he lashed out with his tongue indiscriminately.

'What are you all thinking about? Quartermaster, put your helm over! Mr Bush! Just look at that mizzen tops'l yard! Send the hands aloft this minute! Splice that backstay! You, there! Haven't you coiled those falls yet? Move, damn you! '

'Aye aye, sir! Aye aye, sir! '

The automatic chorus of acknowledgements had a strange note, and in the midst of the bustle Hornblower saw first Bush from one angle and then Prowse from another, both looking at him with strange expressions on their faces.

'What's the matter with you?' he blazed out, and with the last word understanding came to him.

That extinguishing of the fuse appeared to them in monstrous disproportion, as something heroic, even perhaps as something magnificent. They did not see it in its true light as the obvious thing to do, indeed the only thing to do; nor did they know of the instinctive flash of action that had followed his observation of that remaining one-eighth of an inch of fuse. All there was to his credit was that he had seen and acted quicker than they. He had not been brave, and most certainly not heroic.

He returned the glance of his subordinates, and with all his senses still keyed up to the highest pitch he realised that this was the moment of the conception of a legend, that the wildest tales would be told later about this incident, and he was suddenly hideously embarrassed. He laughed, and before the laugh was finished he knew it was a self-conscious laugh, the motiveless laugh of an idiot, and he was angrier than ever with himself and with Chambers of the *Naiad* and with the whole world. He wanted to be away from all this, back in the approaches to Brest, doing his proper work and not engaged in these hare-brained actions that did not forward the defeat of Bonaparte an iota.

Then another thought struck him, occasioned by the discovery that the fuse had burned a hole in his right-hand glove. Those were the gloves Maria had given him on that dark morning when he had walked with her from the George to take *Hotspur* to sea.

XIX

In the Iroise, comfortably sheltered with the wind to the east of south, *Hotspur* was completing her stores again. This was the second time since her refitting in Plymouth that she had gone through this laborious process, refilling her casks from the water-hoys, replacing the empty beef and pork barrels from the victuallers, and coaxing all the small stores she could from the itinerant slop-ship that Cornwallis had put into commission. She had been six months continuously at sea, and was now ready for three more.

Hornblower watched with something of relief the slop-ship bearing away; that six months at sea had barely been sufficient to get his ship clear of all the plagues that had come on board at Plymouth; disease, bed bugs, fleas and lice. The bed bugs had been the worst; they had been hunted from one hiding place in the woodwork to another, scorched with smouldering oakum, walled in with the paint, time after time, and each time that he had thought he had extirpated the pests some unfortunate seaman would approach his division officer and with a knuckling of his forehead would report, 'Please, sir, I think I've got 'em this time.'

He had seven letters from Maria to read – he had opened the last one already to make sure that she and little Horatio were well – and he had already completed this task when Bush came knocking at his door. Sitting at the chart-table Hornblower listened to what Bush had to report; trifles, only, and Hornblower wondered at Bush disturbing his captain about them. Then Bush produced something from his side pocket, and Hornblower, with a sigh, knew what had been the real object of this visit. It was the latest number of the *Naval Chronicle*, come on board with the mail; the ward-room mess subscribed to it jointly. Bush thumbed through the pages, and then laid the open magazine before him, a gnarled finger indicating the passage he had found. It only took Hornblower a couple of minutes to read it; Chambers' report to Cornwallis on the affray off Aber Wrack, which apparently had been published in the Gazette to inform the public regarding the circumstances in which *Grasshopper* had been lost. Bush's finger pointed again to the last four lines. 'Captain Hornblower informs me that *Hotspur* suffered no casualties although she was struck by a five-inch shell which did considerable damage aloft but which fortunately failed to explode.'

'Well, Mr Bush?' Hornblower put a stern lack of sympathy in his voice to warn Bush as much as he could.

'It isn't right, sir.'

This routine of serving so close to home had serious disadvantages. It meant that in only two or three months the fleet would be reading what had appeared in the Gazette and the newspapers, and it was extraordinary how touchy men were about what was written about them. It could well be subversive of discipline, and Hornblower meant to deal with that possibility from the start.

'Would you kindly explain, Mr Bush?'

Bush was not to be deterred. He blunderingly repeated himself. 'It isn't right, sir.'

'Not right? Do you mean that it wasn't a five-inch shell?'

'No, sir. It . . .'

'Do you imply that it didn't do considerable damage aloft?'

'Of course it did, sir, but . . .'

'Perhaps you're implying that the shell really did explode?'

'Oh no, sir. I . . .'

'Then I fail to see what you are taking exception to, Mr Bush.'

It was highly unpleasant to be cutting and sarcastic with Mr Bush, but it had to be done. Yet Bush was being unusually obstinate.

"Tisn't right, sir. 'Tisn't fair. 'Tisn't fair to you, sir, or the ship.'

'Nonsense, Mr Bush. What d'you think we are? Actresses? Politicians? We're King's officers, Mr Bush, with a duty to do, and no thought to spare for anything else. Never speak to me again like this, if you please, Mr Bush.'

And there was Bush looking at him with bewildered eyes and still stubborn.

' 'T'isn't fair, sir,' he repeated.

'Didn't you hear my order, Mr Bush? I want to hear no more about this. Please leave this cabin at once.'

It was horrible to see Bush shamble out of the cabin, hurt and depressed. The trouble with Bush was that he had no imagination; he could not envisage the other side. Hornblower could – he could see before his eyes at that moment the words he would have written if Bush had had his way. 'The shell fell on the deck and with my own hands I extinguished the fuse when it was about to explode.' He could never have written such a sentence. He could never have sought for public esteem by writing it. Moreover, and more important, he would scorn the esteem of a public who could tolerate a man who would write such words. If by some chance his deeds did not speak for themselves he would never speak for them. The very possibility revolted him, and he told himself that this was not a matter of personal taste, but a well-weighed decision based on the good of the service; and in that respect he was displaying no more imagination than Bush.

Then he caught himself up short. This was all lies, all self-deception, refusal to face the truth. He had just flattered himself that he had more imagination than Bush; more imagination, perhaps, but far less courage. Bush knew nothing of the sick horror, the terrible moment of fear which Hornblower had experienced when the shell dropped. Bush did not know how his admired captain had had a moment's vivid mental picture of being blown into bloody rags by the explosion, how his heart had almost ceased to beat – the heart of a coward. Bush did not know the meaning of fear, and he could not credit his captain with that knowledge either. And so Bush would never know why Hornblower had made so light of the incident of the shell, and why he had been so irascible when it was discussed. But Hornblower knew, and would know, whenever he could bring himself to face facts.

There were orders being bellowed on the quarter-deck, a rush of bare feet over the planking, a clatter of ropes against woodwork, and *Hotspur* was beginning to lean over on a new course. Hornblower was at the cabin door bent on finding out what was the meaning of this activity which he had not ordered, when he found himself face to face with Young.

'Signal from the Flag, sir. "*Hotspur* report to Commander-in-Chief." '

'Thank you.'

On the quarter-deck Bush touched his hat.

'I put the ship about as soon as we read the signal, sir,' he explained.

'Very good, Mr Bush.'

When a commander-in-chief demanded the presence of a ship no time was to be wasted even to inform the captain.

'I acknowleged the signal, sir.'

'Very good, Mr Bush.'

Hotspur was turning her stern to Brest; with the wind comfortably over her quarter she was running out to sea, away from France. For the commander-in-chief to demand the attendance of his farthest outpost must be of significance. He had summoned the ship, not merely the captain. There must be something more in the wind than this gentle breeze.

Bush called the crew to attention to render passing honours to Parker's flagship, the flagship of the Inshore Squadron.

'Hope he has as good a ship as us to replace us, sir,' said Bush, who evidently had the same feeling as Hornblower, to the effect that the departure was only the beginning of a long absence from the Iroise.

'No doubt,' said Hornblower. He was glad that Bush was bearing no malice for his recent dressing-down. Of course this sudden break in routine was a stimulant in itself, but Hornblower in a moment of insight realised that Bush, after a lifetime of being subject to the vagaries of wind and weather, could manage to be fatalistic about the unpredictable vagaries of his captain.

This was the open sea; this was the wide Atlantic, and there on the horizon was a long line of topsails in rigid order – the Channel Fleet, whose men and whose guns prevented Bonaparte from hoisting the Tricolour over Windsor Castle.

'Our number from the Commander-in-Chief, sir. "Pass within hail." '

'Acknowledge. Mr Prowse, take a bearing, if you please.'

A pleasant little problem, to set a course wasting as little time as possible, with *Hibernia* close-hauled under easy sail and *Hotspur* running free under all plain sail. It was a small sop to Prowse's pride to consult him, for Hornblower had every intention of carrying out the manoeuvre by eye alone. His orders to the wheel laid *Hotspur* on a steadily converging course.

'Mr Bush, stand by to bring the ship to the wind.'

'Aye aye, sir.'

A big frigate was foaming along in *Hibernia*'s wake. Hornblower looked and looked again. That was the *Indefatigable,* once Pellew's famous frigate – the ship in which he had served during those exciting years as midshipman. He had no idea she had joined the Channel Fleet. The three frigates astern of *Indefatigable* he knew at once; *Medusa, Lively, Amphion,* all veterans of the Channel Fleet. Bunting soared up *Hibernia*'s halliards.

' "All captains," sir!'

'Clear away the quarter-boat, Mr Bush!'

It was another example of how good a servant Doughty was, that he appeared on the quarter-deck with sword and boat cloak within seconds of that signal being read. It was highly desirable to shove off in the boat at least as quickly as the boats from the frigates, even though it meant that Hornblower had to spend longer pitching and tossing in the boat while his betters went up *Hibernia's* side before him, but the thought that all this presaged some new and urgent action sustained Hornblower in the ordeal.

In the cabin of the *Hibernia* there was only one introduction to be made, of Hornblower to Captain Graham Moore of the *Indefatigable*. Moore was a strikingly handsome burly Scotsman; Hornblower had heard somewhere that he was the brother of Sir John Moore, the most promising general in the army. The others he knew, Gore of the *Medusa*, Hammond of the *Lively*, Sutton of the *Amphion*. Cornwallis sat with his back to the great stern window, with Collins on his left, and the five captains seated facing him.

'No need to waste time, gentlemen,' said Cornwallis abruptly. 'Captain Moore has brought me despatches from London and we must act on them promptly.'

Even though he began with these words he spent a second or two rolling his kindly blue eyes along the row of captains, before he plunged into his explanations.

'Our Ambassador at Madrid—' he went on, and that name made them all stir in their seats; ever since the outbreak of war the Navy had been expecting Spain to resume her old rôle of ally to France.

Cornwallis spoke lucidly although rapidly. British agents in Madrid had discovered the content of the secret clauses of the treaty of San Ildefonso between France and Spain; the discovery had confirmed long cherished suspicions. By those clauses Spain was bound to declare war on England whenever requested by France, and until that request was made she was bound to pay a million francs a month into the French treasury.

'A million francs a month in gold and silver, gentlemen,' said Cornwallis.

Bonaparte was in constant need of cash for his war expenses; Spain could supply it thanks to her mines in Mexico and Peru. Every month waggon-loads of bullion climbed the Pyrenean passes to enter France. Every year a Spanish squadron bore the products of the mines from America to Cadiz.

'The next *flota* is expected this autumn, gentlemen,' said Cornwallis. 'Usually it brings about four millions of dollars for the Crown, and about the same amount on private account.'

Eight millions of dollars, and the Spanish silver dollar was worth, in an England cursed by a paper currency, a full seven shillings. Nearly three million pounds.

'The treasure that is not sent to Bonaparte,' said Cornwallis, 'will largely go towards re-equipping the Spanish navy, which can be employed against England whenever Bonaparte chooses. So you can understand why it is desirable that the *flota* shall not reach Cadiz this year.'

'So it's war, sir?' asked Moore, but Cornwallis shook his head.

'No. I am sending a squadron to intercept the *flota,* and I expect you've already guessed that it is your ships that I'm sending, gentlemen. But it is not war. Captain Moore, the senior officer, will be instructed to request the Spaniards to alter course and enter an English port. There the treasure will be removed and the ships set free. The treasure will not be seized. It will be retained by His Majesty's Government as a pledge, to be returned to His Most Catholic Majesty on the conclusion of a general peace.'

'What ships are they, sir?'

'Frigates. Ships of war. Three frigates, sometimes four.'

'Commanded by Spanish naval officers, sir?'

'Yes.'

'They'll never agree, sir. They'll never violate their orders just because we tell 'em to.'

Cornwallis rolled his eyes up to the deck-beams above and then down again.

'You will have written orders to compel them.'

'Then we'll have to fight them, sir?'

'If they are so foolish as to resist.'

'And that will be war, sir.'

'Yes. His Majesty's Government is of the opinion that Spain without eight million dollars is less dangerous as an open enemy than she would be as a secret enemy with that money available. Is the situation perfectly clear now, gentlemen?'

It was instantly obvious. It could be grasped even more quickly than the problem in simple mental arithmetic could be solved. Prize money; one-quarter of three million pounds for the captains – something approaching eight hundred thousand pounds. Five captains. Say a hundred and fifty thousand pounds each. An enormous fortune; with that sum a captain could buy a landed estate and still have sufficient left over to provide an income on which to live in dignity when invested in the Funds. Hornblower could see that every one of the four other captains was working out that problem too.

'I see you all understand, gentlemen. Captain Moore will issue his orders to you to take effect in case of separation, and he will make his own plans to effect the interception. Captain Hornblower—' every eye came round '—will proceed immediately in *Hotspur* to Cadiz to obtain the latest information from His Britannic Majesty's Consul there, before joining you at the position selected by Captain Moore. Captain Hornblower, will you be kind enough to stay behind after these gentlemen have left?'

It was an extremely polite dismissal of the other four, whom Collins led away to receive their orders, leaving Hornblower face to face with Cornwallis. Cornwallis's blue eyes, as far as Hornblower knew, were always kindly, but apart from that they were generally remarkably expressionless. As an exception, this time they had an amused twinkle.

'You've never made a penny of prize money in your life, have you, Hornblower?' asked Cornwallis.

'No, sir.'

'It seems likely enough that you will make several pennies now.'

'You expect the Dons to fight, sir?'

'Don't you?'

'Yes, sir.'

'Only a fool would think otherwise, and you're no fool, Hornblower.'

An ingratiating man would say 'Thank you, sir,' to that speech, but Hornblower would do nothing to ingratiate himself.

'Can we fight Spain as well as France, sir?'

'I think we can. Are you more interested in the war than in prize money, Hornblower?'

'Of course, sir.'

Collins was back in the cabin again, listening to the conversation.

'You've done well in the war so far, Hornblower,' said Cornwallis. 'You're on the way towards making a name for yourself.'

'Thank you, sir.' He could say that this time, because a name was nothing.

'You have no interest at Court, I understand? No friends in the Cabinet? Or in the Admiralty?'

'No, sir.'

'It's a long, long step from Commander to Captain, Hornblower.'

'Yes, sir.'

'You've no young gentlemen with you in *Hotspur*, either.'

'No, sir.'

Practically every captain in the Navy had several boys of good family on board, rated as volunteers or as servants, learning to be sea officers. Most families had a younger son to be disposed of, and this was as good a way as any. Accepting such a charge was profitable to the captain in many ways, but particularly because by conferring such a favour he could expect some reciprocal favour from the family.

A captain could even make a monetary profit, and frequently did, by appropriating the volunteer's meagre pay and doling out pocket money instead.

'Why not?' asked Cornwallis.

'When we were commissioned I was sent four volunteers from the Naval Academy, sir. And since then I have not had time.'

The main reason why young gentlemen from the Naval Academy – King's Letter Boys – were detested by captains was because of this very matter; their presence cut down on the number of volunteers by whom the captain could benefit.

'You were unfortunate,' said Cornwallis.

'Yes, sir.'

'Excuse me, sir,' said Collins, breaking in on the conversation. 'Here are your orders, captain, regarding your conduct in Cadiz. You will of course receive additional orders from Captain Moore.'

'Thank you, sir.'

Cornwallis still had time for a moment more of gossip.

'You were fortunate the day *Grasshopper* was lost that that shell did not explode, were you not, Hornblower?'

'Yes, sir.'

'It is quite unbelievable,' said Collins, adding his contribution to the conversation, 'what a hot bed of gossip a fleet can be. The wildest tales are circulating regarding that shell.'

He was looking narrowly at Hornblower, and Hornblower looked straight back at him in defiance.

'You can't hold me responsible for that, sir,' he said.

'Of course not,' interposed Cornwallis, soothingly. 'Well, may good fortune always go with you, Hornblower.'

XX

Hornblower came back on board *Hotspur* in a positively cheerful state of mind. There was the imminent prospect of a hundred and fifty thousand pounds in prize money. That ought to satisfy Mrs Mason, and Hornblower found it possible not to dwell too long on the picture of Maria as chatelaine of a country estate. He could avoid that subject by thinking about the immediate future, a visit to Cadiz, a diplomatic contact, and then the adventure of intercepting a Spanish treasure fleet in the broad Atlantic. And if that were not sufficiently ample food for pleasant day dreams, he could recall his conversation with Cornwallis. A Commander-in-Chief in home waters had small power of promotion, but surely his recommendations might have weight. Perhaps—?

Bush, with his hand to his hat, welcoming him aboard again, was not smiling. He was wearing a worried, anxious look.

'What is it, Mr Bush?' asked Hornblower.

'Something you won't like, sir.'

Were his dreams to prove baseless? Had *Hotspur* sprung some incurable leak?

'What is it?' Hornblower bit back at the 'damn you' that he nearly said.

'Your servants under arrest for mutiny, sir.' Hornblower could only stare as Bush went on. 'He struck his superior officer.'

Hornblower could not show his astonishment or his distress. He kept his face set like stone.

'Signal from the Commodore, sir!' This was Foreman breaking in. 'Our number. "Send boat."'

'Acknowledge. Mr Orrock! Take the boat over at once.'

Moore in the *Indefatigable* had already hoisted the broad pendant that marked him as officer commanding a squadron. The frigates were still hove-to, clustered together. There were enough captains there to constitute a general court martial, with power to hang Doughty that very afternoon.

'Now, Mr Bush, come and tell me what you know about this.'

The starboard side of the quarter-deck was instantly vacated as Hornblower and Bush walked towards it. Private conversation was as possible there as anywhere in the little ship.

'As far as I can tell, sir,' said Bush, 'it was like this—'

Taking stores on board at sea was a job for all hands, and even when they were on board there was still work for all hands, distributing the stores through the ship. Doughty, in the working-party in the waist, had demurred on being given an order by a bos'n's mate, Mayne by name. Mayne had swung his 'starter', his length of knotted line that petty officers used on every necessary occasion – too frequently, in Hornblower's judgement. And then Doughty had struck him. There were twenty witnesses, and if that were not enough, Mayne's lip was cut against his teeth and blood poured down.

'Mayne's always been something of a bully, sir,' said Bush. 'But this—'

'Yes,' said Hornblower.

He knew the Twenty-Second Article of War by heart. The first half dealt with striking a superior officer; the second half with quarrelling and disobedience. And the first half ended with the words 'shall suffer death'; there were no mitigating words like 'or such less punishment.' Blood had been drawn and witnesses had seen it. Even so, some petty officers in the give and take of heavy labour on board ship might have dealt with the situation unofficially, but not Mayne.

'Where's Doughty now?' he asked.

'In irons, sir.' That was the only possible answer.

'Orders from the Commodore, sir!' Orrock was hastening along the deck towards them, waving a sealed letter which Hornblower accepted.

Doughty could wait; orders could not. Hornblower thought of returning to his cabin to read them at leisure, but a captain had no leisure. As he broke the seal Bush and Orrock withdrew to give him what little privacy was possible when every idle eye in the ship was turned on him. The opening sentence was plain enough and definite enough.

'Sir,

You are requested and required to proceed immediately in HM Sloop *Hotspur* under your command to the port of Cadiz.'

The second paragraph required him to execute at Cadiz the orders he had received from the Commander-in-Chief. The third and last paragraph named a rendezvous, a latitude and longitude as well as a distance and bearing from Cape St Vincent, and required him to proceed there 'with the utmost expedition' as soon as he had carried out his orders for Cadiz.

He re-read, unnecessarily, the opening paragraph. There was the word 'immediately.'

'Mr Bush! Set all plain sail. Mr Prowse! A course to weather Finisterre as quickly as possible, if you please. Mr Foreman, signal to the Commodore. "*Hotspur* to *Indefatigable*. Request permission to proceed." '

Only time for one pacing of the quarter-deck, up and down, and then ' "Commodore to *Hotspur*. Affirmative." '

'Thank you, Mr Foreman. Up helm, Mr Bush. Course sou'west by south.'

'Sou'west by south. Aye aye, sir.'

Hotspur came round, and as every sail began to fill she gathered way rapidly.

'Course sou'west by south, sir,' said Prowse, breathlessly returning.

'Thank you, Mr Prowse.'

The wind was just abaft the beam, and *Hotspur* foamed along as sweating hands at the braces trimmed the yards to an angle that exactly satisfied Bush's careful eye.

'Set the royals, Mr Bush. And we'll have the stuns'l booms rigged out, if you please.'

'Aye aye, sir.'

Hotspur lay over to the wind, not in any spineless fashion, but in the way in which a good sword-blade bends under pressure. A squadron of ships of the line lay just down to leeward, and *Hotspur* tore past them, rendering passing honours as she did so. Hornblower could imagine the feelings of envy in the breasts of the hands over there at the sight of this dashing little sloop racing off towards adventure. But in that case they did not allow for a year and a half spent among the rocks and shoals of the Iroise.

'Set the stuns'ls, sir?' asked Bush.

'Yes, if you please, Mr Bush. Mr Young, what d'you get from the log?'

'Nine, sir. A little more, perhaps – nine an' a quarter.'

Nine knots, and the studding sails not yet set. This was exhilarating, marvellous, after months of confinement.

'The old lady hasn't forgotten how to run, sir,' said Bush, grinning all over his face with the same emotions; and Bush did not know yet that they were going to seek eight million dollars. Nor – and at that moment all Hornblower's pleasure suddenly evaporated.

He fell from the heights to the depths like a man falling from the main royal yard. He had forgotten until then all about Doughty. That word 'immediately' in Moore's orders had prolonged Doughty's life. With all those captains available, and the Commander-in-Chief at hand to confirm the sentence, Doughty could have been court-martialled and condemned within the hour. He could be dead by now; certainly he would have died tomorrow morning. The captains in the Channel Fleet would be unmerciful to a mutineer.

Now he had to handle the matter himself. There was no desperate emergency; there was no question of a conspiracy to be quelled. He did not have to use his emergency powers to hang Doughty. But he could foresee a dreary future of Doughty in irons and all the ship's company aware they had a man in their midst destined for the rope. That would unsettle everyone. And Hornblower would be more unsettled than anyone else – except perhaps Doughty. Hornblower sickened at the thought of hanging Doughty. He knew at once that he had grown fond of him. He felt an actual respect for Doughty's devotion and attention to duty; along with his tireless attention Doughty had developed skills in making his captain comfortable comparable with those of a tarry-fingered salt making long splices.

Hornblower battled with his misery. For the thousandth time in his life he decided that the King's service was like a vampire, as hateful as it was seductive. He could not think what to do. But first he had to know more about the business.

'Mr Bush, would you be kind enough to order the master-at-arms to bring Doughty to me in my cabin?'

'Aye aye, sir.'

The clank of iron; that was what heralded Doughty's arrival at the cabin door, with gyves upon his wrists.

'Very well, master-at-arms. You can wait outside.'

Doughty's hard blue eyes looked straight into his.

'Well?'

'I'm sorry, sir. I'm sorry to put you out like this.'

'What the hell did you do it for?'

There had always been a current of feeling – as Hornblower had guessed – between Mayne and Doughty. Mayne had ordered Doughty to do some specially dirty work, at this moment when Doughty wished to preserve his hands clean to serve his captain's dinner. Doughty's protest had been the instant occasion for Mayne to wield his starter.

'I – I couldn't take a blow, sir. I suppose I've been too long with gentlemen.'

Among gentlemen a blow could only be wiped out in blood; among the lower orders a blow was something to be received without even a word. Hornblower was captain of his ship, with powers almost unlimited. He could tell Mayne to shut his mouth; he could order Doughty's irons to be struck off, and the whole incident forgotten. Forgotten? Allow the crew to think that petty officers could be struck back with impunity? Allow the crew to think that their captain had favourites?

'Damn it all!' raved Hornblower, pounding on the chart-room table.

'I could train someone to take my place, sir,' said Doughty, 'before – before . . .'

Even Doughty could not say those words.

'No! No! No!' It was utterly impossible to have Doughty circulating about the ship with every morbid eye upon him.

'You might try Bailey, sir, the gun-room steward. He's the best of a bad lot.'

'Yes.'

It made matters no easier to find Doughty still so co-operative. And then there was a glimmer of light, the faintest hint of a possibility of a solution less unsatisfactory than the others. They were three hundred leagues and more from Cadiz, but they had a fair wind.

'You'll have to await your trial. Master-at-arms! Take this man away. You needn't keep him in irons, and I'll give orders about his exercise.'

'Good-bye, sir.'

It was horrible to see Doughty retaining the unmoved countenance so carefully cultivated as a servant, and yet to know that it concealed a dreadful anxiety. Hornblower had to forget about it, somehow. He had to come on deck with *Hotspur* flying along with every inch of canvas spread racing over the sea like a thoroughbred horse at last given his head after long restraint. The dark shadow might not be forgotten, but at least it could be lightened under this blue sky with the flying white clouds, and by the rainbows of spray thrown up by the bows, as they tore across the Bay of Biscay on a mission all the more exciting to the ship's company in that they could not guess what it might be.

There was the distraction – the counter irritation – of submitting to the clumsy ministrations of Bailey, brought up from the gunroom mess. There was the satisfaction of making a neat landfall off Cape Ortegal, and flying along the Biscay coast just within sight of the harbour of Ferrol, where Hornblower had spent weary months in captivity – he tried vainly to make out the Dientes del Diablo where he had earned his freedom – and then rounding the far corner of Europe and setting a fresh course, with the wind miraculously still serving, as they plunged along, close-hauled now, to weather Cape Roca.

There was a night when the wind backed round and blew foul but gently, with Hornblower out of bed a dozen times, fuming with impatience when *Hotspur* had to go on the port tack and head directly out from the land, but then came the wonderful dawn with the wind coming from the south west in gentle puffs, and then from the westward in a strong breeze that just allowed studding sails to be spread as *Hotspur* reached southward to make a noon position with Cape Roca just out of sight to leeward.

That meant another broken night for Hornblower to make the vital change of course off Cape St Vincent so as to head, with the wind comfortably over *Hotspur's* port quarter and every stitch of canvas still spread, direct for Cadiz. In the afternoon, with *Hotspur* still flying along at a speed often reaching eleven knots, the look-out reported a blur of land, low-lying, fine on the port bow, as the coastwise shipping – hastily raising neutral Portuguese and Spanish colours at sight of this British ship of war – grew thicker. Then minutes later another hail from the masthead told that the landfall was perfect, and ten minutes after that Hornblower's telescope, trained fine on the starboard bow, could pick up the gleaming white of the city of Cadiz.

Hornblower should have been pleased at his achievement, but as ever there was no time for self-congratulation. There were the preparations to be made to ask permission of the Spanish authorities to enter the port; there was the excitement of the prospect of getting into touch with the British representative; and – now or never – there was the decision to be reached regarding his plan for Doughty. The thought of Doughty had nagged at him during these glorious days of spread canvas, coming to distract him from his day-dreams of wealth and promotion, to divert him from his plans regarding his behaviour in Cadiz. It was like the bye-plots in Shakespeare's plays, rising continually from the depths to assume momentarily equal importance with the development of the main plot.

Yet, as Hornblower had already admitted to himself, if was now or never. He had to decide and to act at this very minute; earlier would have been premature, and later would be too late. He had risked death often enough in the King's service; perhaps the service owed him a life in return – a threadbare justification, and he forced himself to admit to mere self-indulgence as he finally made up his mind. He shut up his telescope with the same fierce decision that he had closed with the enemy in the Goulet.

'Pass the word for my steward,' he said. No one could guess that the man who spoke such empty words was contemplating a grave dereliction from duty.

Bailey, all knees and elbows, with the figure of a youth despite his years, put his hand to his forehead in salute to his captain within sight, and (more important) within earshot of a dozen individuals on the quarter-deck.

'I expect His Majesty's Consul to sup with me tonight,' said Hornblower. 'I want something special to offer him.'

'Well, sir—' said Bailey, which was exactly what, and all, Hornblower had expected him to say.

'Speak up, now,' rasped Hornblower.

'I don't exactly know, sir,' said Bailey. He had suffered already from Hornblower's irascibility – unplanned, during these last days, but lucky now.

'Damn it, man. Let's have some ideas.'

'There's a cut of cold beef, sir—'

'Cold beef? For His Majesty's Consul? Nonsense.'

Hornblower took a turn up the deck in deep thought, and then wheeled back again.

'Mr Bush! I'll have to have Doughty released from confinement this evening. This ninny's no use to me. See that he reports to me in my cabin the moment I have time to spare.'

'Aye aye, sir.'

'Very well, Bailey. Get below. Now, Mr Bush, kindly clear away number one carronade starboard side for the salutes. And isn't that the *guarda costa* lugger lying-to for us there?'

The sun declining towards the west bathed the white buildings of Cadiz to a romantic pink as *Hotspur* headed in, and as health officers and naval officers and military officers came on board to see that Cadiz was guarded against infection and violations of her neutrality. Hornblower put his Spanish to use – rusty now, as he had not spoken Spanish since the last war, and more awkward still because of his recent use of French – but despite its rustiness very helpful during the formalities, while *Hotspur* under topsails glided in towards the entrance to the bay, so well remembered despite the years that had passed since his last visit in the *Indefatigable*.

The evening breeze carried the sound of the salutes round the bay, as *Hotspur's* carronade spoke out and Santa Catalina replied, and while the Spanish pilot guided *Hotspur* between the Pigs and the Sows – Hornblower had a suspicion that the Pigs were Sea Pigs, Porpoises, in Spanish – and the hands stood by to take in sail and drop anchor. There were ships of war lying at anchor already in the bay, and not the Spanish navy, whose masts and yards Hornblower could just make out in the inner harbours.

'Estados Unidos,' said the Spanish naval officer, with a gesture towards the nearer frigate. Hornblower saw the Stars and Stripes, and the broad pendant at the main-topmast-head.

'Mr Bush! Stand by to render passing honours.'

'*Constitution*. Commodore Preble,' added a Spanish officer.

The Americans were fighting a war of their own, at Tripoli far up the Mediterranean; and presumably this Preble – Hornblower could not be sure of the exact name as he heard it – was the latest of a series of American commanders-in-chief. Drums beat and men lined the side and hats were lifted in salute as *Hotspur* crept by.

'French frigate *Félicité*,' went on the Spanish officer, indicating the other ship of war.

Twenty-two ports on a side – one of the big French frigates, but there was no need to pay her further attention. As enemies in a neutral harbour they would ignore each other, cut each other dead, as gentlemen would do if by unlucky chance they met in the interval between the challenge and the duel. Lucky that he did not have to give her further thought, too, seeing that the sight of the *Constitution* was causing modification in his other plans – the bye-plot was intruding on the main plot again.

'You can anchor here, Captain,' said the Spanish officer.

'Helm-a-lee! Mr Bush!'

Hotspur rounded-to, her topsails were taken in with commendable rapidity, and the anchor cable roared out through the hawse. It was as well that the operation went through faultlessly, seeing that it was carried out under the eyes of the navies of three other nations. A flat report echoed round the bay.

'Sunset gun! Take in the colours, Mr Bush.'

The Spanish officers were standing formally in line, hats in hand, as they bowed their farewells. Hornblower put on his politest manner and took off his hat with his politest bow as he thanked them and escorted them to the side.

'Here comes your consul already,' said the naval officer just before he went down.

In the gathering darkness a rowing skiff was heading out to them from the town, and Hornblower almost cut his final farewells short as he tried to recall what honours should be paid to a consul coming on board after sunset. The western sky was blood red, and the breeze dropped, and here in a bay it seemed breathless and stifling after the airy delights of the Atlantic. And now he had to deal with secrets of state and with Doughty.

Recapitulating his worries to himself revived another one. There would now be a break in his letters to Maria; it might be months before she heard from him again, and she would fear the worst. But there was no time to waste in thinking. He had to act instantly.

XXI

With the wind dropping *Hotspur* had swung to her anchors, and now from the stern window of the chart-room USS *Constitution* was visible, revealed by her lights as she rode idly in-slack water.

'If you please, sir,' asked Doughty, as respectful as ever, 'what is this place?'

'Cadiz,' replied Hornblower; his surprise was only momentary at the ignorance of a prisoner immured below – it was possible that some even of the crew still did not know. He pointed through the cabin window. 'And that's an American frigate, the *Constitution*.'

'Yes, sir.'

Until Hornblower had seen the *Constitution* at anchor he had been visualising a drab future for Doughty, as a penniless refugee on the waterfront at Cadiz, not daring to ship as a hand before the mast in some merchant ship for fear of being pressed and recognised, starving at worst as a beggar, at best as a soldier enlisted in the ragged Spanish army. A better future than the rope, all the same. Now there was a better one still. Ships of war never had enough men, even if Preble did not need a good steward.

Bailey came in from the cabin with the last bottle of claret.

'Doughty will decant that,' said Hornblower. 'And Doughty, see that those glasses are properly clean. I want them to sparkle.'

'Yes, sir.'

'Bailey, get for'ard to the galley. See that there's a clear fire ready for the marrow bones.'

'Aye aye, sir.'

It was as simple as that as long as each move was well-timed. Doughty applied himself to decanting the claret while Bailey bustled out.

'By the way, Doughty, can you swim?'

Doughty did not raise his head.

'Yes, sir,' his voice was hardly more than a whisper. 'Thank you, sir.'

Now the expected knock on the door.

'Boat's coming alongside, sir!'

'Very well, I'll come.'

Hornblower hurried out on to the quarter-deck and down the gangway to greet the visitor. Darkness had fallen and Cadiz Bay was quite placid, like a dark mirror.

Mr Carron wasted no time; he hurried aft ahead of Hornblower with strides that equalled Hornblower's at his hastiest. When he sat in a chair in the chart-room he seemed to fill the little place completely, for he was a big heavily built man. He mopped his forehead with his handkerchief and then readjusted his wig.

'A glass of claret, sir?'

'Thank you.' Mr Carron still wasted no time, plunging into business while Hornblower filled the glasses.

'You're from the Channel Fleet?'

'Yes, sir, under orders from Admiral Cornwallis.'

'You know about the situation then. You know about the *flota*?' Carron dropped his voice at the last words.

'Yes, sir. I'm here to take back the latest news to the frigate squadron.'

'They'll have to act. Madrid shows no sign of yielding.'

'Very well, sir.'

'Godoy's terrified of Boney. The country doesn't want to fight England but Godoy would rather fight than offend him.'

'Yes, sir.'

'I'm sure they're only waiting for the *flota* to arrive and then Spain will declare war. Boney wants to use the Spanish navy to help out his scheme for invading England.'

'Yes, sir.'

'Not that the Dons will be much help to him. There isn't a ship here ready for sea. But there's the *Félicité* here. Forty-four guns. You saw her, of course?'

'Yes, sir.'

'She'll warn the *flota* if she gets an inkling of what's in the wind.'

'Of course, sir.'

'My last news is less than three days old. The courier had a good journey from Madrid. Godoy doesn't know yet that we've found out about the secret clauses in the treaty of San Ildefonso, but he'll guess soon enough by the stiffening of our attitude.'

'Yes, sir.'

'So the sooner you get away the better. Here's the despatch for the officer commanding the intercepting squadron. I prepared it as soon as I saw you coming into the Bay.'

'Thank you, sir. He's Captain Graham Moore in the *Indefatigable*.'

Hornblower put the despatch into his pocket. He had been aware for some time of sounds and subdued voices from the cabin next door, and he guessed the reason. Now there was a knock and Bush's face appeared round the door.

'One moment, please, Mr Bush. You ought to know I'm busy. Yes, Mr Carron?'

Bush was the only man in the ship who would dare to intrude at that moment, and he only if he thought the matter urgent.

'You had better leave within the hour.'

'Yes, sir. I was hoping you might sup with me this evening.'

'Duty before pleasure, although I thank you. I'll cross the bay now and make the arrangements with the Spanish authorities. The land breeze will start to make before long, and that will take you out.'

'Yes, sir.'

'Make every preparation for weighing anchor. You know of the twenty-four hour rule?'

'Yes, sir.'

Under the rules of neutrality a ship of one contending nation could not leave a neutral harbour until one whole day after the exit of a ship of another contending nation.

'The Dons may not enforce it on the *Félicité*, but they'll certainly enforce it on you if you give them the opportunity. Two-thirds of *Félicité*'s crew are in the taverns of Cadiz at this moment, so you must take your chance now. I'll be here to remind the Dons about the twenty-four hour rule if she tries to follow you. I might delay her at least. The Dons don't want to offend us while the *flota*'s still at sea.'

'Yes, sir. I understand. Thank you, sir.'

Carron was already rising to his feet, with Hornblower following his example.

'Call the Consul's boat.' said Hornblower as they emerged on to the quarter-deck. Bush still had something to say, but Hornblower still ignored him.

And even when Carron had left there was still an order for Bush with which to distract him.

'I want the small bower hove in, Mr Bush, and heave short on the best bower.'

'Aye aye, sir. If you please, sir—'

'I want this done in silence, Mr Bush, No pipes, no orders that *Félicité* can hear. Station two safe men at the capstan with old canvas to muffle the capstan pawls. I don't want a sound.'

'Aye aye, sir. But—'

'Go and attend to that yourself personally, if you please, Mr Bush.'

No one else dare intrude on the captain as he strode the quarter-deck in the warm night. Nor was it long before the pilot came on board; Carron had certainly succeeded in hastening the slow process of the Spanish official mind. Topsails sheeted home, anchor broken out, *Hotspur* glided slowly down the bay again before the first gentle puffs of the nightly land breeze, with Hornblower narrowly watching the pilot. It might be a solution of the Spaniard's problem if *Hotspur* were to take the ground as she went to sea, and Hornblower determined that should not happen. It was only after the pilot had left them and *Hotspur* was standing out to the south westward that he had a moment to spare for Bush.

'Sir! Doughty's gone.'

'Gone?'

It was too dark on the quarter-deck for Hornblower's face to be seen, and he tried his best to make his voice sound natural.

'Yes, sir. He must have nipped out of the stern window of your cabin, sir. Then he could have lowered himself into the water by the rudder-pintles, right under the counter where no one could see him, and then he must have swum for it, sir.'

'I'm extremely angry about this, Mr Bush. Somebody will smart for it.'

'Well, sir—'

'Well, Mr Bush?'

'It seems you left him alone in the cabin when the Consul came on board, sir. That's when he took his chance.'

'You mean it's my fault, Mr Bush?'

'Well, yes, sir, if you want to put it that way.'

'M'm. Maybe you're right, even if I do say it.' Hornblower paused, still trying to be natural. 'God, that's an infuriating thing to happen. I'm angry with myself. I can't think how I came to be so foolish.'

'I expect you had a lot on your mind, sir.'

It was distasteful to hear Bush standing up for his captain in the face of his captain's self-condemnation.

'There's just no excuse for me. I'll never forgive myself.'

'I'll mark him as "R" on the ship's muster, sir.'

'Yes. You'd better do that.

Cryptic initials in the ship's muster rolls told various stories – 'D' for 'discharged,' 'D D' for 'dead,' and 'R' for 'run' – deserted.

'But there's some good news, too, Mr Bush. In accordance with my orders I must tell you, Mr Bush, in case of something happening to me, but none of what I'm going to say is to leak out to the ship's company.'

'Of course, sir.'

Treasure; prize money, doubloons and dollars. A Spanish treasure fleet. If there were anything that could take Bush's mind off the subject of Doughty's escape from justice it was this.

'It'll be millions, sir!' said Bush.

'Yes. Millions.'

The seamen in the five ships would share one quarter of the prize money – the same sum as would be divided between five captains – and that would mean six hundred pounds a man. Lieutenants and masters and captains of marines would divide one-eighth. Fifteen thousand pounds for Bush, at a rough estimate.

'A fortune, sir!'

Hornblower's share would be ten of those fortunes.

'Do you remember, sir, the last time we captured a *flota*? Back in '99, I think it was, sir. Some of our Jacks when they got their prize money bought gold watches an' *fried* 'em on Gosport Hard, just to show how rich they were.'

'Well, you can sleep on it, Mr Bush, as I'm going to try to do. But remember, not a word to a soul.'

'No, sir. Of course not, sir.'

The project might still fail. The *flota* might evade capture and escape into Cadiz; it might have turned back; it might never have sailed. Then it would be best if the Spanish government – and the world at large – did not know that such an attempt had ever been contemplated.

These thoughts, and these figures, should have been stimulating, exciting, pleasant, but tonight, to Hornblower, they were nothing of the sort. They were Dead Sea fruit, turning to ashes in the mouth. Hornblower snapped at Bailey and dismissed him; then he sat on his cot, too low spirited even to be cheered by the swaying of the cot under his seat to tell him that *Hotspur* was at sea again, bound on a mission of excitement and profit. He sat with drooping head, deep in depression. He had lost his integrity, and that meant he had lost his self-respect. In his life he had made mistakes, whose memory could still make him writhe, but this time he had done far more. He had committed a breach of duty. He had connived at – he had actually contrived – the escape of a deserter, of a criminal. He had violated his sworn oath, and he had done so from mere personal reasons, out of sheer self-indulgence. Not for the good of the service, not for his country's cause, but because he was a soft-hearted sentimentalist. He was ashamed of himself, and the shame was all the more acute when his pitiless self-analysis brought up the conviction that, if he could relive those past hours, he would do the same again.

There were no excuses. The one he had used, that the Service owed him a life after all the perils he had run, was nonsense. The mitigating circumstance that discipline would not suffer, thanks to the new exciting mission, was of no weight. He was a self-condemned traitor; worse still, he was a plausible one, who had carried through his scheme with deft neatness that marked the born conspirator. That first word he had thought of was the correct one; integrity, and he had lost it. Hornblower mourned over his lost integrity like Niobe over her dead children.

XXII

Captain Graham Moore's orders for the disposition of the frigate squadron so as to intercept the *flota* were so apt that they received even Hornblower's grudging approval. The five ships were strung out on a line north and south to the limit of visibility. With fifteen miles between ships and with the northernmost and southernmost ships looking out to their respective horizons a stretch of sea ninety miles wide could be covered. During daylight they beat or ran towards America; during the night they retraced their course towards Europe, so that if by misfortune the *flota* should reach the line in darkness the interval during which it could be detected would be by that much prolonged. The dawn position was to be in the longitude of Cape St Vincent – 9° west – and the sunset position was to be as far to the west of that as circumstances should indicate as desirable.

For this business of detecting the needle of the *flota* in the haystack of the Atlantic was a little more simple than might appear at first sight. The first point was that by the cumbrous law of Spain the *flota* had to discharge its cargo at Cadiz, and nowhere else. The second point was that the direction of the wind was a strong indication of the point of the compass from which the *flota* might appear. The third point was that the *flota*, after a long sea passage, was likely to be uncertain of its longitude; by sextant it could be reasonably sure of its latitude, and could be counted on to run the final stages of its course along the latitude of Cadiz – 36° 30' north – so as to make sure of avoiding the Portuguese coast on the one hand and the African coast on the other.

So that in the centre of the British line, squarely on latitude 36° 30' north, lay the Commodore in the *Indefatigable*, with the other ships lying due north and due south of him. A flag signal by day or a rocket by night would warn every ship in the line of the approach of the *flota*, and it should not be difficult for the squadron to concentrate rapidly upon the signalling ship, a hundred and fifty miles out from Cadiz with plenty of time and space available to enforce their demands.

An hour before dawn Hornblower came out on deck, as he had done every two hours during the night – and every two hours during all the preceding nights as well. It had been a clear night and it was still clear now.

'Wind nor'east by north, sir,' reported Prowse. 'St Vincent bearing due north about five leagues.'

A moderate breeze; all sail to the royals could be carried, although the *Hotspur* was under topsails, stealing along close-hauled on the port tack. Hornblower trained his telescope over the starboard beam, due south, in the direction where *Medusa* should be, next in line; *Hotspur*, as befitted her small importance, was the northernmost ship, at the point where it was least likely for the *flota* to appear. It was not quite light enough yet for *Medusa* to be visible.

'Mr Foreman, get aloft, if you please, with your signal book.'

Of course every officer and man in *Hotspur* must be puzzled about this daily routine, this constant surveillance of a single stretch of water. Ingenious minds might even guess the true objective of the squadron. That could not be helped.

'There she is, sir!' said Prowse. 'Beating sou' by west. We're a little ahead of station.'

'Back the mizzen tops'l, if you please.'

They might be as much as a couple of miles ahead of station – not too unsatisfactory after a long night. It was easy enough to drop back to regain the exact bearing, due north from *Medusa*.

'Deck, there!' Foreman was hailing from the main-topmast-head. '*Medusa*'s signalling. "Commodore to all ships."'

Medusa was relaying the signal from *Indefatigable* out of sight to the southward.

'Wear ship,' went on Foreman. 'Course west. Topsails.'

'Mr Cheeseman, kindly acknowledge.'

Cheeseman was the second signal officer, learning his trade as Foreman's deputy. 'Send the hands to the braces, Mr Prowse.'

It must be a gratifying experience for Moore to manoeuvre a line of ships sixty miles long by sending up and hauling down flags.

'Deck!' There was a different tone in Foreman's voice, not the tone of matter of fact routine. 'Sail in sight on the port bow, nearly to windward, sir. Coming down before the wind, fast.'

Hotspur was still waiting for *Medusa's* signal to come down to indicate the exact moment to wear.

'What do you make of her, Mr Foreman?'

'She's a ship of war, sir. She's a frigate. She looks French to me, sir. She might be the *Félicité*, sir.'

She might well be the *Félicité*, coming out from Cadiz. By now word could easily have reached Cadiz regarding the British cordon out at sea. *Félicité* would come out; she could warn, and divert, the *flota*, if she could get past the British line. Or she could hang about on the horizon until the *flota* should appear, and then interfere with the negotiations. Bonaparte could make great play in the *Moniteur* regarding the heroic French navy coming to the aid of an oppressed neutral fleet. And *Félicité's* presence might have great weight in the scale should it come to a fight; a large French frigate and four large Spanish ones against one large British frigate, three small ones, and a sloop.

'I'll get aloft and have a look at her myself, sir.' This was Bush, in the right place at the right time as usual. He ran up the ratlines with the agility of any seaman.

'Signal's down, sir!' yelled Foreman.

Hotspur should put up her helm at this moment, for all five ships to wear together.

'No, Mr Prowse. We'll wait.'

On the horizon *Medusa* wore round. Now she was before the wind, increasing her distance rapidly from *Hotspur* on the opposite course.

'That's *Félicité* for certain, sir!' called Bush.

'Thank you, Mr Bush. Kindly come down at once. Drummer! Beat to quarters. Clear for action. Mr Cheeseman, send this signal. "Have sighted French frigate to windward." '

'Aye aye, sir. *Medusa's* going out of sight fast.'

'Hoist it, anyway.'

Bush had descended like lightning, to exchange glances for one moment with Hornblower before hurrying off to supervise clearing for action. For that moment there was an enquiring look in his eye. He alone in this ship beside Hornblower knew the objective of the British squadron. If *Hotspur* was parted from the other ships when the *flota* should be sighted she would lose her share of the prize money.

But prize money was only one factor; the *flota* was a primary objective. *Hotspur* would disregard *Medusa's* signals and turn aside from the objective, at her peril – at Hornblower's peril. And Bush knew, too, the disparity of force between *Hotspur* and *Félicité*. A battle broadside to broadside could only end with half *Hotspur's* crew dead and the other half prisoners of war.

'*Medusa's* out of sight, sir. She hasn't acknowledged.' This was Foreman, still aloft.

'Very well, Mr Foreman. You can come down.'

'You can see her from the deck, sir,' said Prowse.

'Yes.' Right on the horizon the Frenchman's topsails and topgallants were plainly in view. Hornblower found it a little difficult to keep them steady in the field of the telescope. He was pulsing with excitement; he could only hope that his face did not reveal him to be as anxious and worried as he felt.

'Cleared for action, sir,' reported Bush.

The guns were run out, the excited guns' crews at their stations.

'She's hauled her wind!' exclaimed Prowse.

'Ah!'

Félicité had come round on the starboard tack, heading to allow *Hotspur* to pass far astern of her. She was declining battle.

'Isn't he going to fight?' exclaimed Bush.

Hornblower's tensions were easing a little with this proof of the accuracy of his judgement. He had headed for *Félicité* with the intention of engaging in a scrambling long range duel. He had hoped to shoot away enough of the *Félicité's* spars to cripple her so that she would be delayed in her mission of warning the *flota*. And the Frenchman had paralleled his thoughts. He did not want to risk injury with his mission not accomplished.

'Put the ship about, if you please, Mr Prowse.'

Hotspur tacked like a machine.

'Full and bye!'

Now she headed to cross *Félicité's* bows on a sharply converging course. The Frenchman, in declining battle, had it in mind to slip round the flank of the British line so as to escape in the open sea and join the Spaniards ahead of the British, and Hornblower was heading him off. Hornblower watched the topsails on the horizon, and saw them swing.

'He's turning away!'

Much good that would do him. Far, fár beyond the topsails was a faint blue line on the horizon, the bold coast of Southern Portugal.

'He won't weather St Vincent on that course,' said Prowse.

Lagos, St Vincent, Sagres; all great names in the history of the sea, and that jutting headland would just baulk *Félicité* in her attempt to evade action. She would have to fight soon, and Hornblower was visualising the kind of battle it would be.

'Mr Bush!'

'Sir!'

'I want two guns to bear directly astern. You'll have to cut away the transoms aft. Get to work at once.'

'Aye aye, sir.'

'Thank you, Mr Bush.'

Sailing ships were always hampered in the matter of firing directly ahead or astern; no satisfactory solution of the difficulty had ever been found. Guns were generally so useful on the broadside that they were wasted on the ends of the ship, and ship construction had acknowledged the fact. Now the cry for the carpenter's crew presaged abandoning all the advantages that had been wrung from these circumstances by shipbuilders through the centuries. *Hotspur* was weakening herself in exchange for a momentary advantage in a rare situation. Under his feet Hornblower felt the crack of timber and the vibration of saws at work.

'Send the gunner aft. He'll have to rig tackles and breechings before the guns are moved.'

The blue line of the coast was now much more sharply defined; the towering headland of St Vincent was in plain view. And *Félicité* was hull-up now, the long, long, line of guns along her side clearly visible, run out and ready for action. Her main-topsail was a-shiver, and she was rounding-to. Now she was challenging action, offering battle.

'Up helm, Mr Prowse. Back the main-tops'l.'

Every minute gained was of value. *Hotspur* rounded-to as well. Hornblower had no intention of fighting a hopeless battle; if the Frenchman could wait he could wait as well. With this gentle breeze and moderate sea *Hotspur* held an advantage over the bigger French ship which was not lightly to be thrown away. *Hotspur* and *Félicité* eyed each other like two pugilists just stepping into the ring. It was such a beautiful day of blue sky and blue sea; it was a lovely world which he might be leaving soon. The rumble of gun trucks told him that one gun-carriage at least was being moved into position, and yet at this minute somehow he thought of Maria and of little Horatio – madness; he put that thought instantly out of his mind.

The seconds crept by; perhaps the French captain was holding a council of war on his quarter-deck; perhaps he was merely hesitating, unable to reach a decision at this moment when the fate of nations hung in the balance.

'Message from Mr Bush, sir. One gun run out ready for action, sir. The other one in five minutes.'

'Thank you, Mr Orrock. Tell Mr Bush to station the two best gun-layers there.'

Félicité's main-topsail was filling again.

'Hands to the braces!'

Hotspur stood in towards her enemy. Hornblower would not yield an inch of sea room unnecessarily.

'Helm a-weather!'

That was very long cannon shot as *Hotspur* wore round. *Félicité's* bow was pointing straight at her; *Hotspur's* stern was turned squarely to her enemy, the ships exactly in line.

'Tell Mr Bush to open fire!'

Even before the message could have reached him Bush down below had acted. There was the bang-bang of the guns, the smoke bursting out under the counter, eddying up over the quarter-deck with the following wind. Nothing visible to Hornblower's straining eye at tne telescope; only the beautiful lines of *Félicité's* bows, her sharply-steeved bowsprit, her gleaming canvas. The rumble of the gun-trucks underfoot as the guns were run out again. Bang! Hornblower saw it. Standing right above the gun, looking straight along the line of flight, he saw the projectile, a lazy pencil mark against the white and blue, up and then down, before the smoke blew forward. Surely that was a hit. The smoke prevented his seeing the second shot.

The long British nine-pounder was the best gun in the service as far as precision went. The bore was notoriously true, and the shot could be more accurately cast than the larger projectiles. And even a nine-pounder shot, flying at a thousand feet a second, could deal lusty blows. Bang! The Frenchman would be unhappy at receiving this sort of punishment without hitting back.

'Look at that!' said Prowse.

Félicité's fore-staysail was out of shape, flapping in the wind; it was hard to see at first glance what had happened.

'His fore-stay's parted, sir,' decided Prowse.

That Prowse was correct was shown a moment later when *Félicité* took in the fore-staysail. The loss of the sail itself made little difference, but the fore-stay was a most important item in the elaborate system of checks and balances (like a French constitution before Bonaparte seized power) which kept a ship's masts in position under the pressure of the sails.

'Mr Orrock, run below and say 'Well done' to Mr Bush.'

Bang! As the smoke eddied Hornblower saw *Félicité* round-to and as her broadside presented itself to his sight it vanished in a great bank of leaping smoke. There was the horrid howl of a passing cannon-ball somewhere near; there were two jets of water from the surface of the sea, one on each quarter, and that was all Hornblower saw or heard of the broadside. An excited crew, firing from a wheeling ship, could not be expected to do better than that, even with twenty-two guns.

A ragged cheer went up from the *Hotspur's* crew, and Hornblower, turning, saw that every idle hand was craning out of the gun-ports, peering aft at the Frenchman. He could hardly object to that, but when he turned back to look at *Félicité* again he saw enough to set the men hurriedly at work. The Frenchman had not yawed merely to fire her broadside; she was hove-to, mizzen topsail to the mast, in order to splice the fore-stay. Lying like that, her guns would not bear. But not a second was to be lost, with *Hotspur* before the wind and the range increasing almost irretrievably.

'Stand by your guns to port! Hands to the braces! Hard-a-starboard!'

Hotspur wore sweetly round on to the port-tack. She was on *Félicité's* port quarter where not a French gun would bear. Bush came running from aft to keep his eye on the port-side guns; he strode along from gun to gun, making sure by eye that elevation and training were correct as *Hotspur* fired her broadside into her helpless enemy. Very long range, but some of those shots must have caused damage. Hornblower watched the bearing of *Félicité* altering as *Hotspur* drew astern of her.

'Stand-by to go about after the next broadside!'

The nine guns roared out, and the smoke was still eddying in the waist as *Hotspur* tacked.

'Starboard side guns!'

Excited men raced across the deck to aim and train; another broadside, but *Félicité's* mizzen topsail was wheeling round.

'Helm a-weather!'

By the time the harassed Frenchman had come before the wind again *Hotspur* had anticipated her; both ships were again in line and Bush was racing aft to supervise the fire of the stern chasers once more. This was revenge for the action with the *Loire* so long ago. In this moderate breeze and smooth sea the handy sloop held every advantage over the big frigate; what had gone on up to now was only a sample of what was to continue all through that hungry weary day of golden sun and blue sea and billowing powder smoke.

The leeward position that *Hotspur* held was a most decided advantage. To leeward over the horizon lay the British squadron; the Frenchman dared not chase her for long in that direction, lest he find himself trapped between the wind and overwhelming hostile strength. Moreover the Frenchman had a mission to perform; he was anxious to find and warn the Spanish Squadron, yet when he had won for himself enough sea room to weather St Vincent and to turn away his teasing little enemy hung on to him, firing into his battered stern, shooting holes in his sails, cutting away his running rigging.

During that long day *Félicité* fired many broadsides, all at long range, and generally badly aimed as *Hotspur* wheeled away out of the line of fire. And during all that long day Hornblower stood on his quarter-deck, watching the shifts of the wind, rapping out his orders, handling his little ship with unremitting care and inexhaustible ingenuity. Occasionally a shot from *Félicité* struck home; under Hornblower's very eyes an eighteen-pounder ball came in through a gunport and struck down five men into a bloody heaving mass. Yet until long after noon *Hotspur* evaded major damage, while the wind backed round southerly and the sun crept slowly round to the west. With the shifting of the wind his position was growing more precarious, and with the passage of time fatigue was numbing his mind.

At a long threequarters of a mile *Félicité* at last scored an important hit, one hit out of the broadside she fired as she yawed widely off her course. There was a crash aloft, and Hornblower looked up to see the main yard sagging in two halves, shot clean through close to the centre, each half hanging in the slings at its own drunken angle, threatening, each of them, to come falling like an arrow down through the deck. It was a novel and cogent problem to deal with, to study the dangling menaces and to give the correct helm order that set the sails a-shiver and relieve the strain.

'Mr Wise! Take all the men you need and secure that wreckage!'

Then he could put his glass again to his aching eye to see what *Félicité* intended to do. She could force a close action if she took instant advantage of the opportunity. He would have to fight now to the last gasp. But the glass revealed something different, something he had to look at a second time before he could trust his swimming brain and his weary eye. *Félicité* had filled away. With every sail drawing she was reaching towards the sunset. She had turned tail and was flying for the horizon away from the pest which had plagued all the spirit out of her in nine continuous hours of battle.

The hands saw it, they saw her go, and someone raised a cheer which ran raggedly along the deck. There were grins and smiles which revealed teeth strangely white against the powder blackened faces. Bush came up from the waist, powder blackened like the others.

'Sir!' he said. 'I don't know how to congratulate you.'

'Thank you, Mr Bush. You can keep your eye on Wise. There's the two spare stuns'l booms – fish the main yard with those.'

'Aye aye, sir.'

Despite the blackening of his features, despite the fatigue that even Bush could not conceal, there was that curious expression in Bush's face again, inquiring, admiring, surprised. He was bursting with things that he wanted to say. It called for an obvious effort of will on Bush's part to turn away without saying them; Hornblower fired a parting shot at Bush's receding back.

'I want the ship ready for action again before sunset, Mr Bush.'

Gurney the Gunner was reporting.

'We've fired away all the top tier of powder, sir, an' we're well into the second tier. That's a ton an' a half of powder. Five tons of shot, sir. We used every cartridge; my mates are sewing new ones now.'

The carpenter next, and then Huffnell the purser and Wallis the surgeon; arrangements to feed the living, and arrangements to bury the dead.

The dead whom he had known so well; there was a bitter regret and a deep sense of personal loss as Wallis read the names. Good seamen and bad seamen, alive this morning and now gone from this world, because he had done his duty. He must not think along those lines at all. It was a hard service to which he belonged, hard and pitiless like steel, like flying cannon-shot.

At nine o'clock at night Hornblower sat down to the first food he head eaten since the night before, and as he submitted to Bailey's clumsy ministrations, he thought once more about Doughty, and from Doughty he went on – the step was perfectly natural – to think about eight million Spanish dollars in prize money. His weary mind was purged of the thought of sin. He did not have to class himself with the cheating captains he had heard about, with the peculating officers he had known. He could grant himself absolution; grudging absolution.

XXIII

With her battered sides and her fished main yard, *Hotspur* beat her way back towards the rendezvous appointed in case of separation. Even in this pleasant latitude of Southern Europe winter was asserting itself. The nights were cold and the wind blew chill, and *Hotspur* had to ride out a gale for twenty-four hours as she tossed about; St Vincent, bearing north fifteen leagues, was the place of rendezvous, but there was no sign of the frigate squadron. Hornblower paced the deck as he tried to reach a decision, as he calculated how far off to leeward the recent gale might have blown *Indefatigable* and her colleagues, and as he debated what his duty demanded he should do next. Bush eyed him from a distance as he paced; even though he was in the secret regarding the *flota* he knew better than to intrude. Then at last came the hail from the mast-head.

'Sail ho! Sail to windward! Deck, there! There's another. Looks like a fleet, sir.'

Now Bush could join Hornblower.

'I expect that's the frigates, sir.'

'Maybe.' Hornblower hailed the main-topmast-head. 'How many sail now?'

'Eight, sir. Sir, they look like ships of the line, some of them, sir. Yes, sir, a three-decker an' some two-deckers.'

A squadron of ships of the line, heading for Cadiz. They might possibly be French – fragments of Bonaparte's navy sometimes evaded blockade. In that case it was his duty to identify them, risking capture. Most likely they were British, and Hornblower had a momentary misgiving as to what their presence would imply in that case.

'We'll stand towards them, Mr Bush. Mr Foreman! Hoist the private signal.'

There were the topsails showing now, six ships of the line ploughing along in line ahead, a frigate out on either flank.

'Leading ship answers 264, sir. That's the private signal for this week.'

'Very well. Make our number.'

Today's grey sea and grey sky seemed to reflect the depression that was settling over Hornblower's spirits.

'*Dreadnought*, sir. Admiral Parker. His flag's flying.'

So Parker had been detached from the fleet off Ushant; Hornblower's unpleasant conviction was growing.

'Flag to *Hotspur*, sir. "Captain come on board." '

'Thank you, Mr Foreman. Mr Bush, call away the quarter boat.'

Parker gave an impression of greyness like the weather when Hornblower was led aft to *Dreadnought*'s quarter-deck. His eyes and his hair and even his face (in contrast with the swarthy faces round him) were of a neutral grey. But he was smartly dressed, so that Hornblower felt something of a ragamuffin in his presence, wishing, too, that his morning's shave had been more effective.

'What are you doing here, Captain Hornblower?'

'I am on the rendezvous appointed for Captain Moore's squadron, sir.'

'Captain Moore's in England by this time.'

The news left Hornblower unmoved, for it was what he was expecting to hear, but he had to make an answer.

'Indeed, sir?'

'You haven't heard the news?'

'I've heard nothing for a week, sir.'

'Moore captured the Spanish treasure fleet. Where were you?'

'I had an encounter with a French frigate, sir.'

A glance at *Hotspur* lying hove-to on the *Dreadnought's* beam could take in the fished main-yard and the raw patches on her sides.

'You missed a fortune in prize money.'

'So I should think, sir.'

'Six million dollars. The Dons fought, and one of their frigates blew up with all hands before others surrendered.'

In a ship in action drill and discipline had to be perfect; a moment's carelessness on the part of a powder boy or a gun loader could lead to disaster. Hornblower's thoughts on this subject prevented him this time from making even a conversational reply, and Parker went on without waiting for one.

'So it's war with Spain. The Dons will declare war as soon as they hear the news – they probably have done so already. This squadron is detached from the Channel Fleet to begin the blockade of Cadiz.'

'Yes, sir.'

'You had better return north after Moore. Report to the Channel Fleet off Ushant for further orders. '

'Aye aye, sir.'

The cold grey eyes betrayed not the least flicker of humanity. A farmer would look at a cow with far more interest than this Admiral looked at a Commander.

'A good journey to you, Captain.'

'Thank you, sir.'

The wind was well to the north of west; *Hotspur* would have to stand far out to weather St Vincent, and farther out still to make sure of weathering Cape Roca. Parker and his ships had a fair wind for Cadiz and although Hornblower gave his orders the moment he reached the deck they were over the horizon almost as soon as *Hotspur* had hoisted in her boat and had settled down on the starboard tack, close-hauled, to begin the voyage back to Ushant. And as she plunged to the seas that met her starboard bow there was something additional to be heard and felt about her motion. As each wave crest reached her, and she began to put her bows down, there was a sudden dull noise and momentary little shock through the fabric of the ship, to be repeated when she had completed her descent and began to rise again. Twice for every wave this happened, so that ear and mind came to expect it at each rise and fall. It was the fished main-yard, splinted between the two spare studding sail booms. However tightly the frapping was strained that held the joint together, a little play remained, and the ponderous yardarms settled backward and forward with a thump, twice with every wave, until mind and ear grew weary of its ceaseless monotony.

It was on the second day that Bailey provided a moment's distraction for Hornblower while *Hotspur* still reached out into the Atlantic to gain her offing.

'This was in the pocket of your nightshirt, sir. I found it when I was going to wash it.'

It was a folded piece of paper with a note written on it, and that note must have been written the evening that *Hotspur* lay in Cadiz Bay – Bailey clearly did not believe in too frequent washing of nightshirts.

'Sir—

The Cabin Stores are short of Capers and Cayenne.

Thank you, Sir. Thank you, Sir.

Your Humble obedient Servant

J. Doughty.'

Hornblower crumpled the paper in his hand. It was painful to be reminded of the Doughty incident. This must be the very last of it.

'Did you read this, Bailey?'

'No, sir. I'm no scholard, sir.'

That was the standard reply of an illiterate in the Royal Navy, but Hornblower was not satisfied until he had taken a glance at the ship's muster rolls and seen the 'X' against Bailey's name. Most Scotsmen could read and write – it was fortunate that Bailey was an exception.

So *Hotspur* continued close-hauled, first on the starboard tack and then on the port, carrying sail very tenderly on her wounded mainyard, while she made her way northward over the grey Atlantic until at last she weathered Finisterre and could run two points free straight for Ushant along the hypotenuse of the Bay of Biscay. It snowed on New Year's Eve just as it had snowed last New Year's Eve when *Hotspur* had baulked Bonaparte's attempted invasion of Ireland. It was raining and bleak, and thick weather closely limited the horizon when *Hotspur* attained the latitude of Ushant and groped her way slowly forward in search of the Channel Fleet. The *Thunderer* loomed up in the mist and passed her on to the *Majestic,* and the *Majestic* passed her on until the welcome word '*Hibernia*' came back in reply to Bush's hail. There was only a small delay while the news of *Hotspur's* arrival was conveyed below to the Admiral before the next hail came; Collins's voice, clearly recognisable despite the speaking-trumpet.

'Captain Hornblower?'

'Yes, sir.'

'Would you kindly come aboard?'

Hornblower was ready this time, so closely shaved that his cheeks were raw, his best coat on, two copies of his report in his pocket.

Cornwallis was shivering, huddled in a chair in his cabin, a thick shawl over his shoulders and another over his knees, and presumably with a hot bottle under his feet. With his shawls and his wig he looked like some old woman until he looked up with his china blue eyes.

'Now what in the world have you been up to this time, Hornblower?'

'I have my report here, sir.'

'Give it to Collins. Now tell me.'

Hornblower gave the facts as briefly as he could.

'Moore was furious at your parting company, but I think he'll excuse you when he hears about this. *Medusa* never acknowledged your signal?'

'No, sir.'

'You did quite right in hanging on to *Félicité*. I'll endorse your report to that effect. Moore ought to be glad that there was one ship fewer to share his prize money.'

'I'm sure he didn't give that a thought, sir.'

'I expect you're right. But you, Hornblower. You could have turned a blind eye to the *Félicité* – there's a precedent in the Navy for turning a blind eye. Then you could have stayed with Moore and shared the prize money.'

'If *Félicité* had escaped round Cape St Vincent there might not have been any prize money, sir.'

'I see. I quite understand.' The blue eyes had a twinkle. 'I put you in the way of wealth and you disdain it.'

'Hardly that, sir.'

It was a sudden revelation to Hornblower that Cornwallis had deliberately selected him and *Hotspur* to accompany Moore and share the prize money. Every ship must have been eager to go; conceivably this was a reward for months of vigilance in the Goulet.

Now Collins entered the conversation.

'How are your stores?'

'I've plenty, sir. Food and water for sixty more days on full rations.'

'What about your powder and shot?' Collins tapped his finger on Hornblower's report, which he had been reading.

'I've enough for another engagement, sir.'

'And your ship?'

'We've plugged the shot holes, sir. We can carry sail on the mainyard as long as it doesn't blow too strong.'

Cornwallis spoke again.

'Would it break your heart if you went back to Plymouth?'

'Of course not, sir.'

'That's as well, for I'm sending you in to refit.'

'Aye aye, sir. When shall I sail?'

'You're too restless even to stay to dinner?'

'No, sir.'

Cornwallis laughed outright. 'I wouldn't like to put you to the test.'

He glanced up at the tell-tale wind-vane in the deck beams above. Men who had spent their whole lives combating the vagaries of the wind all felt alike in that respect; when a fair wind blew it was sheer folly to waste even an hour on a frivolous pretext.

'You'd better sail now,' went on Cornwallis. 'You know I've a new second in command?'

'No, sir.'

'Lord Gardner. Now that I have to fight the Dons as well as Boney I need a vice-admiral.'

'I'm not surprised, sir.'

'If you sail in this thick weather you won't have to salute him. That will save the King some of his powder that you're so anxious to burn. Collins, give Captain Hornblower his orders.'

So he would be returning once more to Plymouth. Once more to Maria.

XXIV

'It really was a magnificent spectacle,' said Maria.

The *Naval Chronicle*, at which Hornblower was glancing while conversing with her, used those identical words 'magnificent spectacle.'

'I'm sure it must have been, dear.'

Under his eyes was a description of the landing of the Spanish treasure at Plymouth from the frigates captured by Moore's squadron. Military precautions had of course been necessary when millions of pounds in gold and silver had to be piled into wagons and dragged through the streets up to the Citadel, but the fanfare had exceeded military necessity. The Second Dragoon Guards had provided a mounted escort, the Seventy-First Foot had marched with the waggons, the local militia had lined the streets, and every military band for miles round had played patriotic airs. And when the treasure was moved on to London troops had marched with it and their bands had marched with them, so that every town through which the convoy passed had been treated to the same magnificent spectacle. Hornblower suspected that the government was not averse to calling the attention of as many people as possible to this increase in the wealth of the country, at a moment when Spain had been added to the list of England's enemies.

'They say the captains will receive hundreds of thousands of pounds each,' said Maria. 'I suppose it will never be our good fortune to win anything like that, dear?'

'It is always possible,' said Hornblower.

It was astonishing, but most convenient, that Maria was quite unaware of any connection between *Hotspur's* recent action with *Félicité* and Moore's capture of the *flota*. Maria was shrewd and sharp, but she was content to leave naval details to her husband, and it never occurred to her to inquire how it had come about that *Hotspur*, although attached to the Channel Fleet off Ushant, had found herself off Cape St Vincent. Mrs Mason might have been more inquisitive, but she, thank God, had returned to Southsea.

'What happened to that Doughty?' asked Maria.

'He deserted,' answered Hornblower; luckily, again. Maria was not interested in the mechanics of desertion and did not inquire into the process.

'I'm not sorry, dear,' she said. 'I never liked him. But I'm afraid you miss him.'

'I can manage well enough without him,' said Hornblower. It was useless to buy capers and cayenne during this stay in Plymouth; Bailey would not know what to do with them.

'Perhaps one of these days I'll be able to look after you instead of these servants,' said Maria.

There was the tender note in her voice again, and she was drawing nearer.

'No one could do that better than you, my darling,' answered Hornblower. He had to say it. He could not hurt her. He had entered into this marriage voluntarily, and he had to go on playing the part. He put his arm round the waist that had come within reach.

'You are the kindest husband, darling,' said Maria. 'I've been so happy with you.'

'Not as happy as I am when you say that,' said Hornblower. That was the base intriguer speaking again, the subtle villain – the man who had plotted Doughty's escape from justice. No; he must remember that his conscience was clear now in that respect. That self-indulgence had been washed away by the blood that had poured over the decks of *Félicité*.

'I often wonder why it should be,' went on Maria, with a new note in her voice. 'I wonder why you should be so kind to me, when I think about – you, darling – and me.'

'Nonsense,' said Hornblower, as bluffly as he could manage. 'You must always be sure of my feelings for you, dear. Never doubt me.'

'My very dearest,' said Maria, her voice changing again, the note of inquiry dying out and the tenderness returning. She melted into his arms. 'I'm fortunate that you have been able to stay so long in Plymouth this time.'

'That was my good fortune, dear.'

Replacing the transoms which Bush had so blithely cut away in *Hotspur's* stern for the fight with *Félicité* had proved to be a laborious piece of work – *Hotspur's* stern had had to be almost rebuilt.

'And the Little One has been sleeping like a lamb all the evening,' went on Maria; Hornblower could only hope that this did not involve his crying all night.

A knock at the door made Maria tear herself away from Hornblower's embracing arm.

'Gentleman to see you,' said the landlady's voice.

It was Bush, in pea-jacket and scarf, standing hesitating on the threshold.

'Good evening, sir. Your servant, ma'am. I hope I don't intrude.'

'Of course not,' said Hornblower, wondering what shift of wind or politics could possibly have brought Bush here, and very conscious that Bush's manner was a little odd.

'Come in, man. Come in. Let me take your coat – unless your news is urgent?'

'Hardly urgent, sir,' said Bush rather ponderously, allowing himself, with embarrassment, to be relieved of his coat. 'But I felt you would like to hear it.'

He stood looking at them both, his eyes not quite in focus, yet sensitive to the possibility that Maria's silence might be a sign that to her he was unwelcome; but Maria made amends.

'Won't you take this chair, Mr Bush?'

'Thank you, ma'am.'

Seated, he looked from one to the other again; it was quite apparent to Hornblower by now that Bush was a little drunk.

'Well, what is it?' he asked.

Bush's face split into an ecstatic grin.

'Droits of Admiralty, sir,' he said.

'What do you mean?'

'Moore and the frigates – I mean Captain Moore, of course, begging your pardon, sir.'

'What about them?'

'I was in the coffee-room of the Lord Hawke, sir – I often go there of an evening – and last Wednesday's newspapers came down from London. And there it was, sir. Droits of Admiralty.'

Wrecks; stranded whales; flotsam and jetsam; Droits of Admiralty dealt with things of this sort, appropriating them for the Crown, and, despite the name, they were of no concern to Their Lordships. Bush's grin expanded into a laugh.

'Serves 'em right, doesn't it, sir?' he said.

'You'll have to explain a little further.'

'All that treasure they captured in the *flota,* sir. It's not prize money at all. It goes to the Government as Droits of Admiralty. The frigates don't get a penny. You see, sir, it was time of peace.'

Now Hornblower understood. In the event of war breaking out with another country, the ships of that country which happened to be in British ports were seized by the Government as Droits of Admiralty; prize money came under a different category, for prizes taken at sea in time of war were Droits of the Crown, and were specifically granted to the captors by an order in Council which waived the rights of the Crown.

The government was perfectly justified legally in its action. And however much that action would infuriate the ships' companies of the frigates, it would make the rest of the navy laugh outright, just as it had made Bush laugh.

'So we didn't lose anything, sir, on account of your noble action. Noble – I've always wanted to tell you it was noble, sir.'

'But how could you lose anything?' asked Maria.

'Don't you know about that, ma'am?' asked Bush, turning his wavering gaze upon her. Wavering or not, and whether he was drunk or not, Bush could still see that Maria had been left in ignorance of the opportunity that *Hotspur* had declined, and he still was sober enough to make the deduction that it would be inadvisable to enter into explanations.

'What was it that Captain Hornblower did that was so noble?' asked Maria.

'Least said soonest mended, ma'am,' said Bush. He thrust his hand into his side pocket and laboriously fished out a small bottle. 'I took the liberty of bringing this with me, ma'am, so that we could drink to the health of Captain Moore an' the *Indefatigable* an' the Droits of Admiralty. It's rum, ma'am. With hot water an' lemon an' sugar, ma'am, it makes a suitable drink for this time o' day.'

Hornblower caught Maria's glance.

'It's too late tonight, Mr Bush,' he said. 'We'll drink that health tomorrow. I'll help you with your coat.'

After Bush had left (being helped on with his coat by his captain flustered him sufficiently to make him almost wordless) Hornblower turned back to Maria.

'He'll find his way back to the ship all right,' he said.

'So you did something noble, darling,' said Maria.

'Bush was drunk,' replied Hornblower. 'He was talking nonsense.'

'I wonder,' said Maria. Her eyes were shining. 'I always think of you as noble, my darling.'

'Nonsense,' said Hornblower.

Maria came forward to him, putting her hands up to his shoulders, coming close so that he could resume the interrupted embrace.

'Of course you must have secrets from me,' she said. 'I understand. You're a King's officer, as well as my darling husband.'

Now that she was in his arms she had to put her head far back to look up at him.

'It's no secret,' she went on, 'that I love you, my dear, noble love. More than life itself.'

Hornblower knew it was true. He felt his tenderness towards her surging up within him. But she was still speaking.

'And something else that isn't a secret,' went on Maria. 'Perhaps you've guessed. I think you have.'

'I thought so,' said Hornblower. 'You make me very happy, my dear wife.'

Maria smiled, her face quite transfigured. 'Perhaps this time it will be a little daughter. A sweet little girl.'

Hornblower had suspected it, as he said. He did not know if he was happy with his knowledge, although he said he was. It would only be a day or two before he took *Hotspur* to sea again, back to the blockade of Brest, back to the monotonous perils of the Goulet.

XXV

Hotspur lay in the Iroise, and the victualler was heaving-to close alongside, to begin again the toilsome labour of transferring stores. After sixty days of blockade duty there would be much to do, even though the pleasant sunshine of early summer would ease matters a little. The fend-offs were over the side and the first boat was on its way from the victualler bringing the officer charged with initiating the arrangements.

'Here's the post, sir,' said the officer, handing Hornblower the small package of letters destined for the ship's company. 'But here's a letter from the Commander-in-Chief, sir. They sent it across to me from the *Hibernia* as I passed through the Outer Squadron.'

'Thank you,' said Hornblower.

He passed the packet to Bush to sort out. There would be letters from Maria in it, but a letter from the Commander-in-Chief took precedence. There was the formal address:

Horatio Hornblower, Esq.
Master and Commander
HM Sloop *Hotspur*

The letter was sealed with an informal wafer, instantly broken.

'My dear Captain Hornblower,

I hope you can find it convenient to visit me in *Hibernia,* as I have news for you that would best be communicated personally. To save withdrawing *Hotspur* from her station, and to save you a long journey by boat, you might find it convenient to come in the victualler that brings this letter. You are therefore authorised to leave your First Lieutenant in command, and I will find means for returning you to your ship when our business is completed. I look forward with pleasure to seeing you.

> Your ob'd't servant,
> Wm. Cornwallis.'

Two seconds of bewilderment, and then a moment of horrid doubt which made Hornblower snatch the other letters back from Bush and hurriedly search through them for those from Maria.

'Best communicated personally' – Hornblower had a sudden secret fear that something might have happened to Maria and that Cornwallis had assumed the responsibility of breaking the news to him. But here was a letter from Maria only eight days old, and all was well with her and with little Horatio and the child to be. Cornwallis could hardly have later news than that.

Hornblower was reduced to re-reading the letter and weighing every word like a lover receiving his first love letter. The whole letter appeared cordial in tone, until Hornblower forced himself to admit that if it was summons to a reprimand it might be worded in exactly the same way. Except for the opening word 'My'; that was a departure from official practice – yet it might be a mere slip. And the letter concerned itself with 'news' – but Cornwallis would call official information 'news' too. Hornblower took a turn up the deck and forced himself to laugh at himself. He really was behaving like a love-lorn youth. If after all these years of service he had not learned to wait patiently through a dull hour for an inevitable crisis the Navy had not taught him even his first lesson.

The stores came slowly on board; there were the receipts to sign, and of course there were the final hurried questions hurled at him by people afraid of accepting responsibility.

'Make up your own mind about that,' snapped Hornblower, and, 'Mr Bush'll tell you want to do, and I hope he'll put a flea in your ear.'

Then at last he was on a strange deck, watching with vast curiosity the handling of a different ship as the victualler filled away and headed out of the Iroise. The victualler's captain offered him the comfort of his cabin and suggested sampling the new consignment of rum, but Hornblower could not make himself accept either offer. He could only just manage to make himself stand still, aft by the taffrail, as they gradually left the coast behind, and picked their way through the Inshore Squadron and set a course for the distant topsails of the main body of the Channel Fleet.

The huge bulk of the *Hibernia* loomed up before them, and Hornblower found himself going up the side and saluting the guard. Newton, the captain of the ship, and Collins, the Captain of the Fleet, both happened to be on deck and received him cordially enough; Hornblower hoped they did not notice his gulp of excitement as he returned their 'Good afternoons.' Collins prepared to show him to the Admiral's quarters.

'Please don't trouble, sir. I can find my own way,' protested Hornblower.

'I'd better see you past all the Cerberuses that guard these nether regions,' said Collins.

Cornwallis was seated at one desk, and his flag-lieutenant at another, but they both rose at his entrance, and the flag-lieutenant slipped unobtrusively through a curtained door in the bulkhead while Cornwallis shook Hornblower's hand – it could hardly be a reprimand that was coming, yet Hornblower found it difficult to sit on more than the edge of the chair that Cornwallis offered him. Cornwallis sat with more ease, yet bolt upright with his back quite flat as was his habit.

'Well?' said Cornwallis.

Hornblower realised that Cornwallis was trying to conceal his mood, yet there was – or was there not? – a twinkle in the china blue eyes; all these years as Commander-in-Chief still had not forged the Admiral into the complete diplomat. Or perhaps they had. Hornblower could only wait; he could think of nothing to say in reply to that monosyllable.

'I've had a communication about you from the Navy Board,' said Cornwallis at length, severely.

'Yes, sir?' Hornblower could find a reply to this speech; the Navy Board dealt with victualling and supplies and such like matters. It could be nothing vital.

'They've called my attention to the consumption of stores by the *Hotspur*. You appear to have been expensive, Hornblower. Gunpowder, shot, sails, cordage – you've been using up these things as if *Hotspur* were a ship of the line. Have you anything to say?'

'No, sir.' He need not offer the obvious defence, not to Cornwallis.

'Neither have I.' Cornwallis smiled suddenly as he said that, his whole expression changing. 'And that is what I shall tell the Navy Board. It's a naval officer's duty to shoot and be shot at.'

'Thank you, sir.'

'I've done all I need to do in transmitting this information.'

The smile died away from Cornwallis's face, and was replaced by something bleak, something a little sad. He looked suddenly much older. Hornblower was making ready to rise from his chair; he could see that Cornwallis had sent for him so that this censure from the Navy Board should be deprived of all its sting. In the Service anticipated crises sometimes resolved themselves into anti-climaxes. But Cornwallis went on speaking; the sadness of his expression was echoed in the sadness of the tone of his voice.

'Now we can leave official business,' he said, 'and proceed to more personal matters. I'm hauling down my flag, Hornblower.'

'I'm sorry to hear that, sir.' Those might be trite, mechanical words, but they were not. Hornblower was genuinely, sincerely sorry, and Cornwallis could hardly think otherwise.

'It comes to us all in time,' he went on. 'Fifty-one years in the Navy.'

'Hard years, too, sir.'

'Yes. For two years and three months I haven't set foot on shore.'

'But no one else could have done what you have done, sir.'

No one else could have maintained the Channel Fleet as a fighting body during those first years of hostilities, thwarting every attempt by Bonaparte to evade its crushing power.

'You flatter me,' replied Cornwallis. 'Very kind of you, Hornblower. Gardner's taking my place, and he'll do just as well as me.'

Even in the sadness of the moment Hornblower's ever observant mind took notice of the use of that name without the formal 'Lord' or 'Admiral'; he was being admitted into unofficial intimacy with a Commander-in-Chief, albeit one on the point of retirement.

'I can't tell you how much I regret it, all the same, sir,' he said.

'Let's try to be more cheerful,' said Cornwallis. The blue eyes were looking straight through Hornblower, extraordinarily penetrating. Apparently what they observed was specially gratifying. Cornwallis's expression softened. Something appeared there which might almost be affection.

'Doesn't all this mean anything to you, Hornblower?' he asked.

'No, sir,' replied Hornblower, puzzled. 'Only what I've said. It's a great pity that you have to retire, sir.'

'Nothing else?'

'No, sir.'

'I didn't know such disinterestedness was possible. Don't you remember what is the last privilege granted a retiring Commander-in-Chief?'

'No, sir.' That was true when Hornblower spoke; realisation came a second later. 'Oh, of course—'

'Now it's beginning to dawn on you. I'm allowed three promotions. Midshipman to Lieutenant. Lieutenant to Commander. Commander to Captain.'

'Yes, sir.' Hornblower could hardly speak those words; he had to swallow hard.

'It's a good system,' went on Cornwallis. 'At the end of his career a Commander-in-Chief can make those promotions without fear or favour. He has nothing more to expect in this world, and so he can lay up store for the next, by making his selections solely for the good of the service.'

'Yes, sir.'

'Do I have to go on? I'm going to promote you to Captain.'

'Thank you, sir. I can't—' Very true. He could not speak.

'As I said, I have the good of the service in mind. You're the best choice I can make, Hornblower.'

'Thank you, sir.'

'Mark you, this is the last service I can do for you. A fortnight from now I'll be nobody. You've told me you have no friends in high places?'

'Yes, sir. No, sir.'

'And commands still go by favour. I hope you find it, Hornblower. And I hope you have better luck in the matter of prize money. I did my best for you.'

'I'd rather be a captain and poor than anyone else and rich, sir.'

'Except perhaps an Admiral,' said Cornwallis; he was positively grinning.

'Yes, sir.'

Cornwallis rose from his chair. Now he was a Commander-in-Chief again, and Hornblower knew himself dismissed. Cornwallis raised his voice in the high-pitched carrying hail of the Navy.

'Pass the word for Captain Collins!'

'I must thank you, sir, most sincerely.'

'Don't thank me any more. You've thanked me enough already. If ever you become an admiral with favours to give you'll understand why.'

Collins had entered and was waiting at the door.

'Good-bye, Hornblower.'

'Good-bye, sir.'

Only a shake of the hand; no further word, and Hornblower followed Collins to the quarter-deck.

'I've a water-hoy standing by for you,' said Collins. 'In a couple of tacks she'll fetch *Hotspur*.'

'Thank you, sir.'

'You'll be in the Gazette in three weeks' time. Plenty of time to make your arrangements.'

'Yes, sir.'

Salutes, the squealing of pipes, and Hornblower went down the side and was rowed across to the hoy. It was an effort to be polite to the captain. The tiny crew had hauled up the big lugsails before Hornblower realised that this was an interesting process which he would have done well to watch closely. With the lugsails trimmed flat and sharp the little hoy laid herself close to the wind and foamed forward towards France.

Those last words of Collins' were still running through Hornblower's mind. He would have to leave the *Hotspur*; he would have to say good-bye to Bush and all the others, and the prospect brought a sadness that quite took the edge off the elation that he felt. Of course he would have to leave her; *Hotspur* was too small to constitute a command for a Post Captain. He would have to wait for another command; as the junior captain on the list he would probably receive the smallest and least important sixth rate in the navy. But for all that he was a Captain. Maria would be delighted.

READ MORE IN PENGUIN

In every corner of the world, on every subject under the sun, Penguin represents quality and variety – the very best in publishing today.

For complete information about books available from Penguin – including Puffins, Penguin Classics and Arkana – and how to order them, write to us at the appropriate address below. Please note that for copyright reasons the selection of books varies from country to country.

In the United Kingdom: Please write to *Dept. EP, Penguin Books Ltd, Bath Road, Harmondsworth, West Drayton, Middlesex UB7 ODA*

In the United States: Please write to *Consumer Sales, Penguin Putnam Inc., P.O. Box 12289 Dept. B, Newark, New Jersey 07101-5289*. VISA and MasterCard holders call 1-800-788-6262 to order Penguin titles

In Canada: Please write to *Penguin Books Canada Ltd, 10 Alcorn Avenue, Suite 300, Toronto, Ontario M4V 3B2*

In Australia: Please write to *Penguin Books Australia Ltd, P.O. Box 257, Ringwood, Victoria 3134*

In New Zealand: Please write to *Penguin Books (NZ) Ltd, Private Bag 102902, North Shore Mail Centre, Auckland 10*

In India: Please write to *Penguin Books India Pvt Ltd, 11 Community Centre, Panchsheel Park, New Delhi 110017*

In the Netherlands: Please write to *Penguin Books Netherlands bv, Postbus 3507, NL-1001 AH Amsterdam*

In Germany: Please write to *Penguin Books Deutschland GmbH, Metzlerstrasse 26, 60594 Frankfurt am Main*

In Spain: Please write to *Penguin Books S. A., Bravo Murillo 19, 1° B, 28015 Madrid*

In Italy: Please write to *Penguin Italia s.r.l., Via Benedetto Croce 2, 20094 Corsico, Milano*

In France: Please write to *Penguin France, Le Carré Wilson, 62 rue Benjamin Baillaud, 31500 Toulouse*

In Japan: Please write to *Penguin Books Japan Ltd, Kaneko Building, 2-3-25 Koraku, Bunkyo-Ku, Tokyo 112*

In South Africa: Please write to *Penguin Books South Africa (Pty) Ltd, Private Bag X14, Parkview, 2122 Johannesburg*

READ MORE IN PENGUIN

A SELECTION OF OMNIBUSES

The Cornish Trilogy   Robertson Davies

'He has created a rich oeuvre of densely plotted, highly symbolic novels that not only function as superbly funny entertainments but also give the reader, in his character's words, a deeper kind of pleasure – delight, awe, religious intimations, "a fine sense of the past, and of the boundless depth and variety of life"' – *The New York Times*

A Dalgliesh Trilogy   P. D. James

Three classics of detective fiction featuring the assiduous Adam Dalgliesh. In *A Shroud for a Nightingale*, *The Black Tower* and *Death of an Expert Witness*, Dalgliesh, with his depth and intelligence, provides the solutions to seemingly unfathomable intrigues.

The Pop Larkin Chronicles   H. E. Bates

'Tastes ambrosially of childhood. Never were skies so cornflower blue or beds so swansbottom ... Life not as it is or was, but as it should be' – *Guardian*. 'Pop is as sexy, genial, generous and boozy as ever, Ma is a worthy match for him in these qualities' – *The Times*

The Penguin Book of New American Voices
Edited by Jay McInerney

'Traditional, well-crafted, poignant tales rub shoulders with ones from the inner city which read like bulletins from a war zone ... At their best [these stories] shake you up, take you some place you've never been, and dump you into some weird life you've never even imagined' – *Mail on Sunday*

Lucia Victrix   E. F. Benson

Mapp and Lucia, *Lucia's Progress*, *Trouble for Lucia* – now together in one volume, these three chronicles of English country life will delight a new generation of readers with their wry observation and delicious satire.

READ MORE IN PENGUIN

A SELECTION OF OMNIBUSES

The Penguin Book of Classic Fantasy by Women
Edited by A. Susan Williams

This wide-ranging and nerve-tingling collection assembles short stories written by women from 1806 to the Second World War. From George Eliot on clairvoyance to C. L. Moore on aliens or Virginia Woolf on psychological spectres, here is every aspect of fantasy from some of the best-known writers of their day.

The Penguin Collection

This collection of writing by twelve acclaimed authors represents the finest in modern fiction, and celebrates sixty years of Penguin Books. Among the stories assembled here are ones by William Boyd, Donna Tartt, John Updike and Barbara Vine.

V. I. Warshawski Sara Paretsky

In *Indemnity Only*, *Deadlock* and *Killing Orders*, Sara Paretsky demonstrates the skill that makes tough female private eye Warshawski one of the most witty, slick and imaginative sleuths on the street today.

A David Lodge Trilogy David Lodge

His three brilliant comic novels revolving around the University of Rummidge and the eventful lives of its role-swapping academics. Collected here are: *Changing Places*, *Small World* and *Nice Work*.

The Rabbit Novels John Updike

'One of the finest literary achievements to have come out of the US since the war . . . It is in their particularity, in the way they capture the minutiae of the world . . . that [the Rabbit] books are most lovable' – *Irish Times*

READ MORE IN PENGUIN

A SELECTION OF OMNIBUSES

Zuckerman Bound Philip Roth

The Zuckerman trilogy – *The Ghost Writer*, *Zuckerman Unbound* and *The Anatomy Lesson* – and the novella-length epilogue, *The Prague Orgy*, are here collected in a single volume. Brilliantly diverse and intricately designed, together they form a wholly original and richly comic investigation into the unforeseen consequences of art.

The Collected Stories of Colette Colette

The hundred short stories collected here include such masterpieces as 'Bella-Vista', 'The Tender Shoot' and 'Le Képi', Colette's subtle and ruthless rendering of a woman's belated sexual awakening. 'A perfectionist in her every word' – *Spectator*

The Collected Stories Muriel Spark

'Muriel Spark has made herself a mistress at writing stories which seem to trip blithely and bitchily along life's way until the reader is suddenly pulled up with a shock recognition of death and judgment, heaven and hell' – *London Review of Books*

The Complete Saki

Macabre, acid and very funny, Saki's work drives a knife into the upper crust of English Edwardian life. Here are the effete and dashing heroes, the tea on the lawn, the smell of gunshot, the half-felt menace of disturbing undercurrents . . . all in this magnificent omnibus.

The Penguin Book of Gay Short Stories
Edited by David Leavitt and Mark Mitchell

The diversity – and unity – of gay love and experience in the twentieth century is celebrated in this collection of thirty-nine stories. 'The book is like a long, enjoyable party, at which the celebrated . . . rub shoulders with the neglected' – *The Times Literary Supplement*

BY THE SAME AUTHOR

Two more omnibuses by C. S. Forester

Captain Hornblower R.N.

In *Hornblower and the* Atropos, Hornblower's first duty in command is to captain the flagship for Lord Nelson's funeral on the Thames (not his idea of thrilling action). But soon his orders come, and he sets sail for the Mediterranean in the *Atropos*. Battle, storm, shipwreck and disease – what were the chances that he would never come back again? *The Happy Return* finds Hornblower sailing South American waters, where he comes face to face with a mad, messianic revolutionary in a novel that ripples with risk and gripping adventure. In *A Ship of the Line*, as Hornblower sails to the Spanish station he must deal with commando raids, hurricanes at sea and the glowering menace of Napoleon's onshore gun batteries.

Admiral Hornblower

From the Mediterranean to Havana – Hornblower's finest battles at sea and on land . . .

In *Flying Colours* he becomes a national hero when he escapes a French firing squad. But the Terror of the Mediterranean becomes Europe's most wanted man, forced to fight alone for England – and liberty. *The Commodore* finds Hornblower returning to the scene of his first naval action: the Baltic. In a gripping adventure in the northern waters he must use all his skill and experience to prevent a catastrophic war. In *Lord Hornblower*, our hero's orders are to suppress a bloody mutiny off Le Havre, with a peerage awaiting him as a prize for a successful mission. Staking his reputation on one bold hunch, the daring Commodore advances into the heart of enemy territory – and comes face to face with death. And in *Hornblower in the West Indies*, a posting abroad for Rear Admiral Hornblower is a relief from the monotony of Britain. But the tattered remnants of the Imperial Guard lie in wait in Central America, threatening further bloodshed – and the destruction of all that Hornblower holds dear.

also published

The African Queen